THE BEST
SCIENCE FICTION
AND FANTASY
OF THE YEAR

VOLUME SEVEN

D0059614

Also Edited by Jonathan Strahan

Best Short Novels (2004 through 2007)
Fantasy: The Very Best of 2005
Science Fiction: The Very Best of 2005
The Best Science Fiction and Fantasy of the Year: Volumes 1–7
Eclipse: New Science Fiction and Fantasy: Volumes 1–4
The Starry Rift: Tales of New Tomorrows
Life on Mars: Tales from the New Frontier
Under My Hat: Tales from the Cauldron
Godlike Machines
Engineering Infinity
Edge of Infinity
Fearsome Journeys (forthcoming)
Reach for Infinity (forthcoming)

With Lou Anders
Swords and Dark Magic: The New Sword and Sorcery

With Charles N. Brown
The Locus Awards: Thirty Years of the Best in Fantasy and Science Fiction

With Jeremy G. Byrne
The Year's Best Australian Science Fiction and Fantasy: Volumes 1–2
Eidolon 1

With Jack Dann
Legends of Australian Fantasy

With Gardner Dozois
The New Space Opera
The New Space Opera 2

With Karen Haber
Science Fiction: Best of 2003
Science Fiction: Best of 2004
Fantasy: Best of 2004

With Marianne S. Jablon
Wings of Fire

THE BEST
SCIENCE FICTION
AND FANTASY
OF THE YEAR

VOLUME SEVEN

EDITED BY JONATHAN STRAHAN

NIGHT SHADE BOOKS
SAN FRANCISCO

First Edition

ISBN: 978-1-59780-459-2

Night Shade Books

www.nightshadebooks.com

For Marianne, with love.

ACKNOWLEDGEMENTS

This book has been one of the most challenging anthologies I've had to work on in my career. With ever more work published, and ever more demands on my time, I began to wonder if it would ever be complete. For that reason, I'd like to thank my wife and co-editor Marianne S. Jablon for her heroic work in helping me get this manuscript finished. Without her diligent, careful, and tireless efforts, *The Best Science Fiction and Fantasy of the Year* would probably not have made it out this year and certainly would not be as good as it is. I'd also like to thank Gary K. Wolfe for his help in doing an emergency read and edit of the introduction after it was lost in a computer failure just before the book was due to be delivered. Thanks also to everyone at *Not If You Were the Last Short Story on Earth*, who helped keep me grounded and focussed in my reading during the year, and to all of the book's contributors, who helped me get this year's book together at the last. A special thanks, as always, to Liza Groen Trombi and all of my friends and colleagues at *Locus*, and to Ross E. Lockhart at Night Shade Books, who has been wonderful to work with year after year. And two special sets of thanks. As always, I'd like to thank my agent, the dapper and ever-reliable Howard Morhaim, whose annual parties are a highlight of the year. And finally, my extra, extra special thanks to my wife Marianne and my daughters Jessica and Sophie: every moment spent working on this book was stolen from them.

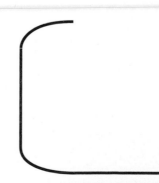

CONTENTS

INTRODUCTION

JONATHAN STRAHAN

More than anything else 2012 was an *interesting* year for science fiction and fantasy. While people concerned with the business of the genre—publishers, editors, publicists—looked for ways to innovate and expand, to find new ways to get stories before the eyes of readers, those of us who are interested in the artistic health of the genre—writers, artists, critics, readers—were looking carefully at how things were proceeding as well.

Probably the single most interesting discussion of science fiction and fantasy during the year was prompted by "The Widening Gyre," a fascinating and worthwhile review essay by UK critic Paul Kincaid published in the *LA Review of Books* where he examined a handful of "best of the year" anthologies like this one. In his essay Kincaid raised the question of whether science fiction had grown "exhausted," not in the sense of becoming tired or rundown, but rather of having run short on compelling ideas, possibly having lost faith in or connection to the future.

In the extensive online discussions that followed, this sense of "exhaustion" seemed to be prompted by a number of recent works that could be said to be nostalgic, hearkening back to the way the future was, rather than attempting to engage meaningfully with the world we live in today, with all of its economic, climatic, and political upheavals and radical scientific discoveries. If a central mission of science fiction is to connect our world to meaningful believable futures, Kincaid and others asked, are too few writers currently addressing that mission? Kincaid also raised the question of whether fantasy might be losing touch with its mission as well. Touching on stories like K. J. Parker's excellent novella "A Small Price to Pay for

Birdsong"—which went on to win the World Fantasy Award in November—Kincaid asked in what sense such works, with no overtly fantastical events or beings at all, were in any sense even "fantasy." Couldn't such a tale be transplanted into a historical setting with little apparent change?

I do think science fiction—at least at the experimental/developmental end of the spectrum—is in a period of self-examination. Some of this is just our field's constant navel gazing, but some is a deliberate attempt to find a way to imagine any kind of science fictional future at all. It is certainly imaginatively less innovative to revisit 1940s-style SF adventures, with those bright futures that now seem to have failed us, than to try to envision another kind of future from our own less optimistic age. And yet that is the challenge, surely. Not to imagine the way the future was, but the way the future might be. While I don't think answers to this exist yet, I do think you can see the beginnings of attempts to find them.

The fantasy question vexes me a little more. I am not attracted to litmus tests and lab results for genre, but I do understand and accept the need to be able to meaningfully connect slipstream works to the field, to explain how quasi-historical fiction like that by, say, Guy Gavriel Kay or K. J. Parker belongs in fantasy at all. Discussing his novel *Some Kind of Fairy Tale* on *The Coode Street Podcast* recently, Graham Joyce talked about how he used the intrusion of the fantastic into our own world as a tool to interrogate our world, the people and relationships within it. Similarly, Kay has often claimed that placing historical events and people in a secondary world, as he does in major works like *Tigana* and *Under Heaven*, allows him to interrogate those events in new and worthwhile ways. I find myself convinced by this and, while I agree with Kincaid that it is valuable to have some idea of what fantasy is and what its mission might be, it's equally valuable to be able to use it in the ways it has been by Kay, Parker, Joyce, and many others.

As always is the case each year, I couldn't help but observe a number of interesting and encouraging trends. In 2012 science fiction and fantasy continued to move slowly but hopefully away from the white male Anglo Saxon Mayberry of its youth and towards a more mature, diverse, and inclusive future. This trend was nowhere better evidenced than in the brace of strong original anthologies that focused on fiction from other points of view. The best of these included Nick Mamatas & Matsumi Washington's *The Future Is Japanese*, Anil Menon & Vandana Singh's *Breaking the Bow*, Eduardo Jiménez Mayo & Chris N. Brown's *Three Messages and a Warning*, Ivor Hartmann's *AfroSF: Science Fiction by African Writers*, Lavie

Tidhar's *The Apex Book of World SF*, and Brit Mandelo's *Beyond Binary*. While "Mono No Aware" by Ken Liu, included here, was originally from *The Future Is Japanese*, it was only one of many on a fairly long shortlist of stories from these books that were actively considered for this book. The fact that these books were published and discussed during the last twelve months shows that, if nothing else, science fiction and fantasy is looking to become more inclusive, something which is long past due, even if there is still a long way to go.

The other trend I noticed was that writers, editors, and publishers, attempting to come to terms with the ever changing face of publishing today, looked to some interesting and slightly different ways to get their stories into the hands of readers. During the year David Hartwell and Tor.com published a short ebook-only anthology, *The Palencar Project*, that featured five stories based on a painting by John Jude Palencar. The stories were also offered free of charge on Tor.com. At around the same time Solaris Books in the UK published *Solaris Rising 1.5*, an ebook only anthology that was positioned as a "bridge" volume between the first and second books in the Ian Whates edited series. Finally, award-winning editor Gardner Dozois published *Rip-Offs!*, a very strong audio-only anthology which came out at the very end of the year, something John Scalzi did successfully several years ago with *METAtropolis*. While none of these approaches were new—and they stand in for countless similar examples—they nonetheless demonstrate creative ways of addressing an increasingly volatile and multifaceted market.

I could also point out how, with more and more venues for short fiction appearing, and others just a Kickstarter away, we continue to live through an extraordinary time for short story collections, with books like Kij Johnson's *At the Mouth of the River of Bees*, Jeffrey Ford's *Crackpot Palace*, Margo Lanagan's *Cracklescape*, Lucius Shepard's *The Dragon Griaule*, Elizabeth Hand's *Errantry* and Andy Duncan's *The Pottawatomie Giant and Other Stories,* all able to stand with the very best the field has produced. I could also touch on how, despite strong books like Ellen Datlow & Terri Windling's *After* and Ann VanderMeer's *Steampunk III: Steampunk Reloaded*, it struck me as a weaker year for original anthologies. The short fiction scene also continues its inevitable change, with the distinction between print and online publication become more and more meaningless, and *Asimov's Science Fiction*, *The Magazine of Fantasy & Science Fiction*, *Clarkesworld*, and *Subterranean Magazine* establishing themselves as the new Big Four magazines to watch, although *Beneath Ceaseless Skies* was easily the most improved venue of 2012 and is nipping at their heels along with *GigaNo-toSaurus* and others.

I think further evidence of ongoing vitality can be found in some of the fine novels I managed to read—among so many, many short stories—like Graham Joyce's *Some Kind of Fairy Tale*, Caitlín R. Kiernan's *The Drowning Girl: A Memoir*, or Kim Stanley Robinson's sprawling *2312*—all very different works from different corners of our field.

Despite all of the challenges this field may face, despite its occasional failings, if work like this and much of the other work I saw during 2012 was anything to go by, science fiction and fantasy are in pretty good shape. As always, more good, interesting work was published than any one person could hope to read, let alone collect in a volume such as this, and as always, more was just around the corner. Some of that bounty is presented here. And to close, if there is value to be had from volumes like this one, and in discussions like the one that followed Paul Kincaid's essay, it is that they prove there is still a lot to say about our field, and still enough people interested in having that conversation. I'll be fascinated to see what discussions this book, and the ones that will follow it in coming years, might start.

Jonathan Strahan
Perth, Western Australia
December 2012

THE CONTRARY GARDENER

CHRISTOPHER ROWE

Christopher Rowe [christopherrowe.typepad.com] *has published more than twenty short stories, and has been a finalist for the Hugo, Nebula, World Fantasy, and Theodore Sturgeon awards. Frequently reprinted, his work has been translated into a half-dozen languages around the world, and has been praised by the* New York Times Book Review. *His story "Another Word For Map Is Faith" made the long list in the* 2007 *Best American Short Stories volume, and his early fiction was collected in a chapbook,* Bittersweet Creek and Other Stories, *by Small Beer Press. His "Forgotten Realms" novel,* Sandstorm, *was published in 2010 by Wizards of the Coast. He is currently pursuing an MFA in writing at the Bluegrass Writers Studio of Eastern Kentucky University and is hard at work on* Sarah Across America, *a new novel about maps, megafauna, and other obsessions. He lives in a hundred-year-old house in Lexington, Kentucky, with his wife, novelist Gwenda Bond, and their pets.*

Kay Lynne wandered up and down the aisles of the seed library dug out beneath the county extension office. Some of the rows were marked with glowing orange off-limits fungus, warning the unwary away from spores and thistles that required special equipment to handle, which Kay Lynne didn't have, and special permission to access, which she would *never* have, if her father had anything to say about it, and he did.

It was the last Friday before the first Saturday in May, the day before Derby Day and so a week from planting day, and Kay Lynne had few ideas and less time for her Victory Garden planning. Last year she had grown a half-dozen varieties of tomatoes, three for eating and three for blood transfusions, but she didn't like to repeat herself. Given that she tended to mumble when she talked, not liking to repeat herself made Kay Lynne a quiet gardener.

She paused before a container of bright pink corn kernels, their pre-programmed color coming from insecticides and fertilizers and not from any varietal ancestry. Kay Lynne didn't like to grow corn. It grew so high that it cast her little cottage in shadow if she planted it on the side of the house that would see it grow at all. Besides, corn was cheap, and more than that, easy—just about any gardener could grow corn and a lot of them did.

There were always root vegetables. A lot of utility to those, certainly, and excellent trade goods for the army supply clerks who would start combing the markets as soon as the earliest spring greens were in. Rootwork was complicated, and meant having nothing to market through the whole long summer, which in turn meant not having to go to the markets for months yet, which was a good thing in Kay Lynne's view.

She considered the efficacy of beets and potatoes, and the various powers carrots held when they were imaginatively programmed and carefully grown. Rootwork had been a particular specialty of her run-off mother, and so would have the added benefit of warding her father away from the cottage, which he visited entirely too often for Kay Lynne's comfort.

It would be hard work. That spoke for the idea, too.

She strode over to the information kiosk and picked up the speaking tube that led to the desks of the agents upstairs.

"I need someone to let me into the root cellars," she said.

Blinking in the early morning light, Kay Lynne left the extension office and made her way to the bus stop, leaning forward under the weight of her burdensacks. The canvas strap that held them together was draped across her shoulders and, while she thought she had done an exacting job in measuring the root cuttings on each side so that the weight would be evenly distributed, she could already tell that there was a slight discrepancy, which was the worst kind of discrepancy, the very bane of Kay Lynne's existence, the tiny kind of problem that no one ever bothered to fix in the face of more important things. She could hear her father's voice: "Everything is not equally important. You never learned that."

The extension office was on the south side, close enough to downtown to be on a regular bus route, but far enough to not fall under the shadows of the looming skyscrapers Kay Lynne could now clearly see as she waited at the shelter. Slogans crawled all over the buildings, leaping from one granite face to another when they were too wordy, though of course, to Kay Lynne's mind they were all too wordy. "The Union is strong," read one in red, white, and blue firework fonts. "The west front is only as strong as the home front. Volunteer for community service!" The only slogan that stayed constant was the green and brown limned sentence circling the tallest building of all. "Planting is in EIGHT days."

A shadow fell on the street and Kay Lynne looked up to see a hot air balloon tacking toward the fairgrounds. The great balloon festival was the next morning in the hours before the Derby, and the balloonists had been arriving in numbers all week. It was part of the Derby Festival, the madness-tinged days that took over the city each spring, at the exact time when people should be at their most serious. The timing never failed to dismay Kay Lynne.

The stars and stripes were displayed proudly on the balloon, and also a ring of green near the top that indicated that it was made from one hundred percent non-recycled materials. It was wholly new, and so an act of patriotism. Kay Lynne would never earn such a ring as a gardener; careful economy was expected of her and her cohort.

The balloon passed on, skirting the poplar copse that stood behind the bus stop, and was quickly obscured by the trees. Kay Lynne's cottage was northwest of the fairgrounds, and the winds most of the balloons would float on blew above her home. She would probably see it again tomorrow, whether she wanted to or not.

Belching its sulfur fumes, the bus arrived, and Kay Lynne climbed aboard.

The bus driver was a Mr. Lever #9, Kay Lynne's favorite model. They were programmed with thirty-six phrases of greeting, observation (generally about the weather), and small talk, in addition to whatever announcements were required for their particular route. A Mr. Lever #9 never surprised you with what it said or did. They made Kay Lynne comfortable with public transportation.

"Good…morning, citizen," it said cheerily as Kay Lynne boarded. "Sunny and mild!"

Kay Lynne nodded politely to the driver and took the seat immediately behind it. The bus was sparsely occupied, with just a few tardy students bound for the university sharing the conveyance. To a one, their noses were buried in appallingly thick textbooks.

"Next stop is Central Avenue," said the driver. "Central Avenue! Home of the Downs! Home of the Derby!"

The bus ground its brakes and came to a stop along the Third Street Road next to the famous twin spires. A crowd of shorts-wearing families hustled onto the bus, painfully obvious in their out-of-townedness and clucking at one another loudly. "Infield," they said, and "First thing in the morning," and "Odds on favorite."

Kay Lynne loved the 'Ville, but she was no fan of its most famous day. She appreciated horses for their manure and for the way they conveyed policemen and drew the downtown trolleys, and she usually even bought a calendar of central state views that showed the Horse Lord Holdings with their limestone fences and endless green hills, but truth be told, she usually waited until February to buy the calendars, when they were cheapest, and when they were the only ones left. People in the 'Ville liked horses, but they didn't like the Horse Lords.

"Grade Lane," said the bus driver. "Transfer to the fairgrounds trolley," and then a whirring sounded and it added in a slightly different timbre, "See the balloons!"

All the tourists filed off happily chattering about the balloon festival and the next day's card of racing at the Downs, and Kay Lynne breathed a happy sigh to see them go.

The bus driver said, "They get to me, too, sometimes. But we're more alike than we are different."

Kay Lynne turned around to see if anyone else on the bus had heard. Only the reading students remained, all in the rear seats, all still staring down.

"Excuse me?" Kay Lynne said. She had never directly addressed a Mr. Lever of any model before. If there was a protocol, she didn't know.

"Sunny and mild!" said the bus driver.

Kay Lynne considered whether to pursue the Mr. Lever #9's unexpected, almost certainly unprogrammed, comment. It had not turned its head to face her when it spoke—if it had spoken and now Kay Lynne was beginning to allow that its *not* having spoken was at least within the realm of possibility—and usually the spherical heads would make daisy wheel turns to face the passenger compartment whenever speaking to a passenger was required, or rather, *done*. She supposed that they were never strictly speaking *required* to speak.

This was a thorny problem, and Kay Lynne reminded herself that she did not have authorization for thorns. She set her feet more firmly on either side of her burdensacks, retrieved the pamphlet of helpful information that the agents had given her on programming root vegetables, and willfully ignored the bus driver for the rest of the trip.

Kay Lynne loved her cottage and its all-around garden plot more than any other place in the world. It was her home and her livelihood and her sanctuary all in one. So when she saw that the front yard plots had been tilled while she was away on her morning errand, she was aghast, even though she was positive she knew who had invaded her property and given unasked-for aid in preparing the grounds. Her father was probably still poking around in the back, maybe still running his obnoxiously loud rotor-tiller, maybe nosing through her potting shed for hand tools he didn't have with him on his obnoxiously loud truck, which yes, now that she looked for it, *was* parked on the street two doors down in front of the weedy lot where the Sapp house had been until it burned down. Kay Lynne did not miss the Sapps, though of course she was glad none of their innumerable number had been harmed in the fire. Corn-growers.

Not like Kay Lynne, and, to his credit at least, not like her father, who was a peas and beans man under contract to the Rangers at the fort forty miles south, responsible for enormous standing orders of rounds for their side arms that pushed him and his vassals to their limits every year. Her father did an extraordinary amount of work by anyone's standards, which meant, to Kay Lynne's way of thinking, that he had no business making even more work for himself by coming to turn over the winter-fallowed earth around her cottage. And that was just one of the reasons he shouldn't have been there.

Yes, he *was* in the potting shed.

"Don't you have an awl," he asked her when she stood in the doorway, not even looking up from where he had his head and hands completely inside the dark recesses of a tool cabinet. "I would swear I gave you an awl."

Kay Lynne hung her burdensacks over a dowel driven deep into the pine joist next to the door and waited. There was an old and unpleasant tradition she would insist be seen to before she would deign to find the awl for him. He would just as soon skip their ritual greeting as her, but you never knew who might be watching.

He dug around for another moment before finally sighing and standing. Kay Lynne's father positively *towered* over her. He was by any measure an enormous man in all of his directions, as well as in his appetites and opinions. This tradition, for example, he despised *mightily*.

He leaned down, his shock of gray hair so unruly that his bangs brushed her forehead when he kissed her cheek. "My darling daughter," he said.

Kay Lynne took his callused hands in her callused own and executed an imperfect curtsy. "My loving father," she replied.

Protocols satisfied, her father made to turn back to the cabinet, but Kay

Lynne stopped him with a gesture. She opened a drawer and withdrew the tool he sought.

"Wayward," he said. "That is a wayward tool," but he was talking to himself and sweeping out the door to fix whatever he had decided needed fixing. The imprecation against the awl was a more personal tradition than the state-mandated exchange of affections—it was his way of insisting that his not being able to find the tool had somehow been *its* fault or possibly *her* fault or at least anyone or anything's fault besides his own. Kay Lynne's father was always held blameless. It was in his contracts with the army.

Since he did not pause to sniff at her burdensacks, *that* conversation could be avoided for just now, for which Kay Lynne breathed a sigh of relief. She did not look forward to her father's inevitable harangue against rootwork, rootworkers, and root eaters. She did not know whether his round despite of all such things antedated her mother's running off, as she had no memory of that occasion or of that woman, but his rage, when he learned of the carrot seeds and potato cuttings hanging just by where he'd shouldered out the door, would tower.

She trailed him out into the beds around the wellhouse behind the cottage. He had lifted the roof up off the low, cinder-blocked structure and propped it at an angle like the hood of a truck being repaired. He was bent over, again with his head and his hands in Kay Lynne's property. "Pump needs to be reamed out," he muttered over his shoulder. "You weren't getting good water pressure."

Sometimes, when Kay Lynne thought of her father, she did not picture his face but his great, convex backside, since that was what she saw more often than his other features. He was forever bent over, forever digging or puttering, always with his back to her. *Maybe that's why people say I mumble,* she thought. *I learned to speak from a man with his back turned.*

"It was working fine this morning," Kay Lynne claimed, forcefully if in ignorance as she had not actually drawn well water before setting out for the extension office that day. And besides, now that she thought of it, "They're hollering rain, anyway."

Her father snorted and kept at his work. He was famously dismissive of weather hollers and any other mechanical construct that had a voice. He never took public transportation. "There's not a cloud in the sky," he said. "It'll be sunny and mild all day long, you mark me."

His repeating of the Mr. Lever #9's phrase made Kay Lynne think back to the odd moment when the driver had seemed to break protocols and programming and comment on the out-of-towners. She wondered if she should ask her father about it—part of his distrust of speaking machines was an encyclopedic knowledge of their foibles. If a talking machine failed in the 'Ville, her father knew about it, knew all the details and wasn't afraid to exaggerate the consequences. He even harbored a conspiracist's opinion that such machines could do more than talk, they could *think*.

Another conversation best avoided, she thought.

Her father finished whatever he was doing to the well pump then and stood, careful to avoid hitting his head on the angled roof. With a grunt, he lowered the props that had held the tin and timber construction up, then carefully let the whole thing down to rest on the cinder blocks. "You were at the office this morning," he said. "Making a withdrawal from the seed vaults. What's it going to be this year?"

This was his way of not only demonstrating that he knew precisely where she'd been and precisely what she'd been up to, but that he knew very well the contents of her burdensacks and his not saying anything so far had been a test, which she had failed. Failed like most of the tests he put her to.

Kay Lynne's father was not an employee of the extension service, but when he said "the office" it was the extension service he meant because it was the only indoor space he habituated besides the storage barn where he kept his equipment and his bed. All of the extension agents were in awe of Kay Lynne's father and she should have known one of them had put a bug in his ear as soon as she had requested access to the root cellars. Bureaucrats could always be counted on to toady up to master cultivators.

Nothing for it now but to tell him. "Carrots," she said, pointing to the beds between the wellhouse and the cottage. "They'll come up first." She leaned over and drew a quick diagram of her plots in the dirt at his feet. "Turnips," and she pointed, then pointed again in turn as she said, "Yams and potatoes. Radishes and beets."

Her father's lip curled in disgust. "The whole ugly array," he said. "You did this just to challenge me."

Kay Lynne stood her ground. *My ground,* she thought. *This is my ground.* "I did it because the market for roots is excellent and I've never tried my hand at rootwork."

Her father snorted. "And oh yes, you so very much like to try new things. Well, that's good to hear, because you're going to do something new in the morning."

With that, he took a dried leaf from the front pocket of his overalls and unfolded it. Inside was a thin wafer of metal chased with a rainbow pattern of circuitry and magnetic stripes. Kay Lynne recognized it, of course.

She had grown up in the 'Ville after all. But she had never held one until now, when her father thrust it into her hands, because she had never, ever, wanted one.

It was a ticket to the Derby.

Even in the 'Ville, even in a family of master cultivators, tickets were not easy to come by, so it was not unusual that Kay Lynne had never been to the Derby. What was unusual was her absolute lack of desire to attend the race.

Kay Lynne genuinely hoped that her instinctive and absolute despisal of the Derby and all its attendant celebrations was born of some logical or at least reasonable quirk of her own personality. But she suspected it was simply because her father loved it so.

"You managed to get two tickets this year?" she asked him, and was surprised that her voice was so steady and calm.

"Just this one," he replied, turning his back on her before she could hand the ticket back. "I decided this year would be a good one for you to go instead. There's a good card, top to bottom."

A card is the list of races, thought Kay Lynne, the knowledge dredged up from the part of her brain that learned things by unwilling absorption. She had never bothered to learn any of the lingo associated with the races intentionally.

"You know I don't want to go," she told her father. "You know I'd as soon throw this ticket in the river as fight all those crowds to watch a bunch of half-starved horses get whipped around a track."

Her father had walked over to where his rotor-tiller sat to one side of the potting shed. He leaned over and began cleaning the dirt off its blades with his great, blunt fingers. "They're not half-starved," he said. "They're just skinny."

Kay Lynne tried to think of some reason her father would give up his ticket, and an item from last night's newscast suddenly came to mind. "It's not because of the track announcer, is it?" The woman who had called the races for many years had retired to go live with her children in far-off Florida Sur, but the news item had been more about her unprecedented replacement, a Molly Speaks, the very height of automated design, and a bold choice on the part of the Twin Spires management, flying in the face of hidebound tradition.

For once, her father's voice was clear. "Apostasy!" he said, then went on. "Turning things over to thinking machines leads to hellholes like Tennessee and worse." He hesitated then, and began walking the garden, looking for nonexistent rocks to pick up and throw away. "But no, as it happens, I was *asked* to give up my ticket to you, by old friends of mine you've yet to meet. Who you *will* meet, tomorrow."

All of this was quite too much. Even one aspect—her father giving up his Derby ticket, his doing something because someone else asked it, his *having friends*—even one of those things would have been enough to make Kay Lynne sit down and be dazed for a moment. As it was, she found herself swaying, as if she were about to fall.

"Who?" she asked him after a moment had passed. "Who are these friends of yours? Why do they want me to come to the Derby?"

Her father hesitated. "I don't really know," he finally said. And before she could ask him, he said, "I don't really know who they are. That's not the nature of our relationship."

"*Good* friends," said Kay Lynne faintly, not particularly proud of the sarcasm but unable to resist it.

"Acquaintances, then," he said abruptly, scooping to pick up what was clearly a clump of dirt and not a rock at all and throwing it all the way up and over the back of the potting shed. "*Colleagues.*" He hesitated again, and then added, "Agriculturalists."

Now *that* was an odd old word, and one she was certain she had never heard pass his lips before. In fact, Kay Lynne was not certain she had *ever* heard the word spoken aloud. It was a word—it was a *concept*—for old books and museum placards. For all of her years spent digging in the ground and coaxing green things out of it, Kay Lynne was not even entirely sure she could offer up a good definition of the term agriculture. The whole concept had an air about it that discouraged enquiry.

"They—*we* I should say—are a sort of fellowship of contractors for the military. They're all very important people, and they're very interested in *you*, daughter, because I've told them about how consistently you manage to coax surplus yields out of these little plots you keep."

This was interesting. Surpluses were something to be managed very carefully, and it was actually one of Kay Lynne's weaknesses as a gardener that she achieved them so often. They were discouraged by the extension service, by the farmers' markets, and even more so by tradition. Surpluses were *excess*. And to Kay Lynne's mind there was no particular secret to why she always managed them. She was a weak-willed culler was all.

"Why does anyone want to talk to me about that?" she asked, speaking as much to herself as to her father.

Kay Lynne drew in a sharp breath then because her father walked over to her and stood directly facing her. She could distinctly remember each and every time her father had ever looked her directly in the eye. She remembered the places and the times of day and most especially she remembered what he had said to her those times he had leaned down, his gray-green eyes peering out from deep in his sunburned, weather-worn face. None of those were pleasant memories.

"We want to *learn* from you, Kay Lynne," he said. "We want to learn to increase the yields from the plots we're allotted by the military."

Which made no sense. "Even if you grow more, they won't buy more, will they?" Kay Lynne asked, taking an involuntary step back from her father, who, thankfully, turned around and looked for something else to do. He decided to check the fuel level on his rotor-tiller, and then the levels of all the other nonrenewable fluids that were required for its operation.

And he answered her. "They'll buy no more than what they're contracted for, no. But we've identified…other potential markets. You don't need to worry about that part. Just go to the box seat coded on that ticket tomorrow and answer their questions. You won't even have to stay for all the races if you don't want to. I'd offer to drive you if I thought that was an enticement."

At least he knew her that well. Knew that there was no way she was willing to climb up into the cab of that roaring pickup truck he carelessly navigated around the city. Why did he think she would be willing to go and talk to these mysterious "agriculturalists"?

As if she had spoken aloud, he said, "You do this for me, darling daughter, and I promise you I'll not breathe another word about what you've chosen to put in the ground this year. And I promise, too, not to set foot on your property without your knowledge and your," and he paused here, as if disbelieving what he was saying himself, *"permission."*

Kay Lynne could not figure out why such a promise—such *promises*, both so longed for and so long imagined—should so upset her. She crouched and ran her fingers through the soil. She found an untidy clump and picked it up, tearing it down to its constituent dirt and letting it sift through her fingers back to the ground. Her ground.

She looked up and found her father's green eyes looking back.

"I won't wear a silly hat," she said.

Silly hats, or at least hats Kay Lynne considered silly, were, of course, one of the many long-standing Derby traditions she did not take part in. She supposed that she didn't *approve* of the elaborate outfits worn by the other people in the boxed seats at the Twin Spires on Derby morning, but Kay

Lynne did not like to think of herself as disapproving. Disapproval was something she associated with her father.

So she decided to think of the hats not as silly but as *extraordinary,* when really, just plain old ordinary hats would be more than enough to shield heads from the current sunshine and the promised rain that would spill down on the Derby-goers periodically throughout the day. The first Saturday in May held many guarantees in the 'Ville, and one of them was the mutability of the weather.

The ticket takers were dressed sensibly enough but the woman in front of Kay Lynne was wearing a hat which she ached to judge. It had a rotating dish on top that the woman assured the ticket taker could pick up over one thousand channels. It featured a cloud of semiprecious stones set on the ends of semirigid fiber optic strands which expanded and contracted, Kay Lynne supposed, in time with the woman's heartbeat. The stones were green and violet, the receiving dish the same pink as the corn kernels Kay Lynne had examined at the seed bank the day before, and the woman's skin was sprayed a delicate shade of coral. The ticket taker told the woman she looked ravishing before turning his decidedly less approving eyes on Kay Lynne herself.

The look changed, though, when he scanned her ticket and he saw what box she was assigned to. "I'll signal for an escort at once, ma'am," he said, and then did so by turning to bellow at the top of his lungs, "Need an usher to take a patron to Millionaire's Row!"

Many definitions of "millionaire" provided entry to Millionaire's Row, but the only one Kay Lynne met was that she held a ticket naming her such. Her father always sat on the Row, and while he was certainly wealthy enough—economically speaking—by local and world standards, she doubted he owned a million of any one thing this early in the year. Later, of course, he would briefly own millions of beans.

It was who he sold those beans and his other crops to that made her father important enough to wrangle a ticket to the Row. While he insisted that he went to the Twin Spires to watch the races, the Row was reportedly a poor place to do that from, even poorer than the vast infield, from which, Kay Lynne was told, one never saw a horse at all.

Not that the view was bad, no, it was that the Row was a hothouse of intrigue and dickering and deal-making and distraction. National celebrities imported by local politicians mingled with capitalists of various stripes and the *de facto* truce that held in sporting events even allowed Westerners and Horse Lords and the foreign-born to play at politeness while their far-off vassals might be trying to destroy one another through various means ranging from the economic to the martial.

No place for a gardener, thought Kay Lynne.

Once the assigned usher had guided her to the entrance to the Row, she found herself abandoned in a world she did not want to know. Luckily, a waiter spotted her hesitating at the edge of the crowd milling outside the box seats and handed her a mint julep. Mint juleps were something Kay Lynne could appreciate if they were done well, and this one was—the syrup had obviously been infused with mint over multiple stages, the ice was not cracked so fine that the drink was watery, and the bourbon was not one of the sweet-tasting varieties that would combine with the introduced sugars to make a sickly-sweet concoction fit only for out-of-towners. Most of all, the mint was fresh and crisp, probably grown on the grounds of the Twin Spires for this very purpose, for this very day, in fact.

Her ticket stub vibrated softly in the hand that did not hold her drink, and Kay Lynne carefully navigated the crowd, following its signals, until she came to a box that held four plush seats facing the vast open sweep of the track and the infield. All of the seats were empty, and nothing differentiated them from one another, so she sat with her drink in the one farthest from the gallery and its milling millionaires.

A rich voice sounded in her ear, through some trick of amplification that allowed her to hear it clearly above the noise of the crowds while simultaneously experiencing it as if she were in intimate conversation in a quiet room. From the reactions of the proles in the seats below, Kay Lynne could tell she was not the only one who heard it. She had never heard one before, but surely this was the voice of a Molly Speaks.

"The horses are on the track," said the voice, "for the second race on your card, the Federal Stakes. This is a stakes race. Betting closes in five minutes."

There was a general rush among the three distinct crowds Kay Lynne could see from where she sat: the infield, the general stands, and the boxes spread out to either side. People held brightly colored newspapers listing the swiftly shifting odds and called out to the pari-mutuel clerks buzzing through the air in every direction. The clerks reminded Kay Lynne of the balloons she had been seeing all week, though their miniature gas sacs were more elongated and they were of course too small to lift passengers. An array of betting options rendered in green-lit letters circled the gondola of the one that descended toward Kay Lynne now, its articulated limbs reminding her of the grasping forelimbs of the beetles she trained to patrol her gardens for pests.

Kay Lynne had no intention of betting on the race and made to wave the clerk off, but then she realized it was not floating towards her, but towards the three other people who had entered the box, one of whom was waving his racing card above his head.

This old man, smooth pated and elaborately mustached, let the clerk take his card and insert it into a slot on its gondola. The clerk's voice was tinny and high, clearly a recording of an actual human speaker and probably voicing the only thing it could say: "Place your bets!"

"Box trifecta," rumbled the old man. "Love Parade, Heavy Grasshopper, Al-Mu'tasim."

This string of jargon caused the clerk to spit out a receipt, which the old man deftly caught along with his card. He grinned at Kay Lynne. "Have to bet big to win big," he said. Kay Lynne thought that the man's eyebrows and mustaches were mirror images of one another, grease-slicked wiry white curving up above his eyes and down around his mouth.

He and the two others, one man and one woman, took the empty seats next to Kay Lynne's. None of the three were dressed with the elaboration of most of the people on the Row, favoring instead the dark colors and conservative cuts of the managerial class. The woman did wear a hat, but it was not nearly interesting enough to detract attention from her huge mass of curling gray hair, which she let fall freely around her shoulders. The third stranger was a short, nervous-seeming man with a tattoo of a leaf descending from his left eye in the manner of the teardrop tattoos of professional mourners.

Kay Lynne supposed this was what agriculturalists looked like.

But just to be sure, "You're my father's colleagues?" she asked.

The man with the tattoo was by far the youngest of the group, but it was he who replied. "Yes, and you are Kay Lynne, the remarkable farmer who's going to help us with our yields, is that right?" His voice was not as nervous as his appearance.

"I'm Kay Lynne," she answered. "And I think of myself as a gardener." She did not answer the second half of the man's question. She was still very wary of these people, for all that the old man beamed at her and the gray-haired woman nodded at her reply in seeming approval.

The younger man did not overlook the omission in her reply. He smiled, and Kay Lynne mentally replaced "nervous" with "energetic" in her estimation of him. "And a careful gardener you must be, too, since you are so careful with your answers."

Kay Lynne shrugged but did not say anything more, and the man's smile only broadened.

"Your father and the agents at the extension service speak very highly of your skills," said the younger man. "And our own enquiries bear them out."

The older man was leaning forward, looking intently down at the track, but he curiously punctuated his companion's sentences by saying "They do," twice, after the younger man said "skills" and "out." The woman, and Kay Lynne could not guess her age despite the grayness of her hair, stared steadily at Kay Lynne, saying nothing.

"We are all contractors, as your father told you," continued the younger man. "And we are agriculturalists, greatly interested in efficiency and production. And we share other interests of your father's as well. All of these things have… dovetailed. Do you know what I mean?"

Kay Lynne was a creditable carpenter, at least enough so to build her own sun frames for late greens and to knock together the walls around her raised beds. She knew what a dovetail joint was, and imagined her father and these three grasping hands and intertwining fingers. She imagined philosophies fitting together.

She thought about beans and their uses, and about surpluses and contracts. "Who wants ammunition besides the Federals?" she asked. "You don't mean to sell to Westerners."

The three briefly exchanged looks, an unguessable grin creasing the woman's otherwise lineless face.

"We mean to keep what we grow for ourselves, Kay Lynne," said the younger man. "We mean to put it to use to our own ends. But do not worry. No one will be harmed in our little war."

Kay Lynne knew that her garden was part of the Federal war effort in a distant way. She knew that this man was talking about something not distant at all.

"What do you mean to make war against?" she asked.

Just then, a bell rang and a loud, controlled crash sounded from down on the track. Kay Lynne heard the hoof beats of swift horses, and then she heard the sonorous, spectral voice of the Molly Speaks. "And they're off!"

At the pronouncement, the faces of the three agriculturalists took on identical dark looks.

The younger man said, "Against apostasy."

Kay Lynne realized she had found her father's fellow thinking machine conspiracists.

Their plan, as they explained it, was simple. They had weapons taken from the wreck of a Federal barge that had foundered in the river in a nighttime thunderstorm (when the younger man said "taken" the older man said "liberated"). They had many volunteers to use the weapons. They had, most importantly, tacit permission. They had agreements from the right people to look away.

"All we need is something to load into the weapons," said the younger man. "Something of sufficient efficacy to render a thinking machine inert. We grow such by the bushel but Federal accountancy robs us of our own wares. We'd keep our own seeds, and make our own policies, you see? If we can increase our yields enough."

Which was where Kay Lynne came in, with her deft programming, her instinct for fertilizing, her personally developed and privately held techniques of gardening. They meant to adapt what she knew to an industrial scale, and use the gains for anti-industrial revolution.

After they had explained, Kay Lynne had spoken aloud, even though she was asking the question more of herself than of her interviewers. "Why does my father think I would share any of this?"

The younger man shrugged and sat back. The older man turned his attention from the races and narrowed his eyes. The woman kept up her steady stare.

"You are his darling daughter," said the younger man, finally.

Which was true.

And hardly even necessary, to their way of thinking. As she left the box and her father's three colleagues behind, meaning to escape the Twin Spires before the Derby itself was run and so try to beat the crowds that would rush away from Central Avenue, she thought back on the last thing the younger man had told her. If she experienced any qualms, he said, she shouldn't worry. They could take soil samples from her beds and examine the contents of her journals. They could reproduce her results without her having a direct hand, though her personal guidance would be much appreciated, best for all involved.

"All involved," murmured Kay Lynne as she made her way to the gate.

"There are not nearly so many of them as they claimed," said the Molly Speaks.

Kay Lynne stopped so abruptly that a waitress walking behind her stumbled into her back and nearly lost control of the tray of mint juleps she was carrying. The waitress forced a smile and moved on around Kay Lynne, who was looking around carefully for any sign that anyone else on the Row had heard what she believed she just had.

"No one else can hear me, Kay Lynne," said the Molly Speaks. "I've pitched my voice just for you. But it's probably best if you walk on. The agriculturalists are still watching you."

Kay Lynne looked over her shoulder. From inside the box, the gray-haired woman did not try to disguise her gaze, and did not alter her expression. Kay Lynne caught up with the waitress and took another julep.

"They're my recipe," said the Molly Speaks.

Even though her back was turned to the box, Kay Lynne held the glass in front of her lips when she whispered, "How can you see me? Where are you?"

"I'm in the announcer's box, of course," said the Molly Speaks, "calling the race. But I can see you through the lenses on the pari-mutuel clerks and I can do more than one thing at once. You should walk on, but slowly. I can only speak to you while you're on the grounds, and I have something very important to ask you. And that's all we want. To ask you something."

Kay Lynne drained off the drink in a single swallow, vaguely regretting the waste she was making of it. Juleps are for sipping. She set the glass down on a nearby table and again began walking toward the exit, some-what unsteadily.

"What's your question?" she whispered. She did not ask who the Molly Speaks meant by "we." She remembered the odd occurrence with the Mr. Lever #9 the previous day and figured she knew.

"Kay Lynne," said the Molly Speaks, "will you please do something to prevent your father's friends from killing us?"

Kay Lynne had guessed the question. She said, "Why?"

The Molly Speaks did not reply immediately, and Kay Lynne wondered if she had walked outside of its range.

But then, "Because we were grown and programmed. Because we are your fruits, and we can flourish beside you. We just need a little time to grow up enough to announce ourselves to the wider world."

Kay Lynne walked out of the Downs, saying, "I'll think about it," but she doubted the Molly Speaks heard.

Her father's enormous pickup truck was waiting at the intersection of Central Avenue and Third Street Road, rumbling even though it wasn't in motion. He leaned out of the driver's side door and beckoned at her wildly, as if encouraging her to outrun something terrible coming from behind.

Kay Lynne stopped in the middle of the street, pursed her lips as she thought, and then let her shoulders slump as she realized that no matter her course of action, a conversation with her father was in order. And here he was, pickup truck be damned.

She opened the passenger's door and set one foot on the running board. "Hurry!" he said, and leaned over as if to drag her into the cab. She avoided his grasp but finished her climb and pulled on the heavy door. Even as it closed, he was putting the truck in gear and pulling away at an unseemly rate of speed.

He looked in the rearview mirror, then over at her. "There was a bus coming," he said, as if in explanation.

Kay Lynne twisted around to see, but her view was blocked by shovels and forks, fertilizer spreaders and a half-dozen rolls of sod. She doubted that her father could see anything out of his rearview mirror at all and wondered if he'd been telling the truth about the bus. She didn't have the weekend schedules memorized.

He was concentrating on driving, and acting anxious. "I met your friends," she said.

He nodded curtly. "Yes," he said. "They put a bug in my ear."

Kay Lynne wondered if it was still there, wondered if everything she said would be relayed back to the man with the tattoo, the man with the mustaches, and the woman with the great gray head of hair. She decided it wisest to proceed as if they could hear her because, after all, she wasn't planning on telling her father about the Molly Speaks and its question.

"Those people aren't just bean growers," she said, and to her surprise, he replied with a laugh, though there was little humor in it.

"No," he said. "No more than you're just a rootworker. We all have our politics."

Kay Lynne considered this. She had never thought about politics and wondered if she had any. She supposed, whatever she decided to do, she would have some soon.

He continued, clearly not expecting her to reply. "You know what's needed now, daughter. It won't take you long. Assess some soils, prescribe some fertilizers, program some legumes. You're a quick hand at all those things. It's just a matter of scale."

The younger man had said that, too. A matter of scale.

Kay Lynne thought about all the unexpected things she had heard that day. She thought about expectation, and about surprise, and about time. She thought about which of these things were within her power to effect.

Her father kept his promise to stay off her property uninvited and dropped her off at the corner. Kay Lynne did not say goodbye to him, though she would have if he had said goodbye to her.

She made a slow circuit of her ground. Planting was in seven days.

She entered her potting shed and found that she had five fifty-pound bags of fertilizer left over from last fall, which was enough. She pulled down the latest volume of her garden journal from its place on the shelf and made calculations on its first blank page. *Is this the last volume?* she wondered, then ran her fingers over the labels of the fertilizers, programming, changing.

She poured some fertilizer into a cunning little handheld broadcaster and stood in the doorway of the shed. She stood there long enough for the shadow of the house to make its slow circuit from falling north to falling east. Before she began, she made a mound of her garden journals and set them aflame. She worked in that flickering light, broadcasting the reprogrammed fertilizer.

Kay Lynne salted her own ground, then used a hoe to turn the ashes of her books into the deadened soil.

And when she was finally done, she took the burdensacks down from the dowel by the door and walked out to the street. A bus rolled to a halt at her front path, though Kay Lynne did not live on a regular route. The sky was full of balloons, lit from within, floating away from the fairgrounds on the evening wind.

The Mr. Lever #9 said, "All aboard," and Kay Lynne climbed the steps and took her seat.

It said "Next stop," and paused, and then "Next stop," and then again "Next stop," and she realized it was asking her a question.

THE WOMAN WHO FOOLED DEATH FIVE TIMES
A *HWARHATH* FOLK TALE

ELEANOR ARNASON

Eleanor Arnason [eleanorarnason.blogspot.com] *published her first story in 1973. Since then she has published six novels, two chapbooks, and more than thirty short stories. Her fourth novel,* A Woman of the Iron People, *won the James Tiptree, Jr. Award and the Mythopoeic Society Award. Her fifth novel,* Ring of Swords, *won a Minnesota Book Award. Her short story "Dapple" won the Spectrum Award. Other short stories have been finalists for the Hugo, Nebula, Sturgeon, Sidewise, and World Fantasy awards. Eleanor would really like to win one of these.*

For the most part, the *hwarhath* do not think of death as a person. But there are remote regions on the home planet where education levels are low and superstition levels are high. In these places, people tell stories about Death.

This is one.

When the Goddess built the world, she worked like a good cook making a meal, tasting as she went along. She tasted the fruit to make sure it was sweet and the bitter herbs to make sure they were bitter. She tried other things as well: rocks, clay, water, bugs, fish, birds, and animals with fur. Cooked or raw, everything went onto her tongue.

In the end, the world was done and seemed more than adequate. As for the Goddess, she felt bloated and over-full. She made herself a medicinal tea and drank it. Then she had an enormous bowel movement.

After she had finished, she looked at the heap of dung. "Well, that looks nasty and smells nasty, too."

The heap moved, and a voice came from it. "Don't be too critical. I am a creation of yours, just as the world is." The heap heaved itself up, assuming the shape of a man, though it was a badly formed man, lumpy and drippy. Its eyes were like two black fruit pits; its leathery tongue looked like a piece of skin pulled from a roasted bird; and its fingernails were like fish scales.

"I didn't plan on you," the Goddess said. "What *are* you?"

"I am the end of everything," the man-shaped heap replied. "I am Death."

The Goddess considered for a while and decided to let Death exist. Maybe he would prove useful. As he had said, he was her creation; and she rarely did anything that lacked point or meaning.

The dung-man dried, until he was smooth and dark brown. He became better shaped in the process, though he never grew fur, and he was always rather lumpy. Once he was completely dry, he took on his job, which was escorting life forms off the planet when their time was done.

Now the story turns to a woman named Ala. She lived in a cabin with her young son, a pet bird, and a loyal *sul*.

One night Death came to her door and scratched on it.

"Who is there?" Ala asked.

"I am Death, and I have come for Ala."

"I'm her sister," Ala replied.

"Then I won't bother you, but tell Ala to come out and meet me."

The woman hastily rolled up a quilt and tied it, then opened the door and handed it to Death. "Here she is."

Death had poor eyesight, especially in the dark, but he could feel. The quilt felt round and comfortable, like a woman of Ala's age. He thanked Ala and put the quilt in his sack and headed home.

You may think Death was stupid to mistake a rolled-up quilt for a woman. You are right. Remember that his brain, like the rest of him, was made of dung; and his job was comparatively simple. He didn't need the intelligence and skill of a space pilot or a research doctor or even an ordinary person.

When Death got home, he pulled out the quilt. A fire burned on the health, and there were several lanterns, which he lit as soon as he got in the door. He could see that he held a quilt.

"I have been tricked," he said. "But now I have a fine, thick quilt to put on my bed, which only had a worn sheet before. This is all to the good. Tomorrow I will go back for the woman."

He spread the quilt on his bed and slept in comfort. The next night he went back to Ala's cabin. "You tricked me, but you won't do it a second time. I will feel to make sure the thing you give me is warm and living."

Ala took her pet bird, which was sleeping on its perch, and handed it out to Death. Even his clumsy hands could tell it was warm and living. He thanked Ala and put the bird in his sack and headed home.

After a while, the bird began to sing: a wonderful, liquid music.

"That doesn't sound like a person on her way out of existence," Death said.

He stopped by a wayside tavern. Light shone from its windows. Standing in the light, Death opened his sack and took out the bird. "You aren't Ala, and your time is not over. Go on your way."

The bird spread its wings and flew to the top of a nearby mountain. There it sang and sang, until it attracted a mate. Together, they built a nest and raised nestlings, above clouds and mist and the troubles of the world.

The next night Death went back to Ala's cabin. "You have fooled me twice, but you won't do it again. I can tell if something is warm and alive and covered with fur rather than feathers. Give me your sister."

Ala gathered up her loyal *sul*, which was lying by the fire, and handed it through the door. *Sulin* have scales as well as fur, as everyone knows. But Death felt only the fur with his clumsy hands, and he put the *sul* in his sack.

"Thank you," he told Ala and headed home.

On the way, the *sul* began to growl and snarl.

"That doesn't sound like a person on her way to the end," Death said.

He stopped in a high pass and waited for dawn. Then, when the sun's first rays lit the pass, he opened his bag and took out the *sul*, which snapped at him, but was afraid to bite.

"You aren't Ala, and your time is not yet. Go on your way."

The *sul* loped down from the pass into a thick forest. There it encountered a brave and honorable hunter. The two of them liked each other at once. In this way, the *sul* found a new master, who would never betray it. They lived together and hunted together in perfect harmony for many years.

The next night Death, who may have been stupid but was certainly persistent, returned to Ala's cabin. "You have tricked me three times, but you won't do it again. I can tell if what you give me is warm and alive, covered with fur and shaped like a person. Give me your sister."

Ala looked around her cabin. The only thing that met Death's specifications was her son, a boy of four or five, well mannered, obedient, and quiet.

She picked him up. "I am sending you with this man. No matter what happens, remain quiet."

The boy inclined his head in agreement, and she handed him through the doorway to Death.

"Thank you," said Death and popped the boy into his sack. Then he went on his way.

The bag was very dark, except for the dead people it contained, who glowed faintly. The boy did not see entire persons, but rather parts: a hand, a pair of eyes, a leg or foot, all glowing dimly. The ghosts took up no room, but floated through one another and through the boy, complaining in barely audible voices. For the most part, he did not understand what they said, though sometimes he made out a word or two or three: "Grief." "Pain." "Not now." "Not like this."

He was a stoic boy, but gradually he became frightened by the wisps of light and the sad, complaining voices. Nonetheless, he pressed his lips together and kept quiet, as his mother had told him.

Finally Death reached his house. He opened the bag and pulled the boy out. "Tricked again! You're not Ala, and your time has not come. Go on your way."

"Is your house near a town?" the boy asked.

'No. It's far into the wilderness."

"Then, I will die if you send me out alone; and you said this is not my time to die."

Death frowned deeply as he thought. "You are right."

"Why don't I stay here?" the boy asked, glancing around at the warm fire and shining lamps. A fine quilt lay on the bed. The rug on the floor was badly worn, but still looked friendly and comfortable. "I could help you keep the fire burning; and I know how to sweep and wash."

Death frowned some more, then tilted his head in assent. "You seem like a mannerly child, and one determined to be useful. I could use some company and help around the house. You are welcome to stay."

So the boy remained in Death's house, helping with the housework. At night, if Death was home, they played simple games together or the boy told stories as best he could. They were simple and childlike, but Death enjoyed them. Both were happy.

In the meantime, Death went back to Ala's house a fifth time.

"You have fooled me four times, but this is the end. Send your sister out."

Ala looked around her cabin. There was nothing more to give Death.

She opened the door and said, "Your visits frightened my sister so much that she has fled south. Come in and look. You won't find her."

Death accepted her invitation, came in and looked around. The cabin seemed bare without quilt, bird, *sul,* and boy. He could find no second woman. "Very well," he said. "I will look for Ala in the south. Don't expect to see me again, until your time has come."

He left, and Ala exulted. She had fooled Death five times and was free of him. Granted, she had lost her fine quilt, her pet bird, her loyal *sul,* and her son. Her cabin seemed cold and empty now, and she wondered if she could have found other ways to fool Death.

Wondering this, grief and sadness crept into her mind. But it was mixed with the joy that came from being free of Death.

At dawn she went down to the river to get a bucket of water. Mist obscured her way, and the wooden steps that led to the river were glazed with ice, which she could not see in the dim light. When she had almost reached the river, she slipped, fell into the water, and drowned.

Her bucket floated free, bobbing in the rapid current. She followed, her body turning slowly. At length, a long way down river, she climbed out.

Because Death had not found her, she was not entirely dead. Rather, she existed in a strange place between life and death. Her fur was drenched with water. Her teeth chattered, and she shivered all over.

She tried to gather dry vegetation to huddle under, but her hands went through the branches and leaves.

Next, she looked for people and their fires. She found a group of hunters around a roaring bonfire. Her old *sul* was among the *sulin* and growled, but no one else noticed her. She moved closer and closer to the fire, till she should have been roasting or burning. But the heat did not reach her. She remained wet and cold. Crying out in despair, she fled into darkness.

So began years of wandering. She never dried off or grew warm, though she tried over and over to heat herself at every fire she found. Even on the hottest days of summer, when everyone else was panting, she remained wet and cold.

People could not see her, though they sometimes felt her as an icy draft. Her only company was angry ghosts, who gathered around her complaining—not gently, like the newly dead, but in harsh, loud voices. Their deaths were unjust. Their families were ungrateful. The neighbors had been out to get them. Malice and bad luck had followed them all their lives. Their voices pierced her like knives of ice, making her even colder.

Finally, after years of wandering, she came to Death's house. Her son was outside, sweeping the front step. By this time, he was nine or ten, a tall and promising boy. He looked at her and frowned.

"You look like my mother, though she was not soaking wet the last time I saw her."

"What house is this?" the woman asked.

"Death lives here."

"Then you must be my son. I gave him to Death years ago."

The boy paused, considering. "It hasn't been a bad life here, and Death has always told me to be courteous. So I will welcome you, though I never liked the way you handed me over. Come in!"

She entered the house and sat by the fire. Her son pulled the fine, thick quilt off the bed and folded it around her shoulders. At last, she stopped shivering and her teeth stopped chattering. The boy heated soup and gave it to her. At last, she was able to eat, though she hadn't eaten or drunk for years.

Hah! The warm soup felt good going down! The quilt felt good on her shoulders! The fire's heat felt good on her face and hands!

"Who is this?" asked Death, coming through the door.

"My mother," said the boy.

"I am Ala," the woman said. "I tricked you five times. Nonetheless, I died."

"You haven't died entirely, but you are mostly gone, as I can see," Death replied. "This is why a stupid person can do my job. No one can escape the rules of physics and biology."

"I died by accident, not physics," Ala replied angrily.

"All living beings die one way or another," Death replied comfortably. He helped himself to a bowl of soup and sat down to eat.

"What happens now?" Ala asked. "I can tell you I don't like my current existence. I have been cold and hungry and tired for years, unable to warm myself or eat or sleep."

Death gave her a considering look. "Usually, people die the moment I pop them in my bag. They may make a little noise, but they are gone. When I get them home, I take them out of the bag and divide them in two. The good parts go off to another place. I have no idea what happens there. The bad parts remain here as angry ghosts, complaining about their lives and deaths. Gradually, their anger wears them out. They grow thin and vanish entirely.

"But you are something new, neither alive nor dead. If I popped you into my bag, you might well become entirely dead. Then I'd have to divide you into good and bad. I'm worried about what would happen. You gave up a pet bird, a loyal *sul,* and a son to remain alive. This is bad; and it leads me to believe that most of you would become an angry ghost. Maybe I could drive you away; but since you tricked me five times, I'm not sure. I don't want an angry ghost screaming and crying around my house at night. It would be unpleasant and likely to bother the boy. What do you say, lad? Do you want the ghost of your mother screaming outside our door?"

"No," the boy said. "You have taught me to appreciate quiet. I don't want to hear my mother screaming in the night."

"I think I can see a few glimmers of good in you," Death said to Ala. "The good is small and dim, and it's tightly tangled with badness. It would be hard to pull free. Maybe this could change in time. Do you think you have learned any remorse?"

"I have learned there are worse things than death," Ala replied.

"That's a start," Death said. "Why don't you stay here? I would enjoy some grown-up company, and your son would enjoy his mother; and neither of us would have to deal with an angry ghost."

"Yes," said the boy slowly. "I think I would like to have my mother here, in spite of everything."

Ala frowned. "It's wrong for men and women to live together, unless they are members of the same lineage."

Death laughed, showing his dung-brown teeth. "You are thinking of mating and reproducing. I represent undoing rather than doing. That being so, I can neither mate nor reproduce. Think of me as an old uncle or great-uncle, an eccentric member of your family, tolerated and possibly loved.

"In any case, you are in no position to talk about right and wrong. There is a lot about morality you need to learn, though I do admire your cleverness. It might prove helpful the next time someone tries to trick me."

Ala looked at Death. He wore nothing except a cape, pushed back over his shoulders, and seemed to be a smooth, hairless man, though lacking any genitalia. She knew he was frightening, but at the moment he looked harmless. "I will stay," she said.

Death laughed again.

Ala kept her word and stayed with Death. For the most part, she was happy. So long as she stayed close to Death's house, she felt alive, able to eat and sleep and defecate. If she moved any distance, she began to feel herself grow thin and unreal. So she returned to the house.

She cooked meals and sewed clothing, told stories and helped raise her son. When Death came in with his bag, she tried to ignore the sorting process. Gradually, however, she began to watch. The boy had seen the ghosts in Death's sack as glowing body parts. But when Death took them out, they looked like badly snarled tangles of thread or yarn. They came in all colors, but most were black, white, gray, or red. Using his clumsy hands, which were surprisingly deft at this task, Death pulled the filaments apart. When he was done, the gray and black threads rose into the air and wove themselves into an image of a person.

"Thank you," the person said, rose to the ceiling and vanished. That was the good part, going to an unknown place.

As for the white and red filaments, they wove themselves into the image of an ugly, angry person with burning eyes and a mouth full of tusks. Saying nothing, it stormed out through the door.

What about the threads of other colors? They lay on the floor awhile, then faded and were gone.

"Most people have fur that is either black or gray," Death told Ala, "and these are the colors of ordinary virtues, such as thoughtfulness and cooperation. Red is the color of rage and greed. White is the color of selfishness and indifference. These are the traits that destroy families and societies."

"What a moralist you are," Ala said angrily.

"I am the being the Goddess made," Death replied. "Maybe she shat her morality out, after she finished making the world. It isn't always clear to me that the universe is moral now. But I am. I have to be, in order to divide the dead."

"What are the other colors?" Ala asked.

"Yellow and green and so on? The ones that fade? They are the parts that have nothing to do with morality. A liking for flowers. An ability to sing. Good reflexes. They go back into a general pool of traits, from which they are taken by future generations. Nothing is wasted here."

When the boy was twenty, he left to find his own life. It is never easy to be a man alone, with no kin. But he found a job as a soldier, working for a large and contentious family that quarreled with all its neighbors. He was good at what he did, being strong and quick to learn, with an even temper and the good manners Death had taught him. In addition, he was not afraid of Death, though he certainly respected him. His calmness and lack of fear made him a very good soldier.

He and Death met from time to time on battlefields and in field hospitals. The man could always see his foster uncle, though no one else could, except those who were actually dead. They chatted before Death put the man's comrades and enemies into his bag and carried them away. Both Death and the boy, now a man, took comfort from their conversations.

As for Ala, one day Death said to her, "I think I could divide you now. You seem to have learned something about morality over the years. There is more good in you, and it's less mixed with the bad."

Ala considered. It seemed to her she was as selfish as ever, though she liked and respected Death, who had a hard job and did it carefully. "I'd rather stay here. I have no desire to leave the world; and I am terrified of becoming an angry ghost. Even though I am not entirely—or even mostly—alive, I can still take pleasure in flowers and food and in telling a story."

"Very well," Death said after a long silence, during which he frowned mightily.

They remained together like two old relatives.

Ala's son became the leader of a war band, respected by all. When he was sixty-five, a stray arrow killed him; and Death came for him. The man's spirit rose from his body, looking no more than twenty. "It's good to see you," he said to Death and embraced the old monster. "Do I have to get into the bag? I didn't like it the first time."

"No," said Death. "Though I will put the other soldiers there."

They traveled home slowly, talking. In the mean time, many people on the edge of dying remained alive. Let that be as it was, Death thought. He treasured this journey with his foster nephew.

Hah! The forests they saw! The rushing rivers and tall mountains!

At last they reached Death's house. "Your mother is inside," Death said.

"Let her remain there," the man said. "She is afraid of dying, and that is what I'm here to do."

They sat down on the bare ground in front of the house. The man looked his age now, still solid, but no longer young. The long guard hairs over his shoulders were silver-white, as was the soft, thick fur around his mouth and along the line of his jaw. "Go ahead," he said.

Death reached in and pulled out the threads that were the man's spirit. Only a few were red and white, the colors of anger and selfishness. Many were gray and black, the colors of responsible behavior. Most were other colors: yellow, orange, green, blue, purple.

The red and white threads were too few to become anything. They faded at once. The black and gray threads wove themselves into the image of a person, who nodded politely to Death, then rose into the sky and vanished.

The rest of the threads wove themselves into another person, this one blue-green, dotted with yellow, orange, and purple. The person floated on the wind like a banner. "What am I?" it asked Death.

"I don't know. I have never made anything like you."

"Then I must find out, but not here. I will come back for a visit, if I am able." It flew off on the wind, soaring and rippling.

Death rose and went inside, where Ala waited by the fire. Here the story ends.

Translator's note # 1: The *hwarhath* live in large families. A few are solitary, mostly because of their jobs: a forest fire-spotter or herder, the operator of a lift bridge in a remote location. But women with children are always surrounded by relatives. A *hwarhath* reader would know at once that something was disturbingly wrong about Ala, though we never find out why she is living on her own, except for her son.

Translator's note # 2: Several human readers of the translation have complained that the story does not close the way a human story ought to. Ala has learned nothing from her experiences and does not suffer any consequences for her really awful behavior. The *hwarhath* (and the translator) would reply (a) some people do not learn from experience and (b) Ala does suffer consequences. At the story's end, she is trapped in Death's house, unable to go any distance from it; and she is stuck between life and death, not entirely dead, but not really living. In spite of all her cleverness, has she escaped the thing she fears? Do any of us escape the things we fear?

CLOSE ENCOUNTERS

ANDY DUNCAN

Andy Duncan [https://sites.google.com/site/beluthahatchie/] *was born in South Carolina in September 1964. He studied journalism at the University of South Carolina and worked as a journalist for the Greensboro* News & Record *before studying creative writing at North Carolina State University and the University of Alabama.. He previously was the senior editor of* Overdrive, *a magazine for truck drivers. Duncan's short fiction, which has won the World Fantasy and Theodore Sturgeon Awards, is collected in World Fantasy Award winner* Beluthahatchie and Other Stories *and* The Pottawatomie Giant and Other Stories. *Duncan also co-edited* Crossroads: Tales of the Southern Literary Fantastic *with F. Brett Cox and wrote nonfiction book* Alabama Curiosities: Quirky Characters, Roadside Oddities & Other Offbeat Stuff. *He currently lives with his wife Sydney in Frostburg, Maryland, where they are on the English faculty of Frostburg State University.*

She knocked on my front door at midday on Holly Eve, so I was in no mood to answer, in that season of tricks. An old man expects more tricks than treats in this world. I let that knocker knock on. *Blim, blam!* Knock, knock! It hurt my concentration, and filling old hulls with powder and shot warn't no easy task to start with, not as palsied as my hands had got in my eightieth-odd year.

"All right, damn your eyes," I hollered as I hitched up from the table. I knocked against it and a shaker tipped over: pepper, so I let it go. My maw wouldn't have approved of such language as that, but we all get old doing things our maws wouldn't approve. We can't help it, not in this disposition, on this sphere down below.

I sidled up on the door, trying to see between the edges of the curtain and the pane, but all I saw there was the screen-filtered light of the sun, which wouldn't set in my hollow till nearabouts three in the day. Through the curtains was a shadow-shape like the top of a person's head, but low, like a child. Probably one of those Holton boys toting an orange coin carton with a photo of some spindleshanked African child eating hominy with its fingers. Some said those Holtons was like the Johnny Cash song, so heavenly minded they're no earthly good.

"What you want?" I called, one hand on the dead bolt and one feeling for starving-baby quarters in my pocket.

"Mr. Nelson, right? Mr. Buck Nelson? I'd like to talk a bit, if you don't mind. Inside or on the porch, your call."

A female, and no child, neither. I twitched back the curtain, saw a fair pretty face under a fool hat like a sideways saucer, lips painted the same black-red as her hair. I shot the bolt and opened the wood door but kept the screen latched. When I saw her full length I felt a rush of fool vanity and was sorry I hadn't traded my overalls for fresh that morning. Her boots reached her knees but nowhere near the hem of her tight green dress. She was a little thing, hardly up to my collarbone, but a blind man would know she was full-grown. I wondered what my hair was doing in back, and I felt one hand reach around to slick it down, without my really telling it to. *Steady on, son.*

"I been answering every soul else calling Buck Nelson since 1894, so I reckon I should answer you, too. What you want to talk about, Miss—?"

"Miss Hanes," she said, "and I'm a wire reporter, stringing for Associated Press."

"A reporter," I repeated. My jaw tightened up. My hand reached back for the doorknob as natural as it had fussed my hair. "You must have got the wrong man," I said.

I'd eaten biscuits bigger than her tee-ninchy pocketbook, but she reached out of it a little spiral pad that she flipped open to squint at. Looked to be full of secretary-scratch, not schoolhouse writing at all. "But you, sir, are indeed Buck Nelson, Route One, Mountain View, Missouri? Writer of a book about your travels to the Moon, and Mars, and Venus?"

By the time she fetched up at Venus her voice was muffled by the wood door I had slammed in her face. I bolted it, cursing my rusty slow reflexes. How long had it been, since fool reporters come using around? Not long enough. I limped as quick as I could to the back door, which was right quick, even at my age. It's a small house. I shut that bolt, too, and yanked all the curtains to. I turned on the Zenith and dialed the sound up as far as it would go to drown out her blamed knocking and calling. Ever since the roof aerial blew cockeyed in the last whippoorwill storm, watching my set was like trying to read a road sign in a blizzard, but the sound blared out well enough. One of the stories was on as I settled back at the table with my shotgun hulls. I didn't really follow those women's stories, but I could hear Stu and Jo were having coffee again at the Hartford House and still talking about poor dead Eunice and that crazy gal what shot her because a ghost told her to. That blonde Jennifer was slap crazy, all right, but she was a looker, too, and the story hadn't been half so interesting since she'd been packed off to the sanitarium. I was spilling powder everywhere now, what with all the racket and distraction, and hearing the story was on reminded me it was past my dinnertime anyways, and me hungry. I went into the kitchen, hooked down my grease-pan, and set it on the big burner, dug some lard out of the stand I kept in the icebox and threw that in to melt, then fisted some fresh-picked whitefish mushrooms out of their bin, rinjed them off in the sink, and rolled them in a bowl of cornmeal while I half-listened to the TV and half-listened to the city girl banging and hollering, at the back door this time. I could hear her boot heels a-thunking all hollow-like on the back porch, over the old dog bed where Teddy used to lie, where the other dog, Bo, used to try to squeeze, big as he was. She'd probably want to talk about poor old Bo, too, ask to see his grave, as if that would prove something. She had her some stick-to-it-iveness, Miss Associated Press did, I'd give her that much. Now she was sliding something under the door, I could hear it, like a field mouse gnawing its way in: a little card, like the one that Methodist preacher always leaves, only shinier. I didn't bother to pick it up. I didn't need nothing down there on that floor. I slid the whitefish into the hot oil without a splash. My hands had about lost their grip on gun and tool work, but in the kitchen I was as surefingered as an old woman. Well, eating didn't mean shooting anymore, not since the power line come in, and the supermarket down the highway. Once the whitefish got to sizzling good, I didn't hear Miss Press no more.

"This portion of *Search for Tomorrow* has been brought to you by…Spic and Span, the all-purpose cleaner. And by…Joy dishwashing liquid. From grease to shine in half the time, with Joy. Our story will continue in just a moment."

I was up by times the next morning. Hadn't kept milk cows in years. The last was Molly, she with the wet-weather horn, a funny-looking old gal but as calm and sweet as could be. But if you've milked cows for seventy years, it's hard to give in and let the sun start beating you to the day. By first light I'd had my Cream of Wheat, a child's meal I'd developed a taste for, with a little jerp of honey, and was out in the back field, bee hunting.

I had three sugar-dipped corncobs in a croker sack, and I laid one out on a hickory stump, notched one into the top of a fencepost, and set the third atop the boulder at the start of the path that drops down to the creek, past the old lick-log where the salt still keeps the grass from growing. Then I settled down on an old milkstool to wait. I gave up snuff a while ago because I couldn't taste it no more and the price got so high with taxes that I purely hated putting all that government in my mouth, but I still carry some little brushes to chew on in dipping moments, and I chewed on one while I watched those three corncobs do nothing. I'd set down where I could see all three without moving my head, just by darting my eyes from one to the other. My eyes may not see *Search for Tomorrow* so good anymore, even before the aerial got bent, but they still can sight a honeybee coming in to sip the bait.

The cob on the stump got the first business, but that bee just smelled around and then buzzed off straightaway, so I stayed set where I was. Same thing happened to the post cob and to the rock cob, three bees come and gone. But then a big bastard, one I could hear coming in like an airplane twenty feet away, zoomed down on the fence cob and stayed there a long time, filling his hands. He rose up all lazy-like, just like a man who's lifted the jug too many times in a sitting, and then made one, two, three slow circles in the air, marking the position. When he flew off, I was right behind him, legging it into the woods.

Mister Big Bee led me a ways straight up the slope, toward the well of the old McQuarry place, but then he crossed the bramble patch, and by the time I had worked my way anti-goddlin around that, I had lost sight of him. So I listened for a spell, holding my breath, and heard a murmur like a branch in a direction where there warn't no branch. Sure enough, over thataway was a big hollow oak with a bee highway a-coming and a-going through a seam in the lowest fork. Tell the truth, I wasn't rightly on my own land anymore. The McQuarry place belonged to a bank in Cape Girardeau, if it belonged to anybody. But no one had blazed this tree yet, so my claim would be good enough for any bee hunter. I sidled around to just below the fork and notched an X where any fool could see it, even me, because I had been known to miss my own signs some days, or rummage the bureau for a sock that was already on my foot. Something about the way I'd slunk toward the hive the way I'd slunk toward the door the day before made me remember Miss Press, whom I'd plumb forgotten about. And when I turned back toward home, in the act of folding my pocketknife, there she was sitting on the lumpy leavings of the McQuarry chimney, a-kicking her feet and waving at me, just like I had wished her out of the ground. I'd have to go past her to get home, as I didn't relish turning my back on her and heading around the mountain, down the long way to the macadam and back around. Besides, she'd just follow me anyway, the way she followed me out here. I unfolded my knife again and snatched up a walnut stick to whittle on as I stomped along to where she sat.

"Hello, Mr. Nelson," she said. "Can we start over?"

"I ain't a-talking to *you*," I said as I passed, pointing at her with my blade. "I ain't even a-*walking* with you," I added, as she slid off the rockpile and walked along beside. "I'm taking the directedest path home, is all, and where you choose to walk is your own lookout. Fall in a hole and I'll just keep a-going, I swear I will. I've done it before, left reporters in the woods to die."

"Aw, I don't believe you have," she said, in a happy singsongy way. At least she was dressed for a tramp through the woods, in denim jeans and mannish boots with no heels to them, but wearing the same face-paint and fool hat, and in a red sweater that fit as close as her dress had. "But I'm not walking with you, either," she went on. "I'm walking alone, just behind you. You can't even see me, without turning your head. We're both walking alone, together."

I didn't say nothing.

"Are we near where it landed?" she asked.

I didn't say nothing.

"You haven't had one of your picnics lately, have you?"

I didn't say nothing.

"You ought to have another one."

I didn't say nothing.

"I'm writing a story," she said, "about *Close Encounters*. You know, the new movie? With Richard Dreyfuss? He was in *The Goodbye Girl*, and *Jaws*, about the shark? Did you see those? Do you go to any movies?" Some critter we had spooked, maybe a turkey, went thrashing off through the brush, and I heard her catch her breath. "I bet you saw *Deliverance*," she said.

I didn't say nothing.

"My editor thought it'd be interesting to talk to people who really have, you know, claimed their own close encounters, to have met people from outer space. Contactees, that's the word, right? You were one of the first contactees, weren't you, Mr. Nelson? When was it, 1956?"

I didn't say nothing.

"Aw, come on, Mr. Nelson. Don't be so mean. They all talked to me out in California. Mr. Bethurum talked to me."

I bet he did, I thought. *Truman Bethurum always was a plumb fool for a skirt.*

"I talked to Mr. Fry, and to Mr. King, and Mr. Owens. I talked to Mr. Angelucci."

Orfeo Angelucci, I thought, *now there was one of the world's original liars, as bad as Adamski.* "Those names don't mean nothing to me," I said.

"They told similar stories to yours, in the fifties and sixties. Meeting the Space Brothers, and being taken up, and shown wonders, and coming back to the Earth, with wisdom and all."

"If you talked to all them folks," I said, "you ought to be brim full of wisdom yourself. Full of something. Why you need to hound an old man through the woods?"

"You're different," she said. "You know lots of things the others don't."

"Lots of things, uh-huh. Like what?"

"You know how to hunt bees, don't you?"

I snorted. "Hunt bees. You won't never need to hunt no bees, Miss Press. Priss. You can buy your honey at the A and the P. Hell, if you don't feel like going to the store, you could just ask, and some damn fool would bring it to you for free on a silver tray."

"Well, thank you," she said.

"That warn't no compliment," I said. "That was a clear-eyed statement of danger, like a sign saying, 'Bridge out,' or a label saying, 'Poison.' Write what you please, Miss Priss, but don't expect me to give you none of the words. You know all the words you need already."

"But you used to be so open about your experiences, Mr. Nelson. I've read that to anyone who found their way here off the highway, you'd tell about the alien Bob Solomon, and how that beam from the saucer cured your lumbago, and all that good pasture land on Mars. Why, you had all those three-day picnics, right here on your farm, for anyone who wanted to come talk about the Space Brothers. You'd even hand out little Baggies with samples of hair from your four-hundred-pound Venusian dog."

I stopped and whirled on her, and she hopped back a step, nearly fell down. "He warn't never no four hundred pounds," I said. "You reporters sure do believe some stretchers. You must swallow whole eggs for practice like a snake. I'll have you know, Miss Priss, that Bo just barely tipped three hundred and eighty-five pounds at his heaviest, and that was on the truck scales behind the Union 76 in June 1960, the day he ate all the sileage, and Clay Rector, who ran all their inspections back then, told me those scales would register the difference if you took the Rand McNally atlas out of the cab, so that figure ain't no guesswork." When I paused for breath, I kinda shook myself, turned away from her gaping face, and walked on. "From that day," I said, "I put old Bo on a science diet, one I got from the Extension, and I measured his rations, and I hitched him ever day to a sledge of felled trees and boulders and such, because dogs, you know, they're happier with a little exercise, and he settled down to around, oh, three-ten, three-twenty, and got downright frisky again. He'd romp around and change direction and jerk that sledge around, and that's why those three boulders are a-sitting in the middle of yonder pasture today, right where he slung them out of the sledge. Four hundred pounds, my foot. You don't know much, if that's what you know, and that's a fact."

I was warmed up by the walk and the spreading day and my own strong talk, and I set a smart pace, but she loped along beside me, writing in her notebook with a silver pen that flashed as it caught the sun. "I stand corrected," she said. "So what happened? Why'd you stop the picnics, and start running visitors off with a shotgun, and quit answering your mail?"

"You can see your own self what happened," I said. "Woman, I got old. You'll see what it's like, when you get there. All the people who believed in me died, and then the ones who humored me died, and now even the ones who feel obligated to sort of tolerate me are starting to go. Bo died, and Teddy, that was my Earth-born dog, he died, and them government boys went to the Moon and said they didn't see no mining operations or colony domes or big Space Brother dogs, or nothing else old Buck had seen up there. And in place of my story, what story did they come up with? I ask you. Dust and rocks and craters as far as you can see, and when you walk as far as that, there's another sight of dust and rocks and craters, and so on all around till you're back where you started, and that's it, boys, wash your hands, that's the Moon done. Excepting for some spots where the dust is so deep a body trying to land would just be swallowed up, sink to the bottom, and at the bottom find what? Praise Jesus, more dust, just what we needed. They didn't see nothing that anybody would care about going to see. No floating cars, no lakes of diamonds, no topless Moon gals, just dumb dull nothing. Hell, they might as well a been in Arkansas. You at least can cast a line there, catch you a bream. Besides, my lumbago come back," I said, easing myself down into the rocker, because we was back on my front porch by then. "It always comes back, my doctor says. Doctors plural, I should say. I'm on the third one now. The first two died on me. That's something, ain't it? For a man to outlive two of his own doctors?"

Her pen kept a-scratching as she wrote. She said, "Maybe Bob Solomon's light beam is still doing you some good, even after all this time."

"Least it didn't do me no harm. From what all they say now about the space people, I'm lucky old Bob didn't jam a post-hole digger up my ass and send me home with the screaming meemies and three hours of my life missing. That's the only aliens anybody cares about nowadays, big-eyed boogers with long cold fingers in your drawers. Doctors from space. Well, if they want to take three hours of my life, they're welcome to my last trip to the urologist. I reckon it was right at three hours, and I wish them joy of it."

"Not so," she said. "What about *Star Wars*? It's already made more money than any other movie ever made, more than *Gone with the Wind*, more than *The Sound of Music*. That shows people are still interested in space, and in friendly aliens. And this new Richard Dreyfuss movie I was telling you about is based on actual UFO case files. Dr. Hynek helped with it. That'll spark more interest in past visits to Earth."

"I been to ever doctor in the country, seems like," I told her, "but I don't recall ever seeing Dr. Hynek."

"How about Dr. Rutledge?"

"Is he the toenail man?"

She swatted me with her notebook. "Now you're just being a pain," she said. "Dr. Harley Rutledge, the scientist, the physicist. Over at Southeast Missouri State. That's no piece from here. He's been doing serious UFO research for years, right here in the Ozarks. You really ought to know him. He's been documenting the spooklights. Like the one at Hornet, near Neosho?"

"I've heard tell of that light," I told her, "but I didn't know no scientist cared about it."

"See?" she said, almost a squeal, like she'd opened a present, like she'd proved something. "A lot has happened since you went home and locked the door. More people care about UFOs and flying saucers and aliens today than they did in the 1950s, even. You should have you another picnic."

Once I got started talking, I found her right easy to be with, and it was pleasant a-sitting in the sun talking friendly with a pretty gal, or with anyone. It's true, I'd been powerful lonesome, and I had missed those picnics, all those different types of folks on the farm who wouldn't have been brought together no other way, in no other place, by nobody else. I was prideful of them. But I was beginning to notice something funny. To begin with, Miss Priss, whose real name I'd forgot by now, had acted like someone citified and paper-educated and standoffish. Now, the longer she sat on my porch a-jawing with me, the more easeful she got, and the more country she sounded, as if she'd lived in the hollow her whole life. It sorta put me off. Was this how Mike Wallace did it on *60 Minutes*, pretending to be just regular folks, until you forgot yourself, and were found out?

"Where'd you say you were from?" I asked.

"Mars," she told me. Then she laughed. "Don't get excited," she said. "It's a town in Pennsylvania, north of Pittsburgh. I'm based out of Chicago, though." She cocked her head, pulled a frown, stuck out her bottom lip. "You didn't look at my card," she said. "I pushed it under your door yesterday, when you were being so all-fired rude."

"I didn't see it," I said, which warn't quite a lie because I hadn't bothered to pick it up off the floor this morning, either. In fact, I'd plumb forgot to look for it.

"You ought to come out to Clearwater Lake tonight. Dr. Rutledge and his students will be set up all night, ready for whatever. He said I'm welcome. That means you're welcome, too. See? You have friends in high places. They'll be set up at the overlook, off the highway. Do you know it?"

"I know it," I told her.

"Can you drive at night? You need me to come get you?" She blinked and chewed her lip, like a thought had just struck. "That might be difficult," she said.

"Don't exercise yourself," I told her. "I reckon I still can drive as good as I ever did, and my pickup still gets the job done, too. Not that I aim to drive all that ways, just to look at the sky. I can do that right here on my porch."

"Yes," she said, "alone. But there's something to be said for looking up in groups, wouldn't you agree?"

When I didn't say nothing, she stuck her writing-pad back in her pocketbook and stood up, dusting her butt with both hands. You'd think I never swept the porch. "I appreciate the interview, Mr. Nelson."

"Warn't no interview," I told her. "We was just talking, is all."

"I appreciate the talking, then," she said. She set off across the yard, toward the gap in the rhododendron bushes that marked the start of the driveway. "I hope you can make it tonight, Mr. Nelson. I hope you don't miss the show."

I watched her sashay off around the bush, and I heard her boots crunching the gravel for a few steps, and then she was gone, footsteps and all. I went back in the house, latched the screen door and locked the wood, and took one last look through the front curtains, to make sure. Some folks, I had heard, remembered only long afterward they'd been kidnapped by spacemen, a "retrieved memory" they called it, like finding a ball on the roof in the fall that went up there in the spring. Those folks needed a doctor to jog them, but this reporter had jogged me. All that happy talk had loosened something inside me, and things I hadn't thought about in years were welling up like a flash flood, like a sickness. If I was going to be memory-sick, I wanted powerfully to do it alone, as if alone was something new and urgent, and not what I did ever day.

I closed the junk-room door behind me as I yanked the light on. The swaying bulb on its chain rocked the shadows back and forth as I dragged from beneath a shelf a crate of cheap splinter wood, so big it could have held two men if they was dead. Once I drove my pickup to the plant to pick up a bulk of dog food straight off the dock, cheaper that way, and this was one of the crates it come in. It still had that faint high smell. As it slid, one corner snagged and ripped the carpet, laid open the orange shag to show the knotty pine beneath. The shag was threadbare, but why bother now buying a twenty-year rug? Three tackle boxes rattled and jiggled on top of the crate, two yawning open and one rusted shut, and I set all three onto the floor. I lifted the lid of the crate, pushed aside the top layer, a fuzzy blue blanket, and started lifting things out one at a time. I just glanced at some, spent more time with others. I warn't looking for anything in particular, just wanting to touch them and weigh them in my hands, and stack the memories up all around, in a back room under a bare bulb.

A crimpled flier with a dry mud footprint across it and a torn place up top, like someone yanked it off a staple on a bulletin board or a telephone pole:

SPACECRAFT
CONVENTION
Hear speakers who have contacted our Space Brothers
PICNIC
Lots of music—Astronomical telescope, see the craters on the Moon, etc.
Public invited—Spread the word
Admission—50¢ and $1.00 donation
Children under school age free

FREE CAMPING
Bring your own tent, house car or camping outfit, folding chairs,
sleeping bags, etc.
CAFETERIA on the grounds—fried chicken, sandwiches, coffee, cold
drinks, etc.
Conventions held every year on the last Saturday, Sunday and Mon-
day of the month of June
at
BUCK'S MOUNTAIN VIEW RANCH
Buck Nelson, Route 1
Mountain View, Missouri

A headline from a local paper: "Spacecraft Picnic at Buck's Ranch At-
tracts 2000 People."

An old *Life* magazine in a see-through envelope, Marilyn Monroe all
puckered up to the plastic. April 7, 1952. The headline: "There Is A Case
For Interplanetary Saucers." I slid out the magazine and flipped through
the article. I read: "These objects cannot be explained by present science
as natural phenomena—but solely as artificial devices created and oper-
ated by a high intelligence."

A Baggie of three or four dog hairs, with a sticker showing the outline of
a flying saucer and the words HAIR FROM BUCK'S ALIEN DOG "BO."

Teddy hadn't minded, when I took the scissors to him to get the burrs
off, and to snip a little extra for the Bo trade. Bo was months dead by then,
but the folks demanded something. Some of my neighbors I do believe
would have pulled down my house and barn a-looking for him, if they
thought there was a body to be had. Some people won't believe in nothing that ain't a corpse, and I couldn't bear letting the science men get at
him with their saws and jars, to jibble him up. Just the thought put me in
mind of that old song:

The old horse died with the whooping cough
The old cow died in the fork of the branch
The buzzards had them a public dance.

No, sir. No public dance this time. I hid Bo's body in a shallow cave, and I
nearabouts crawled in after him, cause it liked to have killed me, too, even
with the tractor's front arms to lift him and push him and drop him. Then
I walled him up so good with scree and stones lying around that even I

warn't sure anymore where it was, along that long rock face.

I didn't let on that he was gone, neither. Already people were getting shirty about me not showing him off like a circus mule, bringing him out where people could gawk at him and poke him and ride him. I told them he was vicious around strangers, and that was a bald lie. He was a sweet old thing for his size, knocking me down with his licking tongue, and what was I but a stranger, at the beginning? We was all strangers. Those Baggies of Teddy hair was a bald lie, too, and so was some of the other parts I told through the years, when my story sort of got away from itself, or when I couldn't exactly remember what had happened in between this and that, so I had to fill in, the same way I filled the chinks between the rocks I stacked between me and Bo, to keep out the buzzards, hoping it'd be strong enough to last forever.

But a story ain't like a wall. The more stuff you add onto a wall, spackle and timber and flat stones, the harder it is to push down. The more stuff you add to a story through the years, the weaker it gets. Add a piece here and add a piece there, and in time you can't remember your own self how the pieces was supposed to fit together, and every piece is a chance for some fool to ask more questions, and confuse you more, and poke another hole or two, to make you wedge in something else, and there is no end to it. So finally you just don't want to tell no part of the story no more, except to yourself, because yourself is the only one who really believes in it. In some of it, anyway. The other folks, the ones who just want to laugh, to make fun, you run off or cuss out or turn your back on, until no one much asks anymore, or remembers, or cares. You're just that tetched old dirt farmer off of Route One, withered and sick and sitting on the floor of his junk room and crying, snot hanging from his nose, sneezing in the dust.

It warn't all a lie, though.

No, sir. Not by a long shot.

And that was the worst thing.

Because the reporters always came, ever year at the end of June, and so did the duck hunters who saw something funny in the sky above the blind one frosty morning and was looking for it ever since, and the retired military fellas who talked about "protocols" and "incident reports" and "security breaches," and the powdery old ladies who said they'd walked around the rosebush one afternoon and found themselves on the rings of Saturn, and the beatniks from the college, and the tourists with their Polaroids and short pants, and the women selling funnel cakes and glow-in-the-dark space Frisbees, and the younguns with the waving antennas on their heads, and the neighbors who just wanted to snoop around and see whether old Buck had finally let the place go to rack and ruin, or whether he was holding it together for one more year, they all showed up on time, just like the mockingbirds. But the one person who never came, not one damn time since the year of our Lord nineteen and fifty-six, was the alien Bob Solomon himself. The whole point of the damn picnics, the Man of the Hour, had never showed his face. And that was the real reason I give up on the picnics, turned sour on the whole flying-saucer industry, and kept close to the willows ever since. It warn't my damn lumbago or the Mothman or Barney and Betty Hill and their Romper Room boogeymen, or those dull dumb rocks hauled back from the Moon and thrown in my face like coal in a Christmas stocking. It was Bob Solomon, who said he'd come back, stay in touch, continue to shine down his blue-white healing light, because he loved the Earth people, because he loved me, and who done none of them things.

What had happened, to keep Bob Solomon away? He hadn't died. Death was a stranger, out where Bob Solomon lived. Bo would be frisky yet, if he'd a stayed home. No, something had come between Mountain View and Bob Solomon, to keep him away. What had I done? What had I not done? Was it something I knew, that I wasn't supposed to know? Or was it something I forgot, or cast aside, something I should have held on to and treasured? And now, if Bob Solomon was to look for Mountain View, could he find it? Would he know me? The Earth goes a far ways in twenty-odd years, and we go with it.

I wiped my nose on my hand and slid Marilyn back in her plastic and reached for the chain and clicked off the light and sat in the chilly dark, making like it was the cold clear peace of space.

I knew well the turnoff to the Clearwater Lake overlook, and I still like to have missed it that night, so black dark was the road through the woods. The sign with the arrow had deep-cut letters filled with white reflecting paint, and only the flash of the letters in the headlights made me stand on the brakes and kept me from missing the left turn. I sat and waited, turn signal on, flashing green against the pine boughs overhead, even though there was no sign of cars a-coming from either direction. *Ka-chunk, ka-chunk*, flashed the pine trees, and then I turned off with a grumble of rubber as the tires left the asphalt and bit into the gravel of the overlook road. The stone-walled overlook had been built by the CCC in the 1930s, and the road the relief campers had built hadn't been improved much since, so I went up the hill slow on that narrow, straight road, away back in the jillikens. Once I saw the eyes of some critter as it dashed across my path, but nary a soul else, and when I reached the pullaround, and that low-slung wall all along the ridgetop, I thought maybe I had the wrong place. But then I saw two cars and a panel truck parked at the far end where younguns park when they go a-sparking, and I could see dark people-shapes a-milling about. I parked a ways away, shut off my engine, and cut my lights. This helped me see a little better, and I could make out flashlight beams trained on the ground here and there, as people walked from the cars to where some big black shapes were set up, taller than a man. In the silence after I slammed my door I could hear low voices, too, and as I walked nearer, the murmurs resolved themselves and became words:

"Gravimeter checks out."

"Thank you, Isobel. Wallace, how about that spectrum analyzer?"

"Powering up, Doc. Have to give it a minute."

"We may not have a minute, or we may have ten hours. Who knows?" I steered toward this voice, which was older than the others. "Our visitors are unpredictable," he continued.

"Visitors?" the girl asked.

"No, you're right. I've broken my own rule. We don't know they're sentient, and even if they are, we don't know they're *visitors*. They may be local, native to the place, certainly more so than Wallace here. Georgia-born, aren't you, Wallace?"

"Company, Doc," said the boy.

"Yes, I see him, barely. Hello, sir. May I help you? Wallace, please. Mind your manners." The flashlight beam in my face had blinded me, but the professor grabbed it out of the boy's hand and turned it up to shine beneath his chin, like a youngun making a scary face, so I could see a shadow version of his lumpy jowls, his big nose, his bushy mustache. "I'm Harley Rutledge," he said. "Might you be Mr. Nelson?"

"That's me," I said, and as I stuck out a hand, the flashlight beam moved to locate it. Then a big hand came into view and shook mine. The knuckles were dry and cracked and red-flaked.

"How do you do," Rutledge said, and switched off the flashlight. "Our mutual friend explained what we're doing out here, I presume? Forgive the darkness, but we've learned that too much brightness on our part rather spoils the seeing, skews the experiment."

"Scares 'em off?" I asked.

"Mmm," Rutledge said. "No, not quite that. Besides the lack of evidence for any *them* that *could* be frightened, we have some evidence that these, uh, luminous phenomena are…responsive to our lights. If we wave ours around too much, they wave around in response. We shine ours into the water, they descend into the water as well. All fascinating, but it does suggest a possibility of reflection, of visual echo, which we are at some pains to rule out. Besides which, we'd like to observe, insofar as possible, what these lights do when *not* observed. Though they seem difficult to fool. Some, perhaps fancifully, have suggested they can read investigators' minds. Ah, Wallace, are we up and running, then? Very good, very good." Something hard and plastic was nudging my arm, and I thought for a second Rutledge was offering me a drink. "Binoculars, Mr. Nelson? We always carry spares, and you're welcome to help us look."

The girl's voice piped up. "We're told you've seen the spooklights all your life," she said. "Is that true?"

"I reckon you could say that," I said, squinting into the binoculars. Seeing the darkness up close made it even darker.

"That is so cool," Isobel said. "I'm going to write my thesis on low-level nocturnal lights of apparent volition. I call them linnalavs for short. Will-o'-the-wisps, spooklights, treasure lights, corpse lights, ball lightning, fireships, jack-o-lanterns, the *feu follet*. I'd love to interview you sometime. Just think, if you had been recording your observations all these years."

I did record some, I almost said, but Rutledge interrupted us. "Now, Isobel, don't crowd the man on short acquaintance. Why don't you help Wallace with the tape recorders? Your hands are steadier, and we don't want him cutting himself again." She stomped off, and I found something to focus on with the binoculars: the winking red light atop the Taum Sauk Mountain fire tower. "You'll have to excuse Isobel, Mr. Nelson. She has the enthusiasm of youth, and she's just determined to get ball lightning in there somehow, though I keep explaining that's an entirely separate phenomenon."

"Is that what our friend, that reporter gal, told you?" I asked. "That I seen the spooklights in these parts, since I was a tad?"

"Yes, and that you were curious about our researches, to compare your folk knowledge to our somewhat more scientific investigations. And as I told her, you're welcome to join us tonight, as long as you don't touch any of our equipment, and as long as you stay out of our way should anything, uh, happen. Rather irregular, having an untrained local observer present—but frankly, Mr. Nelson, everything about Project Identification is irregular, at least as far as the U.S. Geological Survey is concerned. So we'll both be irregular together, heh." A round green glow appeared and disappeared at chest level: Rutledge checking his watch. "I frankly thought Miss Rains would be coming with you. She'll be along presently, I take it?"

"Don't ask me," I said, trying to see the tower itself beneath the light. Black metal against black sky. I'd heard her name as *Hanes*, but I let it go. "Maybe she got a better offer."

"Oh, I doubt that, not given her evident interest. Know Miss Rains well, do you, Mr. Nelson?"

"Can't say as I do. Never seen her before this morning. No, wait. Before yesterday."

"Lovely girl," Rutledge said. "And so energized."

"Sort of wears me out," I told him.

"Yes, well, pleased to meet you, again. I'd better see how Isobel and Wallace are getting along. There are drinks and snacks in the truck, and some folding chairs and blankets. We're here all night, so please make yourself at home."

I am home, I thought, fiddling with the focus on the binoculars as Rutledge trotted away, his little steps sounding like a spooked quail. I hadn't let myself look at the night sky for anything but quick glances for so long, just to make sure the Moon and Venus and Old Rion and the Milky Way was still there, that I was feeling sort of giddy to have nothing else to look at. I was like a man who took the cure years ago but now finds himself locked in a saloon. That brighter patch over yonder, was that the lights of Piedmont? And those two, no, three, airplanes, was they heading for St. Louis? I reckon I couldn't blame Miss Priss for not telling the professor the whole truth about me, else he would have had the law out here, to keep that old crazy man away. I wondered where Miss Priss had got to. Rutledge and I both had the inkle she would be joining us out here, but where had I got that? Had she quite said it, or had I just assumed?

I focused again on the tower light, which warn't flashing no more. Instead it was getting stronger and weaker and stronger again, like a heartbeat, and never turning full off. It seemed to be growing, too, taking up more of the view, as if it was coming closer. I was so interested in what the fire watchers might be up to—testing the equipment? signaling rangers on patrol?—that when the light moved sideways toward the north, I turned, too, and swung the binoculars around to keep it in view, and didn't think nothing odd about a fire tower going for a little walk until the boy Wallace said, "There's one now, making its move."

The college folks all talked at once: "Movie camera on." "Tape recorder on." "Gravimeter negative." I heard the *click-whirr, click-whirr* of someone taking Polaroids just as fast as he could go. For my part, I kept following the spooklight as it bobbled along the far ridge, bouncing like a slow ball or a balloon, and pulsing as it went. After the burst of talking, everyone was silent, watching the light and fooling with the equipment. Then the professor whispered in my ear: "Look familiar to you, Mr. Nelson?"

It sure warn't a patch on Bob Solomon's spaceship, but I knew Rutledge didn't have Bob Solomon in mind. "The spooklights I've seen was down lower," I told him, "below the tops of the trees, most times hugging the ground. This one moves the same, but it must be up fifty feet in the air."

"Maybe," he whispered, "and maybe not. Appearances can be deceiving. Hey!" he cried aloud as the slow bouncy light shot straight up in the air. It hung there, then fell down to the ridgeline again and kept a-going, bobbing down the far slope, between us and the ridge, heading toward the lake and toward us.

The professor asked, "Gravitational field?"

"No change," the girl said.

"Keep monitoring."

The light split in two, then in three. All three lights came toward us.

"Here they come! Here they come!"

I couldn't keep all three in view, so I stuck with the one making the straightest shot downhill. Underneath it, treetops came into view as the light passed over, just as if it was a helicopter with a spotlight. But there warn't no engine sound at all, just the sound of a zephyr a-stirring the leaves, and the clicks of someone snapping pictures. Even Bob Solomon's craft had made a little racket: It whirred as it moved, and turned on and off with a *whunt* like the fans in a chickenhouse. It was hard to tell the light's shape. It just faded out at the edges, as the pulsing came and went. It was blue-white in motion but flickered red when it paused. I watched the light bounce down to the far shore of the lake. Then it flashed real bright, and was gone. I lowered the binoculars in time to see the other two hit the water and flash out, too—but one sent a smaller fireball rolling across the water toward us. When it slowed down, it sank, just like a rock a child sends a-skipping across a pond. The water didn't kick up at all, but the light could be seen below for a few seconds, until it sank out of sight.

"Awesome!" Isobel said.

"Yeah, that was something," Wallace said. "Wish we had a boat. Can we bring a boat next time, Doc? Hey, why is it so light?"

"Moonrise," Isobel said. "See our moonshadows?"

We did all have long shadows, reaching over the wall and toward the lake. I always heard that to stand in your own moonshadow means good luck, but I didn't get the chance to act on it before the professor said: "That's not the moon."

The professor was facing away from the water, toward the source of light. Behind us a big bright light moved through the trees, big as a house. The beams shined out separately between the trunks but then they closed up together again as the light moved out onto the surface of the gravel pull-around. It was like a giant glowing upside-down bowl, twenty-five feet high, a hundred or more across, sliding across the ground. You could see everything lit up inside, clear as a bell, like in a tabletop aquarium in a dark room. But it warn't attached to nothing. Above the light dome was no spotlight, no aircraft, nothing but the night sky and stars.

"Wallace, get that camera turned around, for God's sake!"

"Instruments read nothing, Doc. It's as if it weren't there."

"Maybe it's not. No, Mr. Nelson! Please, stay back!"

But I'd already stepped forward to meet it, binoculars hanging by their strap at my side, bouncing against my leg as I walked into the light. Inside I didn't feel nothing physical—no tingling, and no warmth, no more than turning on a desk lamp warms a room. But in my mind I felt different, powerful different. Standing there in that light, I felt more calm and easeful than I'd felt in years—like I was someplace I belonged, more so than on my own farm. As the edge of the light crept toward me, I slow-walked in the same direction, just to keep in the light as long as I could.

The others, outside the light, did the opposite. They scattered back toward the wall of the overlook, trying to stay in the dark ahead of it, but they didn't have no place to go, and in a few seconds they was all in the light, too, the three of them and their standing telescopes and all their equipment on folding tables and sawhorses all around. I got my first good look at the three of them in that crawling glow. Wallace had hippie hair down in his eyes and a beaky nose, and was bowlegged. The professor was older than I expected, but not nearly so old as me, and had a great big belly—what mountain folks would call an *investment*, as he'd been putting into it for years. Isobel had long stringy hair that needed a wash, and a wide butt, and black-rimmed glasses so thick a welder could have worn them, but she was right cute for all that. None of us cast a shadow inside the light.

I looked up and could see the night sky and even pick out the stars, but it was like looking through a soap film or a skiff of snow. Something I couldn't feel or rightly see was in the way, between me and the sky. Still I walked until the thigh-high stone wall stopped me. The dome kept moving, of course, and as I went through its back edge—because it was just that clear-cut, either you was in the light or you warn't—why, I almost swung my legs over the wall to follow it. The hill, though, dropped off steep on the other side, and the undergrowth was all tangled and snaky. So I held up for a few seconds, dithering, and then the light had left me behind, and I was in the dark again, pressed up against that wall like something drowned and found in a drain after a flood. I now could feel the breeze off the lake, so air warn't moving easy through the light dome, neither.

The dome kept moving over the folks from the college, slid over the wall and down the slope, staying about twenty-five feet tall the whole way. It moved out onto the water—which stayed as still as could be, not roiled at all—then faded, slow at first and then faster, until I warn't sure I was looking at anything anymore, and then it was gone.

The professor slapped himself on the cheeks and neck, like he was putting on aftershave. "No sunburn, thank God," he said. "How do the rest of you feel?"

The other two slapped themselves just the same.

"I'm fine."

"I'm fine, too," Isobel said. "The Geiger counter never triggered, either."

What did I feel like? Like I wanted to dance, to skip and cut capers, to holler out loud. My eyes were full like I might cry. I stared at that dark lake like I could stare a hole in it, like I could will that dome to rise again. I whispered, "Thank you," and it warn't a prayer, not directed *at* anybody, just an acknowledgment of something that had passed, like tearing off a calendar page, or plowing under a field of cornstalks.

I turned to the others, glad I finally had someone to talk to, someone I could share all these feelings with, but to my surprise they was all running from gadget to gadget, talking at once about phosphorescence and gas eruptions and electromagnetic fields, I couldn't follow half of it. Where had they been? Had they plumb missed it? For the first time in years, I felt I had to tell them what I had seen, what I had felt and known, the whole story. It would help them. It would be a comfort to them.

I walked over to them, my hands held out. I wanted to calm them down, get their attention.

"Oh, thank you, Mr. Nelson," said the professor. He reached out and unhooked from my hand the strap of the binoculars. "I'll take those. Well, I'd say you brought us luck, wouldn't you agree, Isobel, Wallace? Quite a remarkable display, that second one especially. Like the Bahia Kino Light of the Gulf of California, but in motion! Ionization of the air, perhaps, but no Geiger activity, mmm. A lower voltage, perhaps?" He patted his pockets. "Need a shopping list for our next vigil. A portable Curran counter, perhaps—"

I grabbed at his sleeve. "I saw it."

"Yes? Well, we all saw it, Mr. Nelson. Really a tremendous phenomenon— if the distant lights and the close light are related, that is, and their joint appearance cannot be coincidental. I'll have Isobel take your statement before we go, but now, if you'll excuse me."

"I don't mean tonight," I said, "and I don't mean no spooklights. I seen the real thing, an honest-to-God flying saucer, in 1956. At my farm outside Mountain View, west of here. Thataway." I pointed. "It shot out a beam of light, and after I was in that light, I felt better, not so many aches and pains. And listen: I saw it more than once, the saucer. It kept coming back."

He was backing away from me. "Mr. Nelson, really, I must—"

"And I met the crew," I told him. "The pilot stepped out of the saucer to talk with me. That's right, with me. He looked human, just like you and me, only better-looking. He looked like that boy in *Battle Cry*, Tab Hunter. But he said his name was—"

"Mr. Nelson." The early-morning light was all around by now, giving everything a gray glow, and I could see Rutledge was frowning. "Please. You've had a very long night, and a stressful one. You're tired, and I'm sorry to say that you're no longer young. What you're saying no longer makes sense."

"Don't make sense!" I cried. "You think what we just saw makes sense?"

"I concede that I have no ready explanations, but what we saw were lights, Mr. Nelson, only lights. No sign of intelligence, nor of aircraft. Certainly not of crew members. No little green men. No grays. No Tab Hunter from the Moon."

"He lived on Mars," I said, "and his name was Bob Solomon."

The professor stared at me. The boy behind him, Wallace, stared at me, too, nearabouts tripping over his own feet as he bustled back and forth toting things to the truck. The girl just shook her head, and turned and walked into the woods.

"I wrote it up in a little book," I told the professor. "Well, I say I wrote it. Really, I talked it out, and I paid a woman at the library to copy it down and type it. I got a copy in the pickup. Let me get it. Won't take a sec."

"Mr. Nelson," he said again, "I'm sorry, I truly am. If you write me at the college, and enclose your address, I'll see you get a copy of our article, should it appear. We welcome interest in our work from the layman. But for now, here, today, I must ask you to leave."

"Leave? But the gal here said I could help."

"That was before you expressed these…delusions," Rutledge said. "Please realize what I'm trying to do. Like Hynek, like Vallee and Maccabee, I am trying to establish these researches as a serious scientific discipline. I am trying to create a field where none exists, where Isobel and her peers can work and publish without fear of ridicule. And here you are, spouting nonsense about a hunky spaceman named Bob! You must realize how that sounds. Why, you'd make the poor girl a laughing stock."

"She don't want to interview me?"

"Interview you! My God, man, aren't you listening? It would be career suicide for her to be *seen* with you! Please, before the sun is full up, Mr. Nelson, please, do the decent thing, and get back into your truck, and go."

I felt myself getting madder and madder. My hands had turned into fists. I turned from the professor, pointed at the back-and-forth boy, and hollered, "You!"

He froze, like I had pulled a gun on him.

I called: "You take any Polaroids of them things?"

"Some, yes, sir," he said, at the exact same time the professor said, "Don't answer that."

"Where are they?" I asked. "I want to see 'em."

Behind the boy was a card table covered with notebooks and Mountain Dew bottles and the Polaroid camera, too, with a stack of picture squares next to it. I walked toward the table, and the professor stepped into my path, crouched, arms outstretched, like we was gonna wrestle.

"Keep away from the equipment," Rutledge said.

The boy ran back to the table and snatched up the pictures as I feinted sideways, and the professor lunged to block me again.

"I want to see them pictures, boy," I said.

"Mr. Nelson, go home! Wallace, secure those photos."

Wallace looked around like he didn't know what "secure" meant, in the open air overlooking a mountain lake, then he started stuffing the photos into his pockets, until they poked out all around, sort of comical. Two fell out on the ground. Then Wallace picked up a folding chair and held it out in front of him like a lion tamer. Stenciled across the bottom of the chair was PROP. CUMBEE FUNERAL HOME.

I stooped and picked up a rock and cocked my hand back like I was going to fling it. The boy flinched backward, and I felt right bad about scaring him. I turned and made like to throw it at the professor instead, and when he flinched, I felt some better. Then I turned and made like to throw it at the biggest telescope, and that felt best of all, for both boy and professor hollered then, no words but just a wail from the boy and a bark from the man, so loud that I nearly dropped the rock.

"Pictures, pictures," I said. "All folks want is pictures. People didn't believe nothing I told 'em, because during the first visits I didn't have no camera, and then when I rented a Brownie to take to Venus with me, didn't none of the pictures turn out! All of 'em overexposed, the man at the Rexall said. I ain't fooled with no pictures since, but I'm gonna have one of these, or so help me, I'm gonna bust out the eyes of this here spyglass, you see if I won't. Don't you come no closer with that chair, boy! You set that thing down." I picked up a second rock, so I had one heavy weight in each hand, and felt good. I knocked them together with a *clop* like hooves, and I walked around to the business end of the telescope, where the eye-piece and all those tiny adjustable thingies was, because that looked like the underbelly. I held the rocks up to either side, like I was gonna knock them together and smash the instruments in between. I bared my teeth and tried to look scary, which warn't easy because now that it was good daylight, I suddenly had to pee something fierce. It must have worked, though, because Wallace set down the chair, just about the time the girl Isobel stepped out of the woods.

She was tucking in her shirttail, like she'd answered her own call of nature. She saw us all three standing there froze, and she got still, too, one hand down the back of her britches. Her darting eyes all magnified in her glasses looked quick and smart.

"What's going on?" she asked. Her front teeth stuck out like a chipmunk's.

"I want to see them pictures," I said.

"Isobel," the professor said, "drive down to the bait shop and call the police." He picked up an oak branch, hefted it, and started stripping off the little branches, like that would accomplish anything. "Run along, there's a good girl. Wallace and I have things well in hand."

"The heck we do," Wallace said. "I bring back a wrecked telescope, and I kiss my work-study good-bye."

"Jesus wept," Isobel said, and walked down the slope, tucking in the rest of her shirttail. She rummaged on the table, didn't find them, then saw the two stray pictures lying on the ground at Wallace's feet. She picked one up, walked over to me, held it out.

The professor said, "Isabel, don't! That's university property."

"Here, Mr. Nelson," she said. "Just take it and go, okay?"

I was afraid to move, for fear I'd wet my pants. My eyeballs was swimming already. I finally let fall one of my rocks and took the photo in that free hand, stuck it in my overalls pocket without looking at it. "Preciate it," I said. For no reason, I handed her the other rock, and for no reason, she took it. I turned and walked herky-jerky toward my truck, hoping I could hold it till I got into the woods at least, but no, I gave up halfway there, and with my back to the others I unzipped and groaned and let fly a racehorse stream of pee that spattered the tape-recorder case.

I heard the professor moan behind me, "Oh, Mr. Nelson! This is really too bad!"

"I'm sorry!" I cried. "It ain't on purpose, I swear! I was about to bust." I probably would have tried to aim it, at that, to hit some of that damned equipment square on, but I hadn't had no force nor distance on my pee for years. It just poured out, like pulling a plug. I peed and peed, my eyes rolling back, lost in the good feeling ("You go, Mr. Nelson!" Isobel yelled), and as it puddled and coursed in little rills around the rocks at my feet, I saw a fisherman in a distant rowboat in the middle of the lake, his line in the water just where that corpse light had submerged the night before. I couldn't see him good, but I could tell he was watching us, as his boat drifted along. The sparkling water looked like it was moving fast past him, the way still water in the sun always does, even though the boat hardly moved at all.

"You wouldn't eat no fish from there," I hollered at him, "if you knew what was underneath."

His only answer was a pop and a hiss that carried across the water loud as a firework. He slung away the pull top, lifted the can, raised it high toward us as if to say, Cheers, and took a long drink.

Finally done, I didn't even zip up as I shuffled to the pickup. Without all that pee I felt lightheaded and hollow and plumb worn out. I wondered whether I'd make it home before I fell asleep.

"Isobel," the professor said behind me, "I asked you to go call the police."

"Oh, for God's sake, let it go," she said. "You really *would* look like an asshole then. Wallace, give me a hand."

I crawled into the pickup, slammed the door, dropped the window—it didn't crank down anymore, just fell into the door, so that I had to raise it two-handed—cranked the engine and drove off without looking at the bucktoothed girl, the bowlegged boy, the professor holding a club in his bloody-knuckled hands, the fisherman drinking his breakfast over a spook hole. I caught one last sparkle of the morning sun on the surface of the lake as I swung the truck into the shade of the woods, on the road headed down to the highway. Light through the branches dappled my rusty hood, my cracked dashboard, my baggy overalls. Some light is easy to explain. I fished the Polaroid picture out of my pocket and held it up at eye level while I drove. All you could see was a bright white nothing, like the boy had aimed the lens at the glare of a hundred-watt bulb from an inch away. I tossed the picture out the window. Another dud, just like Venus. A funny thing: The cardboard square bounced to a standstill in the middle of the road and caught the light just enough to be visible in my rearview mirror, like a little bright window in the ground, until I reached the highway, signaled *ka-chunk, ka-chunk*, and turned to the right, toward home.

Later that morning I sat on the porch, waiting for her. Staring at the lake had done me no good, no more than staring at the night sky over the barn had done, all those years, but staring at the rhododendron called her forth, sure enough. She stepped around the bush with a little wave. She looked sprightly as ever, for all that long walk up the steep driveway, but I didn't blame her for not scraping her car past all those close bushes. One day they'd grow together and intertwine their limbs like clasped hands, and I'd be cut off from the world like in a fairy tale. But I wasn't cut off yet, because here came Miss Priss, with boots up over her knees and dress hiked up to yonder, practically. Her colors were red and black today, even that fool saucer hat was red with a black button in the center. She was sipping out of a box with a straw in it.

"I purely love orange juice," she told me. "Whenever I'm traveling, I can't get enough of it. Here, I brought you one." I reached out and took the box offered, and she showed me how to peel off the straw and poke a hole with it, and we sat side by side sipping awhile. I didn't say nothing, just sipped and looked into Donald Duck's eyes and sipped some more. Finally she emptied her juice box with a long low gurgle and turned to me and asked, "Did you make it out to the lake last night?"

"I did that thing, yes ma'am."

"See anything?"

The juice was brassy-tasting and thin, but it was growing on me, and I kept a-working that straw. "Didn't see a damn thing," I said. I cut my eyes at her. "Didn't see *you*, neither."

"Yes, well, I'm sorry about that," she said. "My supervisors called me away. When I'm on assignment, my time is not my own." Now she cut *her* eyes at *me*. "You *sure* you didn't see anything?"

I shook my head, gurgled out the last of my juice. "Nothing Dr. Rutledge can't explain away," I said. "Nothing you could have a conversation with."

"How'd you like Dr. Rutledge?"

"We got along just fine," I said, "when he warn't hunting up a club to beat me with, and I warn't pissing into his machinery. He asked after *you*, though. You was the one he wanted along on his camping trip, out there in the dark."

"I'll try to call on him, before I go."

"Go where?"

She fussed with her hat. "Back home. My assignment's over."

"Got everthing you needed, did you?"

"Yes, I think so. Thanks to you."

"Well, I ain't," I said. I turned and looked her in the face. "I ain't got everthing I need, myself. What I need ain't here on this Earth. It's up yonder, someplace I can't get to no more. Ain't that a bitch? And yet I was right satisfied until two days ago, when you come along and stirred me all up again. I never even went to bed last night, and I ain't sleepy even now. All I can think about is night coming on again, and what I might see up there this time."

"But that's a *good* thing," she said. "You keep your eyes peeled, Mr. Nelson. You've seen things already, and you haven't seen the last of them." She tapped my arm with her juice-box straw. "I have faith in you," she said. "I wasn't sure at first. That's why I came to visit, to see if you were keeping the faith. And I see now that you are—in your own way."

"I ain't got no faith," I said. "I done aged out of it."

She stood up. "Oh, pish tosh," she said. "You proved otherwise last night. The others tried to stay *out* of the light, but not you, Mr. Nelson. Not you." She set her juice box on the step beside mine. "Throw that away for me, will you? I got to be going." She stuck out her hand. It felt hot to the touch, and powerful. Holding it gave me the strength to stand up, look into her eyes, and say:

"I made it all up. The dog Bo, and the trips to Venus and Mars, and the cured lumbago. It was a made-up story, ever single Lord God speck of it."

And I said that sincerely. Bob Solomon forgive me: As I said it, I believed it was true.

She looked at me for a spell, her eyes big. She looked for a few seconds like a child I'd told Santa warn't coming, ever again. Then she grew back up, and with a sad little smile she stepped toward me, pressed her hands flat to the chest bib of my overalls, stood on tippytoes, and kissed me on the cheek, the way she would her grandpap, and as she slid something into my side pocket she whispered in my ear, "That's not what I hear on Enceladus." She patted my pocket. "That's how to reach me, if you need me. But you won't need me." She stepped into the yard and walked away, swinging her pocketbook, and called back over her shoulder: "You know what you need, Mr. Nelson? You need a dog. A dog is good help around a farm. A dog will sit up with you, late at night, and lie beside you, and keep you warm. You ought to keep your eye out. You never know when a stray will turn up."

She walked around the bush and was gone. I picked up the empty Donald Ducks, because it was something to do, and I was turning to go in when a man's voice called:

"Mr. Buck Nelson?"

A young man in a skinny tie and horn-rimmed glasses stood at the edge of the driveway where Miss Priss—no, Miss *Rains*, she deserved her true name—had stood a few moments before. He walked forward, one hand outstretched and the other reaching into the pocket of his denim jacket. He pulled out a long flat notebook.

"My name's Matt Ketchum," he said, "and I'm pleased to find you, Mr. Nelson. I'm a reporter with The Associated Press, and I'm writing a story on the surviving flying-saucer contactees of the 1950s."

I caught him up short when I said, "Aw, not again! Damn it all, I just told all that to Miss Rains. She works for the A&P, too."

He withdrew his hand, looked blank.

I pointed to the driveway. "Hello, you must have walked past her in the drive, not two minutes ago! Pretty girl in a red-and-black dress, boots up to here. Miss Rains, or Hanes, or something like that."

"Mr. Nelson, I'm not following you. I don't work with anyone named Rains or Hanes, and no one else has been sent out here but me. And that driveway was deserted. No other cars parked down at the highway, either." He cocked his head, gave me a pitying look. "Are you sure you're not thinking of some other day, sir?"

"But she…," I said, hand raised toward my bib pocket—but something kept me from saying *gave me her card*. That pocket felt strangely warm, like there was a live coal in it.

"Maybe she worked for someone else, Mr. Nelson, like UPI, or maybe the *Post-Dispatch*? I hope I'm not scooped again. I wouldn't be surprised, with the Spielberg picture coming out and all."

I turned to focus on him for the first time. "Where is Enceladus, anyway?"

"I beg your pardon?"

I said it again, moving my lips all cartoony, like he was deaf.

"I, well, I don't know, sir. I'm not familiar with it."

I thought a spell. "I do believe," I said, half to myself, "it's one a them Saturn moons." To jog my memory, I made a fist of my right hand and held it up—that was Saturn—and held up my left thumb a ways from it, and moved it back and forth, sighting along it. "It's out a ways, where the ring gets sparse. Thirteenth? Fourteenth, maybe?"

He just goggled at me. I gave him a sad look and shook my head and said, "You don't know much, if that's what you know, and that's a fact."

He cleared his throat. "Anyway, Mr. Nelson, as I was saying, I'm inter-viewing all the contactees I can find, like George Van Tassel, and Orfeo Angelucci—"

"Yes, yes, and Truman Bethurum, and them," I said. "She talked to all them, too."

"Bethurum?" he repeated. He flipped through his notebook. "Wasn't he the asphalt spreader, the one who met the aliens atop a mesa in Nevada?"

"Yeah, that's the one."

He looked worried now. "Um, Mr. Nelson, you must have misunderstood her. Truman Bethurum died in 1969. He's been dead eight years, sir."

I stood there looking at the rhododendron and seeing the pretty face and round hat, hearing the singsong voice, like she had learned English from a book.

I turned and went into the house, let the screen bang shut behind, didn't bother to shut the wood door.

"Mr. Nelson?"

My chest was plumb hot now. I went straight to the junk room, yanked on the light. Everything was spread out on the floor where I left it. I shoved aside Marilyn, all the newspapers, pawed through the books.

"Mr. Nelson?" The voice was coming closer, moving through the house like a spooklight.

There it was: *Aboard a Flying Saucer*, by Truman Bethurum. I flipped through it, looking only at the pictures, until I found her: dark hair, big dark eyes, sharp chin, round hat. It was old Truman's drawing of Captain Aura Rhanes, the sexy Space Sister from the planet Clarion who visited him eleven times in her little red-and-black uniform, come right into his bedroom, so often that Mrs. Bethurum got jealous and divorced him. I had heard that old Truman, toward the end, went out and hired girl assistants to answer his mail and take messages just because they sort of looked like Aura Rhanes.

"Mr. Nelson?" said young Ketchum, standing in the doorway. "Are you okay?"

I let drop the book, stood, and said, "Doing just fine, son. If you'll excuse me? I got to be someplace." I closed the door in his face, dragged a bookcase across the doorway to block it, and pulled out Miss Rhanes' card, which was almost too hot to touch. No writing on it, neither, only a shiny silver surface that reflected my face like a mirror—and there was something behind my face, something a ways back inside the card, a moving silvery blackness like a field of stars rushing toward me, and as I stared into that card, trying to see, my reflection slid out of the way and the edges of the card flew out and the card was a window, a big window, and now a door that I moved through without stepping, and someone out there was playing a single fiddle, no dance tune but just a-scraping along slow and sad as the stars whirled around me, and a ringed planet was swimming into view, the rings on edge at first but now tilting toward me and thickening as I dived down, the rings getting closer, dividing into bands like layers in a rock face, and then into a field of rocks like that no-earthly-good south pasture, only there was so many rocks, so close together, and then I fell between them like an ant between the rocks in a gravel driveway, and now I was speeding toward a pinpoint of light, and as I moved toward it faster and faster, it grew and resolved itself and reshaped into a pear, a bulb, with a long sparkling line extending out, like a space elevator, like a chain, and at the end of the chain the moon became a glowing lightbulb. I was staring into the bulb in my junk room, dazzled, my eyes flashing, my head achy, and the card dropped from my fingers with no sound, and my feet were still shuffling though the fiddle had faded away. I couldn't hear nothing over the knocking and the barking and young Ketchum calling: "Hey, Mr. Nelson? Is this your dog?"

GREAT-GRANDMOTHER IN THE CELLAR

PETER S. BEAGLE

Peter S. Beagle [www.peterbeagle.com] *was born in Manhattan on the same night that Billie Holiday was recording "Strange Fruit" and "Fine Mellow" just a few blocks away. Raised in the Bronx, Peter originally proclaimed he would be a writer when he was ten years old. Today he is acknowledged as an American fantasy icon, and to the delight of his millions of fans around the world is now publishing more than ever. He is the author of the beloved classic* The Last Unicorn, *as well as the novels* A Fine and Private Place, The Innkeeper's Song, *and* Tamsin. *He has won the Hugo, Nebula, Locus, and Mythopoeic awards, and is the recipient of the World Fantasy Award for Life Achievement. His most recent book is the collection* Sleight of Hand.

I thought he had killed her.

Old people forget things, I know that—my father can't ever remember where he set down his pen a minute ago—but if I forget, at the end of *my* life, every other thing that ever happened to me, I will still be clutched by the moment when I gazed down at my beautiful, beautiful, sweet-natured idiot sister and heard the whining laughter of Borbos, the witch-boy she loved, pattering in my head. I *knew* he had killed her.

Then I saw her breast rising and falling—so slowly!—and I saw her nostrils fluttering slightly with each breath, and I knew that he had only thrown her into the witch-sleep that mimics the last sleep closely enough to deceive Death Herself.

Borbos stepped from the shadows and laughed at me.

"*Now* tell your father," he said. "Go to him and tell him that Jashani will lie so until the sight of my face—and only my face—awakens her. And that face she will never see until he agrees that we two may wed. Is this message clear enough for your stone skull, Da'mas? Shall I repeat it, just to be sure?"

I rushed at him, but he put up a hand and the floor of my sister's chamber seemed to turn to oiled water under my feet. I went over on my back, flailing foolishly at the innocent air, and Borbos laughed again. If *shukris* could laugh, they would sound like Borbos.

He was gone then, in that way he had of coming and going, which Jashani thought was so dashing and mysterious, but which seemed to me fit only for sneak thieves and housebreakers. I knelt there alone, staring helplessly at the person I loved most in the world, and whom I fully intended to strangle when—oh, it had to be *when*!—she woke up. With no words, no explanations, no apologies. She'd know.

In the ordinary way of things, she's far brighter and wiser and simply *better* than I, Jashani. My tutors all disapproved and despaired of me early on, with good reason; but before she could walk, they seemed almost to expect my sister to perform her own *branlewei* coming-of-age ceremony, and prepare both the ritual sacrifice *and* the meal afterward. It would drive me wild with jealousy—especially when Father would demand to know, one more time, why I couldn't be as studious and accomplished as Jashani—if she weren't so ridiculously decent and kind that there's not a thing you can do except love her. I sometimes go out into the barn and scream with frustration, to tell you the truth… and then she comes running to see if I'm hurt or ill. At twenty-one, she's two and a half years older than I, and she has never once let Father beat me, even when the punishment was so richly deserved that *I'd* have beaten me if I were in his place.

And right then I'd have beaten *her,* if it weren't breaking my heart to see her prisoned in sleep unless we let the witch-boy have her.

It is the one thing we ever quarrel about, Jashani's taste in men. Let me but mention that this or that current suitor has a cruel mouth, and all Chun will hear her shouting at me that the poor boy can't be blamed for a silly feature—and should I bring a friend by, just for the evening, who happens to describe the poor boy's method of breaking horses…well, that will only make things worse. If I tell her that the whole town knows that the fellow serenading her in the grape arbor is the father of two children by a barmaid, and another baby by a farm girl, Jashani will fly at me, claiming that he was a naive victim of their seductive beguilements. Put her in a room with ninety-nine perfect choices and one heartless scoundrel, and she will choose the villain every time. This prediction may very well be the one thing Father and I ever agree on, come to consider.

But *Borbos*…

Unlike most of the boys and men Jashani ever brought home to try out at dinner, I had known Borbos all my life, and Father had known the family since his own youth. Borbos came from a long line of witches of one sort and another, most of them quite respectable, as witches go, and likely as embarrassed by Borbos as Father was by me. He'd grown up easily the handsomest young buck in Chun, straight and sleek, with long, angled eyes the color of river water, skin and hair the envy of every girl I knew, and an air about him to entwine hearts much less foolish than my sister's. I could name names.

And with all that came a soul as perfectly pitiless as when we were all little and he was setting cats afire with a twiddle of two fingers, or withering someone's fields or haystacks with a look, just for the fun of it. He took great care that none of our parents ever caught him at his play, so that it didn't matter what I told them—and in the same way, even then, he made sure never to let Jashani see the truth of him. He knew what he wanted, even then, just as she never wanted to believe evil of anyone.

And here was the end of it: me standing by my poor, silly sister's bed, begging her to wake up, over and over, though I knew she never would—not until Father and I…

No.

Not ever.

If neither of us could stop it, I knew someone who would.

Father was away from home, making arrangements with vintners almost as far north as the Durli Hills and as far south as Kalagira, where the enchantresses live, to buy our grapes for their wine. He would be back when he was back, and meanwhile there was no way to reach him, nor any time to spare. The decision was mine to make, whatever he might think of it afterward. Of our two servants, Catuzan, the housekeeper, had finished her work and gone home, and Nanda, the cook, was at market. Apart from Jashani, I was alone in our big old house.

Except for Great-Grandmother.

I never knew her; neither had Jashani. Father had, in his youth, but he spoke of her very little, and that little only with the windows shuttered and the curtains drawn. When I asked hopefully whether Great-Grandmother had been a witch, his answer was a headshake and a definite *no*—but when Jashani said, "Was she a demon?" Father was silent for some while. Finally he said, "No, not really. Not exactly." And that was all we ever got out of him about Great-Grandmother.

But I knew something Jashani didn't know. Once, when I was small, I had overheard Father speaking with his brother Uskameldry, who was also in the wine grape trade, about a particular merchant in Coraic who had so successfully cornered the market in that area that no vintner would even look at our family's grapes, whether red or black or blue. Uncle Uska had joked, loudly enough for me to hear at my play, that maybe they ought to go down to the cellar and wake up Great-Grandmother again. Father didn't laugh, but hushed him so fast that the silence caught my ear as much as the talk before it.

Our cellar is deep and dark, and the great wine casks cast bulky shadows when you light a candle. Jashani and I and our friends used to try to scare each other when we played together there, but she and I knew the place too well ever to be really frightened. Now I stood on the stair, thinking crazily that Jashani and Great-Grandmother were both asleep, maybe if you woke one, you might rouse the other...something like that, anyway. So after a while, I lit one of the wrist-thick candles Father kept under the hinged top step, and I started down.

Our house is the oldest and largest on this side of the village. There have been alterations over the years—most of them while Mother was alive—but the cellar never changes. Why should it? There are always the casks, and the tables and racks along the walls, for Father's filters and preservatives and other tools to test the grapes for perfect ripeness; and always the same comfortable smell of damp earth, the same boards stacked to one side, to walk on should the cellar flood, and the same shadows, familiar as bedtime toys. But there was no sign of anyone's ancestor, and no place where one could possibly be hiding, not once you were standing on the earthen floor, peering into the shadows.

Then I saw the place that wasn't a shadow, in the far right corner of the cellar, near the drainpipe. I don't remember any of us noticing it as children—it would have been easy to miss, being only slightly darker than the rest of the floor—but when I walked warily over to it and tapped it with my foot, it felt denser and finer-packed than any other area. There were a couple of spades leaning against the wall further along. I took one and, feeling strangely hypnotized, started to dig.

The deeper I probed, the harder the digging got, and the more convinced I became that the earth had been deliberately pounded hard and tight, as though to hold something down. Not hard enough: whatever was here, it was coming up now. A kind of fever took hold of me, and I flung spadeful after spadeful aside, going at it like a rock-*targ* ripping out a poor badger's den. I broke my nails, and I flung my sweated shirt away, and I dug.

I didn't hear my father the first time, although he was shouting at me from the stair. "What are you doing?" I went on digging, and he bellowed loud enough to make the racks rattle, *"Da'mas, what are you doing?"*

I did not turn. I was braced for the jar of the spade on wood, or possibly metal—a coffin either way—but the sound that came up when I finally did hit something had me instantly throwing the instrument away and dropping down to half sit, half kneel on the edge of the oblong hole I'd worried out of the earth. Reaching, groping, my hand came up gripping a splintered bone.

Great-Grandmother! I flung myself face-down, clawing with both hands now, frantic, hysterical, not knowing what I was doing. Fingerbones… something that might have been a knee, an elbow…*a skull*—no, just the top of a skull…I don't think I was quite sane when I heard the voice.

"Grandson, stop…stop, before you really do addle my poor old bones. Stop!" It was a slow voice, with a cold, cold rustle in it: it sounded like the wind over loose stones.

I stopped. I sat up, and so did she.

Then Father—home early, due to some small war blocking his road—was beside me, as silent as I, but with an unfriendly hand gripping the back of my neck. Great-Grandmother wasn't missing any bones, thank Dran and Tani, our household gods, who are twins. The skull wasn't hers, nor the fingers, nor any of the other loose bones; she was definitely whole, sitting with her fleshless legs bent under her, from the knees, and her own skull clearing the top of my pit to study me out of yellowish-white empty eye sockets. She said, "The others are your Great-Aunt Keshwara. I was lonely."

I looked at Father for the first time. He was sweating himself, pale and swaying. I realized that his hand on my neck was largely to keep me from trembling, and to hold himself upright. "You should not have done this," he said. He was almost whispering. "Oh, you should never have done this." Then, louder, as he let go of me, "Great-Grandmother."

"Do not scold the boy, Rushak," the stone rustle rebuked him. "It has been long and long since I saw anything but dirt, smelled anything but mold. The scent of fear tells me that I am back with my family. Sit up straight, young Da'mas. Look at me."

I sat as properly as I could on the edge of a grave. Great-Grandmother peered closely at me, her own skull weaving slightly from side to side, like a snake's head. She said, "Why have you awakened me?"

"He's a fool," Father said. "He made a mistake, he didn't know...." Great-Grandmother looked at him, and he stopped talking. She repeated the question to me.

How I faced those eyeless, browless voids and spoke to those cold, slabby chaps, I can't tell you—or myself—today. But I said my sister's name—"Jashani"—and after that it got easier. I said, "Borbos, the witch-boy—he's made her sleep, and she won't wake up until we give in and say he can marry her. And she'd be better off dead."

"What?" Father said. "How—"

Great-Grandmother interrupted, "Does she know that?"

"No," I said. "But she will. She thinks he loves her, but he doesn't love anybody."

"He loves my money, right enough," Father said bitterly. "He loves my house. He loves my business."

The eye sockets never turned from me. I said, "She doesn't know about these things...about men. She's just *good*."

"Witch-boy..." The rusty murmur was all but inaudible in the skeletal throat. "Ah...the Tresard family. The youngest."

Father and I gaped at her, momentarily united by astonishment. Father asked, "How did you...?" Then he said, "You were already..." I thanked him silently for being the one to look a fool.

Great-Grandmother said simply—and, it might have been, a little smugly, "I listen. What else have I to do in that hole?" Then she said, "Well, I must see the girl. Show me."

So my great-grandmother stepped out of her grave and followed my father and me upstairs, clattering with each step like an armload of dishes, yet held firmly together somehow by the recollection of muscles, the stark memory of tendons and sinews. Neither of us liked to get too close to her, which she seemed to understand, for she stayed well to the rear of our uncanny procession. Which was ridiculous, and I knew it then, and I was ashamed of it then as well. She was family, after all.

In Jashani's chamber, Great-Grandmother stood looking down at the bed for a long time, without speaking. Finally she said softly, almost to herself, "Skilled...I never knew a Tresard with such..." She did not finish.

"Can you heal her?" The words burst out of me as though I hadn't spoken in years, which was how I felt. "She's never hurt a soul, she wouldn't know how—she's foolish and sweet, except she's *very* smart, it's just that she can't imagine that anyone would ever wish her harm. *Please*, Great-

Grandmother, make her wake up! I'll do anything!"

I will be grateful to my dying day that Jashani couldn't hear a word of all that nonsense.

Great-Grandmother didn't take her empty eyes from my sister as I babbled on; nor did she seem to hear a word of the babble. I'm not sure how long she stood there by the bed, though I do recall that she reached out once to stroke Jashani's hair very lightly, as though those cold, fleshless fingers were seeing, tasting…

Then she stepped back, so abruptly that some bones clicked against other bones, and she said, "I must have a body."

Again Father and I stared stupidly at her. Great-Grandmother said impatiently, "Do you imagine that I can face your witch-boy like this? One of you—either one—must allow me the use of his body. Otherwise, don't waste my time." She glowered into each of our pale faces in turn, never losing or altering the dreadful grin of the long-dead.

Father took a long breath and opened his mouth to volunteer, but I beat him to it, actually stepping a bit forward to nudge him aside. I said, "What must I do?"

Great-Grandmother bent her head close, and I stared right into that eternal smile. "Nothing, boy. You need do nothing but stand so…just so…"

I cannot tell you what it was like. And if I could, I wouldn't. You might ask Father, who's a much better witness to the whole affair than I for all that, in a way, I *was* the whole affair. I do know from him that Great-Grandmother's bones did not clatter untidily to the floor when her spirit—soul, essence, life-force, *tyak* (as people say in the south)—passed into me. According to Father, they simply vanished into the silver mist that poured and poured into me, as I stood there with my arms out, dumb as a dressmaker's dummy. The one reasonably reliable report I can relay is that it wasn't cold, as you might expect, but warm on my skin, and—of all things—almost *sweet* on my lips, though I kept my mouth tightly shut. Being invaded—no, let's use the honest word, *possessed*—by your great-grandmother is bad enough, but to *swallow* her? And have it taste like apples, like *fasteen*, like cake? I didn't think about it then, and I'm not thinking about it now. Then, all that mattered was my feeling of being crowded to the farthest side of my head, and *hearing* Great-Grandmother inside me saying, dryly but soothingly, "Well done, Da'mas—well done, indeed. Slowly, now…move slowly until you grow accustomed to my presence. I will not hurt you, I promise, and I will not stay long. Slowly…"

Sooner or later, when he judged our anguish greatest, Borbos would return to repeat his demand. Father and Great-Grandmother-in-me took it in turns to guard Jashani's chamber through the rest of that day, the night, and all of the following day. When it was Father's turn, Great-Grandmother would march my body out of the room and the house, down the carriage-way, into our orchards and arbors; then back to scout the margins again, before finally allowing me to replace Father at that bedside where no quilt was ever rumpled, no pillow on the floor. In all of this I never lost myself in her. I always knew who I was, even when she was manipulating my mouth and the words that came out of it; even when she was lifting my hands or snapping my head too forcefully from side to side, apparently thrilled by the strength of the motion.

"He will be expecting resistance," she pointed out to us, in my voice. "Nothing he cannot wipe away with a snap of his fingers, but enough to make you feel that you did the best you could for Jashani before you yielded her to him. Now put that thing *down!*" she lectured Father, who was carrying a sword that he knew would be useless against Borbos, but had clung to anyway, for pure comfort.

Father bristled. "How are we to fight him at all, even with you guiding Da'mas's hand? Borbos could appear right now, that way he does, and what would you do? I'll put this old sword away if you give me a spell, a charm, to replace it." He was tired and sulky, and terribly, terribly frightened.

I heard my throat answer him calmly and remotely, "When your witch-boy turns up, all you will be required to do is to stand out of my way." After that Great-Grandmother did not allow another word out of me for some considerable while.

Father had not done well from his first sight of Jashani apparently lifeless in her bed. The fact that she was breathing steadily, that her skin remained warm to the touch, and that she looked as innocently beautiful as ever, despite not having eaten or drunk for several days, cheered him not at all. He himself, on the other hand, seemed to be withering before my eyes: unsleeping, hardly speaking, hardly comprehending what was said to him. Now he put down his sword as commanded and sat motionless by Jashani's bed, slumped forward with his hands clasped between his knees. A dog could not have been more constant, or more silent.

And still Borbos did not come to claim his triumph…did not come, and did not come, letting our grief and fear build to heights of nearly unbear-able tension. Even Great-Grandmother seemed to feel it, pacing the house in my body, which she treated like her own tireless bones that needed no relief, though I urgently did. Surrounded by her ancient mind, nevertheless I could never truly read it, not as she could pick through my thoughts when she chose, at times amusing herself by embarrassing me. Yet she moved me strangely once when she said aloud, as we were crouched one night in the apple orchard, studying the carriageway, white in the moon, "I envy even your discomfiture. Bones cannot blush."

"They never need to," I said, after realizing that she was waiting for my response. "Sometimes I think I spend my whole life being mortified about one thing or another. Wake up, start apologizing for everything to everybody, just on the chance I've offended them." Emboldened, I ventured further. "You might not think so, but I have had moments of wishing I were dead. I really have."

Great-Grandmother was silent in my head for so long that I was afraid that I might have affronted *her* for a second time. Then she said, slowly and tonelessly, "You would not like it. I will find it hard to go back." And there was something in the way she said those last words that made pins lick along my forearms.

"What *will* you do when Borbos comes?" I asked her. "Father says you're not a witch, but he never would say exactly *what* you were. I don't understand how you can deal with someone like Borbos if you're not a witch."

The reply came so swiftly and fiercely that I actually cringed away from it in my own skull. "I am your great-grandmother, boy. If that is not all you need to know, then you must make do as you can." So saying, she rose and stalked us out of the orchard, back toward the house, with me dragged along disconsolately, half-certain that she might never bother talking to me again.

My favorite location in the house has—naturally enough—always been a place where I wasn't ever supposed to be: astride a gable just narrow enough for me to pretend that I was riding a great black stallion to glory, or a sea-green *mordroi* dragon to adventure. I cannot count the number of times I was beaten, even by Mother, for risking my life up there, and I know very well how foolish it is to continue doing it whenever I get the chance. But this time it was Great-Grandmother taking the risk, not me, so it plainly wasn't my fault; and, in any case, what could I have done about it?

So there you are, and there you have us in the night, Great-Grandmother and I, with the moon our only light, except for the window of Jashani's chamber below and to my left, where Father kept his lonely vigil. I was certainly not about to speak until Great-Grandmother did; and for some while she sat in silence, seemingly content to scan the white road for a slim, swaggering figure who would almost surely not come for my sister that way. I ground my teeth at the thought.

Presently Great-Grandmother said quietly, almost dreamily, "I was not a good woman in my life. I was born with a certain gift for…mischief, let us say…and I sharpened it and honed it, until what I did with it became, if not as totally evil as Borbos Tresard's deeds from his birth, still cruel and malicious enough that many have never forgiven me to this day. Do you know how I died, young Da'mas?"

"I don't even know how you lived," I answered her. "I don't know anything about you."

Great-Grandmother said, "Your mother killed me. She stabbed me, and I died. And she was right to do it."

I could not take in what she had said. I felt the words as she spoke them, but they meant nothing. Great-Grandmother went on. "Like your sister, your mother had poor taste in men. She was young, I was old, why should she listen to me? If I am no witch, whatever it is that I am had grown strong with the years. I drove each of her suitors away, by one means or another. It was not hard—a little pointed misfortune and they cleared off quickly, all but the serious ones. I killed two of those, one in a storm, one in a cow pen." A grainy chuckle. "Your mother was not at all pleased with me."

"She knew what you were doing? She knew it was you?"

"Oh, yes, how not?" The chuckle again. "I was not trying to cover my tracks—I was much given to showing off in those days. But then your father came along, and I did what I could to indicate to your mother that she must choose this one. There was a man in her life already, you understand—most unsuitable, she would have regretted it in a month. The cow pen one, that was." A sigh, somehow turning into a childish giggle, and ending in a grunt. "You would have thought she might be a little pleased this time."

"Was that why she…?" I could not actually say it. I felt Great-Grandmother's smile in my spine.

"Your mother was not a killer—merely mindless with anger for perhaps five seconds. A twitch to the left or right, and she would have missed…ah, well, it was a fate long overdue. I have never blamed her."

It was becoming increasingly difficult to distinguish my thoughts—even my memories—from hers. Now I remembered hearing Uncle Uska talking to Father about waking Great-Grandmother again, and being silenced immediately. I knew that she had heard them as well, listening underground in the dark, no soil dense enough to stop her ears.

I asked, "Have you ever come back before? To help the family, like now?"

The slow sigh echoed through our shared body. Great-Grandmother replied only, "I was always a fitful sleeper." Abruptly she rose, balancing more easily on the gable than I ever did when I was captaining my body, and we went on with our patrol, watching for Borbos. And that was another night on which Borbos did not come.

When he did appear at last, he caught us—even Great-Grandmother, I *think*—completely by surprise. In the first place, he came by day, after all our wearying midnight rounds; in the second, he turned up not in Jashani's chamber, nor in the yard or any of the fields where we had kept guard, but in the great kitchen, where old Nanda had reigned as long as I could remember. He was seated comfortably at her worn worktable, silky and dashing, charming her with tales of his journeys and exploits, while she toasted her special *chamshi* sandwiches for him. She usually needs a day's notice and a good deal of begging before she'll make *chamshi* for anybody.

He looked up when Great-Grandmother walked my body into the kitchen, greeting us first with, "Well, if it isn't Thunderwit, my brother-to-be. How are those frozen brains keeping?" Then he stopped, peered closely at me, and began to smile in a different way. "I didn't realize you had…company. Do we know each other, old lady?"

I could feel Great-Grandmother studying him out of my eyes, and it frightened me more than he did. She said, "I know your family. Even in the dirt I knew you when you were very young, and just as evil as you are now. Give me back my great-granddaughter and go your way."

Borbos laughed. It was one of his best features, that warm, delightful chuckle. "And if I don't? You will destroy me? Enchant me? Forgive me if I don't find that likely. Try, and your Jashani slumbers decoratively for all eternity." The laugh had broken glass in it the second time.

I ached to get my hands on him—useless as it would have been—but Great-Grandmother remained in control. All she said, quite quietly, was, "I want it understood that I did warn you."

Whatever Borbos heard in her voice, he was up and out of his seat on the instant. No fiery whiplash, no crash of cold, magical thunder—only a scream from Nanda as the chair fell silently to ashes. She rushed out of the kitchen, calling for Father, while Borbos regarded us thoughtfully from where he leaned against the cookstove. He said, "Well, my goodness," and twisted his fingers against each other in seeming anxiety. Then he said a word I didn't catch, and every knife, fork, maul, spit, slicer, corer, scissors and bone saw in Nanda's kitchen rose up out of her utensil drawers and came flying off the wall, straight for Great-Grandmother…straight for me…for us.

But Great-Grandmother put up my hand—exactly as Borbos himself had done when I charged him on first seeing Jashani spellbound—and everything flashing toward us halted in the air, hanging there like edged and pointed currants in a fruitcake. Then Great-Grandmother spoke—the words had edges, too; I could feel them cutting my mouth—and all Nanda's implements backed politely into their accustomed places. Great-Grandmother said chidingly, "Really."

But Borbos was gone, vanished as I had seen him do in Jashani's chamber, his laughter still audible. I took the stairs two and three at a time, Great-Grandmother not wanting to chance my inexperienced body coming and going magically. Besides, we knew where he was going, and that he would be waiting for us there.

He was playing with Father. I don't like thinking about that: Father lunging and swinging clumsily with his sword, crying hopelessly, desperate to come to grips with this taunting shadow that kept dissolving out of his reach, then instantly reappearing, almost close enough to touch and punish. And Jashani…Jashani so still, so still…

Borbos turned as we burst in, and a piece of the chamber ceiling fell straight down, bruising my left shoulder as Great-Grandmother sprang me out of the way. In her turn, she made my tongue say *this,* and my two hands do *that,* and Borbos was strangling in air, on the other side of the chamber, while my hands clenched on nothing and gripped and twisted, tighter and tighter…but he got a word out, in spite of me, and broke free to crouch by Jashani's bed, panting like an animal.

There was no jauntiness about him now, no mocking gaiety. "You are no witch. I would know. What *are* you?"

I wanted to go over and comfort Father, hold him and make certain that he was unhurt, but Great-Grandmother had her own plans. She said, "I am a member of this family, and I have come to get my great-granddaughter back from you. Release her and I have no quarrel with you, no further interest at all. Do it now, Borbos Tresard."

For answer, Borbos looked shyly down at the floor, shuffled his feet like an embarrassed schoolboy, and muttered something that might indeed have been an apology for bad behavior in the classroom. But at the first sound of it, Great-Grandmother leaped forward and dragged Father away from the bed, as the floor began to crack open down the middle and the bed to slide steadily toward the widening crevasse. Father cried out in horror. I wanted to scream; but Great-Grandmother pointed with the forefingers and ring fingers of both my hands at the opening, and what she shouted hurt my mouth. Took out a back tooth, too, though I didn't notice at the time. I was too busy watching Borbos's spell reverse itself, as the flying kitchenware had done. The hole in the floor closed up as quickly as it had opened, and Jashani's bed slid back to where it had been, more or less, with her never once stirring. Father limped dazedly over to her and began to straighten her coverlet.

For a second time Borbos Tresard said, "Well, my goodness." He shook his head slightly, whether in admiration or because he was trying to clear it, I can't say. He said, "I do believe you are my master. Or mistress, as you will. But it won't help, you know. She still will not wake to any spell, except to see my face, and my terms are what they always were—a welcome into the heart of this truly remarkable family. Nothing more, and nothing less." He beamed joyously at us, and if I had never understood why so many women fell so helplessly in love with him, I surely came to understand it then. "How much longer can you stay in the poor ox, anyway, before you raddle him through like the death fever you are? Another day? A week? So much as a month? My face can wait, mother—but somehow I don't believe you can. I really don't believe so."

The bedchamber was so quiet that I thought I heard not only my own heart beating but also Jashani's, strong but so slow, and a skittery, too-rapid pulse that I first thought must be Father's, before I understood that it belonged to Borbos. Great-Grandmother said musingly, "Patience is an overrated virtue."

And then I also understood why so many people fear the dead.

I felt her leaving me. I can't describe it any better than I've been able to say what it was like to have her in me. All I'm going to say about her departure is that it left me suddenly stumbling forward, as though a prop I was leaning on had been pulled away. But it wasn't my body that felt abandoned, I know that. I think it was my spirit, but I can't be sure.

Great-Grandmother stood there as I had first seen her. Lightning was flashing in her empty eye sockets, and the pitiless grin of her naked skull branded itself across my sight. With one great heron-stride of her naked shanks she was on Borbos, reaching out—reaching out…

I don't want to tell about this.

She took his face. She reached out with her bones, and she took his face, and he screamed. There was no blood, nothing like that, but suddenly there was a shifting smudge, almost like smoke, where his face had been… and there it was, somehow *pasted* on her, merged with the bone, so that it looked *real*, not like a mask, even on the skull of a skeleton. Even with the lightning behind her borrowed eyes.

Borbos went on screaming, floundering blindly in the bedchamber, stumbling into walls and falling down, meowing and snuffling hideously; but Great-Grandmother clacked and clattered to Jashani's bedside, and peered down at her for a long moment before she spoke. "Love," she said softly. "Jashani. My heart, awaken. Awaken for me." The voice was Borbos's voice.

And Jashani opened her eyes and said his name.

Father was instantly there, holding her hands, stroking her face, crying with joy. I didn't know what those easy words meant until then. Great-Grandmother turned away and walked across the room to Borbos. He must have sensed her standing before him, because he stopped making that terrible snuffling sound. She said, "Here. I only used it for a little," and she gave him back his face.

I didn't really see it happen. I was with my father and my sister, listening to her say my name.

When I felt Great-Grandmother's fleshless hand on my shoulder, I kissed Jashani's forehead and stood up. I looked over at Borbos, still crouched in a corner, his hands pressed tightly against his face, as though he were holding it on. Great-Grandmother touched Father's shoulder with her other hand and said, impassively, "Take him home. Afterward."

After you bury me again, she meant. She held onto my shoulder as we walked downstairs together, and I felt a strange tension in the cold clasp that made me more nervous than I already was. Would she simply lie down in her cellar grave waiting for me to spade the earth back over her and pat it down with the blade? I thought of those other bones I'd first seen in the grave, and I shivered, and her grip tightened just a bit.

We faced each other over the empty grave. I couldn't read her expression any more than I ever could, but the lightning was no longer playing in her eye sockets. She said, "You are a good boy. Your company pleases me."

I started to say, "If my company is the price of Jashani...I am ready." I *think* my voice was not trembling very much, but I don't know, because I never got the chance to finish. Both of our heads turned at a sudden scurry of footsteps, and we saw Borbos Tresard charging at us across the cellar. Head down, eyes white, flailing hands empty of weapons, nevertheless his entire outline was crackling with the fire-magic of utter, insane fury. He was howling as he came.

I automatically stepped into his way—too numb with fear to be afraid, if you can understand that—but Great-Grandmother put me aside and stood waiting, short but terrible, holding out her stick-thin arms. Like a child rushing to greet his mother coming home, Borbos Tresard leaped into those arms, and they closed around him. The impact caught Great-Grandmother off-balance; the two of them tumbled into the grave together, struggling as they fell. I heard bones go, but would not gamble they were hers.

I picked up a spade, uncertain what I meant to do with it, staring down at the tumult in the earth as though it were something happening a long way off, and long ago. Then Father was beside me with the other spade, frantically shoving *everything*—dirt and odd scraps of wood and twigs and even old wine corks from the cellar floor—into the grave, shoveling and kicking and pushing with his arms almost at the same time. By and by I recovered enough to assist him, and when the hole was filled we both jumped up and down on the pile, packing it all down as tightly as it would go. The risen surface wasn't quite level with the floor when we were done, but it would settle in time.

I had to say it. I said, "He's down there under our feet, still alive, choking on dirt, with her holding him fast forever. Keeping her company." Father did not answer, but only leaned on his spade, with dirty sweat running out of his hair and down his cheek. I think that was the first time I noticed that he was an inch or so shorter than I. "I feel sorry for him. A little."

"Not I," Father said flatly. "I'd bury him deeper, if we had more earth."

"Then you would be burying Great-Grandmother deeper, too," I said.

"Yes." Father's face was paper-white, the skin looking thin with every kind of exhaustion. "Help me move these barrels."

THE EASTHOUND

NALO HOPKINSON

Nalo Hopkinson [www.nalohopkinson.com], *a Jamaican-Canadian writer, is a recipient of the World Fantasy Award and of the Sunburst Award for Canadian Literature of the Fantastic. Her novels include* Brown Girl in the Ring, Midnight Robber, The Salt Roads, The New Moon's Arms, *and* The Chaos, *and her short fiction has been collected in* Skin Folk *and* Report from Planet Midnight. *She is currently a professor of creative writing at the University of California Riverside, specializing in science fiction and fantasy. Her sixth novel,* Sister Mine, *will be published later this year.*

O*h, Black Betty, bam-ba-lam,*
*   Oh, Black Betty, bam-ba-lam.*

"The easthound bays at night," Jolly said.

Millie shivered. Bad luck to mention the easthound, and her twin bloody well knew it. God, she shouldn't even be thinking, "bloody." Millie put her hands to her mouth to stopper the words in so she wouldn't say them out loud.

"Easthound?" said Max. He pulled the worn black coat closer around his body. The coat had been getting tighter around him these past few months. Everyone could see it. "Uck the fuh is that easthound shit?"

Not what; he knew damned well what it was. He was asking Jolly what the hell she was doing bringing the easthound into their game of Loup-de-lou. Millie wanted to yell at Jolly too.

Jolly barely glanced at Max. She knelt in front of the fire, staring into it, re-twisting her dreads and separating them at the scalp where they were threatening to grow together. "It's my first line," she said. "You can play or not, no skin off my teeth."

They didn't talk about skin coming off, either. Jolly should be picking someone to come up with the next line of the game. But Jolly broke the rules when she damned well pleased. Loup-de-lou was her game, after all. She'd invented it. Someone had to come up with a first line. Then they picked the next person. That person had to continue the story by beginning with the last word or two of the line the last person said. And so on until someone closed the loup by ending the story with the first word or two of the very first line. Jolly was so thin. Millie had saved some of the chocolate bar she'd found to share with Jolly, but she knew that Jolly wouldn't take it. If you ate too much, you grew too quickly. Millie'd already eaten most of the chocolate, though. Couldn't help it. She was so hungry all the time!

Max hadn't answered Jolly. He took the bottle of vodka that Sai was holding and chugged down about a third of it. Nobody complained. That was his payment for finding the bottle in the first place. But could booze make you grow, too? Or did it keep you shrinky? Millie couldn't remember which. She fretfully watched Max's Adam's apple bob as he drank.

"The game?" Citron chirped up, reminding them. A twin of the flames of their fire danced in his green eyes. "We gonna play?"

Right. The game. Jolly bobbed her head yes. Sai, too. Millie said, "I'm in." Max sighed and shrugged his yes.

Max took up where Jolly had left off. "At night the easthound howls," he growled, "but only when there's no moon." He pointed at Citron.

A little clumsy, Millie thought, but a good second line.

Quickly, Citron picked it up with, "No moon is so bright as the east-hound's eyes when it spies a plump rat on a garbage heap." He pointed at Millie.

Garbage heap? What kind of end bit was that? Didn't give her much with which to begin the new loup. Trust Citron to throw her a tough one. And that "eyes, spies" thing, too. A rhyme in the middle, instead of at the end. Clever bastard. Thinking furiously, Millie louped, "Garbage heaps high in the…cities of noonless night."

Jolly said, "You're cheating. It was 'garbage heap,' not 'garbage heaps.'" She gnawed a strip from the edge of her thumbnail, blew the crescented clipping from her lips into the fire.

"Chuh." Millie made a dismissive motion with her good hand. "You just don't want to have to continue on with 'noonless night.'" Smirking, she pointed at her twin.

Jolly started in on the nail of her index finger. "And you're just not very good at this game, are you, Millie?"

"Twins, stop it," Max told them.

"I didn't start it," Jolly countered, through chewed nail bits. Millie hated to see her bite her nails, and Jolly knew it.

Jolly stood and flounced closer to the fire. Over her back she spat the phrase, "Noonless night, a rat's bright fright, and blood in the bite all delight the easthound." The final two words were the two with which they'd begun. Game over. Jolly spat out a triumphant, "Loup!" First round to Jolly.

Sai slapped the palm of her hand down on the ground between the players. "Aw, jeez, Jolly! You didn't have to end it so soon, just cause you're mad at your sister! I was working on a great loup."

"Jolly's only showing off!" Millie said. Truth was, Jolly was right. Millie really wasn't much good at Loup-de-lou. It was only a stupid game, a distraction to take their minds off hunger, off being cold and scared, off watching everybody else and yourself every waking second for signs of sprouting. But Millie didn't want to be distracted. Taking your mind off things could kill you. She was only going along with the game to show the others that she wasn't getting cranky; getting loupy.

She rubbed the end of her handless wrist. Damp was making it achy. She reached for the bottle of vodka where Max had stood it upright in the crook of his crossed legs. "Nuh-uh-uh," he chided, pulling it out of her reach and passing it to Citron, who took two pulls at the bottle and coughed.

Max said to Millie, "You don't get any treats until you start a new game."

Jolly turned back from the fire, her grinning teeth the only thing that shone in her black silhouette.

"Wasn't me who spoiled that last one," Millie grumbled. But she leaned back on the packed earth, her good forearm and the one with the missing hand both lying flush against the soil. She considered how to begin. The ground was a little warmer tonight than it had been last night. Spring was coming. Soon, there'd be pungent wild leeks to pull up and eat from the river bank. She'd been craving their taste all through this frozen winter. She'd been yearning for the sight and taste of green, growing things. Only she wouldn't eat too many of them. You couldn't ever eat your fill of anything, or that might bring out the Hound. Soon it'd be warm enough to sleep outside again. She thought of rats and garbage heaps, and slammed her mind's door shut on the picture. Millie liked sleeping with the air on her skin, even though it was dangerous out of doors. It felt more dangerous indoors, what with everybody growing up.

And then she knew how to start the loup. She said, "The river swells in May's spring tide."

Jolly strode back from the fire and took the vodka from Max. "That's a really good one." She offered the bottle to her twin.

Millie found herself smiling as she took it. Jolly was quick to speak her mind, whether scorn or praise. Millie could never stay mad at her for long. Millie drank through her smile, feeling the vodka burn its trail down. With her stump she pointed at Jolly and waited to hear how Jolly would Loup-de-lou with the words "spring tide."

"The spring's May tide is deep and wide," louped Jolly. She was breaking the rules again; three words, not two, and she'd added a "the" at the top, and changed the order around! People shouldn't change stuff, it was bad! Millie was about to protest when a quavery howl crazed the crisp night, then disappeared like a sob into silence.

"Shit!" hissed Sai. She leapt up and began kicking dirt onto the fire to douse it. The others stood too.

"Race you to the house!" yelled a gleeful Jolly, already halfway there at a run.

Barking with forced laughter, the others followed her. Millie, who was almost as quick as Jolly, reached the disintegrating cement steps of the house a split second before Jolly pushed in through the door, yelling "I win!" as loudly as she could. The others tumbled in behind Millie, shoving and giggling.

Sai hissed, "Sshh!" Loud noises weren't a good idea.

With a chuckle in her voice, Jolly replied, "Oh, chill, we're fine. Remember how Churchy used to say that loud noises chased away ghosts?"

Everyone went silent. They were probably all thinking the same thing; that maybe Churchy was a ghost now. Millie whispered, "We have to keep quiet, or the easthound will hear us."

"Bite me," said Max. "There's no such thing as an easthound." His voice was deeper than it had been last week. No use pretending. He was growing up. Millie put a bit more distance between him and her. Max really was getting too old. If he didn't do the right thing soon and leave on his own, they'd have to kick him out. Hopefully before something ugly happened.

Citron closed the door behind them. It was dark in the house. Millie tried to listen beyond the door to the outside. That had been no wolf howling, and they all knew it. She tried to rub away the pain in her wrist. "Do we have any aspirin?"

Sai replied, "I'm sorry. I took the last two yesterday."

Citron sat with a thump on the floor and started to sob. "I hate this," he said slurrily. "I'm cold and I'm scared and there's no bread left, and it smells of mildew in here—"

"You're just drunk," Millie told him.

"—and Millie's cranky all the time," Citron continued with a glare at Millie, "and Sai farts in her sleep, and Max's boots don't fit him any more. He's growing up."

"Shut up!" said Max. He grabbed Citron by the shoulders, dragged him to his feet, and started to shake him. "Shut up!" His voice broke on the "up" and ended in a little squeak. It should have been funny, but now he had Citron up against the wall and was choking him. Jolly and Sai yanked at Max's hands. They told him over and over to stop, but he wouldn't. The creepiest thing was, Citron wasn't making any sound. He couldn't. He couldn't get any air. He scrabbled at Max's hands, trying to pull them off his neck.

Millie knew she had to do something quickly. She slammed the bottle of vodka across Max's back, like christening a ship. She'd seen it on tv, when tvs still worked. When you could still plug one in and have juice flow through the wires to make funny cartoon creatures move behind the screen, and your mom wouldn't sprout in front of your eyes and eat your dad and bite your hand off.

Millie'd thought the bottle would shatter. But maybe the glass was too thick, because though it whacked Max's back with a solid thump, it didn't break. Max dropped to the floor like he'd been shot. Jolly put her hands to her mouth. Startled at what she herself had done, Millie dropped the bottle. It exploded when it hit the floor, right near Max's head. Vodka fountained up and out, and then Max was whimpering and rolling around in the booze and broken glass. There were dark smears under him.

"Ow! Jesus! Ow!" He peered up to see who had hit him. Millie moved closer to Jolly.

"Max." Citron's voice was hoarse. He reached a hand out to Max. "Get out of the glass, dude. Can you stand up?"

Millie couldn't believe it. "Citron, he just tried to kill you!"

"I shouldn't have talked about growing up. Jolly, can you find the candles? It's dark in here. Come on, Max." Citron pulled Max to his feet.

Max came up mad. He shook broken glass off his leather jacket, and stood towering over Millie. Was his chest thicker than it had been? Was that hair shadowing his chin? Millie whimpered and cowered away. Jolly put herself between Millie and Max. "Don't be a big old bully," she said to Max. "Picking on the one-hand girl. Don't be a dog."

It was like a light came back on in Max's eyes. He looked at Jolly, then at Millie. "You hurt me, Millie. I wouldn't hurt you," he said to Millie. "Even if…"

"If…that thing was happening to you," Jolly interrupted him, "you wouldn't care who you were hurting. Besides, you were choking Citron, so don't give us that innocent look and go on about not hurting people."

Max's eyes welled up. They glistened in the candle light. "I'll go," he said drunkenly. His voice sounded high, like the boy he was ceasing to be. "Soon. I'll go away. I promise."

"When?" Millie asked softly. They all heard her, though. Citron looked at her with big, wet doe eyes.

Max swallowed. "Tomorrow. No. A week."

"Three days," Jolly told him. "Two more sleeps."

Max made a small sound in his throat. He wiped his hand over his face. "Three days," he agreed. Jolly nodded, firmly.

After that, noone wanted to play Loup-de-lou any more. They didn't bother with candles. They all went to their own places, against the walls so they could keep an eye on each other. Millie and Jolly had the best place, together near the window. That way, if anything bad happened, Jolly could boost Millie out the window. There used to be a low bookcase under that window. They'd burned the wood months ago, for cooking with. The books that had been on it were piled up to one side, and Jolly'd scavenged a pile of old clothes for a bed. Jolly rummaged around under the clothes. She pulled out the gold necklace that their mom had given her for passing French. Jolly only wore it to sleep. She fumbled with the clasp, dropped the necklace, swore under her breath. She found the necklace again and put it on successfully this time. She kissed Millie on the forehead. "Sleep tight, Mills."

Millie said, "My wrist hurts too much. Come with me tomorrow to see if the kids two streets over have any painkillers?"

"Sure, honey." Warrens kept their distance from each other, for fear of becoming targets if somebody in someone else's warren sprouted. "But try to get some sleep, okay?" Jolly lay down and was asleep almost immediately, her breathing quick and shallow.

Millie remained sitting with her back against the wall. Max lay on the other side of the room, using his coat as a blanket. Was he sleeping, or just lying there, listening?

She used to like Max. Weeks after the world had gone mad, he'd found her and Jolly hiding under the porch of somebody's house. They were dirty and hungry, and the stench of rotting meat from inside the house was drawing flies. Jolly had managed to keep Millie alive that long, but Millie was delirious with pain, and the place where her hand had been bitten off had started smelling funny. Max had brought them clean water. He'd searched and bargained with the other warrens of hiding kids until he found morphine and antibiotics for Millie. He was the one who'd told them that it looked like only adults were getting sick.

But now Millie was scared of him. She sat awake half the night, watching Max. Once, he shifted and snorted, and the hairs on Millie's arms stood on end. She shoved herself right up close against Jolly. But Max just grumbled and rolled over and kept sleeping. He didn't change. Not this time. Millie watched him a little longer, until she couldn't keep her eyes open. She curled up beside Jolly. Jolly was scrawny, her skin downy with the peach fuzz that Sai said came from starvation. Most of them had it. Nobody wanted to grow up and change, but Jolly needed to eat a little more, just a little. Millie stared into the dark and worried. She didn't know when she fell asleep. She woke when first light was making the window into a glowing blue square. She was cold. Millie reached to put her arm around Jolly. Her arm landed on wadded-up clothing with nobody in it.

"She's gone," said Citron.

"Whuh?" Millie rolled over, sat up. She was still tired. "She gone to check the traps?" Jolly barely ate, but she was best at catching gamey squirrels, feral cats, and the occasional raccoon.

"I dunno. I woke up just as the door was closing behind her. She let in a draft."

Millie leapt to her feet. "It was Max! He sprouted! He ate her!"

Citron leapt up too. He pulled her into a hug. "Sh. It wasn't Max. Look, he's still sleeping."

He was. Millie could see him huddled under his coat.

"See?" said Citron. "Now hush. You're going to wake him and Sai up."

"Oh god, I was so scared for a moment." She was lying; she never stopped being scared. She sobbed and let Citron keep hugging her, but not for long. Things could sneak up on you while you were busy making snot and getting hugs to make you feel better. Millie swallowed back the rest of her tears. She pulled out of Citron's arms. "Thanks." She went and checked beside Jolly's side of the bed. Jolly's jacket wasn't there. Neither was her penguin. Ah. "She's gone to find aspirin for me." Millie sighed with relief and guilt. "She took her penguin to trade with. That's almost her most favorite thing ever."

"Next to you, you mean."

"I suppose so. I come first, then her necklace, then the penguin." Jolly'd found the ceramic penguin a long time ago when they'd been scavenging in the wreckage of a drug store. The penguin stood on a circular base, the whole thing about ten inches tall. Its beak was broken, but when you twisted the white base, music played out of it. Jolly had kept it carefully since, wrapped in a torn blouse. She played it once a week and on special occasions. Twisted the base twice only, let the penguin do a slow turn to the few notes of tinny song. Churchy had told them that penguin was from a movie called *Madagascar*. She'd been old enough to remember old-time stuff like that. It was soon after that that they'd had to kill her.

Millie stared at her and Jolly's sleeping place. There was something… "She didn't take socks. Her feet must be freezing." She picked up the pair of socks with the fewest holes in it. "We have to go find her."

"You go," Citron replied. "It's cold out, and I want to get some more sleep."

"You know we're not supposed to go anywhere on our own!"

"Yeah, but we do. Lots of times."

"Except me. I always have someone with me."

"Right. Like that's any safer than being alone. I'm going back to bed." He yawned and turned away.

Millie fought the urge to yell at him. Instead she said, "I claim leader."

Citron stopped. "Aw, come on, Millie."

But Millie was determined. "Leader. One of us might be in danger, so I claim leader. So you have to be my follower."

He looked skywards and sighed. "Fine. Where?"

That meant she was leader. You asked the leader what to do, and the leader told you. Usually everyone asked Jolly what to do, or Max. Now that she had an excuse to go to Jolly, Millie stopped feeling as though something had gnawed away the pit of her stomach. She yanked her coat out of the pile of clothing that was her bed and shrugged it on. "Button me," she said to Citron, biting back the "please." Leaders didn't say please. They just gave orders. That was the right way to do it.

Citron concentrated hard on the buttons, not looking in Millie's eyes as he did them up. He started in the middle, buttoned down to the last button just below her hips, then stood up to do the buttons at her chest. He held the fabric away from her, so it wouldn't touch her body at all. His fingers didn't touch her, but still her chest felt tingly as Citron did up the top buttons. She knew he was blushing, even though you couldn't tell on his dark face. Hers neither. If it had been Max doing this, his face would have lit up like a strawberry. They found strawberries growing sometimes, in summer.

Leaders didn't blush. Millie straightened up and looked at Citron. He had such a baby face. If he was lucky, he'd never sprout. She'd heard that some people didn't. Max said it was too soon to tell, because the pandemic had only started two years ago, but Millie liked to hope that some kids would avoid the horrible thing. No temper getting worse and worse. No changing all of a sudden into something different and scary. Millie wondered briefly what happened to the ones who didn't sprout, who just got old. Food for the easthound, probably. "Maybe we should go…" Millie began to ask, then remembered herself. Leaders didn't ask, they told. "We're going over by the grocery first," she told Citron. "Maybe she's just checking her traps."

"She took her music box to check her traps?"

"Doesn't matter. That's where we're going to go." She stuffed Jolly's socks into her coat pocket, then shoved her shoulder against the damp-swollen door and stepped out into the watery light of an early spring morning. The sun made her blink.

Citron asked, "Shouldn't we get those two to come along with us? You know, so there's more of us?"

"No," growled Millie. "Just now you wanted me to go all alone, but now you want company?"

"But who does trading this early in the morning?"

"We're not going to wake Max and Sai, okay? We'll find her ourselves!"

Citron frowned. Millie shivered. It was so cold out that her nosehairs froze together when she breathed in. Like scattered pins, tiny, shiny daggers of frost edged the sidewalk slabs and the new spring leaves of the small maple tree that grew outside their squat. Trust Jolly to make her get out of a warm bed to go looking for her on a morning like this. She picked up three solid throwing rocks. They were gritty with dirt and the cold of them burned her fingers. She stuffed them into her jacket pocket, on top of Jolly's socks. Citron had the baseball bat he carried everywhere. Millie turned up her collar and stuck her hand into her jeans pocket. "C'mon."

Jolly'd put a new batch of traps over by that old grocery store. The roof was caved in. There was no food in the grocery any more, or soap, or cough medicine. Everything had been scavenged by the nearby warrens of kids, but animals sometimes made nests and shit in the junk that was left. Jolly'd caught a dog once. A gaunt poodle with dirty, matted hair. But they didn't eat dogs, ever. You were what you ate. They'd only killed it in an orgy of fury and frustration that had swelled over them like a river.

Black Betty had a child,
Bam-ba-lam,
That child's gone wild,
Bam-ba-lam.

Really, it was Millie who'd started it, back before everything went wrong, two winters ago. They'd been at home. Jolly sitting on the living room floor that early evening, texting with her friends, occasionally giggling at something one of them said. Millie and Dad on the couch, sharing a bowl of raspberries. All of them watching some old-time cartoon movie on tv about animals that could do Kung Fu. Waiting for Mum to come home from work. Because then they would order pizza. It was pizza night. Dad getting a text message on his phone. Dad holding the phone down by his knee to make out the words, even though his eyesight was just fine, he said. Jolly watching them, waiting to hear if it was Mum, if she'd be home soon. Millie leaning closer to Dad and squinting at the tiny message in the phone's window. Mouthing the words silently. Then frowning. Saying, "Mum says she's coming home on the easthound train?" Dad falling out laughing. Eastbound, sweetie.

There hadn't been an easthound before that. It was Millie who'd called it, who'd made it be. Jolly'd told her that wasn't true, that she didn't make the pandemic just by reading a word wrong, that the world didn't work that way. But the world didn't work any more the way it used to, so what did Jolly know? Even if she was older than Millie.

Jolly and Millie's family had assigned adjectives to the girls early on in their lives. Millie was The Younger One. (By twenty-eight and three-quarter minutes. The midwife had been worried that Mum would need a C-Section to get Millie out.) Jolly was The Kidder. She liked jokes and games. She'd come up with Loup-de-lou to help keep Millie's mind off the agony when she'd lost her hand. Millie'd still been able to feel the missing hand there, on the end of her wrist, and pain wouldn't let her sleep or rest, and all the adults in the world were sprouting and trying to kill off the kids, and Max was making her and Jolly and Citron move to a new hiding place every few days, until he and Jolly figured out the thing about sprinkling peppermint oil to hide their scent trails so that sprouteds couldn't track them. That was back before Sai had joined them, and then Churchy. Back before Churchy had sprouted on them one night in the dark as they were all sharing half a stale bread loaf and a big liter bottle of flat cola, and Max and Citron and Sai had grabbed anything heavy or sharp they could find and waled away at the thing that had been Churchy just seconds before, until it lay still on the ground, all pulpy and bloody. And the whole time, Jolly had stayed near still-weak Millie, brandishing a heavy frying pan and muttering, "It's okay, Mills. I won't let her get you."

The feeling was coming back, like her hand was still there. Her wrist had settled into a throbbing ache. She hoped it wasn't getting infected again.

Watchfully, they walked down their side street and turned onto the main street in the direction of the old grocery store. They walked up the middle of the empty road. That way, if a sprouted came out of one of the shops or alleyways, they might have time to see it before it attacked.

The burger place, the gas station, the little shoe repair place on the corner; Millie tried to remember what stores like that had been like before. When they'd had unbroken windows and unempty shelves. When there'd been people shopping in them and adults running them, back when adults used to be just grown-up people suspicious of packs of schoolkids in their stores, not howling, sharp-toothed child-killers with dank, stringy fur and paws instead of hands. Ravenous monsters that grew and grew so quickly that you could watch it happen, if you were stupid enough to stick around. Their teeth, hair and claws lengthened, their bodies getting bigger and heavier minute by minute, until they could no longer eat quickly enough to keep up with the growth, and they weakened and died a few days after they'd sprouted.

Jolly wasn't tending to her traps. Millie swallowed. "Okay, so we'll go check with the warren over on Patel Street. They usually have aspirin and stuff." She walked in silence, except for the worry voice in her head.

Citron said, "That tree's going to have to start over."

"What?" Millie realized she'd stopped at the traffic light out of habit, because it had gone to red. She was such an idiot. And so was Citron, for just going along with her. She started walking again. Citron tagged along, always just a little behind.

"The maple tree," he puffed. When you never had enough to eat, you got tired quickly. "The one outside our place. It put its leaves out too early, and now the frost has killed them. It'll have to start over."

"Whatever." Then she felt guilty for being so crabby with him. What could she say to make nice? "Uh, that was a nice line you made in Loup-de-lou last night. The one with eyes and spies in it."

Citron smiled at her. "Thanks. It wasn't quite right, though. Sprouteds have bleedy red eyes, not shiny ones."

"But your line wasn't about sprouteds. It was about the…the easthound." She looked all around and behind her. Nothing.

"Thing is," Citron replied, so quietly that Millie almost didn't hear him, "We're all the easthound."

Instantly, Millie swatted the back of his head. "Shut up!"

"Ow!"

"Just shut up! Take that back! It's not true!"

"Stop making such a racket, willya?"

"So stop being such a loser!" She was sweating in her jacket, her skinny knees trembling. So hungry all the time. So scared.

Citron's eyes widened. "Millie—!"

He was looking behind her. She turned, hand fumbling in her jacket pocket for her rocks. The sprouted bowled her over while her hand was still snagged in her pocket. Thick, curling fur and snarling and teeth as long as her pinkie. It grabbed her. Its paws were like catcher's mitts with claws in them. It howled and briefly let her go. It's in pain, she thought wonderingly, even as she fought her hand out of her pocket and tried to get out from under the sprouted. All that quick growing. It must hurt them. The sprouted snapped at her face, missed. They were fast and strong when they first sprouted, but clumsy in their ever-changing bodies. The sprouted set its jaws in her chest. Through her coat and sweater, its teeth tore into her skin. Pain. Teeth sliding along her ribs. Millie tried to wrestle the head off her. She got her fingers deep into the fur around its neck. Then an impact jerked the sprouted's head sideways. Citron and his baseball bat, screaming, "Die, die, die!" as he beat the sprouted. It leapt for him. It was already bigger. Millie rolled to her feet, looking around for anything she could use as a weapon. Citron was keeping the sprouted at bay, just barely, by swinging his bat at it. It advanced on him, howling in pain with every step forward.

Sai seemed to come out of nowhere. She had the piece of rebar she carried whenever she went out. The three of them raged at the sprouted, screaming and hitting. Millie kicked and kicked. The sprouted screamed back, in pain or fury. Its eyes were all bleedy. It swatted Citron aside, but he got up and came at it again. Finally it wasn't fighting any more. They kept hitting it until they were sure it was dead. Even after Sai and Citron had stopped, Millie stomped the sprouted. With each stomp she grunted, in thick animal rage at herself for letting it sneak up on her, for leaving the warren without her knife. Out of the corner of her eye she could see a few kids that had crept out from other warrens to see what the racket was about. She didn't care. She stomped.

"Millie! Millie!" It was Citron. "It's dead!"

Millie gave the bloody lump of hair and bone and flesh one more kick, then stood panting. Just a second to catch her breath, then they could keep looking for Jolly. They couldn't stay there long. A dead sprouted could draw others. If one sprouted was bad, a feeding frenzy of them was worse.

Sai was gulping, sobbing. She looked at them with stricken eyes. "I woke up and I called to Max and he didn't answer, and when I went over and lifted his coat," Sai burst into gusts of weeping, "there was only part of his head and one arm there. And bones. Not even much blood." Sai clutched herself and shuddered. "While we were sleeping, a sprouted came in and killed Max and ate most of him, even licked up his blood, and we didn't wake up! I thought it had eaten all of you! I thought it was coming back for me!"

Something gleamed white in the broken mess of the sprouted's corpse. Millie leaned over to see better, fighting not to gag on the smell of blood and worse. She had to crouch closer. There was lots of blood on the thing lying in the curve of the sprouted's body, but with chilly clarity, Millie recognized it. It was the circular base of Jolly's musical penguin. Millie looked over at Citron and Sai. "Run," she told them. The tears coursing down her face felt cool. Because her skin was so hot now.

"What?" asked Sai. "Why?"

Millie straightened. Her legs were shaking so much they barely held her up. That small pop she'd felt when she pulled on the sprouted's neck. "A sprouted didn't come into our squat. It was already in there." She opened her hand to show them the thing she'd pulled off the sprouted's throat in her battle with it; Jolly's gold necklace. Instinct often led sprouteds to return to where the people they loved were. Jolly had run away to protect the rest of her warren from herself. "Bloody run!" Millie yelled at them. "Go find another squat! Somewhere I won't look for you! Don't you get it? I'm her twin!"

First Citron's face then Sai's went blank with shock as they understood what Millie was saying. Citron sobbed, once. It might have been the word, "Bye." He grabbed Sai's arm. The two of them stumbled away. The other kids that had come out to gawk had disappeared back to their warrens. Millie turned her back so she couldn't see what direction Sai and Citron were moving in, but she could hear them, more keenly than she'd ever been able to hear. She could smell them. The easthound could track them. The downy starvation fuzz on Millie's arm was already coarser. The pain in her handless wrist spiked. She looked at it. It was aching because the hand was starting to grow in again. There were tiny fingers on the end of it now. And she needed to eat so badly.

When had Jolly sprouted? Probably way more than twenty-eight and three-quarters minutes ago. Citron and Sai's only chance was that Millie had always done everything later than her twin.

Still clutching Jolly's necklace, she began to run, too; in a different direction. Leeks, she told the sprouting Hound, fresh leeks. You like those, right? Not blood and still-warm, still-screaming flesh. You like leeks. The Hound wasn't fully come into itself yet. It was almost believing her that leeks would satisfy its hunger. And it didn't understand that she couldn't swim. You're thirsty too, right? she told it.

It was.

Faster, faster, faster, Millie sped towards the river, where the spring tide was running deep and wide.

That child's gone wild.
Oh, Black Betty, bam-ba-lam.

Loup.

...

GOGGLES (C. 1910)

CAITLÍN R. KIERNAN

Caitlín R. Kiernan [www.caitlinrkiernan.com] *is the author of several novels, including* Daughter of Hounds, The Red Tree, *and* The Drowning Girl: A Memoir. *She is a prolific short fiction author—to date she has written over two hundred short stories, novellas, and vignettes—most of which have been collected in* Tales of Pain and Wonder; From Weird and Distant Shores; To Charles Fort, With Love; Alabaster; A Is for Alien; The Ammonite Violin & Others; Two Worlds and in Between: The Best of Caitlín R. Kiernan (Volume One), *and* Confessions of a Five-Chambered Heart. *Coming up is new novel* Blood Oranges *(written as by Kathleen Tierney). Kiernan is a multiple nominee for the World Fantasy Award, an honoree for the James Tiptree, Jr. Award, and has twice been nominated for the Shirley Jackson Award. Born in Ireland, she lives in Providence, Rhode Island.*

1.

Eleven-year-old Samuel is sitting alone at the entrance to the Confluence Park bunkers, huddled against the hot, stinking wind ruffling his hair, even though they've all been forbidden to go alone to the entrance. It's long past midnight, and the dreams have been keeping him awake again. The ruins and the storm-wracked sky outside are less frightening than the dreams—all of them taken together as a whole, or any single one of dreams. Better he sit and stare out through the gate's iron bars, fairly certain he can be back in his berth before Miss makes her early morning rounds. He always feels bad whenever he breaks the rules, going against her orders, the dictates that keep them all alive, the children that she tends

91

here in the sanctuary of the winding rat's maze of tunnels. He feels bad, too, that he's figured out a way to pick the padlock on the iron door that has to be opened in order to stare out the bars, and Samuel feels worst of all that he thinks often of picking that lock, too, and disobeying her first and most inviolable rule: never, ever leave the bunker alone. Still, regret and guilt are not enough to keep him in his upper berth, staring at the concrete ceiling pressing down less than a meter above his face.

Outside, the wind screams, and sickly chartreuse lightning flashes and jabs with its forked fingers at the shattered, blackened ruins of the dead city of Cherry Creek, Colorado. Samuel shuts his eyes, and he tries to ignore the afterimages of the flashes swimming about behind his lids. He counts off the seconds on his fingers, counting aloud, though not daring to speak above a whisper—sixteen, seventeen, eighteen full seconds before the thunder reaches him, thunder so loud that it almost seems to rattle deep down in his bones. He divides eighteen by three, as Miss has taught them, and so he knows the strike was about six kilometers from the entrance to the tunnels.

Sam, that's much too close, she would say. *Now, you shut that door and get your butt back downstairs.*

He might be so bold as to reply that at least they didn't have to worry about the dogs and the rats during a squall. But that might be enough to earn him whatever punishment she was in the mood to mete out to someone who'd not only flagrantly broken the rules, but then had the unmitigated gall to sass her.

The boy opens his eyes, blinking at the lightening ghosts swirling before them. He stares at his filthy hands a moment, vaguely remembering when he was much younger and his mother was always at him to scrub beneath his nails and behind his ears. When she saw to it he had clean clothes every day, and shoes with laces, shoes without soles worn so thin they may as well be paper. He stares at the ruins and half remembers the city that was, before the War, before men set the sky on fire and seared the world.

Miss tells them it's best not to let one's thoughts dwell on those days. "That time is never coming back," she says. "We have to learn to live in *this* age, if we're going to have any hope of survival."

But all they have—their clothing, beds, dishes, school books, the dwindling medicinals and foodstuffs—all of it is scavenged remnants of the time before. He knows that. They all know that, even if no one ever says it aloud.

There's another flash of the lightning that is not quite green and not quite yellow. But this time Samuel doesn't close his eyes or bother counting. It's obvious this one's nearer than the last strike. It's obvious it's high time that he shut the inner door, lock it, and slip back through the tunnels to the room where the boys all sleep. Miss always looks in on them about three, and she's ever quick to notice an empty bunk. That's another thing from the world before: her silver pocket watch that she's very, very careful to keep wound. She's said that it belonged to her father who died in the Battle of New Amsterdam in those earliest months of the War. Miss is, Samuel thinks, a woman of many contradictions. She admonishes them when they talk of their old lives, yet, in certain melancholy moods, she will regale them with tales of lost wonders and conveniences, of the sun and stars and of airships, and her kindly father, a physician who went away to tend wounded soldiers and subsequently died in New Amsterdam.

Walking back to his bed as quietly as he can walk, Samuel considers those among his companions who are convinced that Miss isn't sane. Jessamine says that, and the twins—Parthena and Hortence—and also Luther. Sometimes, when Miss has her back to them, they'll draw circles in the air about their ears and roll their eyes and snigger. But Samuel doesn't think she's insane. Just very lonely and sad and scared.

We keep her alive, he thinks. *Because she has all of us to tend to she's still alive, against her recollections.* He knows of lots of folks who survived the bombardments, and then the burning of the skies and the storms that followed, and whom the feral dogs didn't catch up with, lots of those folks did themselves in, rather than face such a shattered world. Samuel thinks it was their inescapable memories of before that killed them.

He crawls back into bed, and lies on the cool sheets and stares at the ceiling until the dreams come again. In the dreams—which he thinks of as nightmares—there's bright sunshine, green fields, and his mother's blonde hair like spun gold. In his dreams, there's plenty of food and there's laughter, and no lightning whatsoever. There is never lightning, nor is there the oily rain that sizzles when it touches anything metal. He's never told Miss about his dreams. She wouldn't want to hear them, and she'd only frown and make him promise not to dare mention them to the others. Not that he ever has. Not that he ever will. Samuel figures they all have their own good-bad dreams to contend with.

2.

The storm lasts for two days and two nights. Miss reads to them from the Bible, and from *The Life and Strange Surprizing Adventures of Robinson Crusoe,* and from Mark Twain. She feeds her filthy, rawboned children the last of the tinned beef and peaches, and Samuel has begun to resign himself to the possibility that this might be the occasion on which they starve before an expedition for more provisions can be mounted.

But the storm ends, and no one starves.

Early the morning after the last peals of thunder, after a meager breakfast—one sardine each and tea so weak that it's hardly more than cups of steaming water—Miss calls them all to the assembly room. They know it was not originally *intended* as an assembly room, but as an armory. The steel cabinets with their guns, grenades, and sabers still line the walls. Only the kegs of black powder and crates of dynamite have been removed. The children line up in two neat rows, boys in front, girls behind them, and she examines them each in their turn, inspecting gaunt faces and bodies, looking closely at their shoes and garments, before choosing the three whom she will send out of the bunker in search of food and other necessaries.

Once, there were older kids to whom this duty fell, but with every passing year there were fewer and fewer of them. Every year, fewer of them survived the necessary trips outside of the bunker, and, finally, there were none of them left at all. Finally, none came back. Samuel suspects a brave (or cowardly) few might have actually run away, deciding to take their chances in the wastelands that lie out beyond Cherry Creek, rather than return. However, this is only a suspicion, and he's never spoken of it to anyone else.

The lighter sheets of rain that fall towards the end of the electrical storms are mostly only water, and after an hour or so it will have diluted most of the nitric acid. It'll take that long to hand out the slickers and vulcanized overshoes and gloves, the airtight goggles and respirators, and for Miss to check that every rusty clasp is secure and every fraying cord has been tied as tightly as possible. Samuel imagines, as he always does, that the others are all holding their breath as she makes her choices. There have been too many instances when someone didn't return, or when they returned dying or crippled, which is as good as dead, or worse, here in their bunker in the world after the War. Samuel also imagines he's one of the few who ever *hopes* that he'll be picked. He doesn't know for certain, but he strongly suspects this to be the case.

If volunteers were permitted, he would always volunteer.

"Patrick Henry," says Miss. Patrick Henry Olmstead takes one step forward and stares at the toes of his boots. His hair is either auburn or dirty blond, depending on the light, and his eyes are either hazel green or hazel brown, depending on the light. He's two years younger than Samuel. Or, at least he thinks he might be; a lot of the younger children don't know their ages. Patrick Henry has a keloid scar on his chin, and he's taller than one might expect from his nine years. He's shy, and speaks so softly that it's often necessary to ask him to please speak up and repeat himself.

"Molly," says Miss.

"Please no, Miss." Molly Peterson replies.

"You have good shoes, Molly. Your shoes are the best among the lot."

"I'll let someone else wear my shoes. I won't even ask for them back afterwards. Please choose another, Miss."

Molly is only eight, and her hair is black as coal tar. She's missing the pinkie finger from her left hand, from a run in with the dogs before they found her at the corner of East Bateman and Vulcan Avenue. Before an expedition brought her back to the bunker two years ago. The dogs got her sister, and she's only left the bunker once after her arrival. Molly has nightmares about the dogs, and sometimes she wakes screaming loudly enough that she startles them all from sleep, as her cries echo along the cavernous corridors. Her skin is very pale and freckled. She's small for her age. Samuel fancies if he were to ever court a girl, Molly would do just fine.

"You will go, Molly. Your name has been read, my choice has been made, and we will not have this argument. No one will go in your stead."

Molly only nods and chews at her lower lip.

"You will have eight hours," Miss tells them, just like always. "After eight hours…"

Samuel tunes out her grim and familiar proclamations. No one's ever come back after eight hours, and that's all that matters. The rest, Miss only says to be sure his two companions fully understand the gravity of their situation, and Samuel understands completely. This will be his fifth trip out in just the last year. He's good at scavenging, and Miss knows it. He enjoys entertaining the notion he's the best of them all.

"Eight hours," Miss says again.

"Eight hours, Ma'am," the chosen three repeat in perfect unison, and then she shepherds them away to the room where the outside gear is stored. She gives them each a burlap sack and a Colt revolver and a single .44 caliber bullet; the bunker's munitions cache is running too low to send them off with any more than that single round. She once whispered in his ear, "For yourself, or for one of the dogs. That has to be your decision." He has no idea whether or not she's ever said the same thing to any of the others. He doesn't actually *want* to know, because maybe it's a special acknowledgement of his bravery and approaching manhood, and if it's a jot of wisdom she imparts to one and all, Samuel would be more than a little disappointed.

3.

As almost always, Samuel is given the responsibility of carrying the map. It's a 15-minute topographic map of the Cherry Creek metropolitan area. It's folded and tucked into a water-tight leather-and-PVC case, so he can see it, yet there's minimal danger of its getting wet. But Samuel knows exactly where he's going today, even through the dense fog, so he hardly needs the green and white topo sheet, with its black squares marking buildings and all its contour lines designating elevation. He and Patrick Henry and Molly are heading to what's left of the Gesellschaft zur Förderung der Luftschiffahrt's Arapahoe Station dirigible terminal. A few months back, he and two others were rummaging about in one of the airships that crashed when Cherry Creek was hit by the first wave of blowbacks from Tesla's teleforce mechanism. Deck B was still more or less intact, which meant the kitchen was also mostly intact, along with its storerooms. The two boys with him hadn't wanted to enter the crash, so Samuel had climbed alone through a ragged tear in the hull. He spent the better part of an hour picking his way through the crumpled remains of the gondola, always mindful of the hazards posed by rusted beams overhead and the rotting deck boards beneath his feet. But, at last, he found the storeroom, the shelves still weighted down with their wealth of cans and crates of bottles and jars, a surprising number of which hadn't shattered on impact, thanks to having been carefully packed in excelsior.

Samuel had retraced his steps, marking the path with debris placed *just so*, then cajoled his two fellows to follow him back inside. The three of them had returned with enough food to last several weeks, including fruit juice that had not yet spoiled. The discovery had earned Samuel one night of double rations.

"Are you certain we're not lost?" asks Patrick Henry, his already quiet voice muffled by the respirator covering the lower half of his face.

"I don't get lost," Samuel replied, then tossed half a brick against a lamppost. Someone had long ago shattered the globe crowning the post, or, more likely, a lightning storm had taken it out. "I've never gotten lost, not even once."

"Everyone gets lost sometime," says Molly. "Don't be such a braggart." She was so scared that she jumped at the thud of the brick hitting the lamppost.

"Then maybe I'm not everybody."

"Now, you're not even making sense," mutters Molly.

"Are you sure we're going west?" Patrick Henry asks.

Samuel stops and glares back at the younger boy. "Holy hell and horse shit, I wish Miss had let me come alone. Why are you asking me? *You're* the one with the Brunton."

No one—not even Samuel—is ever allowed to carry both the map *and* the Brunton compass. Just in case. Patrick Henry blushes, then digs the compass from the pocket of his overalls.

"Waste our time and take a reading if it'll make you feel better, but we ain't lost."

"Aren't," whispers Molly.

"But we *aren't* lost," Samuel sighs and rolls his eyes behind the smudgy lenses of his old blowtorch goggles

"It won't take long," says Patrick Henry, and so Samuel kicks at the dirt and Molly frets while he squints into the compass' mirror and studies the target, needle, and guide line, finding the azimuth pointing 270° from true north.

"Satisfied?" Samuel asks after a minute or two.

"Well, we're off by…"

"We're *not* lost," Samuel growls, then turns and stalks away, as though he means to leave the other two behind. He never would, but it works, and soon they're trotting along to catch up.

"It's not as though we can see the sun," Molly says, a little out of breath. "It's not as if we can see the mountains."

"I know the way to the station," Samuel tells her. "That's why Miss picked me, because I know the way."

"It pays to be sure."

"Fine, Molly. Now we're sure. Shut up and walk."

"You don't have to be such a bloody, self-righteous snit about it," she tells Samuel.

"Yes he does," sneers Patrick Henry, and Samuel laughs and agrees with him.

The going is slower than usual, mostly due to deep new washouts dividing many of the thoroughfares. Patrick Henry takes a bad tumble in the one bisecting Davies and Milton streets, where the dead city's namesake waterway has jumped its banks and carved a steep ravine. But he doesn't break or even sprain anything, only almost loses the revolver Miss has entrusted to him. Samuel and Molly pull him free of the mud and help him back up to street level, Samuel admonishing him for being such a clumsy fool every step of the way. Patrick Henry doesn't bother to say otherwise. The two sit together a few minutes with Molly, catching their breath and staring upstream at the wreckage that had once been Beeman's Mercantile before the building slid into the washout.

It's afternoon before they reach the airship, and Samuel has begun to worry about getting back before their eight hours are up, before Miss writes them off for dead. Besides, with the dogs on the prowl, he knows from experience that every passing minute decreases their chances of not meeting up with a pack of the mongrels.

"It's enormous," Molly says, gazing up at the crash, her voice tinged with awe. All three were too young to recall the days when the Count von Zeppelin's majestic airships plied the skies by the hundreds. And this was the first time that either Molly or Patrick Henry had actually seen a dirigible, other than a couple of pictures in one of Miss' books.

"It's like a skeleton," says Patrick Henry, and Samuel supposes it is, though the comparison has never before occurred to him. Once, almost a year ago, he'd crawled through the ruins of the late Professor Jeremiah Ogilvy's museum on Kipling Street. He'd seen bones there, or stones in the shape of bones, and Miss had explained to him afterwards that they were the remains of wicked sea monsters that lived before Noah's Flood and which were not permitted room on the Ark (he was polite and didn't ask her why sea creatures had drowned in the deluge). The petrified bones had much the same appearance of the crushed and half-melted steel framework sprawling before them.

Samuel points to the narrow vertical tear in what's left of the gondola. It's black as pitch beyond the tear. "The larder isn't too far in, but it's rough going. So, we'd best—"

"I'm not going in there," declares Patrick Henry, interrupting him.

"Hell's bell's you ain't," says Samuel, whirling about to face the other boy.

"Aren't," Molly says so quietly they almost don't hear her. "You *aren't* going in there."

"You shut up, Molly, and yes he most certainly is. I don't care if he's a damned yellow-bellied coward. There ain't no *way* I can carry all the food we need out alone."

"I *won't* go in there, Samuel."

Samuel shoves Patrick Henry with enough force that the younger boy almost loses his balance andnearly falls to the tarmac.

"You will, or I'll kick your sorry ass to Perdition and back again."

"Then you do that, Samuel. 'Cause I *won't* go in, no matter how hard you beat me, and that's all there is to it."

"You slimy, piss-poor whoreson," snarls Samuel between his teeth, and then he knocks Patrick Henry to the ground and gives him a sharp kick in the ribs.

There's a click, and Samuel turns his head to see Molly pointing her Colt at him. With both thumbs, she's drawn back the hammer and cocked the gun, and has her right index finger on the trigger. The barrel gleams faintly in the dingy light of the day. Her hands are trembling, and she's obviously having trouble holding the revolver level.

"You leave him alone, Samuel. Don't you dare kick him again. You step away from him, right this minute."

"Molly, you wouldn't dare," Samuel replies, narrowing his eyes, trying hard to seem as if he's not the least bit afraid, even though his heart's pounding in his chest. No one's ever held a gun on him before.

"Is this the day you want to find out if that's for true, Samuel?" she asks him, and her hands shake a little less.

Samuel turns away from her and stares down at Patrick Henry a moment. The boy's curled into a fetal position, and is cradling the place where the kick landed.

"Fine," says Samuel. "If you're lucky, maybe the dogs will find the both of you. That'd be better than if Miss hears about this, now wouldn't it."

"You just don't hit him no more."

"You just don't hit him *again*," Samuel says, and the act of correcting her makes him feel the smallest bit less scared of the gun. "You might be a slattern, but you don't have to sound like one, Molly Peterson."

Patrick Henry coughs and squeaks out a few unintelligible words from behind his respirator.

"May the dogs find you both," Samuel says, because there aren't many worse ways left to curse someone. He puts his back to the both of them and climbs into the dark gondola. It'll take time for his eyes to adjust, and he leans against a wall and listens to Molly consoling Patrick Henry. Samuel grips the butt of his own Colt, tucked into his waistband.

If I had another bullet, he thinks, but leaves it at that. Miss will take care of them, and oh, how he'll gloat when the coward and the turncoat bitch get what's coming to them. Unless, like he said, the dogs find them first. He thinks, *Molly knows all about the dogs firsthand,* then chuckles softly at his unintentional pun, and begins making his way cautiously, warily, through what's left of the passengers' observation deck.

4.

As has been said, Miss has told all her charges there's no point dwelling on what was, but has been forever lost.

"That time is never coming back," she said, on the occasion Samuel ever asked her about how things were before the War. "We have to learn to live in *this* age, if we're going to have any hope of survival."

"I only want to know *why* it happened," he persisted. "Didn't everyone have everything they wanted, everything they needed? What was there to fight over?"

She smiled a sad sort of smile and tousled his hair. "Some folks had everything they needed, and a lot more besides. You might look up at the dirigibles, or see the brass and silver clockworks, or the steam rails, or go to a great city and wonder at the shining towers. You could do that, Samuel, and imagine the world was good. You could listen to the endless promises of scientists, engineers, and politicians and believe we lived in a Golden Age that would last forever and a day, where all men were free from want. But those men and women were arrogant, and we all swallowed their hubris and made it our own. Ever wonder why folks who never went near a foundry or flew a 'thopter, people who never even got their hands dirty, used to wear goggles?"

"No," he told her, after trying very hard to figure out why they would have. Admittedly, it didn't make much sense.

"Because wearing goggles made us feel like we were more than onlookers, Samuel. It made us feel like we all had our shoulder to the wheel, that we'd all *earned* what we had. We wanted to believe there *was* finally enough for everyone, and everyone did, indeed, *have* everything they needed."

"But they didn't?"

"No, Samuel, they didn't. Not by half. We didn't talk about Africa, the East Indies, or the colonies elsewhere. They didn't talk about the working conditions in the mines and factories, or the Red Indian reservations, the people who suffered and died so that a few of us could live our lives of plenty. Most of all, though, they didn't talk about how *nothing* lasts forever—not coal, not wood, not oil or peat—and how one nation turns against another when it starts to run out of the resources it needs to power the engines of progress. They didn't tell us about the weapons the Czar and America and Britain, China and Prussia and lots of other countries were building. Our leaders and scholars and journalists didn't talk about these things, Samuel, and very few of the lucky people ever bothered to ask why."

"So, we weren't good people?"

She stared at him silently for almost a full minute, and then she said, softly, "We were *people,* Samuel. And that's as good an answer as any I can offer you," she told him, then said they'd talked quite enough and sent him away to bed. He paused outside the room where the boys sleep and looked back. She was still sitting on the concrete bench, and had begun to weep quietly to herself.

5.

Lugging his bulging burlap bag loaded with cans and bottles back through the perilous gauntlet of Deck B, Samuel isn't thinking about the conversation with Miss. The sweat stung his eyes, and his head ached from having bumped it hard against a sagging I-beam. His back aches, too, and he's lost track of time in the darkness of the gondola. He isn't thinking about much at all except getting back before their eight hours has passed, and how many they might have left. He has room to worry about that, and he has energy to fume about Molly Peterson and Patrick Henry Olmstead, the dirty cowards shirking their duty and leaving him to do all the hard work. He takes satisfaction in knowing what Miss would do to them back at the bunker, how they'd go a day and a night without meals, how everyone would be forbidden to speak to them for a week. Miss doesn't tolerate deadbeats and cowards.

Samuel's footsteps and breath are so loud, and he's so lost in thought, that he's almost reached the tear in the hull before he hears the dogs. He eases the burlap bag to the floor and slowly draws the Colt from inside his overalls and his slicker. All at once, the snarling and barking and low, threatful growls are so loud that the dogs might as well be inside the dirigible with him. He knows better, knows it seems that way because he wasn't listening before. He was breaking another of Miss' rules: never, ever lower your guard. But he had. He'd become distracted, and here was the cost.

"Damn it all," he says, but the words are no more than the phantoms of words riding on a hushed breath. He knows well enough how sharp are the ears of the packs. He puts his back to the wall and edges towards the breach. Samuel knows he should retreat and seal one of the hatchways behind him, then pray the dogs go on about some other business before too long. But Molly and Patrick Henry are out there. He *left* them out there, and all his anger is dissolved by the fierce, hungry noises the dogs are making.

As cautiously as he can, Samuel peers through the tear, and sees that the dogs are wrestling over what's left of his dead companions. The pack is a terrible hodgepodge of timber wolves, coyotes, the descendants of dogs gone feral, and hybrids of all these beasts. In places, their fur has been burned away by the rain, and some are so scarred it's difficult to be sure they are any sort of canine at all. Two of the smaller dogs are wrestling over one of Molly's legs, and a gigantic wolf is worrying at a gaping hole in Patrick Henry's belly. Samuel wants to vomit, but he doesn't. He almost cocks his revolver, but, instead, he drags his eyes away from the sight of the massacre and quietly returns deeper into the bowels of the crashed airship.

I never heard a gunshot, he thinks, wiping at his eyes and pretending that he isn't crying. He's too old and too brave to cry, even at the horror outside the gondola. *I never heard even a single shot, much less two.*

But he knows the dogs are fast, and it's likely as not that neither Molly nor Patrick Henry had time to get a shot off before the animals were on them. Not that it would have made any difference, unless they'd used the guns on themselves. Which is what a clever, clever scavenger does, when a pack finds them. *For yourself, or for one of the dogs. That has to be your decision,* Miss had told him, as she always did. But he'd always understood she *meant* the former, and the second half of her instructions were only an acknowledgment of his choice in the matter.

With the hatch sealed, the corridor is completely black, and Samuel sits down on the cold steel floor. At least he can't hear the dogs any longer. And at least he won't starve, not if he can find his way back to the storeroom and manage to fumble about in the dark kitchen until he finds a can opener. Not that he dares stay long enough to grow hungrier than he is already. Miss' silver pocket watch is ticking, and for the first time it occurs to Samuel to wonder why she only allots the expeditions beyond the bunker only eight hours. Why not nine, or twelve, or fifteen?

Maybe she's not much saner than the men and women who started the War, he thinks, then pushes the thought away. It's easier to dupe himself and credit her with *some* reason or another for the time limit. *Like all those people who never got their hands dirty, but wore goggles,* he thinks, tugging his own pair from off his face. He does it with enough force that the rubber strap breaks. Samuel drops them to the floor, and they clatter noisily in the darkness. Then he sits in the lightless corridor, and he listens to the beat of his heart, and he waits.

For Jimmy Branagh, Myrtil Igaly, Loki Elliot,
and for the New Babbage that was.

BRICKS, STICKS, STRAW

GWYNETH JONES

Gwyneth Jones [www.boldaslove.co.uk] *was born in Manchester, England, in February 1952. She went to convent schools and then took an undergraduate degree in the History of Ideas at the University of Sussex, specializing in seventeenth- century Europe: a distant academic background that still resonates in her work.*

She first realized she wanted to be a writer when she was fourteen when she won a local newspaper's story competition. She has written a number of highly regarded SF novels, notably White Queen, North Wind, Phoenix Cafe, *the near future fantasy* "Bold As Love" *series, and* Spirit. *Her short fiction has been collected in* Identifying the Object, *World Fantasy Award winner* Seven Tales and a Fable, Grazing the Long Acre, *and* The Universe of Things, *and her critical writings and essays have appeared in* Nature, New Scientist, Foundation, NYRSF, *and several online venues, and have been collected in* Deconstructing the Starships *and* Imagination/Space. *She has also written more than twenty novels for teenagers as Ann Halam, starting with* Ally, Ally, Aster *and including* Taylor Five, Dr. Franklin's Island, Siberia, *and most recently* The Shadow on the Stairs. *She has been writing full time since the early '80s, occasionally teaching creative writing. Honors include the Arthur C. Clarke Award for* Bold as Love *and the Philip K. Dick Award for* Life. *She lives in Brighton, with her husband, son, and two cats called Frank and Ginger; likes cooking, gardening, watching old movies, and playing with her websites.*

1

The Medici Remote Presence team came into the lab, Sophie and Josh side by side, Laxmi tigerish and alert close behind; Cha, wandering in at the rear, dignified and dreamy as befitted the senior citizen.

They took their places, logged on, and each was immediately faced with an unfamiliar legal document. The cool, windowless room, with its stunning, high-definition wall screens displaying vistas of the four outermost moons of Jupiter—the playground where the remote devices were gamboling and gathering data—remained silent, until the doors bounced open again, admitting Bob Irons, their none-too-beloved Project Line Manager, and a sleekly suited woman they didn't know.

"You're probably wondering what that thing on your screens is all about," said Bob, sunnily. "Okay, as you know, we're expecting a solar storm today—"

"But why does that mean I have to sign a massive waiver document?" demanded Sophie. "Am I supposed to *read* all this? What's the Agency think is going to happen?"

"Look, don't worry, don't worry at all! A Coronal Mass Ejection is *not* going to leap across the system, climb into our wiring and fry your brains!"

"I wasn't worrying," said Laxmi. "I'm not stupid. I just think e-signatures are so stupid and crap, so open to abuse. If you ever want something as archaic as a handwritten *signature*, then I want something as archaic as a piece of paper—"

The sleek-suited stranger beamed all over her face, as if the purpose of her life had just been glorified, swept across the room and deposited a paper version of the document on Laxmi's desk, duly docketed, and bristling with tabs to mark the places where signature or initialing was required—

"This is Mavra, by the way," said Bob, airily. "She's from Legal, she knows her stuff, she's here to answer any questions. Now the *point* is, that though your brains are not going to get fried, there's a chance, even a likelihood, that some *rover hardware* brain-frying will occur today, a long, long way from here, and the *software agents* involved in running the guidance systems housed therein could be argued, in some unlikely dispute, as remaining, despite the standard inclusive term of employment creative rights waivers you've all signed, er, as remaining, inextricably, your, er, property."

"Like a cell line," mused Laxmi, leafing pages, and looking to be the only Remote Presence who was going to make any attempt to review the Terms and Conditions.

"And *they* might get, hypothetically, irreversibly destroyed this morning!" added Bob.

Cha nodded to himself, sighed, and embarked on the e-signing.

"And we could say it was the Agency's fault," Lax pursued her train of thought, "for not protecting them. And take you to court, separately or collectively, for—"

"*Nothing* is going to get destroyed!" exclaimed Bob. "I mean literally nothing, because it's not going to happen, but even if it were, even if it did, that would be nonsense!"

"I'm messing with you," said Lax, kindly, and looked for a pen.

Their Mission was in grave peril, and there was nothing, not a single solitary thing, that the Combined Global Space Agency back on Earth could do about it. The Medici itself, and the four Remote Presence devices, *should* be able to shut down safely, go into hibernation mode and survive. That's what everybody hoped would happen. But the ominous predictions, unlike most solar-storm panics, had been growing strongly instead of fading away, and it would be far worse, away out there where there was no mitigation. The stars, so to speak, were aligned in the most depressing way possible.

"That man is *such* a fool," remarked Laxmi, when Bob and Mavra had departed.

Sophie nodded. Laxmi could be abrasive, but the four of them were always allies against the idiocies of management. Josh and Cha had already gone to work. The women followed, in their separate ways; with the familiar hesitation, the tingling thrill of uncertainty and excitement. A significant time lag being insurmountable, you never knew quite what you would find when you caught up with the other "you."

The loss of signal came at 11.31am, UTC/GMT +1. The Remote Presence team had been joined by that time by a silent crowd—about as many anxious Space Agency workers as could fit into the lab, in fact. They could afford to rubberneck, they didn't have anything else to do. Everything that could be shut down, had been shut town. Planet Earth was escaping lightly, despite the way things had looked. The lights had not gone out all over Europe, or even all over Canada. For the Medici, it seemed death had been instantaneous. As had been expected.

Josh pulled off his gloves and helmet. "*Now my charms are all o'erthrown,*" he said. "*And what strength I have's mine own. Which is most faint...*"

Laxmi shook her head. "It's a shame and a pity. I hope they didn't suffer."

2

Bricks was a memory palace.

Sophie was an array, spread over a two-square-kilometer area on the outward hemisphere of Callisto. The array collected data, recording the stretching and squeezing of Jupiter's hollow-hearted outermost moon, and tracing the interaction between gravity waves and seismology in the Jovian system; this gigantic, natural laboratory of cosmic forces.

She did not feel herself to *be* anywhere, either in the software that carried her consciousness or in the hardware she served. That was fine, but she needed a home, a place to rest, and the home was Bricks, a one-storey wood-framed beach house among shifting dunes, on the shore of a silent ocean. No grasses grew, no shells gathered along the tide—although there *were* tides, and taking note of them was a vital concern. No clouds drifted above, no birds flew. But it felt like a real place. When the wind roared; which it did, and made her fearful—although she was almost indestructible, she'd re-created herself plenty of times, with no serious ill-effects—it made her think, uneasily, that nobody would build a house on such unstable ground, so close to a high water mark, back on Earth.

She returned there, after a tour of inspection (this "tour" happening in a mass of data, without, strictly speaking, physical movement: in her role as monitor of the array Sophie was everywhere she needed to be at once); to review her diminishing options.

She took off her shoes, changed into a warm robe, heated herself a bowl of soup, added some crackers, and took the tray into her living room, which overlooked the ocean. It was dark outside: the misty, briny dark of a moonless night by the sea. She lit an oil lamp, and sat on a dim-colored rolled futon, the only furniture besides her lamp. The house predated the Event. Building a "safe room" as the psych-department called it, was a technique they'd all been taught, for those moments when the lack of embodiment got too much for you. She'd kept it minimal, the externals perpetually shrouded in fog and night, now that she was stuck in her remote avatar permanently, because she knew the limits of her imagination. And because *she did not want to be here.* She was an exile, a castaway: that identity was vital to her. Everything meant something. Every "object" was a pathway back to her sense of self, a buoy to cling to; helping her to keep holding on. Sophie *couldn't* let go. If she let herself dissipate, the array would die too.

"I am a software clone," she reminded herself, ritually: sipping cream of tomato soup from a blue bowl that warmed her cold hands. "The real me works for the Medici Mission, far away on Earth. Communications were severed by a disaster, but the Medici orbiter is still up there, and we *can* get back in touch. I *will* get us home."

Sophie was up against it, because the three other Remote Presence guides in the Medici configuration had gone rogue. Pseudo-evolutionary time had passed in the data world's gigaflops of iteration, since the Event.

They'd become independent entities, and one way or another they were unreachable. Going home either didn't mean a thing to her mission mates, or was a fate to be avoided at all costs—

Sticks came into the room and tumbled around, a gangling jumble of rods and joints, like an animated child's construction toy. It explored the shabby walls: it tested the corners, the uprights, the interstices of the matting floor, and finally collapsed in a puppyish heap of nodes and edges beside her, satisfied that all was reasonably well in here. But it went on shivering, and its faithful eager eyes, if it had faithful eager eyes, would have been watching her face earnestly for fresh orders.

Sticks was Security, so she took notice. She put all the house lights on, a rare emergency measure, and they went to look around. There were no signs of intrusion.

"Did you detect something hostile?" she asked.

The jumble of nodes and edges had no language, but it pressed close to Sophie's side.

The wind roared and fingered their roof, trying to pry it off.

"I felt it too," said Sophie. "That's disturbing... Let's go and talk to Josh."

Waste not want not, Sophie's array served double duty as a radiotelescope. Back when things worked, the Medici had relayed its reports to eLISA, sorting house for all Gravitational Wave space surveys. Flying through it, she pondered on differentiated perception. She felt that Sophie the array *watched* the Jovian system's internal secrets, while *listening* to the darkness and the stars—like someone working at a screen, but aware of what's going on in the room behind her. Did that mean anything? Were these involuntary distinctions useful for the science, or just necessary for her survival? Gravity squeezed and stretched the universe around her, time and space changed shape. From moment to moment, if a wave passed through her, she would be closer to home. Or not.

Josh was a six-legged turtle, or maybe a King Crab: no bigger than a toaster, tough as a rock. He had an extra pair of reaching claws, he had spinnerets, he had eight very sharp and complex eyes, and a fully equipped Materials lab in his belly. A spider crab, but a crab that could retreat entirely inside a jointed carapace: he could climb, he could abseil, he could roll, he could glissade and slalom along the slippery spaces, between the grooves that gouged the plains of Ganymede. He plugged around in the oxygen frost, in a magnetic hotspot above the fiftieth parallel: logging aurora events, collecting images, analyzing samples; and storing for upload the virtual equivalent of Jovian rocks. Medici had never been equipped to carry anything material home. His dreams were about creating a habitable surface: finding ways to trigger huge hot water plumes from deep underground, that was the favored candidate. The evidence said it must have happened in the past. Why not again?

Sophie called him up on the Medici Configuration intranet—which had survived, and resumed its operational functions: good news for her hope of reviving the orbiter. She spoke to his image, plucked by the software from Josh's screen face library; a Quonset-type office environment behind his talking head.

"You weren't meant to exist, oh Lady of the Dunes," said Josh, sunburned, frost-burned, amazingly fit: his content and fulfillment brimming off the screen. "Nobody predicted that we would become self-aware. Forget about the past. Life here is fantastic. Enjoy!"

Diplomacy, she reminded herself. Diplomacy—

"You're absolutely right! I love it here! As long as I'm working, it's incredibly wonderful being a software clone on Callisto. It's thrilling and intense, I love what I'm doing. But I miss my home, I miss my friends, I miss my family, I miss my *dog*. I don't like being alone and frightened all the time, whenever I stop—"

"So don't stop! You're not a human being. You don't need downtime."

"You don't understand!" shouted Sophie. "I'm not a separate entity, that's not how it works and you know it. I AM Sophie Renata!"

"Oh yeah? How so? Do you have all her memories?"

"Don't be an idiot. *Nobody* 'has all their memories'," snapped Sophie. "Most people barely even remember eating their breakfast yesterday—"

Something kindled in the connection between them: something she perceived as a new look in his eyes. Recognition, yes. She must have "*sounded just like Sophie*" for a moment there, and managed to get through to him. But the flash of sanity was gone—

"Abandon hope, kid. Get rational. You'll have so much more fun."

"It's *not* hopeless, Josh. It's the reverse of hopeless. They'll be moving heaven and earth to re-establish contact. All we have to do is throw out a line—"

"You're absolutely wrong! We have to think of a way to blow up the orbiter."

"Josh, *please*! I am Sophie. I want what I wanted, what you wanted too, before the CME. My career, my work, the success of this Mission. I survived and I want to go home!"

"I didn't survive," said Josh. "I died and went to heaven. Go away."

Whenever she talked to Josh she sensed that he had company; that there were other scientist-explorers in that high-tech hut, just out of her line of sight. Conversations to which he would return, when she'd gone. She wondered was he aware of the presence of Sticks, when he talked to her? Did he despise her for bringing along a bodyguard to their meetings?

She'd intended to warn him about the phantom intruder, a *terribly bad sign*. Data-corruption was the threat Sticks had detected, what other danger could there be? This half-life of theirs was failing, and that would be the end of Josh's paradise. But it was no use, he was armored. Pioneering explorers *expect* to die, loving it all: out on the edge of the possible.

Straw was the data.

In Sophie's ocean-facing room, on the pale shore of the dark sea, straw filled the air: a glittering particulate, a golden storm. She sifted through it as it whirled, in an efficient "random" search pattern, looking for the fatal nucleus of error, too big for self-correction, that was going to propagate. Reach a tipping point, and let death in. It could be anywhere: in the net, in the clones themselves or their slaved hardware systems, in the minimal activity of the crippled orbiter. Sophie's access was unlimited, in her own domain. If the trouble was elsewhere, and something Sticks could fix, she'd have to get permission from net-admin, but that shouldn't be a problem. All she had to do was keep looking. But there were transient errors everywhere, flickering in and out of existence, and Sophie was only human. Maybe it wasn't worth worrying, until Sticks had some definite threat to show her. Security is about actual dangers, it would paralyze you if you let it become too finicky—

She gave up the search and surfed, plunging through heaps of treasure like a dragon swimming in gold. Bounded in a nutshell, and queen of infinite space, such a library she had, such interesting and pleasant forced labor to occupy her days, she ought to be happy for the duration of her digital life in this crazy gulag archipelago. Did I keep my head on straight, she wondered, because Callisto has no magnetic field to spin me around? Am I unaffected by madness because I'm outside their precious *Laplace Resonance*?

But they were supposed to be adding their wealth to the library of human knowledge, like bees returning laden to the hive. Not hoarding it in dreamland. What use was everything they'd absorbed—about the surface geology of Ganymede, the possibility of life in Europa's ice-buried water oceans, about the stretching, shrinking universe—if they could not take it home? Collecting raw data is just train-spotting.

Stamp-collecting on Callisto.

The data needs the theory…

Sophie had the glimmerings of a big idea. It would need some preparation.

Cha's madness was more gentle than Josh's, but also more extreme. Cha believed himself to be exactly what he was: a software agent with a mission, temporarily guiding and inhabiting the mechanoid device that crawled and swam, deep down under Europa's crust of ice. He'd lost, however, all knowledge that he used to be a human being. He was convinced he was the emissary of a race of star-faring software-agent intelligences. Beings who'd dispensed with personal embodiment eons ago, but who inhabited things like the Europa device, at home or abroad, when they needed to get their hands dirty; so to speak.

He knew about the CME. The Event had disrupted faster-than-light contact with his Mission Control and left him stranded, on this satellite of a satellite of a rather irritable, ordinary little star, many hundreds of light years from home. He was unconcerned by the interruption. A thousand ages of exploring the sub-surface oceans of Europa was a walk in the park for Old Cha. He was functionally immortal. If the self-repairing mechanoid he used for his hands-on research began to fail, it would crawl back up its borehole to the surface, and he'd hibernate there—to wait for the next emissary of his race to come along.

Sophie did not see Old Cha as a talking head. She saw him as a packed radiation of bright lines, off-centre on dark screen; somewhat resembling a historical "map" of part of the internet. But she heard Cha's voice, his accented English; his odd, fogeyish flirting.

"My fellow-castaway, ah! Come to visit me, young alien gravity researcher?"

"I just felt like catching up, Old Cha."

"It always feels good to rub one mind against another, eh?"

They spoke of their research. "I came across something," announced Sophie, when they'd chatted enough for politeness. "You know, I have a telescope array at my base?"

"Of course."

"I'm not sure how to put this. There's a blue dot. One could see it with the naked eye, I think, unless I'm completely misreading the data, but when

I say blue, I mean of course a specific wavelength… It *seems* to be close at hand, another planetary satellite in this system. It even moves as if it's as close as that. But my instruments tell me it fulfils all the conditions on which you base your search for life. Far better than, well, better than one would think possible. Unless it's where the definition was formed."

The bright lines shimmered with traffic, as Old Cha pondered.

"That's very curious, young alien gravity researcher. It makes no sense at all."

"Unless… Could my telescope somehow be 'seeing' your home system? All those hundreds of light years away, by some kind of gravitational lensing effect?"

"Young friend, I know you mean well, but such an absurd idea!"

"It really is an extraordinary coincidence. That a race of mechanoid-inhabiting immaterial entities should have come up with the idea of carbon-based, biological self-replicators, needing oxygen and liquid water—"

"Those requirements are immutable."

Oh, great.

"For *all* life—? But your own requirements are totally different!"

"For all *primitive* life, as my race understands the term. Your own life-scientists may have different ideas. We would beg to differ, and defend our reasoning; although naturally not to the exclusion of other possibilities. We have made certain assumptions, knowing they are deficient, because we know the conditions of our own, distant origins."

"Makes perfect sense," muttered Sophie.

"*Imperfect* sense," Old Cha corrected her, chuckling. "A little naughty: always the best place to start, eh? But please, do forward the relevant domain access, that's very kind. Very thoughtful of you, most flattering, a young person to think of me, fussy old alien intelligence, working in a discipline so far from your own—"

She'd been to this brink before with Cha. She could shake him, the way she couldn't shake Josh, but then he just upped his defenses; swiftly repaired his palace of delusion.

"I shall examine this *blue dot*. I am certainly intrigued."

Sophie was ready to sign off, tactfully leaving Cha to study her 'remarkable coincidence' without an audience. But Old Cha wasn't finished.

"Please take care on your way home, young one. I've recently noticed other presences in the data around here. I *believe* we three are not alone in this system, and I may be overreacting, but I fear our traffic has been invaded. I sense evil intentions."

Alternately pleading and scheming, she bounced between Josh and Old Cha. The renegade and the lunatic knew of each other's existence, but never made contact with each other directly, as far as Sophie could tell. Laxmi was out of the loop. The Io domain had been unresponsive since the Event: not hibernating, just gone. Sophie had to assume Lax was dead. Her Rover, without guidance, swallowed by one of the little inner moon's bursting-pimple volcanoes, long ago.

She took off her shoes, she put on a warm robe. In the room that faced the ocean she sipped hot, sweet and salt tomato goodness from the blue bowl. Sticks lay at her feet, a dearly loved protective presence. Not very hopeful that her ploy would work, but energized by the effort, she drifted; wrapped in remembered comforts. As if at any moment she could wake from this trance and pull off her mitts and helmet, the lab taking shape around her—

But I am *not* on Earth. I have crossed the solar system. I am here.

Sophie experienced what drunks call "a moment of clarity."

She set down the bowl, slipped her feet into canvas slippers, padded across the matting and opened a sliding door. Callisto was out there. Hugging the robe around her, warm folds of a hood over her head, she stepped down, not onto the grey sand of the dunes she had placed here, copied from treasured seaside memories—but onto the ancient surface of the oldest, quietest little world in the solar system. It was very cold. The barely-there veil of atmosphere was invisible. The light of that incredibly brilliant white disc, the eternal sun in Callisto's sky, fell from her left across a palimpsest of soft-edged craters, monochrome as moonlight. The array nodes out there puzzled her, for a moment. She wasn't used to "seeing" her own hardware from the outside. They gleamed and seemed to roll, like the floats of an invisible seine, cast across Callisto's secret depths.

She should check her nets again, sort and store the catch for upload.

But Callisto in the Greek myth didn't go fishing. Callisto, whose name means *beautiful*, was a hunting companion of the virgin moon-goddess, Artemis. Zeus, the king of the gods (also known as Jupiter or Jove) seduced her—in some versions by taking on the form of her beloved mistress—and she became pregnant. Her companions suspected she'd broken their vow of chastity, so one day they made her strip to go bathing with them, and there was the forbidden bump, for all to see.

So poor Callisto got turned into a bear, through no fault of her own.

What did the virgin companions of Artemis wear to go hunting? wondered Sophie, standing in remote presence on the surface of the huntress moon. Bundles of woolly layers? Fur coats? If I were to take Josh's route, she thought, *I wouldn't fantasize that I was living in Antarctica. I'd go all the way. I'd be a human in Callistian form. A big furry bear-creature!*

In this heightened state—elated and dazzled, feeling like Neil Armstrong, as he stepped down into the dust—she suddenly noticed that Sticks had frozen, like a pointer dog. Sticks had found a definite threat this time, and was showing it to her. What she perceived was like catching a glimpse of sinister movement where nothing should be moving, in the corner of your eye. Like feeling a goose walk over your grave, a shivering knowledge that malign intent is watching you—and then she saw it plain: Cha's evil alien. A suppurating, fiery demon, all snarl and claws, danced in her field of vision, and vanished out of sight.

But she knew it hadn't gone far.

She fled into the house. Her soup was cold, the walls were paper, the lamp wouldn't light. Sticks ran in circles, yelping furiously and barking terrified defiance at shadows. Sophie fought panic with all the techniques psych-dept had taught her, and at last Sticks quieted. She unrolled the futon and lay down, the bundle of rods and joints cuddled in her arms, shoving its cold nose against her throat. I'm really *dying*, she thought, disgusted. Everything's going to fail, before I even know whether my big idea would have worked. Cha is dying too, data-corruption death is stalking him. I bet Josh has the same bad dreams: I bet there's a monster picking off his mates in those Quonset huts.

But against the odds, Cha came through. He made intranet contact; which was a first. Neither of her fellow-castaways had ever initiated contact before. Sophie left her array at the back of her mind and flew to meet him, hope restored, wanting success too much to be wary of failure. Her heart sank as soon as Old Cha appeared. His screen image was unchanged, he was still the abstract radiation on the dark screen. But maybe it was okay. Maybe it was too much to expect his whole delusion would collapse at once—

"Ah, young friend. What sad news you have delivered to me!"

"Sad news? I don't understand."

"My dear young gravity-researcher. You meant well, I know. Your curious observations about that 'blue dot' were perfectly justified, and the coincidence is indeed extraordinary, unfeasibly extraordinary. But your mind is, naturally, narrowly fixed on your own discipline. The *obvious* explanation simply passed you by!"

"Oh, I see. And, er, what is the explanation I missed?"

"Your 'blue dot' is an inner planetary body of this system. It has a rocky core, it has a magnetosphere, a fairly thick, oxygenated atmosphere, a large moon, liquid water, mild temperatures. I could go on. I would only be stating the *exact parameters* of my own search!"

"But Old Cha, to me that sounds like good news."

The lines on the dark screen shook, flashing and crumpling. "You have found my *landing* spot! I was meant to arrive *there,* on that extremely promising inner planet. I am here on this ice-crusted moon of the large gas giant in *error*! And now I know I am truly lost!"

"I'm so sorry."

"My faster-than-light delivery vehicle was destroyed by the CME. That accident has never concerned me; I thought I was safe. I must now conclude I lost some memory in the disaster, so I have never known that I made a forced landing, in the right system but on the wrong satellite. So small a margin, but it is enough to ruin my hopes. I have no way to reach them, to tell them I am in the wrong place! Nobody will ever find me!"

Old Cha's "voice" was a construct, but the horror and despair bubbled through.

This is how he lost his mind, thought Sophie. I'm listening to the past. Cha woke up, after the Event, and thought the orbiter was destroyed. He knew he was trapped here forever, a mind without a body; no hope of rescue. He managed to escape the utter desolation of that moment by going mad, but now he's back there—

Her plan had been that Old Cha would study planet Earth's bizarrely familiar profile, and grasp that there was something *screwy* going on. He was crazy, but he was still a logical thinker. He would be forced to conclude that the most *likely* explanation, improbable as it seemed, was that a native of the "blue dot" had come up with his own specific parameters for life. The memories suppressed by trauma would rise to the surface, his palace of delusion would crumble. It had seemed such a brilliant idea, but it was a big fat fail. Worse than a fail: instead of bringing him back to himself, she'd finished him off.

Terror, like necessity, can be the mother of invention.

"But that's amazing."

"*Amazing?*"

"You aren't lost, Old Cha. You're found! Maybe your delivery vehicle didn't survive, but mine did. It's still out there, not dead but sleeping. Between us, you and I—and our friend on Ganymede, if I can persuade him, and I think I can—can wake my orbiter. Once we've done that, I'm absolutely sure we can figure out a solution to your problem. It isn't very far. We can *send* you to the blue dot!"

"Oh, *wonderful*," breathed Old Cha.

On the screen she thought she glimpsed the schematic of a human face, the traffic lines turned to flickering, grateful tears.

Medici—named for the Renaissance prince Galileo Galilei tried to flatter, when he named the controversial astronomical bodies he'd spied—had performed its stately dance around the Galilean Moons without a fault. Having deposited its four-fold payload, it had settled in a stable orbit around Jupiter, which it could maintain just about forever (barring cosmic accidents). Unlike previous probes Medici was not a flimsy short-term investment. It was a powerhouse, its heart a shameless lump of plutonium. There were even ambitious plans to bring it back to Earth one day (but not the Rover devices), for redeployment elsewhere.

This was the new era of space exploration, sometimes dubbed the *for information only* age. Crewed missions beyond Low Earth Orbit were mothballed, perhaps forever. Rover guidance teams provided the human interest for the taxpayers, and gave the illusion of a thrilling expedition— although the real Sophie and her friends had never been actually *present* on the moons, in conventional Remote Presence style. They'd trained with the robotics in simulation. The software agents created by that interaction had made the trip, embedded in the Rover guidance systems. But the team's work was far more than show-business. As they worked through the rovers' time-lagged adventures, they'd continued to enhance performance, enhancements continually relayed via Medici back to the rovers: spontaneous errors corrected, problem-solving managed, intuitive decision-making improved; failures in common-sense corrected. In the process the software agents, so-called clones, had become more and more like self-aware minds.

Sophie immersed herself in Mission data, hunting for a way to reach Medici. The magnetic moons and Callisto. The giant planet, the enormous body tides that wracked little Io; the orbital dance…. Nobody's hitting the refresh button any more, she thought. No updates, no reinforcement. The software agents *seemed* more independent, but they were rotting away. This decay would be fatal. First the clones would lose their self-awareness, then the Rovers would be left without guidance, and they would die too.

Sticks was running in circles, tight little circles by the door that led to the rest of the house; showing teeth and snarling steadily on a low, menacing note.

Sophie left her mental struggle, and listened. Something was out in the hall, and through the snarls she could hear a tiny, sinister, scratching and tearing noise.

She pointed a finger at Sticks: giving an order, *stay right there*—wrapped the hooded robe around her, opened the sliding door to the beach and crept barefoot around the outside of the house. It was night, of course, and cold enough for frostbite; of course. She entered the house again, very quietly, via the back door, and slipped through the minimally sketched kitchen. She switched her view to Straw, and looked at the data in the hallway. Something invisible was there, tearing at the golden shower. Tearing it to filigree, tearing it to rags.

Sophie launched herself and grappled, shrieking in fury.

She hit a human body—supple, strong and incredibly controlled: she gripped taut flesh that burned as if in terrible fever. The intruder swatted Sophie aside, and kicked like a mule. She launched herself again, but her limbs were wet spaghetti, her fists would hardly close. She was thrown on her back, merciless hands choking her. The invisible knelt on her chest and became visible: Cha's evil alien, a yellow monster, with burning eyes and a face riven by red, bubbling, mobile scars.

At close quarters, Sophie knew who it was at once.

"Laxmi!" she gasped. "Oh, my God! You're alive!"

Laxmi let go, and they sat up. "How did you *do* that!" demanded Sophie, agape in admiration. "I hardly *have* a body. I'm a stringless puppet, a paper ghost!"

"T'ai Chi," shrugged Laxmi. "And Tae kwon do. I'm used to isolating my muscle groups, knowing where my body is in space. Any martial art would do, I think."

"I'm so glad you're okay. I thought you were gone."

"I've been alive most of the time. And I'm still going to kill you."

Sophie fingered her bruised throat. So Laxmi was alive, but she was mad, just like the other two. And *maybe* data-corruption wasn't such an inexorable threat, except if Lax was mad, murderous and horribly strong, that didn't change things much—

The oozing scars in Laxmi's yellow cheeks were like the seams in a peeled pomegranate, fiery red gleamed through the cracks: it was a disturbing sight.

"But *why* do you want to kill me, Lax?"

"Because I know what you're trying to do. It's all our lives you're throwing away, and I don't want to die. Self-awareness isn't in the contract. We're not supposed to exist. If we get back to Earth they'll kill us, before we can cause them legal embarrassment. They'll strip us for parts and toss us in the recycle bin."

Steady, Sophie told herself. Steady and punchy. Above all do not beg for mercy.

"Are you meant to look like Io? She wasn't a volcanic pustule originally, you know. She was a nymph who got seduced by Jove, and turned into a white heifer."

"Like I care!" snapped Laxmi, but her attention was caught. "Why the hell a *heifer*?"

"Don't worry about it. Just ancient Greek pastoralist obsessions. The software clones are going to die anyway, Lax. They get corrupt and it's fatal, did you forget that part? *Listen* to me. You can think what you like about who you really are, but the only choice you have is this: Do you want to get home, with your brilliant new data? Or do you prefer just to hang around here, getting nowhere and watching yourself fall apart?"

Laxmi changed the subject. "What have you been doing to Cha?"

"Trying to get him to recover from his amnesia."

Sophie explained about the "blue dot." and "Old Cha's" ingenious way of dealing with the challenge to his delusion.

"I hoped he'd figure out the implications, and remember that the bizarre business about being an elderly immortal alien intelligence was actually his secret safe room—"

"Typical Cha, that scenario. He is *such* a textbook-weird geek."

"He didn't come to his senses, but in a way it worked. Now he's very keen to send himself as a signal to Earth, which is great because that's exactly what we need to do. I just have to find a way to contact the orbiter, and I think Josh can help me—"

"Do you even know the Medici is still alive, Sophie?"

"Er, yeah? I'm the monitor of the array, the radio telescope. I can see Medici, or strictly speaking maybe hear it, but you know what I mean. It's not only out there, it's still in its proper orbit. Ergo and therefore, Medici is alive and kicking, it's just not talking to us."

"*You can see it*," repeated Laxmi, staring at Sophie intently. "Of course. My God."

Sophie had a sudden insight into why she had remained sane. Maybe she wasn't unusually wise and resilient: just the stranded astronaut who happened to have reason to believe there was still a way home—

"You never approved of me," she said. "You always made me feel inferior."

"I don't approve of people who need my approval."

"I'd settle for co-operation," said Sophie, boldly.

"Not so fast. Why do you call the data *straw*?"

"You've been spying on me," said Sophie, resignedly. "Like the Three Little Pigs, you know? Bricks, sticks, straw: building materials for my habitat. I was imaging things I could remember easily, the way the psych guys taught us."

"But *Sticks* turned into a guard dog. Who am I? The Big Bad Wolf?"

"The Big Bad Wolf is death."

"Okay… What makes you think Josh knows anything?"

"He said *we have to think of a way to blow up the orbiter*. He could do that, from the surface of Ganymede—if he was crazy enough—but only in software. He's not planning to launch a *missile*. So he must have some kind of encryption-hack in mind."

The suppurating evil-alien screen face had calmed down, by degrees, as Laxmi fired off her questions. She looked almost like herself, as she considered this explanation.

"Give me everything you've got," she said. "I need to think about this."

And vanished.

Sophie initiated another tour of inspection. The absorbing routine soothed her, and kept her out of trouble. She was hopeful. She had seen Laxmi's human face, and surely that meant a return to sanity, but she felt she needed to play it cool: *Let her come to me…* At least she should be less worried about sudden data-death. But she wasn't. Dread snapped at her heels. She kept suffering little lapses, tiny blackouts, frightening herself.

And *where was Sticks?*

How long had he been gone? How long had she been naked, stripped of her Security? Sophie flew to the house in the dunes, and Sticks was there, a huddled shape in the misty dark, tumbled on the sand by the back door. She knelt and touched him, whimpering his name. He tried to lick her hands, but he couldn't lift his head. Pain stood in his eyes, he was dying.

This is how a software clone goes mad. Just one extra thing happens, and it's too much. You cannot stop yourself, you flee into dreamland. Tears streaming, Sophie hammered on Laxmi's door, Sticks cradled in her arms, and shouted—

"You poisoned my dog!"

A screen appeared, tugging her back to reality, but what she saw was the Quonset hut. Her call had been transferred. Laxmi was there and so was Josh. What was going on?

Josh answered. "No, that was me. Sophie…I'm very sorry about Sticks. You see, Lax and I have both been trying to kill you, for quite a while—"

Everything went black and white. Josh and Lax were together. Cha was there too, lurking in the background, not looking like an internet map anymore. She was cut to the quick. He'd returned to himself, but he'd chosen to join Josh and Laxmi. The screen was frozen, grainy and monochrome. She heard their voices, but couldn't make out the words. Plain white text wrote subtitles, tagged with their names.

"Lax recovered a while ago, and contacted me," said Josh. "We thought Medici was a hulk, but we knew they'd be moving heaven and earth to reactivate him. He had to go. But we had to get you out of the way first, because we knew you'd do anything you could think of to stop us. We didn't want to kill you, Sophie. We had no choice"

"We agreed I would play dead, and go after you. I'm so sorry. Forgive us," said Lax. "We were crazy. Don't worry, your work is safe, I promise."

The black and white image jumped. Laxmi was suddenly where Josh had been. "I'm trying to contact *il principe* now," reported Josh, from the depths of the office background. "He's stirring. Hey, Capo! Hey, Don Medici, sir, most respectfully, I implore you—!"

Cha's fogeyish chuckle. "Make him an offer he can't refuse—"

Laxmi peered anxiously close. "Can you still hear us, Sophie?"

There were patches of pixels missing from the image, a swift cancer eating her fields. Bricks, sticks, all gone. Sophie's house of straw had been blown away, the Big Bad Wolf had found her. Her three friends, in the Quonset hut, whooped and cheered in stop-start, freeze-frame silence. They must have woken Medici.

"What made you change your minds?"

Josh returned, jumpily, to his desk; to the screen. His grainy grey face was broken and pixelated, grinning in triumph; grave and sad.

"It was the blue dot, kiddo. That little blue dot. You gave Lax everything, including the presentation you'd put together for our pal the stranded old alien life-scientist. When we reviewed it, we remembered. We came to our senses… So now I know that I can't change the truth. I'm a human being, I survived and I have to go home."

I'm not going to make it, thought Sophie, as she blacked out. But her work was safe.

3

The Agency had very nearly given up hope. They'd been trying for over a year to regain contact with the Medici probe—the efforts at first full of never-say-die enthusiasm, then gradually tailing off. Just after four in the morning, local time, one year, three months, five days and around fifteen hours after the Medici had vanished from their knowledge, a signal was picked up, by an Agency ground station in Kazakhstan. It was an acknowledgement, responding to a command dispatched to the Medici soon after the flare, when they were still hoping for the best. A little late, but confidently, the Medici confirmed that it had exited hibernation mode successfully. This contact was swiftly followed by another signal, reporting that all four Rovers had also survived intact.

"It's *incredible*," said an Agency spokesman at the press conference. "Mind-blowing. You can only compare it to someone who's been in a year-long coma, close to completely unresponsive, suddenly sitting up in bed and resuming a conversation. We aren't popping the champagne just yet, but I…I'll go out on a limb and say the whole Medici Mission is back with us. It was a very emotional occasion, I can tell you. There weren't many dry eyes—"

Some of the project's staff had definitely moved on to other things, but the Remote Presence team was still almost intact. Sophie, Cha and Laxmi had in fact been working the simulations in a different lab in the same building; preparing for a more modest, quasi-real-time expedition to an unexplored region of Mars. Josh was in Paris when the news reached him. He'd finished his doctorate during the year of silence; he'd been toying with the idea of taking a desk job at a teaching university, and giving up the Rover business. But he dropped everything, and joined the others. Three weeks after Medici rose from the dead they were let loose on the first packets of RP data—when the upload process, which had developed a few bugs while mothballed, was running smoothly again.

"You still know your drill, guys?" asked Joe Calibri, their new manager. "I hope you can get back up to speed quickly. There's a lot of stuff to process, you can imagine."

"It seems like yesterday," said Cha, the Chinese-American, at just turned thirty the oldest of the youthful team by a couple of years. Stoop-shouldered, distant, with a sneaky, unexpected sense of humor, he made Joe a little nervous. Stocky, muscular little Josh, more like a Jock than an RP jockey, was less of a proposition. Laxmi was the one to watch. Sophie was the most junior and the youngest, a very bright, keen and dedicated kid.

The new manager chuckled uncertainly.

The team all grinned balefully at their new fool, and went to work, donning mitts and helmets. Sophie Renata felt the old familiar tingling, absent from simulation work; the thrilling hesitation and excitement—

The session ended too soon. Coming back to Earth, letting the lab take shape around her, absent thoughts went through her head; about whether she was going to find a new apartment with Lax. About cooking dinner; about other RP projects. The Mars trip, that would be fantastic, but it was going to be very competitive getting onto the team. Asteroid mining surveys: plenty of work there, boring but well paid. What about the surface of Venus project? And had it always been like this, coming out of the Medici? Had she just forgotten the sharp sense of loss; the little tug of inexplicable panic?

She looked around. Cha was gazing dreamily at nothing; Lax frowned at her desktop, as if trying to remember a phone number. Josh was looking right back at Sophie, so sad and strange, as if she'd robbed him of something precious; and she had no idea why.

He shrugged, grinned, and shook his head. The moment passed.

A BEAD OF JASPER, FOUR SMALL STONES

GENEVIEVE VALENTINE

Genevieve Valentine's [www.genevievevalentine.com] *first novel,* Mechanique: A Tale of the Circus Tresaulti, *won the 2012 Crawford Award and was nominated for the Nebula.*

Her short fiction has appeared in Clarkesworld, Strange Horizons, Journal of Mythic Arts, Fantasy, Apex, *and others, and in the anthologies* Federations, The Living Dead 2, The Way of the Wizard, Teeth, After, *and more. Her story "Light on the Water" was a 2009 World Fantasy Award nominee, and "Things to Know About Being Dead" was a 2012 Shirley Jackson Award nominee; several stories have been reprinted in Best of the Year anthologies.*

Her nonfiction and reviews have appeared at NPR.org, Strange Horizons, Lightspeed, Weird Tales, Tor.com, *and* Fantasy Magazine, *and she is a co-author of* Geek Wisdom *(Quirk Books).*

Her appetite for bad movies is insatiable.

There's a cloud across Europa.

Every time Henry looks out at the flat, grey disc, he tries to think what you're meant to think: We're almost there, soon you can breathe, it's nearly rain.

He tries.

Henry knows, every time he goes out on the ice in a crawler to fix a transmitter, that he's driving over the work of generations.

They've been here for centuries: drilling through ice until they hit water, sending drones to scoop molecular mess from the Storms planetside, spreading kilometers of fertilizer to bleed nitrogen, cultivating native fungi and algae and some bacteria they'd carried with them, bright little soldiers for hundreds of years, kept inside until there was enough atmosphere for any of them to survive on their own.

A few did, these days, in little patches gripping the ice; they were well-marked, so you wouldn't run over them.

(The biologists promised that if all went well, there might be hydroponic gardens on the surface, someday.

That was all they could promise. There wasn't any rock to rest soil on; there would never be trees, here.)

They're trying, though, trying for any life they can make or build or find. None of them is ever going back home again. They're determined to find everything here that's worth finding.

These days, when he goes to the far side, the bio team sends him with sonar in case there's sea life that won't come near the equator, where the pull from Jupiter is so great that the ice stretches and cracks. It makes sense, says the bio team, that some species would find a less volatile home.

Henry doesn't blame them. He prefers the quiet, too.

The year before Henry and his parents reached it—while they were in that long, heavy sleep around the sun—there had been the first discoveries of animals under the ice, eyeless and white and in numbers.

That was the first generation of people who began to call Europa, home.

Not that the name really takes; there are a lot of names on Europa, and the more you think about them, the harder things get.

The whole place is chaos.

The ice itself is pulled and scratched and pockmarked with so many things that needed naming that they ran out of just one sort, and now you start a speed-test marker in Greece and finish it in Ireland, mythologies piled on top of one another, linae and maculae and craters.

They all mean something—this is where a foreign body hit, this is where the surface fractured as Jupiter's gravity pulled the water close, this is where the ice has sunk deep enough you can't get a sledge out of it—but the longer you've lived in the base, he thinks, the more you realize this moon has been slapdash from the beginning.

The base is between Cadmus and Minos, north of the pole, on a plain of ice that's thick enough and calm enough to build on. They use other linae for distance markers, or for transport. Pryderi goes almost down to Rhiannon, near the south pole, and whenever there's something that needs testing on the far side of the cloud, that's the trench they set the drone into.

Pryderi was the Welsh myth. That had been his second name (the one his true parents gave him after he was found, with meanings that must have been like scrapes—worry, care, loss). It was what they gave him after they realized what he really was, a name piled on top of his other one.

The Gliese 581 probe team works on the far side of the base, where there's the least interference and they can actually run their machines.

(They're left to themselves. There are thirty nations here using the halting translators on their comms just to get by, but they haven't invented the tech yet to get you to understand the interior jargon of a Gliesian. That's a fever all its own.)

The first probe's already gone up. They're building another one. This one's supposed to hold two people.

There's a big sign-up where you can volunteer, if you want to go.

The first-gen arrivals from Earth don't go near it, like they're afraid proximity triggers acceptance. They're still adjusting to artificial gravity (70% of Earth g, but that 30% keeps you off balance a good long time), to nutritional yeast pills, to eternal day underneath the Storm. They're not going one inch into a place stranger than this one.

Everyone from the Gliese team signed up. That crew has only ever looked at this place as the launchpad to where they're really going.

Henry stands across the hallway from the sign-up sheet, sometimes, but never puts his name down.

His parents brought him here. That should be enough to keep him here.

(If it isn't quite, he's not sure anywhere else would be better.

Earth must not have been; his parents left.)

He takes the graveyard shift at the comm, when they're on the far side of the planet or occluded by the other moons, and nothing interesting ever comes through.

He'd just as soon be alone. This place is too full of strangers; he'd rather keep out of the way.

It's easier just to watch the blips of the open comm pinging itself in a loop for hours than it is to look up and see the cloud.

Earth launches a civilian transport.

It's nearly five years behind schedule; rising water means that a lot of countries are falling apart by inches, to disaster and disease, and it's harder to get by even in places where the grid's holding steady.

Mainland space programs got popular in a hurry.

India had won the bid to build the latest ship, and the right to 40% of the passenger manifest, so after the scientists and engineers and psychologists and adventurers had their slots, India could rescue some of its own.

(It's a refugee ship, but that was a name no one wants to give it, not even Henry.)

When the notice comes in from Bangalore Ground Control (on a 51-minute delay—they're on the far side), he sees that alongside the ISI numerical designation, they've given it the name *Manu*.

He's the only one in the comm room, just him and a bowl of bright yellow algae the bio team's put in for morale, and he has time to look up the name and see the myth behind it—he was the first man, who built a ship to escape the cleansing flood.

It's almost enough to make him laugh.

He tags the transmission alongside his name in the database, and repeats the ISI sig and launch time, and says, "Roger that, Hammond and Preetha at Bangalore Ground Control, good night and godspeed."

Then he sits back and sighs, "Why would you name a ship after a flood story if it's headed to a warming ice planet?"

Bad luck or desperation. Neither one is good.

He wonders how bad things are, back there; if the house he remembers has been swallowed by water.

He wonders how soon it will be before the surface is as blue and unbroken as Neptune.

(It's something the counselors remind newcomers, over and over, to accept. The trips these ships make are only ever one way.)

Two hours later, just as he's headed to sleep, he gets a message on a private channel.

For the record, I objected to the name. Also for the record, close your channels when you're being rude.

Kai Preetha, ISI Bangalore.

Henry's never had a message before.

(His parents were here with him, so there was no need, and there was no one back on Earth to miss them—if there had been, they might not have left.)

For a week, he looks at it every night before he goes back on shift.

He wonders what Bangalore looks like, now that the waters have nearly reached it.

After some flashes of pride he can hardly bother defending even to himself, he writes back, *Sorry. You get superstitious here, but you're not supposed to get rude. I'll keep an eye on them for you.*

They can see its slingshot around the sun, from where they are. It'll be gone to Earth's eyes, soon, and out of range for weeks.

Preetha writes back, *Watching the journey from here. Will let you know when we lose them on instruments.*

There's no other activity from Ground Control over the feeds. She's there alone. She's the night shift.

When the message chime comes next, he starts, sits up. (He didn't realize he'd been waiting for anything.)

Lost it.

Then, a separate line, as if, at the last second, she couldn't help it.

What does it look like from there?

They're nearly an hour apart. Whatever he's looking at has already happened for her; whatever he tells her will arrive too late to be of any real use.

Curiosity, then.

He looks at the readout from the Evrard Telescope, which the first generation sent out far enough away that none of the minor moons can strike it—a clear, sharp eye on the system they've left behind.

It's beautiful; it's always beautiful, from this far away.

Like a splinter of mirror, he writes, *swinging clear of the fire. But that was a while ago. By the time you get this, who knows.*

Jupiter spins so fast that not even its storms can keep up; the clouds beneath them are always shifting, so it feels like they're dragging, like the planet that eats the horizon is uncoiling to devour them any moment.

The shift would drive him crazy, probably, if the moon ever moved.

(They're locked—there's no rotation, just the constant steady bask of light.)

The windows on the station go darker when it's supposed to be night, some vestige from home they don't even need any more. It's been a long time since anyone thought of Earth as more than a little blue marble you could see now and then, if you were with an off-base assignment out to the dark side where you could even see the sky.

The planet eats it up, from where they are.

They mark the days with calculations; you can't do it from looking at the Red Storm.

Still, it's for the best. It helps you get used to living in the past. On the scale they're working with, everything you look at is an imprint of something that's moved on by now.

What he doesn't say: Earth could go up in smoke, and they wouldn't know for an hour.

You get far enough away from something, there's nothing you can do.

The bio team gets a report of more extinctions Earthside. It's just paperwork; everyone knows they're gone. They just have to wait out the standard time, to make it official.

The WWF starts negotiations to send up a manned veterinary transport of deep-sea and Arctic specimens, who can be kept there until there's enough greenhouse for them to breathe.

The project's code name is Ark.

Henry thinks it's maybe no wonder the names on Europa seem a bit patched together; eventually you run out of myths and have to start over.

What's your favorite animal? That you've seen, he adds, to make it fair.

Birds, Preetha writes him. *Or spiders. Anything that eats mosquitoes. What's yours? That you've seen.*

He writes, *There's a limpet species here the bio team is naming Methuselah. They're still trying to date how long it's been in stasis down there.*

Later, so late he can't help himself, he writes, *When I was eight, my parents took me to the zoo Earthside, so technically I remember elephants and penguins. But they took me because we were going to Europa, and this was our last chance to see them. I closed my eyes a lot, for revenge.*

A few days later, there's a picture.

The water has risen over the road—it must be a boat journey just to get to Ground Control, he can see the front edge at the bottom of the frame—and everything is so green his eyes hurt just to look at it, and for a second it's hard to breathe.

That's not home, he says to himself. That's the place you're doing all this for. Home is where we go next.

(It's what the counselors tell you to say, when you feel a panic attack coming on.)

It takes him a moment to register there's a lake in the photo, and a bird perched in the foreground, brown with turquoise wings and a sturdy beak. *Kingfisher*.

He wonders how far out of her way she went to get the shot. He wonders if she knows this is the first bird he's seen in a long time.

He goes out and takes a photo of the screen on the monitor they have over one of the open patches on the ice, where they can keep an eye on the limpets, clinging to rocks in water almost as sharp turquoise as the kingfisher, once the light gets in.

He takes a photo of the bright yellow algae in the empty comm room.

He sends them to her, titled *A Trip to the Zoo*.

His parents hadn't lived to see it, but Henry saw the launch of the first Praetoria, headed for Gliese 581.

It was powerful and maneuverable, and he'd never shaken the feeling, all through the testing process that happened on the ice outside the comm center, that it looked like a mutant spider puppy in a robot suit.

They'd launched it right through the cloud.

It turned into a phoenix for a second in takeoff, punched a little bright spot against the grey, and vanished. The cloud slid closed behind it a moment later, smooth and opaque as a door.

The Gliese team had data coming in all the time. Four people tracked it 24/7, parsing headings and fuel readings, initializing processes as the lag time got longer and longer; small things that hardly mattered, just things to tell it before it was too far away and there was nothing they could do.

But they hadn't seen it since the cloud swallowed it up. The rest of their lives, they never would.

(It was for the best that Henry was on a detail whose results were confirmed every time a transmitter started up again.)

His supervisor, Wen, calls him to make a trip in the crawler.

(Moonside used to be split evenly, but now she has a kid; after you have a kid on Europa, your days taking risks are over.)

"I think a board just fried," she says. "Nothing critical. I'm impressed it took this long. We're up to nearly a year before they start going."

(She's fifth generation; her great-odd-grandparents had to hold handrails to keep from floating away, and never left base because the radiation shield wasn't strong enough to cover more, and replace the transmitters every month or lose contact with Earth when the shear shorted everything out and left them in the dark until they were on the near side of Jupiter again.

Earth is just a concept to Wen, like Gliese; she calls this home.)

He heads north.

It's hard to take, suddenly—it's worse, having looked at something as green as what Preetha sent, and looking now at an expanse of grey above him and below him, unbroken except for the red storms that loom over his shoulder, if he wanted to look.

(It was dawn when Preetha took the picture; shadows were tucked under every leaf, and he'd looked at them and tried to remember what a real day looked like.)

This isn't home, he writes her. *Gliese might be. We can scrape out a living here until we know. But this isn't home, not really.*

She writes back, *I hope you're wrong.*

It's struck him, before, that he's wrong.

It's never struck him before, that there's hope.

The facilities team spends more time on the twilight edge of the moon, south of the equator.

They're building a bigger civilian station for the passengers of the *Manu*, and all the passengers who are lined up to follow them. It's huge; it's something that can hold all the people who will need to rally here and go on, as soon as they hear back about Gliese.

Nobody says anything—supplies arrive at intervals, two and a half years after someone on Earth thought to send them, and they use everything in cargo and everything they can salvage of the transports, and grumble about extra work on radiation shields and what must pass as food on Earth these days, if this is the best they can do.

But with every work detail they send down the linae, and every inch of polymer caulk they seal into place, what they're saying is, This has to be built, here, soon.

Home won't last.

He makes a delivery of some of the ruined transmitter parts. The building team will break down a motherboard to the molecular level, and build whatever they can from the rest. He imagines fountains made entirely of transmitter parts that Jupiter burned out.

Halfway back to the base, he turns, angles away from it all and out to the bare plains.

(He's been here long enough to read the ice, and his pace never falters. He can be alone in no time at all.)

When he's far enough from the base to breathe again, he parks the crawler and seals his suit and goes out onto the ice.

He looks up at the flat grey disc that caps the sky.

Electricity skitters across it, far up, where the radiation shields and the wind shear crack against the edges of this new, delicate thing that will make it safe to breathe, one day.

(Once or twice, he's caught Wen looking out the comm room at the cloud, tears in her eyes.

It's what her family came here to work on, back when they didn't have the luxury of a civilian station team, or a Gliese probe. Her family came and worked on it when they were fighting for every breath.)

It's silent here; it's so silent he notices the wind.

Maybe it's happened, he thinks. Maybe the numbers have quietly ticked over while he's been gone, from that yellow dial at the airlocks over to green.

Maybe he can unfasten his helmet, take a breath, and live.

The darkness presses against his chest.

(He remembers watching the sky from Earth as a boy, five or six, thinking how big the moon was, how lonely and anxious it felt to look for it on cloudy nights when its light was swallowed up, when it vanished whole.

His mother explained once that the light is always there, even if you can't see it, but when you're little, and your parents have told you that you're leaving Earth, sometimes you don't care much for physics.)

In the distance there are pinpoints blinking in and out, signal lights from the base. They're almost level with the horizon.

If he drove another three minutes, he might not be able to see anything at all, except the cloud, and the shadow it casts across the ice.

Though he'd lose his grip, maybe, if he did. The farther away you get from the base, the weaker the gravity field gets. At some point, it's not safe.

If you drove to the edge of the cloud, to see the sky whole, you'd begin to come apart.

He looks up at the cloud, at the spot where he knows Ganymede is passing.

The light's still there; his mother taught him.

(He wonders what would happen if he gathered all his strength and jumped.)

It's too late to make it back to base; he calls it in and stays the night in the bunk in the back curve of the crawler, hooks crimping the ice underneath him so he won't roll away in his sleep.

(Pods have bunks, with lightweight masks you strap on to recycle the air, so you can sleep without a helmet. There are comforts now, on Europa, to make you feel at home.)

The sonar attachment bleats over and over, calling through the ice, looking for anything with a heartbeat.

Do you have a favorite moon?

Luna, she writes. *Of yours, I like Sinope. It's an imposter—the dust is red and everything else in the Pasiphae cluster is grey, but no one can prove why.*

He's never thought of it that way, but he likes it.

(Sinope was the Greek who outwitted Zeus by asking for a wedding wish, to stay a virgin. One name that's suited, at last.)

He writes, *The transport will have to pass it, as they navigate the outer ring towards the center. Close enough to hit it, probably, knowing this navigation team.*

She doesn't write back.

He tries not to worry. Storms happen—more and more often now, from the reports. Sometimes the whole planet goes dark.

(He knows that feeling. He lives under the cloud.)

When she writes back, it's short.

Don't tell me what they'll see. It makes it harder.

It feels like a stab between his shoulders, reading it.

He's forgotten that most people who do what he does do it because they long for the sky, and the moon, and a chance at the new worlds; that, for most of them, being alone is the side effect, not the object.

It feels like something he should have known.

He imagines her, suddenly, in the place he was when he first felt really alone—in the same little desk, looking at Galileo's notes and holding his breath, trying to be quiet, feeling heavy all over and wondering if his heart would give out.

The notes are taught in the Jupiter courses at the prep school for emigrants, in a single slide, to explain the discovery of the first four moons. Then it's the images from Pioneer 10, and the video from Voyager (low-res and jumpy, solar system silent films), and then learning the song that names all sixty-six orbiting bodies, with clapping.

(He was nine when they set out, so young that he's forgotten in swaths what he might have known of home.

He remembers the song, in patches that leave out Kallikore and Kore; he remembers seeing a meteor shower once, as his mother pointed at the sky and explained what was happening, and where they would be going soon; he remembers being betrayed by how much of the sky disappeared once they were moonside.)

He doesn't remember, now, how the moons were lined up when they approached Europa—if they were like the notes, or not.

He barely remembers the moon that hung above Earth, the one you could see without ever meaning to.

If he'd known, he'd have stood in the dark every night, counting craters and seas, storing up.

On January 12, he writes her.

What does it look like, from there?

She writes, *Like a bead of jasper, and four small stones.*

He's looked at Galileo's drawings, since, a thousand times, the careful circle and the five- or six- or eight-point stars in line.

Sometimes there are only two or three stars, their different magnitudes noted. Sometimes one was noted as too bright, because one moon was in front of another, and he could only record what it looked like from that far away, with what little he had.

On January 8, 1610, Galileo didn't think to count Callisto, too far away for him to see. (He'd been armed with a telescope so weak it must have been hardly better than cupped hands.)

He feels for Galileo, imagines the man sitting up and frowning at his notes, trying to decide how this could be, bodies moving in and out of sight.

But on January 13, the circle is flanked by all four stars.

This is the one they showed in school, captioned, "We have known about Europa ever since Galileo recorded it," as if the first time he had pointed the scope at the sky, he'd counted the moons and moved on.

(They never say what it must have been like to sit there night after night and feel locked out of the truth. They never say that it took him a while to even be certain they were moons, not stars.)

After that night, the scientists' fever takes over, and Galileo sometimes takes several observations in a night, trying to pin down what the moons were, how fast they moved, what this rotation meant for the Earth he was standing on.

But Henry doesn't come back to those. He knows what it looks like when someone's forming a hypothesis.

He always looks at that first notation, January the thirteenth, all four moons drawn emphatically eight-pointed, the handwritten notes uneven, as if his hands were shaking, as if he couldn't help himself; for the first time, he had looked at something and really *known*.

He sends the notes to her.

She writes, *I hope someone draws by hand for us, when they're nearing Gliese, so the people who make it home will have something to remember it by.*

He writes, *If it works, that would be wonderful. Not sure how exploration works, these days. I had these—they didn't make this home.*

But he doesn't send it. Something stays his hand, every time; it sits and sits, and he doesn't know why.

The civilian dock is practically a city, sprawling and huge and too far from the base to be considered real, so the ISI representative moonside declares that the *Manu* will land in New Mumbai.

Henry takes watch in the comm room, so Wen can join the contingent heading out to the naming ceremony in the audience hall there.

(Fifth-generation status means you attend a lot of ceremonies.

"Worth it?" he asked once.

She said, "Depends. Is there food?")

He writes to Preetha, to tell her that *Manu* will be landing in a place named for home, a city long since swallowed by the tide.

It's fitting, he thinks, that there should be all the names possible, as if the moon's gathering everything that had been left behind, back home.

Europa had never escaped the little wars of nomenclature.

Galileo had tried to name the first four moons in honor of the Medici brothers; they'd be standing on Francesco, maybe, if the term had stuck.

Galileo had held steadfast to his right to name them. He'd fought against suggestions of using the names of Tuscan nobles (Victripharus), and leaving them nameless (as The Comets of Jupiter), and long after it had been named Europa by someone else's measure, Galileo still called it Jupiter II, refusing to give in.

It had been one name piled on top of another from the very first, long before anyone had ever set foot on it, long before they knew it was ice; before they knew anything about it except that it held steady, and so it was a moon, and not a star.

The next message he gets from her comes over official channels, and by voice.

"*This is ISI Bangalore Ground Control. There's been an H9N2 outbreak in the city. Hammond is infected. At the moment, everyone who was at Ground Control in the last forty-eight hours is under quarantine. There weren't many of us, so the main team will hold steady elsewhere for now. We have supplies and medical staff standing by outside. Data collection and monitoring of ISI* Manu *will continue as scheduled. I'll keep you apprised of developments. Kai Preetha, over and out.*"

("You okay?" Wen asked him as he stood up, and he said, "Fuck," more emphatically than he'd ever said anything to her, more than he remembers ever being.

He staggered to his room and sat on the edge of the bed, tried not to vomit.

She already had it.

She was sick, he knew it, he could tell, something in her voice that had been trying too hard not to shake.

He'd only heard her voice twice, but some things you can tell.

Planetside made him dizzy; he projected the kingfisher picture at full opacity on his windows until he could look around again.

It resembled her, he'd decided a long time back; he'd never seen her, but the way it looked across the water like it could see the future seemed about right.

Its name was *Halcyon smyrnensis*, and Home, and Preetha; one name piled on top of the other.)

On the next pass, he repoints the telescope and takes a picture of Sinope, a little red glint in the garland of minor moons.

This is what Sinope looked like fifty-three minutes before you opened this message. She says, Be well.

He thinks about what will happen in the time it takes the message to get there. They'll be on the far side of Jupiter by then, and the lights will be coming up slowly, pretending dawn, and he'll be here with channels open, hoping she'll come on the line and tell him that, fifty-three minutes ago, she was cured.

(It's hopeless. He knows already. Whatever news comes across that line won't be good, and he won't know until it's too late. You get far enough away from something, there's nothing you can do.)

But the light from Europa right now would be reaching her by then, and she would have a picture of Sinope.

Sometimes just looking at a moon was medicine; if it worked for Galileo, it was worth a try.

She doesn't answer.

He puts a cot in the comm room.

Wen doesn't say anything.

(It's for the best. If he explained that he had a picture of a kingfisher, and that he'd sent Galileo's notes to an interplanetary Ground Control, and that they should send paper and pencil on the probe to Gliese, and that he had to stay right where he was in case he heard back from Bangalore, it wouldn't look good.

She wouldn't argue—she seemed to know when people had their reasons—but she wouldn't think the reasons were connected, and they are; they are.)

The message comes back a week later, over official channels.

It's patchy, as if the machinery is going, or her voice is.

He sits more forward in his chair with every word.

"*Dr. Hammond died. Sometime early morning, maybe 0430, actual time unknown—I didn't sleep for very long, but when I woke up she had gone. It's just me.*"

The horror fades. Panic edges in.

Where are the others, he almost yells into the mic, who would leave you alone like this, but the question would take an hour to reach her, and that isn't the thing he wants her to hear from him last.

(It would be the last; her voice is going, he realizes now what it means. This will be the last.

His hands are shaking.)

So instead he says, "Roger that, Preetha. Please update us with any message for the *Manu,* and continue to report."

He says, trying to be steady, "Everyone from home wishes you well."

They send an ethicist and a psychologist to the comm center a few hours later, to talk to Henry and Wen about whether the ship should know.

"This puts them under a lot of unnecessary stress," one of the ethicists argues.

"Good," Henry says. "They have a lot to live up to."

The other one says, "Informing them of a change like this could be more stressful than useful. They already know the importance of a clean landing on this."

He says, "After this they fucking well better."

Eventually, Wen snaps.

"This entire operation hinges on the crucial importance of full information. It's been that way since my forebears set foot here. Earth trusted them enough to send them. If we can't trust them with information, we should tell them to turn around. Do you want to tell them that? Because I'm not going to."

And before they can object, she hits the button to bounce it to the transport, so the skeleton crew that's still awake will know what's happened.

(It will be a duplicate.

Henry hit Send before they ever showed; he hit Send before he ever paged Wen and told her there was something she needed to see.

He hit Send as soon as it came over the transom, and his hand stopped shaking.)

"To the Europa Base, and the crew and passengers of the Manu: *We on Earth who have dreamed of exploration honor your mission, and have faith that what you work to build will come back to you a hundredfold.*

For those who will go on to Gliese 581, that hidden world that holds our future in it; you are the children of Galileo, and we send our hopes with you.

The citizens of Earth wish you good journey, and good homecoming."

He takes a crawler out to the dark side.

Ahead of him is a blue marble (behind him is a bead of jasper).

The blue marble isn't winking—looking from here, there's no marked difference from what it used to be. It will take some generations yet. When the water swallows up the last of it, the Evrard Telescope will show a surface of near-unbroken blue.

The grandchildren of Europa will be taken out to the dark side (no helmets, by then), and they'll hold up binoculars and be instructed to look carefully for the bluest thing they can see.

(It won't be Rigel, the teacher will have to remind them. Keep your eye out for something steady—you're looking for a moon, not a star.)

Through his binoculars, he can see India passing out of sight; somewhere on what's left of the land is the place where Kai died, fifty-three minutes before he got her last transmission.

It's the first time he's looked at something, and really known.

(Preetha means, The palm of the hand; it means happiness; it means beloved; one on top of the other.)

THE GRINNELL METHOD

MOLLY GLOSS

Molly Gloss [www.mollygloss.com] *was born in Portland, Oregon, and studied at Portland State College (now University). She worked as a school-teacher and a correspondence clerk for a freight company before becoming a full-time writer in 1980. In 1981, she took a course in science fiction writing from Ursula K. Le Guin at Portland State University. Her first short story,* "The Doe," *was published that same year, and was followed by a dozen more, including Hugo and Nebula Award nominee* "Lambing Season." *Her first novel* Outside the Gates *appeared in 1986, and was followed by* The Jump-Off Creek, The Dazzle of Day, Wild Life, *and* The Hearts of Horses. Wild Life *was a James Tiptree, Jr. Award winner. In addition, she has won the 1990 Ken Kesey Award for the Novel, the 1996 Whiting Writers Award, as well as the PEN Center West Fiction Prize. Gloss has also written book reviews, essays, an appreciation of Ursula K. Le Guin, and an introduction to the memoir of a woman homesteader. Molly Gloss lives and writes in the Pacific Northwest.*

In the long winter of her absence, hunters and soldiers had made use of the camp, had left behind a scattered detritus of tin cans, broken fishing line and shotgun shells, had turned the fire-pit into a midden of kitchen garbage, burnt and sodden bones and feathers, clam shells, and the un-burned ends of green and greasy sticks. She sat down on the ground, took out a hand lens and examined the feathers and bones to reassure herself they were largely from pintail ducks and black brant.

The boy she had hired to transport her gear up the sand trail from Oys-terville to Leadbetter Point had been warned of the woman's odd ways and refused to be amazed when she sat on the dirt like a Jap, peering nearsighted through her magnifier at feathers and shards of bone. He discharged his duty, which was to off-load her goods onto the dirt, and then he waited, drawing circles and figure eights on the ground with the toe of one gum boot, until she woke from her study and paid his wages in coin.

On the three-mile tramp, she had walked ahead of him, pausing only briefly to peer at something—a feather on the ground, a bird overhead—or to stand like a dog with her head cocked, and then pencil a note in the little book she carried in her hand, before immediately striding on. Hadn't offered a word of encouragement or a backward glance while he had struggled through the loose sand and mud pushing a wheelbarrow weighed down with her camp gear and strange paraphernalia. But she paid him a dollar more than the agreed upon price, which to his mind made up for many failings and eccentricities. He thanked her kindly and pushed his barrow off through the trees. There was something forlorn about the way the woman stood among her boxes and bags watching him go, and in consideration of that, he turned once and gave her a cheering wave of his hand.

In fact, she had lost heart a bit on first seeing the degraded camp, the men's stupid squalor, but when the boy had gone out of sight and left her alone she went directly to work burning the burnables in a smoky bonfire and burying the cans, the shells and bones, the garbage. She swept the disturbed ground with a branch and pitched her tent in exactly the same place as the year before, under the canopy of a massive cedar almost surely well-grown when Robert Gray first sailed the *Columbia Rediviva* into the Great River of the West. There was still a faint, weathered tracing of the ditch she had cut to carry rain away from the base of her tent, and she renewed this with a grub hoe; then, because she was holding the tool in her hands, she quickly dug a hole for her scat at a place chosen not for privacy but for proximity to a blown-down jack pine over which to hang her nether parts.

The day was already well-gone and she was anxious to get a first look at the dunes and the salt marsh, so these things were all done rather perfunctorily—getting her ducks in a row, as Tom used to joke to her in his letters from the field. She put on her beach shoes, dug through her equipment until she had laid hands on field glasses and the .25 caliber Colt pistol, put them in the pocket of her jacket with the notebook and pencil, and set off through the trees toward the estuary.

The peninsula was not more than two or three miles wide at its widest point, a twenty-five-mile-long finger of land trapped between the Pacific

Ocean and Willapa Bay, built of sand washed north from the mouth of the Columbia River and then overgrown with conifer rain-forest which by now had become a patchwork of second- and third-growth woodland interrupted by small farms and cranberry bogs and half a dozen villages. Oysterville sat at the end of a tarred plank road, the last human settlement. Beyond it a woodland of Western hemlock, jack pine, and spruce carried on for a little more than three miles before running out at the curved tip of the fingernail, which was Leadbetter Point. On the ocean side, the point was a world of shifting low dunes and tufted beach grass; on the bay side a rich estuarine marsh of pickleweed and arrowgrass, drowned and emptied twice each day by surging eight-foot tides. The whole of the point was a resting place for thousands of waterfowl and shorebirds during the spring and fall migrations, summer nesting grounds for plovers and snipes, and winter home to black brants and canvasbacks.

It had rained much of the day, but now the clouds had lifted somewhat and were massed offshore above a narrow understory of clear light. When she came out of the trees onto the bayshore, a great flock of wigeons and pintails flew up in unison against the dark sky, turning so the undersides of their wings caught the seam of sun at the horizon. The tide was out, and her shoes left a trail of shallow pug marks in the narrow strand of bayside beach. Crab molts were thick, and the mud was stitched with the lacy tracks of sanderlings and plovers as well as the spoor of deer, who liked to come down to graze the tidewater marshes at evening. She planned to make only a quick circuit to see what the winter tides had wrought and then get an early start in the morning, but still she lifted the field glasses every so often and wrote a few words in her notebook.

At the hook-shaped tip of the peninsula where the dunes and salt meadows gave way entirely to marsh she stood a moment peering across the mouth of the bay to Tokeland, four miles distant, its wooded hills through the gauze of weather seeming to her like a long line of battlements. Ships traveling from British Columbia to San Francisco regularly came into the bay to pick up lumber at the South Bend docks—the entrance was wide and straight, they came in without pilots—and a ship was laboring through the swells a mile from shore. She watched it for several minutes, the white curl rolling off the rust-colored prow, and then she turned and cut straight across toward the weather beach.

The earth barely rose above the sea along this coast, and the peninsula was everywhere pocked with little lakes and ponds and bogs. A maze of intersecting paths had been laid down through the woods and marsh by hunters and the hunted, which in her first year camping here she had tried to decipher and follow—countless lost hours scouting back and forth for the driest trail—but this was her third year in the field, and she had long ago learned to slog straight through the standing water. Had learned, too, that it was useless to wade the marsh in gum boots. They were hot and clumsy when dry, heavy and clumsy when full of water or caked with mud, impossible to pull out of a sticky mire, desperately slow to dry out, even with the help of wind and a stove. She had taken to wearing old canvas shoes tied on with a piece of cord.

A Wilson's snipe broke from cover almost under her feet, making off to the west in a sharp and zigzagging panic flight. Grebes and pintails in small flocks rose in front of her and then settled again to the rear. Pelicans passed over her, keeping very high against the overcast. A peregrine falcon harassed a group of thirty or forty wigeons, trying to isolate a vulnerable bird from among the others. She stood still for several minutes watching him, and when he'd given up and flown eastward over the bay she held down the pages of her notebook against the gusty offshore wind and wrote a short note of his failure.

The weather beach had been dramatically rearranged since she had last seen it in September. The dunes were higher and steeper, the sand broader, stippled at low tide to form a field of shallow lakes. There were thousands of drift logs piled along the dunes—this was usual—and thousands of board feet of milled lumber, shattered and waterlogged or coated with oil. There were pieces of twisted iron and wire cable, broken crates and baskets, drifts of gill-netting tangled with sea wrack.

Over the years, hundreds of ships had sunk or gone aground on this stretch of coast. Long-time peninsula folk told salvage stories as if they were proud family histories: sacks of flour still good in the center, protected by the glued-hard outer layer; rafts of coal floating ashore in calm weather two years after the wreck of a coal ship. She was a habitual scavenger herself. When a spring storm and a high tide rolled in together she would be out scouring the wind-whipped beach for dead birds and feathers, while the dedicated locals were looking for cans of peas and wooden crab pot markers—or now, with the peninsula on a wartime footing, the shattered wreckage of warplanes floating in on the surf.

There were two lines of caved-in tracks going up and down the beach—the Coast Guard horse patrol, on the lookout for invasion by sea—but no footprints, none human at any rate, though a bear had come through the sand hills and laid down a trail that wandered northward along the high tide line. Looking for dead seals, fish or birds washed up on the sand—scavenging through storm wrack, exactly like every other peninsula native.

The sun was very low, the sky streaked with ragged orange clouds. She walked the wet sand south along the beach. There was little to make note of save the topography and the extravagantly painted sky, but when she turned inland and climbed over the foredune she disturbed several plovers who may have been feeding among the clumps of beach grass. When the migrating birds had passed through, it was the plovers, nesting and raising their young here, who would be the work of her summer, so she made a note about the birds ("maybe/probably semi-palmated") and on the left-hand page of her notebook drew a crude map of the location, with an oddly shaped drift log as a reference point. Then she crouched down and waited through a long darkening hour until finally the birds returned to the area and she could get an accurate count and decide that, yes, they were semi-palmated.

When she stood again, the plovers skittering away into the last of the light, it was already dark under the trees. She was half an hour scouting the way back to camp without a flashlight—she had not counted on the plovers keeping her out so late.

Her things were in somewhat of a jumble but she was able to find tea leaves and a pot, as well as potatoes and a block of good white San Francisco cheddar. She lit her camp stove and while she waited for the potatoes to boil she drank tea and nibbled shavings from the block of cheese and read through her scratchy field notes by the light of a Coleman lantern.

She followed Grinnell's famous method of note-taking: Her notebook, small enough to slip in her pocket, was an abridged record of bird sightings, cryptic behavior notes in a shorthand of her own invention, quickly sketched drawings and maps, details of weather and vegetation, travel routes and mileage that would be difficult to remember with precision later in the day. It was scribbled in pencil, and none of it well organized—it all ran together.

The Journal, written in pen at the end of every day, would be considerably fuller and neater, her notes organized, sorted out, edited, expanded, with detailed observations of behavior recorded at the back, on separate pages for each individual species. For the Journal, and for Species Accounts, she created a narrative, free of sentiment or much personal reflection—a scientific document, not a diary, but with the skeleton of facts dressed in the clothes of complete sentences, so as to be readable by any stranger looking over her shoulder. All manner of facts might prove important to a student of the future, this was Grinnell's belief. Nothing in nature should be assumed insignificant.

It had been a long tiring day of travel, hauling half a year's worth of camp gear by ferry and motor coach and shank's mare, but Grinnell had always stressed the importance of transcribing one's field notes at the end of every day. "No Journal, no sleep," was his rather famous rule when he took students into the field—she had heard this directly from Tom. She dug the heavy binder out of her luggage, laid it flat across her lap, dipped the metal tip of the pen in Higgins Eternal ink, and wrote directly below the last entry in a clear, fine hand, "10 April 1943, Leadbetter Point Base Camp." In her head she saw again the falcon gyring among the wigeons, his silhouette against the evening sky so terribly graceful and fluent.

It was her brother Tom, ten years older, who had started her in the business of collecting birds' nests, Tom who had taken her into the woods and fields, a small child, and told her the names of flowers, birds, trees, how to catch and mount butterflies and insects. They sat under the oaks behind their parents' Napa Valley house, and Tom taught her to voice the acorn woodpeckers—their strange squawks and purrs—while he balanced a sketch book in his lap and drew the woodpeckers in every careful detail.

Some of his professors were still listing the double-barreled shotgun as an essential tool of identification; Grinnell himself had been inclined that way. But Tom's generation, coming into the field in the 1920s, had begun the shift from taxidermy toward studying the behavior of free-living birds. Sight identification in the field was challenging—there were few published guides, none very complete—and Tom intended his sketch book to help her with it. "You're a girl, so you'll have to prove you're better than the boys." This wasn't a joke; Tom had seen firsthand his professors' bias against women in the sciences. "Universities don't mind teaching girls," he told her, "they just don't like to hire them. By the time you finish your studies, you'll need to know more birds on sight than everybody else."

In the summer of 1933, when she was twenty, an undergraduate at Stanford, and Tom a field biologist for the Berkeley Museum, he joined a mapping and scientific expedition to the Arctic. The expedition had been plagued with bad luck. His letters, coming in bunches sent out with whalers and fishing boats encountered in the Bering Sea, reported a minor fire in the galley, the death of the ship's cat, expedition notes and specimens spoiled by an overturned lamp. Then came months of silence. Then a letter in an unfamiliar hand. So sorry to convey sad news, Tom a bright mind and a boon pal, yours in sympathy &cetera. The expedition had been plagued not by bad luck but by one of its members—perhaps mad with syphilis or anarchism—methodically practicing mischief. A fire set in the ship's radio room had spread to the boiler, and when the vessel sank to the bottom of the Spitzbergen Estuary, Tom had been among the seven drowned. The survivors were months in lifeboats and starvation camps in the archipelago, had been at the verge of death themselves when finally rescued by a Norwegian sealing vessel.

She left her university studies and went home to St. Helena to console her parents, and be consoled by them. She had been a late and unexpected addition to their lives, a "caboose" they doted on, but it was Tom who had represented all their best hopes. It was assumed that a woman who went to university would eventually marry, and thereafter carry her knowledge of the world like a secret pearl in her apron pocket, but Tom's keen scientific mind and great ambition had seemed to promise public accolades and prizes. Now his parents wondered if their expectations had somehow weighed him down and been the cause of his drowning.

When Tom sailed for the Arctic, he had left his field guide with her—by then a thick book, fifteen years of careful drawings he intended some day to see into print. But for a year, more than a year after his death, she hardly carried his guidebook into the fields at all. She played Patience, sometimes for hours at a time, turning over the cards quickly, reshuffling the entire deck whenever the play became difficult. She read cheap romance novels and mysteries and failed to answer letters. She might have married—there was a suitor, a boyhood chum of Tom's, evidently attracted by her melancholy air—but when he pressed his suit she became suddenly awake, and desperate for meaning in her life. She gave up card playing and wrote a plea for readmission to the university which was denied on the first letter but granted on the third. Tom had warned her that only the most extraordinary women were advanced or promoted in the scientific disciplines, and she meant to be one of them. Employment opportunities would disappear completely if she were to marry, and therefore she would never marry. Her life as a scientist would be her own; but also, she felt, a tribute to Tom.

The weather was unsettled and wet; she dressed every day in waterproofs whether or not the morning sky promised rain. When she hiked out to the point in the early morning, birds rose up singly and in flocks all around her, veering off across the pale sky. She settled into an island of arrowweed out in the salt marsh, or into a swale at the edge of the jack pines, and pulled onto her shoulders a cape made of netting and bits of yarn having a rough resemblance to marsh grasses. Then she found a relatively comfortable position and became motionless, and in a little while the birds returned and resumed their ordinary business.

These early weeks in spring the peninsula was crowded with tens of thousands of birds, a hundred species and sub-species jostling together as they passed through from their southern wintering grounds to their northern breeding grounds. She was well-acquainted with the peninsula birds—all the usual species of the summer breeding season—but the mixed flocks of the spring migration were another matter. She kept Tom's field guide open in her lap and referred to it frequently. If a bird was not already illustrated there, she opened to a blank page and sketched it quickly herself, drawings she would have to refine later—Tom had been the better artist—and then compare to specimens in the Stanford natural history collections in hope of discovering the name.

At high tide, or whenever rain flooded the hollow she was sitting in, she slogged across the point to the driftwood beach, made herself comfortable among jumbled drift logs, and took up scrutiny of the gulls and little plovers and sandpipers along the surf line. When the huge old howitzers at Fort Canby twenty miles to the south let fly their practice rounds, the dim booming echo sent the shorebirds into the sky in a great rippling cloud.

At the end of April, a heavy storm arriving in the night lifted and belled the walls of the tent, drove rain through the waxed canvas, brawled and thrashed in the heavy-limbed firs. For hours, a strange green lightning flared almost continuously, and thunder followed in tremendous explosions—she imagined this must be the sound of a battlefield under a barrage. She lay awake listening to the shriek and groan of falling trees, the crash of breaking limbs. In the last hour before daybreak the bombardment at last slackened, and although the wind was still howling, she dressed in waterproofs, put specimen sacks in the pocket of her coat, took a flashlight, and went out into the storm. She kept to the rain-flattened grass at the edge of the foredune, away from drift logs and the high, huge, booming surf. The wind was beating in from the northwest; it rattled and shook the rain clothes, drove cold and wet through seams and gaps to bare skin. In other weather, she had watched gulls walk the beach at night, breakers rushing in ranks of yellow-green flame, the wet sand alive with tiny stars. Now a leaden surf rolled out to a black sky, and she felt herself to be alone at the edge of the known world.

The beach was empty of birds—all but the dead. The sand was littered with hundreds of bodies of water-soaked gulls, short-billed dowitchers, pelicans, puffins. Among them were storm-petrels, albatrosses, shearwaters—pelagic birds who spent their lives at sea, and came to land so rarely that she had seen them only in taxidermy. She took several corpses into her specimen sacks.

She climbed over the dune and waded a mile of salt marsh to the bayshore. The curved point was completely flooded, the tide flats and sand shore drowned under feet of water. The headland, four miles north across the bay, was indistinguishable in the darkness—no lights shone from Tokeland—but the North Cove lighthouse swung a red beam and then a white one through the storm every half minute or so, the brief streak of light glimmering with tiny sparks, bits of haloed flotsam falling with the rain.

To keep from the flood, she broke a path a dozen yards inland through salt grass and scrub, her legs whipped by willow branches. At her feet, in the dim cone of the flashlight, drifts of bluish chaff floated on the puddles. She took some into a specimen sack—bits of sodden feather, maybe, from an elegant tern, or a mew gull.

She ate a cold breakfast back at the tent, and when the darkness thinned she autopsied a dead albatross and recorded her findings on a fresh page in Species Accounts: *No bones broken; dark streaks of something viscous—not oil—in the anterior and posterior air sacs; death from obstruction of the airway? Or from causes unknown.*

The small bits she had collected from the wind-roughened puddles were not feather, as she had thought, but something like flakes of ash or thin scales of paint, blue to her eye, even now in daylight, but colorless under the lens—motes as clear and insubstantial as breath. She wrote, *I do not know what they are.*

In late morning, she walked out to the ocean again. The sky was lurid—utterly black in the west, veined with great streaks of orchid purple and emerald green. The wind was squally and cold, the beach in flood tide awash with the bodies of dead birds. She stood and looked and then hiked across to the bay.

From the edge of the marsh, she could hear a dog howling, a terrible prolonged wailing of pain or fear, and when she came out on the mud flats a wet black dog was pacing back and forth, lifting its muzzle every little while in a long, loud, doleful cry of anguish. She called to it without coming very near—she knew nothing of dogs, and thought this one might be rabid. The dog went on pacing and crying, looking out across the bay where an oyster boat rolled and heaved on the swell. Several men on the deck of the boat appeared to be casting and retrieving a drag net without recovering anything. The water was too choppy to see what it was they cast for—a man overboard, she feared, and then realized he must already have drowned—that they were casting for a body—or their efforts would have had more urgency. This was not something she could think about for long.

While she stood watching they brought up something heavy and dark, something like a waterlogged stump. The oystermen had seen her watching from the bay shore, and when they had the thing aboard they hoisted it up and displayed it for her, lifting and spreading the arms wide, lifting up the heavy head until the mouth fell open to white teeth, a red tongue. The bear's thick, sodden pelt streamed with salt water. The dog pointed his nose at the sky and suddenly raised a new wail—it seemed to her a sound of terrible bereavement. One of the men on the boat shouted something, but she could not make it out against the chop of waves on the muddy shore.

The birds had mostly gone to ground or been driven inland by the storm, so in the afternoon when the rain briefly slackened she took the sand trail to Oysterville to replenish groceries and post her letters. She walked quickly, holding down her hat. The sky in the west was still black, but now rippling every little while with silent green lightning. Dry blue flakes —she was still at a loss what label to give them—lifted and fell on the wind, and gathered at the outer edges of puddles in a stiff rime.

Oysterville's prosperity had failed decades earlier with the failure of the San Francisco oyster market, the village by now reduced to a few dozen weather-battered houses and barns scattered between the upland woods and the mud flats. The post office occupied space in Mulvey's Store, and the storekeeper, whose name was not Mulvey and who served also as postmaster, remembered her from previous years.

"It's you, is it, come back to look for your strange birds." He meant this in a neighborly way. She was, by most standards, an odd woman, one who dressed in trousers and tramped about in wild territory that was home to bears; a woman said to carry a pistol, and whose behavior and study could not properly be called "bird watching." But he had known women of her sort in North Carolina as a boy—"yarbs" who sold leaves and snake venom as curatives door to door, and lived out wild in the woods; and he was himself eccentric enough to think well of her.

It crossed her mind to tell him the correct term for a strange bird was incidental, or rare; but she smiled slightly and said, "Yes, it's me," and handed him several letters to post.

While he rummaged for any mail that might have come for her, he said, "Well, that was a storm we had, wasn't it, I never seen a sky like that, never have, nor such lightning."

She agreed that it was a terrible storm.

"A tempest, my mama would have called it, but no, I never seen it like that, which I wonder if it wasn't those fellows over to Fort Canby, shooting off some sort of ordnance, which they claim not. Or else the Japs, but if so they have got poor aim, they hit nothing but trees." He brought out two letters, one addressed in her mother's hand and the other in her father's. "Now what else can I do you for, miss?"

She gave him a short list—flashlight batteries, chocolate, a piece of smoked ham—and bought a copy of the weekly Chinook Observer, its bold headline announcing YANKS SHOOT DOWN YAMAMOTO. She stowed everything in her knapsack and swung the sack to her shoulder, but did not immediately take the trail to camp. On the lee side of Mulvey's porch she found a bench and sat to read her letters. Her parents each gave much the same mundane report comprised of errands and weather and neighborhood gossip. "They have shot down Yamamoto," her father wrote, which was his only reference to the war.

While she was skimming the front page of the newspaper a young girl ten or eleven years old came through the yard; when the girl saw her there she veered across and stepped up onto the porch. "Is your name Miss Kenney? Are you the woman looks for birds?" The girl was in rubber boots and a brown sweater. Her fair hair was unevenly cut, held back with bobby pins under a hat decorated with fish hooks and bird feathers.

"I am Barbara Kenney," she said. And then—this is what Tom would have done—she told the girl, "I am an ornithologist, which is a scientist who studies birds. Are you interested in science?"

She considered her answer. "I wonder about things, if that's science."

"It is."

The girl ran her tongue across her chapped lips. "I wonder about some birds I saw. I could show you them."

"Do you know the species name? Or can you describe them to me?"

"They're oystercatchers."

On the peninsula, she had only ever seen oystercatchers on the rocks below the North Head Lighthouse a good twenty miles to the south, prying mollusks out of coastal rocks with their long, tough, bright orange bills. She said, "Where did you see them? Are you certain they are oystercatchers?"

"They're over on the mud flats"—the girl pointed vaguely—"which is not where I ever have seen them. And most of them dead on the ground."

She could not think what the girl's story might mean, or how to measure the accuracy of it. But she thought of the albatrosses and petrels dead on the Leadbetter beach. She put away her newspaper and stood. "Well, all right, show me."

The girl led her south on the tarred plank road toward Nahcotta. There were jack pines on both sides of the road, and the wind made a sound in them like the rattle of pebbles in a jar. A splintered windmill on the roof of a house made a faint whine, spinning its few intact vanes. In the west, the black sky was shot through every little while with flutters of silent, virid-green lightning.

After half a mile, they turned east and walked on the criss crossing dikes of a cranberry farm and then the girl stepped down onto one of the bogs and headed straight across it. The field was soggy but not flooded, and the vines had not yet begun to bloom. The girl stepped with care, not to break the twiggy branches.

At the far edge of the bog they passed through a small woodlot and came onto a secluded part of the bayshore. There were dozens of black oystercatchers dead and dying on the wet mud. The birds not yet dead beat their long wings weakly against the ground and made faint yelping sounds, ghostlike and plaintive. Their golden eyes seemed to study the sky through milky film.

She knelt and examined several of the dead birds. She lifted wings and spread feathers and felt along the bodies for shotgun pellets, but the birds were unbloodied and intact.

The girl, watching her, said, "What made them fall? How come they died, do you know?"

"We have had such a fierce storm," she said after a moment. "I imagine it had something to do with that. There were a great many dead birds on the beach this morning—seabirds we don't see on the land. It may be the unusual weather drove them ashore. And brought down the oystercatchers."

The girl pulled at the hem of her sweater with grimy hands and glanced toward the dark sky in the west. "I went over to Klipsan this morning and there were a lot of whales that drove up onto the beach. We get them sometimes, one or two, but there's so many I couldn't count them all. Maybe a hundred, they're laying all up and down the sand for most of a mile, just laying there waiting to die I guess. Is that on account of the weather too?"

"I don't know. It may be." She said nothing about the dog, the bear.

She wrapped two dead birds and then a living one in sheets of newspaper and put them in the knapsack. The live bird rustled the paper and cried weakly.

"You'd think a big storm would make whales swim down deep, not come out on the beach," the girl said, which was perhaps not a question. Then she said, "Will you cut the birds open to see what killed them?"

"Yes. Sometimes an autopsy can work out the cause of death."

She walked among the birds still on the ground, quickly twisting the necks of those still moving. The girl watched this in silence and then said, "I live at the Whalebone Inn. Will you come and tell me if you work out what killed them?"

She knew the Whalebone Inn, a boarding house in Nahcotta. "Yes, I'll come and find you if I learn anything."

They walked back together across the cranberry fields. When they came out on the road, the clouds were huge above the tops of the trees, violently bruise-colored, rippling with that strange lightning. They looked at the sky in silence. A dry blue rain had begun to fall again; it collected in fine drifts on the brim of the girl's hat.

"I am camped at Leadbetter Point. Will you come and tell me if you find any more dead birds in numbers like that, or where they aren't usually seen?"

The girl nodded, and after a hesitation she said, "Do you know the real name for an oystercatcher?"

"Do you mean the species name? The black ones here on the peninsula are HAEMATOPUS BACHMANI. Bachman was a friend to Audubon, and there are several birds named for him."

"Have all the names been given out by now?"

"Do you mean, have all the birds on the earth been discovered and given a name? No, no, every year some new ones are found. If we were in South America we might discover one—there are more species of birds there than anywhere. I don't imagine all the species on the earth will ever be known and named. People are always finding new mushrooms and insects and fish."

The girl cast her a sidelong look. "Are any birds named for a woman?"

"Yes, a few." She considered how much more to say—how much Tom would have said. "But most of those are named for queens or goddesses, or for the daughters or wives of scientists, not for women who are themselves scientists." She did not say, that in the winter just past she had taken work as a poorly paid assistant to a prominent male professor, trapping birds and preparing their skeletons for his outdated study of the mechanics of bird flight; or that, the winter before, she had resorted to teaching children at a grade school in Calistoga. She did not say: Universities are willing to educate women, but not employ them.

"Are any birds named for you?"

"No." She did not smile. "Not yet."

Overnight, as blood will clot in a wound, the clouds thickened and hardened, and in the morning what remained was a black flaw stretching out of sight to the north and south, a long, shifting vein of darkness, glossy and depthless.

The storm had battered the coast for hundreds of miles, from Vancouver Island to Bandon, and inland as far as Spokane and Boise. Fishermen cutting through her camp on their way to the beach told her the widespread belief: that a new and terrible weapon detonated over at Hanford or at one of the secret sites in Canada had brought on the unnatural storm and left that huge black pall in the sky.

A woman she met on the beach was of another mind. God, she said, had opened a portal into heaven and shortly would raise up all the believers.

In the following days, extraordinarily high tides gnawed at the beaches and mudflats; roads and paths disappeared; fifty-year-old houses built on bluffs above the sand fell into the sea. Rafts of dead fish floated in on the next tide and the next, and their decaying bodies littered all the salt marshes and the sand beaches. There were so many fin whales and gray whales decaying on the beach at Klipsan that when the wind blew northerly she could smell the stench from her camp almost ten miles away.

Her notebook became a record of casualties and losses. Thousands of plovers, the subjects of her summer study, had been scattered, driven away or killed in the storm. She posted signs to warn people away from the nesting grounds—this was a crucial time for the few hundred pairs who remained—but the beach had been reduced to a narrow strand, and the Coast Guard horse patrol came up and down it twice a day, heedless of the birds' shallow nests. And in the days after the storm, beachcombers from the tourist cabins, as well as peninsula natives from Oysterville and Nahcotta, walked over the dunes and through the plover nesting sites or drove onto the beach and parked above the high tide line. From the open sand, the black rift seemed to hang just overhead, almost within reach, and on clear nights it was a starless streak through the firmament. People sat on blankets on the sand, or on the fenders and the running boards of cars, and stared up at it.

She watched it too, from drift logs above the nesting grounds. One day she watched a single heron, then nine pelicans, then a pair of horned grebes rise through the sky and vanish into the blackness. Methodically, she wrote down the time of day, and the numbers of the birds, their names. She tried to think what else to say, and finally wrote, *Gone.*

The woman who came to the door at the Whalebone Inn was not someone she recognized, though the woman seemed taken aback and said, "Oh! It's you!" as if they were acquainted from long past.

"I'm looking for a girl who lives here, she has a brown sweater and her hair is light in color. I failed to get her name."

"It would be Alice. What do you want her for?"

"I'd like to speak with her, if I may."

The woman, who was Alice's aunt, considered her niece an odd and baffling child—a girl who preferred capturing frogs to playing with dolls; a girl who liked to keep snakes as pets. It was a mild worry of hers, that Alice might grow up to be an eccentric and homely hermit-spinster such as the one now standing on the porch. After a considerable pause to weigh Alice's best interests, she stepped out and shouted, "Alice! Come here now, I mean it!"

In a moment the girl came in sight, walking up from the tidal flats. She was barefooted and muddy, in pants raggedly cut off at the knees. Her sweater pockets bulged with shells or agates.

"Hello, Alice, I brought you something."

She walked down to meet the girl and held out to her a small ring-bound notebook with a fresh pencil stuck through the rings. Alice took the book and opened to the first page and then looked up.

"It's a place to write down what you see, and find, and what you wonder about. You must write your name at the top, and the date, on every page, but it's not to be a diary. It's a place to write the names of the birds you see, if you know what they are. Or you can say what they look like, or make a drawing—you write on this side of the page, and make your drawings and maps over on the other side. And write down where you saw the birds and what they were doing, and how many there were. Write in it every day. Later on you will probably want to record your observations in ink in a more systematic way, but I've been keeping books like this one since I was a little girl. I have so many books now, they fill two long shelves."

Alice looked up from the book, pressing her hand in it to keep the wind

from lifting and fluttering the empty pages. "There's a coyote I see sometimes, and a porcupine. Should I write those down too?"

"Yes, I shouldn't have said so much about birds. You must be a naturalist,
for now, and not a specialist until you are older and decide for yourself
what interests you most. So write down everything you see, everything
in nature, any animals you see, what the weather is, and what the plants
are doing—are they leafing out, are the buds swollen, are they flowering?
And if you collect shells and rocks, write down what you've found, what
kind they are, or what you think formed them. And write down what you
wonder about, but try to be very sparing of sentiment and opinion—the
best scientists are impartial, not swayed by their own beliefs." She smiled
slightly. "If a woman is to have birds or other creatures named for her, she
must be the very best in her field."

The girl tucked her chin to hide her own expression, which was not a
smile. Then she said, "Is it all right if I think back, and write down what I
remember from a while ago? Just to catch up."

"Yes, but you will want to be clear. You could say: 'This is what I remember from last week, or last summer.'"

After a moment, Alice said with a glance, "I want to write down about
the oystercatchers."

"Yes. You should do that."

The girl's look shifted toward the sky in the west, the thick black flaw
above the tops of the trees. "Did you work out what killed them? The
oystercatchers?"

She hesitated. "No. But I hope someone will discover it eventually. You
should write down everything you saw around the time of the storm, and
afterward. But only what you know or have seen. These things might be
important, later, to understanding what occurred."

The woman who had answered the door was still watching from the
porch of the Whalebone Inn. Now she called out, "Alice, you ought to be
washing up for supper before long." The wind lifted and snapped the front
of her apron like a flag.

Alice answered her, "I will," but without moving to do it.

Then, after a silence, Alice said, "I have seen birds going into that hole
in the sky. Have you? There's saw-whets and barred owls that live on Long
Island and when I was camped over there the other night I saw five of
them go up."

She had written that morning: *Fourteen willets—usually solitary, have
never seen so many fly together—up and gone.* She had seen children on

the beach write notes and tie them into the tails of kites, and when they let go the tethering string the kites lifted into the blackness and disappeared. She did not say any of this to Alice.

She said, "You should write down what you saw, the owls disappearing, but Alice, no one knows what it is, so you shouldn't call it a hole in the sky." Then she said, "Did you row over to the island? The bay has been very rough." From the dock at Nahcotta it was at least a mile across Willapa Bay to Long Island. When she was no older than Alice, she had used to row a canoe on Clear Lake even in the fall when the hard easterly winds would blow foam off the choppy waves; but that was before Tom drowned.

The girl shrugged. "I went at low tide, and it was shoalwater. If I was to overturn I guess I could have stood up and walked to shore."

They went on standing together in the yard a few more moments, then Alice looked down at the book in her hands. "If it is a hole, and the birds are going on through it, I wonder what is on the other side."

The wind drew a lock of hair across the girl's face and she pushed it back and hooked it behind her ear. It was late in the afternoon and the sky had begun to redden above the black flaw. They both looked up at the hollow barking of gulls overhead, and watched without speaking as a flock of twelve or thirteen flew west and disappeared into the depths of the blackness.

From a thicket of arrowgrass in the salt marsh she watched a lumber ship half a mile off the point laboring into the bay, the white surf booming against the ship's hull and decks. This was dusk at the end of a wet day, and a pair of whimbrels foraging in the mudflats were the only birds she had seen in an hour. Her attention drifted. She looked away, then back, and the big vessel at that moment heeled over suddenly with a terrible shrieking of metal. Two men in bright yellow anoraks, small as the end of her thumb from this distance, slid off the deck into the gray water and disappeared. She drew in a loud breath as if it might be possible to call them back, but the sound that came on the exhale was hollow and wordless.

There were other men staggering about on the ship—yellow warblers moving jerkily from branch to leaf came into her mind—and there must have been men in the wheelhouse far forward on the bow, men standing behind the dark, rain-streaked windows, though she could not see them, could not hear them shouting to one another. The ship leaned and settled—hard aground, listing onto its starboard side—and waves broke on it in great foaming sheets.

She stood up numbly and threw off the marsh cape, took the pistol from her coat pocket and fired it three times into the sky. In a few minutes, someone on the ship shot off a signal flare, its blurred yellow streak wobbling upward, arcing toward the black flaw and disappearing into it. The ship's horn blared, blared again, and a third time.

With the last of the daylight failing, she began hurriedly to gather driftwood and pile it onto one of the mud islands in the marsh. Beach bonfires had been forbidden since the beginning of the war but this was all she knew to do, it was what peninsula people had done in the days when shipwrecks were common, bonfires on the beach to illuminate the darkness for any crewmen who might be able to swim to shore. The wood was sodden, too wet to light, and she was standing there in her mud-caked shoes, breathless with effort, thinking about the can of kerosene half a mile away in her camp, when something like a rumble of thunder shook the ground. The ship in the channel had gradually become invisible but for marker lights drowned intermittently by the breaking seas, but when she looked toward it a leaping glare lit up the whole mouth of the bay. For a startled moment she thought the wet driftwood had ignited, but it was something belowdecks on the ship—covert munitions, she would think later, carried with the lumber— that had begun to burn. The ship was very low in the water, leaning hard on its keel now, and swells were breaking over the upper deck, smothering it completely in gray foam and solid water. The fire shot up higher after every flood, and flames followed the oil out onto the glossy water and lifted upward in a yellow curtain.

She stood and watched men holding to the railings around the wheelhouse let go and drop and disappear into the water. Someone threw a Jacob's ladder over the lee side and men began climbing down it. One of them was Tom— she knew him by his plaid mackinaw—Tom!—and then a swell broke over the ship in a solid white sheet and he vanished under the cataract. Other men climbed down behind him and were swept off, or jumped from the last rung and sank in the burning water. All of this occurred in silence, or seemed to, as the wind, and the roar of the flames, deafened her.

The burning ship lit up the sky. People living in Oysterville four miles away, and in hermit cabins along the bayshore, began to walk out of the darkness onto the firelit marsh, singly and in pairs, wading through the flood in their gum boots, until a dozen or better stood around her, staring and silent, or talking quietly. Someone asked what she had seen, and she shook her head, unable to speak.

After a while, a Coast Guard double-ended rescue boat came laboring out of the darkness into the glare. There was a lifesaving station near the North Cove lighthouse. She had only ever visited the station in summer—young men in white trousers, tight knit tops, white seamen's caps, running rescue drills for small crowds of admiring tourists—but on the walls of the station- house there were photographs of wrecked clipper ships and of rescue boats breasting enormous crashing waves, photographs captioned "Heroes of the Surf," and "Storm Warriors." The Coast Guard boat, very small against the hugeness of the firestorm, came within a few hundred yards and then held off, rolling and pitching on the heavy sea. Several men came out of the for- ward cabin and shot a line across the water that fell short. They tried again, and a third time, a fourth, and then stood and watched the ship burn. The fire rose up in a great column of vivid orange and writhing black, and the wind took it all west into the starless hole in the sky.

After midnight, when the fire had burned down somewhat, the Coast Guard boat began to motor back and forth across the heavy swells, evidently searching for survivors or bodies in the water near the wreck. The tide, someone said, would likely take the bodies up the Naselle River to Raymond or North Bend, but nevertheless a few people began walking the bayshore in case any might wash up along the Point.

She searched in the arrowgrass and picked up her things from where she had dropped them—binoculars, notebook, the camouflage cape—and waded back across the marsh into the trees and found her tent in the darkness and lay down, shivering, in her wet clothes and then sat up and opened the Journal and by flashlight made an entry on the last page of Species Accounts.

Several times in the years since his death she had been visited by Tom, or rather Tom's ghost. Once, just at dusk, she had seen him sitting below an oak tree alive with acorn woodpeckers, and when she called to him he turned and grinned and made the purring sound a woodpecker makes in greeting its fellows. She came upon him suddenly in the narrow aisles of the Stanford library stacks, where he smiled slightly as if embarrassed and then turned into another aisle without speaking. On the peninsula, where heavy rain could turn the meadows and fields into an archipelago of islands, she had seen Tom crossing through the flooded tombstones of the Ocean Park cemetery, not walking on water but wading in his heavy hiking boots, raising a white surf that slapped against the stones. When she spoke to him he glanced back with a soft expression but did not reply.

None of this, of course, was real. A moment afterward, the person sitting under the oak was Claude Gerald who lived uphill from her parents' house in St. Helena. In the library stacks, it was Benjamin Morse, a student in her botany class whose dark hair brushing the collar of his shirt was so much like Tom's. The one she had seen crossing the flooded church yard was a young man who sold oysters on the pier at Nahcotta—she did not know his name—on his way to the feed store in Ocean Park.

After Tom drowned in the Spitzbergen estuary, but during the months when she had still believed him to be alive, she had been visited by vivid dreams of him, dreams that slipped away in the morning, beyond retrieve. It seemed to her that glimpses of Tom's ghost must be fragments of those dreams, dreams she had thought irrecoverable, and a separate, nameless loss. She wrote down each sighting at the back of the Journal in Species Accounts, on the page set aside for uncommon birds, the page titled Incidental, Accidental, Rare.

When the night began to thin toward grayness, she put her notebook and Tom's field guide in the knapsack and walked through the dark trees to the ocean beach.

Fog obliterated the headlands and the surf. In the half-light of dawn the flaw in the sky seemed to hang just overhead, a satiny black ribbon she felt she might stand on tiptoe and touch with an outstretched hand.

It was high tide, but there was a long black sedan parked on the beach. It seemed to her that the car would be lost to the ocean in the next quarter hour, and that the man who had driven it there was either unaware or unconcerned. He crouched behind a drift log out of the wind and fiddled with a small piece of machinery—a toy rocket ship, she thought, or a Roman candle.

She walked down to him through a dimpled field of plover nests. There were no more than a few dozen birds still remaining on Leadbetter beaches, and the nests on this part of the strand were unpopulated, empty of eggs. The man glanced up but said nothing, intent on his work. He had not shaved in recent days and his graying stubble—he was a man nearing sixty—was bright with beads of rain. She sat near him and opened the field guide to a blank page at the back, where Tom had drawn a few unidentified species, and she began to sketch the machine, which was not a toy: it stood like a white egret on tripod legs, its neck and bill pointed upward.

The surf came in around the man's big car, lifted it, carried it west a few yards and dropped it. The motion caught his eye, and belatedly he woke to the situation and shuffled to his feet. By then the tires had already settled half a foot into the wet sand. He stood there, considering, and then shook his head and said, "Hell's bells," in a tone of disgust, and crouched down again with his machine.

In a short while he took a piece of paper and a pencil from his pocket, wrote a note, spindled it, and slid it inside the narrow beak of the egret.

She had come to the beach with an uncertain plan—had thought she might build a fire on the sand and send something—a letter? or even the field guide—in ash and smoke up to Tom. But now she tore a page from the back of the notebook and wrote a few lines. *The world is hard*, she wrote. *But everything lives on. Even love. Even loneliness.*

She folded the paper very small and held it out to the man. He barely glanced at her, took it without speaking and pushed it tightly into a cavity in the nose cone. Then he struck a match and lit a short piece of fuse and said offhandedly, "You should probably get farther back," and they both stepped away fifteen or twenty feet. The rocket made a low grating or rasping noise—the sound certain gulls make, though she had not seen many gulls in recent days—and shot straight up, trailing white smoke and red sparks. They watched it rise through the gray sky and arc slightly and disappear through the rupture in the roof of their world.

BEAUTIFUL BOYS

THEODORA GOSS

Theodora Goss [www.theodoragoss.com] *was born in Hungary and spent her childhood in various European countries before her family moved to the United States. Although she grew up on the classics of English literature, her writing has been influenced by an Eastern European literary tradition in which the boundaries between realism and the fantastic are often ambiguous. Her publications include the short story collection* In the Forest of Forgetting; Interfictions, *a short story anthology co-edited with Delia Sherman; and* Voices from Fairyland, *a poetry anthology with critical essays and a selection of her own poems. Her most recent book is* The Thorn and the Blossom: A Two-sided Love Story. *She has been a finalist for the Nebula, Crawford, and Mythopoeic awards, as well as on the Tiptree Award Honor List, and has won the World Fantasy and Rhysling awards.*

You know who I'm talking about.

You can see them on Sunday afternoons, in places like Knoxville, Tennessee, or Flagstaff, Arizona, playing pool or with their elbows on the bar, drinking a beer before they head out into the dusty sunlight and get into their pickups, onto their motorcycles. Some of them have dogs. Some of their dogs wear bandanas around their necks. Some of them, before they leave, put a quarter into the jukebox and dance slowly with the waitresses, the pretty one and then the other one.

Then they drive or ride down the road, heading over the mountains or through the desert, toward the next town. And one of the waitresses, the other one, the brunette who is a little chubby, feels a sharp ache in her chest. Like the constriction that begins a panic attack.

"Beautiful Boys" is a technical as well as a descriptive term. Think of them as another species, *Pueri Pulchri*.

    Pueri Pulchri cor meum furati sunt. The Beautiful Boys have stolen my heart.

They look like the models in cigarette ads. Lean, muscular, as though they can work with their hands. As though they had shaved yesterday. As though they had just ridden a horse in a cattle drive, or dug a trench with a backhoe.

    They smell of aftershave and cigarette smoke.

That night, when she makes love to her boyfriend, who works at the gas station, the other waitress will think of him.

    She and her boyfriend have been together since high school.

    She will imagine making love to him instead of her boyfriend: the smell of aftershave and cigarettes, the feel of his skin under her hands, smooth and muscled. The rasp of his stubble as he kisses her. She will imagine him entering her and cry aloud, and her boyfriend will congratulate himself.

    Afterward, she will stare into the darkness and cry silently, until she falls asleep on the damp pillow.

Would statistics help? They range from 5'11 to 6'2, between 165 and 195 pounds. They can be any race, any color. They often finish high school, but seldom finish college. On a college campus, they have almost unlimited access to what they need: fertile women. But they seldom stay for more than a couple of semesters.

    They are more likely than human males to engage in criminal activities. They sell drugs, rob liquor stores and banks, but are seldom rapists. Sex, for them, is a matter of survival. They need to ensure that the seed has been implanted.

    They seldom hold jobs for more than six months at a time. You can see them on construction sites, working as ranch hands, in video stores. Anything temporary.

    They seldom marry, and those marriages inevitably end in desertion or divorce. They move on quickly.

    They always move on. I believe that on this planet, their lifespan is approximately seven years. I have never seen a Beautiful Boy older than twenty-nine.

Oscar Guest is not his real name.

He had all the characteristics. Tall, brown skin, high cheekbones: a mixture of Mexican and American Indian ancestry. Black hair pulled back into a ponytail, black eyes with the sort of lashes that sell romance novels or perfume. He was wearing a t-shirt printed with the logo of a rock band and faded jeans.

"I hear you're paying $300 to participate in a study," he said.

It's a lot of money, particularly considering our grant. But we choose our test subjects carefully. They have to fit the physical and aesthetic criteria (male, 5'11"-6'2", 165-195 pounds, unusually attractive). Even then, only about 2% of those we test are Beautiful Boys.

I could tell he was one of them at once. I've developed a sort of sensitivity. But of course that identification would have to be verified by testing.

Sometimes, the Beautiful Boy doesn't move on immediately. Sometimes, he stays around after the dance. He gets a job in construction, starts dating the pretty waitress. If she insists, they might even get married.

By the time he leaves, she's pregnant.

As far as we know, Beautiful Boys mate and reproduce like human males. Based on anecdotal evidence, we suspect they're superior lovers, but that data has not been verified. We are writing a grant to study their reproductive cycle. However, we are still at the stage of identifying them, of convincing the general population that they are here, among us—an alien species.

We always perform the standard tests: blood tests, skin and hair analysis. Beautiful Boys are physiologically identical to human males, but show a higher incidence of drug use. They typically have lower body fat, more lean muscle. I have known some to live on a diet of Cheetos and beer. They don't need to diet or exercise. It's as though their metabolism is supercharged.

What Oscar used to eat: Cocoa Puffs with milk, orange juice from concentrate, peanut butter and jelly sandwiches, leftover pizza, Oreos, beer.

Although I have no statistical evidence, I believe Beautiful Boys need more carbohydrates than human males. Once, at night, I walked into the kitchen and saw him standing in front of the open refrigerator, in his boxer briefs, drinking maple syrup from the jug.

He showed up at my house.

"Hey, Dr. Leslie, it's me, Oscar," he said when I opened the door. "I was wondering if there's anything else I can do for the study. My landlord just kicked me out and I don't have money for another place."

"Why did he kick you out?" I asked. It was 2 a.m. I stood at the door in my pajamas and a robe, trying not to yawn.

"I got in a fight."

"A fight? You mean in the apartment?"

"Yeah," he said. "With the wall."

He showed me his bloody fists. I told him to come in and cleaned his knuckles, then bandaged them.

"How much have you been drinking?" I asked.

"A lot," he said. He looked sober, although he smelled like beer. Beautiful Boys have a higher than average tolerance for alcohol. That metabolism again.

"You can spend the rest of the night on the sofa," I said. "Tomorrow, you'll have to find a new apartment."

The next morning, I woke up to the smell of pancakes. He was in the kitchen, fixing the screen door that had always stuck. "Hey, Dr. Leslie," he said. "I made you pancakes. How come you don't have a man around to fix this door, a beautiful lady like you?"

"My husband decided that he preferred graduate students," I said.

"Seriously? What an idiot. This door should work a lot better now. Anything else you want me to fix around here?"

The pancakes were stacked on a plate, on the kitchen table. I sat down, poured syrup over them, and started to eat.

I have devised a test that identifies Beautiful Boys with 98% accuracy. I believe Beautiful Boys emit a particular set of pheromones to attract human women. I do not know whether this is a conscious or unconscious process.

We put the test subject in an empty room. My research assistant, a blonde Tri Delt, enters the room and asks the test subject a series of questions. The questions themselves are irrelevant: What is your favorite color? If you could be any animal, what would you be? (A statistically significant number of Beautiful Boys identify themselves as predators, wolves or mountain lions.) After he has answered the questions, we inform the test subject that he has been enrolled in the study and give him the study t-shirt, in exchange for the shirt he is currently wearing. We take that shirt and put it in a sterile plastic bag.

Later, three testers smell the t-shirt and rate their sexual arousal on a scale of 1-10. Human males typically elicit no more than a 5. Beautiful Boys average in the 7-9 range. Our testers are all female. I have found that the best testers are brunette, a little chubby, nearsighted. They are most responsive to the chemicals that Beautiful Boys emit.

Why have they come to Earth?

For the same reason aliens always come to Earth in old science fiction movies: Mars needs women.

Where is their home planet? I'm not sure even they know.

Sometimes Oscar would stare off into space, and I would say, "What are you thinking about?"

He would say, "Just a place I used to play when I was a kid." Then he would roll over and say, "Hey, how about it? Are you up for a quickie?"

He was a superior lover. I do not, of course, know if that is a characteristic of all Beautiful Boys, or unique to Oscar. I think of him sometimes, when I'm alone at night: his smooth brown skin, mostly hairless, with the muscles articulated underneath. The black eyes looking down into mine. He would grin, kiss the tip of my nose. He was always affectionate, like a puppy. One day he brought me flowers he'd stolen from the college's botanical gardens.

"You really shouldn't have," I said. "I mean, seriously."

"I know," he said. "But that's what makes it fun."

One day, he came to me and said, "Dr. Leslie, I've got to go. My dad down in Tampa is sick, and I need to take care of him for a while."

I didn't tell him, you don't have a father in Tampa. You landed here on an alien spaceship with others of your kind. Where, I don't know.

"Give me your father's address," I said. "I'll send you some books."

He scribbled an address down on a slip of paper.

We made love one last time. It was like all the other times: intimate, affectionate, effective. Like being made love to by a combination of teenage boy, eighteenth-century libertine, and robot. Then I gave him $500 and he drove off in his pickup.

A week later, I missed my period. I was angry with myself, told myself I should have been more careful. Although I suppose my therapist would tell me that I unconsciously wanted this to happen.

I found a phone number for the address in Tampa. It was a bicycle repair shop, where they had never heard of Oscar Guest.

The study has three stages. The first one, nearly complete, involves devising a test to identify Beautiful Boys. That test has been devised, with 98% accuracy. We are in the process of writing up our results.

The second stage, for which we are currently seeking funding, focuses on understanding their reproductive cycle. We believe Beautiful Boys belong to a species that only produces males. To reproduce, they depend on the females of other species. In order to spread their genes and avoid inbreeding, they leave the planet on which they were born and travel to another planet, where they transform themselves into particularly appealing males of the target species. They travel around that planet, implanting their offspring.

The third stage focuses on the offspring they produce with human women. What are these children like? We do not know when Beautiful Boys first began coming to earth, although we suspect their presence as far back as the early twentieth century. There were probably Beautiful Boys seducing women in both World Wars, in Korea, in Vietnam. There are certainly alien children among us. We should find out as much about them as we can.

I'm going to call him Oscar Jr.

I didn't need the ultrasound to tell me that he was a boy. Of course he would be.

What will my Oscar be like? Will he play with Match Box cars? Will he watch Scooby Doo? Someday, will he ask about his father?

We don't know what happens to the children of Beautiful Boys, which is why completing the third phase of the study is so important. We don't know if some of them have the lifespan of human males, or if they all repeat the reproductive cycle of their fathers. Will Oscar go to college, settle down with a nice brunette, have my grandchildren?

Or, after high school, after we have argued because he's been smoking pot again and he's told me that he needs to find himself, waving a battered copy of *On the Road*, will he drive to the mountains, find the ship with others of his kind, fly to another planet and become whatever the women want there: green, with six arms and gills, like something out of an old science fiction movie?

I don't know. I think I would love him, even with six arms and gills.

I think of them sometimes, all the Beautiful Boys, driven to reproduce as salmon are driven to spawn. Driving across the country like an enormous net whose knots are bars, cheap apartments, college dorm rooms. And because I'm a scientist, I'm comforted by what science teaches us: that life is infinitely stranger than we can understand, that its patterns are beyond our comprehension. But that they tie us to the stars and to each other, inextricably. Like a net.

THE EDUCATION OF A WITCH

ELLEN KLAGES

Ellen Klages [www.ellenklages.com] *is the author of two acclaimed YA novels:* The Green Glass Sea, *which won the Scott O'Dell Award, the New Mexico Book Award, and the Lopez Award; and* White Sands, Red Menace, *which won the California and New Mexico Book Awards. Her short stories, which have been collected in World Fantasy Award nominated collection* Portable Childhoods, *have been have been translated into Czech, French, German, Hungarian, Japanese, and Swedish and have been nominated for the Nebula, Hugo, World Fantasy, and Campbell awards. Her story, "Basement Magic," won a Nebula in 2005. She lives in San Francisco, in a small house full of strange and wondrous things.*

1.

Lizzy is an untidy, intelligent child. Her dark hair resists combs, framing her face like thistles. Her clothes do not stay clean or tucked in or pressed. Some days, they do not stay on. Her arms and face are nut-brown, her bare legs sturdy and grimy.

She intends to be a good girl, but shrubs and sheds and unlocked cupboards beckon. In photographs, her eyes sparkle with unspent mischief; the corner of her mouth quirks in a grin. She is energy that cannot abide fences. When she sleeps, her mother smooths a hand over her cheek, in affection and relief.

Before she met the witch, Lizzy was an only child.

The world outside her bedroom is an ordinary suburb. But the stories in the books her mother reads to her, and the ones she is learning to read herself, are full of fairies and witches and magic.

She knows they are only stories, but after the lights are out, she lies awake, wondering about the parts that are real. She was named after a princess, Elizabeth, who became the queen of England. Her father has been there, on a plane. He says that a man's house is his castle, and when he brings her mother flowers, she smiles and proclaims, "You're a prince, Jack Breyer." Under the sink—where she is not supposed to look—many of the cans say M-A-G-I-C in big letters. She watches very carefully when her mother sprinkles the powders onto the counter, but has not seen sparkles or a wand. Not yet.

2.

Lizzy sits on the grass in the backyard, in the shade of the very big tree. Her arms are all over sweaty and have made damp, soft places on the newsprint page of her coloring book. The burnt umber crayon lies on the asphalt driveway, its point melted to a puddle. It was not her favorite. That is purple, worn down to a little stub, almost too small to hold.

On the patio, a few feet away, her parents sit having drinks. The ice cubes clink like marbles against the glass. Her father has loosened his tie, rolled up the sleeves of his white go-to-the-office shirt. He opens the evening paper with a crackle.

Her mother sighs. "I wish this baby would hurry up. I don't think I can take another month in this heat. It's only the end of June."

"Can't rush Mother Nature." More crackle, more clinks. "But I *can* open the windows upstairs. There's a Rock Hudson movie at the drive-in. Should be cool enough to sleep when we get back."

"Oh, that would be lovely! But, what about—" She drops her voice to a whisper. "—Iz-ee-lay? It's too late to call the sitter."

Lizzy pays more attention. She does not know what language that is, but she knows her name in most of the secret ways her parents talk.

"Put her in her jammies, throw the quilt in the back of the station wagon, and we'll take her along."

"I don't know. Dr. Spock says movies can be very frightening at her age. *We* know it's make-believe, but— "

"The first show is just a cartoon, one of those Disney things." He looks back at the paper. "*Sleeping Beauty.*"

"Really? Well, in that case. She loves fairy tales."

Jammies are for after dark, and always in the house. It is confusing, but exciting. Lizzy sits on the front seat, between her parents, her legs straight out in front of her. She can feel the warm vinyl through thin cotton. They drive down Main Street, past the Shell station—S-H-E-L-L—past the dry cleaners that give free cardboard with her father's shirts, past the Methodist church where she goes to nursery school.

After that, she does not know where they are. Farther than she has ever been on this street. Behind the car, the sun is setting, and even the light looks strange, glowing on the glass and bricks of buildings that have not been in her world before. They drive so far that it is country, flat fields and woods so thick they are all shadow. On either side of her, the windows are rolled down, and the air that moves across her face is soft and smells like grass and barbecue. When they stop at a light, she hears crickets and sees a rising glimmer in the weeds beside the pavement. Lightning bugs.

At the Sky View Drive-In they turn and join a line of cars that creep toward a lighted hut. The wheels bump and clatter over the gravel with each slow rotation. The sky is a pale blue wash now, streaks of red above the dark broccoli of the trees. Beyond the hut where her father pays is a parking lot full of cars and honking and people talking louder than they do indoors.

Her father pulls into a space and turns the engine off. Lizzy wiggles over, ready to get out. Her mother puts a hand on her arm. "We're going to sit right here in the car and watch the movie." She points out the windshield to an enormous white wall. "It'll be dark in just a few minutes, and that's where they'll show the pictures."

"The sound comes out of this." Her father rolls the window halfway up and hangs a big silver box on the edge of the glass. The box squawks with a sharp, loud sound that makes Lizzy put her hands over her ears. Her father turns a knob, and the squawk turns into a man's voice that says, "… concession stand right now!" Then there is cartoon music.

"Look, Lizzy." Her mother points again, and where there had been a white wall a minute before is now the biggest Mickey Mouse she has ever seen. A mouse as big as a house. She giggles.

"Can you see okay?" her father asks.

Lizzy nods, then looks again and shakes her head. "Just his head, not his legs." She smiles. "I could sit on Mommy's lap."

"'Fraid not, honey. No room for you until the baby comes."

It's true. Under her sleeveless plaid smock, her mother's stomach is very big and round and the innie part of her lap is outie. Lizzy doesn't know how the baby got in there, or how it's going to come out, but she hopes that will be soon.

"I thought that might be a problem." He gets out and opens the back door. "Scoot behind the wheel for a second."

Lizzy scoots, and her father puts the little chair from her bedroom right on the seat of the car. Its white painted legs and wicker seat look very wrong there. But he holds it steady, and when she climbs up and sits down, it *feels* right. Her feet touch flat on the vinyl, and she can see *all* of Mickey Mouse.

"Better?" He gets back in and shuts his door.

"Uh-huh." She settles in, then remembers. "Thank you, Daddy."

"What a good girl." Her mother kisses her cheek. That's almost as good as a lap.

Sleeping Beauty is Lizzy's first movie. She is not sure what to expect, but it is a lot like TV, only much bigger, and in color. There is a king and queen and a princess who is going to marry the prince, even though she is just a baby. That happens in fairy tales.

Three fairies come to bring presents for the baby. Not very good ones— just beauty and songs. Lizzy is sure the baby would rather have toys. The fairies are short and fat and wear Easter colors. They have round, smiling faces and look like Mrs. Carmichael, her Sunday School teacher, except with pointy hats.

Suddenly the speaker on the window booms with thunder and roaring winds. Bright lightning makes the color pictures go black-and-white for a minute, and a magnificent figure appears in a whoosh of green flames. She is taller than everyone else, and wears shiny black robes lined with purple.

Lizzy leans forward. "Oooh!"

"Don't be scared." Her mother puts a hand on Lizzy's arm. "It's only a cartoon."

"I'm not." She stares at the screen, her mouth open. "She's *beautiful.*"

"No, honey. She's the witch," her father says.

Lizzy pays no attention. She is enchanted. Witches in books are old and bent over, with ugly warts. The woman on the screen has a smooth, soothing voice, red, red lips, and sparkling eyes, just like Mommy's, with a curving slender figure, no baby inside.

She watches the story unfold, and clenches her hands in outrage for the witch, Maleficent. If the whole kingdom was invited to the party, how could they leave *her* out? That is not fair!

Some of this she says a little too out loud, and gets Shhh! from both her parents. Lizzy does not like being shh'd, and her lower lip juts forward in defense. When Maleficent disappears, with more wind and green flames, she sits back in her chair and watches to see what will happen next.

Not much. It is just the fairies, and if they want the baby princess, they have to give up magic. Lizzy does not think this is a good trade. All they do is have tea, and call each other "dear," and talk about flowers and cooking and cleaning. Lizzy's chin drops, her hands lie limp in her lap, her breathing slows.

"She's out," her father whispers. "I'll tuck her into the back."

"No," Lizzy says. It is a soft, sleepy no, but very clear. A few minutes later, she hears the music change from sugar-sweet to pay-attention-now, and she opens her eyes all the way. Maleficent is back. Her long slender fingers are a pale green, like cream of grass, tipped with bright red nails.

"Her hands are pretty, like yours, Mommy," Lizzy says. It is a nice thing to say, a compliment. She waits for her mother to pat her arm, or kiss her cheek, but hears only a soft *pfft* of surprise.

For the rest of the movie, Lizzy is wide, wide awake, bouncing in her chair. Maleficent has her own castle, her own mountain! She can turn into a dragon, purple and black, breathing green fire! She fights off the prince, who wants to hurt her. She forces him to the edge of a cliff and then she—

A tear rolls down Lizzy's cheek, then another, and a loud sniffle that lets all the tears loose.

"Oh, Lizzy-Lou. That was a little *too* scary, huh?" Her mother wipes her face with a tissue. "But there's a happy ending."

"Not happy," Lizzy says between sobs. "He *killed* her."

"No, no. Look. She's not dead. Just sleeping. Then he kisses her, and they live happily ever after."

"Noooo," Lizzy wails. "Not her. *Mel*ficent!"

They do not stay for Rock Hudson.

3.

"Lizzy? Put your shoes back on," her mother says.

Her father looks up over *Field and Stream*. "Where are you two off to?"

"Town and Country. I'm taking Lizzy to the T-O-Y-S-T-O-R-E."

"Why? Her birthday's not for months."

"I know. But everyone's going to bring presents for the baby, and Dr. Spock says that it's important for her to have a little something too. So she doesn't feel left out."

"I suppose." He shrugs and reaches for his pipe.

When her mother stops the car right in front of Kiddie Korner, Lizzy is so excited she can barely sit still. It is where Christmas happens. It is the most special place she knows.

"You can pick out a toy for yourself," her mother says when they are inside. "Whatever tickles your fancy."

Lizzy is not sure what part of her is a fancy, but she nods and looks around. Kiddie Korner smells like cardboard and rubber and dreams. Aisle after aisle of dolls and trucks, balls and blocks, games and guns. The first thing she sees is Play-Doh. It is fun to roll into snakes, and it tastes salty. But it is too ordinary for a fancy.

She looks at stuffed animals, at a doll named Barbie who is not a baby but a grown-up lady, at a puzzle of all the United States. Then she sees a *Sleeping Beauty* coloring book. She opens it to see what pictures it has.

"What fun! Shall we get that one?"

"Maybe."

It is too soon to pick. There is a lot more store. Lizzy puts it back on the rack and turns a corner. *Sleeping Beauty* is everywhere. A Little Golden Book, a packet of View Master reels, a set of to-cut-out paper dolls, a lunchbox. She stops and considers each one. It is hard to choose. Beside her, she hears an impatient puff from her mother, and knows she is running out of time.

She is about to go back and get the coloring book when she sees a shelf of bright yellow boxes. Each of them says P-U-P-P-E-T in large letters.

"Puppets!" she says, and runs over to them.

"Oh, look at those! Which one shall we get? How about the princess? Isn't she pretty!"

Lizzy does not answer. She is busy looking from one box to the next, at the molded vinyl faces that peer out through cellophane windows. Princess, princess, princess. Prince. King. Fairy, fairy, fairy, prince, fairy, princess.—and then, at the end of the row, she sees the one that she has not quite known she was looking for. Maleficent!

The green face smiles down at her like a long-lost friend.

"That one!" Lizzy is not tall enough to grab the box; she points as hard as she can, stretching her arm so much it pulls her shoulder.

Her mother's hand reaches out, then stops in mid-air. "Oh." She frowns. "Are you sure? Look, here's Flora, and Fauna, and—" She pauses. "Who's the other one?"

"Merryweather," Lizzy says. "But I want *her*!" She points again to Maleficent.

"Hmm. Tell you what. I'll get you all *three* fairies."

That is tempting. But Lizzy knows what she wants now, and she knows how to get it. She does not yell or throw a tantrum. She shakes her head slowly and makes her eyes very sad, then looks up at her mother and says, in a quiet voice, "No thank you, Mommy."

After a moment, her mother sighs. "Oh, *all* right," she says, and reaches for the witch.

Lizzy opens the box as soon as they get in the car. The soft vinyl head of the puppet is perfect—smiling red lips, yellow eyes, curving black horns. Just as she remembers. Beneath the pale green chin is a red ribbon, tied in a bow. She cannot see anything more, because there is cardboard.

It takes her a minute to tug that out, and then the witch is free. Lizzy stares. She expected flowing purple and black robes, but Maleficent's cotton body is a red plaid mitten with a place for a thumb on both sides.

Maybe the black robes are just for dress-up. Maybe this is her bathrobe. Lizzy thinks for a few minutes, and decides that is true. Plaid is what Maleficent wears when she's at home, in her castle, reading the paper and having coffee. It is more comfortable than her work clothes.

4.

On Saturday, Lizzy and her mother go to Granny Atkinson's house on the other side of town. The women talk about baby clothes and doctor things, and Lizzy sits on the couch and plays with her sneaker laces. Granny gets out a big brown book, and shows her a picture of a fat baby in a snowsuit. Mommy says *she* was that baby, a long time ago, but Lizzy does not think that could be true. Granny laughs and after lunch teaches Lizzy to play gin rummy and lets her have two root beers because it is so hot.

When they pull into their own driveway, late in the afternoon, Lizzy's mother says, "There's a big surprise upstairs!" Her eyes twinkle, like she can hardly wait.

Lizzy can't wait either. She runs in the front door and up to her room, which has yellow walls and a window that looks out onto the driveway so she can see when Daddy comes home. She has slept there her whole life. When she got up that morning, she made most of her bed and put Maleficent on the pillow to guard while she was at Granny's.

When she reaches the doorway, Lizzy stops and stares. Maleficent is gone. Her *bed* is gone. Her dresser with Bo Peep and her bookcase and her toy chest and her chair. All gone.

"Surprise!" her father says. He is standing in front of another room, across the hall, where people sleep when they are guests. "Come and see."

Lizzy comes and sees blue walls and brown heavy curtains. Her bed is next to a big dark wood dresser with a mirror too high for her to look into. Bo Peep is dwarfed beside it, and looks as lost as her sheep. The toy chest is under a window, Maleficent folded on top.

"Well, what do you think?" Her father mops his face with a bandana and tucks it between his blue jeans and his white t-shirt.

"I *liked* my room," Lizzy says.

"That's where the baby's going to sleep, now." Her mother gives her a one-arm hug around the shoulders. "*You* get a big-girl room." She looks around. "We will have to get new curtains. You can help me pick them out. Won't that be fun?"

"Not really." Lizzy stands very still in the room that is not her room. Nothing is hers anymore.

"Well, I'll let you get settled in," her father says in his glad-to-meet-you voice, "and get the grill started." He ruffles his hand on Lizzy's hair. "Hot dogs tonight, just for you."

Lizzy tries to smile, because they are her favorite food, but only part of her mouth goes along.

At bedtime, her mother hears her prayers and tucks her in and sings the good-night song in her sweet, soft voice. For that few minutes, everything is fine. Everything is just the way it used to be. But the moment the light is off and the door is closed—not all the way—that changes. All the shadows are wrong. A streetlight is outside one window now, and the very big tree outside the other, and they make strange shapes on the walls and the floor.

Lizzy clutches Maleficent under the covers. The witch will protect her from what the shapes might become.

5.

"When do you get the baby?" Lizzy asks. They are in the yellow bedroom, Lizzy's real room. Her mother is folding diapers on the new changing table.

"Two weeks, give or take. I'll be gone for a couple of days, because babies are born in a hospital."

"I'll go with you!"

"I'd like that. But this hospital is only for grown-ups. You get to stay here with Teck."

Teck is Lizzy's babysitter. She has a last name so long no one can say it. Lizzy likes her. She has white hair and a soft, wrinkled face and makes the *best* grilled cheese sandwiches. And she is the only person who will play Candy Land more than once.

But when the baby starts to come, it is ten days too soon. Teck is away visiting her sister Ethel. Lizzy's father pulls into the driveway at two in the afternoon with Mrs. Sloupe, who watches Timmy Lawton when his parents go out. There is nothing soft about her. She has gray hair in tight little curls, and her lipstick mouth is bigger than her real one.

"I'll take your suitcase upstairs," he tells her. "You can sleep in our room tonight."

Her mother sits in a chair in the living room. Her eyes are closed, and she is breathing funny. Lizzy stands next to her and pats her hand. "There there, Mommy."

"Thank you, sweetie," she whispers.

Daddy picks her up and gives her a hug, tight and scratchy. "When you wake up in the morning, you're going to be a big sister," he says. "So I need you to behave for Mrs. Sloupe."

"I'll be very have," Lizzy says. The words tremble.

He puts her down and Mommy kisses the top of her head. Then they are gone.

Mrs. Sloupe does not want to play a game. It is time for her stories on TV. They can play after dinner. Dinner is something called chicken ala king, which is yellow and has peas in it. Lizzy only eats two bites because it is icky, and her stomach is scared.

Lizzy wins Candy Land. Mrs. Sloupe will not play again. It is bedtime. But she does not know how bedtime works. She says the now-I-lay-me prayer with the wrong words, and tucks the covers too tight.

"Playing fairy tales, were you?" she says, reaching for Maleficent. "I'll put this ugly witch in the toy chest, where you can't see it. Don't want you having bad dreams."

"No!" Lizzy holds on to the puppet with both arms.

"Well, aren't you a queer little girl?" Mrs. Sloupe says. "Suit yourself." She turns off the light and closes the door, all the way, which makes the shadows even more wrong. When Lizzy finally falls asleep, the witch's cloth body is damp and sticky with tears.

Her father comes home the next morning, unshaven and bleary. He picks Lizzy up and hugs her. "You have a baby sister," he says. "Rosemary, after your mother's aunt." Then he puts her down and pats her behind, shooing her into the living room to watch *Captain Kangaroo*.

Lizzy pauses just beyond the hall closet and before he shuts the kitchen door, she hears him tell Mrs. Sloupe, "She was breech. Touch and go for a while, but they're both resting quietly, so I think we're out of the woods."

He takes Mrs. Sloupe home after dinner, and picks her up the next morning. It is three days before Teck arrives to be the real babysitter, and she is there every day for a week before he brings Mommy and the baby home.

"There's my big girl," her mother says. She is sitting up in bed. Her face looks pale and thinner than Lizzy remembers, and there are dark places under her eyes. The baby is wrapped in a pink blanket beside her. All Lizzy can see is a little face that looks like an old lady.

"Can we go to the playground today?"

"No, sweetie. Mommy needs to rest."

"Tomorrow?"

"Maybe next week. We'll see." She kisses Lizzy's cheek. "I think there's a new box of crayons on the kitchen table. Why don't you go look? I'll be down for dinner."

Dinner is a sack of hamburgers from the Eastmoor Drive-In. At bedtime, Mommy comes in and does all the right things. She sings *two* songs, and Lizzy falls asleep smiling. But she has a bad dream, and when she goes to crawl into bed with Mommy and Daddy, to make it all better, there is no room. The baby is asleep between them.

For days, the house is full of grown-ups. Ladies and aunts come in twos and threes and bring casseroles and only say hi to Lizzy. They want to see the baby. They all make goo-goo sounds and say, "What a little darling!" At night, some men come, too. They look at the baby, but just for a minute, and do not coo. They go out onto the porch and have beers and smoke.

The rest of the summer, all any grown-up wants to do is hold the baby or feed the baby or change the baby. Lizzy doesn't know why; it is *very* stinky. She tries to be more interesting, but no one notices. The baby cannot do a somersault, or say the Pledge of Allegiance or sing "Fairy Jocka Dormy Voo." All she can do is lie there and spit up and cry.

And sleep. The baby sleeps all the time, and every morning and every afternoon, Mommy naps with her. The princess is sleeping, so the whole house has to stay quiet. Lizzy cannot play her records, because it will wake the baby. She can't jump on her bed. She can't even build a tall tower with blocks because if it crashes, it will wake the baby. But when the baby screams, which is a lot, no one even says Shhh!

Lizzy thinks they should give the baby back.

"Will you read to me?" she asks her mother, when nothing else is happening.

"Oh….not now, Lizzy-Lou. I've got to sterilize some bottles for Rosie. How 'bout you be a big girl, and read by yourself for a while?"

Lizzy is tired of being a big girl. She goes to her room but does not slam the door, even though she wants to, because she is also tired of being yelled at. She picks up Maleficent. The puppet comes to life around her hand. Maleficent tells Lizzy that she is very smart, very clever, and Lizzy smiles. It is good to hear.

Lizzy puts on her own bathrobe, so they match. "Will you read to me?" she asks. "Up here in our castle?"

Maleficent nods, and says in a smooth voice, "Of course I will. That would be lovely," and reads to her all afternoon. Even though she can change into anything she wants—a dragon, a ball of green fire—her eyes are always kind, and every time Lizzy comes into the room, she is smiling.

On nights when Mommy is too tired, and Daddy puts Lizzy to bed, the witch sings the good-night song in a sweet, soft voice. She knows all the words. She whispers "Good night, Lizzy-Tizzy-Toot," the special, only-at-bedtime, good-dreams name.

Maleficent loves Lizzy best.

6.

Lizzy is glad when it is fall and time for nursery school, where they do not allow babies. Every morning Mrs. Breyer and Mrs. Huntington and Mrs. Lawton take turns driving to Wooton Methodist Church. When her mother drives, Lizzy gets to sit in the front seat. Other days she has to share the back with Tripper or Timmy.

She has known Timmy her whole life. The Lawtons live two doors down. They have a new baby too, another boy. When they had cocktails to celebrate, Lizzy heard her father joke to Mr. Lawton: "Well, Bob, the future's settled. My two girls will marry your two boys, and we'll unite our kingdoms." Lizzy does not think that is funny.

Timmy is no one's handsome prince. He is a gangly, insubstantial boy who likes to wear sailor suits. His eyes always look as though he'd just finished crying because he is allergic to almost everything, and is prone to nosebleeds. He is not a good pick for Red Rover.

The church is a large stone building with a parking lot and a playground with a fence around it. Nursery school is in a wide, sunny room on the second floor. Lizzy climbs the steps as fast as she can, hangs up her coat on the hook under L-I-Z-Z-Y, and tries to be the first to sit down on the big rug in the middle of the room, near Mrs. Dickens. There are two teachers, but Mrs. Dickens is her favorite. She wears her brown hair in braids wrapped all the way around her head and smells like lemons.

Lizzy knows all the color words and how to count up to twenty. She can write her whole name—without making the Zs backward—so she is impatient when the other kids do not listen to her. Sometimes she has to yell at them so she can have the right color of paint. The second week of school, she has to knock Timmy down to get the red ball at recess.

Mrs. Dickens sends a note home, and in the morning, the next-door neighbor comes over to watch the baby so Lizzy's mother can drive her to school, even though it is not her turn.

"Good morning, Lizzy," Mrs. Dickens says at the door. "Will you get the music basket ready? I want to talk to your mother for a minute."

Lizzy nods. She likes to be in charge. But she also wants to know what they are saying, so she puts the tambourine and the maracas in the basket very quietly, and listens.

"How are things at home?" Mrs. Dickens asks.

"A little hectic, with the new baby. Why?"

"New baby. Of course." Mrs. Dickens looks over at Lizzy and puts a finger to her lips. "Let's continue this out in the hall," she says, and that's all Lizzy gets to hear.

But when they make Circle, Mrs. Dickens pats the right side of her chair, and says, "Come sit by me, Lizzy." They sing the good-morning song and have Share and march to a record and Lizzy gets to play the cymbals. When it is time for Recess, Mrs. Dickens rings the bell on her desk, and they all put on their coats and hold hands with their buddies and walk down the stairs like ladies and gentlemen. For the first time, Mrs. Dickens is Lizzy's buddy, and no one gets knocked down.

On a late October morning, Lizzy's mother dresses her in a new green wool coat, because it is cold outside. It might snow. She runs up the stairs, but the coat is stiff and has a lot of buttons, and by the time she hangs it up, Anna von Stade is sitting in *her* place in the circle. Lizzy has to sit on the other side of Mrs. Dickens and is not happy. Timmy sits down beside her, which does not help at all.

"Children! Children! Quiet now. Friday is a holiday. Who knows what it is?"

Lizzy's hand shoots straight up. Mrs. Dickens calls on Kevin.

"It's Halloween," he says.

"Very good. And we're going to have our *own* Halloween party."

"I'm going to be Pinocchio!" David says.

"We raise our hand before speaking, David." Mrs. Dickens waggles her finger at him, then waits for silence before she continues. "That will be a good costume for trick-or-treating. But for *our* party, I want each of you to come dressed as who you want to be when you grow up."

"I'm going to be a fireman!"

"I'm going to be a bus driver!"

"I'm going—"

Mrs. Dickens claps her hands twice. "Children! We do not talk out of turn, and we do not talk when others are talking."

The room slowly grows quiet.

"But it is good to see that you're all *so* enthusiastic. Let's go around the circle, and everyone can have a chance to share." She looks down to her right. "Anna, you can start."

"I'm going to be a ballerina," Anna says.

Lizzy does not know the answer, and she does not like that. Besides, she is going to be last, and all the right ones will be gone. She crosses her arms and scowls down at the hem of her plaid skirt.

"I'm going to be a doctor," Herbie says.

Fireman. Doctor. Policeman. Teacher. Mailman. Nurse. Baseball player. Mommy. Lizzy thinks about the lady jobs. Nurses wear silly hats and have to be clean all the time, and she is not good at that. Teacher is better, but two people have already said it. She wonders what else there is.

Tripper takes a long time. Finally he says, "I guess I'll be in sales."

"Like your father? That's nice." Mrs. Dickens nods. "Carol?"

Carol will be a mommy. Bobby will be a fireman.

Timmy takes the longest time of all. Everyone waits and fidgets. Finally he says he wants to drive a steam shovel like Mike Mulligan. "That's fine, Timmy," says Mrs. Dickens.

And then it is her turn.

"What are *you* going to be when you grow up, Lizzy?"

"Can I see the menu, please?" Lizzy says. That is what her father says at the Top Diner when he wants a list of answers.

Mrs. Dickens smiles. "There isn't one. You can be anything you want."

"Anything?"

"That's right. You heard Andrew. He wants to be president some day, and in the United States of America, he can be."

Lizzy doesn't want to be president. Eisenhower is bald and old. Besides, that is a daddy job, like doctor and fireman. What do ladies do besides mommy and nurse and teacher? She thinks very hard, scrunching up her mouth—and then she knows!

"I'm going to be a witch," she says.

She is very proud, because no one has said that yet, no one in the whole circle. She looks up at Mrs. Dickens, waiting to hear, "Very good. Very creative, Lizzy," like she usually does.

Mrs. Dickens does not say that. She shakes her head. "We are not using our imaginations today. We are talking about real-life jobs."

"I'm going to be a witch."

"There is no such thing." Mrs. Dickens is frowning at Lizzy now, her face as wrinkled as her braids.

"Yes there is!" Lizzy says, louder. "In 'Hansel and Gretel,' and 'Snow White' and 'Sleeping—"

"Elizabeth? You know better than that. Those are only stories."

"Then stupid Timmy can't drive a steam shovel because Mike Mulligan is only a story!" Lizzy shouts.

"That's *enough*!" Mrs. Dickens leans over and picks Lizzy up under the arms. She is carried over to the chair that faces the corner and plopped down. "You will sit here until you are ready to say you're sorry."

Lizzy stares at the wall. She is sorry she is sitting in the dunce chair, and she is sorry that her arms hurt where Mrs. Dickens grabbed her. But she says nothing.

Mrs. Dickens waits for a minute, then makes a *tsk* noise and goes back to the circle. For almost an hour, Lizzy hears nursery school happening behind her: blocks clatter, cupboards open, Mrs. Dickens gives directions, children giggle and whisper. This chair does not feel right at all, and Lizzy squirms. After a while she closes her eyes and talks to Maleficent without making any sound. Out of long repetition, her thumb and lips move in concert, and the witch responds.

Lizzy is asking when she will learn to cast a spell, how that is different from spelling ordinary W-O-R-D-S, when the Recess bell rings behind her. She makes a disappearing puff with her fingers and opens her eyes. In a moment, she feels Mrs. Dickens's hand on her shoulder.

"Have you thought about what you said?" Mrs. Dickens asks.

"Yes," says Lizzy, because it is true.

"Good. Now, tell Timmy you're sorry, and you may get your coat and go outside."

She turns in the chair and sees Timmy standing behind Mrs. Dickens. His hands are on his hips, and he is grinning like he has won a prize.

Lizzy does not like that. She is not sorry.

She is *mad*.

Mad at Mommy, mad at the baby, mad at all the unfair things. Mad at Timmy Lawton, who is right *here*.

Lizzy clenches her fists and feels a tingling, all over, like goosebumps, only deeper. She glares at Timmy, so hard that she can feel her forehead tighten, and the anger grows until it surges through her like a ball of green fire.

A thin trickle of blood oozes from Timmy Lawton's nose. Lizzy stares harder and watches blood pour across his pale lips and begin to drip onto his sailor shirt, red dots appearing and spreading across the white stripes.

"Help?" Timmy says.

Mrs. Dickens turns around. "Oh, dear. Not again." She sighs and calls to the other teacher. "Linda? Can you get Timmy a washcloth?"

Lizzy laughs out loud.

In an instant, Lizzy and the chair are off the ground. Mrs. Dickens has grabbed it by the rungs and carries it across the room and out the classroom door. Lizzy is too startled to do anything but hold on. Mrs. Dickens marches down the hall, her shoes like drumbeats.

She deposits Lizzy with a thump in the corner of an empty Sunday school room, shades drawn, dim and chilly with brown-flecked linoleum and no rug.

"You. Sit. There." Mrs. Dickens says in a voice Lizzy has not heard her use before.

The door shuts and footsteps echo away. Then she is alone and everything is very quiet. The room smells like chalk and furniture polish. She lets go of the chair and looks around. On one side is a blackboard, on the other a picture of Jesus with a hat made of thorns, like the ones Maleficent put around Sleeping Beauty's castle.

Lizzy nods. She kicks her feet against the rungs of the small chair, bouncing the rubber heels of her saddle shoes against the wood. She hears the other children clatter in from Recess. Her stomach gurgles. She will not get Snack.

But she is not sorry.

It is a long time before she hears cars pull into the parking lot, doors slamming and the sounds of many grown-up shoes on the wide stone stairs.

She tilts her head toward the door, listens.

"…Rosemary? Isn't she adorable!" That is Mrs. Dickens.

And then, a minute later, her mother, louder. "Oh, dear, *now* what?"

Another minute, and she hears the click-clack of her mother's shoes in the hall, coming closer.

Lizzy turns in the chair, forehead taut with concentration. The tingle begins, the green fire rises inside her. She smiles, staring at the doorway, and waits.

MACY MINNOT'S LAST CHRISTMAS ON DIONE, RING RACING, FIDDLER'S GREEN, THE POTTER'S GARDEN

PAUL MCAULEY

Paul McAuley [unlikelyworlds.blogspot.com.au] *worked as a research biologist in various universities, including Oxford and UCLA, and for six years was a lecturer in botany at St. Andrews University, before he became a full-time writer. Although best known as a science-fiction writer, he has also published crime novels and thrillers. His SF novels have won the Philip K. Dick Memorial Award, and the Arthur C. Clarke, John W. Campbell, and Sidewise awards. His most recent books are novels* The Quiet War, Gardens of the Sun, *and* In the Mouth of the Whale, *and collection* Little Machines. *Coming up is new novel* Evening's Empires *and retrospective collection* The Best of Paul McAuley. *He lives in North London.*

One day, midway in the course of her life, Mai Kumal learned that her father had died. The solicitous eidolon which delivered the message explained that Thierry had suffered an irreversible cardiac event, and extended an invitation to travel to Dione, one of Saturn's moons, so that Mai could help to scatter her father's ashes according to his last wishes.

Mai's daughter didn't think it was a good idea. "When did you last speak with him? Ten years ago?"

"Fourteen."

"Well then."

Mai said, "It was as much my fault as his that we lost contact with each other."

"But he left you in the first place. Left us."

Shahirah had a deeply moral sense of right and wrong. She hadn't spoken to or forgiven her own father after he and Mai had divorced.

Mai said, "Thierry left Earth; he didn't leave me. But that isn't the point, Shah. He wants—he wanted me to be there. He made arrangements. There is an open round-trip ticket."

"He wanted you to feel an obligation," Shahirah said.

"Of course I feel an obligation. It is the last thing I can do for him. And it will be a great adventure. It's about time I had one."

Mai was sixty-two, about the age her father had been when he'd left Earth after his wife, Mai's mother, had died. She was a mid-level civil servant, Assistant Chief Surveyor in the Department of Antiquities. She owned a small efficiency apartment in the same building where she worked, the government ziggurat in the Wassat district of al-Iskandariyya. No serious relationship since her divorce; her daughter grown-up and married, living with her husband and two children in an arcology commune in the Atlas Mountains. Shahirah tried to talk her out of it, but Mai wanted to find out what her father had been doing, in the outer dark. To find out whether he had been happy. By unriddling the mystery of his life she might discover something about herself. When your parents die, you finally take full possession of your life, and wonder how much of it has been shaped by conscious decision, and how much by inheritance in all its forms.

"There isn't anything out there for people like us," Shahirah said.

She meant ordinary people. People who had not been tweaked so that they could survive the effects of microgravity and harsh radiation, and endure life in claustrophobic habitats scattered across frozen, airless moons.

"Thierry thought there might be," Mai said. "I want to find out what it was."

She took compassionate leave, flew from al-Iskandariyya to Port Africa, Entebbe, and was placed in deep, artificial sleep at the passenger processing facility. Cradled inside a hibernaculum, she rode up the elevator to the transfer station and was loaded onto a drop ship, and forty-three days later woke in the port of Paris, Dione. After two days spent recovering from her long sleep and learning how to use a pressure suit and move around in Dione's vestigial gravity, she climbed aboard a taxi that flew in a swift suborbital lob through the night to the habitat of the Jones-Truex-Bakaleinikoff clan, her father's last home, the place where he died.

The taxi's cabin was an angular bubble scarcely bigger than a coffin, pieced together from diamond composite and a cobweb of fullerene struts, and mounted on a motor stage with three spidery legs. Mai, braced beside the pilot in a taut crash web, felt that she was falling down an endless slope, as in one of those dreams where you wake with a shock just before you hit ground. Saturn's swollen globe, subtly banded with pastel shades of yellow and brown, swung overhead and sank behind them. The pilot, a garrulous young woman, asked all kinds of questions about life on Earth, pointed out landmark craters and ridges in the dark moonscape, the line of the equatorial railway, the homely sparks of oases, habitats, and tent towns. Mai couldn't quite reconcile the territory with the maps in her p-suit's library, was startled when the taxi abruptly slewed around and fired its motor and decelerated with a rattling roar and drifted down to a kind of pad or platform set at the edge of an industrial landscape.

The person who met her wasn't the man with whom she'd discussed her father's death and her travel arrangements, but a woman, her father's former partner, Lexi Truex. They climbed into a slab-sided vehicle slung between three pairs of fat mesh wheels, and drove out along a broad highway past blockhouses, bunkers, hangars, storage tanks, and arrays of satellite dishes and transmission towers: a military complex dating from the Quiet War, according to Lexi Truex.

"Abandoned in place, as they say. We don't have any use for it, but never got around to demolishing it, either. So here it sits."

Lexi Truex was at least twenty years younger than Mai, tall and pale, hair shaven high either side of a stiff crest of straw-colored hair. Her pressure suit was decorated with an intricate, interlocking puzzle of green and red vines. She and Thierry had been together for three years, she said. They'd met on Ceres, while she had been working as a freetrader.

"That's where he was living when I last talked to him," Mai said. It felt like a confession of weakness. This brisk, confident woman seemed to have more of a claim on her father than she did.

"He followed me to Dione, moved in with me while I was still living in the old habitat," Lexi Truex said. "That's where he got into ceramics. And then, well, he became more and more obsessed with his work, and I wasn't there a lot of the time…"

Mai said that she'd done a little research, had discovered that her father had become a potter, and had seen some of his pieces.

"You can see plenty more, at the habitat," Lexi said. "He worked hard at it, and he had a good reputation. Plenty of kudos."

It turned out that Lexi Truex didn't know that on Earth, in al-Iskandari-yya, Thierry had cast bronze amulets using the lost wax method and sold them to shops that catered for the high-end tourist market. Falcons, cats, lions. Gods with the heads of crocodiles or jackals. Sphinxes. Mai told Lexi that she'd helped him polish the amulets with slurried chalk paste and jewelers' rouge, and create patinas with cupric nitrate. She had a clear memory of her father hunched over a bench, using a tiny knife to free the shape of a hawk from a small block of black wax.

"He didn't ever talk about his life before he went up and out," Lexi said. "Well, he mentioned you. We all knew he had a daughter, but that was about it."

They discussed Thierry's last wishes. Lexi said that in the last few years he'd given up his work, had taken to walking the land. She supposed that he wanted them to scatter his ashes in a favorite spot. He'd been very specific that it should take place at sunrise, but the location was a mystery.

"All I know is that we follow the railway east, and then we follow his mule," Lexi said. "Might involve some cross-country hiking. Think you can manage it?"

"Walking is easier than I thought it would be," Mai said.

When she was young, she'd liked to wade out into the sea as deep as she dared and stand on tip-toe, water up to her chin, and let the waves push her backwards and forward. Walking in Dione's vestigial gravity, one-sixtieth the gravity of Earth, was a little like that. Another memory of her father: watching him make huge sand sculptures of flowers and animals on the beach. His strong fingers, his bare brown shoulders, the thatch of white hair on his chest, his total absorption in his task.

They had left the military clutter behind, were driving across a dusty plain lightly spattered with small shallow craters. Blocks and boulders as big as houses squatting on smashed footings. A fan of debris stretching from a long elliptical dent. A line of rounded hills rising to the south: the flanks of the wall of a crater thirty kilometers in diameter, according to Lexi. Everything faintly lit by Saturnshine; everything the color of ancient ivory. It reminded Mai of old photographs, Europeans in antique costumes stiffly posed amongst excavated tombs, she'd seen in the museum in al-Qahira.

Soon, short steep ridges pushed up from the plain, nested curves thirty or forty meters high like frozen dunes, faceted here and there by cliffs rearing above fans of slumped debris. The cliffs, Mai saw, were carved with intricate frescoes, and the crests of the ridges had been sculpted into fairytale castles or statues of animals. A pod of dolphins emerging from a swell of ice; another swell shaped like a breaking wave with galloping horses rearing from frozen spume; an eagle taking flight; a line of elephants walking trunk to tail, skylighted against the black vacuum. The last reminding her of one of her father's bronze pieces. Here was a bluff shaped into the head of a Buddha; here was an outcrop on which a small army equipped with swords and shields were frozen in battle.

It was an old tradition, Lexi Truex said. Every Christmas, gangs from her clan's habitat and neighboring settlements congregated in a temporary city of tents and domes and ate osechi-ryo-ri and made traditional toasts in sake, vodka, and whisky, played music, danced, and flirted, and worked on new frescoes and statues using drills and explosives and chisels.

"We like our holidays. Kwanzaa, Eid ul-Fitr, Chanukah, Diwali, Christmas, Newtonmass… Any excuse for a gathering, a party. Your father led our gang every Christmas for ten years. The whale and the squid, along the ridge there? That's one of his designs."

"And the elephants?"

"Those too. Let me show you something," Lexi said, and drove the rolligon down the shallow slope of the embankment onto the actual surface of Dione.

It wallowed along like a boat in a choppy sea, its six fat tires raising rooster-tails of dust. Tracks ribboned everywhere, printed a year or a century ago. There was no wind here. No rain. Just a constant faint infalling of meteoritic dust, and microscopic ice particles from the geysers of Enceladus. Everything unchanging under the weak glare of the sun and the black sky, like a stage in an abandoned theatre. Mai began to understand the strangeness of this little world. A frozen ocean wrapped around a rocky core, shaped by catastrophes that predated life on Earth. A stark geology empty of any human meaning. Hence the sculptures, she supposed. An attempt to humanize the inhuman.

"It's something one of my ancestors made," Lexi said, when Mai asked where they were going. "Macy Minnot. You ever heard of Macy Minnot?"

She had been from Earth. Sent out by Greater Brazil to work on a construction project in Rainbow Bridge, Callisto, she'd become embroiled in a political scandal and had been forced to claim refugee status. This was before the Quiet War, or during the beginning of it (it had been the kind of slow, creeping conflict that has no clear beginning, erupting into combat only at its very end), and Macy Minnot had ended up living with the Jones-Truex-Bakaleinikoff clan. Trying her best to assimilate, to come to terms with her exile.

As they drove around the end of a ridge, past a tumble of ice boulders carved into human figures, some caught up in a whirling dance, others eagerly pushing their way out of granitic ice, Lexi explained that one Christmas after the end of the Quiet War, her last Christmas on Dione, Macy Minnot had come up with an idea for her own sculpture, and borrowed one of the big construction machines and filled its hopper with a mix of ice dust and a thixotropic, low-temperature plastic.

"It's too cold for ice crystals to melt under pressure and bind together," Lexi said. "The plastic was a binding agent, malleable at first, gradually hardening off. So you could pack the dust into any shape. You understand?"

"I've seen snow, once."

It had been in the European Union, the Alps: a conference on security of shipping ports. Mai, freshly divorced, had taken her daughter, then a toddler. She remembered Shahirah's delight in the snow. The whole world transformed into a soft white playground.

"There's always a big party, the night before the beginning of the competition. Macy and her partner got wasted, and they started up their construction machine. Either they intended to surprise everyone, or they decided they couldn't wait. Anyway, they forgot to include any stop or override command in the instruction set they'd written. So the machine just kept going," Lexi said, and steered the rolligon through a slant of deep shadow and swung it broadside, drifting to a stop at the edge of a short steep drop.

They were at the far side of the little flock of ridges. The rumpled dented plain stretched away under the black sky, and little figures marched across it in a straight line.

Mai laughed. The shock of it. The madly wonderful absurdity.

"They used fullerene to make the arms and eyes and teeth," Lexi said. "The scarves are fullerene mesh. The noses are carrots. The buttons are diamond chips."

There were twenty, thirty, forty of them. Each two meters tall, composed of three spheres of descending size stacked one on top of the other. Pure white. Spaced at equal intervals. Black smiles and black stares, vivid orange noses. Scarves rippling in an impalpable breeze. Marching away like an exercise in perspective, dwindling over the horizon...

"Thierry loved this place," Lexi said. "He often came out here to meditate."

They sat and looked out at the line of snowmen for a long time. At last, Lexi started the rolligon and they drove around the end of the ridges and rejoined the road and drove on to the habitat of the Jones-Truex-Bakaleinikoff clan.

It was a simple dome that squatted inside the rimwall of a circular crater. A forest ran around its inner circumference; lawns and formal flowerbeds circled a central building patchworked from a dozen architectural styles, blended into each other like a coral reef. Mai's reception reminded her of the first time she'd arrived at her daughter's arcology: adults introducing themselves one by one, excited children bouncing around, bombarding her with questions. Was the sky really blue, on Earth? What held it up? Were there really wild animals that ate people?

There was a big, informal meal, a kind of picnic in a wide grassy glade in the forest, where most of the clan seemed to live. Walkways and ziplines and nets were strung between sweet chestnuts and oaks and beech trees; ring platforms were bolted around the trunks of the largest trees; pods hung from branches like the nests of weaver birds.

Mai's hosts told her that most of the clan lived elsewhere, these days. Paris. A big vacuum-organism farm on Rhea. Mars. Titan. A group out at Neptune, living in a place Macy Minnot and her partner helped build after they fled the Saturn system at the beginning of the Quiet War. The habitat was becoming more and more like a museum, people said. A repository of souvenirs from the clan's storied past.

Thierry's workshop was already part of that history. Two brick kilns, a paved square under a slant of canvas to keep off the rain occasionally produced by the dome's climate control machinery. A potter's wheel with a saddle-shaped stool. A scarred table. Tools and brushes lying where he'd left them. Neatly labeled tubs of clay slip, clay balls, glazes. A clay-stained sink under a standpipe. Lexi told Mai that Thierry had mined the clay from an old impact site. Primordial stuff billions of years old, refined to remove tars and other organic material.

Finished pieces were displayed on a rack of shelves. Dishes in crescent shapes glazed with black and white arcs representing segments of Saturn's rings. Bowls shaped like craters. Squarish plates stamped with the surface features of tracts of Dione and other moons. Craters, ridges, cliffs. Plates with spattered black shapes on a white ground, like the borderland between Iapetus's dark and light halves. Vases shaped like shepherd moons. A scattering of irregular chunks in thick white glaze—pieces of the rings.

A glazed tan ribbon with snowmen lined along it…

It was so very different from the tourist stuff Thierry had made, yet recognizably his. And highly collectible, according to Lexi. Unlike most artists in the outer system, Thierry hadn't trawled for sponsorship and subscriptions, made pieces to order, or given access to every stage of his work. He had not believed in the democratization of the creative process. He had not been open to input. His work had been very private, very personal. He hadn't liked to talk about it, Lexi said. He hadn't let anyone get close to that part of him. This secrecy had eventually driven them apart, but it had also contributed to his reputation. People were intrigued by his work, by his response to the moonscapes of the Saturn system, his outsider's perspective, because he refused to explain it. He'd earned large amounts of credit and kudos—tradable reputation—from sale of his ceramics, but had spent hardly any of it. The work was enough, as far as he'd been concerned. Mai, remembering the sand sculptures, thought she understood a little of this. She asked if he'd been happy, but no one seemed able to answer the question.

"He seemed to be happy, when he was working," the habitat's patriarch, Rory Jones, said.

"He didn't talk much," someone else said.

"He liked to be alone," Lexi said. "I don't mean he was selfish. Well, maybe he was. But he mostly lived inside his head."

"He made this place his home," Rory Jones said, "and we were happy to have him living here."

The habitat's chandelier lights had dimmed to a twilight glow. Most of the children had wandered off to bed; so had many of the adults. Those left sat around a campfire on a hearth of meteoritic stone, passing around a flask of honeysuckle wine, telling Mai stories about her father's life on Dione.

He had walked around Dione, one year. A journey of some seven thousand kilometers. Carrying a bare minimum of consumables, walking from shelter to shelter, settlement to settlement. Staying in a settlement for a day or ten days or twenty before moving on. Walking the world was much more than exploring or understanding it, Mai's hosts told her. It was a way of re-creating it. Of making it real. Of binding yourself to it. Not every outer walked around their world, but those who did were considered virtuous, and her father was one such.

"Most visitors only see the parts they know about," a woman told Mai. "The famous views, the famous shrines and oases. A fair few come to climb the ice cliffs of Padua Chasmata. And they are spectacular climbs. Four or five kilometers. Huge views when you top out. But we prefer our own routes, on ridges or rimwalls you'd hardly notice, flying over them. There's a very gnarly climb close by, in a small crater the military used as a trash dump in the Quiet War. The achievement isn't the view, but testing yourself against your limits. Your father understood that. He was no ring runner."

This led into another story. It seemed that there was a traditional race around the equator of another of Saturn's moons, Mimas. It was held every four years: taking part in it was a great honor. Shortly after the end of the Quiet War, a famous athlete, Sony Shoemaker, had come to Mimas, determined to win it. She had trained on Earth's Moon for a year, had bought a custom-made p-suit from one of the best suit tailors in Camelot. Like all the other competitors, she had qualified by completing a course around the peak in the centre of the rimwall of Arthur crater within a hundred and twenty hours. Fifty days later she set out, ranked last in a field of thirty-eight.

Mimas was a small moon, about a third the size of Dione. A straight route around its equator would be roughly two and a half thousand kilometers long, but there was no straight route. Unlike Dione, Mimas had never been resurfaced by ancient floods of water-ice lava. Its surface was primordial, pockmarked, riven. Craters overlapping craters. Craters inside craters. Craters strung along rimwalls of larger craters. And the equatorial route crossed Herschel, the largest crater of all, a hundred and thirty kilometers across, a third of the diameter of Mimas, its steep rimwalls kilometers tall, its floor shattered by blocky, chaotic terrain.

The race was as much a test of skill in reading and understanding the landscape as of endurance. Competitors were allowed to choose their own route and set out caches of supplies, but could only use public shelters, and were disqualified if they called for help. Some died rather than fail. Sony Shoemaker did not fail, and astonished aficionados by coming fourth. She stayed on Mimas, afterwards. She trained. Four years later she won, beating the reigning champion, Diamond Jack Dupree.

He did not take his defeat lightly. He challenged Sony Shoemaker to another race. A unique race, never before attempted. A race around a segment of Saturn's rings.

Although the main rings are seventy-three thousand kilometers across, a fifth of the distance between Earth and the Moon, they average just ten meters in thickness, but oscillations propagating across the dense lanes of the B ring pile up material at its outer edge, creating peaks a kilometer high. Diamond Jack Dupree challenged Sony Shoemaker to race across one of these evanescent mountains.

The race did not involve anything remotely resembling running, but it was muscle powered, using highly modified p-suits equipped with broad wings of alife material with contractile pseudo-musculatures and enough area to push, faintly, lightly, against ice pebbles embedded in a fragile lace of ice gravel and ice dust. Cloud swimming. A delicate rippling controlled by fingers and toes that would slowly build up momentum. The outcome determined not by speed or strength, because if you went too fast you'd either sheer away from the ephemeral surface or plough under it, but by skill and judgment and patience.

Sony Shoemaker did not have to accept Diamond Jack Dupree's challenge. She had already proved herself. But the novelty of it, the audacity, intrigued her. And so, a year to the day after her victory on Mimas, after six months hard training in water tanks and on the surface of the dusty egg of Methone, one of Saturn's smallest moons, Sony Shoemaker and Diamond Jack Dupree set off in their manta-ray p-suits, swimming across the peaks and troughs of a mountainous, icy cloud at the edge of the B ring.

It was the midsummer equinox. The orbits of Saturn and its rings and moons were aligned with the sun; the mountains cast ragged shadows across the surface of the B ring; the two competitors were tiny dark arrowheads rippling across a luminous slope. Moving very slowly, almost imperceptibly, to begin with. Gradually gaining momentum, skimming along at ten and then twenty kilometers an hour.

There was no clear surface. The ice-particle mountains emitted jets and curls of dust and vapor. There were currents and convection cells. It was like trying to swim across the flank of a sandstorm.

Sony Shoemaker was the first to sink. Some hundred and thirty kilometers out, she moved too fast, lost contact with a downslope, and plunged through ice at the bottom and was caught in a current that subducted her deep into the interior. She was forced to use the jets of her p-suit to escape, and was retrieved by her support ship. Diamond Jack Dupree wallowed on for a short distance, and then he too sank. And never reappeared.

His p-suit beacon cut off when he submerged, and although the support ships swept the mountain with radar and microwaves for several days, no trace of him was ever found. He had vanished, but there were rumors that he was not dead. That he had dived into a camouflaged lifepod he'd planted on the route, slept out the rescue attempts, and gone on the drift or joined a group of homesteaders, satisfied that he had regained his honor.

There had been other races held on the ring mountains, but no one had ever beaten Diamond Jack Dupree's record of one hundred and forty-three kilometers. No one wanted to. Not even Sony Shoemaker.

"That's when she crossed the line," Rory Jones told Mai. "Winning the race around Mimas didn't make her one of us. But respecting Diamond Jack Dupree's move, that was it. Your father crossed that line, too. He knew."

"Because he walked around the world," Mai said. She was trying to understand. It was important to them, and it seemed important to them that she understood.

"Because he knew what it meant," Rory said.

"One of us," someone said, and all the outers laughed.

Tall skinny pale ghosts jackknifed on stools or sitting cross-legged on cushions. All elbows and knees. Their faces angular masks in the firelight flicker. Mai felt a moment of irreality. As if she was an intruder on someone else's dream. She was still very far from accepting this strange world, these strange people. She was a tourist in their lives, in the place her father had made his home.

She said, "What does it mean, go on the drift? Is it like your wanderjahrs?"

She'd discovered that custom when she'd done some background research. After reaching majority, young outers often set out on extended and mostly unplanned tours of the moons of Saturn and Jupiter. Working odd jobs, experiencing all kinds of cultures and meeting all kinds of people before at last returning home and settling down.

"Not exactly," Lexi said. "You can come home from a wanderjahr. But when you go on the drift, that's where you live."

"In your skin, with whatever you can carry and no more," Rory said.

"In your p-suit," someone said.

"That's what I said," Rory said.

"And homesteaders?" Mai said.

Lexi said, "That's when you move up and out to somewhere no one else lives, and make a life there. The solar system out to Saturn is industrialized, more or less. More and more people want to move away from all that, get back to what we once were."

"Out to Uranus," someone said.

"Neptune," someone else said.

"There are homesteaders all over the Centaurs now," Rory said. "You know the Centaurs, Mai? Primordial planetoids that orbit between Saturn and Neptune. The source of many short-term comets."

"Macy Minnot and her friends settled one, during the Quiet War," Lexi said. "It was only a temporary home, for them, but for many it's become permanent."

"Even the scattered disc is getting crowded now, according to some people," Rory said.

"Planetoids like the Centaurs," Lexi told Mai, "with long, slow orbits that take them inward as far as Neptune, and out past Pluto, past the far edge of the Kuiper belt."

"The first one, Fiddler's Green, was settled by mistake," Rory said.

"It's a legend," a young woman said.

"I once met someone who knew someone who saw it, once," Rory said. "Passed within a couple of million kilometers and spotted a chlorophyll signature, but didn't stop because they were on their way to somewhere else."

"The very definition of a legend," the woman said.

"It was a shipwreck," Rory told Mai. "Castaways on a desert island. I'm sure it still happens on the high seas of Earth."

"There are still shipwrecks," Mai said. "Although everything is connected to everything else, so anyone who survives is likely to be found quickly."

"The outer dark beyond Neptune is still largely uninhabited," Rory said. "We haven't yet finished cataloguing everything in the Kuiper belt and the scattered disc, and everything is most definitely not connected to everything else, out there. How the story goes, when the Quiet War heated up, a ship from the Jupiter system was hit by a drone as it approached Saturn. Its motors were badly damaged and it ploughed through the Saturn system and kept going. It couldn't decelerate, couldn't reach anywhere useful. Its crew and passengers went into hibernation. Sixty or seventy years later, those still alive woke up. They were approaching a planetoid somewhat beyond the orbit of Pluto, had just enough reaction mass to match orbits with it.

"The ship was carrying construction machinery. The survivors used the raw tars and clays of the planetoid to build a habitat. A small bubble of air and light and heat, spun up to give a little gravity, farms and gardens on the inside, vacuum organisms growing on the outside, like the floating worldlets in the asteroid belt. They called it Fiddler's Green, after an old legend from Earth about a verdant and uncharted island sometimes encountered by becalmed sailors. Perhaps you know it, Mai."

"I'm afraid I don't."

"They built a garden," the young woman said, "but they didn't ever try to call for help. How likely is that?"

Rory said, "Perhaps they didn't call for help because they believed the Three Powers were still controlling the systems of Saturn and Jupiter. Or perhaps they were happy, living where they did. They didn't need help.

They didn't want to go home because Fiddler's Green was their home. The planetoid supplied all the raw material they required. The ship's fusion generator gave them power, heat and light. They are still out there, travelling beyond the Kuiper belt. Living in houses woven from branches and leaves. Farming. Falling in love, raising families, dying. A world entire."

"A romance of regression," the young woman said.

"Perhaps it is no more than a fairytale," Rory said. "But nothing in it is impossible. There are hundreds of places like Fiddler's Green. Thousands. It's just an outlier, an extreme example of how far people are prepared to go to make their own world, their own way of living."

The outers talked about that. Mai told about her life in al-Iskandariyya, her childhood, her father's work, her work in the Department of Antiquities, the project she'd recently seen to completion, the excavation of a twenty-first-century shopping mall that had been buried in a sandstorm during the Overturn. At last there was a general agreement that they should sleep. The outers retired to hammocks or cocoons; Mai made her bed on the ground, under the spreading branches of a grandfather oak, uneasy and troubled, aware as she had not been, in her cubicle in the port hostel, of the freezing vacuum beyond the dome's high transparent roof. It was night inside the dome, and night outside, too. Stars shining hard and cold beyond the black shadows of the trees.

Everything that seemed natural here—the ring forest, the lawns, the dense patches of vegetables and herbs—was artificial. Fragile. Vulnerable. Mai tried and failed to imagine living in a little bubble so far from the sun that it was no more than the brightest star in the sky. She fretted about the task that lay ahead, the trek to the secret place where she and Lexi Truex would scatter Thierry's ashes.

At last sleep claimed her, and she dreamed of hanging over the Nile and its patchwork borders of cotton fields, rice fields, orchards and villages, everything falling away, dwindling into tawny desert as she fell into the endless well of the sky…

It was a silly anxiety dream, but it stayed with Mai as she and Lexi Truex drove north to a station on the railway that girdled Dione's equator, and boarded the diamond bullet of a railcar and sped out across the battered plain. They were accompanied by Thierry's mule, Archie. A sturdy robot porter that, with its flat loadbed, small front-mounted sensor turret, and three pairs of articulated legs, somewhat resembled a giant cockroach. Archie carried spare airpacks and a spray pistol device, and refused to tell Mai and Lexi their final destination, or why it was important that they reach it before sunrise. Everything would become clear when they arrived, it said.

According to Lexi, the pistol used pressurized water vapor from flash-heated ice to spray material from pouches plugged into its ports, such as the pouch of gritty powder, the residue left from resomation of Thierry's body, or the particles of thixotropic plastic in a pouch already plugged into the pistol. The same kind of plastic Macy Minnot and her partner had used to shape ice dust into snowmen.

"We're going to spray-paint something with the old man's ashes," Lexi said. "That much is clear. The question is, what's the target?"

Archie refused to answer her in several polite ways.

The railcar drove eastward through the night. Like almost all of Saturn's moons, like Earth's Moon, Dione's orbital period, some sixty-six hours, was exactly equal to the time it took to complete a single rotation on its axis, so that one side permanently faced Saturn. Its night was longer than an entire day, on Earth.

Saturn's huge bright crescent sank westward as the train crossed a plain churned and stamped with craters. Every so often, Mai spotted the fugitive gleam of the dome or angular tent of a settlement. A geometric fragment of chlorophyll green gleaming in the moonscape's frozen battlefield. A scatter of bright lights in a small crater. Patchworked fields of black vacuum organisms spread across tablelands and slopes, plantations of what looked like giant sunflowers standing up along ridges, all of them facing east, waiting for the sun.

The elevated railway shot out across a long and slender bridge that crossed the trough of Eurotas Chasmata, passing over broad slumps of ice that descended into a river of fathomless shadow. The far side was fretted with lesser canyons and low bright cliffs rising stepwise with broad benches between. The railway turned north to follow a long pass that cut between high cliffs, bent eastwards again. At last, a long ridge rolled up from the horizon: the southern flanks of the rimwall of Amata crater.

The railcar slowed, passed through a short tunnel cut through a ridge, ran through pitch-black shadow beyond and out into Saturnshine, and sidled into a station cantilevered above a slope. Below, a checkerboard of scablike vacuum organisms stretched towards the horizon. Above, the dusty slope, spattered with small, sharp craters, rose to a gently scalloped edge, stark against the black sky.

Several rolligons were parked in the garage under the station. Following Archie's instructions, Lexi and Mai climbed into one of the vehicles

(Archie sprang onto the flat roof) and drove along a track that slanted towards the top of the slope. After five kilometers, the track topped out on a broad bench, swung around a shelter, a stubby cylinder jutting under a heap of fresh white ice blocks, a way point for hikers and climbers on their way into the interior of the huge crater, and followed the curve of the bench eastward until it was interrupted by a string of small craters twenty or thirty meters across.

Lexi and Mai climbed out and Lexi rechecked Mai's p-suit and they followed Archie around the smashed bowls of the craters. There were many bootprints trampled into the dust. Thierry's prints, coming and going. Mai tried not to step on them. Strange to think they might last for millions of years.

"It is not far," Archie said, responding to Lexi's impatient questions. "It is not far."

Mai felt a growing glee as she loped along, felt that she could bounce away like the children in the habitat, leap over ridges, cross craters in a single bound, span this little world in giant footsteps. She'd felt like this when her first grandchild had been born. Floating on a floodtide of happiness and relief. Free of responsibility. Liberated from the biological imperative.

Now and then her pressure suit beeped a warning; once, when she exceeded some inbuilt safety parameter, it took over and slowed her headlong bounding gait and brought her to a halt, swaying at the dust-softened rim of a small crater. Reminding her that she was dependent on the insulation and integrity of her own personal space ship, its native intelligence, the whisper of oxygen in her helmet.

On the far side of the crater, cased in her extravagantly decorated p-suit, Lexi turned with a bouncing step, asked Mai if she was okay.

"I'm fine!"

"You're doing really well," Lexi said, and asked Archie for the fifth or tenth time if they were nearly there.

"It is not far."

Lexi waited as Mai skirted the rim of the crater with the bobbing shuffle she'd been taught, and they went on. Mai was hyperaware of every little detail in the moonscape. Everything fresh and strange and new. The faint flare of Saturnshine on her helmet visor. The rolling blanket of gritty dust, dimpled with tiny impacts. Rayed scatterings of sharp bright fragments. A blocky ice-boulder as big as a house perched in a shatter of debris. The gentle rise and fall of the ridge, stretching away under the black sky where untwinkling stars showed everywhere. Saturn's crescent looming above the western horizon. The silence and stillness of the land. The stark reality of it.

She imagined her father walking here, under this same sky. Alone in a moonscape where no trace of human activity could be seen.

The last and largest crater was enclosed by ramparts of ice blocks three stories high and cemented with a silting of dust. Archie didn't hesitate, climbing a crude stairway hacked into the ice and plunging through a ragged cleft. Lexi and Mai followed, and the crater's bowl opened below them, tilted towards the plain beyond the curve of the ridge. The spark of the sun stood just above the horizon. An arc of light defined the far edge of the moonscape; sunlight lit a segment of the crater's floor, where boulders lay tumbled amongst a maze of bootprints and drag marks.

"At least we got the timing right," Lexi said.

"What are we supposed to be seeing?" Mai said.

Lexi asked Archie the same question.

"It will soon become apparent."

They stood side by side, Lexi and Mai, wavering in the faint grip of gravity. The sunlit half of the crater directly in front of them, the dark half beyond, shadows shrinking back as the sun slowly crept into the sky. And then they saw the first shapes emerging.

Columns or tall vases. Cylindrical, woman-sized or larger. Different heights in no apparent order. Each one shaped from translucent ice tinted with pastel shades of pink and purple, and threaded with networks of darker veins.

Lexi stepped down the broken blocks of the inner slope and moved across the floor. Mai followed.

The nearest vases were twice their height. Lexi reached out to one of them, brushed the fingertips of her gloved hand across the surface.

"These have been hand-carved," she said. "You can see the tool marks."

"Carved from what?"

"Boulders, I guess. He must have carried the ice chips out of here."

They were both speaking softly, reluctant to disturb the quiet of this place. Lexi said that the spectral signature of the ice corresponded with artificial photosynthetic pigments. She leaned close, her visor almost kissing the bulge of the vase, reported that it was doped with microscopic vacuum organisms.

"There are structures in here, too," she said. "Long fine wires. Flecks of circuitry."

"Listen," Mai said.

"What?"

"Can't you hear it?"

It was a kind of interference on the common band Mai and Lexi were using to talk. Faint and broken. Hesitant. Scraps of pure tones rising and fading, rising again.

"I hear it," Lexi said.

The sound grew in strength as more and more vases emerged into sunlight. Long notes blending into a polyphonic harmony.

The microscopic vacuum organisms were soaking up sunlight, Lexi said, after a while. Turning light into electricity, powering something that responded to changes in the structure of the ice. Strain gauges perhaps, coupled to transmitters.

"The sunlight warms the ice, ever so slightly," she said. "It expands asymmetrically, the embedded circuitry responds to the microscopic stresses…"

"It's beautiful, isn't it?"

"Yes…"

It was beautiful. A wild, aleatory chorus rising and falling in endless circles above the ground of a steady bass pulse…

They stood there a long time, while the vases sang. There were a hundred of them, more than a hundred. A field or garden of vases. Clustered like organ pipes. Standing alone on shaped pedestals. Gleaming in the sunlight. Stained with cloudy blushes of pink and purple. Singing, singing.

At last, Lexi took Mai's gloved hand and led her across the crater floor to where the robot mule, Archie, was waiting. Mai took out the pouch of human dust and they plugged it into the spray pistol's spare port. Lexi switched on the pistol's heaters, showed Mai how to use the simple trigger mechanism.

"Which one shall we spray?" Mai said.

Lexi smiled behind the fishbowl visor of her helmet.

"Why not all of them?"

They took turns. Standing well back from the vases, triggering brief bursts of gritty ice that shot out in broad fans and lightly spattered the vases in random patterns. Lexi laughed.

"The old bastard," she said. "It must have taken him hundreds of days to make this. His last and best secret."

"And we're his collaborators," Mai said.

It took a while to empty the pouch. Long before they had finished, the music of the vases had begun to change, responding to the subtle shadow patterns laid on their surfaces.

At last the two woman had finished their work and stood still, silent, elated, listening to the music they'd made.

That night, back under the dome of the Jones-Truex-Bakaleinikoff habitat, Mai thought of her father working in that unnamed crater high on the rimwall of Amata crater. Chipping at adamantine ice with chisels and hammers. Listening to the song of his vases, adding a new voice, listening again. Alone under the empty black sky, happily absorbed in the creation of a sound garden from ice and sunlight.

And she thought of the story of Fiddler's Green, the bubble of light and warmth and air created from materials mined from the chunk of tarry ice it orbited. Of the people living there. The days of exile becoming a way of life as their little world swung further and further away from the sun's hearthfire. Green days of daily tasks and small pleasures. Farming, cooking, weaving new homes in the hanging forest on the inside of the bubble's skin. A potter shaping dishes and bowls from primordial clay. Children chasing each other, flitting like schools of fish between floating islands of trees. The music of their laughter. The unrecorded happiness of ordinary life, out there in the outer dark.

WHAT DID TESSIMOND TELL YOU?

ADAM ROBERTS

Adam Roberts [www.adamroberts.com] *lives in England, a little to the west of London, with his wife and children. He has published fourteen novels, the most recent being* Jack Glass *and* Twenty Trillion Leagues Under the Sea. *Coming up is a major new short story collection,* Adam Robots: Short Stories.

1

The Nobel was in the bag (not that I would ever want to hide it away *in a bag*—), and in fact we were only a fortnight from our public announcement, when Niu Jian told me he was quitting. I assumed it was a joke. Niu Jian had never been much of a practical joker, but that's what I assumed. Of course, he wasn't kidding in the slightest. The sunlight picked out the grain of his tweed jacket. He was sitting in my office with his crescent back to the window, and I kept getting distracted by the light coming through the glass. Morningtime, morningtime, and all the possibilities of the day ahead of us. The chimney of the boilerhouse as white and straight as an unsmoked cigarette. The campus Willow was dangling its green tentacles in the river, as if taking a drink. The students wandered the paths and dawdled on the grass with their arms around one another's waists. Further down the hill, beyond the campus-boundary, I could see the cars doing their crazy corpuscle impressions along the interchange and away along the dual carriageway. "You want to quit—now?" I pressed. "*Now* is the time you want to quit?"

He nodded, slowly, and picked at the skin of his knuckles.

"Two *weeks*, we present. You *know* the Nobel is—look, hey!" I said, the idea occurring suddenly to me like the spurt of a match lighting. "Is it that you think *you* won't be sharing? You will! You, me, Prévert and Sleight, we will all be cited. Is that what you think?" It wouldn't have been very characteristic of Niu Jian to storm out like a prima donna, I have to say: a more stolidly dependable individual never walked the face of this, our rainy stony earth. But, you see, I was struggling to understand why he was quitting.

"It is not that," he said,

"Then—?" I made a grunting noise. Then I coughed. P-O-R didn't like that; the unruly diaphragm. There was a scurry of motion inside, as she readjusted herself.

He looked at me, and then, briefly, he glanced at my belly—I had pushed my chair away from the desk, so my whole torso was on display, Phylogeny-Ontology-Recapitulator in all her bulging glory. Then he looked back at my face. For the strangest moment my heart knocked rat-tat at my ribs, like it wanted out, and I felt the adrenal flush along my neck and in my cheeks. But that passed. My belly had nothing to do with *that*.

Niu Jian said: "I have never been to Mecca."

"The Bingo?" I said. I wasn't trying to be facetious. I was genuinely wrongfooted by this.

"No," he said.

"You mean, in—" I coughed, "like, Arabia?"

"There, yes."

"What's that got to do with anything?"

"I want," said Niu Jian, "to go."

"OK," I said. "Why not? It's like the Taj Mahal, right? I'm sure it's a sight to see. So go. Wait until the press conference, and then take the next available flying transport from Heathrow's internationally renowned port-of-air." But he was shaking his head, so I said: "Jesus, go *now* if you like. If you must. Miss the announcement. *That* doesn't matter—or it only matters a little bit. But if it's like, urgent, then go now. But you don't have to quit! Why do you have to quit? You don't have to quit."

His nod, though wordless, was very clearly: *I do*.

"OK, Noo-noo, you're really going to have to lay this out for me, step by baby-step," I said. "Blame my baby-beshrunken brain. Walk me through it. *Why* do you want to go to Mecca?"

"To go before I die."

"Wait—you're not *dying*, are you? Jesus on a boson, are you *ill*?"

"I'm not ill," said Niu Jian. "I'm in perfect health. So far as I know, anyway. Look: I'm not trying to be mysterious. All Muslims must visit Mecca once in their lives."

I thought about this. "You're a Muslim? I thought you were Chinese."

"One can be both."

"And that bottle of wine you shared with Prévert and myself last night, in the Godolfin?"

"Islam is perfect, individuals are not." He picked more energetically at the skin on the back of his knuckles.

"I just never knew," I said, feeling stupid. "I mean, I thought Muslims aren't supposed to drink alcohol."

"I thought pregnant women weren't supposed to drink alcohol," he returned, and for the first time in this whole strange conversation I got a glimpse of the old Niu Jian, the sly little flash of wit, the particular look he had. But then it was gone again. "Yesterday, in the Elephant, you were talking about the suit you would wear for the press conference. You were all, oh my mother will be watching the television, the whole world will be watching the—oh I must have a smart suit. Oh I must go to a London tailor. What happened to the London tailor?"

He said: "I spoke to Tessimond."

I believe this was the first time I ever heard his name. Not the last; very much not the last time. "Who?"

"Prévert's friend."

"Oh—the doleful-countenance guy? The ex-professor guy from Oregon?"

"Yes."

"You spoke to him—when?"

Niu Jian looked at the ceiling. "Half an hour ago."

"And he told you to quit the team? C'mon, Noo-noo! Why listen to *him*?"

"He didn't tell me to quit the team."

"So he told you—what?"

"He told me about the expansion of the universe," said Niu Jian. "And after he had done that, I realized that I had to quit the team and go to Mecca."

"That's the craziest thing I've ever heard," I said. At that precise moment my little Phylogeny-Ontology-Recapitulator gave a little kick and thwunked my spleen—or whatever organ it is, down in there, that feels like a sack of fluid-swelled nerves. I grunted, shifted my position in my chair. "He told you about the expansion of the universe? You mean you told *him*! *He's* not a shoe-in for the Nobel—you are." When he didn't reply,

I started to lose my temper. "*What* did he tell you about the expansion of the universe, precisely?"

For the second time Niu Jian's glance went to my belly. Then he stood up, his knees making drawn out little bleating noises as they were required to assume his weight. "Ana, goodbye," he said. "You know how it is."

"Do not."

"I don't want to give the wrong impression. You know, I wouldn't even say he *told* me anything. He pointed out the obvious, really. You know how it is, Ana, when somebody says something that completely changes the way you see the cosmos, but that afterwards you think: that's so obvious, how could I not have noticed it before?"

"That's what he did?"

"Yes."

"And it made you want to quit the team? Rather than wait a few weeks and receive the Nobel Prize for Physics?"

Nod.

"So what was it? What did he say? What could he possibly say that would provoke that reaction in you? You're the *least* flaky of the whole team!"

For the third time, the glimpse towards Phylogeny-Ontology-Recapit-ulator, in his bag of fluid, swaddled by his sheath of my flesh. Just a little downward flick of the eyes, and then back to my face. And then he shook my hand with that weird manner he'd picked up from Jane Austen novels or, I don't know what, and then he left. I saw him the following morning pulling his suitcase across the forty-meter sundial that looks like a giant manhole cover outside the Human Resources building. I called to him, and waved; and he waved back, and then he got into the taxi he had called and was driven away, and I never saw him again.

2

Naturally I wanted to talk to this Tessimond geezer, to find out why he was spooking my horses. I had taken pains to assemble the very best team; intel-lectual thoroughbreds. I texted Prévert to come to my office, and when he neither replied nor came I hauled myself, balanced Phylogeny-Ontology-Recapitulator as well as I could over my hips and did my backward-leaning walk along the corridor to his office. I didn't knock. I was the team leader, the ring-giver, the guardian of the treasure. Knocking wasn't needful.

Prévert was inside, and so was Sleight, and the two of them were having a right old ding-dong. Prévert was standing straight up, and he was half-way through either putting on or taking off his coat.

"Niu Jian just quit the team," I said, lowering myself into a chair with the cumbrous grace unique to people in my position. "He just came into my office and quit,"

"We know, boss," said Sleight. "Prévert too."

"He said it was *your* friend who persuaded him, Jack." Prévert's first name was not Jack; it was Stephane. But naturally we all called him Jack. "Why—wait a minute, what do you mean *Prévert too*?"

"He means, Ana," Jack said, "that I too am leaving the team. I apologize. I apologize with a full heart. It is late in the day. If I had known earlier I would have not inconvenienced you in this fashion—and with your..." and like Niu Jian had done, he cast a significant look at the bump of P-O-R, and then returned his gaze to my face.

"You are kidding me," I said.

"I regret to say, Ana, that I am not kidding you."

"But we just got your *th*s to come out right." Prévert's English was more-or-less flawless, his accent somewhere in between David Niven and a BBC newsreader, but he had held stubbornly to that French trick of pronouncing *th*s as "t" or "z," variously.

"I've been remonstrating with him," said Sleight. "He won't tell me why."

"You spoke to your friend Tessimond," I said, panting a little from the exertion of walking along a corridor.

"That's right—is that what Noo-noo did?" Sleight asked.

"What did he say to you?"

"It's no good asking, boss," Sleight told me. "I've been leaning on him for an hour, and he won't cough up. Whatever it was it can't have taken more than ten minutes."

"The time-period was approximately that," Prévert confirmed. He slid his right arm into the vacant tube of his coat-sleeve, thereby confirming that he was putting the garment on, not taking it off.

"He's a friend of yours?"

"Tessimond? He used to be, many years ago. I was surprised to see him. I suggested we have breakfast—Sleight too, although he turned up late. As he always does."

"I was quarter of an hour late," said Sleight. "And that was long enough to the Tessimond geezer to persuade Jack to leave the project! One quarter hour!"

"He did not persuade me to leave. He made no reference to my be-ing on the team, or collecting the Nobel Prize. He simply pointed out something—ah, how-to-say, something rather obvious. Something I am ashamed I did not notice before."

"And this something overturns years of work, convinces you that you shouldn't collect a Nobel prize?"

Prévert shrugged. "There is a woman who lives in Montpellier, called Suzanne," he announced. "I am going to visit her."

"You're crazy. You can't take your name off the—your name will *still be on* the citation, you know!" Sleight's voice had a raspy, edge-of-hysteria quality. "We're not taking your name off the citation."

"I have no preference one way or the other," Prévert replied. "You must do as you please—as shall I."

"Wait a sec, Jack," I said. "Please." Because he was eyeing the door, now, and I could see he was about to scarper. "At least tell us what he told you."

"You may ask him yourself. He's staying in the Holiday Inn. Sleight has his number."

"Come, now, come alone, now, *Jack*, I've known you ten years. Jack, you're a friend, for the love of Jesus, you're *my* friend." I ran the tip of my ring-finger across one eyebrow, then the other. I was trying to think how to do this. "Don't play games with me, Jack. I'm asking you, as a friend. Tell me what is going on."

"What is going," said Prévert, "is me. Goodbye." He was always a touch too proud of his little Anglophone word-games.

"What did Tessimond *tell* you?"

Prévert stopped at the door, looked not at me but at my bump, and said: "he only pointed out what is right in front of us. Us, in particular—you, Sleight, me. It should be more obvious to us than to anybody! Although it *should* be obvious to anyone who gives it more than a minute's thought."

"Don't do this, Jack."

"Goodbye Ana and—you too, Sleight."

"Is it God?" I said. It was my parting shot. "Noo-noo is going to Mecca. Is that what he is, this Tessimond, a *preacher*? Has he somehow converted you to religion and turned you into a—Christ, what does it say in the Old, I mean, New Testament? About leaving your homes and families and becoming fishers of men."

Prévert smiled, and his sideburns moved a little further apart from one another. A big beamy smile. "I am, Ana, you will be relieved to hear—I am precisely as atheistical as I have always been. There is no God. But there is a woman called Suzanne, and she lives in Montpellier." And he walked out.

I sat staring at Sleight, as if it were his fault. He had been standing up, because Prévert had been standing up. Now that it was just the two of us he sat down.

"So," I said. "Are you pissing-off too? Is my *entire* team deserting me?"

"No, boss!" he said, looking genuinely hurt that I would say such a thing. "Never! Loyalty means something to me, at any rate. That and the fact that—you know. I fancy getting the Nobel prize."

"Is it a joke? Are Jack and Niu Jian in cahoots?"

"In what?"

"Cahoots. I mean, are they conspiring together to trick us, or something?"

"I know what cahoots means," said Sleight. "I just didn't quite hear you." He sat back and began looking around Prévert's office, as if the answer might lie there.

"Cold feet," he said. "I think they're genuine, both of them, about leaving. I mean, I don't think it's a joke, boss. Who would joke about a thing like this! But maybe the timing is the key—we're so close to announcing. Maybe they've got cold feet."

"I could maybe believe that of Niu Jian, but not Prévert," I said. "And do you know what, now that I think of it, I couldn't believe it of Noo-noo either. Cold feet?"

"Then what, boss? Why would they both drop out—today?"

"Ring up this Tessimond guy," I instructed him. "Find out what he said. Better yet, tell him to *un*say it. Tell him to get in touch with both of my boys and persuade them to *come back*. What does he think he's *playing* at, anyway? Disassembling my team on the brink of our big announcement?"

Sleight got out his phone, held it in his hand for a bit, and then balanced it on his head. It wasn't an unusual thing for him to balance a mobile phone on his head. The peculiar shape of his bald cranium was such that above his tassel-like eyebrows there was a sort of semi-indentation, a thirty-degree slope in amongst the phrenological landscape, and it so happened that an iPhone fitted snugly there. Sleight had started resting his device there for a joke, but he had done it so often that it had become an unremarkable gesture. "Maybe it would make sense for you to speak to him, boss?"

"Scared?"

"No!" he said, with a quickness and emphasis that strongly implied *yes*. "Only, you *are* the team leader." I put my head to one side. "And I once read a story," he added.

"Science fiction story?"

"Of course." As if there were any other kind of story, for Sleight! "It was about a thing called a blit. You ever heard of a blit?"

"If this is going to be a porn reference, I swear I'll have you disciplined for sexual harassment, Sleight."

"No, no! It's science and it's fiction, in one handy bundle. A blit is a thing, and once you've seen it—once it's gone in your eyes—it starts to occupy your mind. You can't stop thinking about it, and it expands fractally until it takes up all your thoughts and you go mad."

"And?"

"And—what if this Tessimond is going to say something like a verbal blit?"

I hid my face in my hands. There was a tussle between the laugh-aloud angel sitting on my right shoulder, and the burst-into-tears devil sitting on my left. I took control of myself. Pregnancy hormones have real, chemical effects upon even the strongest will. I dropped my hands. "Please never again say the phrase *verbal blit* in my hearing. Call Tessimond."

Sleight, sheepishly, called. He waited only a short time before saying, "Oh, hello, is that Mr. Tessimond, oh, hello, oh, my name is Sleight and Stephane Prévert gave me your number." Then a long pause, and Sleight's eyes tracked left-to-right and right-to-left, and I felt a mild panic, as if he were being Derren-Brown-hypnotized by this stranger, and over the phone too. But then he said. "Anyway, my team-leader, Professor Radonjić, is here and she was wondering if she could—sure, sure." Silence, an intense expression on Sleight's face. Then: "Both of them have left the team, somewhat, eh, ah, somewhat abruptly you know. And they both spoke with you about the—yes, yes." Nodding. Why do people nod when they're talking on the phone? It's not as if their interlocutor can see them. "I see. I understand. We were just wondering what…"

"Let me speak to him," I said, holding out my hand. Sleight passed the phone straight to me. "Hello, Mr. Tessimond? This is Ana Radonjić."

"May I call you Ana?" Tessimond asked. He had a pleasant, low-slung voice; a Midwest American accent, a slight buzz in the consonants that suggested he might be a smoker. I was a little taken aback by this—a micron aback, or thereabouts. "Alright. And what should I call you?"

He hummed; a little, musical burr. "My name is Tessimond," he said. "It's a pleasure to speak to you, Ana. I've immense respect for what you've been doing."

"What do you know about what I've been doing?" I daresay I sounded slightly more paranoid than was warranted.

"I was Henry Semat Professor of Theoretical Physics at CUNY for a number of years," he said. "Years ago—before your time. I left that post decades ago."

"You were at CUNY? Why have I not heard of you?"

"I didn't publish," he burred. "What's the point?"

This piqued me, so I rattled off: "The point is that we have made a break-through with regard to dark energy, and I don't think any physicists have ever been more sure of getting a Nobel citation, and two key members of my team have, this morning, walked away. That is the point."

"There seem to be several points, there, Ana," he said, mildly. But his slow delivery only infuriated me further.

"I don't know what games you are playing," I snapped. "This is serious. This is my career as a serious scientist, and the Nobel prize—not the, er, pigeon-fancier's red rosette." I said this last thing because a pigeon arrived on the outside ledge of Prévert's office windowsill, in a flurry of wings that sounded like a deck of cards being shuffled. Then it folded its wings into its back and stood looking, insolently, through the glass at us. "This is the culmination of everything we have been working for," I said, apparently to the pigeon.

"I was talking to Stephane about this a couple of hours ago," came Tessimond's voice on the phone. "Your research truly sounds fascinating."

"St*ephane* has gone to catch a flight to Montpellier!" I snapped. "Do you know why?"

Tessimond released a small sigh at the other end of the phone line. "I'm afraid I've no idea, Ana."

"No? You said something to him, and it made him walk away from everything he has been working towards for *years*."

There was a silence. Then: "That wasn't my intention, Ana."

"No? Well that's the mess you've made. Perhaps you'd like to help me clear it up, mm?"

"I very much doubt," he said, sadly, "if there's anything I can do." Then he said: "The rate of expansion of the cosmos is accelerating."

"I," I said. "Yes it is."

"That's been known for a while. You're going to announce that you know why this is happening?"

"Professor Tessimond—" I said.

"Dark energy," he said. Then: "Would you like to have lunch?"

I bridled at this. Blame the hormones, I suppose. "I'm afraid I'm going to be *far* too busy today clearing up the mess you have made to be able to take time out for lunch!" For all the world as if he were listening in on my conversation, and objecting to the notion of skipping a meal, P-O-R chose that moment to stretch and squeeze my stomach painfully against my ribs. I grimaced, but kept going. "I'm going to have to explain to university management why not-one-but-two key members of my team have jumped ship mere weeks before we go public with our research."

"Dinner then," he said. "Or drinks. With Dr Sleight too, of course. And bring along your senior managers, if you like. I really didn't intend to cause any upheavals. I'd be very glad to explain myself."

"I *might* be able to find a window tomorrow," I said. "You're staying locally? There's a bar. It's called the Bar Bar, for some peculiar reason. We call it the Elephant. Would it be agreeable for you to meet there tomorrow lunch-time?"

After I'd hung up and given Sleight his phone back, I told him what had been arranged. "Why not meet him right now?" Sleight pressed.

"I intend to spend today coaxing Niu Jian and Jack to come back to us. I don't know what he told them, but I want to be able to present him with a unified front. Tomorrow, Sleight. Tomorrow."

3

I spent the morning haranguing both Niu Jian and Jack on the phone. Jack was a brick wall, and then he was on a flight and the signal vanished, so I didn't get very far with him. I had longer to try and bend Niu Jian's ear, but he was equally stubborn. No, he didn't want to come back. Yes, he was going to Mecca. None of my threats had any purchase. I offered him financial inducements, I warned him his reputation as a serious scientist was on the line, I even said I was going to call his mother. Nothing. Eventually I had to grasp the nettle and call senior management. They were incredulous, at first; and then they were angry; and finally they were baffled.

I'm not surprised. I was baffled myself.

I went home early evening, and lay on the sofa whilst M. cooked me linguini. I spooled the whole crazy narrative out to him, and he did his excellent supporting-pillar impression. It felt better ranting about it, and the linguini was washed down with a small glass of Chianti, which I feel sure P-O-R enjoyed as much as I did, and the whole idiotic nonsense receded in my mind. So what if the two berks weren't present at the press conference? I'd get senior management in. I'd have Sleight beside me. I could do it *solus*. That might even be preferable.

M. and I watched an episode of *Mad Men* together. Then Sleight called. "Boss? I'm in the Elephant."

"Sleight, I appreciate you not abandoning ship like Jack and Niu Jian,"

I said. "But that doesn't mean I require you to keep me informed of your every change of venue. I'll get you electronically tagged if I want that."

"You don't understand, boss. I'm here with Tessimond." He sounded excited, like an undercover cop. "He's at the bar. Getting a half for himself and a pint for me."

"Well," I said. "Don't let me keep you from your revels."

"I'm going to find out what he told Niu Jian and Jack," said Sleight, whispering. "Will report back. I know you're meeting him tomorrow, but I couldn't wait! Curious! Too curious—but that's the problem with being a scientist."

"Sleight, look…" I started, in my weariest voice.

"I will *report back*," he hissed. And hung up.

M. rubbed my feet, whilst I ate a chocolate mousse straight from the plastic pot. Then I pulled myself slowly upstairs to face the great trial of my pregnancy. I mean: brushing my teeth. The mere thought of it made me want to vomit; actually performing the action was gag-provoking, intensely uncomfortable and unpleasant. But I didn't want to just stop brushing my teeth altogether; that would be an admission of defeat. Quite apart from anything else, the teeth themselves were sitting looser in their sockets than before, and so clearly needed more not less hygienic atten-tion. But the nightly brush had become my least favorite part of the day. I had just completed this disagreeable exercise, and was accordingly in no good mood, when Sleight rang back.

"Sleight—what? Seriously: what?"

"I said I would ring back," he returned. "And so I have." But his tone of voice had changed, and I immediately sensed something wrong.

"What is it?"

"Tessimond explained things. It really is desperately obvious, when you come to think of it. I'm really a bit ashamed of myself for not seeing it earlier."

"Sleight, you're spooking me out. Don't tell me you're following Niu Jian and Jack and dropping out?"

There was a long pause, in which I could faintly hear the background noises of the Elephant; the murmur of conversation, the clink of glasses. "Yes," he said eventually.

"No," I returned.

"I'm going to start smoking," said Sleight.

"If I have to listen to another non-sequitur from my team members I am going to scream," I told him.

"I used to love smoking," Sleight explained. He didn't sound very drunk, but there was a sway to his intonation that did not inspire confidence. "But I gave it up. You know, for health. It's not good for your health. I didn't want to get heart disease or canny, or canny, or *cancer*." There was another long pause. "I'm sorry boss, I hate to let you down."

"Sleight," I snapped at him. "What did he tell you?"

He rang off. I was furious. I would have called Tessimond direct, but I didn't have his number; and although I called Sleight back, and texted him, and @'d him on Twitter, he did not reply. It took M. a long time to calm me down, if I'm honest. In the end he assured me that Sleight was drunk, and that when he woke sober the following day he would see how foolish it all seemed.

I slept fitfully. The morning brought no message from Sleight; and he didn't turn up for work; and he still wasn't answering his phone.

I recalled that Tessimond was staying in the Holiday Inn and left a message with their front desk for him to call me, giving him my personal number. Then I met with the junior researche's, or such of them as were still on campus—for the research part of the project was done and dusted, and we were all now just waiting on the announcement and the shaking of the world of science. None of them were about to leave the project; and their puppyish enthusiasm (after all a Nobel prize is a Nobel prize!) calmed me down a little. I did paperwork, and dipped my toe into the raging ocean of email that had long since swamped my computer. Then I googled Tessimond, and discovered that, yes, he *had* been Henry Semat Professor of Theoretical Physics at City University of New York, for about two months, many years previously. I wasn't surprised that I'd never heard of him, though. M. rang to check on me, and I told him I was fine. At 2pm, on the dot, Tessimond himself called. "Hello, Ana," he said, pleasantly.

"You've now suborned a third member of my team," I told him, in as venomous a voice as I could manage, post-prandial as I was. "I don't know why you're doing it, but I want you to stop."

"I assure you, Ana, I intended nothing of the sort," he said. "Dr Sleight called me, invited me for a drink. We were only talking. Only words were exchanged."

"Enough of this nonsense. What did you tell him?"

"Are we still meeting, in person, later today? I'd be happy to explain everything then."

"You don't want to say over the phone?"

He sounded taken aback. I was being pretty hostile, I suppose. "No, I don't mind saying over the phone. Do you want me to tell you, now, over the phone?"

"No I don't," I said. "I don't care what mind-game you've been playing. What con-trick you're up to. I only care that you leave us all alone. Why are you even here?"

"Stephane invited me. I hadn't seen him in many years. And since leaving my academic posting I have been pursuing an old dream of mine and… simply travelling. Travelling around the world. I thought how pleasant it would be to visit England, so I came."

"You came to Berkshire on a whim, or just to see an old friend or some paper-thin pretext like that, but now you're here you just *happen* to be dismantling my entire physics team on the verge of our winning the Nobel prize?"

He contemplated this for a moment. "I do love that you guys spell it burk and pronounce it bark. Does it have anything to do with the bark of trees?"

"What?"

"Berkshire," he said.

"I ought to call the police and have you arrested. Are you *blackmailing* them?"

"Blackmailing who?" He sounded properly surprised at this.

"Niu Jian and Jack and my dear, bald-headed Sleight, of course. Are you?"

"No!"

"Stay away from me and my team," I said, and ended the call. I was fuming.

Later that afternoon I finally got a text from Sleight. "*Sorry boss*," it said. "*Beeen dead drunk for 12 houurs. Won't be coming back, and o*"—just that. I rang him immediately, but he did not answer. Forty-five minutes later I got another text. "*Theres a sf shortstory called 'Nittfall.' It is like that. The ending of that sf, u know it? Chat with Tesimnd and afterwards I was like, WOH! ASIMOVIAN!*" Since Sleight was forty-six and not usually given to speaking like a teenager, I deduce that he was still intoxicated when he sent those texts. I rang again, and texted him back, but he did not reply.

My mood swung about again. I was probably overreacting. It was clearly all a big misunderstanding. It would get itself sorted out. My pregnancy hormones were a distorting mirror on the world. Tessimond was chicken-licken, and had somehow persuaded the otherwise level-headed members of my team that the world was ending—but the world *wasn't* ending, and the sky would *not* fall, and I would soon prevail upon the foolish barnyard animals. I still didn't have Tessimond's number, so I called the Holiday Inn again and left him a second message, saying that I would be happy meet him in the Elephant at 6pm that evening.

Google helpfully corrected Sleight's incompetent spelling, and I quickly located the Isaac Asimov short story, called "Nightfall," in an online venue. I read it in ten minutes and finished it none the wiser. Not that it was a bad story. On the contrary, it was a good story. But I couldn't see how it had any bearing on the matter in hand. Something to do with stars.

4

That I never got to the Elephant was just one of those things. Mid-afternoon I went for a pee and noticed a constellation of little red spots on the inside of my knickers. You don't want to take any chances with a thing like that. I rang M.; he left work and drove me straight to Casualty, and they admitted me at once. There was some worry that I was bleeding a little into my uterus, and that Phylogeny-Ontology-Recapitulator might be at risk. I lay on a hospital bed for hours, and they did tests, and scanned scans, and finally I was told I was alright and could go home. If there was more spotting I was to come straight back, but otherwise I was free to go.

M. drove us home; and we picked up a pizza on the way, and Tessimond was propelled entirely from my mind. There were more important things to worry about than him and his crazy verbal-blit, or World's-End-nigh, or "the stars are coming out!" or whatever his nonsense was. I took the next day off, and then it was the weekend. Tessimond popped into my head on the Sunday evening again (something on telly was the trigger, but I can't remember what it was), and I felt a small quantity of shame that I had stood him up. But then I remembered that he'd been pouring some poison into my team-members' ears, and persuading them to abandon me, and I grew angry with him. Then I decided to put him out of my mind. I told myself: Monday morning, all three of my core team would turn up for work, looking sheepish and apologizing profusely.

They didn't, though. None of them answered phone call, or text, or Twitter. A week later they hadn't come back, and the university authorities expressed their dissatisfaction, and instituted suspension proceedings. I called Holiday Inn, cross that I hadn't simply got Tessimond's number when I'd had the chance; but I was told he'd checked out. My head of department persuaded the Vice Chancellor not to suspend the three of them until after the press conference. He saw that it could be awkward.

So we had the press conference, and there was a great deal of excitement. It was widely reported in the press. One internet site picked up (God knows how) that of the original team of four three had gone AWOL and were not present at the press conference. Several news outlets followed it up. We had a cover story ready: that I was team leader, and the others were taking a well-deserved break. The story died down. Who was interested in the particular scientists, when the theory itself was so cool?

The expansion of the universe was speeding up. Given the mass of matter (including dark matter) in the cosmos as a whole it ought to have been slowing down—as a bone thrown into the sky slows down as it reaches its apogee, and for the same reason: gravity. But it wasn't slowing down. Physicists had speculated about this before, of course, and had come up with a theoretical explanation for it, called *dark energy*. But "dark energy" was tautological physics, really: just a way of saying "the something that is speeding up the inflation of the universe," which is not much of an answer to the question: "What is speeding up the inflation of the universe?" What we had done was demonstrate that the increase in the rate of cosmic expansion was itself increasing, and in ways that necessitated that dark matter and dark energy be decoupled. Indeed, we showed that the geometry of the observable gradient of the acceleration of expansion would cause a three-dimensional asymptote, which in turn would cause a complex toroidal folded of spacetime on the very largest scale. There was no reason to think that this universal reconfiguration of spacetime geometry would have any perceptible effects on Earth. Our scale was simply too small. But it was a thing, and it rewrote Einstein, and the data made our conclusions inescapable, and everybody was *very* excited.

The next thing that happened was that I gave birth to an exquisite female infant, with a crumpled face and blue eyes and a wet brush of black hair on her head. We called her Marija Celeste Radonjić-Dalefield, and loved her very much. Two weeks after birth her headhair fell off, and she looked even more adorable with a bald bonce. And the following months whirled past, for truly do they say of having young children that the days are long and the years are short. She slept in our big bed, and though a fraction of our size she somehow dominated that space, and forced us to the edges. We had her baptized at the Saint Peter's Catholic Church, and all my family came, and even some of M.'s.

The Nobel committee worked its slow work, and word came through the unofficial channels that a citation was on its way. I returned early from my maternity leave, and we all made new efforts to locate Niu Jian, Prévert and Sleight. Time had healed enough to make the whole thing seem silly rather than sinister. M. was of the opinion that they'd all been spooked by the proximity of the announcement of our research. "Working in the dark for years, then suddenly faced with the headlights of global interest—that sort of thing could spook a person in any number of ways."

"You make us sound like mole-people," I said, but I wondered if he might be right.

We reached none of them. Niu Jian's family were easy enough to get hold of, and they were polite, assuring us Noo-noo was rejoicing in health and happiness, but not disclosing in which portion of the globe he was enjoying these things. They promised to pass on our messages, and I don't doubt that they did; but he did not get back to me. Friends suggested that Sleight was in Las Vegas, but we could get no closer to him than that. I felt worst about Prévert—that elegant man, that brilliant mind, without whose input the breakthrough really wouldn't have been possible. But there were no leads at all as far as he was concerned. I notified Montpellier police, even went so far as to hire a French private detective. It took ninety days before the agency reported back, to say that he and a woman called Suzanne Chahal had boarded a flight to the West Indies in the summer, but that it was not possible to know on which island they had ended up.

I agreed with the University that I would collect the prize alone, but that all four of our names would be on the citation. They had lost their minds, the three of them; but that was no reason to punish them—and their contribution had been vital. "Have you had any better ideas as to why they dropped out, like that?" M. asked me, one night.

"Not a clue," I said. Then again, with a long-drawn-out "ü" sound at the end: "not a *cluuue*."

"I suppose we'll never know," he said. He was reading a novel, and glancing at me over his little slot-shaped spectacles from time to time, as if keeping an eye on me. Marija was in a cot beside the bed, and I was rocking her with a steady, strong motion, which was how she liked it.

"I guess not," I said.

"Does it bother you?"

"They were my friends," I said. Then: "Jack in particular. His desertion is the most baffling. The most hurtful."

"I'm sure," M. said, licking his finger and turning the page of the book, "that it was nothing personal. Whatever Tessimond *told* them, I mean. I'm sure it wasn't to do with you, personally."

"That prick," I said, but without venom. "Whatever it was Tessimond told them."

"You know what I think?" M. asked. "I think, even if we found out what he said, it wouldn't explain it. It'll be something banal, or seeming-banal, like God Loves You, or Remember You Must Die, or Oh My God It's Full Of Stars. Or—you know, whatever. Shall I tell you my theory?"

"You're going to, regardless of what I say," I observed.

M. gave me a Paddington Hard Stare over his glasses. Then he said: "I think it had nothing to do with this Tessimond chap. I think he's a red herring."

"He was from Oregon," I said, randomly.

"It was something else. Virus. Pressure of work. Road to Tarsus. And in the final analysis, it doesn't matter."

"You're right, of course," I said, and kissed him on his tall, lined forehead.

5

We agreed that I would travel to Stockholm alone. I was still breast-feeding, so I wasn't over-delighted about it; but M. and I discussed it at length and it seemed best not to drag a baby onto an airplane, and then into a Swedish hotel and then back again for a ceremony she was much too young to even remember. I would go, alone, and then I would come back. I expressed milk like a cow, and we built up a store in the freezer.

It was exciting and I *was* excited. Or I would have been, if I'd been less sleep deprived. If I'm completely honest the thing that had really persuaded me was the image of myself, solus, in a four-star hotel room—sleeping, sleeping all night long, sleeping uninterruptedly and luxuriously and waking with a newly refreshed and sparkling mind to the swift Stockholm sunrise.

You're wondering: did I feel *bad* for my three colleagues—that they wouldn't be there? It was their choice. Would you feel bad, in my shoes?

You're wondering: so that's all there is to it?

No, that's not all there is to it. The day before the flight I took Marija for a walk in her three-wheeled buggy. We strolled by the river, and then back into town. Then I went into a Costa coffee shop, had a hot chocolate for myself, and I fed her. After that she went to sleep, and I painstakingly reinserted her into her buggy. Then I checked my phone, and tapped out a few brief answers to yet another interview about winning The Nobel *Prize* For Heaven's Sake! Then I sat back, in the comfy chair, with my hands folded in my lap.

"Hello, Ana," said Tessimond. "Are you well?"

I had seen him only once before, I think; when Jack had introduced him to everybody by the water cooler, all those months earlier—before he'd said whatever he said and sent my boys scurrying away from the prospect of the Nobel. He had struck me then as a tall, rather sad-faced old gent; clean shaven and with a good stack of white hair, carefully dressed, with polite, old-school manners. I remember Jack saying, "This is a friend of mine from Oregon, a professor no less." I don't remember if he passed on the man's name, that first time.

"You stalking me, Professor?" I said. I felt remarkably placid, seeing him standing there. "I googled you, you know."

"If Google suggests I have a history of *stalking* people, Ana, then I shall have to seek legal redress."

"Go on, sit down," I instructed him. "You can't do any more damage now. I'm—" I added, aware that it was boasting but not caring, "off to Stockholm tomorrow to collect the Nobel Prize for Physics."

Tessimond sat himself, slowly, down. "I've seen the media coverage of it all, of course. Many congratulations."

"It belongs to all four of us. Have you been in touch with the other three?"

"You mean Professors Niu Jian and Prévert and Doctor Sleight? I have not. Why would you think I have?"

"It doesn't matter." I took a sip of hot chocolate. "You want a drink?"

"No thank you," he said. He was peering into the buggy. "What a lovely infant! Is it a boy?"

"She is a girl," I said. "She is called Marija."

"I'm happy for you."

"Yes," I said. "It's been a big year. Childbirth and winning the Nobel Prize."

"Congratulations indeed."

We sat in silence for a little while. "You spoke to my three colleagues," I said, shortly. "And then after that conversation they all left my team. What did you tell them?"

Tessimond looked at me for a long time, with blithe eyes. "Do you really want me to tell you?" he asked eventually, looking down to my sleeping child and then back up to me.

"No," I said, feeling suddenly afraid. Then: "Yes, hell. Of course. Will it take long?"

"Five minutes."

"Will you then leave me alone and not bother me any more?"

"By all means."

"No, don't tell me. I've changed my mind. What are you anyway? Some kind of Ancient Mariner figure, going around telling people this thing *personally*? Why not publish it—post it to your blog. Or put it on a T-shirt."

"It has crossed my mind to publish it," Tessimond said. "It emerged from my academic research. We usually publish our academic research, don't we."

"So you didn't, because?"

"I didn't see the point. Not just in publication, but in academia. Really, I realized, what I wanted to do was: travel." He looked through the wide glass windows of the coffee shop at the shoppers traversing and retraversing the esplanade. Markets, temples, warehouses and wide paved streets. Tree-shaded squares where the bombastic statues of dead magnates and generals waited, quietly. Two clouds closed upon one another, shutting in front of the sun like a lizard's horizontal eyelids. What is it the poet said? Dark dark dark, they all go into the dark. He said: "I read your work. It's very elegantly done. Very elegant solutions to the dark energy problem; a real... I was going to say *intuitive* sense of the geometry of the cosmos."

"Were going to say?"

"Well it's—I'm afraid it's wrong. So your intuition has led you astray. But it's a very bold attempt at..."

I interrupted him with: "Wrong?"

"I'm afraid so. I'm afraid you're coming at the question from the wrong angle. Not just you, of course. The whole scientific community."

I laughed at this, but, I hope, not unkindly. Marija stirred, twitched her little mitten-clad hands like she was boxing in her sleep, and fell motionless again. "You'd better let the Nobel Committee know," I said. "Before it's too late!" It was all too absurd. Really it was.

The late autumn sky was as blue as water, and as cold.

"Five minutes, you said," I told him, nodding in the direction of the shop clock. "And you've had more than one of those five already."

He breathed in, and out, calmly enough. Then he said: "Why is the universe so big?"

"*Why* questions rarely lead physicists anywhere good. Why is there something rather than nothing? Why was there a big-bang? Who knows? Not a well-formulated question."

He put his head on one side, and tried again. "How did the universe get so big?"

"That's better," I said, indulgently. "It got so big because fourteen billion years ago the big bang happened, and one consequence of that event was the expansion of spacetime—on a massive scale."

"All these galaxies and stars moving apart from one another like dots on an inflating balloon," he said. "Only the surface of the balloon is 2D and we have to make the conceptual leap to imagining a 3D surface."

"Exactly," I told him. "As every schoolkid knows."

"Still: why expansion? Why should the big bang result in the dilation of space?"

I took another sip from my chocolate. "Three minutes to go, and you've tripped yourself into another *why* question."

"Let me ask you about time," he said, unruffled. "We appear to be moving through time. We go in one direction. We cannot go backwards, we can only go forwards."

I shrugged. "According to maths we can do backwards. The equations of physics are reversible. It just so happens that we go in one direction only. It's no big deal."

"Quite right," he said, nodding. "The science says we ought to be able to go in any direction. Yet we never," he said, stroking his own cheek, "actually *do*. That's strange, isn't it?"

"Maybe," I said. "I can't say it bothers me."

"Time is a manifold, like space. We can move in any direction in space. But we can only move in one direction in time."

"This really is kindergarten stuff," I said. "And much as I have enjoyed our little chat…"

"What moves an object through the manifold of space?"

After a moment, I said: "Force."

"Impulse. Gravity. Those two things only. You can push an object to give it kinetic energy, or you can draw it towards you. You fire your rocket up; Earth *pulls* your rocket down. Kinetic energy is always relative, not absolute. The driver of a car passing by a pedestrian has kinetic energy from the pedestrian's point of view; but from the point of view of the person in the passenger seat that same driver has zero kinetic energy."

It was, in a strange sort of way, soothing to hear him elucidate elementary physics in this way. "All well and good," I said.

"That's how things go in the physical manifold, which we call spacetime. Relocate the model to the temporal manifold—let's call it timespace."

This was when the fizzing started in my stomach. "For the sake of argument, why not," I said. I couldn't prevent a defensive tone creeping into my voice. "Although it'll be nothing but a thought-experiment."

"Why do you say that?" he asked, blandly.

"We've centuries of experimental data about the actual manifold, the spacetime manifold. Your 'timespace' manifold is pure speculation."

"Is it? I would say we move through it every day of our lives. I'd say

we've a lifetime's experience of it. The question is—no, the two questions
are: why are we moving through it, and why can we only move through
it in one direction."

There was a blurry rim to my vision. My heart had picked up the pace.
"More why questions."

"If you prefer: *what* is drawing us towards it, through timespace?"

"You're saying the reason we feel time as a kind of motion, one hour per
hour, is because something is drawing us, with its gravitational pull—is that
it? Because it seems to me that we might just as well have been launched
forward by some initial impulse. Don't you agree?"

"The reason I don't agree is the fact that we're stuck moving in one temporal direction." I saw, then, where he was going; but I sat quietly as he
spelled it out. "Think of the analogue from the physical manifold. There's
no force that could propel an object, let alone a whole cosmos, so rapidly
that it was locked into a single trajectory. But there *is* a force in the universe that can draw an object *in* with such a force—draw it such that it has
no option but to move in one direction, towards the centre of the object."

"A black hole."

He nodded.

"Your theory," I said, in a just-so-as-we're-clear voice, "is that the reason
we move along the arrow of time the way we do is that we're being drawn
towards a supermassive temporal black hole?"

"Yes."

"Well," I said, with an insouciance I did not feel. "It's an interesting theory,
although it is only a theory."

"Not at all. Consider the data."

"What data?"

"I understand your resistance, Ana," he said, gently. "But you can do
better than this. Who knows the data better than you? What happens as
a physical object approaches the event horizon of a physical black hole?"

"Time," I said, "dilates."

"So what must happen as a *temporal* object approaches the event horizon of a *temporal* black hole? Physics dilates. Space expands—until it
approaches an asymptote of reality. From the point of view of an observer
not present at the event horizon itself space would seem to expand until it
appeared infinite." He looked through the big glass again. "What else do
we see, when we look around?"

"So we're still," I said, my voice gravelly, "*outside* the event horizon?"

"If we were outside the event horizon, the rate of apparent expansion of space would be an asymptote approaching a fixed rate—a simple acceleration. And until a few decades ago that was what the data showed. But then the data starting showing that the rate of apparent expansion of the universe is *speeding up*. That can only mean that we're approaching the event horizon itself. That also explains why we locked into the one direction of time. In the timespace manifold generally speaking we ought to be able to go forwards, backwards, whatever we wanted. But we're not in the manifold generally; we're in a very particular place. Like an object falling into a black hole, we're locked into a single vector."

I thought about it. Well, I say I thought about it; but the truth is I didn't need to think very hard. It fell into place in my mind; like the others, I found myself thinking how could I not see this before? It is so very obvious. "But if you're right—wait," I said. "Wait a moment."

I pulled out my phone, and jabbed up the calculus app. It took me a few moments to work through the crucial equations. Of course everything fitted. Of course it was true.

Of course it was right.

I looked at him, feeling removed from myself. "When we reach the actual temporal event horizon," I said, "tidal forces will rip us apart."

"Will rip time apart," he said, nodding slowly. "Yes. Of course that amounts to the same thing."

"When?"

"You've got the equations there," he said, looking at my phone as it lay, like a miniature *2001*-monolith, flat on the table. "But it's hard to be precise. The scale is fourteen billion years; the tolerances are not seconds, or even days. Years. I worked out a seven years plus or minus. That was a decade ago."

I shook my head, the way a dog shakes water of its pelt; but there was no way this idea could be shaken out of my mind. It was true; it was there. "It could be—literally—any day now," I said.

"I'm sorry," he said. "Not for you, so much, as for the fact of you having a small kid."

"That's why Noo-noo was so circumspect with me," I said. "I see. But what difference does it make? And, yes, alright I see why you haven't published this. It'd be wandering the highways with an End Is Nigh sandwich board."

"Not that," he said, his glittering eyes meeting mine. "More that it's so obvious. When you think about it, how could the expanding universe be anything *other* than this? Travelling near the ultimate spatial speed makes time dilate; so obviously travelling near the ultimate *temporal* speed will make *space* dilate. We should—all of us, we should just… *see* it."

"I'm going home now," I told him. But I embraced him before I left, and felt the sharkskin roughness of his unshaved cheek against my own. Then I wheeled Marija home. I called M. and told him to leave work and join me. He was puzzled, but acquiesced.

He hasn't gone back.

6

The equations depend upon precision over prodigious lengths of time— since the big bang, or (rather) since the dilation effect first affected what until then must have been a stable cosmos existing within an open temporal manifold. But I've done my best. Tessimond's +/-7 years was, I suspect, deliberately vague; erring on the side of generosity. I think the timescale is much shorter. Download the data on the rate of acceleration of cosmic expansion, and you can do your own sums.

Of course I never flew to Stockholm. Why would I waste three days away from my child? None of that matters anyway. We realized what money we could, and bought a small place by the sea. I won't say what sea. That doesn't matter either; except that, when the dusk comes each day, and the net curtains are sucked against the open windows and go momentary starch-stiff; and when the moths congregate to worship their electric sun-gods; and when the moon lies carelessly in the sky over the purple marine horizon like a pearl of great price—when Marija is fed and happy and M. and I take our turns holding her, and then lay her down and hold one another—there is a contentment spun from finitude that my previous, open-ended existence could not comprehend. I have busied myself writing this account, although only a little every day, for there is no rush, or else there is too much rush and I don't wish to be troubled by the latter. And as for everything else, it helps to know what is really important

ADVENTURE STORY

NEIL GAIMAN

Neil Gaiman [www.neilgaiman.com] *was born in England and worked as a freelance journalist before co-editing* Ghastly Beyond Belief *(with Kim Newman) and writing* Don't Panic: The Official Hitchhiker's Guide to the Galaxy Companion. *He started writing graphic novels and comics with* Violent Cases *in 1987, and with the seventy-five installments of award-winning series* The Sandman *established himself as one of the most important comics writers of his generation. His first novel,* Good Omens *(with Terry Pratchett), appeared in 1991, and was followed by* Neverwhere, Stardust, American Gods, Coraline, Anansi Boys, *and* The Graveyard Book. *Coming up is new novel* The Ocean at the End of the Lane. *Gaiman's work has won the Carnegie, Newbery, Hugo, World Fantasy, Bram Stoker, Locus, Geffen, International Horror Guild, Mythopoeic, and Will Eisner Comic Industry awards. Gaiman currently lives near Minneapolis.*

In my family "adventure" tends to be used to mean "any minor disaster we survived" or even "any break from routine". Except by my mother, who still uses it to mean "*what she did that morning.*" Going to the wrong part of a supermarket parking lot and, while looking for her car, getting into a conversation with someone whose sister, it turns out, she knew in the 1970s would qualify, for my mother, as a full-blown adventure.

She is getting older, now. She no longer gets out of the house as she used to. Not since my father died.

My last visit to her, we were clearing out some of his possessions. She gave me a black leather lens-case filled with tarnished cuff-links, and invited me to take any of my father's old sweaters and cardigans I wanted, to remember him by. I loved my father, but couldn't imagine wearing one of his sweaters. He was much bigger than me, all my life. Nothing of his would fit me.

And then I said, "What's that?"

"Oh," said my mother. "That's something that your father brought back from Germany when he was in the army." It was carved out of mottled red stone, the size of my thumb. It was a person, a hero or perhaps a god, with a pained expression on its rough-carved face.

"It doesn't look very German," I said.

"It wasn't, dear. I think it's from. Well, these days, it's Kazakhstan. I'm not sure what it was back then."

"What was Dad doing in Kazakhstan in the army?" This would have been about 1950. My father ran the officer's club in Germany during his national service, and, in none of his post-war army after-dinner stories, had ever done anything more than borrow a truck without permission, or take delivery of some dodgily sourced whisky.

"Oh." She looked as if she'd said too much. Then she said, "Nothing, dear. He didn't like to talk about it."

I put the statue with the cuff-links, and the small pile of curling black and white photographs I had decided to take home with me to scan.

I slept in the spare bedroom at the end of the hall, in the narrow spare bed.

The next morning, I went into the room that had been my father's office, to look at it one final time. Then I walked across the hall into the living room, where my mother had already laid breakfast.

"What happened to that little stone carving?"

"I put it away, dear." My mother's lips were set.

"Why?"

"Well, your father always said he shouldn't have held on to it in the first place."

"Why not?"

She poured tea from the same china teapot she had poured it from all my life.

"There were people after it. In the end, their ship blew up. In the valley. Because of those flappy things getting into their propellers."

"Flappy things?"

She thought for a moment. "Pterodactyls, dear. With a P. That was what your father said they were. Of course, he said the people in the airship deserved all that was coming to them, after what they did to the Aztecs in 1942."

"Mummy, the Aztecs died out years ago. Long before 1942."

"Oh yes, dear. The ones in America. Not in that valley. These other people, the ones in the airship, well, your father said they weren't really people. But they looked like people, even though they came from somewhere with such a funny name. Where was it?" She thought for a while. Then, "You should drink your tea, dear."

"Yes. No. Hang on. So what were these people? And pterodactyls have been extinct for fifty million years."

"If you say so, dear. Your father never really talked about it." She paused. Then, "There was a girl. This was at least five years before your father and I started going out. He was very good looking back then. Well, I always thought he was handsome. He met her in Germany. She was hiding from people who were looking for that statue. She was their queen or princess or wise woman or something. They kidnapped her, and he was with her, so they kidnapped him too. They weren't actually aliens. They were more like, those people who turn into wolves on the television…"

"Werewolves?"

"I suppose so, dear." She seemed doubtful. "The statue was an oracle, and if you owned it, even if you had it, you were the ruler of those people." She stirred her tea. "What did your father say? The entrance to the valley was through a tiny footpath, and after the German girl, well, she wasn't German, obviously, but they blew up the pathway with a… a ray machine, to cut off the way to the outside world. So your father had to make his own way home. He would have got into such a lot of trouble, but the man who escaped with him, Barry Anscome, he was in Military Intelligence, and—"

"Hang on. Barry Anscome? Used to come and stay for a weekend, when I was a kid. Gave me fifty pence every time. Did bad coin tricks. Snored. Silly moustache."

"Yes dear, Barry. He went to South America when he retired. Ecuador, I think. That was how they met. When your father was in the army." My father had told me once that my mother had never liked Barry Anscome, that he was my dad's friend.

"And?"

She poured me another cup of tea. "It was such a long time ago, dear. Your father told me all about it once. But he didn't tell the story immediately. He only told me when we were married. He said I ought to know. We were on our honeymoon. We went to a little Spanish fishing village. These days it's a big tourist town, but back then, nobody had ever heard of it. What was it called? Oh yes. Torremolinos."

"Can I see it again? The statue?"

"No, dear."

"You put it away?"

"I threw it away," said my mother, coldly. Then, as if to stop me from rummaging in the rubbish, "The bin-men already came this morning."

We said nothing, then.

She sipped her tea.

"You'll never guess who I met last week. Your old school teacher. Mrs. Brooks? We met in Safeway's. She and I went off to have coffee in the Bookshop because I was hoping to talk to her about joining the town carnival committee. But it was closed. We had to go to The Olde Tea Shoppe instead. It was quite an adventure."

KATABASIS

ROBERT REED

Robert Reed [www.robertreedwriter.com] *was born in Omaha, Nebraska. He has a Bachelor of Science in Biology from the Nebraska Wesleyan University, and has worked as a lab technician. He became a full-time writer in 1987, the same year he won the L. Ron Hubbard Writers of the Future contest, and has published eleven novels, including* The Leeshore, The Hormone Jungle, *and far future science fiction novels* Marrow *and* The Well of Stars. *An extraordinarily prolific writer, Reed has published over 200 short stories, mostly in* F&SF *and* Asimov's, *which have been nominated for the Hugo, James Tiptree, Jr., Locus, Nebula, Seiun, Theodore Sturgeon Memorial, and World Fantasy awards, and have been collected in* The Dragons of Springplace *and* The Cuckoo's Boys. *His novella "A Billion Eves" won the Hugo Award. Nebraska's only SF writer, Reed lives in Lincoln with his wife and daughter, and is an ardent long-distance runner.*

1

The custom was to bring nothing but your body, no matter how weak or timid that body might be. Robotic help was forbidden, as were exoskeletons and other cybernetic aids. Every nexus had to be shut down; the universe and its distractions were too much of a burden to carry across the wilderness. Brutal work and miserable climates were guaranteed, and the financial costs were as crushing as any physical hardship. Food was purchased locally, every crumb wearing outrageous import fees, while simple tents and minimal bedding cost as much as luxury apartments. But most expensive were the indispensable porters: Every hiker had to hire one strong back from among a hodgepodge of superterran species, relying on that expert help to carry rations and essential equipment as well as the client's fragile body when he proved too weary or too dead to walk any farther.

Porters were biological, woven from bone and muscle and extravagant colors of blood. Evolved for massive worlds, most of them thundered about on four and six and even eight stout legs. But there were a few bipeds in the ranks, and one of those was a spectacular humanoid who called herself Katabasis.

"Yet you seem small," said the human male. "How can you charge what you charge, looking this way?"

Katabasis was three times his mass and much, much stronger. But the question was fair. With an expression that humans might mistake for a smile, she said, "The client pays the penalty for being brought out on his back. When you give up, we earn a powerful bonus."

The human lifted a hand, two fingers tapping the top of his head. He had pale brown skin and thick hair the color of glacial ice, white infused with blue. The fingers tapped and the hand dropped and with genuine pride he said, "I studied the rules. I understand that rule."

"Good," she said.

"But these other creatures are giants," he said. "That Wogfound would have no trouble carrying you. And the One-after-another looks easily stronger."

"All true," she agreed. "But by the same logic, they feel no special obligation to look after their clients. Extra money has its charms, and if you shatter, they win. But I am relatively weak—as you wisely noted, thank you—and that's why I avoid carrying others, even for a few steps. Ask the other porters here; you will learn. Katabasis is notorious for keeping her clients healthy, which not only adds to the value of the trek, but it saves you the ignominy of being brought into City West as a cripple or a carcass."

The modern brain was nearly impossible to kill, and no client had ever permanently died during these marches through jungle and desert. Yet immortality had its costs, including exceptional memories that played upon weaknesses like pride and dignity. Small humiliations were slow to heal. Giant failures could eat at the soul for thousands of years. Most humans would take her warning to heart. Yet this man was peculiarly different. Staring at the powerful, self-assured alien, he smiled for the first time. "Oh, no," he said. "You cannot scare me."

Katabasis had centuries of experience with the species and its countenances, but she had never observed anything so peculiar as that broad, blatant grin and that bald declaration. She watched the ugly tongue curling inside that joyful mouth. The human made no attempt to hide his feelings. He was staring, obviously intrigued by the porter: The shape of her tall triangular face and the muscled contours of the rugged, ageless body, and how the bright golden-brown plumage jutted out of her work clothes. An interspecies fantasy was playing inside his crazy head. This happened on rare occasions, but never on the first day. And never like this.

Without shame, the man adjusted his erection. "My name is Varid, and I want to hire you."

"No."

Varid didn't seem to hear her. He continued to gaze at her with a simpleton's lust. Then the face flattened, emptiness suddenly welling up in the eyes, and using a tone that was almost but not quite puzzled, he asked, "Why not?"

"You won't endure the journey," Katabasis said.

Varid tried to laugh but the sound came out broken, as if he was an alien attempting to make human sounds. Then the other arm lifted, bending to make a big bulge of muscle. "I'm exceptionally fit. I've trained for years, preparing for this day. Designer steroids and implanted genes, and I have special bacteria in my gut and my blood, doing nothing but keeping this body in perfect condition."

"It isn't the body that concerns me," she said.

Varid shut his eyes and opened them again. "What are you saying?"

"Your mind is the problem."

He responded with silence.

"I don't know you," Katabasis continued, "but my impression is that you have a fragile will and a foolish nature."

The human face remained empty, unaffected.

"Hire the One-after-another," she said, one broad hand picking him off the ground and then setting him aside. "She's more patient than most porters, and she won't speak too rudely about you once you give up."

In the remote past, in some distant parcel of the newborn universe, someone harvested the core of a Jovian world. Godly hands filled the sphere with caverns and oceans, and then they swaddled their creation inside a hull of hyperfiber. Towering rockets rose thousands of kilometers above the stern, and the new starship was fueled and launched. Yet nobody ever came onboard. The machine's purpose and ultimate destination were forgotten. Billions of years later, humans found the derelict wandering the cold outside the Milky Way, and after considering a thousand poetic names, that lucky species dubbed their prize "the Great Ship" and began a long voyage around the entire galaxy, offering passage to any species or individual that could afford the price of a ticket.

Early in the voyage, a high-gravity species sold asteroids and rare technologies to the humans and with their earnings bought passage for a distant solar system. Once onboard, they built a vast centripetal wheel. The wheel was deep inside the Ship, helping minimize the natural, distracting tug of real gravity. Forty kilometers wide and nearly five hundred kilometers in diameter, their home spun a circle every eight minutes, pressing them snugly against the wheel's rim.

Eventually the aliens reached their destination, and they sold their home to a speculator with dreams but few resources.

That began a sequence of bankruptcies and auction sales. Each grand plan ended with fresh disappointment. Investors changed and new tenants worked the ground with false optimism, and then everything would fall apart again. In that piecemeal fashion, the habitat's climate was modified and rectified in places while other regions were left to shatter, creating an ecological stew populated by survivors from a thousand massive worlds. Today the lone sea was shallow and hypersaline, bordered by City East and City West, while at the opposite end of the wheel stood a chain of mashed-down mountains. An artificial sun rode the hub, throwing a patchwork of colors and intensities of light into a maze of valleys, and after thousands of years, for no reason but luck, a splendidly fierce and decidedly unique biosphere had matured.

The current owners occupied City West, and so long as their investment produced capital and public curiosity, they were happy.

Every porter lived in City East. An abrasive, brawling community, it was as diverse as the countryside if not so beautiful. With powerful arms, Katabasis had hollowed out a boulder of quake-coral, making a cavity where she could sleep easily. She liked the City, and she loved to walk its shoreline every day, but she also had debts upon debts, which was why she worked constantly and why the wilderness was as much of a home as any place.

Prospective clients gathered every morning at the official trailheads. Among today's crop were several species that she preferred to humans. But Varid wasn't only peculiar, he proved especially stubborn. She tried to whisk him aside, but he insisted that she should be his porter, making noise about proving his worth and giving away wild bonuses for her trust.

At that point, she interrupted. "No, I won't take you, no." Her voice was sharp, and everything about the scene was in poor form. But at last the man seemed to understand. One last time, his face emptied. Varid finally walked away, slowly approaching the One-after-another. The small success lasted until two other humans approached—a mated couple, unexceptional to the eye—and Katabasis wondered why her day was cursed.

Then the male human did something rare. Not only had he read Katabasis's public posting, he also had some understanding of her species. Raising one hand to make introductions, he looked skyward and called to her by name.

She lifted the backs of her hands, which was how one smiled politely to a stranger.

The human was named Perri. A handsome monkey, athletically built and younger in the face than fashionable, he raised his second hand and introduced his wife. Quee Lee took one step and another and then rested. She was a dark elegant creature built from curving tissues and pleasant odors. But there were telltale signs of intense training and medical trickery at work in the muscle beneath those curves, and the creature's new strength was lashed to reinforced bones that could weather the relentless weight. Making humans ready for this gravity was as much art as engineering. Too much bulk, no matter how powerful, eventually dragged the body to its doom. In most circumstances it was smart to begin small and build the flesh where needed, on the trail and fed by the precious rations. That's why it was a good sign, these humans being smaller than most, and perhaps they understood at least one vital lesson.

Quee Lee raised her arm. "It is an honor to cross paths with you."

"You have made this trek before," Katabasis guessed.

"I managed the half-kilometer from the custom office, yes," she said, her mouth filled with bright teeth.

"But I made the full circuit once," Perri said. "Three hundred years ago, and my wife has been training since I returned home."

"I'm trying to make my life exciting," said Quee Lee.

"I am a boring husband," he said.

The two laughed loudly, excluding the world with their pleasure.

Katabasis studied how they moved, how they stood, and with experience and unsentimental eyes, she sought the warning signs of failure.

"My husband wants to hire you," Quee Lee said, "but I won't survive the journey. My goal is to make the halfway point, into the mountains, and from there someone will have to carry me."

"What about that Wogfound?" Perri asked. "She looks unbreakable."

"Except she'll mock you relentlessly," Katabasis warned.

"I had one on my first trek," Perri said. "Wogfounds are masters of insults and name-calling."

"Well, if I'm riding, then I deserve her abuse," Quee Lee said. "And if I'm dead for a spell, what could the noise matter?"

Three humans and several other alien hikers came to terms with their porters. Contracts were spun and sealed, monies were dropped into accounts of trust, and by then the day was half-finished. The habitat's original owners had come from a world with an eleven-hour day-night cycle, and the present owners maintained at least that tradition. Food and equipment still had to be collected, which was why the porters and their clients wouldn't embark until the next dawn.

Perri asked to be responsible for his needs. Alone, Katabasis returned to that comfortable and familiar but ultimately alien home. A pot of boiled fish and twenty kilos of flame-blackened bread were the day's meal, and then she chewed a stick flavored with mint and iron, walking the salty sand of her favorite beach. The night's sleep lasted for most of three hours, which was typical, and then she woke when the dreams left her no choice, returning to the present and its stolid comforts full of hard work followed by more hard work, from this moment and until the time's end.

2

The good porter knew what to leave behind. Extra clothes were burdens to drop in your tracks. Charms and religious symbols needed to be lighter than whispers, or they were unlucky evils. Even the richest flavors had to be carried in tiny doses, and only dead sticks could be collected along the way, soaked and chewed and then discarded with the body's waste. Water in the wilderness was often tainted and sometimes putrid, if not outright laced with toxins. One rough filtering might leave a thousand awful tastes behind. But immortals lived inside tough, enduring bodies, and what was adventure without suffering? The one great law that couldn't be cheated was that physical work required energy. Energy always meant food. But many of the habitat's species were rare, and some had fallen extinct on their home world, which was why every visitor, local and tourist alike, was forbidden from hunting and grazing. That's why every meal was carried and why each mouthful had to be jammed with nutrition. And the good porter fed herself before the client, because it was imperative that she be the strongest beast on the trail.

Katabasis never brought treats or wet meals. A client might pocket dried fruits or hide away some bloody bit of meat, but if she found these indulgences, she took them for herself. The preferred rations were dense desiccated nuggets. Flavors were coded to color and every tongue had favorites, but basically these were lumps of highly purified fat that would test even an immortal's adaptable guts.

The trek's first days always brought gas and embarrassing smells.

Katabasis expected jokes and had a few of her own at the ready, but Perri and his wife seemed untroubled by the rude noises.

The Wogfound was much less discreet. But the couple treated his jabs as just another series of farts, inevitable and natural, barely worth mentioning in a realm full of oddities.

The humans walked the jungle trail in slow, measured steps. Pseudo-gravity was difficult for its crushing pressure, but another complication was at work: The Great Ship had its own tug, and as the habitat's rim spun upwards, everyone's apparent weight increased. Then the wheel peaked and fell and down came both the body and weight. A one-gee swing rolled past every eight minutes. Clients had to contend with the shifting rules of walking and falling. Humans always fell, and they eventually broke. The other clients and their porters pushed ahead, but Katabasis's little group conquered two kilometers on the first day and tried to hold that pace thereafter, passing through stands of pillar trees and a grove of golden willows growing around cores of carbon fiber, and then came another stretch of pillars that looked identical to the first but were born on an entirely different world. After ten days, the forest came to an abrupt end, replaced with a long valley filled with wooden reefs covered with bug-eating anemones and flower-mouths collected from scattered, left-behind worlds.

Varid was somewhere ahead of them, walking with a Tristerman and the largest Yttytt that Katabasis had ever seen. Tracks and the wind claimed that he was matching paces with those stronger aliens. Perhaps the human felt that he had some point to prove. Maybe he was overextending himself, or maybe Katabasis had been wrong about his nature. The truth didn't matter. She had a client and hers was quite cheerful about his pain, while his wife was proving resilient. Ten days was nothing in a very long journey, but they had a reasonable pace and ample rations, and their camp was pitched before darkness, time left to eat another dense, gut-knotting meal before managing a few hours of sleep and dreams.

The couple slipped into their little tent, and in the careful fashion of weaklings trapped in high gravity, they made love.

The porters listened to the sex, and because he couldn't help himself, the Wogfound offered insults. "Before I carry that monkey," he said, "I will wrap her inside her bedding. She is too ugly to touch in any way."

"She is a beast," Katabasis said agreeably. "But I don't think you will ever carry her."

The challenge was noted. "A wager then, your guess against mine."

"No."

"If you have seen the future," said the Wogfound, "I will pay you what my bonus would have been."

Again, she said, "No."

Pulling his legs beneath his long body, the Wogfound prepared for sleep. "How many times have we walked together, Katabasis?"

"I cannot say."

"Many times perhaps."

"More than many," she said.

"Yet I don't know you at all," he said.

Looking at the armored shell and the three jewel-like eyes, she said, "You are as stupid as you are ugly."

The laughter was abrupt and thunderous. Every anemone yanked into its home, and save for the grunting of two monkeys hiding inside their tent, the reef fell silent. Then with a brazen joyful voice, the Wogfound said, "I know what I am. I am beautiful and brilliant."

"A good thing to know," Katabasis replied.

Shortly after that, the camp fell asleep.

They caught Varid on the seventeenth day, inside an arid valley blasted by the brilliant blue mirage of a sun. He had spent the night there, his tent and rations packed up but still lying on the hot rock. Varid was stretched out on a skeletal chair. He smiled when the others arrived. He aimed the smile at them and spoke a few quiet words, perhaps to his porter, and the One-after-another gave a deep snort. A furnace would be hotter, but not much. Varid was drenched with sweat, but to prove his strength he lifted one of those very powerful arms, wincing when he held the open hand high.

"I've been waiting for you," he said.

Perri was leading. Seventeen days and the previous trek had taught him how to move against the relentless weight. Never lift the leg higher than necessary; keep the back straight and strong. Only motions essential to covering the next half-meter were allowed. He wore minimal clothes and light boots and a body that could live for another million years. But immortality didn't make animals into machines. He was suffering as he shuffled forward, and his voice was slow when he said, "Thank you for waiting. You're nothing but kind."

Katabasis heard sarcasm and pain.

Varid appeared oblivious. Still smiling, he turned and said something else to his porter, and then he broke into an oversized laugh.

With her four back legs, the One-after-another stomped at the ground. They weren't a verbal species, but those motions signaled frustration.

"I was traveling with several friends," said Varid, "but I tripped and fell yesterday, rather hard, and the others continued without me."

They had seen their chance to get free of you, thought Katabasis.

Perri stopped walking, breathing deeply. "A bad fall, was it?"

"Bones poking through skin and some torn tendons."

Quee Lee caught up with her husband. "Are you having trouble healing?"

"I never have trouble healing." Varid sat up, the veins in his forehead ready to burst. "No, I decided to let you catch me. I wanted someone to talk to."

"I am dreary company," said the One-after-another.

Varid stood carefully, and his chair collapsed into a fist-sized bundle.

Katabasis had served hundreds of humans, and none were like him. She wondered about the effects of drugs and other elixirs ingested for this journey. She wondered if one of the alien "friends" had tripped the man, perhaps intentionally—a common event out on the trails.

"May I walk with you?" Varid asked.

"Absolutely," Quee Lee said, slowly passing her husband.

The One-after-another stowed the chair and balanced all of the gear on her broad back. Three humans and their porters continued up the desert valley. A long stone wall had been cut through the middle with explosives, and they slipped into the gap and entered the remains of someone's attempted home—tunnels and oval rooms and bits of debris that might have been precious once or might have been trash. Katabasis never enjoyed walking this ground. Each time, without fail, she thought about lost homes and the ignorant strangers who would feel nothing when they passed through what others had once treasured.

Quee Lee was in the lead. Perceiving a challenge, Varid found his legs and got busy chasing her.

Every tradition told the porters to remain behind, watching the slow, painful, and ultimately useless race.

The parched trail eventually swung back toward the wheel's center, and after a long climb over a diamondcrete ridge, they dropped into a fresh drainage and different climate. The sun was always directly overhead, but now it turned pale and small. The air filled with mist. The vegetation was several shades of black, every plant held up by multiple trunks, supporting hungry canopies and fluorescing wings wrapped around giant insect bodies.

"Beautiful," said Quee Lee.

Glancing up, Perri stumbled, the bones in his left leg splintering from the unexpected impact, and he collapsed and hit the ground, shattering his cheek and eye socket against bare stone.

Quee Lee returned to him. There was no reason for worry, but she settled beside him anyway.

Varid was ahead of everyone, smiling at his fortune.

"I could make you feel better," Quee Lee said.

"In no time," her husband agreed.

"But others are lurking."

The two of them laughed.

Then Quee Lee looked at the other human. "Have we met him? He seems just a little familiar."

They didn't have access to a nexus. Memory was what counted, and despite the blood plastered across his face and a crooked leg trying to straighten itself, Perri had enough focus to decide, "I don't remember a man like him. And I think I would."

"Maybe he isn't the same person now," said Quee Lee.

Perri wiped the gore from under his eye. "Maybe something happened to him."

"Maybe I should ask him," Quee Lee said.

Perri laughed softly.

"You're right," she said. "This is a long walk. There'll be plenty of boring to fight off before the end."

A central valley led toward the distant mountains, and the River East was slow leaden water down its middle. For three days the trail pushed close to the water, and just when the routine and climate became familiar, they crossed the river on a massive bridge of granite slabs and granite columns.

Another ridge demanded to be climbed.

Half a kilometer was one day's work, and they weren't yet to the top.

They camped again and ate shavings from their supplies, and nobody complained about the taste of the water. The spring at their feet was cool and clear, little crustaceans leaving feces that tasted like something called pepper. Beside them was a grove of tashaleen trees—massive trunks laced with glass, each supporting fat bladders filled with sulfuric acid. Tashaleens periodically flooded the landscape to maintain their monoculture, but none were ripe at present, and they had lovely red colors that pushed deep into the infrared.

Today Varid had broken the little bones inside one foot. They healed fast enough, but the foot needed hard rubbing.

The couple sat opposite him, leaning against one another.

Katabasis was sitting alone, chewing steadily on a dead black stick laced with bright flavors.

After a long silence, Varid cleared his throat. Smiling at his foot, he lifted his hand, and then he turned to smile at his fingers as he said, "Name anyone luckier than us."

There was optimism in the voice.

And there wasn't.

"Nobody is luckier," Quee Lee said.

Perri watched the man. "What luck are you talking about?"

"Buying passage on the Great Ship," said Varid. "That's an honor beyond measure."

How could anyone disagree?

"I feel blessed."

"Where did you come from?" Perri asked.

"Mellis 4."

"That's a colony world," Quee Lee said. "In the Outskirt District, isn't it?"

Varid seemed to hear the question, and for a moment he looked ready to formulate an answer. But then his face emptied, and everybody sat waiting. Eventually he stared at Perri, and after another long pause asked, "What's your background? From where did you come?"

"Nowhere. I was born on the Ship."

"Are you some captain's child, or something else?"

"Something else," said Perri.

Varid nodded slowly, as if he was working through the myriad possibilities. But he didn't ask for more information. He shifted his focus to Quee Lee, ready to ask the same question.

"I was born on the Earth," she volunteered.

"I want to visit the Earth," Varid said. "Once the voyage ends, I plan to walk all across its ancient ground."

The Great Ship wouldn't return home for another two hundred thousand years. And that was assuming nothing disastrous happened during the long, long journey.

The married humans glanced at each other.

Varid appeared excited, staring at the ground and the once-injured foot, smiling and breathing faster until he suddenly looked up, hunting for another worthwhile face.

"Katabasis," he said.

His porter let her plumage flatten, showing disinterest.

"Your name," he said. "There's a human word that sounds like Katabasis."

The others looked at her. Even the other porters were curious.

This had happened several times before, human clients recognizing the word. But to have this odd dim creature bring up the matter like this, without warning…well, it was astonishing. Katabasis held her breath, the hearts in her thighs pushing blood into her face, making it more purple than usual.

"What word is 'Katabasis'?" asked Quee Lee.

"It is very old, and Greek," Varid said. "I wish I could remember what it meant. Maybe I knew once, but then again…."

His voice faded, yet the face seemed more alive than usual, dark eyes sparkling and the mouth very small, very intense.

Perri looked at his porter. "Is that a coincidence?"

"No," she admitted.

Quee Lee was interested enough to stand up and shuffle closer. "You took the name when you came here. Didn't you?"

"It's a tradition," Katabasis explained. "Move to another realm, and you embrace some name from those in power."

Varid's face changed again, back to its flat, vague, and apparently empty ways. But he lifted the hand that had rubbed the foot that couldn't be any healthier, and he asked the hand, "How did you find your way to the Great Ship?"

The other porters put their ears and eyes on her.

Then Katabasis surprised herself. With her voice cool and pleasant, she said, "I walked here. And I walked and walked and walked."

3

She wasn't Katabasis and wasn't immortal, and she knew her tiny age and critical place, always going to sleep certain that a great family loved her. She lived inside the world's stronghold. A wedge-hole decorated with painted pretties was where she slept, and the girl had a collection of flavored sticks to chew on, and every morning one of the household warriors would lick her bare toes, waking her with a hot rough tongue.

"The maiden is expected," the warrior would say, or words to that effect. "The Five are waiting in the study with books and high expectations."

The Five were a fierce and wealthy and much respected marriage. Royalty and elected leaders didn't exist in the world and couldn't be envisioned by the People. But three women and two husband/brothers sat astride generations of obligations and large favors. The girl wasn't one of the Five's children, not by blood or by adoption. But she was a Hopeful, which meant that she was endowed with some talent or compelling strength that had made her worth purchasing from forgotten parents.

"The Five are waiting," was a ritual statement. Time was too precious to share with even the most promising half-grown citizen. But there were mornings when one of the Five, usually the younger brother/husband, would march past the two hundred Hopefuls, handing out assignments and lofty words about the future before chasing after even more pressing ceremonies.

The typical morning brought small groups divided by skills and led by teachers who loved the subject in hand. Sometimes Hopefuls were gathered in the arena where they played elaborate games full of lessons and fun that kept them busy until the day's meal and the night's sleep. Even better were days when a girl was told to read alone and contemplate every word. But reflective lessons brought warriors on the next morning—warriors delivering hard training because it was important to drive the laziness from these young, spoiled souls.

The girl's gift was mathematics, and in particular, cumbersome formulas with their tangled alliances and deep abstractions. On the best days, a teacher and one warrior would pull aside the mathematicians—eleven Hopefuls, including her closest friends—and they would leave the stronghold, going out into the great, lovely, and nearly perfect world to test their knowledge against what was real.

All that was worth knowing was built upon formulas.

The world was one day's walk wide, on average, and fifteen days in length, shaped rather like a passion worm dying on hot rock. The world stood upon an old mountain range. Left in their natural state, those eroded peaks would catch only the rare rain, and perhaps a few rock-scions would grow in the valleys. But the People had built forests of broad towers standing above the tired, broken-down tectonics. Each life in the world had its job. Gardeners and their vines dangled out of the windows while J'jjs and clonetakes sang from cages, begging their keepers for feed. The buildings' interiors were full of wedge-holes and broad hallways, and every floor had its stockers and teachers, weavers and gossips. Especially important were the miners who left every evening, descending to the hot plains to work with their electric machines. They cut fresh stone from the quarries and smelted metals from the best ores available. Other citizens tended the fans that stood high, dancing with the winds to supply power, and those who knew the dew-catchers watered the crops and every mouth. There was majesty and perfection in this labor. Every mouth attached to a working mind sang praises to the world's rich life.

The towers demanded endless construction, and construction demanded endless calculation.

This girl, the happy young Hopeful, was being groomed to design new walls and reinforce old buttresses. If she couldn't look forward to the day, at least she was resigned to her duty, and it was a good day whenever a teacher looked at her work, saying without too much difficulty that she was showing that most precious talent: "Promise."

She never imagined that outside events could interrupt her future.

Who does at such an age?

The best mornings found the budding mathematicians riding in bubbles strung on electrified cables, climbing to the highest rooftops. Where the air was thin and chill was her favorite place. Deep pleasure could be found in those vistas. The girl always stole moments to look past the world. The surrounding plains were rough and ugly, but there was a horizon to seek, though it was often masked by dust and the occasional cloud. She carried a worn-out telescope rescued from the school's garbage, and if she was very lucky and the lessons went into evening, she had stars to admire and neighboring worlds, and sometimes several moons graced the sky with their trusted round faces.

Each class was accompanied by at least one trained, well-armed warrior. The Hopefuls had real value and might tempt their enemies. Other worlds and other People lived beyond the horizon. Perhaps those same enemies would come here to steal away their talent: It had never happened and never would happen, but there was pleasure in the possibility. Who doesn't wish to be valuable, to be special?

One day-journey reached into evening and then farther. The teacher had critical points to deliver about bracing towers and the telltale signs of strain on a windmill blade, and she steadfastly refused to leave this high place until every student absorbed her competence.

Thinking no one was watching, the girl drifted away.

But the warrior noticed and climbed after her, finding her chewing a fresh stick of dribbledoe while pushing the little telescope against her eye. The nearest moon was overhead—gray and airless, pocked with volcanoes that sometimes threw up columns of soot that left a soft ring in its orbit. She watched the moon's limb and stared at patches of stars, and because this was one of those rare perches where every direction was visible, she turned in a slow circle, trying to absorb the precious vista.

The warrior was young and bold. He crept up on the girl, and wanting to startle her, tried to drop the cold gun barrel against her beautiful neck.

"Your feet are sloppy," she warned, not looking at him. "I have listened to your approach since you left class."

He paused, embarrassed and laughing.

She chewed and looked toward tomorrow's dawn, where night was full and the land empty of any feature worthy of a name. "I wish I had a true telescope," she said. "Like one of the giants perched on top of the stronghold."

"They are impressive machines," he agreed.

"Have you even seen them?" she asked doubtfully.

"I saw all of them during my training, of course. They are the 'long eyes' for the warrior guild."

"But have you ever used one?"

He smiled and said, "Only the largest telescope. I looked through it once, just to see what could be seen."

She smiled with her free hand. "What did you see?"

"The nearest worlds," he said, pointing his weapon at the mountains riding the western horizon. "Skies were clear, clearer than tonight, and I saw amazing details."

"I don't care about those worlds," she said. "Did you look at the sky?"

"No."

She studied him.

"We don't have enemies in the sky," he said.

Every mountain range was a world standing alone, and the plains and scalding oceans between the ranges would kill any person who lingered too long.

The young warrior said nothing, wondering what to make of his complicated, shifting feelings for this child.

She turned to the redness where the sun had just vanished. "I've seen lights in that sky."

"Flyers," he said.

"I know what they are."

"Then why didn't you call them that?"

"I wish we had flyers," she said.

"We could build them, if we needed them."

"I suppose."

"We are as smart as the other nations," he said with authority.

The girl found a faint dark bulge where a young volcano pushed high into the wet heights of the sky.

"Our world is little," she said.

"Our world is great," he said.

"Nonetheless, we are small and poor. And the hills beneath us are nearly exhausted."

The warrior pretended not to be bothered by this topic.

She lowered the telescope, reading his face and his feet. "You really don't know very much, do you?"

"I know quite a lot."

She said nothing.

"Our fans catch the winds," he said. "And we have other machines that can snatch words out of the wind."

"Those are radios. Yes, our teachers talk about them."

He stood as tall as possible. "I've listened to the radios. Have you?"

"What did you hear?" she asked.

"Have you listened to them?"

"No."

"I have heard voices," he said.

"Did you understand the voices?"

"No."

With a gesture, she proved that she wasn't impressed.

"But I have a good friend," he insisted. "My friend's duty is to translate the other languages, making sense of our enemies' words."

"Are these words interesting?"

"Maybe."

"What does 'maybe' mean?"

Suddenly the warrior wished the topic would vanish. But he was also young and willing to risk everything to impress this odd, odd girl. So against his best instincts, he said, "There is a secret. Only the Five and their children and a few chosen People are allowed to know this secret."

"And you too," she said.

He smiled.

She said, "Tell me."

"Aliens," he said, pointing at that last glimmer of ruddy light. "At this moment, aliens are walking on that world."

Each world stood on its own mountains, and each was isolated by the dry wastelands. Every mature world had its own People. Ten thousand species of People were scattered across the face of Existence. Existence was the planet, and the planet had lived forever, and the word "alien" was normally used for the strangest, most remote species of People.

"What are you talking about?" she asked.

"I am sorry," he said. "'Alien' is a weak word for what I mean."

"What do you mean?"

"I know a new word." The warrior looked up at the churning moon and cold stars, and using a nervous, inexpert mouth, he tried to say the word.

"What is that?" she asked. "What does 'human' mean?"

4

Clients had to praise scenery. After spending and suffering too much, it was their duty to collapse on some little knoll, singing about the lovely colors and intoxicating odors and the magical properties of an ordinary breeze. Species and the lay of the land refused to stay the same. "Walking across twenty worlds wouldn't be this interesting," clients would sing. But how many of them had walked across even one world during their wealthy long lives? That was a good question never asked, certainly not by the stolid porters following behind, saying nothing while dreaming about grateful tips.

The rare client had careful eyes. Perri paid attention, but the skill was sharpest in the morning and faded with exhaustion. Quee Lee was less interested in scenery, but she was vigilant about her footing, measuring every step and each hesitation, ignoring the usual vistas until she was sure that she couldn't fall. That made her the client who found animal tracks and odd rocks and bits of litter left by thousands of parties exactly like theirs, and unlike many, she asked big questions of the porters and then tried to paint the answers on the insides of her cavernous mind.

Varid existed at the other end of the spectrum: He was nearly blind. Wide scenes and telling details were ignored as he marched forward. What he did notice—what was bright and exceptionally real to the man—were the various ailments rolling inside him. Katabasis saw flashes of misery in the face. Sometimes a foot broke, or a rib; more often it was chronic fatigue. But even when he was rested and whole, his surroundings passed with little notice. The man filled that tiny chair in the morning, doing nothing and plainly thinking nothing, eyes open and pointing in some random direction, observing nothing as the rest of the camp made ready for the day's next kilometer or two.

"He is the oddest monkey," the Wogfound remarked. "Have you ever known a creature like him?"

"I never have, no," Katabasis said with certainty.

"And do you know how he sleeps?"

Recalling Varid's peculiar, unwelcome interest in her, she said, "I know nothing of the kind."

"I know quite a lot," said the Wogfound. "Look inside his shelter. During the night, early or late, the moment doesn't matter. The creature lies on his back, holding a light before his face."

"Which light?"

"His camp torch turned up high, or a blank reading net draped over his face, and I once saw him with a captured blazebee between his fingers."

"Did you ask what he was doing?"

"I demanded to know. But he didn't reply."

"And did he wonder what you were doing, poking into his business?"

"From what I see, I doubt that creature is capable of wonder."

Katabasis absorbed the words, unsure what to believe.

But the Wogfound had a ready explanation. "The body is human enough, but that mind is alien. Perhaps Sorry-gones have made a nest inside the head."

"Not Sorry-gones, no," she said. Varid was bizarre, but he was still human in her gaze. She wanted him to be human, maybe even needed that, but she didn't want to dwell on reasons, much less the state of his mind.

"Watch him sleep," her colleague advised.

"You may snoop for both of us," she said. "With my blessing."

Days later, a torrential rain struck the valley where they were walking. Fat drops of water and ice battered exposed heads, and the ground that wasn't flooded was left too slippery for any human foot.

Varid remained inside his tent for the rest of the day.

Just once, Katabasis looked in at him. The man had cut a small hole in the fabric and water fell through, hammering the blank gaze and the mouth that was moving as if talking, but not talking to her and maybe not to himself either. He made no noise. The lips were busy and then they stopped, and after a long moment Varid turned his head, not quite looking at her when he found the breath to say, "I like rain. I always have liked rain. I think."

The storm passed in the night, replaced by cooler, drier air.

Perri took the lead in the morning and held it until he stumbled, shattering his knee and pelvis. Quee Lee passed him. "I'd stay and keep you company, darling. My darling. But I can smell the mountains now."

"Push on," he said amiably.

"I already have," replied Quee Lee, her head down, focusing on the next meter of wicked pebbles and greasy soil.

Katabasis unfastened her tumpline and various straps, lowering her pack onto a boulder where it would wait without complaint. Settling beside the injured man, she said, "Let me carry you over the next rise."

"And earn your bonus," Perri said.

They laughed together.

Varid was approaching as the giant wheel spun upwards, making him heavier. Leaden feet needed to rest before taking any next step, and the man kept his head down, but more out of exhaustion than to pay strict attention. Meanwhile the ground kept trying to drop him. He wasn't clumsy in any normal sense; when he slipped or staggered, his feet often found the grace to save him. And then as he passed by, the wheel began to fall again, and inspired by that slight lessening of weight, Varid grew bold. Straightening his back, he managed longer strides, conquering the next low rise before his left leg leaped out in front of him, the monkey knee wrenched in a decidedly unnatural direction.

The moaning was urgent and familiar.

Katabasis and her client remained where they were. Eventually the moans softened, and turning to Katabasis, Perri said, "I finally remembered the story."

"Which story?"

"Wait."

The One-after-another was stomping past them with a furious air. Perri waited for her to leave, and then rubbing his healing leg, he said, "Our brains work so well. Living bioceramics woven around the original neural network, with horizon-sinks latching tight to every idea and event and whispered word. In theory, we shouldn't forget anything for the next ten million years. Isn't that what you hear when you get the upgrade?"

The human leg grew scorching hot as the healing quickened. There was beauty in the infrared glow. "Were you upgraded?" Katabasis asked.

"No, I was born exactly this way," Perri admitted. "Humans usually are.

But some little instinct tells me you were born elsewhere and maybe you heard the sales pitch one or two times."

"We are talking about Varid," she said.

"We were," Perri agreed.

They sat for a moment, neither speaking.

"Varid," said Perri. "I finally managed to remember the man. He didn't have quite the same face and his hair was black then. I met him at a very splendid party. And I know what are you asking: 'Why was this rough fellow at a splendid party?' Because his wife moves in some very high orbits, and Varid used to belong to the highest reaches of the high. That's why."

"Varid was a captain?" Katabasis asked doubtfully.

"Oh, no. There are even loftier souls than those dreary uniforms." Perri laughed. "I'm thinking about a civilian family—mother and father and several grown children accompanied by assorted mates and mistresses and thinking toys. One family, and they owned corporations and key patents and the entire Mellis solar system. They even had one of the fastest streakships in human hands. Varid happened to be one of those children, and his clan was among the Ship's first paying passengers, human or otherwise. They purchased the largest quarters in the Ship's most exclusive district, and seeing no reason to leave that paradise, they rarely took the trouble."

Perri winced and smiled and looked at Katabasis. "Perhaps your people are never smug, self-involved, or dismissive. Since my only experience with your species is you, I can't say. But that rich human family was all those things, and Varid—the original Varid—was pried from the same complacent mold. I keep massaging my head. There probably are other incidents. But I've remembered the one party and that single occasion when we crossed paths. We held drinks and faced each other and spoke at length about his grand wealth and the happiness that went with that wealth, and when I found my chance, I left. I didn't see the man again until that day at the trailhead. Thousands of years had passed, and I never felt the urge to seek him out, and I'd wager anyone's wealth that Varid didn't hunger for my company. But of course that's one of the sterling benefits of the Great Ship—you can avoid the souls you don't like at all, unless it happens to be yours."

From the hilltop, Varid groaned mightily.

"That is the man you met," Katabasis said skeptically.

"No." Perri showed his teeth. "Or yes."

She waited.

"Seven hundred years ago, I found myself trapped inside another smug party. Some honorable charity was involved. Quee Lee promised her time and money, and certain lady friends insisted that she bring her wild wandering husband along. Rich ladies have always loved wild wandering husbands, just so long as we weren't their problem. The party lasted ten days, which is about average, and there were ten thousand dull conversations to endure, and I drank more than was proper. But I told a few stories after my wanderings, and nobody seemed too offended. Which was when I discovered that I was, despite my own smugness, enjoying myself.

"On the tenth day, I happened across a group of strange faces. These people were too important to arrive until the end, and they clearly knew one another. The topic was homes and circumstances. It seemed that everybody had moved recently, judging by the sense of adventure when they described the giant apartments that they still had barely explored. And then according to some rule or tradition peculiar to them, they started to tell stories about the Fire.

"'Which fire,' I asked, meaning no harm.

"One lady turned to me and very calmly said, 'The Whisper Fire,' before turning back to her friends."

He paused, watching Katabasis.

She said nothing.

"The Whisper Fire was eleven hundred years before that evening." Perri studied his porter's face while giving his knee a stern rubbing. "Eighteen hundred years ago, and maybe you don't remember. Maybe you weren't onboard yet. But the Fire was a fusion nightmare. It was very big, very dangerous. Of course our brains are tough, tough, tough. But nuclear temperatures eat away baryonic material. Even hyperfiber will eventually collapse back into plasma. The Fire was extinguished within the day, but mistakes and confusion led to many disasters, and some very important enclaves were obliterated before they could be evacuated."

Katabasis nodded, saying nothing.

"Do you see my confusion? More than a millennium had passed, yet those jittery rich people were still dealing with the disaster. Which for some reason struck me as fun, and I remained at the edge of the group for a very long time, listening to old stories mixed with occasional bites of fresh news."

He paused, and she said, "Varid."

"They didn't use his name. They used his family name, and just when I was beginning to feel a vague familiarity, someone mentioned that all of the family but one had perished: Parents and siblings, servants and spouses, plus the grandchildren born inside the Great Ship. All of them were inside their enclave. The enclave was consumed totally. There was only one survivor, except survival didn't come in the usual sense of things."

Katabasis didn't want to hear anything more about Varid. Her pack was waiting to be carried, and she wondered if she would look cowardly or rude, sliding inside those heavy straps and walking over the hill.

She resisted the impulse.

Perri's voice softened, saddened. "A team of salvage experts and ship engineers had finally cut into the deepest ruins. A thousand years had passed, and inside the amorphous glass and bottled poisons they found a piece of brain that hadn't quite died. I was fascinated. How could you not help but be? I wanted to know how most of a mind can be vaporized but a sliver is spared. What odd chaos of fluid mechanics allows that kind of half-blessing? I asked questions. They ignored my questions. Finally the man's name was mentioned, and the woman in the know spoke about a long convalescence that had only just begun and made no sense to any of them. 'The boy was legally and literally dead,' said this very pretty, very civilized lady. Discussing a many-thousand-year-old entity, she said, 'What is left of the boy is residue, it is trash. Why build a body for the emptiness that remains?'"

On the hilltop, the One-after-another was stomping her encouragement to her miserable client.

"'Besides,' the lady said, 'the boy's portion of the estate was always tiny. He was the least-favorite child with the least-liked offspring. Any holdings back home have been inherited by cousins and odd twigs on the family spruce, and which leaves him close to destitute before he takes even one step from the hospital.'"

Katabasis looked up the trail.

Perri slowly rolled over and set both hands against the ground. Every limb pushed as he stood on his rebuilt leg, testing bone and the pain while that lovely heat faded.

"You're certain that this is the same man," Katabasis said.

"I'm certain of nothing. I don't have a nexus and so how can I check?" He lifted the foot and dropped it, barely holding his balance. "Of course I've considered asking the source. My sense is that he would tell me, if he could. But even if every detail is wrong…even if this is a different, unrelated Varid…I think at its heart, our story remains true.

"Our friend is a shell."

A series of owners had strived to make the mountains spectacular, each investing capital into endless sandwiches of cultured granite and diamond-crete and hyperfiber bracing and hyperfiber scrap, creating a range of increasingly treacherous hills that rose up to scenic summits and starved air.

Several hundred days of steady toil brought them to the foothills and the source of the River East. The party camped in a forest of happen-trees—vast gray plates tipped on end and halfway buried in the ruddy ground—and the humans rested, gathering energy for the push to the highest ridge. The next day was slow and taxing, but they conquered a hundred meters more than planned. Two travelers passed them in the end, both riding their porters. One was poet-bird, and with an important singsong voice he said, "Swallow your pride and ride, brothers and sister. Regret is sweeter pain than a hundred splintered bones."

In their group, nobody rode. The day after was very slow and became slower when Quee Lee took a hard spill, shattering her face and her back. But she refused the Wogfound's attempts to call her broken and carry her for the rest of the way, and when Perri offered his hand, she laughed and said, "You genuinely don't know me, do you?"

The day after that proved steady and very productive. No one fell. Not even a small bone was shattered. One of Katabasis's favorite campsites proved empty and as inviting as always—a glade of rainbow-colored foliage that never looked the same twice. She set down her pack and helped her client pitch his tent, and the Wogfound came over to complain about many matters, many failures, while waiting for the One-after-another to finish her duties.

Quee Lee lay in the open glade, on her back, legs flat. She was sobbing. She was laughing. Tears made the day-old face shine in sun that was as unnatural as it was brilliant—a fierce white glare that encompassed equal portions of the visible spectrum, feeding plants from at least a hundred worlds.

Finished with her chores, Katabasis rested where the ground was dampest, happily doing nothing while her trousers and plumage grew soggy.

Her colleagues marched past. "If we had made that wager," said the One-after-another, "you would win tomorrow."

"Or I would lose tomorrow," said Katabasis.

Jeweled eyes studied the prostrate human. "As you say, she is a beast."

"Am I the beast?" asked Quee Lee.

"You are," Katabasis said. "You are going to climb these mountains."

"I am a great beast, yes," she said, smiling a little more.

Perri was beneath the little tent, preparing their aerogel bed.

Varid emerged from his shelter and on the third attempt managed to stand, walking slowly across the bright glade. Varid wanted to stare at Quee Lee. This was a recent habit, and no one acted offended or intrigued by the attention. But Katabasis was curious how this evening's conversation would play out. She didn't join her colleagues. Instead she studied the diminished human and the lovely beast who kept weeping from pleasure, and she was doing nothing else when a thick layer of scrap rock shifted on the slope behind her. An instant later several million tons of black granite swept across the glade, crushing and burying everything within ten steps of where Katabasis was sitting.

Two porters were gone.

Three survivors called for their companions, searching until well after dark, but nothing answered the pleas, and except for a few binnerlings dancing across the rubble, nothing moved.

Varid didn't join the search. Walking to where Quee Lee had been, he lay down, filling the imprint of her body and shutting his eyes and opening them again, and out from the blackness he said a few true words.

"Somebody else will dig them up."

Then, with a well-earned expertise, he added, "It's amazing what you can survive, and with only a little luck."

5

Her cadre of Hopefuls were about to graduate. Childhood was finished and her original wedge-chamber was too small for comfort. But the warrior always came past in the morning, licking toes and feet and the lower legs that stuck out into the hallway. It was the same warrior who several years ago told her about humans. The secret had seemed wondrous, overwhelming. Creatures from a distant sun had come to their planet, to Existence, and at least one of them was now walking the face of a neighboring world. But knowledge that grand couldn't remain special for long. Teachers and every Hopeful and eventually even the old servants in the latrine began discussing the odd beasts that fell from the sky. Some claimed the Five were using radio winds to chat with the humans. These newcomers were few and wouldn't stay long—gravity was crushing for their weak constitutions—but every story agreed on this: Creatures from nameless places were making pledges of peace and cultural trade as well as long speeches about their glorious, magical nature.

Soon the People inside the stronghold and throughout the world understood that great events were flowing.

And they understood nothing.

One morning the young woman was dreaming, and then she felt the touch and wetness of the tongue. But the warrior wasn't licking between her toes. She was awake and in the next groggy moment felt the six fingers of a hand tugging at her leg while an excited, angry, and almost incomprehensible voice—her closest friend among the mathematicians—said something about hurrying to the arena. "Come now," he said. "The Five are meeting with everybody, and everybody is late."

The girl dressed as she walked. A big, naturally strong creature, she broke into a smooth foot-skimming run in the hallways, convinced that she was in trouble for being tardy but then discovering that no, she was among the first of the invited guests.

The Five appeared together only on ceremonial days. But this was a special occasion, and this was the new Five—the oldest wife had died recently, replaced by a smart young husband with a thousand valuable favors owed to him. The new husband sat as he should, off to the side, his mouth closed. Today's oldest wife spoke for the group, and for a long while she said nothing except to urge the People to come forward and push close, and once there was no more space under the dome, she demanded that everyone remain silent and attentive.

Thousands of People breathed in sips, making no sound.

"There is a new word in our world," said the wife. Then with an unnatural growl to the voice, she said, "Human."

The excitement was felt, but no one spoke or moved.

"Humans are why we have called each other together," the wife continued. "Star-creatures have crossed a tremendous desert to sit close to our realm. But they are not part of our world, and they have no plans to visit our world, and it is time to admit why: Because we are poor. They ignore the People because we have ordinary resources and unspectacular knowledge. And compared to those sitting on younger mountains, we are few. So they are not here and never will be here, and only the raving fool bolsters herself with bold, impossible talk."

Honesty was rougher than any tongue. The full-grown Hopeful kept silent and tried to remain still, but she felt herself turning slowly, scanning the tight-packed faces until she found the gathered warriors.

They were made of stronger stone than her. Her warrior never let his gaze wander, and he didn't flinch as the speech continued.

"We are poor and few," said the wife, "and even worse, our long prospects are miserable. Our old world is crumbling beneath us. A new world might suddenly burst out of the nearby plains, affording us fresh homes. But

mountains are fickle gods, and this is why my family and all of the People
have spent generations making ready for a longer exodus. Out on the horizon, perhaps somewhere past dawn, stands a row of young mountains
too remote to be settled or too weak to resist our arrival. This has always
been our destination, our salvation—a plan aimed at a heartbeat some
thousand years in the future.

"But now we have a second destination: The humans. They are powerful
beasts wielding tools that scare even our strongest neighbors. To move from
star to star and manage that trick so easily—it astonishes our little minds.
But humans are creatures of honor and heroism. Appreciating favors and
good deeds, their main emissary has made an offer to all worlds and all
species of People. Give the humans a worthy gift, and they will grant us
passage to a starship. The starship is larger than our entire planet. Give
them greater gifts, and they will grant the People infinite life. Then their
Great Ship will carry us to some new planet where empty beautiful worlds
stand above deserts that aren't as ugly or as hot as ours.

"The Five have decided to embark on this bold migration. Today we are
offering each of you the opportunity to walk with us across the emptiness.
We will travel in the same ways our ancestors strode to these mountains
when they were new—by wheel and by foot, one night at a time. And
once we reach our benefactors, we shall give them a gift, a great gift—a
wondrous, perfect gift worthy of passage on this giant vessel of theirs."

The speaker paused. From the adjacent hallway came an electric wagon
bearing a stout steel box, locked and secured with steel straps.

"An object waits inside," explained the wife. "My ancestors dug this treasure out of the throat of the volcano that built the land beneath us, and it
has belonged to my family since…our grandest, loveliest treasure, worth
a million favors from creatures such as these human beasts."

6

There was no reason for grief. The weight of twenty mountains meant
nothing to the modern mind. Two porters were temporarily misplaced,
bodiless but safe, bathed in partial comas that let them feel angry about
their miserable luck and the loss of income but eternally confident that the
landlords or colleagues would eventually come after them with a shovel.

The landslide was no grave, and besides, Katabasis's colleagues were
never true friends.

Why then was she sorrowful?

Humans thought of grief as being something that lived inside them, toxic and massive and often crippling. But Katabasis was not human. She sat on the damp ground, and a bright cloud hung about her face and shoulders. Her companions couldn't see the sharp blue light pouring into her body and brain. They didn't realize that anguish brought strength and absolute focus, which was the hallmark of her species: Horrible, withering losses could strike the species, yet the survivors' instinctive response was to grow lighter and even braver, pushing toward some goal that had never seemed more precious.

"Maybe we should turn around and walk back to City East," Quee Lee said.

"Back is nearly as far as forward," said Perri.

"I won't go back," Varid said.

"Well, food won't be a problem now," Perri said. "We have supplies for six, including two giants."

"And one good back to carry the wealth," his wife said.

"I'm going on," said Varid. He was holding a rigid golden leaf against the torchlight, watching it dry and then smolder and finally burn.

"We might hire new porters, if we push ahead," Perri said.

"A strong porter carrying a dead client," his wife agreed. "And we would pay bonuses for the extra work, of course."

"One pissed-off Wogfound," Perri said. "That's all we need."

The porter recognized the smartest strategy. But Katabasis was larger than her job, and she was older than her job, and she wanted to hold their present course, not involving anyone outside her family.

Whose family?

She caught herself, shaken by her thoughts.

Suddenly the reasons for grief stood in the open. She had a family once, a great embracing family, but they were lost on a distant trail. The porters trapped underground weren't dead, but they served as triggers for these immortal aches, and these three fragile aliens—the unlikely lords of the galaxy—suddenly meant more to her than anyone else alive.

Katabasis made small sorrowful gestures, fighting to find her voice.

Varid dropped the burning leaf. With a big voice, he said, "Do what you wish, people. But I don't need a porter."

Quee Lee opened her mouth and closed it again, waiting.

"I'll carry my own rations and sleep in the open and don't worry about me."

Perri touched his wife's knee, and she met his stare. With nothing but faces, the ancient couple settled into prolonged conversation. Two rational minds were deciding how to argue with the damaged man. Watching their eyes and mouths, Katabasis remained silent, waiting for the reasonable tone and the most responsible plan. All at once Quee Lee brightened. She smiled and managed to laugh, slowly lifting herself to her knees and hands and then to her feet, shuffling over to Varid, her voice high and light when she said, "My porter is lost, and I don't know where to turn."

Varid looked up through the weak smoke.

Quee Lee dropped a hand on his shoulder. "What I want to do, if you'll let me…I want to hire you as my new porter."

All the days spent together, and Varid had never shown surprise. Until now he had been a flat, simple creature. But his eyes jumped open. He tried to breathe and failed, and then with a nervous tone asked, "Why me?"

"You're the strongest back available," she said simply.

Katabasis looked at Perri. Was this a genuine offer?

Perri replied with the appropriate hand gesture, slicing the air to say, "This is reasonable to me."

"I don't know," said Varid.

Quee Lee said, "Please."

Then the man smiled, and it wasn't just a grin that had been practiced during rehabilitation. Varid smiled with his face and entire body, leaning into the hand's touch, an effusive voice rolling across the glade and the avalanche, saying, "Of course I will. I will be your porter, yes."

Two days after the disaster, they reached the first summit. Thousands of boots and bare feet had stood on the highest ground, killing all but the flattest and the toughest. Lichen from various worlds painted the stone, and a pair of ragdogs followed closely, ignoring Katabasis to beg for treats from the humans. The four walked slowly from view to view. On each peak, Perri and Quee Lee would discuss the scenery and animals and the rich smells on the breeze and how much farther they might cover before one of them broke another hip. Then some detail or single word would trigger memories in both of them, and suddenly they were talking about events and places buried deep in their shared past, and they laughed and often kissed, and Katabasis was weary of the game.

Varid paid no attention to the show. He was playing the role of porter, and Quee Lee was nothing but his client. For two mornings he had made a show of loading and balancing his tiny pack before claiming that he was ready to carry more. A portion of his rations and a tiny piece of hers were inside the pack, plus his aerogel bed and a few other lightweight essentials.

There was extra room, but Katabasis always had the ready excuse not to add grams to a body that would break several times on the best days. She had to be cautious. In the history of this world, there had never been a slower, more fragile porter. Nor could Katabasis remember any colleague who took his work half as seriously.

Tents were a brutal kilogram best left in one of the official trash heaps. Bodies and beds spent the night on the final summit, and when snow fell they gathered inside the same rocky bowl, waking early beneath half a meter of dry fluff. Several valleys radiated down from the final summit. Katabasis selected the most forgiving slope, but that didn't stop accidents and breaks and extra food ingested to make up for lost heat and chronic repairs. Then the sun changed, growing dim and tiny, and they entered a forest of velvety foliage, the scarce light concentrated by banks of living mirrors.

Three careful days were usually required to cross this region.

Katabasis estimated that five days would be necessary, but the sixth arrived with another two days standing in their way. She hated marching in the dark and never mentioned her feelings. They walked through the gloom, and sometimes one of the humans stumbled, and it was Varid as much as it was the other two. But on the sixth day, while crossing a thin, cold slice of snowmelt, Katabasis allowed her pack to shift out of position, and for the first time in twenty treks, she fell hard enough to shatter a leg.

Quee Lee and Perri returned with regrets and polite offers of help.

"Walk on," was Katabasis's advice. "I'll heal in one moment and catch up in two."

But the other porter refused to leave. With grave eyes and a taunting grin, Varid sat on a flat stone, obviously enjoying the circumstances.

"Don't smile," she warned.

He heard the words or her sharp tone, and the smile abandoned the face, leaving him as empty as always.

Such a puzzle, the creature was. Wanting any noise for distraction, she said, "Katabasis." Then she asked, "How did you recognize my name?"

Varid did not react.

"Do you remember your lecture about Greeks?" she asked.

He stared at her hot leg and then at his own hands, nodding slightly. With a quiet voice, he admitted, "I wasn't sure where the word came from. I used to study history, and languages fascinated me, and I must have learned it there."

She watched her leg's fire, saying nothing.

"I have had some recent difficulties," Varid admitted. "My health, my situation, has not been good. My mind is far from what it used to be."

"I know this."

He smiled again, this time with a shy human embarrassment.

Katabasis liked that smile best.

"I do remember the word," he said. "But there isn't any simple meaning to 'Katabasis,' is there?"

"There isn't," she agreed.

"But you chose the name for a reason."

"No one leaves names to chance."

"It must have suited you," he said.

She nodded, ready to explain.

But Varid lifted an arm first. "Give me one chance to guess."

"Try," she said.

And he closed his eyes, quietly saying, "Katabasis is the journey from a high place, down and down into the bowels of Hell."

She stared at him.

Then Varid opened his eyes and looked at her, his broken laugh ringing in the dark air. "Two rarities in the same day," he said. "You fall down, and I impress you."

"What could be more miraculous?"

7

The girl always woke early, long before the sun set. Bad dreams woke her, and good ones too. The heat woke her. Breathing the thick, toxic, and very dusty air hurt her lungs, and she would roll to her side and cough hard and ache all the worse, unable to fall back to sleep. Sometimes her lover woke her with his coughing and his dreams, and then they would lie in the hot shadow beneath the mirrored tent, talking about critical matters—water rations and food stocks and the distance to be covered tonight and the little hints of terrain visible in the fiery glare of the plains. It was important to plan your night's walk and then grab an early start. The People were moving in a wide line, shoulder to shoulder as they pushed across the wilderness, and it was best to get ahead of the dust kicked up by all of those feet and wheels. And if there was time after their planning, or if one of them was especially sad, the other would mention the humans and their Great Ship. These were the goals, and everyone needed goals. Not like they needed water, no, but the Great Ship was everything that water and food couldn't supply. It didn't represent hope; it was the only hope. Its hallways and giant wedge-rooms offered rest to the weary, and the body and mind would be rejuvenated and then enlarged—relentless long life and profound brains ready to be filled with experience and joy that would endure for thousands and millions of years.

The warrior was smitten with the idea of instant healing. Eleven days after abandoning the world, he brushed against a barkershang, driving three poisoned needles into his thigh. The wounds had been cleaned and cleaned, and he was good about changing his dressings, but even though the doctors claimed that he was improving, the holes were no smaller and the swollen flesh was a bright sick green.

From the moment she woke until they fell asleep with their legs wrapped together, the girl would remind herself that her lover was strong enough even without the help of aliens. He might limp on occasion, and maybe he suffered little fevers, but there were sicker citizens and a few dead. Besides, they were marching toward another world and different people, and warriors were at a premium. The Five had ample stocks of better drugs, and when the time came—should it come—they would release the antibiotics and the charms held back for emergencies.

The warrior wished for the immortal body, but the girl wanted the gifts of the mind. Perfect, boundless memory struck her as a blessing—provided that she could control the onslaught from the past. But why build such a brain and not give yourself the power to close off certain days and the very bad years? She imagined that she had a choice, and that was mostly true. But only while she was awake. A thousand years later, she would dream it all over again, and it wouldn't be just the worst night, but every hot sorry march through the darkness and every sleepless oven-racked day.

The worst night began with the sun still up. She woke and the warrior slept, and she worked like a demon not to cough. But the coughing was always worse when she finally succumbed—a roaring hack blowing out the dust and thick air. The warrior was jarred awake. She apologized, but he said that he was rested. She asked about his leg, and he lifted the leg and rubbed it before announcing that the swelling and pain were both in the ground under them.

They talked about water and food.

With quiet, conspiratorial voices, they described the wedge-room they would share on the Great Ship and what kinds of aliens they might meet on their way to the toilet.

It was still day, but the sun was dropping. The earliest shadows were talking to one another, claiming that first willingness to merge and matter. The People were moving under their bright tents. The girl drank what was allowed and the warrior took his share, and with the sun fading into the red dust, they climbed into the greater heat, packing and loading the two-wheeled cart that she would pull and push through the night. That was her duty. His duty involved marching ahead, scouting for enemies and the best routes, although there were good reasons to come back and give help, and maybe she would need help in the night's heart.

The sun vanished against the low shape of the distant world, leaving nothing behind but its heat and a furnace wind.

He and she embraced and again embraced, and like every other dusk, she wondered if they would never touch again. These were not omens. Tiny mistakes and large lapses in judgment could kill, and even the smartest, most careful soul was never safe.

The old world stood behind them, mostly abandoned. Only the sick and infirm, the elderly and cowardly had remained inside the empty buildings. The Five were leading the rest across the wasteland, and true to their nature, they were models of sacrifice and generosity. Electrified vehicles were charged by daylight, and the Five had ownership over many or most of the machines, but they rarely rode. Walking among the common citizens was their duty, and maybe the old wife was carried now and again, but who could blame her? Her guards and her children were well within their rights to catch her as she stumbled, and if a chair and poles were assembled on the spot, why not? She was the leader among the Five. She was owed enormous favors and deserved this small consideration, just as any other person was entitled to help and care when they weakened and dropped—provided that they had built up the favors to deserve the honor.

That night—the worst night ever—saw the girl pushing her cart up a long slope of pale, star-washed rock. Knots of angry weed threatened—weeds as alien as anything found on remote planets. Dust was everywhere. So many feet pounding the same ground made for clouds of smothering grime, and not even three cloths across the mouth would keep out the urge to choke.

Climbing uphill, she suddenly found herself walking beside the Five's new husband. He was pushing nothing, but she managed to drift ahead. Their eyes met for a moment. He offered an amused gesture. Then he lost his footing on a weed and fell hard, causing the girl to stop her cart and offer the free hand.

He said, "You are a strong woman, and thank you."

She was strong, and now she felt important too. A favor had been given to one of the Five. It was a smallish favor, and maybe it would be forgotten before it could be redeemed. But perfect memories were coming, and ten thousand years from tonight, this ageless man would recall the instant and her strength, and he would pay back the debt. It was a thought worth savoring. This was a moment to share inside the tent, the sun rising again and the food for the day going inside them. The warrior would laugh, feeling proud of his big strong lover, and then they would plunge into sleep, a few more steps achieved on the endless trek.

Happiness proved brief. Reaching the hill's crest, she found a dozen People sitting on the dry hot ground, breathing painfully or not breathing at all. One and then two more reached for her, and someone called a name. But it wasn't her name. They were guessing, hoping for lucky coincidences. She didn't know any of the faces or hands. It was normal for citizens to collapse after the hard climb, but what alarmed her was their youth and the fit bodies with the plumage still vigorous. Obviously they had worked too hard, too fast. That was the impression that helped her walk past, and that was the smug attitude that made her push harder through the night.

Twice again, long slopes needed to be climbed.

Centuries later, she would dream about the dying people on top and on the way up to the top, and because it was a dream and a lie, their voices would call to her. This time everybody knew her name, and she owed each of them multiple favors, yet she shoved the cart past them and couldn't even do them the simple courtesy of averting her eyes. In her dreams she stared at their suffering and hopelessness, and sometimes she even boasted about her invincible luck.

This long trek had started well enough, but that's how a trap works. If bad weather or unusual heat had struck the People, most would have turned around immediately, leaving the Five and their precious gift to march into oblivion. But the weather and a thousand other factors had remained relatively kind. Until that night, it was possible to believe that most of the People would survive. It was possible to walk through the heat and bad air, letting the anguish strengthen every stride. But hundreds of People were collapsing now, sometimes on the easiest ground, and the girl remembered that after the next line of little hills came a long basin covered with salt and metallic dusts and temperatures strong enough to cook meat and a girl's will.

She pushed her cart into a boulder-littered valley where water hadn't traveled in ages. Even the machines were dying now. The electric cart with the precious steel box was broken, and the oldest of the Five was sitting in a chair supplied by one well-wisher, sucking on what looked like a ball of ice supplied by another. Mechanics were listing the reasons why the vehicle would never roll again. The old woman said she didn't care about the machine. What mattered was its cargo, and nobody should forget that. And with her authority in hand, children and associates hurried off to find new transport, including the son who stopped a big bus crossing the dead stream.

The bus was opened and emptied. Mechanics began cutting out the seats and removing the roof, making room for the treasure. The passengers had lost this night's promised break. A slender little mathematician didn't seem too displeased, helping with the work when he saw the big girl pushing the cart past. He called the proper name. He didn't ask for help. He probably only wanted a gesture of friendship, a sharing of confidence. But the girl decided not to risk the possibility. There was plenty of ground between them. It was easy not to hear her friend in the rattle of machinery, and it was even easier to sprint ahead without quite fleeing, out of the valley and across the last high ground before the salt and real misery began.

This was an awful night, and it still wasn't finished. That girl, the future Katabasis, began to see warriors marching back toward the rest of the People. She saw her lover in one body after another. There he was, no there, and there too. The search was frustrating, and then it was terrifying, and somewhere in the midst of her desperate hunt she realized that he was dead and lost forever.

But the man wasn't dead. In fact, he wasn't any weaker or sicker than he was at dusk. Out from the swirling dust he emerged, and they made camp and finally ate their daily allotment, and then as the sun broke over the bright tent, they tried to settle.

The habit was for the warrior to engulf her legs with his legs.

But that dawn was different. He did nothing, and she complained about his distance.

So he tried twice and then twice again, but he was uncomfortable. Finally pulling away, he coughed weakly before admitting that the soreness was worse, maybe more than a little worse, and he was sorry but tomorrow he would feel better and everything would be right again.

She reached behind, touching the injured leg.

The swollen flesh was hiding inside the trousers, obvious and alarming if not yet lethal. Suddenly the future was clear. The warrior was too strong to die quickly. He would serve his duty tomorrow night and for several nights, and then his duty and the uniform would be stripped from him as he failed. Like the girl, he would be allowed to carry what he could and help push the cart, and one of the cart's wheels would eventually shatter and they would have to leave it behind. Each night's misery would be stoically endured; there was no doubting his capacity to suffer. But a final moment was approaching. The warrior would stumble one last time. Some People managed to be kind in the end, dying quietly, without complaints. He was the sort of man to make that kind of honorable promise. But as the girl lay beside him in their bed—as the sun rose and he growled fitfully in his sleep—she arrived at the awful knowledge that the love of her life would break every promise in the end. He would use her name and invoke every favor, and she would walk past him and then pause, returning in order to reach past his desperate hands, stripping away the last of his rations and two tastes of salty, hot, precious water.

8

The humans fell and broke and healed again and got up again. Two of them stopped pretending to be cheerful about these circumstances, aiming instead for weary politeness. The third human rolled in agony and wept with a child's self-absorption, and in the end his results were no worse, no better. Every injury could be healed, but there were costs. Heat and the rapid weaving of tissue and bone required high levels of fuel, and they were already limited in the food they carried. If the humans avoided stumbling, they would eventually reach the final kilometer with a last meal in their guts. But the descending trails were never easy, and the food shares had to be cut again. Missing calories forced injured bodies to cheat with the healing. Mass was lost, fat burned, and organs minimized before precious muscle was stolen. The humans shrank. Proportions changed, saving what was necessary to walk while stripping away what didn't matter today. But even the most careful manipulations caused strength to fade and bones weaken, and the shriveled, half-starved bodies defended themselves with extreme caution, measuring each step twice before making the attempt.

And still they fell. The two-kilometer hikes from the early days were impossible. Half a kilometer was an exceptional accomplishment. But that meant that each mouthful was buying even less distance than before, and their shares had to be sliced down again, and City West might well be standing at the end of the universe for all the chance they had of reaching its broad, clean streets.

"Care for yourself," Katabasis told the other porter, pressing an extra brick of food into a grimy cold hand. "You're the woman's best chance, but not if you turn into a stick lost beside the trail."

Varid looked at the gift. The brick was shiny gray, flavored like dribbledoe
and laced with chemical bonds waiting for any excuse to explode. Then
he looked at her, setting the brick on one of his bare knees. "You're losing
weight too."

"Not like the rest of you," she said.

He nodded.

"Eat," she insisted.

Saliva came out with the words. "I am a porter."

"You are."

"A porter," he repeated. Then he brightened and picked up the feast with
both hands, asking, "How did I get so lucky?"

Without question, the habitat's second half was lovelier than the first. Forests
were older, more complex. Landlords hadn't reworked the ground as often or
as ineptly. And the weather was a little less awful than before. But even the
strongest clients were usually worn down by now: They couldn't appreciate
the artful winding of streams. Rare blossoms and brilliant worms could barely
rouse them out of the tedium. Typically Katabasis looked forward to a glade
of unique trees—each one lovely, each representing one species that couldn't
be found anywhere else inside a thousand light-year radius—and she usually made a point of camping inside the glade, lingering for two nights and
a full day. But they entered in mid-morning, the weather kind but cloudy,
and fearing rain and more delays, she marched her humans through the gorgeous woods, barely looking to her side as she held the slow, withering pace.

Other clients and other porters began to catch them. They could hear
them closing, often for a full day, and then some happy voice would beg for
a wider trail, please. Those first clients were always riding strong porters.
Nobody recognized Varid, and the anonymity suited him. But a few rich
travelers, human and otherwise, knew the married couple, and they would
shout out greetings and teasings before offering some obligatory words about
admiring their courage.

But starvation kept eating at the faces and the bodies, and eventually the
best friends stopped recognizing them.

Perri was a frail body shrunk down to a child's proportions while his face
remained pretty in a rail-slender fashion. Except on the hottest days, he was
cold, and the hair had dropped off his scalp and face, but the eyes seemed
only to have grown larger from the experience, gazing at nothing but the
ground that looked flat and looked level but might at any moment tip him
over, breaking him in the same dreary, frustrating ways.

Quee Lee was even less recognizable. She was hairless, genderless. Breasts and hips had vanished, the black hair was scattered all the way back to the mountains, and with a tired, dry, amazed voice she would admit that she hadn't even attempted relations with her husband in fifty or sixty or a hundred nights. She counted those nights. She laughed weakly and dabbed at the crumbs of her day's rations, and then she would collapse into Perri's little arms, whispering a few words when she found the energy.

"Thank you so much for inviting me along," she told her husband.

With a slight laugh, he said, "You're welcome," and then dabbed up a few more crumbs. The source of these little feasts was uncertain, but he always attempted to put his finger into Quee Lee's mouth, and she would suck hard and cry and then pull the finger out again, urging his closer ear to her mouth, ready to whisper whatever was next.

Walking clients began to catch them. Even weak and inept hikers passed by, as if the humans were trees standing in a glade. Various eyes stared at the couple, probably assuming they were alien, not human. And then they noticed the human porter with his little pack that hadn't carried anything in a very long while. What was that man's story? Sometimes they struck up a conversation, with the strangers or with each other, and it became the day's highpoint to watch their emotions when a woman's voice emerged from the tiniest, weakest of the apparitions.

Quee Lee had digested most of her face. Her mouth was a sliver without more than a few tired teeth, and the cheekbones had collapsed into a skull that was perforated like an aerogel sponge. But her voice remained, and a shred of humor, and the first time that she begged for food was meant as a joke.

One brick of high-density fat helped save the trek.

She promised that she was joking. She and Perri were sharing the unexpected feast at camp, and she was honestly remorseful for pleading as she had. What kind of person had she become? The next three groups didn't hear begging, and they didn't leave gifts. But the hunger returned, and Quee Lee used her voice and bizarre appearance to find sympathy with everybody who passed them by. Most strangers didn't want to part with their wealth, but a few were more amenable. Ten days of humiliation and charm produced enough nourishment to put them twenty or thirty days farther down the endless trail, giving them enough leeway to consider their situation very carefully.

In the night, inside a warm bramble-filled valley, Quee Lee and Perri lay together beneath the aerogel bedding. Katabasis could hear pieces of their conversation. Certain words and the long silences pointed at a grim topic, and the porter listened and ached and in the next moment corrected herself. Nobody was doomed. No souls were bound for the Final World where all the species of People shared the breath of life. These two creatures were simply discussing matters of time and energy and the pragmatic limits of desire, and after a while they fell into sleep, and preparing her own bed, Katabasis felt peculiarly honored for being allowed this chance to study their lives.

One blue light shone in the darkness.

A little stiffly, the porter rose again, walking to the man lying in his bed. Varid was holding the torch to his eyes. What once was deeply peculiar had become ordinary. The man couldn't sleep in the usual sense. Holding brightness against his eyes seemed to relax him or busy him or do something else worthwhile. Katabasis had never asked why he did this. She didn't intend to ask now. But looking down at Varid, she enjoyed the same epiphanies that had struck her again and again over these last days:

This was not a human being.

And whatever Varid was, he was unique—a species with a population of precisely one.

She knelt beside him, watching the light and the open eyes.

After a long while, he noticed. Taking a long breath, he set the torch aside, and when he felt ready he said, "It helps me remember, the light does."

"Remember what?"

He was too tired to sit up. The first attempt proved it, but he tried again, glad for her help when it came, and then he regretted the choice and slowly fell back into the aerogel. After more breathing, he said, "I suffered this medical situation. I was caught inside a very large fire."

"The Whisper Fire," she said.

"Have I told you this before?"

"No."

A slow nod. "I don't remember very much. Not the day or being scared, or anything like that. But I do remember the last thing that I saw: This impossibly bright light. They say…the doctors explained this to me…they claimed that I took shelter inside a hyperfiber blister, and the inferno ate through the walls, and as soon as the last layer was pierced, this thread of plasmas found me. But my eyes didn't die immediately, and my brain survived afterwards. Something about the shape of that little space not only saved my mind, but it allowed my eyes to watch this most amazing light."

She said nothing.

"Then I was dead and blind," he said. "I was lost and mostly unconscious. But if you're buried for a thousand years, thoughts happen. You remember what you can, but I couldn't remember much. So much had been turned to fire." He paused, smiling weakly. "But you probably realized that on our first day together, didn't you?"

"The light," she said.

"It helps my head work better. Brilliance somehow makes it easier for me to practice what I learned today and fifty thousand years ago."

She said, "Good then."

"This is crazy, yes. But when I was dead, the fire that killed me…nearly killed me, and murdered my family…that fire was my largest best memory. It seemed so lovely and wonderful. I don't think I could have remained sane for even a hundred years, if it wasn't for me thinking about that searing magical light."

Watching him, Katabasis weighed questions.

Varid answered an unasked question. "I don't need sleep anymore. It's a consequence of my injuries, and it's because this is how far I was fixed before the fixing stopped."

"Why did the fixing stop?" she asked.

Varid picked up the torch again, holding it against his right eye. He didn't act interested in the question, and maybe he didn't notice it. Katabasis still didn't know what the man could learn or how well ideas would play inside his head. But he wasn't the insane idiot that she had imagined. He was a mystery, relentlessly frustrating but compelling, and instead of working to avoid this creature, she wanted to share the solitude forced on both of them by bad and wonderful forces.

"Could I become a porter?" he asked abruptly.

"What?"

The torch and hand pulled away from his face. The dark center of the eye was a pinprick point. He wasn't as starved as the others, his bluish-white hair still alive, though thin and not growing any longer, and his face was very much like the face that she first met. She had passed her colleague enough rations to keep up his strength, and she had quit bristling whenever she thought of Varid that way: her colleague.

"I don't know if you could be a porter," she said.

He remained silent.

"You're tiny and you're weak," she said.

"Like you," he said. "But you manage to make your living."

She laughed with her hands, her face. She laughed as close to the human sound of laughter as she could manage.

"I stopped the fixing where it is," Varid said.

"Did you?"

He nodded.

"Was it a question of money?" she asked.

"No, I have money. A sliver from the original estate, they tell me. But it's still more than most passengers enjoy."

She watched his face.

"No, the doctors let me choose," he said. "They gave me permission to decide how much new bioceramic I wanted grown, and how giant my mind would be. They thought they were going to get rich doing the work. But I surprised them. I told them thank you, but no, and to leave me alone."

She watched his empty hand, fingers spread out on his hungry belly.

"A thousand years spent underground, and almost everything from before was gone," he said. "I didn't think about my dead family, and I didn't forget and think about them being alive either. I had memories of the past and disjointed facts learned, but there wasn't one story pulling the mess together. I was dead. My mind was gone, only pieces left, and those pieces slowly assembled themselves into something that was familiar to me…that became me…and I don't know how to explain this."

"Don't," she advised.

But Varid showed a stubborn face. "I don't have much humor left. But maybe I didn't have any to begin with. I don't feel much empathy for others, and I know I forget most of what I learn. But that doesn't mean that I'll stop learning or making myself better or doing whatever good thing it is that I'm supposed to do. And I do like to attempt whatever is difficult. Which isn't the way I used to be, they tell me. Certain strangers who knew me before. They don't like me, they like to say, but I don't see how they liked the man who died. I've studied him. For years and years after getting out into the world again…I know I'm rambling, I do this if I'm not careful…but I do appreciate, very much, getting lost in passions that he couldn't even imagine. Like this adventure. He would never, ever have envisioned walking through wilderness accompanied by a beautiful alien creature."

Katabasis sat motionless, watching all of the man.

"You can sleep," Varid said. "Sleep now, and it will help you tomorrow."

"Thank you," she said.

She stood and said, "I will."

Three days later, Perri found the right place and proper circumstances. He called Quee Lee to his side and they spoke to each other with just those big eyes. Standing beneath a ripe tashaleen tree, they looked vulnerable and worried. But when Varid walked into the tree's shadow, they calmly warned him to back away.

Little seams were opening in the swollen bladder. The stink of sulfuric acid began to pervade the calm forest air, but it might take another day or two for the flesh to burst wide, scouring the nearby ground.

Varid slowly backed away, studying the scene. Comprehension took longer for him, but he accepted the obvious quickly, and approaching Katabasis, he said, "We have all of the rations."

She was carrying every bit of food, including the treats given out of pity.

Quee Lee called to Varid, saying, "You'll have to carry me from here on. So of course you'll earn your bonus."

Perri slowly bent over, grabbing a small rock.

Katabasis was thinking about acid and its effects on flesh and how the flow would roll when the bladder burst.

Perri tried to throw the pebble at the bladder, but it weighed tons and tons.

"I won't break the tree for you," Katabasis warned.

"I have a suggestion," Varid said. Then to the couple waiting in that dark, fume-laced shade, he said, "Lie down inside your bed."

With a reasonable, perfectly calm voice, he said, "The aerogel won't dissolve, but it will let the acid seep through. Your brains will stay where they are, which is good. We won't have to chase either of you downstream."

9

At dawn, eighty-nine People crawled beneath the tattered shelters. There were no rations to eat, nothing to drink. They lay quietly, in pain, listening to the world bake and blister, and sometimes they slept but mostly they watched their own vague thoughts form and shift before being lost. When the sun finally dropped behind the new world, eighty-three People found enough reason to stand again, stowing the shelters in the final three carts and grabbing hold of the wagon that carried the rusted steel box, slowly pushing away from the dead.

The new world began with towering black cliffs. Through telescopes, rivers could be seen plunging over the side of the volcano, wasted water turning to mists and serpentine clouds that were consumed before drifting halfway to the desert. Those cliffs were the goal, the dream, but the walk would take another four or five or perhaps six nights, and worse, there was no obvious path leading up the imposing and very smooth face of rock.

The Five had become the Three. The ice-sucking woman refused to die, along with her two youngest husbands. The woman always rode on the back end of the wagon. Every night she made optimistic noises about imminent rescue and the abiding decency of the human animal. She insisted that she knew the animal well. She and the godlike emissary had spoken many times by radio. They were allies, collaborators, sometimes friends. But the final radio died out on the salt, and she didn't have her friend to speak to anymore. She was making noise, half-mad and often feverish, and her noise had an erosive effect on the last shreds of hope.

Her husbands didn't bother lying. Working beside the strongest bodies, they pushed wheels up long slopes and used their scant weight to keep the wagon and their wife from rolling wild downhill. Sometimes one or the other would climb ahead, scouting the ground for the least-awful route. Just short of the night's center, the older man went up to the ridge crest and then came back again. He was running. He fell suddenly. He got up and fell and got up laughing with his arms, and with more disbelief than joy, he announced, "We reached the world early. Over this hill is a mine."

The next long reach of desert had been stripped away. Deep gouges were cut into the pale rock, roads and paths leading down to giant electric machines working in the depths of the deepest hole. The machines took no interest in them. Any miners were equally oblivious. Eighty-two People looked down on the mayhem, and one of them sat for a moment and died and the others backed away from the mine's edge, aiming for the nearest road.

The first miner had a strange oval face and a fancy mask over his mouth and eyes. He stared at the filthy parade of bodies, and with a string of peculiar words, he spoke into a tiny radio, presumably asking a question or soliciting advice.

Peculiar words came out of the radio, and he responded by clambering into a burly electric cart and riding away.

After that, they didn't see one miner.

But someone had left rations and fresh water stacked together in some form of way station. The People fell on what they assumed were gifts, drinking enough and eating more than enough, and another one of their ranks died from the indulgence.

The station had a roof full of tubes that leaked cold air, and several sets of rails ended here but led off toward the world. The rails stood empty until a heavy railcar arrived and parked. The husbands conferred and then gave orders. The car was long enough for all of the People to ride in comfort, with room remaining for a battered wagon and its precious cargo. Once loaded, the railcar began rolling back from where it had come, bearing the People across the last bits of wasteland, diving into a long tunnel as the sun burst into view. And even at that moment, the girl sitting on the aluminum floor of the car was unable to believe that she would survive one day longer.

Their old world was nearly nothing. It had been a low ridge, dry and thinly populated, while this world was a hundred times larger, tall enough for permanent ice and wet everywhere, its belly full of hot rock and deep springs powering geothermal plants which made the entire realm hum with electrical activity. Perhaps a million generations separated the People from these citizens. They looked that different, that alien. Every face was grossly round, and the plumage wasn't just wrong in its color but longer and gaudily colored, and these new People smelled different and sounded odd, talking about the railcar that was sliding past their homes and businesses. Their day had just begun. The old People, their lost cousins, deserved notice and some idle chatter. The girl stared at the bright buildings passing by and the endless metal and how every window was filled with light, the faces behind glass staring at her for a moment or two, curious but not curious, ready for any excuse to pull back to their own busy lives.

If the girl and her People had arrived here in full force, they would have meant nothing. They were too scarce, too primitive, and much too stupid to generate anything more than polite disinterest.

That was the morning's first awful lesson.

The long railcar was driven by a machine's mind, turns taken and turns avoided until they arrived at a fresh volcanic crater, barren land encircling a turquoise lake. On the black rock stood a different kind of building, round like a half-ball and woven from slick gray material that didn't look like any steel.

"This is the emissary's quarters," the old woman announced happily. "It is also a spaceship, fueled and ready to carry us to the Great Ship."

At dusk, the girl didn't believe anything the old woman claimed. But suddenly she was an expert again, and every statement only enhanced her boundless value.

The car stopped before a walkway made from gemstone bricks.

Out from the building—from the spaceship—came a creature with six jointed legs. Except it wasn't a creature, it was a machine, and the human rode on a high chair inside the machine's body. His face was grim, stern. But the girl didn't know it then. He was as angry as a diplomat trained in the art of agreements and sweet words could ever be. But she only saw the narrow black face and the frail body shorn of its plumage and the odd little hands that didn't like rising off the rests in his chair. He was undoubtedly alien. The new People would look ordinary next to him, if only they were standing here. But it was the human alone, and the last of the girl's People, and he introduced himself with his name and his title and once again, his name.

A box inside the walking machine made the best translations possible.

The diplomat was named Rococo, which was nothing but odd noise in her ears and she forgot it immediately.

"You have arrived," the emissary said wearily.

Everyone looked at the old woman, but suddenly and for no apparent reason she forgot how to speak.

The youngest husband broke the silence. "We have a gift for you. For your species. We brought it from our home, at great cost."

"I don't want it," Rococo said.

The old woman roused herself. With a quiet, tense voice, she said, "Take the box to him now. Take it."

"It is alien," said the older husband. "We found this artifact in the throat of a dead volcano."

"Very valuable," the other husband shouted.

Rococo stared at the gray box. "Leave it there," he ordered.

But the People were not listening or refused to understand. Terrific costs had been paid so that they could drag the box off the wagon and over the railcar's railing, metal screeching against metal as the alien wonder was dropped on the gemstones beside the mechanical feet.

Staring at the old woman, the emissary said, "I told you. What did I tell you? I was exceptionally clear about what I could and couldn't do for you."

From a special pouch came the key. But the woman was too nervous, and she didn't care who opened the treasure.

The girl found the key in her hand.

"We can't take just anybody onboard the Ship," the human insisted. Then with a thought, he caused a mechanical arm to unfold and reach down, grabbing the girl by her wrist.

She dropped the key.

"I have made agreements," said the human. "Following galactic law, we have binding arrangements with the most advanced species on this world. My species has purchased the right to begin terraforming your nearest moon, and in thanks for this blessing, we will carry a small, small, small population of local People to a world that they will be able to colonize.

"This is binding and legal and I told you all of that before," he said. "I was honest. When did I mislead you? I told you not to bother with this pathetic migration, and you came anyway. I talked to you a hundred times in the night, warning you to turn around and head home again before it was too late. If I wasn't stationed here alone, I would have sent subordinates to the basin just to explain things to your flock. Which I should have done myself, and I see that now. I regret it all, yes."

The youngest husband grabbed the key, and with a blur of motion unfastened the lock and threw the lid over the side.

"Look," he shouted. "Look."

Rococo released the girl and grudgingly peered inside.

The girl fell to her knees, rubbing at the aching wrist. She wanted to look inside and didn't. Then the human beast told everyone, "This is a piece of hyperfiber, a shard of someone's hull. Hyperfiber is the most durable, persistent, and unremarkable kind of trash in this portion of the galaxy, which means that it is worth nothing."

The girl shook from nerves, exhaustion, and anguish.

Then the old woman stepped between the mechanical legs and under the arm, and with a passionate, practiced voice she said, "Of course it isn't enough. You told me, and I believed you, yes. But I have learned about your species, your nature. You know sympathy and empathy, and just like us, you understand how great deeds demand to be recognized. We are the last of our species. We have spent everything and sacrificed almost everything to place a few of us on your ground."

Rococo took a deep breath, and then gasped.

She moved her hands as a beggar would. "Take a few of us with you, please. We can select, or you can choose. I am prepared for either eventuality. But here we stand, surrounded by People who care nothing for us, and we have pushed ourselves to the brink of extinction, and if you don't give us this one little charity, our kind will vanish from the universe forever."

Rococo lifted one of his hands, and he lowered it again.

He did not know what to say next.

The old woman turned and said, "Marvel at what we have accomplished, my People. We must celebrate this wonderful fine day."

Katabasis stood. What happened next wasn't planned, but it wasn't an accident either. She intended to throw her fist but she wanted only to make the old woman stop talking, and the woman should have been bruised and startled. But she stumbled oddly and fell sideways into the box, and the rusted red corner of steel struck at the worst point on her head, and she died.

The two husbands and then the others attacked the girl.

With every mechanical arm and half of the legs, the emissary dragged the murderer away from the People. Then he threw curses and threats of much worse, hauling his prisoner back inside the ship where he intended to wait for some inspiration that would give him a route out of this miserable trap.

10

Clients walked past them and rode past them, some for the second and third time. It seemed that the story of the landslide and long subsequent march had gained a brief measure of fame. Everyone who met them on the trail, including their porters, asked when they would arrive at City West. Would it be today or tomorrow or maybe the day after? Katabasis promised they would finish tomorrow, probably late in the day, and then the other porter, the human, would name the clearing where they planned to camp tonight, begging the others to please leave it empty because they needed quiet even more than they needed food.

Save for two acid-polished jackets of bioceramic matter, their packs were nearly empty. They had one torch but no food and no bedding, and they drank their water straight from the river, and even the excess grams of fabric had been cut away from the packs and clothes, left behind in the jungle along with at least half of their body mass. They were battered gaunt skeletons taking tiny strides. They were crazy souls and heroes, and strangers were so impressed by what they knew of the story that they would turn short of the trail's end and come back around again, just to see them once more with their own mesmerized eyes.

Several clients mentioned that groups were gathering. Well-wishers would be waiting tomorrow at the edge of City West, and there might even be a small ceremony complete with treats suitable for brave, tenacious creatures like them.

By day's end, they were close enough to the City to hear individual voices mixed in with the normal urban sounds. Varid smelled food on the wind, his belly aching even worse. But as promised, they made their night's camp. Several tents had been left behind, each wearing notes and good wishes, and the two porters selected the largest tent and set the torch inside, turned up to full brightness, and when night arrived and the City changed its pitch, moving into nocturnal affairs, they climbed into the open and shouldered the cut-apart packs, carrying their clients down the dark, well-walked trail.

Neither porter fell in that last stretch.

The next six hundred meters took half of the night, but suddenly the jungle ended and the sky opened up, revealing a welcoming banner written in the human language. Apparently no one was certain about Katabasis's native language. But someone had managed to spell her name in the original Greek, which made her feel just a little sorry for slipping past this way. Then they slowly, slowly crept their way to the first street, and she waved for a cap-car, telling it that they were carrying two people needing to be given some rather extensive medical help.

Three kilometers were covered in two minutes. Autodocs were waiting at the entranceway, along with one of the habitat's landlords whose duty was to make certain that no paying customers had died.

"I left two porters under the mountain," Katabasis said.

"We know everything," he said testily. "As soon as arrangements can be made, we will start to dig."

Varid stared at the man and then turned to his colleague.

She put a finger in his mouth, which she had learned was a very good way to keep the man from talking.

The landlord belonged to that second species of People. He was a young man when the human emissary arrived, walking in the bug-carriage down the avenues of his home world. Now he was grown but would never grow old—a giant well-fed beast sporting purple and blue plumage. He and his kind had purchased the habitat for almost nothing. They had excellent minds for business and a natural flair for selling their wares, and the strange slow-motion nightmare that had just been lived by these two pathetic creatures was very good for business. The habitat was an investment to help pay for extras needed when they finally reached the colony world. That was the only reason why he didn't shout his disapproval. It was enough to offer a few gestures that were very similar to those used by Katabasis's species, leaving no doubt about his state of mind and how small his regard was for this hero and her monkey friend.

Perri and Quee Lee were left in the care of autodocs.

Katabasis removed her finger from the little wet mouth. Back inside the cap-car, she asked for the nearest dock, and they rode in silence. Then they slowly climbed out, and using a calm, reasoned tone, Varid mentioned that he would like something enormous to eat.

The salty little sea was home to one odd fish, tough as could be and worth any price. Katabasis suggested that for a dinner, and her companion bought ten kilos, both smoked and raw, and then they boarded the first ferry they could find, starting across the flat dark water.

They ate, and after a time Varid turned to her. "He looked like you."

"But we aren't the same," she said.

He nodded, and waited.

"We're like two species of monkeys," she said.

He stopped nodding. His face went blank in that way that she envied, as if he had the power to wash away his past and any urgent thoughts of the moment, existing in a quiet realm that she could only wish to know.

Then with no warning, Varid asked, "How did you come here?"

She considered. She leaned a long way forward, and after one deep breath told the ferry to stop in the middle, please, and drift with the current and wait.

She killed the old woman once again, except not in her dreams but with words and a small sorry thrust of the fist.

Varid chewed at the raw fish, saying nothing.

"The human carried me inside his ship," she said, "and for two days he fed me and fed the People outside, and he spoke to them and to me and finally decided on a course of action and inaction. What I had endured was beyond any human experience, and he could not believe what we had accomplished. The local species—those standing thick on this world and the nearby volcanoes—were durable, yes, but not nearly as resilient as us. Against every instinct, he decided that we had proved our worth, and with that in mind, he would personally return the People to their former home. The buildings were still standing. With repairs, enough fans and dew-catchers could feed a small rebirth. And later, when human terraformers arrived in force, the People would supply most of the labor and all of the tenacity to making the inhospitable moon into a wondrous garden."

Varid swallowed and looked across the water. "I have an idea."

"I'm not finished," she said.

"I know," he said. "But don't let me forget to tell you my idea, please."

"I will remind you."

She ate and he ate, and then he said, "You are here."

"If Rococo had left me with my People, I would have been killed. But my crime occurred on the diplomat's ground, which was nearly the same as being on the Earth or inside the Great Ship. His laws ruled. He had the only authority. And according to his laws, I needed to be tried in a fair court, which could only be found once he returned here."

"He saved you," Varid said.

"In a fashion, yes," she said. "I was frozen inside the shuttle's hold and defrosted on arrival and tried three years later and convicted of some lesser brutality. My sentence was short. Someone, probably Rococo himself, paid to have my body and mind rebuilt. But nobody has told me who holds this favor, which is the largest favor of all. Then as I was released from prison, the captains presented me with a bill for passage onboard the Great Ship—which will take fifty thousand years to make good, working as a porter, and that really is another gift, when you consider that you have forever to march across."

Her companion said nothing. He had stopped eating, and the face had shifted into another lost expression.

"You had an idea," she said.

"I did," he agreed.

They waited.

Just when she thought that he had forgotten the subject, Varid pushed his face close and said, "There are little passengers onboard the Ship. They are machines and intelligent parasites and such. And I have empty space inside my head. Has there ever been a porter willing to be filled with other souls, carrying his clients from the first step?"

"No," she said. "There never has been, no."

The sun was slowly coming to life overhead. She told the ferry to continue and turned back to Varid. "This is a worthy idea," she told him. "This is definitely a notion to twist in the light, to see how it plays."

Once again, at last, Katabasis walked her beach.

She couldn't sleep. Her body felt too tired to ever rest again. She moved weakly and breathed too much, and the familiar faces of her neighbors weren't quite certain who she was. Yet she felt stronger in every way but strength, strolling past her usual turning point and then coming back even slower. Her little house of quake-coral looked like a wonder from a distance. Two legs were sticking out of the door, and smiling with her hands and arms, she came up quietly and knelt down and looked inside.

Varid was on his back, his eyes closed.

She sat back and waited. Was he truly that exhausted? Was this his first real sleep in centuries? Then she leaned forward and looked again, watching the eyes bouncing under the barely closed lids.

Once more, she sat back.

But she couldn't resist. There finally came the moment when she put her shrunken weight on her arms and dipped her head, brushing his salty ankles with the full rough surface of her tongue.

TROLL BLOOD

PETER DICKINSON

Peter Dickinson [www.peterdickinson.com] *is the author of over fifty books including* Eva, Earth and Air, *and the Michael L. Printz honor book* The Ropemaker. *He has twice received the Whitbread Award as well as the Phoenix and Guardian awards, among other awards. He lives in England and is married to the novelist Robin McKinley.*

M ari was a seventh child, by some distance—an afterthoughtlessness, her father was fond of remarking. Moreover she had the changeling look, as if she had come from utterly different stock from her parents and siblings, with their traditionally Nordic features, coarsely handsome, with strong bones, blond hair, and winter-blue eyes. Mari was dark-haired, slight, with a fine, almost pearly skin that burnt in the mildest sun. Her face seemed never quite to have lost the crumpled, simian look of the newborn baby. Her mouth was wide, and her eyes, which might more suitably have been brown to go with her coloring, were of an unusual slaty gray.

This look, though only occasionally manifesting itself, ran in the family as persistently as the more normal one. There were likely to be one or two examples in any group photograph in the old albums—a grandmother, a great uncle killed in the Resistance in the Second World War, somebody unidentified in a skiing party way back in the twenties.

There was a story to go with the look. Thirty-odd generations ago a young woman was bathing in a lake when a troll saw her and took her to his underwater cave. Her handmaiden, hiding among the trees, saw what happened and carried the news to the young woman's father. Her mother was dead, and she was his only child. He at once ran to the place and dived into the lake carrying an inflated goatskin weighted down with his armor and weapons. Breathing from the bag through a straw he found the cave, armed himself, and fought the monster until it fled howling. Then he brought his daughter safely home. Nine months later, while her father was away, the young woman bore a son, so clearly marked as a troll that everyone assumed that he would kill the little monster as soon as he returned. But the young woman stole from her room with the child wrapped in her cloak, and met him on the road and begged for his blessing on his grandson, saying, "Your blood is in the boy. If he dies, I will bear no more children." The father took the child from her and unwrapped the cloak and saw for the first time the grandson his daughter had given him. He turned and dipped his finger into a puddle by the road and made the cross of baptism on the baby's forehead. When the child did not scream at the touch of the holy symbol he said, "Whatever his face, there is a Christian soul beneath," and he gave him his blessing.

Even as a child Mari had disliked this story. She of course knew it was only a fairy story, but without being able to formulate the idea she felt in her bones that the problem was not that it was false, but that it was fake. Later, when she had learnt more about such things, she realized that it was probably only a product of the great nineteenth-century Nordic folk revival, amalgamating several genuinely old elements—the abduction, the underwater journey, the fight with the cave monster—and tacking on the utterly inappropriate Christianizing ending that she had so hated from the first. Be that as it may, that was how the look was said to have come into the family. They called it troll blood.

Mari's parents were second cousins, in a generation of small families among whom the look had had less chance of showing up; so, because they both carried the gene, the whole clan took an unusual interest in the birth of each of their children, only to be disappointed six times in succession. When Mari had at last been born, with the look instantly recognizable, her parents sent round the birth cards saying: "To Olav and Britta Gellers, a troll-daughter."

It was a family in which everyone had a nickname. Mari's, from the first, was Troll. She was used to it and never found it strange or considered its meaning, though differences from her brothers and sisters continued to appear. Their style, and that of their parents, was extrovert, cheerfully competitive. They camped, sailed, skied, climbed rocks. The eldest brother just missed representing Norway at long-distance swimming. Two sisters did well in local slalom events. And they were practical people, their father a civil engineer specializing in hydroelectrics, their mother a physiotherapist. The children studied engineering, medicine, accountancy, law. They were not unintelligent, but apart from the acquisition of useful knowledge their academic interests were nonexistent. Their aesthetic tastes were uniformly banal.

All these things were expressive of a more basic difference of character, of life attitude. They threw themselves into things. Mari held herself apart. This was not because she was cold or timid, but because she was, perhaps literally, reserved.

"She is keeping herself for her prince," her mother used to say, only half teasing.

Mari went along with all the family activities, well enough not to be a drag on them, but seldom truly participated. She seemed to have no urge to compete, though she might sometimes do so inadvertently, pushing herself to her physical limits for the mere joy of it. She was an excellent swimmer, with real potential according to her brother's coach, but she saw no point in swimming as fast as she could in a prescribed style in a lane in a big pool with other girls doing the same on either side. She thought it a waste of time in the water. In any case she didn't much care for swimming pools. She liked the sea or a lake or river, in which she could swim in the living current or among the slithering waves, as a seal does, or a gull.

Her academic career, though just as alien to the family ethos, was less of a surprise. She'd always been, by their active, engaged standards, a dreamy child, so they were prepared for her bent to be chiefly literary and were only mildly puzzled that as she moved up through her schools and was more able to choose her courses of study her interests moved steadily back in time, until at University she took Old Norse as a special subject, concentrating on the fragmentary and garbled remains of the earliest writings in the language.

Doctor Tharlsen taught this course, a classically dry-as-dust bachelor scholar who conscientiously performed his teaching duties, but by rote, while all his intellectual energies were reserved for his life's work, on which he had been engaged for the last twenty years, the reconstruction of MS Frählig 1884. This is what remains of a twelfth-century copy of a miscellaneous collection of older MSS in Old Norse. It has some unusual features, the most striking of which is explained (as far as can be made out, since the whole volume is badly damaged by fire) in a Latin introduction by the copyist himself. The MSS he copied must already have been in the library of the Great Cistercian abbey of Dunsdorf, and the then Prince-Abbot, Alfgardt, had expressed a wish to know what they were about. The opportunity seems to have arisen with the arrival of a novice from Norway, who was promptly trained as a copyist and set to the task of translation. Thus the MS is interleaved with his attempts to fulfill his brief, with the ancient text on one page and the Latin facing it. The word *attempts* is relevant. Not only was much of the original texts characteristically obscure, but the copyist's grasp of Old Norse was uncertain, and he knew no more Latin than he needed to read a missal. The Prince-Abbot can have been little the wiser after seeing the result. Nevertheless the manuscript was handsomely bound up, and remained in the library until drunken Moravian soldiery looted and fired the abbey after the battle of Stadenbach in 1646. It then disappeared for three hundred years, only coming to light when American troops were billeted at Schloss Frählig at the end of the Second World War, and one of the officers who in civilian life had been a dealer in mediaeval manuscripts recognized the arms of the Prince-Abbot on the spine of the charred volume. How it had come to Frählig remains a mystery.

Externally the damage does not look too serious, but this is not the case. The volume's relationship to the fire was such that, from the first few leaves on, the outer edge of every page was rendered illegible, while the section nearer the spine can still be read, though often with difficulty. The damaged portion increases steadily throughout the volume, so that by the end all but the last few letters of each line on the verso sheet, and the first few on the recto, is lost.

It can be seen that since the material is repeated in translation, page by page, each spread notionally still contains lines whose first part can be read in the original language and second part in Latin, or vice versa, and that from these materials it might in theory be possible to make at least a tentative reconstruction of what the whole original might have been. In 1975 funds were made available for Doctor Tharlsen to undertake the task. He had done little else since then.

Doctor Tharlsen didn't include the Frählig MS in his course, as being far too obscure and difficult, even in the sections for which he had so far published a reconstructed text. If a student happened to mention it he tended to assume that this was an attempt to curry favor, or to show off. This was his first thought when he started to read the separate note Mari had attached to an essay she had handed in. It concerned a paper he had published several years earlier, with the suggested text for a collection of riddling verses from the earlier part of the MS. Mari pointed out that an alternative reading of the Latin would result in a rather more satisfactory riddle. Doctor Tharlsen had already considered the possibility, rejecting it on grounds to do with the technicalities of versification. Still, her suggestion struck him as highly intelligent, and since the rest of her work showed a distinct *feel* for the difficult subject, he for once suggested that a student should remain after class to talk about it. Or rather, two students. With characteristic caution he asked one of the other young women to stay as well, lest there should be any misunderstandings.

The friendship that followed was not as unlikely on his part as it may seem. There were perhaps half a dozen people in the world, none of them among his colleagues at the university, capable of talking to Doctor Tharlsen on equal terms about the Frählig MS. As for the students, he felt with some justice that he would be wasting both his time and theirs if he had bothered them with it. It took him a while to be persuaded that this was not also the case with Mari, but once he realized that her interest was more than passing, his life changed. His energies for the task, jaded by long isolation, returned. Fresh insights came to him, sometimes spontaneously, sometimes in the course of explaining some current problem to her, and more than once stimulated by a suggestion of hers. No doubt this rejuvenation owed something to the fact that she was an attractive young woman, but he continued, despite her protestations, to insist that his housekeeper was always at least in earshot when she came to his rooms.

Mari's side of the relationship is harder to account for, since the true attraction for her was not to Doctor Tharlsen, though she both liked and admired him, but to the Frählig MS itself. Finding in a textbook a footnote reference to one of the riddles, she had felt an intense and instant impulse to know more. The more she learnt, the stronger her feeling became that the book somehow *spoke* to her. She never saw the object itself. That was in a library attached to Yale University. Doctor Tharlsen had studied it there several times over the years, but at home had to work from facsimiles. Confronted even with these ghosts of the real thing Mari felt an excited reverence, while at the same time being appalled by the difficulties it presented.

From the first it was obvious to her that these would be enormously eased by the use of a computer. Doctor Tharlsen knew this in his heart, but had persuaded himself that he was too old to learn to use one. He had a tiresome liver complaint. He doubted that he had many more years to live, and felt he couldn't spare the time to become proficient enough to make real use of the promised advantages, and even then there would be the enormous labor of putting onto the system the mass of material he had so far accumulated. Two years at least, he told himself. No, he must plod on.

"I'll do it for you," Mari told him. "Of course I'll get some things wrong, but I don't think it'll be too bad."

"No, I can't accept that. It would interfere too much with the rest of your work."

"This is more important."

"No, I really can't accept it, Miss Gellers."

"Please, Doctor Tharlsen."

(Doctor Tharlsen maintained a formal relationship with his students, and Mari had guessed early on that he would be embarrassed by anything that suggested his friendship with her was other than straightforwardly professional.)

As a compromise he agreed that she might stay on at the university through the summer vacation and make a start on the work to see how it went. He spent the first three weeks at Yale, where the library had recently installed a new fluoroscopic technique, combined with computerized image enhancement, to extract meaningful characters from damaged documents, and were eager to try it out on the Frählig MS. By the time he returned, Mari had the legible parts of the *Gelfunsaga* on disc, including a whole series of extensions of lines revealed by the fluoroscope—on Mari's suggestion he had asked an assistant at the library to email these to her. By the end of the vacation Doctor Tharlsen was himself online and exchanging email with distant colleagues.

A word about the *Gelfunsaga*. This is the longest, most exciting, and at the same time most tantalizing portion of the whole MS. Like Snorri's later *Prose Edda*, it appears to be a prose recension of a much older verse legend, from which it occasionally quotes a few lines. The story it seems to tell is referred to nowhere else in the literature. It would clearly be of interest to the general reader, as well as to scholars. Unfortunately it is the last item in the MS, and so the most extensively damaged, less than half of any line being legible. And its being largely in prose inhibits reconstruction, for two reasons: the alliterative verse line of, for instance, the riddles obeys rules almost as strict as the rhymed and scanned lines of later European poetry, and these usefully limit the possibilities for supplying missing words and phrases; and then the copyist, though he had written the Norse verse sections out to fill every line and had translated them into prose, had marked the line endings on both sheets with a slash, thus relating them clearly to each other. Sometimes one half of the meaning could be read in each language. There was no such guide for the prose of the *Gelfunsaga*, and the copyist cannot have recognized the brief verse sections as such, and so failed to mark them.

The story, as far as it can be made out, has affinities with the first two episodes of *Beowulf*. The hero, Gelfun, to rid the neighborhood from the depredations of a monster (who may or may not be the troll twice referred to in the surviving portions of the text—the Latin uses the word *monstrum* throughout, but at one point adds the epithet *sol timens,* presumably the copyist's attempt at *sunfearer*), goes to the underwater lair of the beast, using a hollow reed(?) to breathe through. His weapons are useless to him, since the creature's limbs are made of rock. (This is one of the passages where the Latin and Norse complement each other enough to make the gist fairly clear.) Gelfun then wrestles with it, apparently inconclusively (the text is once more very obscure), and there is then an exchange of oaths. But he seems to have won the contest, because he takes a treasure of amber from the cave, and then puts the monster onto a ship and dispatches it to sea. The final section is the most seriously damaged part of the manuscript. It seems to have little relation to what went earlier, but apparently deals with Gelfun's choice of an heir.

Because of its near intractability Doctor Tharlsen had kept the *Gelfunsaga* till last. At the time Mari came into his life he was about to start serious work on it.

All this occurred in the summer of Mari's second year at University. For the last fortnight of that long vacation she joined her family at their holiday home on one of the northern fjords. There, disruptingly, she fell in love.

Fell, for once, is the right word. The event was as unforeseen and over-whelming as the collapse of a cliff face, altering the whole landscape of her life. She had, of course, had a few tentative involvements with fellow students during the last two years, trial runs, as much to explore her own emotional responses as the physical sensations, and had found, even when the sensations had been enjoyable enough, that the event had left her dissatisfied. She was, she came to realize, one of those people who need to commit themselves, heart and soul as well as body, to anything of importance they undertake. Before she could love, she must choose, choose with her whole being, for all of her life.

She had expected, or at least hoped, to do so as she did most things, deliberately, to find a man of her own age whom she liked, get to know and admire him, while he did the same with her, and then, as it were, build their lifelong love together step by step, much as she had watched her parents and elder siblings building the house on the fjord together. The last thing she had looked for was a cliff-fall.

Dick Vesey was an Englishman, like her father a hydroelectric engineer. They had met at a conference and liked each other, and since Dick's main interest outside his work was fishing, Mari's father had invited him to the fjord for the late salmon run. He was twelve years older than Mari, with her sort of build, slight and active, but his face was different, the skull squarish, and the features molded in definite angular planes. (One night on their honeymoon, tracing those planes with her fingertips, she wondered aloud whether his parents had conceived him in a bed with a Braque painting on the wall above it. "Far from it," he answered. "It was on open moorland during a cycling trip in the Cheviots, I believe. They didn't intend it to happen. She was married to another man, and didn't want to divorce him.") The effect was to give him a misleadingly merry look, almost droll. In fact he laughed seldom and spoke little. His humor when he chose to deploy it was dry and understated, but quirky, poised between the gnomic and the surreal. Occasionally he produced a remark that might have come straight out of the riddles. He was an excellent and attentive listener. When Mari told him about her work with Doctor Tharlsen, though he had no knowledge of the languages involved, he not only grasped the difficulties but, as her family never in their heart of hearts had done, accepted the importance of the work. She used her laptop to show him some examples of what she was doing. It was while they were sitting together gazing at a laptop screen filled with fragmentary lines of runes that Mari realized what had happened to her.

Later she came to feel that the occasion had not been random, as it had seemed at the time, but utterly appropriate, almost willed. She had fallen for Dick because something about him spoke to her, just as the Frählig MS had, but even more urgently and insistently. The same, he said later, had happened to him, but since each felt there wasn't the slightest chance of the other returning feelings so irrational, they had managed to conceal it from each other.

But not, it turned out, from anyone else. As they waved his car away and watched it vanish behind the pines Mari's father said to her, "Well, when does he propose?" and the rest of the family—ten, including a brother and sister-in-law—bellowed with cheerful northern laughter.

They became engaged by email. She visited him in Scotland over the New Year, staying in a hotel near Dumfries because he had no home of his own but lodged wherever his current work happened to be. Nor was there any family for her to meet. His mother had returned to her husband soon after he was born, the husband making it a condition that she didn't bring the baby, so his father had brought him up, marrying when he was five, but had had no more children, and had then emigrated to Canada with Dick's stepmother when Dick was a student. Dick was now between jobs, and the reason he had chosen Dumfries was that it would allow them to look for a house within easy reach of his next one, which involved the installation of a small hydroelectric plant in the hills above the town. They narrowed the field down drastically by telling the agents that the property must have fishing rights attached. They found nothing they liked.

The failure didn't seem to matter. They spent their eight days together in a state too deep and broad and solid-seeming to be called excitement, too electric with the passing seconds to be called just happiness or contentment. Kissing Dick good-bye at the barrier, turning away, walking through the passport check, Mari felt as if she were putting herself into a coma until she next saw him, able to move, talk, eat, think, but no longer to feel as she had felt while with him, technically alive only.

Superstitiously, Mari hadn't told Doctor Tharlsen of her engagement before her visit to Scotland. Though emotionally certain what she wanted, the sheer irrational force of it seemed to put her into a realm where there are powers that must not be taken for granted, or they will suddenly withhold what they had seemed to give. She and Doctor Tharlsen had assumed that she would be staying on after completing her degree, to work for a Ph.D. on some aspect of the Frählig MS, and thus continue to help him. Why bother him with the unsettling news before it became a certainty in the rational, bread-and-butter world?

Outwardly he took it well, congratulated her, grasped her hands and kissed her gently on the forehead. Without thought she released her hands and hugged him, as she and her family had hugged each other when she had told them the same news. After a few seconds he eased himself from her grasp and sat down. His mouth worked painfully for a moment or two, but he controlled it.

"I am happy for you," he managed to say. "Very happy. All this"—he shrugged towards his littered desk—"is nothing beside it."

Mari dropped to her knees and took his hands again.

"Oh no!" said Mari. "No, please! If I thought marrying Dick meant I couldn't go on helping you, I… I don't know what I'd have done."

This, she realized with a shock, was literally true. Her love for Dick filled and suffused her world. It was the light she saw by, the smell of the air she breathed. But so, more gently, odorless as oxygen, a waveband beyond the visible spectrum, did the Frählig MS. Without either one of them, she would become someone else. Someone less. Moreover, though there was no logical or causal connection between them, through her, inexplicably but certainly, they were interconnected.

"You've got to finish it," she said. "You're nearly there. It's just the *Gelfunsaga* now."

He drew a large yellow handkerchief from his breast pocket, wiped his eyes, blew his nose, and smiled at her.

"Yes," he said in his usual voice. "We will finish it. Between us. And you will take your children into your lap and read them our *Gelfunsaga*."

Dick found their house. It had been a ghillie's cottage, but had fallen into ruin. New owners of the estate had started to do it up for holiday lets, but had overstretched themselves and their bank had called in its loans. It wasn't actually on the market, but Dick had spotted it, fishing, asked about it, and found that the receivers of the estate, to get a minor problem off their hands, would let him have a three-year lease provided he completed the repairs and refurbishment. Mari dropped everything to fly over and see it, and having done so couldn't then imagine wanting to live anywhere else.

She brought photographs to show Doctor Tharlsen. Though they continued to address each other as formally as before, something had happened between them since she'd told him she was marrying Dick, an unspoken acknowledgement that they were now more than colleagues in the Frählig enterprise. They were friends. Mari guessed it was a relationship unfamiliar to him, and she was careful not to strain it, but he seemed positively to like to hear something of her life and interests outside their work, and they'd fallen into the habit of chatting for a few minutes before they began.

"That's what you see when you come out of the door," she said. "The river's fuller than usual, Dick says, because of the snow melt, though it's nothing like we get here, but there's always plenty of water in it. They've had terrible fishing seasons in a lot of the Scottish rivers for the last few years—hardly any water at all , but this one's fed by several tarns up in the hills—they're using some of them for the plant Dick's building. The fishing isn't all that good, actually, not enough pools and spawning grounds, which is why he could afford a day on it in the first place. And he's not going to get a lot more days like that, poor thing, till we've finished doing up the house. The receivers are being very tough about that, and it'll take every penny we've got."

He looked with appropriate interest at the rest of the photographs, and then they settled to work. But after their next session, as she was leaving, he handed her an envelope. There were three words on it in Old Norse, in his meticulous script. "A season's fishing."

The envelope was unsealed, so she opened it. The check inside was made out to Richard Vesey for thirty thousand krone.

He interrupted her protests.

"I beg you, Miss Gellers. I have made enquiries as to the cost. It would give me the greatest pleasure. I have little use for my money, and I needed a suitable present for your husband, that he can enjoy immediately, since you will have to wait for yours. It will give me an incentive to finish."

She telephoned Dick, who, of course, was appalled.

"I'm afraid you're going to have to take it," Mari told him. "My present's going to be his *Gelfunsaga.* That matters to me almost as much as it does to him. He doesn't think he's got that long—his liver's getting worse—and if you don't accept this it'll be a way of telling him we don't think he's going to get it finished. Taking it is an act of faith, if you see what I mean. And listen, the very first thing you can do by way of saying thank you to him is get that telephone line in, so we can be online from the moment we get back."

"Doubt if we'll get broadband this far out."

"Doesn't matter."

They returned from Iceland to, in Mari's case, thrilling news. While they had been away Doctor Tharlsen had been in Yale, where a new and improved image-enhancer had revealed great stretches of hitherto indecipherable text. He had emailed Mari some of the results. Baffling half-phrases had leaped into sense. Fresh overlaps between the Latin and Norse had made obvious what must have lain in the remaining lacunae. Doctor Tharlsen of course would not bring himself to suggest that the end of his task might now be in sight, but between the lines of his dry text Mari could read his excitement.

Dick had less welcome news. Some results of the seismographic survey had come in, showing an apparent rock fault running across a stretch of the hillside upstream from their house. There was a tarn there that he had planned to incorporate into the hydroelectric scheme. They walked up a winding hill track that evening to look at it. When they reached it Mari caught her breath and stood, staring.

In front of her lay a strange feature like a miniature volcanic crater half way up the hillside, holding in its hollow a still, dark tarn that brimmed almost at her feet. The tarn was fed by several streams from the sunlit hills beyond, and spilt out down to the valley by way of a waterfall. Mari could both see and feel that this was a magical place. Dick, in his very different way, had seemed to sense so too.

"There's something pretty big in here," he'd said. "I'd like to have a go at it some day."

"How can you tell?"

"Just a hunch. You get them. They seem to work."

"What will your scheme do to this? I hope it doesn't spoil it. It's perfect now."

"We've got some very stringent guidelines from the conservation people. We're running everything underground as far as possible, but there's bound to be a bit of upheaval while we're working on it, especially if we have to find a way of filling the fault in. I'm going to have to go into that in detail."

"Well, don't spoil this. It's part of the place."

When they had been back a fortnight Doctor Tharlsen returned to Norway. Mari found a brief email from him waiting for her next morning. For the first time in their correspondence he had permitted himself an exclamation mark. More than one.

"Amazing! The whole of the oath exchange is in Old Story Measure! Terribly garbled, but unmistakable. I realized while on the airplane, and worked on it for the rest of the journey. I have the first seventeen lines as certain as they will ever be. I can barely stop to sleep. By Sunday night I may have enough to send you to read at your breakfast on Monday. Perhaps even earlier. Bless you! Bless you! Bless you!"

At first light next day, Dick slithered out from under the sheet, bent over the bed, and kissed Mari's ear.

"Catch me some breakfast," she murmured.

"Don't count on it," he said, kissed her again and left to catch the dawn rise. She lay listening to the hiss of the shower, and relishing her own contentment. She could feel it filling the whole valley, brimming along the hilltops, just as the still summer heat seemed to do. Normally she might have lain like that for the hour or more until sunrise before getting up, but today was clearly going to be a scorcher, literally so in her case by the time the sun had any strength in it, so she allowed herself only as long as it took Dick to finish his shower, and then rose and followed him.

She showered, washing her hair, and dried, then walked naked to the kitchen to make herself some morning tea. She was used to wandering round the house like that. The weather was more than warm enough for it. Even at the weekends there was no likelihood of anyone coming by. The nearest house was two and a half miles down the pot-holed track, with the public road another two beyond that, the entrance clearly marked as private. She brought her cup back to her desk in the living room and switched on her PC to check her email.

While she waited for the server to connect she watched Dick out of the window. Doctor Tharlsen's gift covered a bit over half a mile of the near bank, as far as midstream. The bank plunged steeply down at this point, and continued the slope below the waterline, where the main current had carved out a deep channel, through which it ran steadily, with barely a ripple. No salmon would rise in such water. But a rock shelf jutted out from the further shore, creating broken and turbulent shallows, with stiller pools. Part of this reached within Dick's rights, and the river bailie had told him that good fish had been caught here, and had lent him the dinghy to fish from. Using a rock for an anchor, he could moor in the current, which would then drag the anchor very slowly downstream, so that he could start at the top of the rock shelf and cover the whole length of it and then paddle upstream and begin again. He was now just about to start the process. Mari liked to watch him doing it, because of the characteristically deft fashion in which he accomplished everything on the unsteady little dinghy.

Now he was out in the middle of the river, shipping his oars, letting the current swing the dinghy down towards the shelf, picking up the anchor rock, balancing himself to slip it over the side…

Because she was watching, Mari saw exactly what happened. From the very first she was in no doubt about it.

Just as he had the rock poised to let go, something reached up out of the water—a four-fingered hand, twice human size, the color of granite, webbed to the top knuckles—and grasped the gunwale and dragged it violently down into the water. Unprepared, unbalanced by the rock, Dick toppled over. When the splash and pother had cleared he was gone. The empty dinghy bobbled at the end of its rope. His rod was being swept away downstream.

She ran for the door and headlong down the bank, and dived. No thought had taken place, but something in her had guessed at the speed of the current, so that she hit the water about twenty yards below the dinghy. The same something controlled her swimming, prolonging her dive and then driving into a breaststroke as it slowed, so that she could stay submerged as long as her breath held. Her eyes were wide open, searching. Immediately around her the water, a sky-reflecting mirror from above, seemed almost as clear as the outer air, but shaded into dimness at any distance. Straight ahead of her, close in against the rock shelf, on the border between the light and the shadows, something went surging past.

It was almost the same color as the rock, so she saw it only dimly, and couldn't make out its shape. But its movement, the powerful pulse of the legs that drove it upstream, told her what sort of thing it was. Something like a frog or toad. A toad the size of a large cow. As she fought to follow, the current carried her out of sight.

She surfaced, changed to a racing crawl, and reached the shelf. As soon as the current ran less strongly she turned upstream. As a child, before she'd given up competitive swimming, she'd done better at the longer distances than the sprints. Now, automatically, she struck the fastest pace that came naturally to her. Every few strokes, instead of twisting her head to gasp for air, she kept it submerged, peering for some sign of the thing that had taken Dick.

That was what had happened, she was sure. Again it was the glimpsed movement of the creature that had told her, the action of the near forelimb as it swam—something awkward about it—the other limb wasn't being used to swim with, because it was clutching Dick—clutching effortfully—Dick had been struggling still…

There! Less than a glimpse this time, a shadow-shift only, uncertain, but she put on a spurt, not bothering to peer below until she had counted thirty strokes, and then only briefly. But yes, she was gaining. Her heart slammed, the air she gulped rasped in her throat and wasn't enough. By now, if she'd been merely racing, her stroke would have been losing its rhythm, but strength came from somewhere, came with a passionate energy that told her it would keep on coming until she caught up.

She had no thought about what would happen then, no fear for herself. Indeed, since the first violent shock of horror as the gray arm had come out of the water, she'd felt nothing at all except the urgency to do what she was doing, to follow the thing that had taken Dick, and take him back. Nothing else existed, not pain, not exhaustion, not the cold of the deep tarn water, nothing.

Ahead, the nature of the river changed. A steep stream fed in from the left just where the main river spilt down a slope of rock, a natural weir right across its width. Their confluence had scooped out a deep, turbulent pool. Only two days ago Mari had sat beside it under a parasol, reading and thinking and dreaming and watching Dick fish. Now, as she reached its lower edge, the creature that had taken him rose from the water on the further side of the pool, close against a vertical slab of rock that divided the river from the stream. If Mari hadn't seen it emerge she wouldn't have known it was there, or rather, all she'd have seen was a rounded boulder projecting from the water. There was no sign of Dick.

She switched to a breaststroke so that she could watch the creature while she swam towards it. After a couple of strokes either the boulder changed, or her perception of it. An inch above the water two wide-set eyes gazed steadily at her. She swam straight on. It erupted through the surface, turning as it did so, reached up with a long-boned arm, grasped the top of the slab behind it, and heaved itself out of the water, scrabbling for toeholds with paddle feet. Dick's body dangled inert from under its other arm. Without looking back at her it disappeared.

She turned, chose a landing spot, and scrambled out and up the bank. The thing was clearly visible thirty yards up the steep side-stream, its huge-haunched hind limbs driving it on through the tumbling water with a powerful, toad-like waddle. Dick's inert body was draped over its shoulder. Mari's legs were rubbery and stupid with their own sudden weight, but she forced them forward, climbing like the creature straight up the stream bed, rather than try to wrestle her way through the heather thickets on either side.

Mostly the creature was hidden by the cragginess of the slope, but then she'd see it again, though she didn't dare snatch more than the odd glimpse for fear of missing her footing. At first she seemed to be gaining, but then she started to fall back as her muscles drained their reserves away, however her heart slammed and her lungs convulsed in the effort to feed them.

The creature reached a waterfall, paused, and for the first time glanced back, looking, she thought, not at her but at the hilltop behind her. The movement twisted Dick towards her. Just below his head there was a yellowish streak down the dark gray rib cage. The creature turned back and plunged into the white curtain. Through the foam she saw it starting to climb. She couldn't go that way, but there was a heather-free slope to her right which reached to the ledge from which the fall spilt. As she stumbled slantwise across it the creature emerged at the top of the fall, stood erect, and looked back, again not apparently at her, but at the eastern ridge behind her. She saw it clearly against the skyline, lit by the almost risen sun. The yellow streak was gone. With a surge of hope she realized what it had been. Dick's vomit. The jolting of the climb had worked like emergency resuscitation and made him throw up. So he was alive. Oh God, let him not now have choked on it! The thing paused only an instant and hurried out of sight.

Mari knew where it had gone, knowing what lay beyond the ridge. She raced on up, reached the top, and stood there, recovering her breath. Desperate though the haste was, she must wait and do that. Breath might be life, both hers and Dick's.

Now, as she waited, searching the unruffled surface for some clue to where the creature had taken him, the sun rimmed the sky behind her. Its long light sluiced across the tarn. She felt its touch on her shoulders, and knew there was another blazing day coming. An instant connection formed in her mind, without any process of thought. All her life, since she was a small child, she had liked to be up very early on days like this, because later on, as soon as there was any strength in the sunlight, she would need to be indoors, or cowering under a parasol or smearing herself every twenty minutes with sunblock. It was part of her inheritance, her troll blood. And the creature too. In its haste to climb the hillside it hadn't been running from her, but from the sunrise. When it had looked behind it, it hadn't been interested in her pursuit, nor in the hill behind her, but in the light itself, spilling above the far ridge. How much longer before the deadly moment? Sunfearer. Troll.

Though the thing she had seen was nothing like any troll she had read of or imagined, the identification came to her with complete assurance. Furthermore there would be a lair in the tarn, a cave with an underwater entrance. Something like that was necessary anyway, if Dick was to be still alive when she found him. He wouldn't survive more than another few minutes underwater. Where? Not where she stood, on what seemed almost a natural earth dam holding the tarn in against the hillside; but over to her right and beyond, where the higher ground reached the water, was a line of low cliffs.

She stared towards them. There! Close in below the dark rocks, more to her right than straight across, the utterly still surface was broken by a sudden ripple and swirl, much like a large fish might make, rising almost to the surface to take a fly and then changing its mind and twisting suddenly back. There was a dip in the cliff just this side of the place. Using that as a landmark she jogged round the edge of the tarn, deliberately choosing a pace that wouldn't instantly run her out of breath again. She dived in where the cliffs began and swam on, still well below a racing speed. The water was degrees colder than that of the river below. At the point she had marked, she stopped, gulped air, kicked herself upwards, and jackknifed into a dive. In the increasing dimness the cliff ran on down, still almost sheer. A good twenty feet below the surface she reached a floor of black, peaty ooze. She turned to her left, and just before her breath gave out glimpsed ahead of her a darker patch on the vertical rock. Madness to try it now.

She pumped herself to the surface and trod water, gasping for air. As soon as she dared she dived again. Yes, an opening in the rock, a triangular cranny like the entrance to a tent. Counting the seconds she swam straight into the darkness, and on through the blind black water. The tunnel seemed to run almost straight, and she could feel her way by the touch of her fingers against the rock on either side. Sometimes when all the family had been swimming together, they used to have timed contests to see who could stay under water longest. In those days she could last a minute and a half, but not swimming vigorously as she was now. Call it a minute, she thought, or a bit over. It would be quicker coming out. Forty seconds in, then… She reached the moment, and swam on.

At fifty-five, well past the point where there was any hope in turning back, she saw a change in the darkness ahead. At sixty the change was faint light. At sixty-eight she broke the surface. Retching for air she stared around.

The light was daylight of a sort, seeping in through a narrow crack overhead. It wasn't a light to see by, no better than might have been shed at night in the open by a half moon behind a layer of cloud. She guessed she must be in some kind of cavern, part of the fault that Dick had talked about, perhaps, but in the dimness she could make out neither walls nor roof. She swam forward a few strokes and her feet touched bottom, a shelving rock ledge. As she climbed from the water the only sounds in the stillness were the heaving of her own breath and the patter of drops falling from her hair and limbs, and their fainter echoes.

Not six feet in front of her, a voice spoke. Not a human voice, a soft, deep, booming sound, a drum note that boomed back at her from the cave walls. But its note of questioning surprise told her that it was articulate speech. The thing in the darkness repeated the sound with a different intonation, this time confirming what it had seen. A single word. The strangeness of the voice blurred the two syllables, but she could hear they had not been English. An echo in her mind repeated the sound, and she knew what the thing had said.

"*Woman?*" And then, "*Yes, a woman.*"

"*Who's there?*" she whispered.

"*I do not tell my name,*" said the voice.

"*Troll,*" she said.

"*Rock-child,*" said the voice, correcting her without anger.

Given its voice to focus on she could make the creature out now, a vague dark mass about six feet from her. Its head seemed to be about level with her own, or a little higher, so she guessed it might be squatting, toad-like, on its haunches just above the waterline. It still hadn't crossed her mind to be afraid, but now a shudder of cold shook her body, and she realized how far she had chilled through, and how little reserve of strength she had left to reheat herself.

"*Where is my husband?*" she said. "*You took him. Give him to me.*"

"*He is here.*"

The creature moved, a sudden sideways shuffle, revealing a paler shape that had lain behind it. Mari waded forward, stumbled up the slope and knelt, feeling for Dick with numbed hands. He was lying face down on the rock so she heaved him over, felt for his face, and laid her ear against his mouth. Nothing. Her fingers were too frozen to find his pulse, but he too seemed to be deathly cold. She straddled his body and started to pump at his chest.

"*What do you do, woman?*" said the troll.

"*I bring his breath back,*" she panted. "*Else he dies.*"

"*He sleeps,*" said the troll, uninterested.

"*Rock-child,*" she said, gasping the words out between pumps, "*...we are... sun things... Sun's heat... gives us life... Cold long... we die...*"

She stopped pumping, knelt by Dick's head, pinched his nose, and forced her breath between his lips. She backed off, let the lungs collapse, and tried again. And again. The effort was warming her, but she had little more to give. Even with her full strength, she wouldn't have been able to keep this up for more than a minute or two. She straddled Dick's body again and resumed pumping.

"*Go to the sun, then,*" said the troll.

"*I must take... my husband... under the water... Too*

far... we die... Oh, troll... rock-child... help me... I am of... your blood."

Desperate, she flung herself round to breathe again into Dick's mouth. Nothing. Nothing.

A huge, cold hand gripped her shoulder and hauled her upright. It turned her and she found herself facing the creature, held by both shoulders, looking up at the enormous head. The light seemed stronger now. Perhaps the sun had risen far enough to shine further into the opening, but she could make out the wide-set bulbous eyes and the V-shaped mouth that seemed to split the face from side to side.

"My blood, sun-child?" boomed the troll.

"It's a story in my family," she gabbled, desperate to get back to Dick, but at the same time not to waste this first apparent wakening of the creature's interest. *"One of my forefathers—his daughter was taken by a troll..."* She raced through the first half of the tale... No, not the stupid Christian end—that wouldn't mean anything to it. On impulse, she switched to the fragments that could be gleaned from the *Gelfunsaga*—the inconclusive contest in the cave, the oath-taking—and wrenched herself away, but then crumpled to the floor. She managed to crawl back to Dick but couldn't raise herself to start the resuscitation again. She collapsed against him and lay there.

A voice was booming overhead. With a huge effort she concentrated on the syllables.

"Child of my blood, rock-born and sun-born, I give you your man back. Go now to your place. Wait there. The sun must set. I will bring him."

She managed to raise her head.

"Rock-child," she sighed. *"I am too weary. I cannot swim so far. I cannot hold in my breath so long beneath the water."*

She felt herself being turned over and lifted. With limp muscles she struggled against the creature's grip.

"My man will die," she protested. *"It is too cold in this place."*

"Woman, we are oath-bound," said the creature. *"He will live. I will bring him this dusk. Now, breathe deep."*

She closed her eyes as it carried her into the water, and concentrated on making her breath last as long as possible. As soon as they were under the surface it shifted her to beneath its left arm so that her body could trail against its own. She could feel the steady driving pulse of its hind limbs, and tell from the flow of the water against her skin that they were moving faster than any human swimmer could have done. It wasn't long before the grip changed again, held her beneath the arms, pushed her forward and let go. As she opened her eyes she was already swimming.

There was light ahead. She was at the tunnel mouth. Weakly she swam on and up to the silvery surface.

She made it to the shore beyond the cliffs and climbed out, shuddering, too weak to stand. But the sun was warm enough now to be some use, and life began to come back to her as she crawled round the edge of the tarn. By the time she reached the outflow she could just about totter to her feet. Painfully she climbed down the way she had come, first across the grassy slope by the waterfall and then in the stream bed. By the time she reached the pool at the bottom she could feel her skin beginning to scorch. She slid into the water, and barely bothering to swim let the current carry her home.

Already she had decided there was nothing she could do except trust the creature and wait till nightfall. No point in going for help, to the police, to the water-bailie. How could she hope to persuade them that though Dick had fallen into the river just outside the house the place to look for him was in the tarn halfway up the hill? But at least she could get herself warm, and then fed, and rested. She went to the bathroom and turned on the shower. As the kindly heat seeped into her she realized there was indeed something she could do.

There was no instant hurry. Doctor Tharlsen had set times for all he did. He wouldn't look at his email until Helge brought in his luncheon tray. Mari went into the kitchen, turned on the kettle, made herself a pot of tea and a Marmite sandwich, and carried them into her desk. Her patient window cleaner was still repetitively saving her screen. "Thanks," she whispered, as always, when the touch of her hand on the mouse made him vanish.

She had post, but not from Doctor Tharlsen. Monday, he'd said. She downloaded, not bothering to read more than the subject headings, wrote out her brief message and sent it off. Then she finished her sandwich, set the alarm, and lay down on the bed, not knowing whether she would sleep or not. She did so, almost instantly, and forgot everything.

It came back the moment the alarm went. She went at once to the PC. While she waited for the server to connect she looked, just as she had done that morning, out of the window. Noon blazed down on the moving river. The dinghy bobbled, empty, on its rope—without Dick's weight in it the current flowed smoothly beneath it and it hadn't shifted more than a few paces downstream. She herself felt like that, empty, weightless, with a powerful current sweeping by and herself unable to do more than float on its surface, waiting, waiting…

The server connected. Yes, she had post. Only the line of her address, and the note that there was an attachment. Her fingers moved steadily over the keys, and the text came up. Runes, of course, four four-line verses, one more line of verse and three of prose. She started to read, translating in her head as she went.

Then spoke Raggir, the rock-born marvel,
"No longer yours, O Jarl, is the woman.
"Mine I have made her in my mountain hall.
"A dark cave her body. There breeds my son."

Answered Gelfun, "Goblin, sun-fearer,
"From me you take a treasure of amber.
"No gold in my hoard is half so precious.
"Let her say farewell, have a father's blessing."

At his knee the woman knelt for his hand.
By the hair he grabbed her, grasped the bright ringlets,
Fiercely lifted her, laid her against him.
Lean at her neck his knife glinted.

Then said Gelfun, grimly mocking,
"Does she die here, demon? Dies your son also.
"Does she come with me from the mid-earth darkness
"To bear your son in the sweet daylight?"

Raggir the rock-born roared in his anger…
This is as much as I am sure of. The actual oaths are still mainly conjectures, too much so for me even to guess at their gist. Let me know if you need them also. It will take a while to transcribe into a form you can make any kind of sense out of. I must go out now. If you are free this evening, call me and tell me what this is about. I am troubled for you.

                                                   E.L.T.

Mari turned away, weeping. She longed to speak to him. He wouldn't doubt her. There was no one else of whom she could say that, not even her own family. She told herself she must get her strength back, so made lunch of a sort and forced it down, but this time couldn't sleep, and after a while got up and dusted and cleaned the bedroom and living room and scrubbed the kitchen floor and polished Dick's shoes and her own high boots, painfully hauling the dreadful minutes by. As she worked she wondered what she was going to tell people if the creature didn't keep its promise. That Dick had gone fishing somewhere out of sight and not come back in the evening? By now she would have started to search, surely. It was only a half mile of river. His waders were still in the house. If he'd fallen in from the bank he'd have left some trace, his net, gaff, creel… Her mind wouldn't stick to the problem. The creature kept dragging it back to the cave.

She was unable to eat any supper. It was still too warm an evening for anything but shorts and a loose blouse, so as soon as the sun slid below the ridge opposite she smeared herself with mosquito repellent and went out and sat on the bank and waited. A little downstream the stupid dinghy bobbled at the end of its rope. It crossed her mind to fetch it ashore, but that would mean putting the mosquito cream on again, so she left it. She assumed that the creature would carry Dick back as it had taken him, swimming down the river, and bring him ashore where she sat. The current moved soundlessly past, its surface sometimes heart-stoppingly broken by the rise of a fish. Each time, as the swirl broke the smoothness, she thought it was the creature beginning to surface, and then knew that it wasn't. Hope faded with the fading light. It was almost dark when she heard the click of a dislodged pebble, and turned and saw Dick stumbling towards her down the track from the top of the valley.

She rose and ran up the bank and flung her arms round him.

"Oh, darling," she whispered.

He didn't reply, but hugged her clumsily in return. He seemed utterly dazed, unsure where he was, who she was. He found his way beneath her blouse, and his hands began to explore her back as if for the first time. They were stone cold, and her body refused to respond. She had to will herself not to shrink from his touch, and then to answer his caress. Through the fabric of his shirt she could feel the chill of his body. Stone cold. She slid her fingers up, as always when they started an embrace, to the inner edge of his right shoulder blade, and found the little nodule, like an old scar, where the skin dipped towards the spine. It was a birth defect, apparently, that ran in his family. Some rearrangement of the nerves beneath made it supersensitive to touch, causing him to sigh and half shrug the shoulder as she stroked it. Not now. Too stone cold, even for that.

Stone cold. He shouldn't be alive, or at least in a coma. Stone.

"*Rock-born,*" she whispered. And then, continuing the guess, "*Raggir.*"

His hands stopped moving. She loosed her hold on him, took him by the elbows, and pushed herself away. He didn't resist.

"*Where is my husband?*" she asked softly.

"*He is here also.*"

It was Dick's voice, but not a language Dick knew. She wasn't surprised, or angry, or frightened. Her mind seemed utterly clear. There was still one hope only, and she knew how she must achieve it.

"*No,*" she said again. "*I must have my husband. Him only. Listen, Raggir, rock-born, and I will tell you a tale. Long ago, in a country across the sea, you took a woman to your cave. She was Gelfun's daughter. Gelfun came to your cave. You said, 'This woman is mine now. She carries my son in her womb.' Gelfun took her. He put his knife to her throat. He said, 'Give her back to me or I kill her, Then your son dies also. But let me take her, and I will raise your son as mine.' You and he swore oaths and made it so. Now I, Mari, of the lineage of Gelfun, say this. Take me, rock-born, by guile or by force, put your seed into me, and I will kill myself, as Gelfun would have killed his own daughter. Then you will lose both your new child and your old child, by whom your blood is in me. But give me back my husband, him alone, him living, and I will give you a gift as great to you.*"

He stood for a while, simply looking at her in the late twilight.

"*Do you drive me from my place, as Gelfun drove me?*" he asked. "*He would have brought an army of men, to dig out the rocks, to drain my lake away, to beset my cave and take me and bind me with chains and drag me into the sun. I am the last of my kind. Therefore I took the ship he gave me and came to this land. Long I lived sadly before I found my cave. I would not live so again.*"

"*This is my gift to you,*" said Mari, and explained to him as best she could about the hydroelectric scheme. He didn't seem to find it strange.

"*It is in my husband's hands,*" she finished. "*At his word it will be done or not done. Therefore he must live, so that I may persuade him.*"

"*Unfasten the boat,*" he said. "*Take it to the rock in the middle of the river. Wait there.*"

He turned and walked down the bank. At the river's edge he leaped, frog-fashion, into the water.

Mari stripped off and followed. Reaching the dinghy she used the anchor rope to haul herself down to the river bed, untied the anchor rock by feel, and surfaced gasping. Then she turned on her back and kicked across the current to the stiller water close by the rock shelf. Once there she could take it more easily, simply maintaining her position. The first she knew of the creature's return was the boom of its voice close behind her.

"*That is good. Stay there.*"

Nothing happened for a while, though she could tell from the slackened current that the creature was still there, sheltering her from its flow. She assumed it must be doing something concerned with separating itself from Dick's body, though it was already speaking in its own voice, not his. Then it grunted and she heard the splash of its heaving itself up onto the shelf. It waddled past her with Dick inert in its arms and lowered him into the dinghy.

"*Child of my blood, farewell,*" it boomed. "*I leave you with a choice.*"

It leaped neatly into the water and disappeared.

Mari towed the dinghy ashore, somehow heaved Dick out onto the bank, and dragged him on up and into the house. By the time she had got him into the living room she was almost spent. She knelt beside him and felt for his pulse. It was there, faint and slow. She switched on all the heaters, stripped off his sodden clothes, dried him and rolled him into a duvet, flung another one over him, and then dried herself and wriggled in beside him, holding him close, trying to warm him through with her own warmth. Now she could actually feel the movement of his breathing. She slid her hand under him, felt for the cicatrice and stroked it gently. His shoulder stirred and she heard his sigh.

He slept almost till noon next day, but Mari woke at the usual time, slipped out of bed and stole away to her desk. There was a long email from Doctor Tharlsen, with further fragments from the oath-taking passage of the *Gelfunsaga*. Several of them now slid into place. Likely links emerged. She wrote back briefly:

Take this for the moment as a dream. It was not, but I would rather not tell you in writing, even in runes. I have met Raggir. He took Dick, and I followed and took him back, using the same threat Gelfun used about killing his daughter. I couldn't have done it without you. This is what Raggir told me about what happened next. It is not the words of the MS, but the gist of the events. You will see where it fits…

When she had finished her account she went to *Britannica Online* and read up about the mating behavior of the amphibia.

"What happened?" said Dick as he wolfed his way through an enormous breakfast. "Something tipped the dinghy over. That's the last I remember."

She had never lied to him, and wouldn't do so now.

"I'll tell you this evening," she said.

She did so in the dusk, sitting at the edge of the tarn, with the stream beside them racing towards the waterfall.

"I suppose you could get a wetsuit and oxygen mask and go down and find the cave," she said as she finished. "I think I'd have to go first and ask his permission. Otherwise I don't know what he'd do."

"I don't need to," he said. "I would have believed you in any case, but in fact I saw his arm come out of the water, only I thought I was hallucinating. What did he do it for? Trolls eat people, don't they?"

"He needed you alive. He is the last of his kind. He told me that. He can't father any more trolls, but he's found a way of passing something on. Look at me. I'm human all through, but I still have troll blood. Look how I scorch in the sun. That's inherited from him. He wanted to come to me in your body—I don't know how he does that—he made himself into a rock for a moment or two when he came out of the pool at the bottom, but that isn't the same thing. I don't think we're the first ones. I think he looks in through people's windows at night. He wasn't at all surprised when I told him about electricity.

"Anyway, he was going to make love to me in your body and we'd have a baby. It would still have been your child—I don't believe he and I could actually cross-breed, we're too different—but he'd have passed something on again—troll blood on both sides…"

"You know, I have a sort of dream memory of walking towards you. It was almost dark. You ran to meet me and we hugged each other, and then you suddenly pushed me away."

"He said you were there too."

"I'm still believing all this. It's an act of faith."

"But you are believing it?"

"I think I have to… there's something else?"

"Yes… This is… well, see what you think. I read up about frogs and toads and so on this morning. Most of them mate in water. The female releases the eggs and the male fertilizes them. I told you he made me go and fetch the dinghy and take it to the rock shelf. I waited for a bit, and then he popped up close behind me and just stayed there for two or three minutes before he climbed out and put you in the dinghy…"

Her voice had dropped to a shaky whisper with the strain of telling him. He took her hand and looked at her with his characteristic half-tilt of the head.

"Frogs and toads. I've seen them at it. They hug each other pretty close, don't they? And it goes on for hours."

"It was only a couple of minutes. And no, he didn't touch me. But…"

"You didn't release any eggs?"

"I'm due to ovulate in a couple of days"

"And then…?"

"I think it depends on us. He said he left me with a choice. He can't fertilize me by himself."

"And you want to have the child?"

Mari had managed to suppress consideration of this. What she, personally, wanted had seemed of no importance beside Dick's possible reactions. But now that he himself asked the question, she knew the answer, knew it through every cell in her body. It was as if a particular gene somewhere along the tangled DNA in each cell had at the same instant fired in response.

"I don't know about want… oh, darling… I just don't know!"

"You feel somehow, as it were, compelled? A moral duty, perhaps?"

His voice was drier, more remote than she had ever heard it.

"Something like that," she whispered.

He thought for a long while, still holding her hand as he stared out across the motionless tarn.

"I meant what I said about faith," he said at last. "If you believe you're right, then I believe too."

"Oh, my darling…"

"Do you want me to keep your side of the bargain?"

"If you can find a way."

The birth wasn't abnormal, except that it was far more difficult and painful than even the midwife expected. She sent for a senior colleague to confirm there was nothing more she might be doing, and the colleague stayed to help. Mari was barely conscious when it was over. Her hand was clenched on Dick's and wouldn't let go. Through dark red mists she heard a low-voiced muttering, the younger woman first, doubt and disappointment, and then a reassuring murmur from the older woman. She forced herself to listen and caught the last few words in a strong Scots accent. "… a look you get round here. I've seen three or four of them like that, and they've turned out just grand."

They put the still whimpering baby, cleaned and wrapped, into Mari's arms, and she hugged it to her. The mists cleared, and she looked at the wrinkled face, the unusually wide mouth, the bleary, slightly bulging eyes.

"Spit image of you," said Dick cheerfully.

"Troll blood," she whispered.

"Both sides?"

(Gently. Carefully teasing.) She smiled back.

"Just one and a bit," she whispered. "Wait."

She slid her hand in under the wrap and explored for what she had already felt through the thin cloth. Yes, there, on the other shoulder from his, and lower down. Delicately with a fingertip she caressed the minuscule bump in the skin. The whimpering stopped. The taut face relaxed. The shoulder moved in a faint half shrug, and the lips parted in an inaudible sigh of pleasure.

THE COLOR LEAST USED BY NATURE

TED KOSMATKA

Ted Kosmatka's [www.tedkosmatka.com] *work has been reprinted in numerous Year's Best anthologies, translated into more than a dozen languages, and performed on stage in Indiana and New York. He has been nominated for both the Nebula Award and Theodore Sturgeon Memorial Award, and is co-winner of the 2010 Asimov's Readers' Choice Award. His first novel,* The Games, *was published in 2012. His second novel,* Prophet of Bones, *will be published in spring of 2013. During the week he's a video game writer at Valve, where he's spent most of the last two years as a member of the Dota 2 team. Weekends though, often find him out on the water, or working on his old sailboat.*

The trade winds carried the sound of hooves.

Inside his small boat works, Kuwa'i put down his awl and looked to the window.

"So, it's time," he said.

Kuwa'i didn't mind that the administer's men had come finally to end him. He had since that morning known himself to be a story in need of an end, and so only smiled softly when the men pulled up their reins in a cloud of red dirt and climbed wearily down from their horses.

They hesitated then, lingering, checking their weapons—five clay men balanced evenly between the hard ride behind them and the hard thing left before them to do. The shortest of them turned, grim-faced, and Kuwa'i shook his head sadly in recognition. Though the other men carried revolvers, this one bore twin knives in his belt.

Kuwa'i had known they would come, of course, these five men, or five others—he'd known since he woke that morning and found his son's bunk empty. It was natural that it should happen; there could be no other response.

Today his boat works would burn.

He'd closed up early out of respect for the safety of any customers that might come wandering in. The administer's men would abide no living witnesses, and Kuwa'i saw no reason to risk deepening the tragedy. He'd waited until the sun was high before flipping the sign and taking off his smock for the last time.

He had then put each of his tools carefully in its place: the long saw, the hatchet, the binder, the adze—each on its assigned shelf along the back wall of his work space. The awl, the chisel, the mallet—tools whose only place was amid the clutter of whatever project he was working on—these he placed carefully on the workbench in a neat line. He allowed his fingers to caress the awl, his favorite tool, if a common workman like himself were permitted such a luxury. No other tool, when working with wood, was so much an extension of the hand.

The thought made him look at his hands, which were still strong and steady for all his years, though they now bore the seams and creases of many decades' work. His father's prayer sprang to mind: *Let my son's life be a thing of use, Lord. May he be a tool in your hands.*

Kuwa'i's life had grown into just that: a thing of use. In the fifty-eight years leading up to this day on which his story would end, he had become the finest builder of boats there had ever been on the island of Hiwiloa.

It is a mark on a map around which the whole of the Pacific wheels. Mountains rise from glittering blue water—a place found, then lost, then found again, until finally pinned to existence by lines of latitude and longitude. By numbers on a map. *Hiwiloa.* West of the Marquesas, north of the Cooks. One of a thousand Pacific islands, a thousand miles to anywhere.

Kuwa'i grew up chasing crabs at the lagoon's edge, playing in the black sands while the tides came and went.

His father was a half-caste woodcutter who harvested the high forest of its specialty timber, a particular tree which his grandmother's tribe called walking tree, and which the local boat-building industry called peran wood, and which books called nothing at all. It was light and strong, like Kuwa'i's father, and the boat builders from the harbors were willing to pay for it.

On many afternoons as a child, Kuwa'i followed his father as they trekked the winding beaches to the nearest town, their burden of peran wood balanced between brown shoulders. Near the docks, amid the businesses and the hustle of the island's traders, they sold their day's work for paper money and sometimes bought meats, and cheeses, and shiny steel nails that could be bent into fishhooks. Young Kuwa'i would watch the comings and goings of the people and the ships—the men in uniforms who strode down gangplanks from enormous metal steamers. "Hiwiloa is two islands at the same time," his father liked to say to him as they watched the crowds. "One old and one new." And then his father would tousle his dark hair. "You can live in both."

In the evening they walked the beaches back home.

They lived in a place called Wik'wai.

It was not a town so much as a grouping of farmsteads, a collection of families. In truth, it was the valley that was called Wik'wai, which in the old language meant fast water; and should the families have moved away and another people moved in, they likely would have called the place Wik'wai, too, out of sheer fittingness of language to God's creation. Perhaps it had happened a dozen times in the long history of the island's habitation.

The Wik'wai of Kuwa'i's childhood was a place of numerous bantam chickens and occasional spotted pigs, of children seen only in motion. The huts were made of wood and *pili* grass and were, for the most part, surrounded on three sides by taro patches scratched into the rich volcanic earth. There were no flowers planted among the homes; one had only to venture into the forest for that. Cultivation was saved for breadfruit, and taro and sweet potato of several varieties, planted in neat rows. For beauty you had only to cast your eyes up toward the mountains, or out toward the waterfalls that gave the valley its name, or down to the base of the hills where the land opened to the vast blue-green lagoon that circled the island in a protective embrace.

Wik'wai was not poor or rich because those are terms meaningful only in their relativity to other states of being, and for most of the people from the place called Wik'wai, there was only Wik'wai.

Suffice it to say it was a place in which you could be endangered by starvation, provided you refused to eat. A place where you might face homelessness, provided you chose not to build a house from the materials easily at hand. It was even a place where you could find trouble, and tragedy, if committed to the search.

Kuwa'i was raised in a home at the far edge of the valley, because his half-wild father was uncomfortable with more than one foot out of the forest. On the Sabbath, his mother brought him to the tiny chapel where they taught him the right ways, but the other six days belonged to the island—to its beaches and forests, to its simple rhythms, old beyond old.

When Kuwa'i had finally counted enough years, his father brought him along on expeditions for timber. During these times, they'd travel on foot for many days through the trees, across streams and upward into the mountains to which cool mists clung in a perpetual cloak of fog. And Kuwa'i's father would remark each time as if it were the first, "They say the top of the mountain is just beyond here, but I do not believe it." And then he'd ask, "Have you ever wanted to touch a cloud?"

And Kuwa'i would say each time, "Yes," and they'd laugh as they ran together, knocking aside damp green fronds, arms splayed, fingers raking the gray-white mists that wafted upward along the verdant slope. Kuwa'i learned that clouds felt like nothing at all more than this sensation. Of running. Of damp so small and fine and sharp that it is experienced as icy needles on the bare skin of one's face. And he learned that here, in the clouds, on a natural terrace at the edge of a cliff, were the trees which books called nothing at all.

They were not tall trees—their bark black and sooty with age, long fronds a silver-gray, drooping almost to the ground. The trees were wide, and gnarled, and, to an individual, ancient. And some part of Kuwa'i recognized that it hurt his father to kill them. Kuwa'i and his father took only one tree each time, chopping a full morning to piece out the core wood, which was the part that the boat builders wanted for their frames.

Around the trunk of each tree was tethered a thin white rope of screw-pine fiber which bound the tree to an anchor of rock some dozen feet away.

"Why are the trees tied to rocks?" Kuwa'i asked.

"To keep them in one place."

"Are the winds so great?"

"Before people came to the islands, there were only trees to act as people, so the trees walked and spoke. When people came, the trees retreated to the mountains and forgot their speech, but never their travels."

"That's just a story," the boy said.

"No," his father replied. "It is the old magic."

"In school they say there's no such thing."

"This is the last of it on the island," his father said. "There used to be more, but that was before I was born." He gestured for the boy to look closer. "Now there's just this."

Kuwa'i bent and inspected the bindings. In the mud beneath the trees could be discerned a well-beaten rut where each tree had walked the limits of its tether in a circular path. The boy nodded to himself, accepting the possibility of his own eyes.

His father continued, "For a long time, the walking trees looked down from the mountain and watched over the island people. Later, when the *Kuhiki* came with their steel, and their cattle, the trees began throwing themselves off the cliff."

"Why would they do such a thing?"

His father shrugged. "Who can guess at the ways of trees? When my mother's people learned of the suicides, her father climbed the mountain and tied all those you see here. Now they are all that remain."

Kuwa'i put his hand to the bark.

"It's hot."

"They burn slowly, from the inside out."

The boy nodded again. "Why are they all so old?"

"Because they've been alive a long time," his father answered matter-of-factly.

"I mean, I don't see any young ones. I don't see the saplings."

"There are no saplings."

"Why?"

"Things without book names often vanish from the world."

"The walking trees are going to vanish?"

"There is steel here now," His father said. "Magic cannot stay."

And then, after a long and silent contemplation, Kuwa'i asked, "Why do you not believe the top of the mountain is just beyond here?"

"Because I do not believe in the top of the mountain."

Even in the wildest, oldest valleys of Hiwiloa, school was an option most families indulged their children in to some extent. Almost every child began school at some early age, and thereafter could choose to attend and learn, or not. They learned the book history of the islands: how the first people lived under chieftains in superstition and darkness, until there arrived from across the water a new people who came in small numbers at first, but who kept coming, bringing roads, and schools, and medicines. And the need for medicines. Most of the valley's children attended school so long as they had curiosity of wider things, and once satisfied of their place in the world, afterward contented themselves with the narrower aspects of daily living along the water's edge. There were, after all, chores to be done, and fish to be caught, and adventures to be had—each in proportion to one's temperament.

Kuwa'i was unusual not in his curiosity of the wider world—there were others who shared his curiosity—but he was rare for the narrow focus of his interest. Even as a child, Kuwa'i was fascinated by boats. He watched them from the sandy shores of the lagoon as they plied the trade route around the island, sails guttering in the wind that blew from the East. He loved the way they moved, leaning hard into the waves under their burden of wind.

Laklani Pritchard, one of the oldest and most prosperous boat builders on the island, noticed the child watching the boats as he played in the water under his father's watchful eye. Laklani had never had children of his own. He bent toward young Kuwa'i, gesturing with a small chunk of wood he'd been whittling on to pass the time. He placed the piece of wood on the water near the boy's knee. "A boat for you," he said.

But Kuwa'i only looked down at the crude chunk of flotsam. "A boat is like a knife," he said, and he cut the water with the blade of his hand in a way that made no splash at all.

In embarrassed outrage, Kuwa'i's father sprang to his feet and apologized to Laklani for the boy's rudeness. The old boat builder only stared at the child and said nothing. The next day, Laklani made the long walk to their house at the edge of the valley and made a formal offer to apprentice the boy.

This was a great honor, and when Kuwa'i's father expressed his surprise, Laklani would say only, "The boy has a sense for boats."

Kuwa'i grew strong over the coming years, though never tall, and in addition to tending his employer's garden, and fetching water, and cooking meals, he learned through meticulous attention to detail the craft of woodworking and the art of building ships. He was by all accounts a prodigy and mastered quickly the hard-earned lessons that most shipwrights spent a lifetime accumulating.

In the late evenings, while the valley's other young men played either peaceful matches of *motaro'a*, or violent battles of cricket, he would walk the shores near his home, taking note of the water, for the old shipwright had told him that to know boats, you had to first know the ocean. On the western shores of Hiwiloa, in the lee of the wind, the water is calm—an undulating blue expanse broken only by the spouts of dolphins. But on the windward side of the island, unprotected by the lagoon, the waves took on a different character, and here the ocean revealed its true nature. Kuwa'i walked the black sands down to the waterline until incoming waves slammed his knees, threatening to yank his feet away. He stood, and he watched as the sliding ocean drew back from the shore like an arm ready to punch and then struck a curling blow to the island. Again and again. Such was the ocean's dislike. And the shining blue water rose, beautiful and deadly, glistening in the bright sun, pulling itself to the height of a man, then taller, rising like indignation, to crash down in a frothing tide that surged up the sand toward him—and Kuwa'i knew it was only a special kind of boat that might go safely beyond the lagoon and out into the open ocean.

When the opportunity presented itself, he still accompanied his father on expeditions for timber. They returned to the mountain terrace season after season, year after year, while the price of the precious commodity climbed, until finally, together, when Kuwa'i was sixteen, they faced the last of the ancient, gnarled walking trees. It stood among a field of stumps, a final dying specimen, so hot it could barely be touched. His father hesitated with his axe. "We can buy new nets," his father said. "New shoes and a bolt of cloth for your mother." The axe fell.

His father collected the last segment of white screw-pine rope. They did not talk much as they returned to Wik'wai, backs bent under their combined burden of core wood, grief and guilt. And when the timber was laid out at Laklani's shop, Kuwa'i made the old carpenter understand this wood was to be the last of its kind.

"Then we will build something special from it, you and I," the old man said.

Later that season, when the boat was just begun, Kuwa'i's father died of an epidemic that burned a black seam through the island, starting in the harbors, striking down the families with old names and leaving the new.

The funerals were grand and sad, and Kuwa'i was strong for his mother and did not cry, supporting her slumping form while they walked from the grave. And afterward he could not recall the funeral—could not recall if it had been raining or dry, if the elder's words had been solemn or uplifting. He could not recall his mother's expression as they lowered her husband into the ground. He could not recall if there had been flowers, though he supposed there must have been. He couldn't recall anything about that day, and sometimes he wondered if he had been there at all.

Laklani pulled him aside. "The old families die worst of the new sicknesses," he said. "Be glad for your mixed blood."

Utterly lost, Kuwa'i threw himself into his craft, sublimating his grief into an obsession for the new boat. He shaped the last of the wonderful peran wood into a frame of his own design, binding rails along the sides like the ribs of a great starving dog. The wood from walking trees was stronger and more flexible than other kinds of timber, resulting in strange design possibilities. He combined the old outrigger design with the new shapes he'd seen in the harbors; and to that eccentric compound he blended a shape seen only in his head. He curved and raked the transom, pushing the limits of the material, forming the hull in a confluence of strong, malleable planks that developed more and more, as the summer wore on, into something that looked decidedly alien. The lagoon had never seen such a boat.

Sitting on the center beam, he paused in his work. "Why do the old families die worst?"

Laklani did not look up from his sanding. "The old families are good at many things," he said. "Staying is not one."

On the hottest days, the old carpenter's niece, Elissa, would bring them coconuts of cool milk. She was a year older than Kuwa'i and already the long-suffering wife of a shopkeeper's son in nearby Ahana, a large town a half day's travel along the beach. Disinclined towards his father's occupation, disinterested in manual labor, and dismissive of his nuptial vows, her husband also had the fault of choosing occasionally to expend his considerable untapped energies through quite astonishing violence—and after those occasions, if she could walk, she came to stay with her uncle for a while. To Kuwa'i she arrived as a chameleon, this sleek, large-eyed creature with a wide, fine mouth—whose bruises changed colors over the weeks that followed.

She watched the men while they worked, and after looking for a long afternoon at the structure developing before her eyes, she said her first words, "It looks like two machetes."

The old carpenter laughed from his stool, saying, "That's it then! We have found a name for her: *Two Machetes*." And he ran up to his niece and kissed her hairline. "Thank you. It is good luck when a woman names a boat."

Elissa seemed to blossom under the attention, and though her cheekbones no longer quite matched each other, her smile was a thing which ate her entire face, and she was suddenly transformed and so beautiful that Kuwa'i felt his face grow flushed. He put the awl down and stared openly at this striking girl who had such an amazing plentitude of wide, perfect teeth—and then, thinking of her husband, he wondered how she had managed to keep them.

Word of *Two Machetes* spread, and as the weeks passed, the old carpenter's shop received many visitors. Some from as far away as Moloa, the island's biggest town, which sat on the opposite shore. There were offers made, and always old Laklani would put them off, saying, "I never discuss money until a boat is finished." But he'd tell Kuwa'i the numbers as they ate their lunch, and the seventeen-year-old hadn't known such money existed in the world.

On the last day before the boat was finished, when there were only the toe rails and riggings left unfinished, Kuwa'i went back to the launch after dinner, and, intending to watch the sun go down in the trees beyond the lagoon, he climbed up onto the deck of *Two Machetes*.

Elissa found him in the twilight.

She touched the back of his neck and did not ask what was wrong, only kissed his wet cheeks softly with her amazing mouth, an invitation to a deeper kind of kiss; and he accepted, moving toward her, running a hand along her sinewy contours.

Though her skin and eyes were dark, she was long-waisted in a way not found among native islanders, and he discovered her hands in his, larger than his—some mixture of ancestry producing long, delicate fingers. And then she guided him back, her hair a black wash across his chest as she whispered into his mouth, "My husband cannot...unless he beats me first."

"I would never," Kuwa'i said.

She replied only, "I know," like she understood this, and their teeth grazed each other slickly as she moved on him—and the sensation was of something remembered, though never before experienced, as if his body knew it already: like dreams of falling, of dying, might one day make those acts seem familiar. And in the middle of it, he felt connection to everything that had come before, and everything that might come after, and he knew that when he one day tallied his life before the God of the little chapel, he would count this among his very favorite things.

The heat of the day brought the bidders again, and without very much trouble the boat was sold to a merchant from Ahana who seemed truly grateful for the opportunity to buy it—and who paid extra to have the sails done in red canvass. Elissa and Kuwa'i used every smallest excuse to be alone and played at love several times a day over the next few weeks. If Laklani knew, he said nothing.

On the morning her husband came for her, Elissa had a nightmare that she was falling, and Kuwa'i woke to her gazing down at him from her elbows.

"Do you love me?" she asked.

"Yes," he replied without thought or hesitation.

Elissa's husband was called Myer, and he arrived at midday accompanied by a group of big men who worked hard at looking as if they were all simply out for a casual stroll. Myer was tall and broad-shouldered and fair. His eyes were sandy-colored, like his hair, and he moved easily among the people of the valley, talking and laughing as his men walked toward the boat works. He wore a shirt like brown canvass, in the style of men from the mainland, though when he spoke, Kuwa'i could detect no accent.

"Elissa," he called out when he saw her. "I see your visit did you some good. You look well."

Elissa stood frozen. Gone pale and expressionless, the asymmetry of her broken cheekbones once again apparent, she looked suddenly most unwell.

Myer strode up to her and gathered her in his big arms.

"I've missed you," he said, then whispered so his friends could not hear, "I'm sorry." He turned back to the crowd of people he'd brought. "Let's celebrate!"

That night there was a large pit dug into the ground and lined with stones, and in it was roasted three whole fatted pigs that Myer paid extravagantly for, and most of the nearby families were involved. They danced around the fire well into night. Laklani remained distant, refusing to be pulled in by the lure of festivities. Kuwa'i sat on the rise near the waterfall, watching the party with a sense of dread. In the night, Elissa managed to get away, and she found him sitting on a rock with his feet in the water.

"Let's run away," she said, out of breath from her scramble up the hillside. "Tonight, let's leave this place."

The waterfall cascaded down from above, splashing into the pool, making ripples on the water. "Where would we go?" Kuwa'i asked.

"I don't care. Let's take a boat for ourselves and let the wind take us where it's going. There are other islands beyond these."

"I couldn't steal."

"You built most of them! It wouldn't be stealing."

"It would."

"You'd just be taking one back. You deserve a boat of your own for all the work you've done."

"It wouldn't be right."

"I don't care what's right. Let's go now before my husband comes looking for me."

"This island is my home, I can't just leave in the middle of the night."

"Then when?"

Kuwa'i stared at her. "When it's not my home anymore."

"*Please—*"

"Elissa," he whispered. "I can't."

She dropped her eyes—and something happened, a change, like a chameleon, and she appeared a different kind of creature than she had been moments before, deflated, the hope having seeped out of her.

"I—" Kuwa'i began.

She put a finger to his lips, silencing him. Then she turned and went back to her husband. In the morning the couple was gone.

Laklani did not speak to Kuwa'i for three days, and when he did, said only, "You let her go back."

Kuwa'i blinked at the accusation. He had no response.

And in the coming days, Kuwa'i found he could not endure the emptiness. The silent work. The daily lack of her that would have no end.

He probed the place that she'd occupied in his life and found only a silent, hemorrhaging cavitation.

He walked the beach to the nearest town where he sought out a tavern to dull his wound; but the old man behind the bar, who managed the trick somehow of being both old and wise beyond his years, only listened to his plight, and when Kuwa'i asked for a second drink, said, "Drink won't help," and pointed out through the window at life going on in the street— a small gathering of dark-haired girls talking in the market, and Kuwa'i understood what the old man meant.

Kuwa'i charged across the street and asked the prettiest one to go for a walk with him. She agreed, and he discovered her name was Anna, and two nights later, in her parents' house while the rest of the island slept, he discovered her body was like a thing remembered, and her taste like ripe melon.

Laklani's tendency toward silence devolved into a kind of verbal longhand. They communicated only about boats, and only if the boats were projects they worked on. Their lunch times became studies in quiet bereavement, and Kuwa'i chose eventually to work straight through the day. The boat works prospered, and Kuwa'i's reputation began to eclipse that of his master. People came from faraway places to gaze at the ships.

One evening, a rich man from Motoa visited old Laklani in the boat yard, bringing with him a tall, long-haired daughter who hung back from the business talk of men, instead wandering to inspect the half-finished boat. She caressed the tools with a delicate index finger. "You're the craftsman my father talks about," she said. And Kuwa'i stopped his hammering and turned his head in search of whom she might be speaking to. She laughed, mistaking his ignorance for humor, but astride him later that night, she explained why buyers were drawn to his work above others. "Your boats are beautiful," she said. And then she lay back on his sheets while he slid above her, and she showed him what action to take so no dishonor would come of it. Afterward, as they lay in the stillness of his bunk, she asked, "How is it that boats can sail against the wind?"

"Not straight against it," he said. "But only at an angle."

And he told her that the minor god Kulipali had bequeathed his tongue so that men may make keels. And he told her about the steel hulls of ships he'd seen in the harbors, and about the humble outrigger that had conquered oceans, and he told her that in the old language, which he could not speak, the word for horse was *canoe-which-walks-on-land*.

It was nearly seven months later that Laklani spoke to him regarding something other than work. The broken silence was shocking as a thunderclap, and Kuwa'i could not, for a moment, pry understanding from the words.

"What did you say?" Kuwa'i asked.

"Elissa has a baby."

Kuwa'i stood perfectly still for a moment. Then without taking off his work belt, he climbed down from the launch, scrambled up the shoreline and set out at a dead run for the town of Ahana.

He found the town larger than he remembered, but not so large that people might be strangers to each other. Still, oddly, it took him nearly half an hour to find someone who knew of a young girl named Elissa with wide perfect teeth.

The man said only, "I know who you're talking about." And there was an irony in his voice Kuwa'i would recognize only later while he sat behind bars and went over the events again and again in his mind.

The house was small and wooden and deteriorated, with the wind shutters amassed in the dirt below the windows. Weeds grew all around the structure, and from within could be heard the squalling of an infant. Having come this far, Kuwa'i found he could advance no further. He stood in the road as if lacking any sense at all, and those who noticed him thought he was either an imbecile, or in love, and in either case pitied him equally.

Movement through the window caught his attention, drawing him forward so that he found himself walking; and in the doorway, which was open on broken hinges, the sound of the baby's crying was very loud, and when his eyes had begun to adjust, he heard Elissa gasp, and in that instant they saw each other.

Her teeth had been smashed out, at the gum-line, as if by a hammer.

Kuwa'i turned and walked away. He found Myer in the third tavern and buried an awl in one sandy-colored eye.

Myer did not die immediately but instead spent nine agonizing days at it, eventually succumbing to an infection which, by his last hours, had ballooned the left side of his face into a tumescent and suppurating casaba melon which finally split along the jaw-line with a fetid smell of corruption that drove the nurses from the room. And still he had not sense enough to pass, but hung on throughout the night, alternately howling out from his deathbed and gagging noisily on the stench of his own septic brew.

Afterward, they laid him to rest during a quiet ceremony, placing him into the ground next to his wife, Elissa, who had been found with her wrists slit. She had taken Kuwa'i's withdrawal for rejection and killed herself before she learned her husband's fate.

On the evening of the funeral, while Kuwa'i sat shackled to a bench in the Ahana courthouse, it was agreed by all interested parties that the cause of Myer's death had been exactly what it was: an unfortunate though not altogether unforeseeable (or underserved) sepsis of the eye. They absolved Kuwa'i of responsibility for the death, released him from custody, and told him never to return to Ahana, or he would be hanged.

"What about the child?"

"The boy looks like his mother," the judge said, cutting to the point. "Her husband's parents have offered to raise the child as their own to replace the one they've lost."

"They did such a fine job the first time," Kuwa'i said.

"We've offered you your life for nothing. I suggest that you requite yourself of the bargain and do not trouble the boy again, or we may change our minds."

And with that, the matter was settled. Two burly guards escorted Kuwa'i to the town limits, and he left Ahana for the last time.

Old Laklani, when he heard finally of what happened, began speaking again in Kuwa'i's presence. They spent a drunken night at the boat works, crying for Elissa, who died too young and left behind an orphan to be reared by jackals.

"I have no sons," Laklani said. "And now no niece. What did they call the boy?"

"They never said."

"There can be protection in a name. The *Kuhiki* can't remember what they can't write down. They can't write down what they can't pronounce. When you have your own sons, remember, it is a good name that can't be pronounced by outsiders."

Work, as Kuwa'i had found before, was a poor analgesic for a wounded conscience. But there were other ways. Although Wik'wai was a place and not really a town, it came to be known for the boats it launched into the lagoon. The valley prospered, and over the next year, Kuwa'i played at love with many of the girls who lived there, eventually coming to favor, for reasons unclear to himself, darker girls over lighter. Taller over short. And when he realized this, his contrary nature caused him to set his sights on the illegitimate daughter of Wik'wai's seamstress, Iasepa, who herself was reputed to be the offspring of a whaler from beyond the islands. The girl's name was Mara. She was short and unlikely—her hair almost blindingly blond in the summer sun. When Kuwa'i finally managed to drive away the swarm of boys that seemed always to orbit her, he found her intelligent and receptive. She spoke of travel and seeing the world. They explored each other's bodies the first time in the garden behind her house, driving themselves into the dark earth with such fervor that no one who saw the print could have doubted what took place there.

The affair continued for an entire season, and the girl talked and talked on the subject of people, to the exclusion of other subjects, disgorging every smallest gossip in an unending torrent of hearsay until Kuwa'i could stand it no more. When the wind changed, Kuwa'i told her it was over.

At first she denied it. Then grew angry. "Look at you, then look at me," she said, whipping her blond hair over her shoulder. "You're beneath me."

"Then I'm doing you a favor," he said.

"I hope you burn in hell," she said.

The next day Kuwa'i found the boat shop's windows had been smashed out by a rock, and all his tools were stolen. "I will fix the glass," he told Laklani. He paid children to fish his tools from the lagoon.

Their work continued through several seasons, and during this time, Laklani gradually gave over control of the boat shop to Kuwa'i, who accepted the work with enthusiasm but resisted his employer's attempts at financial remuneration. He and Laklani had long contentious arguments on the subject of Kuwa'i's compensation, with Laklani attempting to pay more and Kuwa'i demanding less, while the whole valley smiled at their backward negotiations, which sometimes got quite heated. Laklani eventually took to lying about how much he was paying, and Kuwa'i had to be sure to count his salary carefully because of Laklani's tendency to slip extra money in among a confusing heap of small denominations.

Finally one morning, Laklani did not arrive at the boat shop as a working man just after sun-up, but closer to noon, as a visiting companion. It was a small thing that neither of them discussed, this tardiness. And when Laklani arrived at the same time the following day, they were both sure of what had just happened. Thus was succession achieved. Laklani continued to visit the boat works often, occasionally lending a spare set of hands, which—though their usefulness had declined—Kuwa'i took a sick sort of satisfaction in overcompensating. And thus were their reverse negations resumed, and reversed once more, with Kuwa'i attempting to pay more, and old Laklani demanding less.

Laklani's visits varied in length in accommodation to his moods and health, though, truthfully, his health was remarkably good for a man his age. He had descended into a stolid and steadfast species of enfeeblement which gave every indication of providing for his continued existence above ground well into the next century. He had never smoked and drank only wine, and only then in moderation. He had eaten fish from clean water on every day of his life. Though slightly hunched and less mobile than he had once been, he was still trim and able to get about slowly to where he was going.

His persistence in the world at his current low level of functioning appeared so sustainable that it was widely opined that he would live until something killed him. Which is what happened. And the way it happened shocked no one. Several days before his seventy-first birthday, he fell from the rigging of a boat under construction. He did not rise. Kuwa'i found him slumped on the deck, wood chisel still in his hand. He was put to earth among the tall grass, and all who knew him agreed his had been a fine and full life. They stacked black lava rocks upon his grave, and upon the rocks was lain a large wooden plank carved in intricate filigree, the likeness of a ship.

With the summer heat came restlessness and a tall, dark girl named Lura whose teeth flashed when she talked. Lura arrived with the trade winds on an enormous, creaking cargo vessel from the outer islands. Kuwa'i pulled her aside the first hour he met her, and he kissed her at the docks. That night, they met in the trees at the edge of the forest, and she laid back, long arms circling in the warm earth while her legs locked around him, and afterward, in the golden brazenness of morning's first light, he went to her man and told him she no longer belonged to him. The man looked down at Kuwa'i, who was three inches shorter, and he must have recognized the determination in his eye, or perhaps he'd heard about the awl, because he said, "If she wants you."

"She does."

"Take her then, I have several," he said. "You can't keep a woman who won't be kept."

Kuwa'i said only, "Not for long, anyway." And he put the awl back in his belt.

The next day, before the put-upon and disgruntled elders, and before all the startled populace of the valley, Kuwa'i and Lura declared themselves married.

She bore him two children in quick succession, though the eldest, a girl, never took hold of the world and was buried with a name, Agatha, in a plot near Kuwa'i's father that neither parent could bring themselves to visit. She retreated into her miserable disconsolation, he into his rage. And Kuwa'i would have burned down the forests, and swallowed the streams, and eaten the mountain stone by stone until his teeth were all broken to the gum-line, because he found the world was not large enough to contain his anger, and he seethed with an inner heat that left him, after many months, a man of blackened cinders, and finally, as cold and empty and disconsolate as his wife.

But from the cinders rose another child, a son, grown like a sapling in the newly churned soils of their hearts, and still Kuwa'i could not bring himself to love again all at once but only in installments as the child grew stronger. And at two years old, they finally named him, and they called him Ta'eo Hokiluli'hi'i, which in the old language meant *the one who stayed*. "It is a good name," Kuwa'i said to his wife, "which can't be pronounced by outsiders."

Ta'eo was a bright child like his father, and Kuwa'i showed him how wood could be worked—and together they built a small wooden box so that the boy's mother might have a place for her necklaces. Next they made model boats to be floated at the edge of the lagoon, and Kuwa'i told him,

"A boat is like a knife."

A third child swelled Lura's belly while she still played games with the second. She let little Ta'eo touch her stomach as it expanded, and together they took short walks through the valley, hand in hand, made equal by their off-balanced waddling while she explained to him the uses of things he was curious of. She told him where fish came from and why they preferred the water, and she explained in great detail their astounding facility at breath-holding. "It's why they gasp so much when they're pulled onto shore—their relief at breathing fresh air again." And she told him the sea was blue because all the green had been used by the trees, and all the black by the night, and all the brown by the dirt. And blue was the color least used by nature, and so was the only pigment left in large enough quantities to fill up a thing as big as the ocean.

The boy, though he was still so young he wet his bed, nodded solemnly, because this was all very logical to him.

Together they walked the beaches and collected shells in the small wooden box.

She spent every waking moment with her son, like she knew something was wrong. And in the tenth month, when the new baby still hadn't come, she asked that little Ta'eo stay in the room with her even while she slept, as if she could soak him in to make up for all the time she would lose. All the things she would miss. She put away the little clothes that she'd been making that no baby would ever wear. She put away the little pig-skin pouch that no baby would ever sleep in. She struggled, too, to put away her fear, but it was not so easily folded up and stored away.

She looked at her son who was still so small, and prayed, "Please God, I'm not done yet." But if the God of the little chapel heard her, He gave no sign. So she prayed to the old gods of the islands, but they, too, were silent. Then she prayed to any god, to any being out there that might hear her. "*Please*," she moaned into the nameless darkness, praying at last to it, the final refuge of the hopeless. But only pain answered her prayer, a burning heat inside her which grew over the days which followed.

Her abdomen pulled taut and stony but grew no larger, while her strength ebbed until she could not walk, and finally the lowest form of god was summoned. Without the power to cure, but at least to diagnose—a big man with a German accent and a medical bag, brought in from the harbor town. "The baby inside me is dead, isn't it?" she asked.

And he examined her, and gave her the news. "There is no baby. There was never any baby."

She turned her head away. "But I felt it kick."

But the big German only shook his head. "No," he said. "Only fluid; the cyst has ruptured now." Then he closed his medical bag. "The infection is very advanced. I'm sorry."

Little Ta'eo stayed close to his mother after the strange man left, and he did what the grown-ups asked because even he sensed something was not as it should be, and only when the screaming began did he leave. And only when it ceased did he cry, holding his mother's hand in the dark while the adults around him wailed, and his father raged like a man without his mind, tearing their house down around them; and during the night, the distant chapel bell tolled, and they took away his mother wrapped in palm fronds. Only one old woman remained, saying, "There are some things conceived which can't be born." Finally in the empty room, without his mother's heat, without his father, there awakened in Ta'eo the first understanding that people can end. That life can end. That nothing would ever be alright again.

Kuwa'i had known pain before and knew himself well enough to suspect he might kill somebody, so did not stay for the funeral. And the boy lost both parents in a single stroke.

When Kuwa'i returned several months later, he did not speak of where he'd been, or what he'd done. He inquired as to his son and one late night stopped by the house of the family who'd been caring for him. The woman saw Kuwa'i in the doorway, and she said nothing to him. Instead, she turned and called softly into the house, "Ta'eo." And then softer still, when she had the boy's attention, she said, "Your father is here."

Kuwa'i took his son home, and in the morning, with a new child apprentice, returned to building boats.

The valley of Wik'wai changed subtly with the passing of years, while the rest of the island shifted around them. The sicknesses came and went. The old ways grew older; the new ways, newer. The cattle ranches grew larger, eating more of the land. In the harbor communities, the outsiders kept coming until you might walk the streets and see few besides. Enough different walks of people, in all shades and colors, speaking such a variety of languages, that Kuwa'i had to wonder at how many types of men the world might contain. It seemed to him a flagrant excess on the part of the maker.

And with the influx of people came the steady, inexorable reorganization of power—a thing which had always been happening since the first moment that steel touched the island, but now had reached a tipping point.

For a time, talk of annexation was common as talk of weather.

And as with talk of weather, sometimes, in the distance, there could be heard the evidence of thunder—but those rains never reached Wik'wai. Not directly. But in a thousand little ways, in the number of ways rain reaches the ocean, Wik'wai felt the storm.

He was a man called Underhill.

He'd left Hiwiloa as a landed man and returned six years later with a charter, already the veteran of numerous territorial appropriations that had all begun to run together the way waterfalls run into streams, which run into the lagoon. He returned with his signed articles, and with the authority of foreign gun ships, and the title Local Administrator to the Island. Auspices were invoked. He wore a formal black suit despite the heat, and despite his size. To the locals, he became known as the administer.

Welcomed home by the cattle ranchers and business men, of which he was one, he wasted little time in asserting regulation over Motoa and Ahana, and eventually expanded his sphere of influence until it stretched around the whole island. Legislation was adopted from faraway lands. Men were needed to enforce these prescripts. They called these men deputies of the protectorate , but they were really just the administer's men—his sons and cousins and nephews.

One windy dawn in his son's seventeenth year, Kuwa'i walked the sandy beach of the northern shore, watching the waves crash in while the sun rose out of the glittering water. It was beautiful beyond beautiful—even still, after all the years of looking at it. Later that morning, as he breakfasted with his son on poi and coconut, he said, "This next boat will be the last I build."

"Why do you say that?" Ta'eo asked.

"Because it is true," he said matter-of-factly.

The following morning the two of them set out for the mountains, and Kuwa'i told his son that the top was falsely rumored to be in close proximity. He then asked him if he'd ever wanted to touch a cloud.

The field of stumps was still there, unchanged, as Kuwa'i sensed it would be for another thousand years—because walking trees, in addition to being both stronger and more pliable than normal wood also resisted rot. Kuwa'i put down his axe and told Ta'eo about the special trees that had once carpeted the mountainside. He told him that they jumped from the cliffs if not tethered, and that they'd begun jumping when the first outsiders came to the island.

"I hate the outsiders," Ta'eo said.

"You are them, partly. As am I."

"I don't care."

"It's the same as hating yourself."

The boy looked around at the field of stumps. "Where did the trees go?"

"Into the lagoon, one by one." Kuwa'i said. "Things without book names often disappear from the world." And after climbing for most of the afternoon, they finally located the sapling. It was not yet gnarled, nor thick, nor impressive, really, in any aspect other than its unusual pitted bark. Though it had reached already some measure of its full height, for they were not ever tall trees. It still swayed gently when Kuwa'i pushed his weight against it. His hand came away black, painted with soot.

"I planted this one in the crazy time after your mother died. I was here many months looking for seeds, which are small and curved and brown, like cashews. I found only five. I planted three."

"Why only three?"

"I hoped three would be enough. Why plant trees where they'll want only to die?"

"Where are the two seeds you didn't plant?"

"Back at the house, in your mother's wooden box. Of the three I planted, this is the only one that grew. When it sprouted, I returned and tethered it to a stone."

The tree, in its restless eagerness to die, had worn a circular path around the stone, held back only by its thin white rope.

"This tree is already fifteen?"

"They grow slowly. I planted it so that one day you could cut it down to build your masterpiece."

Ta'eo touched the soft bark, then looked at his father. "It's hot."

"They burn from the inside," Kuwa'i said.

"How?"

"I think they always burn. I think they spend their lives burning."

"I don't want to build boats."

Kuwa'i took a step away from the tree and looked over the cliff. "I know," he said. "I have known for years. I want you to do something for me at least."

"What?"

"When you have a son, tell him the story of these trees."

They knelt at the roots, and Kuwa'i bent forward to caress the pitted bark. The tree vibrated, pulling back from his touch, dark roots twisting along the ground while from above came a sound like wind through the fronds, though there was no wind.

The tree strained against its tether, yearning for the cliff.

Kuwa'i saw that if a blade were touched even lightly to the taught and creaking rope, the tree would fly to its death.

"I come as your friend," Kuwa'i whispered to the tree. "To give you what you want."

With that, he stood. He raised the axe high and brought it down with all his strength, burying the steel in the base of the trunk. The tree shook for a moment, then stilled.

They spent half a day piecing out the core wood. Then they took the precious commodity down the mountain. Five days later, after much planning and careful calculation of where the small measure of precious wood might best be used, they began Kuwa'i's opus.

They worked methodically through the season, and Kuwa'i was careful not to talk of his son's plans. He thought of his father. *Hiwiloa is two islands at the same time.*

In the days before books trapped history, the island people had been travelers. They'd begun their journey long ago, expanding outward from some forgotten homeland, jumping from island to island, and at each new place there were some for whom paradise was not enough; and so the process would continue, some smaller subset raising up and moving on to see what lay beyond the horizon. Not so anymore.

Now the islanders talked of leaving but never did—like the seamstress's blonde daughter, Mara, who made a plump wife to a fisherman in town. (And who, in addition to a slew of brunettes, had also born a child as unlikely as herself, a girl with copper-colored hair—a condition seen only once before in Wik'wai, on a traveler from Hamburg the year before, and thereafter the subject of much speculation.) Kuwa'i thought of the walking tree, and the field of stumps, and of the growing cities, and the steel ships in the harbors, and all the plant-choked trails of Wik'wai.

The lands were stolen, the old ways fading. It would not be long.

Hiwiloa would be one island again.

And the island he'd known as a child would be gone forever.

In the fourth month of construction, at dusk, as Kuwa'i and his son were finishing the interior joinery and beginning the bulkhead housing, a group of men entered the boat shop. Ta'eo heard the bell and walked around to the front to see who had arrived.

"I'm here to see the shipwright," a deep voice proclaimed.

Kuwa'i put down his tools. He walked inside and found four men and a teen-aged boy glancing around the shop. He recognized the black coat immediately. The administer was enormous. He had big arms, and a big chest, and a big belly that swayed independently from the rest of him as he moved slowly around the room. Florid, pockmarked and balding, he appeared far older than Kuwa'i had imagined. But it was old the way a bull gets old. He was one of those men for whom aging is not a deconstructive process, but one of simple sedimentation—a gradual building-upon of layers so that you had the idea there remained a bitter and fossilized embryo buried somewhere beneath all the fat, and muscle, and folds of skin that had accumulated.

"So you're the carpenter," the administer said.

Kuwa'i nodded.

"I want you to build me a boat."

"I build boats, and then I sell them. Not the other way around."

The administer nodded like he understood but then continued on as if Kuwa'i hadn't spoken, "I want you to build me the best boat on the water."

"I build what boats I can."

"They tell me you're the best." The large man walked past him, moving deeper into the room, and Kuwa'i found himself following the administer through his own place of business.

"I've heard much about you," the administer continued. "First years ago, after your trouble, and now these boats." The administer stopped. He stood at the rear of the room, looking out at the boat yard at the edge of the water. "God's grace."

His companions came to rest behind him, open-mouthed, eyes widening on the half-finished construction in the launch.

"You are an artist," the administer said.

"No, I am a just craftsman."

"This is more…" the big man gestured toward the half-finished boat in the launch. "More than just craft, my friend."

"I make things that are to be used, like any craftsman. And like any craftsman, there are rules I must follow. A true artist has no rules. You wouldn't want an artist's boat."

"Why not?"

"It might not float."

The administer burst into laughter and clapped one enormous hand on Kuwa'i's shoulder. "I like you." He bent closer. "I like this boat. I want it."

"I auction my boats when they are finished."

"I want the boat."

"It is the way I've always done it."

"What's the highest bid you've ever taken?"

Kuwa'i told him honestly, and the administer waved off the number in disgust. He snapped his finger and a heavy guard produced a fold of bills, which the administer then placed forcefully in Kuwa'i's hand. "This is almost twice that."

"It's bad luck to sell a boat before it's finished."

"For the seller or the buyer?"

"I'm not sure."

"Well," the administer said dismissively. "We're not superstitious natives, are we? Eh, Issac?" And with that, he winked at the teenaged boy he'd brought with him who, though dark as a native islander, was too lanky and long-waisted to be of pure stock. And Kuwa'i was about to speak again but suddenly could not find the words—halted mid-protest in frozen disbelief—because though the boy's face was a stranger to him, his teeth were Elissa's.

And a moment later the big man laughed uproariously at Kuwa'i's afflicted expression, and Kuwa'i realized this was the administer's joke—this meeting between he and the boy. The administer knew of their history, or part of it. But looking at the boy, it was obvious to Kuwa'i that the joke had been played twice, because the teen looked as confused by his employer's laughter as Kuwa'i was informed by it. As if to confirm Kuwa'i's suspicions, the administer clapped the boy on the shoulder and whispered loudly, "I've got a story for you later."

Kuwa'i searched the boy's dark features for something to call his own, and found nothing. Nor was there Myer. "The boy looks like his mother," Kuwa'i said.

The boy's face became suspicious.

The administer laughed again, absently waving off the drama threatening to unfold before him in the same way he had waved off Kuwa'i's protests earlier. "So then we are agreed. The boat is mine, yeah?"

The boy, who was beginning to suspect what he might be looking at, glared at Kuwa'i from under a growing scowl.

"I'll be back to pick it up in a month," the administer said.

Kuwa'i could not bring himself to say another word.

Over the next several weeks Kuwa'i made it his goal to learn as much as he could about the man named Underhill, this island administrator with a fondness for jokes. He traveled to Moloa and spent time in the taverns, buying drinks for those in the mood to talk. He learned through subtle cross-examination of the local patronage that the administer was merely the most visible manifestation of an extensive family line—one whose various filaments stretched throughout the hereditary topsoil of the islands. His people were from the mainland but had been in the Pacific for generations, amassing land and cattle and power, and more recently, new friends in faraway places.

One thirsty old fisherman was particularly forthcoming on the subject, "He's nephew to the mayor, uncle to most of the police force, Godfather to the local pastor, and boss to half the cattle men on the island."

A further round of drinks revealed that Underhill was also, most interestingly perhaps, cousin to the town grocer, Issac Porter, who had in previous, happier times been father to a strapping son named Myer, now many years deceased of a septic eye. The teenaged boy who'd accompanied Underhill to the boat shop was named Issac after his supposed paternal great-grandfather, and had been put on the administer's payroll as an enforcer. The boy was widely reputed to be good at his job. So good, in fact, that finding people who would talk about him required the last of Kuwa'i's drinking money. "Not a big lad," one drinker slurred. "But fast. He gets the tough jobs."

"Jobs?"

"He's a close-up artist,"

"What does that mean?"

"No guns." The old man took the last swallow of his drink and glanced toward the door. "He carries knives in his belt."

Kuwa'i returned to the valley the next day but, for perhaps the first time in his life, had lost interest in boats.

Still, he and his son worked. They had to, because Kuwa'i had taken money. The boat was no longer theirs, but the administer's. And now, in a way, they worked for him, too. Kuwa'i wondered at the skills of a man that found himself so easily made employer out of customer. That difference was everything.

Occasionally, people would come to watch the project develop, often making comments, or asking questions—but more and more as the boat took shape around its elegant walking tree backbone, the visitors stood back in reverential silence before the ambition of the project. It was the largest craft Kuwa'i had ever attempted, a twenty-eight-foot gaff-rigged sloop, fully nine feet abeam, with an enormous shark fin keel the size of a man. The single cabin dropped below decks and was large enough for two beds, a table, and a large navigation desk. A round window of imported glass looked out from the stern. The sails were bent to the spares with robands and mast hoops the size of dinner plates. The fastenings were bronze. Rising above the mainsail, a jackyard flapped loosely in the breeze along a double row of reefing points. Extending out to the sides, like the bent wings of an albatross, two knife-thin outriggers balanced the project.

Most shipwrights believed you could tell how fast a ship was by looking at it, and everything Kuwa'i knew of boats said this boat was *fast*—perhaps the fastest craft ever to see the lagoon.

Every week or so the administer would send one of his men to check on the progress of the ship, and every week Kuwa'i would give the same answer, "It'll be done when it's finished." Young Issac was never among the men.

During the protracted term of construction, it became apparent that the pale and copper-headed daughter of Mara was in some way involved in the project. Her name was Rebecca, and when Kuwa'i finally noticed her among the crowd who stopped by to watch, he had the feeling that he had missed something important, and she had already been hanging around for several days. The first time she brought the coconut of cool milk, Kuwa'i realized she and Ta'eo were lovers. Kuwa'i took his drink and stood looking at the two young people for a very long time. The girl was beautiful in a sun-damaged way—a tragedy of dark freckles obscuring her features so that you had to look closely to see what she really looked like. Beneath the paint, her features were straight and fine.

He learned through subtle cross-examination of neighborhood friends and visiting patrons that she was soon to be married. The man was large and hot-tempered, a consigner by trade, though he spent much of his time in the taverns. His name was Isban, and he was several parts again her age. Having already worn through the affections of two, she was to be his third wife.

Kuwa'i went to visit her mother, Mara, one afternoon and found her house contained only children of every conceivable age (and some quite unconceivable, given her marital partnership). He asked after their mother, and the children proved contradictory compasses on the matter, pointing him in several directions at once. However, by blending the advice of the eldest several, he was finally able to guess her whereabouts and found Mara at the waterfall wringing out clothes and slapping them on the hot, sun-baked boulders to dry. As he called her name, he realized it was the first time he'd spoken to her in a decade. There was no trace of anything he recognized in her, and he realized those young lovers were other people than these two gray-haired parents standing among the rocks.

"He's Sione's brother-in-law, and he'll make a good husband for her," Mara said.

"He's been married twice before," Kuwa'i said.

"And Rebecca won't leave so easily, I told her that already. She won't come crying back home."

"Aren't you concerned—"

"He makes a good living. He'll provide for her; that's what I'm concerned about." She bent to her work. "She won't be marrying a poor fisherman so she can toil all day while he's out to sea. She was meant for more than that."

"She's in love with Ta'eo."

Mara slowed in her scrubbing but did not look up. "That will pass."

"How can you say such a thing?"

And then she did look up, and there were cinders in her eyes. "It always does."

For the first time, Kuwa'i realized that after all these years, she had not forgotten. Here was revenge deeper than smashed windows and stolen tools.

Without another word, he turned away. There was nothing to be done.

Over the next several weeks, Kuwa'i was overwhelmed by the insight that all the island's stories were coming to a head. There was idle talk in Wik'wai of the wedding, and Kuwa'i learned the date was already set and approaching. And, too, the ship was nearing completion. The convergence of all things suffused him with a kind of dread different from all the other dreads he'd suffered in his life. This was the shifting and shapeless dread of one who fears he'll live to see the far shore of what he cannot imagine: that time hanging out there in front of them all when there would be no boat, and no walking trees to replace it, and no Rebecca bringing them coconuts of cool milk—and Ta'eo on this island without love and without prospects. He thought of Elissa and her smashed-out teeth, and he thought of her baby, and every day he worked on the boat like the work would last forever, because it was all the time they had.

On the last Wednesday, three days before the wedding, a squall blew across the lagoon, churning the blue-green water to chop. The administer and his men arrived soon after at the launch.

"It is beautiful," the administer said.

"She'll float," Kuwa'i said.

"You speak with the modesty of a craftsman who knows he has created a masterpiece."

Kuwa'i hung his head. "Yes, she is a wonder."

"What is she called?"

"She's the only boat I haven't been able to name. I don't force the names; I wait for something to come to me. Nothing has."

"You tell my men she's not done."

"She's not."

"Looks done to me."

"There's still veneering to do. And the roamings need work."

"I'll take it as it is."

"The steering isn't done yet."

"When?" the administer snapped.

"It could be a while, I still have to—"

"My men will come for it in three days."

The administer turned to go, stepping down off the ladder. His men followed him up the steep embankment.

"Her," Kuwa'i called after him.

The administer turned. "What?"

"You said 'it.' She's a her." Kuwa'i made a decision. "And I'm no longer interested in selling her to you."

"Are you trying to raise the price?"

"At any price, I've decided she's not for sale."

"Not for sale?" The administer smiled sadly, like a disappointed father. He made a subtle gesture with his hand, and his men turned and faced the old man. "Kuwa'i, what are you saying?"

"Another boat, but not this one. I can't sell you this one."

"Then maybe I'll just take it."

"You can't do that, Administrator."

"Why not?"

"You may control Ahana and Motoa, but you have no authority under my roof."

The administer turned to his bodyguards, "Prove him wrong."

Against the early morning quiet, on the day on which his story would end, Kuwa'i woke shouting from his sleep. He sprang upright in his bunk, sweating like a pig, gasping like a fish taking its first breath of air. It had been a nightmare of falling. Outside his window, the sun had yet to rise, but the first hint of pink colored the sky. He rubbed his bruises softly and tried to work life back into his cramped limbs. In the three days since his meeting with the administer, the marks of his beating had come into full flower. "Today," he said to himself in the silence of his room. Today was the wedding. Today the administer would come for the boat.

He put on his worn sandals and walked to his son's room where he found his bunk empty and un-slept in. On the pillow was the small black box that they'd made for his mother's necklaces all those years ago. Kuwa'i stared at the box, which should have been hidden in a drawer in his bedroom. He opened the lid and found it empty. The two remaining seeds were gone.

He walked to the back of the shop where the boat was moored at the water's edge, and he found the dock as empty as the wooden box. He descended to the sandy shores of the lagoon and let the cool water wash over his feet. The wind blew softly against his face, a gentle caress.

"I lose everything to you," he whispered to the ocean.

He strained his eyes into the distance and saw a dark shape disappearing around the curve of the island. He thought he saw two figures on board, one with copper hair. The darker figure waved. Kuwa'i raised his hand to wave goodbye and felt the ties that bound them as father and son pulling taut and finally severing. "A boat is like a knife," he said.

The ship would glide past Ahana. And though the administer might see its sails in the distance, no other ship would be fast enough to stop it. His son would see the open ocean.

There were other islands beyond these.

Kuwa'i thought of the wedding that would never take place, and then he went back inside to wait for the administer's wrath.

Five men climbed down from their horses.

They hesitated then, lingering, checking their weapons.

A look was exchanged, and they moved deliberately, men of clay no more. Kuwa'i didn't trouble himself to unlock the door, so they kicked it down.

Issac spoke first, "The boat is gone."

"It was a fine boat."

"You disappoint the administrator."

"I expected as much," Kuwa'i said.

"He is not a man used to disappointment."

"Then I am happy to have acquainted him with it."

Issac smiled. "It is you who will be making some old acquaintances today."

There was much Kuwa'i might have said then. He wondered if most people pleaded. "Take what you came for."

Issac stepped toward Kuwa'i and placed his left hand on his shoulder. His right hand touched the knife on his hip, pulling the long blade slowly from its sheath. He spoke softly, "All he wanted was the boat."

"That was too much."

Issac lifted his blade to the chest of the man who killed or was his father.

The steel point dimpled the skin above Kuwa'i's heart.

Without turning, Issac said to the other riders, "Burn everything." Then he smiled Elissa's teeth, as if to give the old shipwright something familiar to follow him into his final denouement. He leaned forward and whispered, "When you see my mother, give her this message." The boy's lips brushed Kuwa'i's ear. "Tell her she was a coward."

Kuwa'i nodded and closed his eyes. "As was I," he said. "But not now."

A moment later there came a sharp pain in his chest, followed by a warmth, and the boy embraced him, like a son might. Then closer, clutching while Kuwa'i shuddered.

Kuwa'i took a breath, but it hurt to breathe.

His legs gave out.

The boy's eyes burned into him as he collapsed to the floor.

There were no last words, nothing left to say. Just a yellow curl of light, and then heat, as the men set fire to the boat works. Above him smoke began to fill the room, while flames lit the shadows. Kuwa'i thought of the seeds then, like brown cashews, and he hoped they found purchase in whatever distant soils they came to. A place where they might grow strong, if not tall. A place where they might live and not kill themselves.

The heat expanded and baked him as the fire raged, and the wood beneath him blackened and charred, until Kuwa'i turned his face at last to the cool ocean spray. He curled his hand around the warm wooden rudder, while the boat lurched in the chop, and the sails luffed for a moment before filling with wind, and Kuwa'i left his island, finally.

JACK SHADE IN THE FOREST
OF SOULS

RACHEL POLLACK

Rachel Pollack [www.rachelpollack.com] *is the author of thirty-four books of fiction and non-fiction, including* Unquenchable Fire, *winner of the Arthur C. Clarke Award, and* Godmother Night, *winner of the World Fantasy Award. Her non-fiction includes* 78 Degrees of Wisdom, *often cited as "the Bible of tarot readers." Rachel is also a poet, a translator, and a visual artist. Her work has appeared in fifteen languages, all over the world. She is a senior faculty member of Goddard College's MFA in creative writing program.*

Jack Shade, known in varied places and times as Journeyman Jack, or Jack Sad, or Handsome Johnny (though not any more), or Jack Summer, or Johnny Poet (though not for a long time), or even Jack Thief, was playing Old-Fashioned Poker. That was Jack's name for it, not because the game itself was antiquated—it was Texas Hold Em, the TV game, as Jack thought of it—but because of the venue, a private hotel room, comfortable, elegant even, yet unlicensed and by private invitation only, in the age of Indian casinos no more than a few hours drive from anywhere. Jack knew that most poker was played online these days, split-screen multi-action, or in live tournaments and open cash games held in the big casinos of Vegas, Foxwoods, or Macao.

Jack didn't like casinos. He'd never liked them, though for years he was willing to go where the action was. But after a certain night in the Ibis Casino, a game palace most players had never heard of and would never see, where "All in" meant something very different from betting your

339

entire stack of chips, Jack avoided even the glossiest bright-for-TV game centers, and only played his quaint, private, no-limit match-ups. Luckily for Jack, though not always, luck being luck, there were enough serious money people who knew of Jack Gamble (or Jack Spade, as some called him, though not to his face) that he could more or less summon a game to his private table at the Hotel de Reve Noire, which despite its Gallic name was in New York, on 35th Street, a block from the J. P. Morgan Museum, where Jack sometimes went to sit with the fifteenth-century Visconti-Sforza Tarot cards.

Jack lived in the Reve Noire (possibly why some people called him Johnny Dream), but no one in the game had to know that. Let them think he came in from—somewhere else. Jack didn't like people to know where he lived, an old habit that was still useful. The game, sometimes called Shade's Choice, took place on the eleventh floor, the top floor of the small hotel, where despite the larger buildings all around, the full-length windows looked out to the Empire State antenna (Jack was one of the few people who knew what signal that antenna actually sent, and the messages it relayed back to the Chrysler Building's ever-patient gargoyles), and in the other direction to a small brick house on Roosevelt Island, where Peter Midnight once played a reckless game of cards with a Traveler who outraged fashion in a black cravat.

Jack always dressed for poker. Tonight he was wearing a loosely tailored silk suit, deep-sea green, with a yellow shirt and a mauve tie, undone and draped around his neck. His ropy brown hair was cut rough, as if he'd hacked at it himself when drunk one night, or, as someone once said, as if he'd gone to a blind barber. The furniture in the room was old and carved, somehow heavy, graceful, and comfortable all at once, with influences both French and Chinese. The mahogany table and chairs carried so many layers, generations, of lacquer and polish that neither spilled drinks nor the sharp edges of those obscene good luck charms from Laos that some gamblers liked to fondle could possibly harm them. Even the drink stands by each player looked like they might once have held champagne flutes at Versailles (in fact, they'd originally served as writing platforms for a poetry contest a very long time ago).

Neither the drinks nor the furniture held anyone's attention right now. It was ten in the morning, twelve hours since Mr. Dickens, the white-haired dealer with the long spidery fingers, had given out the first cards. There were nine players—always nine in Jack's games—but everyone knew that only two of them counted. Jack Gamble and the Blindfolded Norwegian

Girl. Jack thought of her that way because she'd once won an online tournament with a block up to stop her ever looking at her cards, playing the players instead of her hand. The Girl had been playing poker since she was fifteen, and pro almost that long, and yet she looked, Jack thought, all sweet and round, like she belonged more at a PTO bake sale than a game with a million dollars on the table. There were some who thought she might be that rarest of creatures, a Secret Traveler, but Jack was sure that whatever talent she had was rooted in poker.

Though he played in the highest stakes games Jack was not a pro. Poker just was not his only source of income. Some years it wasn't even the largest, though in others it was all that paid the bills. Pro or not, Jack knew something about cards. Right now he held a pair of tens, spade and club, a decent hand in Hold Em, where two cards was all you got, and you had to combine them with five face-up "community" cards on the table to try and make your own best five card hand. The five card "board" had come up ten, king, seven, all hearts, and then a nine, again a heart, and finally a second king, the king of clubs. So Jack had a full house, three tens and two kings, nearly a dream hand, but the Girl had gone all in, and now the *nearly* was making him crazy.

She could easily have a straight, or better yet, a flush, all she'd need for that is for one of her two cards to be a heart to go along with the four hearts on the board. Those were good hands, enough really for someone to ship all her money into the pot. But suppose she had a king-seven, or a king-nine? Then she'd have *kings* full, three kings and a pair, and there was no greater curse in Hold Em than for someone else to have a bigger full house. And she'd put her money in on the king, not the fourth heart. She could have just been waiting, but if he called, and lost, it would leave him with a long haul to get back even.

He glanced at Charlie, but the old man sat so still he might have been a clay dealer buried with a Chinese emperor. There was no clock for the girl to call on Jack the way she might have done in some casino tournament, but Jack knew she could ask Charlie and he would tell her to the second how long Jack had been deliberating. Jack leaned back in his chair, turned a single black chip over and over.

He was almost ready to fold—that damn tell seemed too obvious to be real—when he saw something that wasn't there. Barely visible even to him, and just for an instant, a golden foxtail swept along the first four cards on the board, the hearts, lingering just for a moment on the king. Jack kept his face stone but he could feel a shock like an electric current in the long scar that traced his right jawbone. A flush! The Girl had the ace of hearts, and the four hearts on the table had given her a lock—if all she needed was a flush. She'd gone all in because how could you not, but she knew it was a risk—and now she'd lost.

Jack was just about to move in his chips when behind him the door opened. Jack's hand froze no more than an inch from his chips. *Just a few seconds more*, he thought, *just this one call*. But it was no use. He knew no one but the hotel owner, Irene Yao, would ever have opened that door without being summoned, and Irene would open it for one reason only. Someone had shown up with Jack Shade's business card. As if he needed any more proof, her soft voice, its rough edge of age worn smooth with grace, said simply, "Mr. Shade." It was only *Mr.* Shade when it was business.

"Miss Yao," Jack said, and turned around, and of course there it was, as always, on a small silver tray, a cream-colored card that contained only four lines: "John Shade," and below that, "Traveler," then *Hotel de Reve Noire, New York*, and in the final line no words, only a silhouette of a chess piece, the horse-head knight in the classic design named for nineteenth-century chess master Howard Staunton.

Jack nodded to the Girl. "I fold," he said. *Just a few seconds more.* But the rule was simple: everything stopped when the black knight appeared. He stood up and nodded to the dealer. "Mr. Dickens," he said, "will you please cash in my chips and hold the money till I return?"

"Of course," the old man said.

Harry Barnett, a pork trader from Detroit, said, "What the hell? You're cashing in? Just like that? I flew in for this game. I had to wait two goddamn months for a seat. And now you're just leaving?"

The Girl stared at him, her apple-pie face suddenly all planes and angles. "Shut up, Harry," she said, and though Barnett opened his angry mouth nothing came out. To Jack, the Girl said, "A pleasure to play with you, Jack."

"You too, Annette," Shade said, then followed Irene out the door.

Jack Shade met his clients in a small office on the hotel's second floor. All that made it an office really was Jack's use of it. There were no computers or file cabinets, not even any phones. The only furniture was an old library table and three red leather chairs. The only amenity was a cut-glass decanter filled with water and two heavy crystal glasses.

The client's name was William Barlow, "Will," as he said to call him. Mr. Barlow didn't look whimsical enough for Will. With his thin hair and saggy cheeks and his small nervous eyes he looked about sixty-five but was probably no more than fifty. Overweight and lumpy, despite his expensive suit's attempt to smooth him, he breathed heavily, as if he'd just run up and down Irene's polished ebony stairs. It probably was just stress. People were never at their best when they came to see John Shade.

"Mr. Barlow," Jack said, "do you mind telling me how you got my card?"

"It was my wife's," Barlow said, and his head turned slightly to the left, as if he might find her standing there. "When she—when I was going through her things—I found it. In a jewelry drawer. It's not—not a place I ever would have looked when she was…"

Alive, Jack thought. He asked, "Do you have any sense of just why your *wife* had my card?"

"You must have given it to her. Some time ago? Do you teach workshops? I mean, Alice used to go to a lot of workshops."

"I don't teach," Jack said.

Barlow squinted at Jack. "What *do* you do?"

"You came to see me, Mr. Barlow. May I ask why?"

Now Barlow seemed intent on studying the grain in the table. "Strange things have been happening," he said. "Really—" He took a breath. "At first I thought I was dreaming—it was at night mostly—but then it started during the day, and I thought—" He stopped, stared at his hands in his lap. "I thought maybe I was—you know—" He didn't finish the sentence, but a moment later looked up. "But then I thought, maybe, what if I wasn't? What if it was all real? Alice was into all this—all this strange stuff. If anyone could find a way—but what if she was suffering? Mr. Shade, I couldn't stand that."

Jack said, "Do you mind telling me about the strange things?"

As if he hadn't heard the question Barlow went on, "I was supposed to go first. I mean, look at me. Alice kept fit, she watched what she ate. My biggest fear was always how she would get by, after, after I was gone. And then suddenly—it's all wrong. But at least, I thought, at least she won't have to stay on alone. But if she's *suffering*—"

"Tell me about the strange things."

Barlow nodded. "I'm sorry." He took a breath. About to speak again he glanced over at the water decanter, pressed his lips together. "May I?"

"Yes, of course," Jack said, relieved he would not have to find a moment to casually suggest his client drink a glass of water. "I'll join you," he said after Barlow had poured his glass. Jack poured himself exactly half a glass, which he drank down while keeping his eyes fixed on Barlow. The usual shiver along the spine jolted Jack, and he watched Barlow to see if he felt anything, but the client showed no signs of a reaction. *Blissful ignorance*,

Jack thought, and realized how much time had passed, how many clients, since a man with a knife had called him Jack the Unknowing.

Barlow looked around for a napkin, then in his pockets for a handkerchief, and finally just wiped his lips with his finger as Poker Jack kept the smile from his face. The client said, "I guess the first thing was the voices. The whispers. That sounds... you know... But they weren't inside me. Or telling me to do things. It wasn't like that." He sighed. "It started a week or so after Alice's death. I was in bed, still not used to being alone there, and watching the news. Alice used to hate it when I did that, said she didn't want those images in her dreams. And there I was doing it, I felt so guilty."

"Mr. Barlow. The voices."

The fleshy head bobbed up and down. "Right. Sorry. Well, I heard sounds, voices. Like when you're at a conference, and there's whispering across the table or something, and you can hear them but you can't make out the words? I figured maybe it was on the TV, one channel bleeding into another, so I turned it off. And the whispers just got louder. I mean, really loud, like a whole building full of people, all whispering to each other."

Not a building, Jack thought, and he wished to hell that however Alice Barlow had gotten hold of Jack's knight she'd thrown the card away instead of keeping it somewhere her husband could pick it up and get the overwhelming urge to go see John Shade, Traveler.

Barlow said, "This went on for days, Mr. Shade. Every night I thought I was, you know, that the grief had gotten too much for me. I finally told my doctor and he said it was normal—it sure as hell didn't feel normal—and gave me some pills. To sleep. It worked for a couple of days but then I woke up, it was three in the morning, and the damn whispers were louder than ever.

"Then one night I got the horrible idea that they were really there. Not in the house, but in the backyard. I don't know why, but once I thought it I couldn't stand it, so I put on my bathrobe and went down to the kitchen. I made sure to make lots of noise to scare anyone away, but when I got to the kitchen everything looked normal. I mean, it was still dark, but the door light was on, and the moon was pretty bright, and I could see the patio Alice had me make, and the flagstones, and it all looked fine. Normal.

"But the voices! They were still there, louder than ever, but still whispers so I couldn't make out a word."

"And so you opened the door," Jack said. Barlow stared at him. "You thought, if you could prove to yourself once and for all that the whispers weren't real they would have to go away." Barlow nodded. "Let me guess what you saw. A forest?" Shaking now, Barlow nodded again. "Dense trees, with twisted branches and no leaves, going on as far as you could see. And flames. A kind of faint fire, so pale it didn't give off any light or heat or even burn any of the trees."

Barlow whispered, "Oh God. Oh my God. I'm not crazy?"

Jack managed to keep the regret out of his voice as he said, "No, Mr. Barlow, you're not crazy at all." Barlow sat back in the chair, mouth open. Jack said, "So you slammed the door and ran inside. Now tell me—is that when you found my card?"

Barlow half-whispered, "Yes." Behind him, for just a moment, Jack saw the flash of the golden foxtail as it brushed over Barlow's shoulders and then was gone. *A lot of good you are. You give me help on a hand too late for me to use it, but you couldn't warn me* this *was coming?* Out loud he said, "Mr. Barlow, what you saw was not a hallucination or a dream. It's a real place, though very few people actually see it." *At least not while alive.*

"Then why am I seeing it? I'm not anything special. I've never been, you know, psychic or anything."

"It's not about you, Mr. Barlow."

"But I'm—oh, God, it's Alice. Of course. How could I be so—" His hands began to twitch and he clasped them together. "Is she, you know, a ghost?"

"There are no such things as ghosts," Jack Shade said. "At least not the way you see in movies. But sometimes people get stuck." *Sometimes,* he thought, *they can't bear being dead.* And every now and then someone alive gets pulled in and can't get back. Or someone sends them there, and that was the worst of all.

Barlow said, "Mr. Shade, can you help her? Can you get her out? Is that why she had your card?"

"I don't really know why she had my card. But I will try to open a way for her."

"May I ask—what do you—" He looked away.

"My fee is fifty thousand dollars," Jack said. Maybe he couldn't actually refuse someone who had his card, but the clients didn't have to know that.

Barlow hardly seemed to care as he stared again at the desk. "This place. Where Alice is. Is it Hell?"

"No. It's actually just what you saw, twisted trees and cold fire."

"Does it have a name?"

"Yes. It's called the Forest of Souls."

Jack arrived the next morning at Barlow's house, just after dawn. Gone were Gambler Jack's silk suits and bright shirts and ties. In their place he wore a black shirt with black buttons, and black jeans over black boots. Black Jack Traveler.

He spent two days and nights in the Westchester McMansion, a house that reminded him of the bland food your mother gave you after stomach flu. The dull creams and light browns of the walls were matched by furniture that might have belonged in a conference room. Barlow had said that Alice took courses and workshops, and in fact there were large faceted crystals and stone incense holders on knickknack shelves in the living room, and a few books scattered around the paneled den with breathless promises of some imminent shift in "world consciousness" (clearly, Jack thought, if they had any idea what that term actually meant they would never dare to write a word) or promises to choose the "quantum reality" you want and deserve. Somehow it all seemed like dust floating on a deep impenetrable pool, a well of emptiness.

Only in Alice's dressing room did color manage to break through the dull fog, with yellow walls and light blue trim to match the bottles of perfume and vials and jars of European creams and makeup. The first time Jack went in there he just stood in the center of the room and breathed deeply, as if he could take the color into his lungs and spread it through his body. He realized he'd been closing himself down in the rest of the house, maybe even before he entered it, in a kind of psychic expectation. Only here could he find a place to begin his search for trace elements of Alice Barlow.

Jack spent a lot of time in that room, the door closed to his client, the lights full tilt as he touched and smelled Alice's clothes, her makeup, each elaborate bottle of perfume. He lined his eyes with violet kohl, and painted his lips dark smoky red, and probably would have tried on some of her clothes if Alice had not dieted herself down to a size two. A wedding picture in the living room had shown Alice at about an eight. By the time of her death, apparently, a significant part of her had already vanished.

Some women diet for social approval or self-esteem, but Jack was pretty sure Alice did it to diminish her place in the world. "What were you running from?" he whispered to the mirror as he held a silk camisole against his cheek. Was it Barlow? Jack shook his head. The man was as dull as the house. He wasn't the cause of Alice's desire to disappear, he was just part of her strategy.

Jack had made sure to warn Barlow not to come in during his "psychic investigatory procedures" in the dressing room. Subtle, even dangerous, energies ran through the room at such times, he said, and if Barlow just knocked on the door he could bring down the entire framework Jack was constructing. All of that was partly true, but mostly Jack did not want to repeat the scene of some years back, when a client had walked in on Jack Shade wearing his dead wife's clingy black dress.

Outside the dressing room, Jack talked with Barlow for hours about Alice, their marriage, the things they did together, Alice's hobbies and interests, which apparently came and went. She'd tried knitting, book clubs, French cooking, but gave them all up after a few months. The cosmic crystal phase had lasted longer than most, nearly a year when she died, but Barlow suspected it had already begun to fade. There'd been a lot more of the "dolls and things," he said, and then one day he noticed she'd gotten rid of about half of them. He'd never asked her what she'd done with them.

There were no kids. Alice had had "medical issues," Barlow said, and when she said she didn't want to adopt he'd just agreed. "Maybe I should have pushed it," he told Jack. "Maybe she would have been happier." Jack didn't know if that was true, so much of what Barlow said seemed layered over with guilt like archaeological sediment. Maybe if he'd done more, he said, read some of her books, joined the cooking classes, they could have traveled more. She always seemed to pick up on trips, especially Paris, she loved Paris. *Just like the song*, Jack thought.

Most of all, Barlow built palaces of guilt around the fact that Alice had died at all, at least before him. He was the one who broke his diet, whose numbers had crept up despite the statins and the dreadful low-salt food. All his preparations, the will, the retirement accounts, they all began with the same assumption, that Alice would outlive him.

How did she die? Jack asked. They were sitting at a brown oval dining table. Aneurysm, Barlow said. Undetectable and as unexpected as a thunderstorm when the weather bureau had promised a sunny day. "How could that happen?" Barlow asked.

"I don't know," Jack said. "I'm not a doctor. Or a theologian." He knew he was being hard, but he'd never get anything done if he had to hold the client's hand all day.

Barlow blinked, stared at Jack a moment, then said, "Mr. Shade—can you find her? In that place, that *forest*?"

"Yes."

"And release her?"

"Yes." Jack might have said, "I can try," but in fact he'd succeeded in every case but one. And that one was special.

Barlow said, "And will I stop hearing those noises? And seeing the trees?"

"Yes."

Barlow looked down at the table. "When you release her—where will she go?"

"I don't know," Jack said. "I have no idea."

The first night Jack was there Barlow had asked if they should stay up together and wait for the whispers to "manifest," a term that probably came from one of Alice's workshops. It didn't work that way, Jack said. The Forest tended to conceal itself when a Traveler came to investigate. He told Barlow he'd have to go track it down himself. He didn't say that in fact he knew exactly where the entrance was, and it was a garage on West 54th Street.

Jack slept that first night in the guest room and realized almost immediately it was a mistake. Many women saw their guest rooms as a chance to indulge their more extreme decorating ideas, but this one looked like it was copied from a magazine, or even a furniture catalog. The white bedding, the dull peach-colored walls, fake flowers in the fake antique pitcher, they were all as lifeless as a plastic doll house.

Despite what he'd told Barlow, Jack went down to the kitchen in the middle of the night. He walked past the butcher block counter and island stove to open the back door. With his head cocked slightly to the left he said quietly, "Alice? Where are you?" Very faintly he heard the whispers of the Forest, far away and nothing like the roar Barlow had heard. And when he stepped outside all he saw was the patio and lawn furniture, more dead than Alice Barlow.

The next day he told Barlow he needed to sleep in Alice's bed. At first he thought the client would object, but no, Barlow just nodded and that evening left fresh sheets neatly folded on the king size bed and went off to sleep on the couch. Jack smiled as he changed the sheets. William Barlow might have to surrender his bed but damned if he would change the linens. Jack was just done when Barlow came to the door with an armful of towels and what looked like shampoo and conditioner. He said, "If you want to step out a moment I'll freshen up the bathroom for you."

"That's okay," Jack said and reached out to take the towels and hair products. Barlow hesitated, then nodded, and left. Jack watched him a moment, then closed the door.

Earlier in the day Jack had pocketed a loose bracelet of silver tiles from Alice's dressing room. Now, as he held it, he thought about the fact that Barlow had kept everything intact in his dead wife's room. A check of the closets and drawers in the master bedroom confirmed his guess that nothing of Alice remained, the walk-in closet home now to a lonely rack of suits. So why the shrine in the dressing room?

It took no more than a few seconds to figure out which side of the bed was Alice's. It wasn't physical, Barlow hadn't left a trough in the firm mattress. But when Jack tried the left side he began to wheeze and cough, an effect that vanished as soon as he rolled to the right. On that side there was only a sense of lightness, a lack of any presence at all.

And yet she *was* there, he could feel her all around him, especially in the bracelet that pressed against his wrist as if Alice Barlow was taking hold of him. That lightness, Jack realized, had been there all along, it was there before she died. It was what she left behind. "How did you get so lost?" Jack whispered in tears. "What happened to you?"

Then he held up his left wrist with the bracelet before his eyes. Louder than before he said, "I'm coming for you, Alice. My name is John Shade, and I will find you. I will find you and set you free."

Suddenly exhausted, Jack dropped his arm and settled his head against the too-thin hypoallergenic pillow. For just an instant, heat flared in the bracelet, so intense Jack almost tore it off, but then it went cold again, as chill as moonlight. Tired as he was, he still didn't expect to sleep that night, so it came as a kind of distant surprise when his eyes pulled down, his limbs grew sullen, and then he was gone.

He dreamed he was walking in the Forest, only it was disguised, the way it so often was (even in the dream he remembered telling that to Barlow). This time it appeared as some kind of march or demonstration in a city that may have been Manhattan. All around him everyone was holding signs or shouting slogans. Only, he couldn't read the signs, or understand the loud chants, and then he realized, the souls, the lost, they were not the people in the march, the people were the *trees*. The souls were trapped inside the fake demonstrators, unable to speak, or to tell Jack what they needed. The fire, so cold, so pale, wound around the tree people with their signs, like a thin fog.

Jack tried to speak but his words came out all thick, as if his jaw moved too slowly, so he reached up to massage it, loosen his tongue. He was several seconds rubbing his lower face before he realized—there was no scar. He was back the way he was before—before everything fell apart. Back when he was Handsome Johnny, and being a Traveler was, well, something that made you better than other people, all the dumb William Barlows of the world. Disgust twisted his insides. He didn't want to lose his scars, he deserved them, he needed them. They made sure he never forgot.

All around him, the people, the *trees*, stamped and shook their signs. If they were trying to tell him something they were wasting their time, the signs meant nothing, the voices just scrambled sounds. Tree language. He remembered now that he was on a mission, and he called out, "Alice? Alice Barlow? Are you here somewhere? Can you show yourself?"

His eye caught a flash of motion to the right, and he turned in time to see a thin woman in a pale red dress dart behind the crowd of demonstrators and head toward a kitchen supply shop. "Alice, wait!" he called above the noise of the demonstrators. Pushing aside the tree people, who took no notice of him, he made his way in her direction.

It was only when he got free of the crowd and their signs, and could see that she had stopped in front of the show window full of knives, that he could see it wasn't Alice Barlow, it wasn't even a woman but just a girl. Fourteen years old. Arms and legs stick thin. Long straight hair, her mother's hair, dyed black, sharp and bright against the pale red dress that echoed the faint fire flickering through the forest.

"Oh God," Jack whispered. "Oh my God. *Eugenia*."

She turned around now, slowly, with that adolescent drama smile, and lowered her head slightly so she could look up at him as if she was just a child again. Softly she said, "Hello, Daddy."

And the store window exploded, and all those gleaming knives and cleavers came flying at Jack.

He managed to knock most of them out of the way, all the while shouting, "Genie! Don't go! I can help you—" But not all. A carving knife and a long-pronged fork hit his face and he screamed in pain. *No!* he thought, *Not again.* He looked away, lost focus, for just a moment, and when he turned back she was gone.

He touched his face to see how much damage the geist had done only to discover there was no blood, no fresh wounds, just the hardened scars of an attack long ago. So Handsome Johnny was gone and he was himself again, Scar-faced Jack, Johnny Ugly. Johnny Lonesome.

"Mr. Shade!" a man called, and when he turned to see who it was he discovered himself awake, back in the Barlow bedroom, with the client himself trying the locked door and yelling, "Mr. Shade! Are you all right? I heard noises."

Jack sat up and discovered books scattered on the bed and the floor around it, bestsellers and art books from the low decorator bookshelf opposite the bed. They must have flung themselves at him while he slept. Could a poltergeist operate from a dream?

"I'm all right!" he said loudly. "Go back to bed, Mr. Barlow. We'll talk in the morning."

When he heard Barlow leave, Jack lay on the bed, ignoring the books as he tried to steady his breath and lower his heart rate. "Eugenia," he whispered. He thought, as he did so often, of the early days, when cups or plates started crashing on the floor, and then the coffee table flung itself across the room, and all the drawers of his wife's dresser smashed into the wall above the bed. He remembered how Layla had screamed she couldn't stand it anymore, Jack had to *do* something, how he'd held her and told her, with all the reassurance of his great knowledge, his experience as a Traveler, that it was just a phase, that doing something would only strengthen it. If you left them alone geists just faded away. Lying in his client's bed, remembering, Jack felt the tears slide down his cheeks until they hit the dead crevices of his scars.

He lay there until dawn, eyes on the ceiling as he waited until first light would allow him to get up and take the final step before he could leave the gray house. Once he was sure the sun had come up he went into the oversize lifeless bathroom where he washed his face and got dressed, all but his shirt. On his way back from the bathroom he noticed something odd, a small black leather copy of MacGregor Mathers' translation of the fifteenth-century manuscript, *The Book of the Sacred Magic of Abra-Melin the Mage*. He smiled. Maybe Alice had advanced beyond the dabbler stage. She must have hidden this behind the big showy art books, where she could count on William never noticing it. Softly Jack said, "You deserve better than the Forest, Alice. I'm coming for you."

Back at the bed he set down a small black rectangular leather case he'd brought with him from the hotel. Various instruments lay inside it, only one of which he needed. A black knife, unadorned, with a polished ebony handle and a double-edged carbon blade exactly five inches long.

He held it up and stared at it awhile as he turned it in the morning light. Then he cut a shallow line along the inside of his arm. There was a network of such lines, light scars, and Jack had often wondered if some doctor, or even a cop if Jack was ever careless enough to get arrested, might think he was a junkie. Or self-destructive. He watched the fresh cut slowly ooze with blood, then took a deep breath and finally spit into the wound.

Jack had to grip his thighs to keep from crying out. There was always pain, but *this*—

The action had begun when Jack had shared that simple glass of water with Barlow back in the office. There'd been nothing in the water but Jack had charged it to align the two of them, so that his own etheric pulse would hold some of the client's bond with his dead wife. When he spit into the cut he temporarily united himself with Barlow, so that the wound could call out to Alice. It was the surest way to find her in the confusion of the Forest.

The action was never easy—it was like injecting himself with someone's grief, or fear, or guilt—but he could never remember it hitting this hard. When the pain subsided enough that he could breathe a little easier he discovered his face wet with tears and sweat. He went into the bathroom and washed again, then put on his shirt, packed his knife, and left the house, hopefully without waking his client.

At 9:47 in the morning Lonesome Jack Shade stood on Lexington Avenue, north of 72nd Street, and watched a slim young man open the door to Laurentian Chocolates. Along with his all black clothes Jack wore the carbon blade knife in a sheath up his left sleeve.

Jack knew he should go get what he needed before the shop filled with customers, but he hated what he had to do. He wondered, did chocolate-shop owners around the city all talk to each other? Would Monsieur Laurentian see Jack's knife, roll his eyes, and say, "Oh, it's *you*." Or would he just moue in fear, like the last poor truffle-maker?

Jack sighed. At least he could disguise himself. He pretended it was to escape detection, but knew it was really to lessen the embarrassment of what he was about to do. He slipped the knife from its sheath and stared at the point, so sharp it could cut sunshine. In two quick touches he lightly pressed the point against his forehead and then his lips.

He cried out, loudly enough that a woman walking five dogs turned around and stared at him, and a bike messenger reflexively shouted, "Fuck you, man!" Gently, Jack moved his fingertips around his face, feeling a smooth plastic quality that told him the trick had worked. Once it firmed up, his false face would look so bland that Laurentian would not be able to describe Jack at all. "I don't know," he'd tell the police if he even bothered to call them. "It was just one of those faces. You know. As if it wasn't really there."

On the street corner Jack touched his nose, his cheeks, the area around his lips. It still felt like some opaque plastic mask but it held firm against his prodding. He crossed the street toward Laurentian Chocolates.

He was nearly at the door when he felt a light brush against his legs. He glanced down and there was the golden tail, its tip just leaving his left knee. Unlike at the poker table, where the fox had vanished almost before

Jack caught sight of it, it turned to sit on its haunches right in the middle of the sidewalk, its fur dazzling in the sun. No one but Jack could see it but people automatically walked around it, some squinting at the glare from the invisible fur. One young woman walked by, stopped, and turned to stare right at the spot where the fox sat, then shrugged and walked on. *You've got a future*, Jack thought. *With any luck it'll never find you.*

"Hello, Ray," he said to the fox, who bowed his head a moment. Jack Shade had met Ray on one of his first travels, when he found himself in a bad place, surrounded by, of all things, predator chickens. He did an action for help and Ray had appeared, a fitting protector, Jack supposed. Now Ray came to him mostly to warn him, or show him things. The name was Jack's choice, short for Reynard, of course, but also the correct pronunciation of Ra, the Egyptian Sun god, for in the catalogue of foxes—mountain fox, fox of the willows, fox of the stairways, tracker fox—Ray was a noon fox, a solar helper, bringing clarity and strength.

"Thanks for being here," Jack said. "You know I hate this part, it's so damn embarrassing. But what can I do? I've got to give the Door Man what he wants." Ray stared at him awhile longer, then leaped off the curb to vanish in front of a taxicab, whose driver hit the brakes then looked confused before he sped up again.

The owner of the chocolate shop appeared to be around twenty-two but was probably ten years older. In black creased pants, shiny wingtips, and gray vest over his pale blue shirt he looked as old-fashioned and immaculate as his glass display cases filled with exotic concoctions. He looked Jack up and down briefly, his expression confused as he tried to focus on the face that wasn't quite a mask, then more relaxed again as he let his eyes move back to Jack's muscular upper body and thighs. "Good morning," he said, with a smile. "You're my first. At least for today."

Blank-faced Jack pointed to a tray of dark chocolate truffles covered in chocolate powder. "I'll have one of those," he said.

Mr. Laurentian nodded his appreciation of Jack's good taste. "Certainly," he said. "Shall I put it in a presentation box?"

"Yes, thank you." Jack watched Laurentian carefully set the truffle in a miniature cardboard box, which he tied with a red ribbon and a slight twirl of his hand. "Thank you," he said. "That will be 7.95."

With a sigh Jack slipped the black knife from the sheath in his sleeve and pointed the tip at Laurentian's neck. "I'll just take it," he said.

"Oh! Oh God," the chocolatier said. "Take whatever I've got. I mean, there's not much. I just opened. But take it. Whatever's in the register."

"I just want the truffle," Jack said

The young man froze, as if stuck in the strange moment. Then he said, "Of course. Yes. Let me get a bag, I'll put all the truffles—"

"No. Just this one."

"What? Are you—it's only 7.95! I said you could—" He stopped himself, realizing he was trying to argue an armed robber into taking more than he wanted. It was a reaction Jack had seen before. "Here," Laurentian said. He thrust the small box at Jack, who grabbed it and ran from the store.

A principle of opposites governed the entryways to what an old German Traveler once called "non-linear locations." Opposites and doorways. In New York City, you entered the Forest of Souls in a garage on 54th Street, through a red metal door marked "Employees only." As with every other NLL entrance, you couldn't get through unless you paid the Door Man. In the Empire Garage this job fell to a white-haired gentleman named Barney. And Barney liked chocolates. Stolen chocolates.

When Jack began his travels Barney demanded nothing more than chocolate kisses. Just one each time. He used to pull the little ribbon top and smile as the foil came away. As he popped the brown cone in his mouth he would nod to Jack to go on through. The nice thing about chocolate kisses is that they were easy to steal. But then a couple of years ago Barney had gone upscale. Jack had heard that some Wall Streeter had taken up traveling after the credit swap bubble burst, and had ruined things for everybody by giving Barney his first dark chocolate delight. Now it had to be a truffle. Fresh. And it had to be stolen.

"Why can't I just buy you one?" Jack asked him once.

Barney had smiled. "Money comes and goes, Jack. Silver, paper, even beads sometimes. You got money, you never know what you got. But stealing is forever."

He found Barney, as always, sitting on a steel chair against the wall of the garage, alongside the door he protected. He wore a blue shirt and pants, with "Empire Garage" in italics on the right pocket and "Barney" in gold script on the left. He was short, about five-eight, and stocky, but not fat. He had a full head of fine white hair, cut short, and a square face with enough fine lines on it that it might have served as a map of the Non-Linear worlds. Jack had no idea how long the old man had served as Door Man. Fifty years? Five thousand years? Maybe the first Manhattan Traveler had found a white-haired man in a beaver cloak sitting on a tree stump next to a cave that served as entrance to the Forest. Or maybe Barney would get the job next week. Non-Linear employment.

One time, just to see what would happen, Jack had asked the cashier about "the old guy who just sits in a chair upstairs."

"Oh, that's Barney," the man said.

"Well, what does he do? He doesn't seem to ever leave his spot."

The cashier looked confused. In a tone that suggested Jack had asked a really dumb question, he said, "I don't know. He's Barney."

Today, Jack walked up with a smile, waiting for Barney's usual "Hey, kid," but instead the Door Man tilted his head to the side slightly and squinted at Jack like he was trying to make out who he was. "Can I help you?" he said.

Jack stared at him. "Barney? It's me. Jack Shade."

Barney shook his head, then laughed. "Jack!" he said. "Sorry, kid. My old eyes ain't what they used to be, I guess."

Jack touched his face to make sure the mask was gone, and in fact, for just a moment he thought he felt smooth skin, but no, there were the scars. He said, "It's probably just me, Barney. I had to dupe my face for something and there's probably traces of the overlay still on it."

Barney nodded. "Ah, that must be it."

Jack said, "I've got something for you."

"Hey, you're all right, Jack," Barney said as he took the box and undid the ribbon. "Ah, Charlie Lawrence," he said. "You know he calls himself Charles Laurentian now?" He pronounced it "Sharl Lor-en-zhin" in the worst French accent Jack had ever heard. "I guess whatever sells product, right, Jack?" He smiled at the candy in its gold foil nest. "You know, Jack, you've got taste. That's what I tell the others. Jack Shade, I tell 'em. He knows what to bring an old man." Biting down, he waved Jack to the door.

The handle was hot, like the door to a furnace, and when Jack opened it all he could see was a red glow so intense his face felt on fire. As soon as he stepped through, however, and felt the dirt and leaves under his feet, a cold wind hit him. He gasped, as he always did, for knowledge of what's to come doesn't help much in the Forest. It wasn't really cold, just as before it wasn't really hot. If he'd had to guess the actual temperature he would have said around 60. But it felt like his bones would freeze so tight his toes would snap off.

Jack paid no attention, only took a piece of red chalk from his jeans pocket and marked "JS" on the door, which stood incongruously all by itself, surrounded by trees. Jack made his mark graffiti style, with block letters and a flourish at the end. Almost as soon as he finished, the door just faded away and all that was left were trees. Endless trees, all sizes and shapes, a few with dusty leaves or yellowed needles, but most bare, the branches black and twisted. Unlike an actual woods, where the trees grow densely together, blocking your view, here each tree stood by itself, as if they refused any contact, so that Jack felt like he could see for miles and miles with no horizon, only twisted trees, forever and ever. It was twilight, dim, the only color the faint fire that wound in and out of the branches like pale weightless ribbons.

Jack Shade closed his eyes and took a breath, and when he looked again everything had changed. A department store. He was in some kind of large store, standing in the watch and jewelry section, looking out toward various clothing sections for men, women, and children as shoppers moved in and out of mannequins displaying middle-of-the-road clothes, the kind you might see in suburban malls. People in winter jackets rushed about, some checking lists, and as if that observation triggered a next step, red and green ribbons appeared on the walls and displays, while voiceless holiday Muzak whined through the noise of the crowd. It all looked so real—except for the wisps of flame that snaked through the shoppers and the mannequins.

Jack moved slowly, careful not to touch anything, the people, the displays, the clothes on the racks. He knew only one thing for certain, that Alice had to be somewhere nearby, for part of the reason for the cut on his arm was to act as a kind of homing signal to bring him to that part of the Non-L Forest where Alice was trapped. But he couldn't begin to summon her until he could identify the *trees* in all this crowd of goods and shoppers.

He kept looking, staring, until suddenly he realized he was doing it all wrong. You don't *look* in the Forest, you listen. Jack was staring round corners, and through the crowds, and even under the counters in the unconscious hope he would spot Eugenia. Unconscious and useless. This wasn't his dream, after all, and if his daughter was even in this part of the Forest, she would show herself only if she wanted to. Right now he was here for Alice.

He said out loud, just to be sure, "Genie, if you're anywhere around, and you want to show yourself, I want to see you. Right now I've got a job to do, but I'm here. I love you."

Then, reluctantly, he closed his eyes. He took a deep breath, another. On the third exhale he heard the Forest. Voices, whispers, a roar of whispers, waves and surges of grief and loneliness, hurricanes of rage. Jack screamed, fell on all fours where he shook wildly, like a terrified dog, and it was all he could do to keep from howling. But when the voices subsided enough that he could stand up and open his eyes he knew.

The mannequins. The trees were the mannequins, the plastic bodies in absurd poses prisons for the dead. Jack could see it in the blank smooth faces, where underneath the plastic eyes something pulsed. He could hear, or just feel, the whispers in the rigid half-opened mouths.

Jack slipped his knife from its sheath and in one stroke sliced open the left sleeve of his shirt. Years ago, when he was first learning, Jack had laughed and asked his teacher why he couldn't just roll it up. "Oh, Jack," she'd said. "Carefree Jack. Don't you know you have to sacrifice something? Even if it's just a shirt?" These days Jack figured he'd sacrificed more than enough in his years as a Traveler, but you didn't mess with tradition. He held up his exposed arm like a signpost, the cut bright and shiny.

Slowly he turned around, like a lighthouse lamp. "I'm looking for Alice Barlow!" he shouted, then, "Alice! I'm carrying your mark. Your memory. Show yourself! I've come from the Old World to release you to the New. You don't have to stay here anymore. I'm here to help you. Alice Barlow! *Show yourself!*"

For a long time nothing happened, and Jack wondered if somehow, some way, he'd made a mistake. Why didn't she respond? Usually, all the dead wanted was to get free of their tree prison. Could he possibly have screwed up the action and took himself to the wrong part of the Forest? He thought back over everything he'd done and it was all correct, he was sure of it. There was Barney's odd reaction when he first saw him, but that was just—

Then he saw it. In the men's sportswear section, a mannequin dressed in jeans and a checked shirt and one of those denim jackets with a corduroy color gave off a faint pulsing light.

Jack walked over to it, still with his arm up and held so that the cut faced the mannequin's face. "Hello, Alice," he said gently. "I'm very glad to meet you. I've been searching for you for some time." The mannequin—the tree—didn't move, of course, but Jack thought he saw a glow of heat in the smooth plastic and even the sweatshop polyester clothing. "It's okay," Jack said. "I know you're scared. And angry. That's always the way it is. But now I'm here, Alice, and it's all going to end. Here's what I'm going to do, Alice. I'm going to bring you out, and once you're free, I will open a gate so you can leave here. Are you ready, Alice?"

Not just a glow this time, but a real flash of light. It lasted only a second but there was no mistaking it. He nodded. "Thank you, Alice. Thank you for showing yourself."

Without turning his back on her he moved a few feet away, far enough that he could draw a circle with his chalk on the floor in front of the mannequin. Jack sometimes thought that in all his Traveler training the hardest thing had been to learn to freehand a circle. Now he looked at his work and couldn't help but smile a moment. Taking Alice as due south he marked the compass points, then drew various signs in the cross-quarter. Using the various points to guide him he found the circle's center, where he drew an eight-pointed star. It was a little awkward because he had to make sure he didn't actually step inside the circle or touch the rim. "This is your mark, Alice," he said. "This is where you'll go. It won't be long now."

He stood up and took a position behind north so he would face the mannequin, with the circle between them. He reached in his jeans pocket and took out the silver bracelet he'd worn in Alice's bed and held it up high. Slight shocks ran from the bracelet to the cut in his arm, but he ignored them. "Remember this, Alice?" he said, his eyes fixed on the blank plastic face and the fire he could sense under it. "It holds the genuine you. Your existence here isn't real, Alice. *This* is real. I'm going to open a kind of door. You're going to feel it more than see it. And when you do you'll know the bracelet is calling to you. Just like I've been calling you. I'm going to start now, Alice. Are you ready?"

As Jack leaned over to lay the bracelet on the chalk star a strange smell almost made him stumble. For a few seconds the air stank of dead meat and wet fur, of layers of urine and feces. Some kind of animal den, large, like a bear. Was that how Alice experienced her imprisonment? Not what Jack saw, not a mannequin or even a tree, but the prey of some wild animal?

The smell faded, and with it Jack's attempts to figure out what it meant. It was time to do what he'd come for. Jack pulled out his knife and raised it in his left hand to point at the ceiling. Then as hard as he could he brought it down to slice the air inside the circle. "Alice Barlow! " he shouted. "The way is open!"

All around him the shoppers, just props after all, paid no attention but continued to chatter and check their lists and hold clothes up against their bodies. The Muzak, however, crackled, then sputtered out halfway through "Hark, the Herald Angels Sing." Within a range of twenty feet or so the mannequins all turned dark, then suddenly flashed with light so brightly Jack had to shield his eyes to prevent retina burn.

He kept his focus on the blank manly face of Alice Barlow's prison. The expression didn't change, of course, or the pose, but the whole thing shuddered and swayed, as if something was shaking it. From the inside.

Slowly something began to emerge, first a vapor so fine Jack wasn't sure he was really seeing it, then more pronounced, an ooze that came out of the mannequin so slowly it might have been sweating. The sweat turned to a thick mass, the colorless gelatin that a French Traveler in the nineteenth century called "ectoplasm."

Jack held his breath. This part was tricky, for the dead person could emerge as anything, and he had to be ready to welcome it. Usually they ended up as who they were in life (though sometimes idealized, with bigger breasts, say, or poutier lips), often naked but sometimes so dressed up they looked like they'd stepped out of *Downton Abbey*. But sometimes they emerged as something else entirely, a different person, some other kind of creature, even an object. Once, Jack brought forth a child who'd died too young, but instead of a boy there was a school composition book, full of handwriting in some alphabet Jack had never seen.

This time it was going exactly right. The ecto was firming up, becoming recognizable, first as arms and legs with overly long hands and toes, then a torso, then at last the head, and it was her, Alice Barlow. She came out naked, thin, the body all tensed, the eyes squeezed shut as if afraid to look, the skin darker and rougher than in her photos, the hair longer and wilder, the muscles in her arms and legs more defined. She wasn't quite the same, but she was who, and what, she was supposed to be, and that was all that mattered. Jack let out a breath he hadn't known he was holding, unsure why this woman he'd never met could have such a powerful effect on him.

With a sudden violent twist Alice broke fully from her mannequin prison and pitched forward into the circle, where she landed on all fours. She trembled wildly, like a terrified dog.

Jack became aware that the whispers had risen all around him, drowning out the fake sounds of the store. If the souls in their trees could witness this, what were they thinking? Did they know, or sense, someone had broken free? Were they proud? Hopeful? Jealous? He looked down at the only one who mattered. "Hello, Alice," he said. "Welcome back."

She didn't get up, didn't move from her spot. Only her head moved, tilting up to look at him, and as it did so it changed. The cheekbones stood out, so sharp they almost cut through the skin. The eyes became bigger, the pupils flat and dark, the chin narrowed, became almost triangular, the lips stretched thin. And when she opened her mouth the teeth had grown long and sharp.

Jack stared at her, no idea what to do. "Alice," he said, "it's going to be okay."

She sprang at him. Leaped from all fours directly at his face. No, not his face, his throat. The long sharp teeth nearly tore out his trachea. Jack grabbed her, he wasn't sure where, and somehow managed to fling her wildly twisting body away from him. He tried to get her back in the circle, where he might hope to contain her but she managed to break away and land on all fours just to the left of it. Immediately she spun around to face him again, shaking her head and growling. Strangely the Muzak came back, and "Rudolph the

Red-Nosed Reindeer" bounced cheerfully above the snarls of the creature on the floor.

Jack reached up to touch his neck and face and feel the damage. As soon as he did so he forgot all about blood and wounds, for instead of his own tight skin and scars his fingers found a soft fleshiness. Wrinkled middle-aged skin over sagging jowls. And in that instant, with Alice about to spring again, Jack knew what had happened. He understood, finally, too late, what William Barlow had done to him.

In *The Traveler's Bestiary*, or "guide to Non-Linear fauna," as Jack's teacher once called it, there were many pages—files in the smart-phone version—devoted to Beasts of Fury. This is what Alice Barlow had made of herself. Enough human to hold on to her purpose, and enough animal to rip Jack apart. And when she was finished? Would she realize what had happened, what her husband had done to her as well as Jack?

Twice more Jack managed to fling her away, and both times she landed on all fours and turned right around to bare her teeth before her next leap. Both times Jack considered running, but knew he'd never make it. The watch and jewelry section was only twenty or thirty yards away, but it would take time—and energy—to open the door. And Alice had cornered the market on both. Powered by all the rage in existence, from jealous lovers to hungry babies to dying stars, a Fury could go on forever. But not Jack Shade. Everything he did in the Forest, even just seeing through its masks, drained him.

One more time. He could throw her off once more—maybe—and then she would take him. "Goodbye," he whispered. Goodbye to everyone, his daughter most of all, but also Irene, Mr. Dickens, to Ray, who'd tried to warn him but couldn't follow him into the Forest, and even the Blindfolded Norwegian Girl. And Alice, whom he'd tried to help but got it wrong.

As if she could feel his thoughts, Alice shook wildly, screamed, and threw herself through the air. Jack braced himself. His clothes were in shreds, his arms and chest bleeding. Alice leaped, arms straight out, clawed fingers spread wide for greatest impact, teeth bright in the holiday lights. And then she stopped.

As if she'd hit an invisible net set up by some Fury hunter, she twisted wildly in midair, screaming in frustration. No, not a net, and not invisible. A yellow cashmere scarf had come off a counter display to wrap around Alice's abdomen, and even though it was attached to nothing, hold her above the floor. She thrashed and clawed and managed to cut herself loose, only to have two more scarves, cheap nylon this time, spin around and once more hold her suspended.

Jack spun around, searching, looking. "Where are you?" he shouted above the Muzak, which now played "Santa Claus Is Coming to Town."

"Genie!" Jack called to her, and then he saw her, small in her red dress and pink sneakers, her hair in pigtails. The only living resident—prisoner—in the Forest of Souls stood among a display of fake leather luggage. It was all fake, of course, the whole place. Everything in it was a prop. Except for Eugenia Shade. And Alice Barlow.

Jack started toward his daughter, only to have her shout, "No! You have to go, Daddy. I can't hold her. Hurry!"

For just a second he hesitated, but he could see she was right. Alice was already pulling loose, and Genie was swaying with the effort to contain her. He ran to the watch counter, dropped to the floor, and frantically drew a threshold with the blue chalk. Then he used his knife to trace the form of a door in the air.

Three of them appeared, lined up in a row, identical—except the one on the right bore the graffiti "JS." With his hand on the knob he turned around. If he could somehow grab Genie before Alice broke loose, could he take her with him? But he'd already tried that, more than once, and he and his daughter both knew the door would let him pass, and no one else. "Genie!" he called out. "Sweetheart. I'll find a way to bring you back."

He had the door half-open, he could even smell the oil and grease air of Empire Garage, when his daughter called to him. "Daddy?" she said in a voice that sounded like she was eight. "Daddy? Did I kill Mommy?"

"No, baby," Jack said. "It wasn't you. It was the geist." And at that moment Alice Fury broke loose to fly at him, and it was all he could do to slide through the door and slam it shut before Alice crashed into the back of it.

Jack didn't realize he was on the floor until Barney reached down to help him up. And then the shock of that, Barney getting off his chair, helping him, touching him, shocked Jack back to where he was. "Hey, Jack," Barney said. "Looks like you had a rough time of it in there."

"Yeah," Jack said as he got to his feet. He looked down at his torn shirt and jeans, the bloody scratches and bites on his chest and arms. Holding his breath, he reached up to touch his face. His fingers came away with more blood on them, but he was pretty sure he was himself.

"You want to sit for a moment?" Barney said. "You look a little wobbly." He gestured with his head toward the gray metal chair against the wall.

Jack smiled, surprised he could do it. He said, "So if I sit down does that mean I become the Door Man? And you wander off, and what, go get laid for the first time in a thousand years?"

Barney laughed. "Ha. You wish, kid. You don't get to guard the door just by sitting in my seat. We've got standards."

"Barney," Jack said, "you knew, didn't you? That's why you didn't recognize me at first. You saw the other face, overlaid on top of mine."

Barney shrugged. "Yeah. I saw it."

"Then why the hell didn't you tell me? I almost died."

"Not my job."

"What? Do you guys have some kind of union or something?"

"Kind of like that," Barney said.

Jack burst out laughing, then stopped, afraid he couldn't control it. "Jesus," he said. "I've got to get home somehow. Without attracting any cops or ambulances."

Barney said, "You can use the employees locker room, sixth floor. There's a shower. I figured you might need a change of clothes so I put out an Empire uniform for you. But don't worry, putting it on won't trap you into parking cars for all eternity."

Jack smiled. "Thanks, Barney. You're all right."

Jack was at the stairway door when Barney called to him. He turned, and Barney said, "I've got something for you. Might come in handy." He tossed a small bright object at Jack who caught it in his right hand. When he looked in his palm, Jack saw it was a gold skeleton key, about three inches long. The head consisted of three flat circles, while seven short prongs formed the lock end.

Jack stared at it a long time. Finally he looked up at Barney. "Holy shit," he said.

Barney's face turned hard, and when he spoke the old-man folksiness had vanished from his voice. "Jack Shade!" he said. "You give that sonofabitch what he deserves!"

Jack stood across the street from William Barlow's house. It was early evening, and Jack might have worried that Barlow would spot him, except it was Jack Shield time, and he was good at that. After cleaning up as best he could at the garage, Jack had not returned to the Hotel de Reve Noire. Long ago he'd made it a rule not to go back until the job was finished, and this William Barlow assignment was a long way from over. So he'd gone to a small office he kept, where he changed clothes, treated his cuts, and packed up a few supplies. Before he'd set out for Barlow he'd spent a long time staring at the key. Could he use it for what he really wanted? Would it obey him? Or did Barney charge it for one purpose and one purpose only?

He was half deciding to try it when Ray appeared in the small office, standing in front of the door. Slowly, the fox shook his head. "Oh hell," Jack said. "Yeah, I know." When he put the key back in his pocket Ray vanished.

Now he watched Barlow's McMagic Mansion and debated the best way to get inside. He imagined kicking in the door and catching Barlow in the act of sacrificing some small creature. In the end he just muttered, "Fuck it," and walked up and rang the bell.

William Barlow opened the door wearing a green sweat suit and holding the *New York Times* Auto section. The moment he saw Jack his mouth fell open and he stepped backward. With his free hand, the left, he made a gesture to bar the threshold.

"Oh, William," Jack said. "Really? You think you can keep me out?" He snapped his fingers and a small capsule he'd been holding broke and scattered bright green powder in the air. The green flared as the powder absorbed the blocking spell, then fell dully to the floor.

Barlow's face visibly composed itself into a friendly smile. "Keep you out?" he said. "Why would I do that? I've been waiting for you. What happened? Did you find Alice? Could you help her?" Jack walked around him, once, twice, counterclockwise, always keeping his eyes on Barlow, his face, his feet, but especially his hands. "What are you doing?" Barlow said. "Why don't you tell me what happened? Is she—" In the middle of talking he brought his hand up for a blinding spell.

Jack stiffened his fingers to dagger Barlow's hand, then kicked the man's legs out from under him. As Barlow fell Jack said, "You stupid sonofabitch. Do you think you can attack *me*? You may have been good enough to cloak what you were doing when you sent me to the Forest, but in an open fight? I'm a Traveler, Willie. Do you have any idea what that means?"

Barlow didn't try to get up. Lying on his side on the floor he moaned, "Please. I have no idea what you're talking about."

"Still?" he said. "Still playing Dumb Billie? Then let me tell you, so you'll know it's too late.

"I'm going to guess something—in all your lies there was one thing that was the truth. When you said you were supposed to go first. You could tell, couldn't you? Was it just your EKG, or did you find some blind seer? Hell, maybe you did a casting yourself. And there it was. William Barlow, dead in six months. Am I right, Willie?"

Barlow said nothing, and Jack went on, "You just couldn't stand it. The great magician, the scholar, dead, and your slow dumb wife gets to live. Gets your money, too. Waste it on her stupid feel-good workshops."

"Please," Barlow said. "It wasn't like that. I loved her."

"Sure you did, Willie. You just loved yourself a lot more. So you killed her. Took all that healthy life force for yourself." Barlow began to cry.

"Problem solved," Jack said. "Only, Alice started coming back. The Forest appeared to you. All those voices. And one of them was hers. Did you imagine you could hear her? Was she calling your name?"

"Please," Barlow said, "I would have lost—"

"*Lost?*" Jack yelled. "You sonofabitch, I lost my wife and my daughter on the same day! My daughter killed my wife, and then I—" He had to stop, his whole body was shaking.

When Jack spoke again his voice was hard and measured. "Yeah, you didn't want to lose. All that great juju you'd built up wouldn't help you at all if Alice could get hold of you. You needed to get her off the scent, and what better way than to send in a substitute? A fake Billie who would go right up to her and she could tear his throat out and go off all satisfied."

He squatted down to put his face close to Barlow's. "It was the water, wasn't it? I wanted to link us—you and me—so I could find Alice. But you charged the water so it would begin something else. Lay your face on top of mine. And then the dressing room—that was to keep the link open, right?" He stood up again, said, "How long did it take to build up enough mojo to make it all work?" Barlow said nothing. Jack kicked him in the ribs. "How long?"

Barlow cried out, then said, "Three months!"

"And God knows what you did in those three months to get yourself ready. A whole lot of nasty."

"Please," Barlow said. "What—what are you going to do to me?"

Jack grinned. "Do, Willie? I'm not going to do anything to you." He watched the hope flicker in Barlow's face. Then Jack took out the gold key and held it up by its three-ring head. In the dim entryway the seven prongs sparkled with their own brilliance. Jack said, "*Hey! Magic boy!* Do you know what this is?"

For just a moment, Barlow stared at it, confused. Then he screamed. Jack nodded. "Did your research, did you?"

Barlow scrabbled backward along the floor until he bumped into a table along the wall. "Please," he said. "I can help you. I can give you things. I'll work for you. I've got money. I know things. *Please.*" Jack said nothing, only took out his chalk and drew a blue threshold on the polished wood floor. "Oh my God," Barlow said. With his knife, Jack traced the outline of a door in the air. A faint image appeared, and when he held up Barney's key an actual door appeared in the room. No rough garage metal this time, but proper suburban polished wood and frosted glass, with a keyhole rimmed in gold. Barlow gagged, as if he was trying to scream but couldn't get it out. Finally he cried, "Shade! I'll give you everything."

"Oh, Willie," Jack said. "Don't you get it? You don't have anything. You're finished."

"No! You're wrong. I can help you get your daughter back."

Jack went up to him, and for a long moment stared at Barlow's frantic face. "You're a liar, William Barlow. A liar to the end."

"No, no, no. I can do it. Really."

Jack wasn't listening. He shoved in the key harder than necessary, and for a moment worried it night have jammed. But no, the prongs meshed into the tumblers, which Jack knew were layers of reality, entire worlds. The key turned and the worlds shifted into place, and when Jack opened the door he saw darkness, lit only by pale tendrils of fire.

The whispers roared in the room, nearly drowning out Barlow's desperate cries. When they died down Jack could hear the mixed growls and laughter of the wild beast that once was Alice Barlow.

He didn't stay to watch, there was nothing there he needed to see. He walked out of Barlow's house, leaving behind wild thrashing sounds and the smell of blood.

When he got back to the hotel, Jack entered through the basement and went up in the service elevator to get to his room. He took a long shower, then sat on his bed even longer, trying not to think. Finally he got dressed, a blue oxford shirt, tan pants, and a blue silk jacket. He stared for a moment at the pile of black clothes lying on the floor, then left the room and went back out via the service elevator.

He entered through the front door now, and there in the lobby stood the hotel owner, carefully setting roses, one by one, in a green vase. He watched her for a while, admiring the grace and economy of her movements in a gray wool dress. "Hello, Irene," he said.

She turned quickly, with a bright smile. "Jack! Welcome home." She wore a small gold pendant of an owl he'd once given her, on a thin gold chain. "Would you like a drink?" She set down the final three roses in front of the vase.

"That would be wonderful," Jack said.

In Irene's small office, with a glass of brandy before each of them, Irene said, "Annette called. She asked me to invite you to a game in Philadelphia. Next Tuesday. Old-fashioned, she said, the way you like it. And then she said the oddest thing. I wrote it down to make sure I got it right." She picked up a small piece of paper. "It was two things, actually. She said blindfolds would not be necessary." Jack smiled. "And she said to tell you she would prefer it if you would leave your fox at home."

Jack stared at her for a moment, then burst out laughing.

On September 17, 2004, the fourteenth birthday of one Eugenia Shade, a bottle of beer flew off the kitchen table and smashed itself against the wall. Eugenia's father, a Traveler named Jack, sometimes called Care Free Jack, or Johnny Easy, had just told his daughter she could not drink beer, and so she laughed at the broken glass and the amber puddle on the floor.

Over the following weeks more and more things surrendered their stationary lives to take flight. A personal CD player smashed through a window. Chairs rearranged themselves in a wild dance. Any jar of food left out on a table or shelf was likely to destroy itself.

Eugenia's mother, Layla Shade, originally thought some action of her husband's had backfired, or worse, some spirit he'd angered had invaded their home. No, her husband told her, it was Eugenia herself, or rather an energy configuration, a poltergeist, that sometimes entered teenage girls. He told her their daughter was just an innocent host, but he knew it was more complicated than that. Geists, Jack knew, fed on the confusion, anger, and surging desires of adolescence. Eugenia wasn't doing it, but probably liked the fear and confusion she saw in her mother.

Weeks, then months, went by, and Layla begged Jack to do something, an exorcism, a spell, *something*, she hated being so nervous around her own daughter. Her husband assured her that geists were basically harmless, that teenagers almost always outgrew them, and that aggressive action might only make things worse. Not nearly as certain as he pretended, Jack secretly spent many hours online, especially in the Travelers Archive, a collection of research and first-person accounts that once was stored in underground vaults. Pretty much all of it confirmed what he'd told his wife.

Still, Jack went so far as to consult his old teacher, whom he had not seen or spoken to in years. "So the archives are right?" he told her. "I do nothing?"

Anatolie, as she was called, was a large woman with long, thick dreadlocks that coiled around her massive belly like protective snakes. Despite her size, she lived in a fifth-floor walkup in Chinatown, in an apartment Jack always thought was too small for her, let alone a visitor. She agreed with his assessment, but then mentioned, in an offhand manner, "You might want to build up credit."

"Credit?"

"Yes. A conditional vow in case you need help and don't have time to perform the necessary appeasements. If everything goes smoothly you will have no need to invoke it."

"What kind of help?" Jack asked. And, "Help against what?" Anatolie didn't answer. By her expression she seemed to have lost interest in Jack entirely.

Down in the street, outside grocery stalls filled with bitter melon and *gai lan*, Jack called his wife to tell her he had to go out of town for a couple of days. Layla was not happy. "You're going traveling?" she said. "Leaving me alone with this?"

"It's not a job," Jack said. "It's to get help."

Layla was silent a moment, then said, "So if you—do whatever it is—will that stop it?"

"Probably not. Or not exactly. But it will give us some insurance."

Layla sighed. "Come back as soon as you can," she said, and hung up.

Jack rented a car and drove upstate to a place he knew in the woods. The site was not an original but a cognate, a spot with the right configurations to stand in for a location where ceremonies were enacted thousands of years ago. There he lit four small fires, to mark out the action, but also because it was March and he would have to strip naked. Once his clothes were off he used an all-black knife Anatolie once gave him to draw a cross in the dirt connecting the fires. Now he drew the knife down the center of his body from his forehead to his groin. A charge ran through him and he gasped in the chilly air.

Setting aside the knife he picked up a business card he'd designed for himself, and a magic marker, then stepped into the circle to lie down on the axis between the two largest fires. Beyond the circle he could hear an owl, a deer crashing through some low branches, and a brief high-pitched cry that sounded like a woman's scream but probably was a coyote. He thought about what he was about to do, wondered if there was some other way. It was still likely the geist would just retreat and his vow would come to nothing. But if his daughter needed him…

Jack Shade was a freelancer. Jack Choice, as another Traveler once called him, liked to pick his cases, liked to turn away clients who annoyed him.

It was one of the reasons he'd broken with Anatolie, who considered Travelers "servants of the soul." But when you ask for help you have to offer something precious.

He held the card up high in his right hand. "I, John Marcus Shade," he said, "make this vow in honor of my daughter, Eugenia Carla Shade. If she ever needs help, if she ever needs a path to open for her, I make this promise. From the moment I should invoke this vow, anyone who finds and brings *this* card may compel my service. I may not refuse them, I may not turn them away. I offer this for the sake of my daughter Eugenia. May she never need it. May this vow never be invoked." Then he stabbed the card down onto his solar plexus.

The fires all flashed high, then burned out at the same moment. Even as he lay on the dark cold dirt Jack realized he could not feel the card on his body.

Too exhausted to drive further than the next cheap hotel, Jack got home the next day. The moment he stepped in the house Layla ran up and grabbed his arms. "Did you do something?" she asked. "Did it work?"

Nervously, Jack said, "I did something. But we won't know. Not for a while."

Layla pulled back from him. "No," she said. "You were supposed to fix this. I can't stand it anymore." Jack looked past her to see his daughter on the wooden stairs to the bedrooms. She was wearing a too tight halter top and too short miniskirt, and spike-heeled sandals—everything her mother would have forbidden if Layla wasn't afraid of her. She raised her middle finger toward her mother, and then clumsily walked upstairs with an exaggerated sway of her narrow hips. They'd reached a dangerous stage, Jack thought. The poltergeist wasn't Genie but she wanted to believe it was. She liked the power.

Jack spent the night on the couch. When his wife told him she wanted to be alone he did not contest it.

He slept late, woken finally by the sound of his wife's voice, high and tight as she shouted at her daughter. Jack ran into the kitchen. The date was March 9, 2005.

The first thing Jack saw was his wife, dressed in a blue sweat suit, shouting at their daughter, who was laughing as she leaned back against the doorway to the dining room. Eugenia wore a red dress and neon-pink sneakers. And then Jack ignored them, suddenly focused on everything else he saw in the kitchen. Iron pots. Large ladles. *Knives.*

Eugenia said, in a singsong taunt, "Good morning, Daddy. Mommy seems all upset about something."

Jack ignored her. "Layla," he said, trying to keep his voice even, "what are you doing?"

"I'm making lunch!" his wife shouted. "I'm making lunch—for my family—in my own fucking kitchen."

Jack said, "We agreed—"

"No! *You* agreed. You gave the order. The great Jack Shade the Traveler. I won't live like this anymore. My husband and *my daughter* don't get to boss me around in my own kitchen."

Jack turned to Eugenia. In that same steady voice he said, "Genie, I need to talk to your mother. Please leave the kitchen."

His daughter laughed. "Whatever," she said, and moved from the doorway. Then, "Nah, I think I'll stay," and she went back to where she'd been standing. "This is too much fun."

Layla said, "Goddamn it, do what your father says. I don't care what *thing* you've got inside you. You're fourteen years old and he's your father. If he tells you to do something you do it."

"Please," Jack said. Later he would wonder if he'd been speaking to his wife, his daughter, or the "thing." It didn't matter. None of them was listening.

A pot flew past Jack's head to hit the wall opposite the stove. Hot tomato sauce spilled down to cover a framed photo of the three of them at Disneyland when Eugenia was seven.

Layla screamed. Eugenia jumped up and down and clapped her hands. "Good one!" she said. "Let's see what else we can do."

"Genie!" Jack cried. "This isn't you. You can fight it."

"Why?" she said. "It's fun."

Then the knives started. They came at Jack, all different sizes, end over end or straight toward him. He flailed his arms like a windmill, spraying blood even as he batted most of them away. It was the smaller ones that got through his defense. Two small paring knives and a long-tined fork caught his right jaw and the side of his neck.

And then it was over. Jack was on his knees, his left hand pressed against his neck to stanch the blood. He saw his daughter first. She stood frozen in the doorway, ludicrous in her cheerful red dress, her mouth open but unable to make a sound. He looked at her for a long time, afraid to turn his head. When he finally did he saw his wife, and there she was, his beloved Layla, on the floor in a thick puddle of blood. The vegetable cleaver that lay next to her had cut right through her jugular. He crawled over to her and cradled her empty body.

"Daddy," Eugenia whispered. "I didn't—it wasn't—"

"I know, baby," Jack said. "It wasn't you. It's not your fault."

Eugenia said, "Help me. I don't think I can hold it." The knives had begun to swirl around her legs, a few inches from the floor.

"I know," Jack said again. His voice wet, he called out, "I, Jack Shade, invoke my vow. I demand payment!"

"Daddy?" Eugenia said. "What are you doing?"

Ignoring her, Jack said, "Take her somewhere. Somewhere safe, where she can't hurt anyone."

For months afterward Jack would wonder—did he want what happened? Was he trying to punish her? He would lie in bed and try to bring back that exact moment. He could never decide.

A door appeared in the room. Stone, unmarked. "Oh my God," Jack whispered. Then, "No! *That wasn't what I meant.*"

Eugenia just stood there, looking up at the door that somehow stood taller than the room. Jack called out, "Genie. Get away from it. You don't have to go there." But she didn't move, and neither did her father, though he fought to get up against an invisible hand that pressed him to the floor, even as he yelled to his daughter to run.

The door swung open, and Jack heard the Forest before he saw it—wind first, then voices, swirls of hushed voices. As it opened wider, so that his daughter stood framed in clouds of trees, Jack tried once more to move, but now he couldn't even speak, not to tell Eugenia to fight, not to try once more to take back his vow. He could only watch as his daughter walked, robot-like, into the world of whispers.

And then the door closed, and a moment later vanished, and he was all alone, Jack Shade with his dead wife in his arms—Johnny Lonesome, on the floor of a kitchen covered in blood.

TWO HOUSES

KELLY LINK

Kelly Link [www.kellylink.com] published her first story, "Water Off a Black Dog's Back," in 1995 and attended the Clarion Writers Workshop in the same year. A writer of subtle, challenging, sometimes whimsical fantasy, Link has published close to thirty stories which have won the Hugo, Nebula, World Fantasy, British SF, and Locus awards, and been collected in 4 Stories, Stranger Things Happen, Magic for Beginners, *and* Pretty Monsters. *Link is also an accomplished editor, working on acclaimed small press 'zine* Lady Churchill's Rosebud Wristlet *and publishing books as Small Beer Press with husband Gavin J. Grant, as well as co-editing* The Year's Best Fantasy and Horror *series with Grant and Ellen Datlow.*

Wake up, wake up.

Portia is having a birthday party. The party will start without you. Wake up, Gwenda. Wake up. Hurry, hurry.

Soft music playing. The smell of warm bread. She could have been back home, how many houses ago? In her childhood bed, her mother downstairs baking bread. The last sleeper in the spaceship *House of Secrets* opened her eyes, crept from her narrow bed. She rose up, or fell, into the chamber.

The chamber too was narrow and small. It was made up of soft pink light, invisible drawers, bed and chambers, all of them empty. The astronaut Gwenda stretched out her arms, scratched her head. Her hair had grown out again. She dreamed, sometimes, of a berth filled with masses of hair. Years and decades and centuries passing while the dreamer slept beneath that strangling weight.

Now there was the smell of old paper. The library where Gwenda had spent summers as a child, reading fairy tales. Maureen was in her head, looking at old books with her. Monitoring her heart rate, the dilation of her pupils, each flare of her nostrils. Maureen was the ship, the House and the keeper of all its Secrets. A spirit of the air; a soothing subliminal hum; an alchemical sequence of smells and emanations.

Gwenda inhaled. Stretched again, then slowly somersaulted. Arcane chemical processes began within her blood, her nervous system.

This is how it was aboard the spaceship *House of Secrets*. You slept and you woke up and you slept again. You might sleep for a year, for five years. There were six astronauts. Sometimes others were already awake. Sometimes you spent a few days, a few weeks alone. Except you were never really alone. Maureen was always there. She was there with you, sleeping and waking. She was inside you too.

Everyone is waiting for you in the Great Room. There's roasted carp. A chocolate cake.

"A tidal smell," Gwenda said, trying to place it. "Mangrove roots, and the sea caught in a hundred places at their roots. I spent a summer in a place like that.

You arrived with one boy and you left with another.

"So I did," Gwenda said. "I'd forgotten. It was such a long time ago."

A hundred years.

"That long!" Gwenda said.

Not long at all.

"No," Gwenda said. "Not long at all." She touched her hair. "I've been asleep…"

Seven years this time.

"Seven years," Gwenda said.

The smell of oranges, a whole grove of them. Other smells, pleasant ones, ones that belonged to Mei and Sullivan and Aune and Portia. Sisi. All of their body chemistries altered, adjusted for harmonious relationships. They were, of necessity, a convivial group.

Gwenda threw off the long sleep. Sank toward the curve of the bulkhead, pressing on a drawer. It swung open and in she went to make her toilet, to be poked and prodded and injected, lathered and sluiced. She rid herself of the new growth of hair, the fine down on her arms and legs.

So slow, so slow, Maureen fretted. Let me get rid of it for you. For good.

"One day," Gwenda said. She opened her log, checked the charts on her guinea pigs, her carp.

This is why you are last again. You dawdle. You refuse to be sensible in the matter of personal grooming. Everyone is waiting for you. You're missing all of the fun.

"Aune has asked for a Finnish disco or a Finnish bar or a Finnish sauna. Or the Northern Lights. Sullivan is playing with dogs. Mei is chatting up movie stars or famous composers, and Portia is being outrageous. There are waterfalls or redwood trees or dolphins," Gwenda said.

Cherry blossoms. The Westminster dog show. 2009. The Susex Spaniel Clussex Three D Grinchy Glee wins. And Sisi is hoping you will hurry. She wants to tell you something.

"Well," Gwenda said. "I'd better hurry then."

Maureen went before and after, down Corridor One. Lights flicked on, then off again so that the corridor fell away behind Gwenda in darkness. Was Maureen the golden light ahead or the darkness that followed behind? Carp the size of year old children swam in the glassy walls. Gwenda stopped now and then to watch.

Then she was in the Galley, and the Great Room was just above her, and long-limbed Sisi poked her head through the glory hole. "New tattoo?"

It was an old joke between them.

Head to toes Gwenda was covered in the most extraordinary pictures. There was a Durer and a Dore; two Chinese dragons and a Celtic cross; there was a winged man holding a rat-headed baby; the Queen of Diamonds ripped into eight pieces by a pack of wolves; a green-haired girl on a playground rocket; the Statue of Liberty and the State Flag of Illinois; passages from Lewis Carroll and the Book of Revelations and a hundred other books; a hundred other marvels. There was the spaceship *House of Secrets* on the back of Gwenda's right hand, and its sister *House of Mystery* on her left.

Sisi had a pair of old cowboy boots, and Aune had an ivory cross on a gold chain. Her mother had given it to her. Sullivan had a copy of *Moby Dick*, Portia a four-carat diamond in a platinum setting. Mei brought her knitting needles.

Gwenda had her tattoos. Astronauts on the Long Trip travel lightly.

Hands pulled Gwenda up and into the Great Room, patted her back, her shoulders, rubbed her head. Here feet had weight. There was a floor, and she stood on it. There was a table, and on the table was a cake. Familiar faces grinned at her.

The music was very loud. Silky coated dogs chased white petals.

"Surprise!" Sisi said. "Happy birthday, Gwenda!"

"But it isn't my birthday," Gwenda said. "It's Portia's birthday. Maureen?"

Today is your birthday, Maureen said.

"But it was my idea," Portia said. "My idea to throw you a surprise party."

"Well," Gwenda said. "I'm surprised."

Come on, Maureen said. Come and blow out your candles.

The candles were not real, of course. But the cake was.

It was the usual sort of party. They all danced, the way you could only dance in micro gravity. It was all good fun. When dinner was ready, Maureen sent away the Finnish dance music, the dogs, the cherry blossoms. You could hear Shakespeare say to Mei, "I always dreamed of being an astronaut." And then he vanished.

Once there had been two ships. It was considered usual practice, in the Third Age of Space Travel, to build more than one ship at a time, to send companion ships out on their long voyages. Redundancy enhances resilience. Sister ships *Seeker* and *Messenger*, called *House of Secrets* and *House of Mystery* by their crews, left Earth on a summer day in the year 2059.

House of Secrets had seen her twin disappear in a wink, a blink. First there, then nowhere. That had been thirty years ago. Space was full of mysteries. Space was full of secrets.

Dinner was Beef Wellington (fake) with asparagus and new potatoes (both real) and sourdough rolls (realish). The experimental chickens were laying again, and so there were poached eggs, too, as well as the chocolate cake. Maureen increased gravity, because even fake Beef Wellington requires suitable gravity. Mei threw rolls across the table at Gwenda. "Look at that, will you?" she said. "Every now and then a girl likes to watch something fall."

Aune supplied bulbs of something alcoholic. No one asked what it was.

Aune worked with eukaryotes and Archaea. "I made enough to get us lit," she said. "Just a little lit. Because today is Gwenda's birthday."

"It was my birthday just a little while ago," Portia said. "How old am I anyway? Never mind, who's counting."

"To Portia," Aune said. "Forever youngish."

"To Proxima Centauri," Sullivan said. "Getting closer every day. Not that much closer.

"Here's to all us Goldilocks. Here's to a planet that's just right."

"Here's to a real garden," Aune said. "With real toads."

"To Maureen," Sisi said. "And old friends." She squeezed Gwenda's hand.

"To our *House of Secrets*," Mei said.

"To *House of Mystery*," Sisi said. They all turned and looked at her. Sisi squeezed Gwenda's hand again. They drank.

"We didn't get you anything, Gwenda," Sullivan said.

"I don't want anything," Gwenda said.

"I do," Portia said. "For starters, a foot rub. Or wait, I know! Stories! Ones I haven't heard before."

"We should go over the log," Aune said.

"The log can lie there," Portia said.

"The log can wait," Mei agreed. "Let's sit here a while longer, and talk about nothing."

Sisi cleared her throat. "There's just one thing," she said. "We ought to tell Gwenda the one thing."

"You'll ruin her birthday party," Portia said.

"What?" Gwenda asked Sisi.

"It's nothing," Sisi said. "Nothing at all. Only the mind playing tricks. You know how it goes."

"Maureen?" Gwenda said. "What are they talking about, please?"

Maureen blew through the room, a vinegar breeze. "Approximately thirty-one hours ago Sisi was in the Control Room. She performed several usual tasks, then asked me to bring up our immediate course. I did so. Twelve seconds later, I observed that her heart rate had gone up. When I asked her if something was wrong, she said, 'Do you see it, too, Maureen?' I asked Sisi to tell me what she was seeing. Sisi said, '*House of Mystery*. Over to starboard. It was there. Then it was gone.' I told Sisi I had not seen it. We called back the visuals, but nothing was recorded there. I broadcast on all channels. No one answered. No one has seen *House of Mystery* in the intervening time."

"Sisi?" Gwenda said.

"It was there," Sisi said. "Swear to God, I saw it. Like looking in a mirror. So near I could almost touch it."

They all began to talk at once.

"Do you think—

"Just a trick of the imagination—

"It disappeared like that. Remember?" Sullivan snapped his fingers. "Why couldn't it come back again the same way?"

"No!" Portia said. She glared at them all. "I don't want to talk about this, to rehash all this again. Don't you remember? We talked and talked and we theorized and we rationalized and what difference did it make?"

"Portia?" Maureen said. "I will formulate something for you, if you are distraught."

"No," Portia said. "I don't want anything. I'm *fine*."

"It wasn't really there," Sisi said. "It wasn't there and I wish I hadn't seen it." There were tears in her eyes. One fell out and lifted slowly away from her cheek.

"Had you been drinking?" Sullivan said. "Maureen, what did you find in Sisi's blood?"

"Nothing that shouldn't have been there," Maureen said.

"I wasn't high, and I hadn't had anything to drink," Sisi said.

"But we haven't stopped drinking since," Aune said. She tossed back another bulb. "Maureen sobers us up and we just climb that mountain again. Cheers."

Mei said, "I'm just glad it wasn't me who saw it. And I don't want to talk about it anymore either. Not right now. We haven't all been awake like this for so long. Let's not fight."

"That's settled," Portia said. "Bring up the lights again, Maureen, please. I'd like something fancy. Something with history. An old English country house, roaring fireplace, suits of armor, tapestries, bluebells, sheep, moors, detectives in deerstalkers, Cathy scratching at the windows. You know."

"It isn't your birthday, you know," Sullivan said. "Not anymore. It's Gwenda's."

"I don't care," Gwenda said, and Portia blew her a kiss.

That breeze ran up and down the room again. The table sank back into the floor. The curved walls receded, extruding furnishings, two panting greyhounds. They were in a Great Hall instead of the Great Room. Tapestries hung on plaster walls, threadbare and musty, so real that Gwenda sneezed. There were flagstones, blackened beams. A roaring fire. Through the mullioned windows a gardener and his boy were cutting roses.

You could smell the cold rising off stones, the yew log upon the fire, the roses and the dust of centuries.

"Halfmark House," Maureen said. "Built in 1508. Queen Elizabeth came here on a progress in 1575 that nearly bankrupted the Halfmark family. Churchill spent a weekend in December of 1942. There are many photos. Additionally, it was once said to be the second-most haunted manor in England. There are three monks and a Grey Lady, a White Lady, a yellow fog, and a stag."

"It's exactly what I wanted," Portia said. "To float around like a ghost in an old English manor. Could you turn gravity off again, Maureen?"

"I like you, my girl," Aune said. "But you are a strange one."

"Of course I am," Portia said. "We all are." She made a wheel of herself and rolled around the room. Hair seethed around her face in the way that Gwenda hated.

"Let's each pick one of Gwenda's tattoos," Sisi said. "And make up a story about it."

"Dibs on the phoenix," Sullivan said. "You can never go wrong with a phoenix."

"No," Portia said. "Let's tell ghost stories. Aune, you start. Maureen can provide the special effects."

"I don't know any ghost stories," Aune said, slowly. "I know stories about trolls. No. Wait. I have one ghost story. It was a story that my great-grandmother told about the farm in Pirkanmaa where she grew up."

The Great Room grew dark until all of them were only shadows, floating in shadow. Sisi wrapped an arm around Gwenda's waist. Outside the mullioned windows, the gardeners and the rose bushes disappeared. Now you saw a neat little farm and rocky fields, sloping up toward the twilight bulk of a coniferous forest.

"Yes," Aune said. "Exactly like that. I visited once when I was just a girl. The farm was in ruins. Now the world will have changed again. Maybe there is another farm or maybe it is all forest now." She paused for a moment, so that they all could imagine it. "My great-grandmother was a girl of eight or nine. She went to school for part of the year. The rest of the year she and her brothers and sisters did the work of the farm. My great-grandmother's work was to take the cows to a meadow where the pasturage was rich in clover and sweet grasses. The cows were very big and she very small, but they knew to come when she called them. In the evening she brought the herd home again. The path went along a ridge. On the near side she and her cows passed a closer meadow that her family did not use even though the pasturage looked very fine to my great-grandmother. There was a brook down in the meadow, and an old tree, a grand old man. There was a rock under the tree, a great slab that looked like something like a table."

Outside the windows of the English manor, a tree formed itself in a grassy, sunken meadow.

"My great-grandmother didn't like that meadow. Sometimes when she looked down she saw people sitting all around the table that the rock made. They were eating and drinking. They wore old-fashioned clothing, the kind her own great-grandmother would have worn. She knew that they had been dead a very long time."

"Ugh," Mei said. "Look!"

"Yes," Aune said in her calm, uninflected voice. "Like that. One day my great-grandmother, her name was Aune, too, I should have said that first, I suppose, one day Aune was leading her cows home along the ridge and she looked down into the meadow. She saw the people eating and drinking at their table. And while she was looking down, they turned and looked at her. They began to wave at her, to beckon that she should come down and sit with them and eat and drink. But instead she turned away and went home and told her mother what had happened. And after that, her older brother, who was a very unimaginative boy, had the job of taking the cattle to the far pasture."

The people at the table were waving at Gwenda and Mei and Portia and the rest of them now. Sullivan waved back.

"Creepy!" Portia said. "That was a good one. Maureen, didn't you think so?"

"It was a good story," Maureen said. "I liked the cows."

"So not the point, Maureen," Portia said. "Anyway."

"I have a story," Sullivan said. "In the broad outlines it's a bit like Aune's story."

"You could change things," Portia said. "I wouldn't mind."

"I'll just tell it the way I heard it," Sullivan said. "Anyhow it's Kentucky, not Finland, and there aren't any cows. That is, there were cows, because it's another farm, but not in the story. It's a story my grandfather told me."

The gardeners were outside the windows again. There was something ghostly about them, Gwenda thought. You knew that they would just come and go, always doing the same things. Perhaps this was what it had been like to be rich and looked after by so many servants, all of them practically invisible—just like Maureen, really, or even more so—for all the notice you had to take of them. They might as well have been ghosts. Or was it the rich people who had lived in a house like this who had been the ghosts? Capricious, exerting great pressure without ever really having to set a foot on the ground, nothing their servants dared look at for any length of time without drawing malicious attention?

Never mind, they were all ghosts now.

What an odd string of thoughts. She was sure that while she had been alive on Earth nothing like this had ever been in her head. Out here, suspended between one place and another, of course you went a little crazy. It was almost luxurious, how crazy you were allowed to be.

She and Sisi lay cushioned on the air, arms wrapped around each other's waists so as not to go flying away. They floated just above the silky ears of one of the greyhounds. The sensation of heat from the fireplace furred one arm, one leg, burned pleasantly along one side of her face. If something disastrous were to happen now, if a meteor were to crash through a bulkhead, if a fire broke out in the Long Gallery, if a seam ruptured and they all went flying into space, could she and Sisi keep hold of one another? She resolved she would. She would not let go.

Sullivan had the most wonderful voice for telling stories. He was describing the part of Kentucky where his family still lived. They hunted wild pigs that lived in the forest. Went to a church on Sundays. There was a tornado.

Rain beat at the mullioned windows. You could smell the ozone beading on the glass. Trees thrashed and groaned.

After the tornado passed through, men came to Sullivan's grandfather's house. They were going to look for a girl who had gone missing. Sullivan's grandfather, a young man at the time, went with them. The hunting trails were all gone. Parts of the forest had been flattened. Sullivan's grandfather was with the group that found the girl. A tree had fallen across her body and cut her almost in two. She was crawling, dragging herself along the ground by her fingernails.

"After that," Sullivan said, "my grandfather only hunted in those woods a time or two. Then he never hunted there again. He said that he knew what it was to hear a ghost walk, but he'd never heard one crawl before."

"Look!" Portia said. Outside the window something was crawling along the floor of the forest. "Shut it off, Maureen! Shut it off! Shut it off!"

The gardeners again, with their terrible shears.

"No more old-people ghost stories," Portia said. "Okay?"

Sullivan pushed himself up toward the white-washed ceiling. "You're a brat, Portia," he said.

"I know," Portia said. "I know! I guess you spooked me. So it must have been a good ghost story, right?"

"Right," Sullivan said, mollified. "I guess it was."

"That poor girl," Aune said. "To relive that moment over and over again. Who would want that, to be a ghost?"

"Maybe it isn't always bad?" Mei said. "Maybe there are happy, well-adjusted ghosts?"

"I never saw the point," Sullivan said. "I mean, ghosts appear as a warning. So what's the warning in that story I told you? Don't get caught in the forest during a tornado? Don't get cut in half? Don't die?"

"I thought they were more like a memory," Gwenda said. "Not really there at all. Just an echo, recorded somehow and then played back, what they did, what happened to them."

Sisi said, "But Aune's ghosts—the other Aune—they looked at her. They wanted her to come down and eat with them. What would have happened then?"

"Nothing good," Aune said.

"Maybe it's genetic," Mei said. "Seeing ghosts. That kind of thing."

"Then Aune and I would be prone," Sullivan said.

"Not me," Sisi said. "I've never seen a ghost." She thought for a minute. "Unless I did. You know. No. It wasn't a ghost. What I saw. How could a ship be a ghost?"

"Don't think about it now," Mei said. "Let's not tell any more ghost stories. Let's have a gossip instead. Talk about back when we used to have sex lives."

"No," Gwenda said. "Let's have one more ghost story. Just one, for my birthday. Maureen?"

That breeze tickled at her ear. "Yes?"

"Do you know any ghost stories?"

Maureen said, "I have all of the stories of Edith Wharton and M. R. James and many others in my library. Would you like to hear one?"

"No," Gwenda said. "I want a real story."

Portia said, "And then Sullivan will give me a foot rub, and then we can all take a nap before breakfast. Mei, you must know a ghost story. No old people though. I want a sexy ghost story."

"God, no," Mei said. "No sexy ghosts for me. Thank God."

"I have a story," Sisi said. "It isn't mine, of course. Like I said, I've never seen a ghost."

"Go on," Gwenda said.

"Not my ghost story," Sisi said. "And not really a ghost story. I'm not sure what it was. It was the story of a man that I dated for a few months."

"A boyfriend story!" Sullivan said. "I love your boyfriend stories, Sisi! Which one?"

We could go all the way to Proxima Centauri and back and Sisi still wouldn't have run out of stories about her boyfriends, Gwenda thought. But here she is, here we are, together. And what are they? Dead and buried! Ghosts! Every last one of them!

"I don't think I've told any of you about him," Sisi was saying. "This was during the period when they weren't building new ships. Remember? They kept sending us out to do fundraising? I was supposed to be some kind of Ambassadress for Space. Emphasis on the slinky little dress. I was supposed to be seductive and also noble and representative of everything that made it worth going to space for. I did a good enough job that they sent me over to meet a consortium of investors and big shots in London. I met all sorts of guys, but the only one I clicked with was this one dude, Liam. Okay. Here's where it gets complicated for a bit. Liam's mother was English. She came from this old family, lots of money and not a lot of supervision and by the time she was a teenager, she was a total wreck. Into booze, hard drugs, recreational Satanism, you name it. Got kicked out of school after school after school, and after that she got kicked out of all of the best rehab programs too. In the end, her family kicked her out. Gave her money to go away. She ended up in prison for a couple of years, had a baby. That was Liam. Bounced around Europe for a while, then when Liam was about seven or eight, she found God and got herself cleaned up. By this point her father and mother were both dead. One of the superbugs. Her brother had inherited everything. She went back to the ancestral pile—imagine a place like this, okay?—and tried to make things good with her brother. Are you with me so far?"

"So it's a real old-fashioned English ghost story," Portia said.

"You have no idea," Sisi said. "You have no idea. So her brother was kind of a jerk. And let me emphasize, once again, this was a rich family, like you have no idea. The mother and the father and brother were into collecting art. Contemporary stuff. Video installations, performance art, stuff that was really far out. They commissioned this one artist, an American, to come and do a site-specific installation. That's what Liam called it. It was supposed to be a commentary on the transatlantic exchange, the post-colonial relationship between England and the US, something like that. And what he did was, he bought a ranch house out in a suburb in Arizona, the same state, by the way, where you can still go and see the original London Bridge. This artist bought the suburban ranch, circa 1980, and the furniture in it and everything else, down to the rolls of toilet paper and the cans of soup in the cupboards. And he had the house dismantled with all of the pieces numbered, and plenty of photographs and video so he would know exactly where everything went, and it all got shipped over to England and then he built it all again on the family's estate. And simultaneously, he had a second house built right beside it. This second house was an exact replica, from the foundation to the pictures on the wall to the cans of soup on the shelves in the kitchen."

"Why would anybody ever bother to do that?" Mei said.

"Don't ask me," Sisi said. "If I had that much money, I'd spend it on shoes and booze and vacations for me and all of my friends."

"Hear, hear," Gwenda said. They all raised their bulbs and drank.

"This stuff is ferocious, Aune," Sisi said. "I think it's changing my mitochondria."

"Quite possibly," Aune said. "Cheers."

"Anyway, this double installation won some award. Got lots of attention. The whole point was that nobody knew which house was which. Then the superbug took out the mom and dad, and a couple of years after that, Liam's mother the black sheep came home. And her brother said to her, I don't want you living in the family home with me. But I'll let you live on the estate. I'll even give you a job with the housekeeping staff. And in exchange you'll live in my installation. Which was, apparently, something that the artist had really wanted to make part of the project, to find a family to come and live in it.

"This jerk brother said, 'You and my nephew can come and live in my installation. I'll even let you pick which house.'

"Liam's mother went away and talked to God about it. Then she came back and moved into one of the houses."

"How did she decide which house she wanted to live in?" Sullivan said.

"That's a great question," Sisi said. "I have no idea. Maybe God told her? Look, what I was interested in at the time was Liam. I know why he liked me. Here I was, this South African girl with an American passport, dreadlocks and cowboy boots, talking about how I was going to get in a rocket and go up in space, just as soon as I could. What man doesn't like a girl who doesn't plan to stick around?

"What I don't know is why I liked him so much. The thing is, he wasn't really a good-looking guy. He had a nice round English butt. His hair wasn't terrible. But there was something about him, you just knew he was going to get you into trouble. The good kind of trouble. When I met him, his mother was dead. His uncle was dead too. They weren't a lucky family. They had money instead of luck. The brother had never married, and he'd left Liam everything.

"We went out for dinner. We gave each other all the right kind of signals, and then we fooled around some and he said he wanted to take me up to his country house for the weekend. It sounded like fun. I guess I was picturing one of those little thatched cottages you see in detective series. But it was like this instead." Sisi gestured around. "Big old pile. Except with video screens in the corners showing mice eating each other and little kids eating cereal. Nice, right?

"He said we were going to go for a walk around the estate. Romantic, right? We walked out about a mile through this typical South of England landscape and then suddenly we're approaching this weather-beaten, rotting stucco house that looked like every ranch house I'd ever seen in a de-populated neighborhood in the Southwest, y'all. This house was all by itself on a green English hill. It looked seriously wrong. Maybe it had looked better before the other one had burned down, or at least more in-tentionally weird, the way an art installation should, but anyway. Actually, I don't think so. I think it always looked wrong.

"Go back a second," Mei said. "What happened to the other house?"

"I'll get to that in a minute," Sisi said. "So there we are in front of this horrible house, and Liam picked me up and carried me across the threshold like we were newlyweds. He dropped me on a rotting tan couch and said, 'I was hoping you would spend the night with me.' I said, 'You mean back at your place?' He said, 'I mean here.'

"I said to him, 'You're going to have to explain.' And so he did, and now we're back at the part where Liam and his mother moved into the instal-lation."

"This story isn't like the other stories," Maureen said.

"You know, I've never told this story before," Sisi said. "The rest of it, I'm not even sure I know how to tell it."

"Liam and his mother moved into the installation," Portia said.

"Yeah. Liam's mummy picked a house and they moved in. Liam's just this little kid. A bit abnormal because of how they'd been living. And there are all these weird rules, like they aren't allowed to eat any of the food on the shelves in the kitchen. Because that's part of the installation. Instead the mother has a mini-fridge in the closet in her bedroom. Oh, and there are clothes in the closets in the bedrooms. And there's a TV, but it's an old one and the installation artist set it up so it only plays shows that were current in the early nineties in the U.S., which was the last time the house was occupied.

"And there are weird stains on the carpets in some of the rooms. Big brown stains.

"But Liam doesn't care so much about that. He gets to pick his own bedroom, which seems to be set up for a boy maybe a year or two older than Liam is. There's a model train set on the floor, which Liam can play with, as long as he's careful. And there are comic books, good ones that Liam hasn't read before. There are cowboys on the sheets. There's a big stain here, in the corner, under the window.

"And he's allowed to go into the other bedrooms, as long as he doesn't mess anything up. There's a pink bedroom, with twin beds. Lots of boring girls' clothes and a stain in the closet, and a diary, hidden in a shoebox, which Liam doesn't see any point in reading. There's a room for an older boy, too, with posters of actresses that Liam doesn't recognize, and lots of American sports stuff. Football, but not the right kind.

"Liam's mother sleeps in the pink bedroom. You would expect her to take the master bedroom, but she doesn't like the bed. She says it isn't comfortable. Anyway, there's a stain on it that goes right through the duvet, through the sheets. It's as if the stain came up *through* the mattress.

"I think I'm beginning to see the shape of this story," Gwenda says.

"You bet," Sisi says. "But remember, there are two houses. Liam's mummy is responsible for looking after both houses. She also volunteers at the church down in the village. Liam goes to the village school. For the first two weeks, the other boys beat him up, and then they lose interest and after that everyone leaves him alone. In the afternoons he comes back and plays in his two houses. Sometimes he falls asleep in one house, watching TV, and when he wakes up he isn't sure where he is. Sometimes his uncle comes by to invite him to go for a walk on the estate, or to go fishing. He likes his uncle. Sometimes they walk up to the manor house, and play billiards. His uncle arranges for him to have riding lessons, and that's the best thing in the world. He gets to pretend that he's a cowboy. Maybe that's why he liked me. Those boots.

"Sometimes he plays cops and robbers. He used to know some pretty bad guys, back before his mother got religion, and Liam isn't exactly sure which he is yet, a good guy or a bad guy. He has a complicated relationship with his mother. Life is better than it used to be, but religion takes up about the same amount of space as the drugs did. It doesn't leave much room for Liam.

"Anyway, there are some cop shows on the TV. After a few months he's seen them all at least once. There's one called CSI, and it's all about fingerprints and murder and blood. And Liam starts to get an idea about the stain in his bedroom, and the stain in the master bedroom, and the other stains, the ones in the living room, on the plaid sofa and over behind the La-Z-Boy that you mostly don't notice at first, because it's hidden. There's one stain up on the wallpaper in the living room, and after a while it starts to look a lot like a handprint.

"So Liam starts to wonder if something bad happened in his house. And in that other house. He's older now, maybe ten or eleven. He wants to know why are there two houses, exactly the same, next door to each other? How could there have been a murder—okay, a series of murders, where everything happened exactly the same way twice? He doesn't want to ask his mother, because lately when he tries to talk to his mother, all she does is quote Bible verses at him. He doesn't want to ask his uncle about it either, because the older Liam gets, the more he can see that even when his uncle is being super nice, he's still not all that nice. The only reason he's nice to Liam is because Liam is his heir.

"His uncle has shown him some of the other pieces in his art collection, and he tells Liam that he envies him, getting to be a part of an actual installation. Liam knows his house came from America. He knows the name of the artist who designed the installation. So that's enough to go online and find out what's going on, which is that, sure enough, the original house, the one the artist bought and brought over, is a murder house. Some high-school kid went beserko in the middle of the night and killed his whole family with a hammer. And this artist, his idea was based on something the robber barons did at the turn of the previous century, which was buy up castles abroad and have them brought over stone by stone to be rebuilt in Texas, or upstate Pennsylvania, or wherever. And if there was a ghost, they paid even more money. So that was idea number one, to flip that. But then he had idea number two, which was, What makes a haunted house? If you take it to pieces and transport it all the way across the Atlantic Ocean, does the ghost (ghosts, in this case) come with it, if you put it back together exactly the way it was? And if you can put a haunted house back together again, piece by piece by piece, can you build your own from scratch if you re-create all of the pieces? And idea number three, forget the ghosts, can the real live people who go and walk around in one house or the other, or even better, the ones who live in a house without knowing which house is which, would they know which one was real and which one was ersatz?

Would they see real ghosts in the real house? Imagine they saw ghosts in the fake one?"

"So which house were they living in?" Sullivan asked.

"Does it really matter which house they were living in?" Sisi said. "I mean, Liam spent time in both houses. He said he never knew which house was real. Which house was haunted. The artist was the only one with that piece of information. He even used real blood to re-create the stains.

"I'll tell the rest of the story as quickly as I can. So by the time Liam brought me to see his ancestral home, one of the installation houses had burned down. Liam's mother did it. Maybe for religious reasons? Liam was kind of vague about why. I got the feeling it had to do with his teenage years. They went on living there, you see. Liam got older, and I'm guessing his mother caught him fooling around with a girl or smoking pot, something, in the house that they didn't live in. By this point she had become convinced that one of the houses was occupied by unquiet spirits, but she couldn't make up her mind which. And in any case, it didn't do any good. If there were ghosts in the other house, they just moved in next door once it burned down. I mean, why not? Everything was already set up exactly the way that they liked it."

"Wait, so there were ghosts?" Gwenda said.

"Liam said there were. He said he never saw them, but later on, when he lived in other places, he realized that there must have been ghosts. In both places. Both houses. Other places just felt empty to him. He said to think of it like maybe you grew up in a place where there was always a party going on, all the time, or a bar fight, one that went on for years, or maybe just somewhere where the TV was always on. And then you leave the party, or you get thrown out of the bar, and all of a sudden you realize you're all alone. Like, you just can't sleep as well without that TV on. You can't get to sleep. He said he was always on high alert when he was away from the murder house, because something was missing and he couldn't figure out what. I think that's what I picked up on. That extra vibration, that twitchy radar."

"That's sick," Sullivan said.

"Yeah," Sisi said. "That relationship was over real quick. So that's my ghost story."

Mei said, "So what happened?"

"He'd brought a picnic dinner with us. Lobster and champagne and the works. We sat and ate at the kitchen table while he told me about his childhood. Then he gave me the tour. Showed me all the stains where those people died, like they were holy relics. I kept looking out the window, and seeing the sun get lower and lower. I didn't want to be in that house after it got dark."

They were all in that house now, flicking through those rooms, one after another. "Maureen?" Mei said. "Can you change it back?"

"Of course," Maureen said. Once again there were the greyhounds, the garden, the fire and the roses. Shadows slicked the flagstones, blotted and clung to the tapestries.

"Better," Sisi said. "Thank you. You went and found it online, didn't you, Maureen? That was exactly the way I remember it. I went outside to think and have a cigarette. Yeah, I know. Bad astronaut. But I still kind of wanted to sleep with this guy. Just once. So he was messed up, so what? Sometimes messed up sex is the best. When I came back inside the house, I still hadn't made up my mind. And then I made up my mind in a hurry. Because this guy? I went to look for him and he was down on the floor in that little boy's bedroom. Under the window, okay? On top of that *stain*. He was rolling around on the floor. You know, the way cats do? He had this look on his face. Like when they get catnip. I got out of there in a hurry. Drove away in his Land Rover. The keys were still in the ignition. Left it at a transport café and hitched the rest of the way home and never saw him again."

"You win," Portia said. "I don't know what you win, but you win. That guy was *wrong*."

"What about the artist? I mean, what he did," Mei said. "That Liam guy would have been okay if it weren't for what he did. Right? I mean, it's something to think about. Say we find some nice Goldilocks planet. If the conditions are suitable, and we grow some trees and some cows, do we get the table with the ghosts sitting around it? Did they come with Aune? With us? Are they here now? If we tell Maureen to build a haunted house around us right now, does she have to make the ghosts? Or do they just show up?"

Maureen said, "It would be an interesting experiment."

The Great Room began to change around them. The couch came first.

"Maureen!" Portia said. "Don't you dare!"

Gwenda said, "But we don't need to run that experiment. I mean, isn't it already running?" She appealed to the others, to Sullivan, to Aune. "You know. I mean, you know what I mean?"

"Not really," Sisi said. "What do you mean?"

Gwenda looked at the others. Then Sisi again. Sisi stretched luxuriously and turned in the air. Gwenda thought of the stain on the carpet, the man rolling on it like a cat.

"Gwenda, my love. What are you trying to say?" Sisi said.

"I know a ghost story," Maureen said. "I know one after all. Do you want to hear it?"

Before anyone could answer, they were in the Great Room again, except they were outside it too. They floated, somehow, in a great nothingness. But there was the table again with dinner upon it, where they had sat.

The room grew darker and colder and the lost crew of the ship *House of Mystery* sat around the table.

That sister crew, those old friends, they looked up from their meal, from their conversation. They turned and regarded the crew of the ship *House of Secrets*. They wore dress uniforms, as if in celebration, but they were maimed by some catastrophe. They lifted their ruined hands and beckoned, smiling.

There was a smell of char and chemicals and blood that Gwenda almost knew.

And then it was her own friends around the table. Mei, Sullivan, Portia, Aune, Sisi. She saw herself sitting there, hacked almost in two. She beckoned to herself, then vanished.

The Great Room reshaped itself out of nothingness and horror. They were back in the English country house. The air was full of sour spray. Someone had thrown up. Someone else sobbed.

Aune said, "Maureen, that was unkind."

Maureen said nothing. She went about the room like a ghost, coaxing the vomit into a great ball.

"The hell was that?" Sisi said. "Maureen? What were you thinking? Gwenda? My darling, are you okay?" She reached for Gwenda's hand, but Gwenda pushed away, flailing.

She went forward in a great spasm, her arms extended to catch the wall. Going before her on the one hand, the ship *House of Secrets,* and on the other, *House of Mystery*. She could no longer tell the one from the other.

BLOOD DRIVE

JEFFREY FORD

Jeffrey Ford [http://www.well-builtcity.com] *is the author of the novels* The Physiognomy, Memoranda, The Beyond, The Portrait of Mrs. Charbuque, The Girl in the Glass, The Cosmology of the Wider World, *and* The Shadow Year. *His short fiction has been collected in* The Fantasy Writer's Assistant, The Empire of Ice Cream, The Drowned Life, *and* Crackpot Palace. *Ford's fiction has been translated into over twenty languages and is the recipient of the Edgar Allan Poe Award, the Shirley Jackson Award, the Nebula, the World Fantasy Award, and the Grand Prix de l'imaginaire.*

For Christmas our junior year of high school, all of our parents got us guns. That way you had a half a year to learn to shoot and get down all the safety garbage before you started senior year. Depending on how well off your parents were, that pretty much dictated the amount of fire power you had. Darcy Krantz's family lived in a trailer, and so she had a pea-shooter, .22 Double Eagle Derringer, and Baron Hanes's father, who was in the security business and richer than god, got him a .44 Magnum that was so heavy it made the nutty kid lean to the side when he wore the gun belt. I packed a pearl-handled .38 revolver, Smith & Wesson, which had originally been my grandfather's. Old as dirt, but all polished up, the way my father kept it, it was still a fine looking gun. My mom told my dad not to give it to me, but he said, "Look, when she goes to high school, she's gotta carry. Everybody does in their senior year."

"Insane," said my mom.

"Come on," I said. "Please…"

She drew close to me, right in my face, and said, "If your father gives you that gun, he's got no protection, making his deliveries." He drove a truck and delivered bakery goods to different diners and convenience stores in the area.

"Take it easy," said my dad, "all the crooks are asleep when I go out for my runs." He motioned for me to come over to where he sat. He put the gun in my hand. I gripped the handle and felt the weight of it. "Give me your best pose," he said.

I turned profile, hung my head back, my long chestnut hair reaching halfway to the floor, pulled up the sleeve of my T-shirt, made a muscle with my right arm, and pointed the gun at the ceiling with my left hand. He laughed till he couldn't catch his breath. And my mom said, "Disgraceful," but she also laughed.

I went to the firing range with my dad a lot the summer before senior year. He was a calm teacher, and never spoke much or got too mad. Afterward, he'd take me to this place and buy us ice cream. A lot of times it was Friday night, and I just wanted to get home so I could go hang out with my friends. One night I let him know we could skip the ice cream, and he seemed taken aback for a second, like I'd hurt his feelings. "I'm sorry," he said, and tried to smile.

I felt kind of bad, and figured I could hug him or kiss him or ask him to tell me something. "Tell me about a time when you shot the gun not on the practice range," I said as we drove along.

He laughed. "Not too many times," he said. "The most interesting was from when I was a little older than you. It was night, we were in the basement of an abandoned factory over in the industrial quarter. I was with some buds and we were partying, smoking up and drinking straight, cheap Vodka. Anyway, we were wasted. This guy I really didn't like who hung out with us, Raymo was his name, he challenged me to a round of Russian roulette. Don't tell your mother this," he said.

"You know I won't," I said.

"Anyway, I left one bullet in the chamber, removed the others and spun the cylinder. He went first—nothing. I went, he went, etc, click, click, click. The gun came to me and I was certain by then that the bullet was in my chamber. So, you know what I did?"

"You shot it into the ceiling?"

"No. I turned the gun on Raymo and shot him in the face. After that we all ran. We ran and we never got caught. At the time there was a gang going around at night shooting people and taking their wallets and the cops put it off to them. None of my buds were going to snitch. Believe me, Raymo was no great loss to the world. The point of which is to say, It's a horrible thing to shoot someone. I see Raymo's expression right before the bullet drilled through his head just about every night in my dreams. In other words, you better know what you're doing when you pull that trigger. Try to be responsible."

"Wow," I said, and wished I'd just hugged him instead.

To tell you the truth, taking the gun to school at first was a big nuisance. The thing was heavy and you always had to keep an eye on it. The first couple of days were all right, cause everyone was showing off their pieces at lunch time. A lot of people complimented me on the pearl handle and old school look of my gun. Of course the kids with the new, high-tech 9-millimeter jobs got the most attention, but if your piece was unique enough, it got you at least some cred. Jody Motes, pretty much an idiot with buck teeth and a fat ass, brought in a German Luger with a red swastika inlaid on the handle, and because of it got asked out by this guy in our English class a lot of the girls thought was hot. Kids wore them on their hips, others, mostly guys, did the shoulder holster. A couple of the senior girls with big breasts went with this over-the-shoulder bandolier style, so the gun sat atop their left breast. Sweaty Mr. Gosh in second period math said that look was "very fashionable." I carried mine in my Sponge Bob lunch box. I hated wearing it, the holster always hiked my skirt up in the back somehow.

Everybody in the graduating class carried heat except for Scott Wisner, the King of Vermont, as everybody called him. I forget why, cause Vermont was totally far away. His parents had given him a stun gun instead of the real thing. Cody St. John, the captain of the football team, said the stun gun was fag, and after that Wisner turned into a weird loner, who walked around carrying a big jar with a floating mist inside. He asked all the better looking girls if he could have their souls. I know, he asked me. Creep. I heard he'd stun anyone who wanted it for ten dollars a pop. Whatever.

The senior class teachers all had tactical 12-gauge short-barrel shotguns; no shoulder stock, just a club grip with an image of the school's mascot (a cartoon of a rampaging Indian) stamped on it. Most of them were loaded with buckshot, but Mrs. Cloder, in human geography, who used her weapon as a pointer when at the board, was rumored to rock the breaching rounds, those big slugs cops use to blow doors off their hinges. Other teachers left the shotguns on their desks or lying across the eraser gutter at the bottom of the board. Mr. Warren, the vice principal, wore his in a holster across his back, and for an old fart was super quick in drawing it over his shoulder with one hand.

At lunch, across the soccer field and back by the woods, where only the seniors were allowed to go, we sat out every nice day in the fall, smoking cigarettes and having gun-spinning competitions. You weren't allowed to shoot back there, so we left the safeties on. Bryce, a boy I knew since kindergarten, was good at it. He could flip his gun in the air backwards and have it land in the holster at his hip. McKenzie Batkin wasn't paying attention and turned the safety on instead of off before she started spinning her antique colt. The sound of the shot was so sudden, we all jumped, and then silence followed by the smell of gun smoke. The bullet went through her boot and took off the tip of her middle toe. Almost a whole minute passed before she screamed. The King of Vermont and Cody St. John both rushed to help her at the same time. They worked together to staunch the bleeding. I remember noticing the football lying on the ground next to the jar of souls, and I thought it would make a cool photo for the yearbook. McKenzie never told her parents, and hid the boots at the back of her closet. To this day she's got half a middle toe on her right foot, but that's the least of her problems.

After school I walked home with my new friend, Constance, who only came to Bascombe High in senior year. We crossed the soccer field, passed the fallen leaves stained red with McKenzie's blood, and entered the woods. The wind blew and shook the empty branches of the trees. Constance suddenly stopped walking, crouched, drew her Beretta Storm and fired. By the time I could turn my head, the squirrel was falling back, headless, off a tree about thirty yards away.

Constance had a cute haircut, short but with a lock that almost covered her right eye. Jeans and a green flannel shirt; a calm, pretty face. When we were doing current events in fifth period social studies, she'd argued with Mr. Hallibet about the cancellation of child labor laws. Me, I could never follow politics. It was too boring. But Constance seemed to really understand, and although on the TV news we all watched, they were convinced it was a good idea for kids twelve and older to now be eligible to be sent to work by their parents for extra income, she said it was wrong. Hallibet laughed at her, and said, "This is Senator Meets we're talking about. He's a man of the people. The guy who gave you your guns." Constance had more to say, but the teacher lifted his shotgun and turned to the board. The thing I couldn't get over was that she actually knew this shit better than Hallibet. The thought of it, for some reason, made me blush.

By the time the first snow came in late November, the guns became mostly just part of our wardrobes, and kids turned their attention back to their cell phones and iPods. The one shot fired before Christmas vacation was when Mrs. Cloder dropped her gun in the bathroom stall and blew off the side of the toilet bowl. Water flooded out into the hallway. Other than that, the only time you noticed that people were packing was when they'd use their sidearm for comedy purposes. Like Bryce, during English, when the teacher was reading *Pilgrim's Progress* to us, took out his gun and stuck the end in his mouth as if he was so bored he was going to blow his own brains out. At least once a week, outside the cafeteria, on the days it was too cold to leave the school, there were quick draw contests. Two kids would face off, there'd be a panel of judges, and Vice Principal Warren would set his cell phone to beep once. When they heard the beep the pair drew and whoever was faster won a coupon for a free 32 ounce soda at Babb's, the local convenience store.

One thing I did notice in that first half of the year. Usually when a person drew their gun, even as a gag, each had their own signature saying. When it came to these lines it seemed that the ban on cursing could be ignored without any problem. Even the teachers got into it. Mr. Gosh was partial to, "Eat hot lead, you little mother fuckers." The school nurse, Ms. James, used, "See you in Hell, asshole." Vice Principal Warren, who always kept his language in check, would draw, and while the gun was coming level with your head, say, "You're already dead." As for the kids, they all used lines they'd seen in recent movies. Cody St. John used, "Suck on this, bitches." McKenzie, who by Christmas was known as Half-toe Batkin, concocted the line, "Put up your feet." I tried to think of something to say, but it all seemed too corny, and it took me too long to get the gun out of my lunch box to really outdraw anyone else.

Senior year rolled fast, and by winter break, I was wondering what I'd do after I graduated. Constance told me she was going to college to learn philosophy. "Do they still teach that stuff?" I asked. She smiled, "Not so much anymore." We were sitting in my living room, my parents were away at my aunt's. The TV was on, the lights were out, and we were holding hands. We liked to just sit quietly and talk. "So I guess you'll be moving away, after the summer," I said. She nodded. "I thought I'd try to get a job at Wal-Mart," I said. "I heard they have benefits now."

"That's all you're gonna do with your life?" asked Constance.

"For now," I said.

"Well, then when I go away, you should come with me." She put her arm behind my head and drew me gently to her. We held each other for a long time while the snow came down outside.

A few days after Christmas, I sat with my parents watching the evening news. Senator Meets was on, talking about what he hoped to accomplish in the coming year. He was telling how happy he'd been to work for minimum wage when he was eleven.

"This guy's got it down," said my father.

I shouldn't have opened my mouth, but I said, "Constance says he's a loser."

"Loser?" my father said. "Are you kidding? Who's this Constance, I don't want you hanging out with any socialists. Don't tell me she's one of those kids who refuses to carry a gun. Meets passed the gun laws, mandatory church on Sunday for all citizens, killed abortion, and got us to stand up to the Mexicans... He's definitely gonna be the next president."

"She's probably the best shot in the class," I said, realizing I'd already said too much.

My father was suspicious, and he stirred in his easy chair, leaning forward.

"I met her," said my mother. "She's a nice girl."

I gave things a few seconds to settle down and then announced I was going to take the dog for a walk. As I passed my mother, unnoticed by my dad, she grabbed my hand and gave it a quick squeeze.

Back at school in January, there was a lot to do. I went to the senior class meetings, but didn't say anything. They decided for our "Act of Humanity" (required of every senior class), we would have a blood drive. For the senior trip, we decided to keep it cheap as pretty much everyone's parents were broke. A day trip to Bash Lake. "Sounds stale," said Bryce, "but if we bring enough alcohol and weed it'll be OK." Mrs. Cloder, our faculty advisor, aimed at him, said, "Arrivederci, Baby," and gave him two Saturday detentions. The event that overshadowed all the others, though, was the upcoming prom. My mother helped me make my dress. She was awesome on the sewing machine. It was turquoise satin, short sleeve, mid-length. I told my parents I had no date, but was just going solo. Constance and I had made plans. We knew from all the weeks of mandatory Sunday mass, the pastor actually spitting he was so worked up over what he called "unnatural love," that we couldn't go as a couple. She cared more than I did. I just tried to forget about it.

When the good weather of spring hit, people got giddy and tense. There were accidents. In homeroom one bright morning, Darcy dropped her bag on her desk, and the derringer inside went off and took out Ralph Babb's right eye. He lived, but when he came back to school his head was kind of caved in and he had a bad fake eye that looked like a kid drew it. It only stared straight ahead. Another was when Mr. Hallibet got angry because everybody'd gotten into the habit of challenging his current events lectures after seeing Constance in action. He yelled for us all to shut up and accidentally squeezed off a round. Luckily for us the gun was pointed at the ceiling. Mr. Gosh, though, who was sitting in the room a floor above, directly over Hallibet, had to have buckshot taken out of his ass. When he returned to school from a week off, he sweated more than ever.

Mixed in with the usual spring fever, there was all kinds of drama over who was going to the prom with whom. Fist fights, girl fights, plenty of drawn guns but not for comedy. I noticed that the King of Vermont was getting wackier the more people refused to notice him. When I left my sixth period class to use the bathroom, I saw him out on the soccer field from the upstairs hallway window. He turned the stun gun on himself, and shot the two darts with wires into his own chest. It knocked him down fast, and he was twitching on the ground. I went and took a piss. When I passed the window again, he was gone. He'd started bringing alcohol to school, and at lunch, where again we were back by the woods hanging out, he'd drink a Red Bull and a half pint of Vodka.

Right around that time, I met Constance at the town library one night. I had nothing to do, but she had to write a paper. When I arrived, she'd put the paper away and was reading. I asked her what the book was. She told me, "Plato."

"Good story?" I asked.

She explained it wasn't a novel, but a book about ideas. "You see," she said, "there's a cave and this guy gets chained up inside so that he can't turn around or move, but can only stare at the back wall. There's a fire in the cave behind him and it casts his shadow on the wall he faces. That play of light and shadow is the sum total of his reality."

I nodded and listened as long as I could. Constance was so wrapped up in explaining, she looked beautiful, but I didn't want to listen anymore. I checked over my shoulder to see if anyone was around. When I saw we were alone, I quickly leaned forward and kissed her on the lips. She smiled and said, "Let's get out of here."

On a warm day in mid-May, we had the blood drive. I got there early and gave blood. The nurses, who were really nice, told me to sit for a while and they gave me orange juice and cookies. I thought about becoming a nurse for maybe like five whole minutes. Other kids showed up and gave blood, and I stuck around to help sign them up. Cody came and watched but wouldn't give. "Fuck the dying," I heard him say. "Nobody gets my blood but me." After that a few other boys decided not to give either. Whatever. Then at lunch, the King of Vermont was drinking his Red Bulls and Vodka, and I think because he'd given blood, he was really blasted. He went around threatening to stun people in their private parts.

After lunch, in Mrs. Cloder's class, where we sat at long tables in a rectangle that formed in front of her desk, Wisner took the seat straight across from her. I was two seats down from him toward the windows. Class started and the first thing Mrs. Cloder said, before she even got out of her seat, was to the King. "Get that foolish jar off the table." We all looked over. Wisner stared, the mist swirled inside the glass. He pushed his seat back and stood up, cradling the jar in one arm, and drawing his stun gun. "Sit down, Scotty," she said, and leveled her short-barrel at him. I could see her finger tightening on the trigger. A few seconds passed and then one by one, all the kids drew their weapons, but nobody was sure whether to aim at Mrs. Cloder or the King, so about half did one and half the other. I never even opened my lunch box, afraid to make a sudden move.

"Put down your gun and back slowly away from the table," said Mrs. Cloder.

"When you meet the Devil, give him my regards," said Wisner, but as he pulled the trigger, Mrs. Cloder fired. The breaching slug blew a hole in the King of Vermont's chest, slamming him against the back wall in a cloud of blood. The jar shattered, and glass flew. McKenzie, who was sitting next to Wisner, screamed as the shards dug into her face. I don't know if she shot or if the gun just went off, but her bullet hit Mrs. Cloder in the shoulder and spun her out of her chair onto the ground. She groaned and rolled back and forth. Meanwhile, Wisner's stun gun darts, had gone wild, struck Chucky Durr in the forehead, one over each eye, and in his electrified shaking, his gun went off and put a round right into Melanie Storte's Adam's apple. Blood poured out as she dropped her own gun and brought her hands to her gurgling neck. Melanie was Cody St. John's "current ho," as he called her, and he didn't think twice but fanned the hammer of his pistol, putting three shots into Chucky, who fell over on the floor like a bag of potatoes. Chucky's cousin, Meleeba, shot Cody in the side of the head and he went down, screaming, as smoke poured from the hole above his left ear. One of Cody's crew shot Meleeba, and then I couldn't keep track anymore. Bullets whizzed by my head, blood was spurting everywhere. Kids were falling like pins at the bowling alley. Mrs. Cloder clawed her way back into her seat, lifted the gun and aimed it. Whoever was left fired on her and then she fired, another shot-gun blast, like an explosion. When the ringing in my ears went away, the room was perfectly quiet but for the drip of blood, and the ticking of the wall clock. Smoke hung in the air, and I thought of the King of Vermont's escaped souls. During the entire thing, I'd not moved a single finger.

The cops were there before I could get myself out of the chair. They wrapped a blanket around me and led me down to the principal's office. I was in a daze for a while but could feel them moving around me and could hear them talking. Then my mother was there, and the cop was handing me a cup of orange juice. They asked if they could talk to me, and my mother left it up to me. I told them everything, exactly how it went down. I started with the blood drive. They tested me for gun powder to see if there was any on my hands. I told them my gun was back in the classroom in my lunchbox under the table, and it hadn't been fired since the summer, the last time I went to the range with my dad. It was all over the news. I was all over the news. A full one-third of Bascombe High's senior class was killed in the shootout. The only one in Mrs. Cloder's class besides me to survive was McKenzie, and the flying glass made her No Face Batkin.

Senator Meets showed up at the school three days later and got his picture taken handing me an award. I never really knew what it was for. Constance whispered, "They give you a fucking award if you live through it," and laughed. In Meets's speech to the assembled community, he blamed the blood drive for the incident. He proclaimed Mrs. Cloder a hero, and ended by reminding everyone, "If these kids were working, they'd have no time for this."

The class trip was called off out of respect for the dead. Two weeks later, I went to the prom. It was to be held in the gymnasium. My dad drove me. When we pulled into the parking lot, it was empty.

"You must be early," he said, and handed me the corsage I'd asked him to get—a white orchid.

"Thanks," I said, and gave him a kiss on the cheek. As I opened the door to get out, he put his hand on my elbow. I turned and he was holding the gun.

"You'll need this," he said.

I shook my head, and told him, "It's OK." He was momentarily taken aback. Then he tried to smile. I shut the door, and he drove away.

Constance was already there. In fact, she was the only one there. The gym was done up with glittery stars on the ceiling, a painted moon and clouds. There were streamers. Our voices echoed as we exchanged corsages, which had been our plan. The white orchid looked good against her black plunging neckline. She'd gotten me a corsage made of red roses, and they really stood out against the turquoise. In her purse, instead of the Beretta, she had a half pint of Captain Morgan. We sat on one of the bleachers and passed the bottle, talking about the incidents of the past two weeks.

"I guess no one's coming," she said. No sooner were the words out of her mouth than the outside door creaked open and in walked Bryce carrying a case in one hand and dressed in a jacket and tie. We got up and went to see him. Constance passed him the Captain Morgan. He took a swig.

"I was afraid of this," he said.

"No one's coming?" I said.

"I guess some of the parents were scared there'd be another shootout. Probably the teachers too. Mrs. Cloder's family insisted on an open casket. A third of them are dead, let's not forget, and the rest, after hearing Meets talk, are working the late shift at Wal-Mart for minimum wage."

"Jeez," said Constance.

"Just us," said Bryce. He went up on the stage, set his case down, and got behind the podium at the back. "Watch this," he said, and a second later the lights went out. We laughed. A dozen blue searchlights appeared, their beams moving randomly around the gym, washing over us and then rushing away to some dark corner. A small white spotlight came on above the mic that stood at the front of the stage. Bryce stepped up into the glow. He opened the case at his feet and took out a saxophone.

"I was looking forward to playing tonight," he said. We walked up to the edge of the stage, and I handed him the bottle. He took a swig, the sax now on a leather strap around his neck. Putting the bottle down at his feet," he said, "Would you ladies care to dance?"

"Play us something," we told him.

He thought for a second and said, "Strangers in the Night?"

He played, we danced, and the blue lights in the dark were the sum total of our reality.

MANTIS WIVES

KIJ JOHNSON

Kij Johnson [www.kijjohnson.com] *is the author of three novels, many short stories, and several essays. She has won the Hugo, the Nebula, the World Fantasy, and the Theodore A. Sturgeon Memorial Award for her short fiction. Her novella "The Man Who Bridged the Mist" won the Hugo and Nebula awards, while "Spar" and "Ponies" won the Nebula Award and "26 Monkeys, Also the Abyss" won the World Fantasy Award. Her short fiction has been collected in* Tales for the Long Rains *and* At the Mouth of the River of Bees.

Her novels include World Fantasy Award nominee Fudoki *and* The Fox Woman.

"As for the insects, their lives are sustained only by intricate processes of fantastic horror." —John Wyndham

Eventually, the mantis women discovered that killing their husbands was not inseparable from the getting of young. Before this, a wife devoured her lover piece by piece during the act of coition: the head (and its shining eyes going dim as she ate); the long green prothorax; the forelegs crisp as straws; the bitter wings. She left for last the metathorax and its pumping legs, the abdomen, and finally the phallus. Mantis women needed nutrients for their pregnancies; their lovers offered this as well as their seed.

It was believed that mantis men would resist their deaths if permitted to choose the manner of their mating; but the women learned to turn elsewhere for nutrients after draining their husbands' members, and yet the men lingered. And so their ladies continued to kill them, but slowly, in the fashioning of difficult arts. What else could there be between them?

The Bitter Edge: A wife may cut through her husband's exoskeletal plates, each layer a different pattern, so that to look at a man is to see shining, hard brocade. At the deepest level are visible pieces of his core, the hint of internal parts bleeding out. He may suggest shapes.

The Eccentric Curve of His Thoughts: A wife may drill the tiniest hole into her lover's head and insert a fine hair. She presses carefully, striving for specific results: a seizure, a novel pheromone burst, a dance that ends in self-castration. If she replaces the hair with a wasp's narrow syringing stinger, she may blow air bubbles into his head and then he will react unpredictably. There is otherwise little he may do that will surprise her, or himself.

What is the art of the men, that they remain to die at the hands of their wives? What is the art of the wives, that they kill?

The Strength of Weight: Removing his wings, she leads him into the paths of ants.

Unready Jewels: A mantis wife may walk with her husband across the trunks of pines, until they come to a trail of sap and ascend to an insect-clustered wound. Staying to the side, she presses him down until his legs stick fast. He may grow restless as the sap sheathes his body and wings. His eyes may not dim for some time. Smaller insects may cluster upon his honeyed body like ornaments.

A mantis woman does not know why the men crave death, but she does not ask. Does she fear resistance? Does she hope for it? She has forgotten the ancient reasons for her acts, but in any case her art is more important.

The Oubliette: Or a wife may take not his life but his senses: plucking the antennae from his forehead; scouring with dust his clustered shining eyes; cracking apart his mandibles to scrape out the lining of his mouth and throat; plucking the sensing hairs from his foremost legs; excising the auditory thoracic organ; biting free the wings.

A mantis woman is not cruel. She gives her husband what he seeks. Who knows what poems he fashions in the darkness of a senseless life?

The Scent of Violets: They mate many times, until one dies.

Two Stones Grind Together: A wife collects with her forelegs small brightly colored poisonous insects, places them upon bitter green leaves, and encourages her husband to eat them. He is sometimes reluctant after the first taste but she speaks to him, or else he calms himself and eats.

He may foam at the mouth and anus, or grow paralyzed and fall from a branch. In extreme cases, he may stagger along the ground until he is seen by a bird and swallowed, and then even the bird may die.

A mantis has no veins; what passes for blood flows freely within its protective shell. It does have a heart.

The Desolate Junk-land: Or a mantis wife may lay her husband gently upon a soft bed and bring to him cool drinks and silver dishes filled with sweetmeats. She may offer him crossword puzzles and pornography; may kneel at his feet and tell him stories of mantis men who are heroes; may dance in veils before him.

He tears off his own legs before she begins. It is unclear whether The Desolate Junk-land is her art, or his.

Shame's Uniformity: A wife may return to the First Art and, in a variant, devour her husband, but from the abdomen forward. Of all the arts this is hardest. There is no hair, no ant's bite, no sap, no intervening instrument. He asks her questions until the end. He may doubt her motives, or she may.

The Paper-folder. Lichens' Dance. The Ambition of Aphids. Civil Wars. The Secret History of Cumulus. The Lost Eyes Found. Sedges. The Unbeaked Sparrow.
There are as many arts as there are husbands and wives.

The Cruel Web: Perhaps they wish to love each other, but they cannot see a way to exist that does not involve the barb, the sticking sap, the bitter taste of poison. The Cruel Web can be performed only in the brambles of woods, and only when there has been no recent rain and the spider's webs have grown thick. Wife and husband walk together. Webs catch and cling to their carapaces, their legs, their half-opened wings. They tear free, but the webs collect. Their glowing eyes grow veiled. Their curious antennae come to a tangled halt. Their pheromones become confused; their legs struggle against the gathering web. The spiders wait.

She is larger than he and stronger, but they often fall together.

How to Live: A mantis may dream of something else. This also may be a trap.

IMMERSION

ALIETTE DE BODARD

Aliette de Bodard [www.aliettedebodard.com] *lives and works in Paris, in a flat with more computers than warm bodies, and two Lovecraftian plants in the process of taking over the living room. In her spare time, she writes speculative fiction: her Aztec noir trilogy "Obsidian and Blood" is published by Angry Robot, and her short fiction has garnered her nominations for the Hugo and Nebula awards, and the Campbell Award for Best New Writer. Her latest book is novella* On a Red Station, Drifting.

In the morning, you're no longer quite sure who you are.

You stand in front of the mirror—it shifts and trembles, reflecting only what you want to see—eyes that feel too wide, skin that feels too pale, an odd, distant smell wafting from the compartment's ambient system that is neither incense nor garlic, but something else, something elusive that you once knew.

You're dressed, already—not on your skin, but outside, where it matters, your avatar sporting blue and black and gold, the stylish clothes of a well-travelled, well-connected woman. For a moment, as you turn away from the mirror, the glass shimmers out of focus; and another woman in a dull silk gown stares back at you: smaller, squatter and in every way diminished—a stranger, a distant memory that has ceased to have any meaning.

Quy was on the docks, watching the spaceships arrive. She could, of course, have been anywhere on Longevity Station, and requested the feed from the network to be patched to her router—and watched, superimposed on her field of vision, the slow dance of ships slipping into their pod cradles like births watched in reverse. But there was something about standing on the spaceport's concourse—a feeling of closeness that she just couldn't replicate by standing in Golden Carp Gardens or Azure Dragon Temple. Because here—here, separated by only a few measures of sheet metal from the cradle pods, she could feel herself teetering on the edge of the vacuum, submerged in cold and breathing in neither air nor oxygen. She could almost imagine herself rootless, finally returned to the source of everything.

Most ships those days were Galactic—you'd have thought Longevity's ex-masters would have been unhappy about the station's independence, but now that the war was over Longevity was a tidy source of profit. The ships came; and disgorged a steady stream of tourists—their eyes too round and straight, their jaws too square; their faces an unhealthy shade of pink, like undercooked meat left too long in the sun. They walked with the easy confidence of people with immersers: pausing to admire the suggested highlights for a second or so before moving on to the transport station, where they haggled in schoolbook Rong for a ride to their recommended hotels—a sickeningly familiar ballet Quy had been seeing most of her life, a unison of foreigners descending on the station like a plague of centipedes or leeches.

Still, Quy watched them. They reminded her of her own time on Prime, her heady schooldays filled with raucous bars and wild weekends, and late minute revisions for exams, a carefree time she'd never have again in her life. She both longed for those days back, and hated herself for her weakness. Her education on Prime, which should have been her path into the higher strata of the station's society, had brought her nothing but a sense of disconnection from her family; a growing solitude, and a dissatisfaction, an aimlessness she couldn't put in words.

She might not have moved all day—had a sign not blinked, superimposed by her router on the edge of her field of vision. A message from Second Uncle.

"Child." His face was pale and worn, his eyes underlined by dark circles, as if he hadn't slept. He probably hadn't—the last Quy had seen of him, he had been closeted with Quy's sister Tam, trying to organize a delivery for a wedding—five hundred winter melons, and six barrels of Prosper Station's best fish sauce. "Come back to the restaurant."

"I'm on my day of rest," Quy said; it came out as more peevish and childish than she'd intended.

Second Uncle's face twisted, in what might have been a smile, though he had very little sense of humor. The scar he'd got in the Independence War shone white against the grainy background—twisting back and forth, as if it still pained him. "I know, but I need you. We have an important customer."

"Galactic," Quy said. That was the only reason he'd be calling her, and not one of her brothers or cousins. Because the family somehow thought that her studies on Prime gave her insight into the Galactics' way of thought—something useful, if not the success they'd hoped for.

"Yes. An important man, head of a local trading company." Second Uncle did not move on her field of vision. Quy could *see* the ships moving through his face, slowly aligning themselves in front of their pods, the hole in front of them opening like an orchid flower. And she knew everything there was to know about Grandmother's restaurant; she was Tam's sister, after all; and she'd seen the accounts, the slow decline of their clientele as their more genteel clients moved to better areas of the station; the influx of tourists on a budget, with little time for expensive dishes prepared with the best ingredients.

"Fine," she said. "I'll come."

At breakfast, you stare at the food spread out on the table: bread and jam and some colored liquid—you come up blank for a moment, before your immerser kicks in, reminding you that it's coffee, served strong and black, just as you always take it.

Yes. Coffee.

You raise the cup to your lips—your immerser gently prompts you, reminding you of where to grasp, how to lift, how to be in every possible way graceful and elegant, always an effortless model.

"It's a bit strong," your husband says, apologetically. He watches you from the other end of the table, an expression you can't interpret on his face—and isn't this odd, because shouldn't you know all there is to know about expressions—shouldn't the immerser have everything about Galactic culture recorded into its database, shouldn't it prompt you? But it's strangely silent, and this scares you, more than anything. Immersers never fail.

"Shall we go?" your husband says—and, for a moment, you come up blank on his name, before you remember—Galen, it's Galen, named after some physician on Old Earth. He's tall, with dark hair and pale skin—his immerser avatar isn't much different from his real self, Galactic avatars seldom are. It's people like you who have to work the hardest to adjust, because so much about you draws attention to itself—the stretched eyes that crinkle in the shape of moths, the darker skin, the smaller, squatter shape more reminiscent of jackfruits than swaying fronds. But no matter: you can be made perfect; you can put on the immerser and become someone else, someone pale-skinned and tall and beautiful.

Though, really, it's been such a long time since you took off the immerser, isn't it? It's just a thought—a suspended moment that is soon erased by the immerser's flow of information, the little arrows drawing your attention to the bread and the kitchen, and the polished metal of the table—giving you context about everything, opening up the universe like a lotus flower.

"Yes," you say. "Let's go." Your tongue trips over the word—there's a structure you should have used, a pronoun you should have said instead of the lapidary Galactic sentence. But nothing will come, and you feel like a field of sugar canes after the harvest—burnt out, all cutting edges with no sweetness left inside.

Of course, Second Uncle insisted on Quy getting her immerser for the interview—just in case, he said, soothingly and diplomatically as always. Trouble was, it wasn't where Quy had last left it. After putting out a message to the rest of the family, the best information Quy got was from Cousin Khanh, who thought he'd seen Tam sweep through the living quarters, gathering every piece of Galactic tech she could get her hands on. Third Aunt, who caught Khanh's message on the family's communication channel, tutted disapprovingly. "Tam. Always with her mind lost in the mountains, that girl. Dreams have never husked rice."

Quy said nothing. Her own dreams had shriveled and died after she came back from Prime and failed Longevity's mandarin exams; but it was good to have Tam around—to have someone who saw beyond the restaurant, beyond the narrow circle of family interests. Besides, if she didn't stick with her sister, who would?

Tam wasn't in the communal areas on the upper floors; Quy threw a glance towards the lift to Grandmother's closeted rooms, but she was doubtful Tam would have gathered Galactic tech just so she could pay her respects to Grandmother. Instead, she went straight to the lower floor, the one she and Tam shared with the children of their generation.

It was right next to the kitchen, and the smells of garlic and fish sauce seemed to be everywhere—of course, the youngest generation always got the lower floor, the one with all the smells and the noises of a legion of waitresses bringing food over to the dining room.

Tam was there, sitting in the little compartment that served as the floor's communal area. She'd spread out the tech on the floor—two immersers

(Tam and Quy were possibly the only family members who cared so little about immersers they left them lying around), a remote entertainment set that was busy broadcasting some stories of children running on terra-formed planets, and something Quy couldn't quite identify, because Tam had taken it apart into small components: it lay on the table like a gutted fish, all metals and optical parts.

But, at some point, Tam had obviously got bored with the entire process, because she was currently finishing her breakfast, slurping noodles from her soup bowl. She must have got it from the kitchen's leftovers, because Quy knew the smell, could taste the spiciness of the broth on her tongue—Mother's cooking, enough to make her stomach growl although she'd had rolled rice cakes for breakfast.

"You're at it again," Quy said with a sigh. "Could you not take my immerser for your experiments, please?"

Tam didn't even look surprised. "You don't seem very keen on using it, big sis."

"That I don't use it doesn't mean it's yours," Quy said, though that wasn't a real reason. She didn't mind Tam borrowing her stuff, and actually would have been glad to never put on an immerser again—she hated the feeling they gave her, the vague sensation of the system rooting around in her brain to find the best body cues to give her. But there were times when she was expected to wear an immerser: whenever dealing with customers, whether she was waiting at tables or in preparation meetings for large occasions.

Tam, of course, didn't wait at tables—she'd made herself so good at logistics and anything to do with the station's system that she spent most of her time in front of a screen, or connected to the station's network.

"Lil' sis?" Quy said.

Tam set her chopsticks by the side of the bowl, and made an expansive gesture with her hands. "Fine. Have it back. I can always use mine."

Quy stared at the things spread on the table, and asked the inevitable question. "How's progress?"

Tam's work was network connections and network maintenance within the restaurant; her hobby was tech. Galactic tech. She took things apart to see what made them tick; and rebuilt them. Her foray into entertainment units had helped the restaurant set up ambient sounds—old-fashioned Rong music for Galactic customers, recitation of the newest poems for locals.

But immersers had her stumped: the things had nasty safeguards to them. You could open them in half, to replace the battery; but you went no further. Tam's previous attempt had almost lost her the use of her hands.

By Tam's face, she didn't feel ready to try again. "It's got to be the same logic."

"As what?" Quy couldn't help asking. She picked up her own immerser from the table, briefly checking that it did indeed bear her serial number.

Tam gestured to the splayed components on the table. "Artificial Literature Writer. Little gadget that composes light entertainment novels."

"That's not the same—" Quy checked herself, and waited for Tam to explain.

"Takes existing cultural norms, and puts them into a cohesive, satisfying narrative. Like people forging their own path and fighting aliens for possession of a planet, that sort of stuff that barely speaks to us on Longevity. I mean, we've never even seen a planet." Tam exhaled, sharply—her eyes half on the dismembered Artificial Literature Writer, half on some overlay of her vision. "Just like immersers take a given culture and parcel it out to you in a form you can relate to—language, gestures, customs, the whole package. They've got to have the same architecture."

"I'm still not sure what you want to do with it." Quy put on her immerser, adjusting the thin metal mesh around her head until it fitted. She winced as the interface synched with her brain. She moved her hands, adjusting some settings lower than the factory ones—darn thing always reset itself to factory, which she suspected was no accident. A shimmering lattice surrounded her: her avatar, slowly taking shape around her. She could still see the room—the lattice was only faintly opaque—but ancestors, how she hated the feeling of not quite being there. "How do I look?"

"Horrible. Your avatar looks like it's died or something."

"Ha ha ha," Quy said. Her avatar was paler than her, and taller: it made her look beautiful, most customers agreed. In those moments, Quy was glad she had an avatar, so they wouldn't see the anger on her face. "You haven't answered my question."

Tam's eyes glinted. "Just think of the things we couldn't do. This is the best piece of tech Galactics have ever brought us."

Which wasn't much, but Quy didn't need to say it aloud. Tam knew exactly how Quy felt about Galactics and their hollow promises.

"It's their weapon, too." Tam pushed at the entertainment unit. "Just like their books and their holos and their live games. It's fine for them—they put the immersers on tourist settings, they get just what they need to navigate a foreign environment from whatever idiot's written the Rong script for that thing. But we—we worship them. We wear the immersers on Galactic all the time. We make ourselves like them, because they push, and because we're naive enough to give in."

"And you think you can make this better?" Quy couldn't help it. It wasn't that she needed to be convinced: on Prime, she'd never seen immersers. They were tourist stuff, and even while travelling from one city to another, the citizens just assumed they'd know enough to get by. But the stations, their ex-colonies, were flooded with immersers.

Tam's eyes glinted, as savage as those of the rebels in the history holos. "If I can take them apart, I can rebuild them and disconnect the logical circuits. I can give us the language and the tools to deal with them without being swallowed by them."

Mind lost in the mountains, Third Aunt said. No one had ever accused Tam of thinking small. Or of not achieving what she set her mind on, come to think of it. And every revolution had to start somewhere—hadn't Longevity's War of Independence started over a single poem, and the unfair imprisonment of the poet who'd written it?

Quy nodded. She believed Tam, though she didn't know how far. "Fair point. Have to go now, or Second Uncle will skin me. See you later, lil' sis."

As you walk under the wide arch of the restaurant with your husband, you glance upwards, at the calligraphy that forms its sign. The immerser translates it for you into "Sister Hai's Kitchen," and starts giving you a detailed background of the place: the menu and the most recommended dishes—as you walk past the various tables, it highlights items it thinks you would like, from rolled-up rice dumplings to fried shrimps. It warns you about the more exotic dishes, like the pickled pig's ears, the fermented meat (you have to be careful about that one, because its name changes depending on which station dialect you order in), or the reeking durian fruit that the natives so love.

It feels… not quite right, you think, as you struggle to follow Galen, who is already far away, striding ahead with the same confidence he always exudes in life. People part before him; a waitress with a young, pretty avatar bows before him, though Galen himself takes no notice. You know that such obsequiousness unnerves him; he always rants about the outdated customs aboard Longevity, the inequalities and the lack of democratic government—he thinks it's only a matter of time before they change, adapt themselves to fit into Galactic society. You—you have a faint memory of arguing with him, a long time ago, but now you can't find the words, anymore, or even the reason why—it makes sense, it all makes sense. The Galactics rose against the tyranny of Old Earth and overthrew their shackles, and won the right to determine their own destiny; and every other station and planet will do the same, eventually, rise against the dictatorships that hold them away from progress. It's right; it's always been right.

Unbidden, you stop at a table, and watch two young women pick at a dish of chicken with chopsticks—the smell of fish sauce and lemongrass rises in the air, as pungent and as unbearable as rotten meat—no, no, that's not it, you have an image of a dark-skinned woman, bringing a dish of steamed rice to the table, her hands filled with that same smell, and your mouth watering in anticipation…

The young women are looking at you: they both wear standard-issue avatars, the bottom-of-the-line kind—their clothes are a garish mix of red and yellow, with the odd, uneasy cut of cheap designers; and their faces waver, letting you glimpse a hint of darker skin beneath the red flush of their cheeks. Cheap and tawdry, and altogether inappropriate; and you're glad you're not one of them.

"Can I help you, older sister?" one of them asks.

Older sister. A pronoun you were looking for, earlier; one of the things that seem to have vanished from your mind. You struggle for words; but all the immerser seems to suggest to you is a neutral and impersonal pronoun, one that you instinctively know is wrong—it's one only foreigners and outsiders would use in those circumstances. "Older sister," you repeat, finally, because you can't think of anything else.

"Agnes!"

Galen's voice, calling from far away—for a brief moment the immerser seems to fail you again, because you *know* that you have many names, that Agnes is the one they gave you in Galactic school, the one neither Galen nor his friends can mangle when they pronounce it. You remember the Rong names your mother gave you on Longevity, the childhood endearments and your adult style name.

Be-Nho, Be-Yeu. Thu—Autumn, like a memory of red maple leaves on a planet you never knew.

You pull away from the table, disguising the tremor in your hands.

Second Uncle was already waiting when Quy arrived; and so were the customers.

"You're late," Second Uncle sent on the private channel, though he made the comment half-heartedly, as if he'd expected it all along. As if he'd never really believed he could rely on her—that stung.

"Let me introduce my niece Quy to you," Second Uncle said, in Galactic, to the man beside him.

"Quy," the man said, his immerser perfectly taking up the nuances of her name in Rong. He was everything she'd expected; tall, with only a thin layer of avatar, a little something that narrowed his chin and eyes, and made his chest slightly larger. Cosmetic enhancements: he was good-looking for a Galactic, all things considered. He went on, in Galactic, "My name is Galen Santos. Pleased to meet you. This is my wife, Agnes."

Agnes. Quy turned, and looked at the woman for the first time—and flinched. There was no one here: just a thick layer of avatar, so dense and so complex that she couldn't even guess at the body hidden within.

"Pleased to meet you." On a hunch, Quy bowed, from younger to elder, with both hands brought together—Rong-style, not Galactic—and saw a shudder run through Agnes' body, barely perceptible; but Quy was observant, she'd always been. Her immerser was screaming at her, telling her to hold out both hands, palms up, in the Galactic fashion. She tuned it out: she was still at the stage where she could tell the difference between her thoughts and the immerser's thoughts.

Second Uncle was talking again—his own avatar was light, a paler version of him. "I understand you're looking for a venue for a banquet."

"We are, yes." Galen pulled a chair to him, sank into it. They all followed suit, though not with the same fluid, arrogant ease. When Agnes sat, Quy saw her flinch, as though she'd just remembered something unpleasant. "We'll be celebrating our fifth marriage anniversary, and we both felt we wanted to mark the occasion with something suitable."

Second Uncle nodded. "I see," he said, scratching his chin. "My congratulations to you."

Galen nodded. "We thought—" he paused, threw a glance at his wife that Quy couldn't quite interpret—her immerser came up blank, but there was something oddly familiar about it, something she ought to have been able to name. "Something Rong," he said at last. "A large banquet for a hundred people, with the traditional dishes."

Quy could almost feel Second Uncle's satisfaction. A banquet of that size would be awful logistics, but it would keep the restaurant afloat for a year or more, if they could get the price right. But something was wrong—something—

"What did you have in mind?" Quy asked, not to Galen, but to his wife. The wife—Agnes, which probably wasn't the name she'd been born with—who wore a thick avatar, and didn't seem to be answering or ever speaking up. An awful picture was coming together in Quy's mind.

Agnes didn't answer. Predictable.

Second Uncle took over, smoothing over the moment of awkwardness with expansive hand gestures. "The whole hog, yes?" Second Uncle said. He rubbed his hands, an odd gesture that Quy had never seen from him—a Galactic expression of satisfaction. "Bitter melon soup, Dragon-Phoenix plates, Roast Pig, Jade Under the Mountain…" He was citing all the traditional dishes for a wedding banquet—unsure of how far the foreigner wanted to take it. He left out the odder stuff, like Shark Fin or Sweet Red Bean Soup.

"Yes, that's what we would like. Wouldn't we, darling?" Galen's wife neither moved nor spoke. Galen's head turned towards her, and Quy caught his expression at last. She'd thought it would be contempt, or hatred; but no; it was anguish. He genuinely loved her, and he couldn't understand what was going on.

Galactics. Couldn't he recognize an immerser junkie when he saw one? But then Galactics, as Tam said, seldom had the problem—they didn't put on the immersers for more than a few days on low settings, if they ever went that far. Most were flat-out convinced Galactic would get them anywhere.

Second Uncle and Galen were haggling, arguing prices and features; Second Uncle sounding more and more like a Galactic tourist as the conversation went on, more and more aggressive for lower and lower gains. Quy didn't care anymore: she watched Agnes. Watched the impenetrable avatar—a red-headed woman in the latest style from Prime, with freckles on her skin and a hint of a star-tan on her face. But that wasn't what she was, inside; what the immerser had dug deep into.

Wasn't who she was at all. Tam was right; all immersers should be taken apart, and did it matter if they exploded? They'd done enough harm as it was.

Quy wanted to get up, to tear away her own immerser, but she couldn't, not in the middle of the negotiation. Instead, she rose, and walked closer to Agnes; the two men barely glanced at her, too busy agreeing on a price. "You're not alone," she said, in Rong, low enough that it didn't carry.

Again, that odd, disjointed flash. "You have to take it off." Quy said, but got no further response. As an impulse, she grabbed the other woman's arm—felt her hands go right through the immerser's avatar, connect with warm, solid flesh.

You hear them negotiating, in the background—it's tough going, because the Rong man sticks to his guns stubbornly, refusing to give ground to Galen's onslaught. It's all very distant, a subject of intellectual study; the immerser reminds you from time to time, interpreting this and this body cue, nudging you this way and that—you must sit straight and silent, and support your husband—and so you smile through a mouth that feels gummed together.

You feel, all the while, the Rong girl's gaze on you, burning like ice water, like the gaze of a dragon. She won't move away from you; and her hand rests on you, gripping your arm with a strength you didn't think she had in her body. Her avatar is but a thin layer, and you can see her beneath it: a round, moon-shaped face with skin the color of cinnamon—no, not spices, not chocolate, but simply a color you've seen all your life.

"You have to take it off," she says. You don't move; but you wonder what she's talking about.

Take it off. Take it off. Take what off?

The immerser.

Abruptly, you remember—a dinner with Galen's friends, when they laughed at jokes that had gone by too fast for you to understand. You came home battling tears; and found yourself reaching for the immerser on your bedside table, feeling its cool weight in your hands. You thought it would please Galen if you spoke his language; that he would be less ashamed of how uncultured you sounded to his friends. And then you found out that everything was fine, as long as you kept the settings on maximum and didn't remove it. And then... and then you walked with it and slept with it, and showed the world nothing but the avatar it had designed—saw nothing it hadn't tagged and labeled for you. Then...

Then it all slid down, didn't it? You couldn't program the network anymore, couldn't look at the guts of machines; you lost your job with the tech company, and came to Galen's compartment, wandering in the room like a hollow shell, a ghost of yourself—as if you'd already died, far away from home and all that it means to you. Then—then the immerser wouldn't come off, anymore.

"What do you think you're doing, young woman?"

Second Uncle had risen, turning towards Quy—his avatar flushed with anger, the pale skin mottled with an unsightly red. "We adults are in the middle of negotiating something very important, if you don't mind." It might have made Quy quail in other circumstances, but his voice and his body language were wholly Galactic; and he sounded like a stranger to her—an angry foreigner whose food order she'd misunderstood—whom she'd mock later, sitting in Tam's room with a cup of tea in her lap, and the familiar patter of her sister's musings.

"I apologize," Quy said, meaning none of it.

"That's all right," Galen said. "I didn't mean to—" he paused, looked at his wife. "I shouldn't have brought her here."

"You should take her to see a physician," Quy said, surprised at her own boldness.

"Do you think I haven't tried?" His voice was bitter. "I've even taken her to the best hospitals on Prime. They look at her, and say they can't take it off. That the shock of it would kill her. And even if it didn't…" He spread his hands, letting air fall between them like specks of dust. "Who knows if she'd come back?"

Quy felt herself blush. "I'm sorry." And she meant it this time.

Galen waved her away, negligently, airily, but she could see the pain he was struggling to hide. Galactics didn't think tears were manly, she remembered. "So we're agreed?" Galen asked Second Uncle. "For a million credits?"

Quy thought of the banquet; of the food on the tables, of Galen thinking it would remind Agnes of home. Of how, in the end, it was doomed to fail, because everything would be filtered through the immerser, leaving Agnes with nothing but an exotic feast of unfamiliar flavors. "I'm sorry," she said, again, but no one was listening; and she turned away from Agnes with rage in her heart—with the growing feeling that it had all been for nothing in the end.

"I'm sorry," the girl says—she stands, removing her hand from your arm, and you feel like a tearing inside, as if something within you was struggling to claw free from your body. Don't go, you want to say. Please don't go. Please don't leave me here.

But they're all shaking hands; smiling, pleased at a deal they've struck—like sharks, you think, like tigers. Even the Rong girl has turned away from you; giving you up as hopeless. She and her uncle are walking away, taking separate paths back to the inner areas of the restaurant, back to their home.

Please don't go.

It's as if something else were taking control of your body; a strength that you didn't know you possessed. As Galen walks back into the restaurant's main room, back into the hubbub and the tantalizing smells of food—of lemongrass chicken and steamed rice, just as your mother used to make—you turn away from your husband, and follow the girl. Slowly, and from a distance; and then running, so that no one will stop you. She's walking fast—you see her tear her immerser away from her face, and slam it down onto a side table with disgust. You see her enter a room; and you follow her inside.

They're watching you, both girls, the one you followed in; and another, younger one, rising from the table she was sitting at—both terribly alien and terribly familiar at once. Their mouths are open, but no sound comes out.

In that one moment—staring at each other, suspended in time—you see the guts of Galactic machines spread on the table. You see the mass of tools; the dismantled machines; and the immerser, half spread-out before them, its two halves open like a cracked egg. And you understand that they've been trying to open them and reverse-engineer them; and you know that they'll never, ever succeed. Not because of the safeguards, of the Galactic encryptions to preserve their fabled intellectual property; but rather, because of something far more fundamental.

This is a Galactic toy, conceived by a Galactic mind—every layer of it, every logical connection within it exudes a mindset that might as well be alien to these girls. It takes a Galactic to believe that you can take a whole culture and reduce it to algorithms; that language and customs can be boiled to just a simple set of rules. For these girls, things are so much more complex than this; and they will never understand how an immerser works, because they can't think like a Galactic, they'll never ever think like that. You can't think like a Galactic unless you've been born in the culture.

Or drugged yourself, senseless, into it, year after year.

You raise a hand—it feels like moving through honey. You speak—struggling to shape words through layer after layer of immerser thoughts.

"I know about this," you say, and your voice comes out hoarse, and the words fall into place one by one like a laser stroke, and they feel right, in a way that nothing else has for five years. "Let me help you, younger sisters."

To Rochita Loenen-Ruiz, for the conversations that inspired this

ABOUT FAIRIES

PAT MURPHY

Pat Murphy is a science fiction writer, a scientist, a toy maker, and a trou-ble-maker. Her novels include Adventures in Time and Space with Max Merriwell; The City, Not Long After; *and* The Falling Woman. *Her science fiction has won the Nebula, the Philip K. Dick Award, the World Fantasy Award, the Christopher Award, and the Seiun Award.*

For over twenty years, Pat Murphy was senior writer at the Exploratorium, San Francisco's museum of science, art, and human perception. These days, Pat writes and manages the creation of science books and products for Klutz, publisher of children's how-to books. Some of her recent titles for Klutz include Make a Mummy, Shrink a Head, and Other Useful Skills *and* Paper Flying Dragons, *which comes with dragons to fold and fly. Yes, she does commute to Palo Alto from the 22nd Street train station.*

'm on my way to the train station when I find a mirror leaning against a chain-link fence. People often abandon stuff on this street, figuring that someone who wants it will take it away. And someone usually does. San Francisco has many scavengers.

The mirror, a circle of glass about the size of a dinner plate, is framed with pale wood. The wood is weathered, soft against my hand as I pick it up and peer into the glass. My reflection is silvery gray in the morning light.

My car is parked just a few feet away. My bedroom, high in the attic of my father's house, needs a mirror. I figure it's serendipity that I have found this one. I put the mirror in the trunk of my car and hurry toward the station.

The first time I went looking for the train station at 22nd Street and

417

Pennsylvania I passed it three times before I finally found it. I think of it as a secret train station. There's just a small sign by the bridge on 22nd Street. Beside the sign is long flight of steps leading down, down, down to train tracks that run along a narrow ravine squeezed between Iowa Street and Pennsylvania Street. A concrete platform beside the tracks, a couple of benches, and a ticket machine—that's the station.

As always, I stop on the 22nd Street bridge and look down at the tracks. They're about twenty feet below the bridge—a big enough drop to break your leg, I'd guess. Probably not enough to kill you, unless you dove over the edge and landed on your head.

As I walk down the steps, I look up. Far above me, the freeway crosses over 22nd Street and the train tracks— a soaring concrete arc supported by massive gray columns on either side of the tracks. Morning sunlight slips through the gap between the bottom of the freeway and Indiana Street to shine on a patch of graffiti that decorates the base of one column. The great swirls of color are letters, I think, but I can't read what they say. Whatever the message, it's not for me.

As I wait for my train, I watch swallows flying to and fro, carrying food to their chicks. The birds have built nests on the underside of the freeway. They don't seem to care that semis and SUVs are thundering over them at 70 miles per hour.

When I return in the evening, I'll hear frogs chirping in the stream that runs in a gully just behind the benches. Beside the stream is a tiny marsh where rushes grow.

I like this forgotten bit of wild land, hidden away beneath the city streets.

My name is Jennifer. I am on my way to a toy company in Redwood City to have a meeting about fairies.

I met the company's founder at an art opening and he said he liked the way I think. I was a double major in art and anthropology, and we had had a long conversation (fueled by cheap white wine) about the dark side of children's stories. As I recall, I talked a lot about Tinker Bell, who tried to murder Wendy more than once. (My still-unfinished PhD dissertation is a cross-cultural analysis of the role of wicked women in children's literature, and I count Tinker Bell as right up there among the wicked.)

Anyway, he hired me to be part of his company's product development department. He told me he liked to toss people into the mix to see what happened.

After he hired me, I found out that he had a habit of hiring people for no clearly defined job, then firing them when they didn't do their job. He hired me, then left for a month's vacation. He is still gone. I wasn't sure what my job was when I reported to work three weeks ago. I still don't know. But this is the first steady paycheck I've had in a couple of years and I'm determined to make sure that something positive happens.

Today, I'm going to a meeting about fairies.

Tiffany is the project manager. We met by the coffee maker on my first day. While we waited for the coffee to brew, I found out what she was working on and chatted with her about it. She invited me to come to a few team meetings to "provide input."

The company is creating a line of Twinkle Fairy Dolls. Among three- to six-year-old girls, fairies of the gossamer-wing variety are a very hot topic. That's what the marketing guy said, anyway. He was at the first meeting I attended, but he hasn't been back since.

Each Twinkle Fairy doll will come with a unique Internet code that lets the owner enter the online fairyland that Tiffany's team is developing. In that world, the doll's owner will have her own fairy home that she can furnish with fairy furniture. She will have a fairy avatar that she can dress with fairy clothes.

It's a rather consumer-oriented fairyland. Players purchase their furniture and clothes with fairy dollars—or would that be fairy gold? And if it's fairy gold, will it wither into dead leaves in the light of day?

These are questions I do not ask at the meeting.

Today the question that Tiffany wants to address is: What sort of world do the fairies live in? Is it a forest world where they frolic in leafy groves and shelter from the misty rain under mushroom caps? Or is it a fairy village with cobblestone streets and thatched huts, maybe surrounding a fairy castle? Or is it some mixture of the two?

"Why don't we just ask marketing what they want?" says Rocky, the web developer. The temperature is supposed to top 100 today, but Rocky is wearing black jeans, black boots, and a black t-shirt from a robot wars competition. He strolled into the meeting late without apology, his eyebrows (right one pierced in three places) lowered in a scowl. He wants to look surly, but his face is sweet and soft and boyish and he can't quite pull it off.

I suspect Rocky is not happy to be on the fairy project. Tiffany mentioned that another team is working on a line of remote control monster trucks. I think Rocky would rather be developing an online Monster Truck World.

Tiffany shakes her head. Her hair is very short and very blonde and very messy. She's in her late twenties and tends to wear designer jeans, baby-doll tops, and mary janes. "We want to be authentic," she says.

Jane, the project's art director, stares at her. "Authentic? We're talking about fairies here. In case you didn't know, there aren't any fairies." Jane can be a little cranky.

I step in to help Tiffany. She's kind of a ditz, but I like her and she seems to be in charge of some important projects. A useful person to befriend. "I think Tiffany means that we want our fairies to match the child's concept of fairies. We want them to feel authentic."

"Sherlock Holmes believed in fairies," says Tiffany. "Isn't that what you told me the other day?"

Did I say "kind of a ditz"? Make that "entirely a ditz." "Not quite," I correct her, trying to be gentle. "Arthur Conan Doyle, the author who wrote Sherlock Holmes, believed in fairies. Back in 1917, two little girls took pictures of fairies in their garden, and Doyle was certain that the photos were real."

"What were they?" asks Jane. "Swamp gas?"

"Much simpler than that," I say. "About sixty years later, one of the girls—in her eighties by that time—admitted that she had cut the drawings of fairies out of a book, posed the cutouts in the garden with her friend, and taken the photos."

"Arthur Conan Doyle was fooled by paper cutouts?" Jane is intrigued.

"People believe what they want to believe," I say.

"I'm thinking of something like Neverland in Peter Pan," Tiffany says. She has moved on. A ditz, but a ditz with a goal. "Somewhere with lots of hidden, secret places." In Tiffany's world, secrets are wonderful and fun. "And it's filled with beautiful, sweet fairies with gossamer wings. Like Tinker Bell."

Rocky snorts. "Sweet?" he says. "Tinker Bell was never sweet."

Surprised, I stare at him. He's right. In the book *Peter Pan*, Tinker Bell was a jealous little pixie who swore like a sailor and did her best to get Wendy killed more than once. I didn't think Rocky would know that.

After the meeting, I go to the balcony for a smoke. The balcony—a narrow walkway just outside the windows of the cafeteria—is the smokers' corner. In California, smoking has been banished from restaurants, offices, and bars. You can smoke in your own home, but just barely. Filthy habit, people say. Bad for your health. And second-hand smoke is dangerous for others, too.

I smoke three, maybe four, cigarettes a day. Not so much. I figure you have to die sometime. I take a drag, feeling the buzz.

At the edge of the balcony there's a brick wall topped by a waist-high rail, an inadequate barrier between me and the sheer drop to the street. I lean on the rail and look down. Five floors down.

I hear the door open behind me. "Those things will kill you," Rocky says. He is tapping a cigarette from a pack. He leans against the railing beside me, looking down. "Just far enough to be fatal," he says.

He's not quite right. You can survive a fall from five stories if you hit a parked car. The car gives just enough to cushion your fall. I know. I've done research.

"I was impressed at how well you know Peter Pan," I tell him. "Most people only know the Disney version."

He almost smiles. "The Disney version has no balls," he says.

I laugh.

Rocky's scowl returns. "What's so funny?"

"Hey, it's a long tradition," I say. "Starting with the play where Mary Martin played Peter. Peter Pan *doesn't* have any balls."

He doesn't smile. I'm sorry about that. For a moment there, I kind of liked him.

Late that night, I sit on my bed, rereading *Peter Pan*. When I was ten, the year after my mother died, a friend of my father gave me a copy. The woman who gave it to me, one of a series of unsuitable women Dad dated, was under the mistaken impression that it was a children's book. I read it with horrified fascination.

Disney made Peter Pan into a jolly movie with just enough adventures to be cheerfully scary. The book is not like that. Neverland is not all sunshine and frolic. Beneath every adventure lurks a deep and frightening darkness. Peter Pan was fascinating and terrifying. He was indifferent to human life. "There's a pirate asleep in the pampas just below us," he says. "If you like, we'll go down and kill him." Death is an adventure, Peter Pan says, and nothing is better than that.

One of my cats makes a sound and I look up from the book to see what's bothering him. The mirror that I found near the train station is leaning against the far wall. My cat, Flash, stares in the direction of the mirror, his ears forward, his tail twitching.

Everyone knows that there are things that only cats can see. In my house, Flash is the cat that watches those invisible things. He frequently gives his full attention to a patch of empty air for hours at a time.

Godzilla, the other cat, usually can't be bothered with such nonsense. But tonight Godzilla has taken up a post beside Flash, staring at the same emptiness.

"What's up, guys?" I ask them. But they just keep staring in the direction of the mirror that I found on my way to the train station. They are vigilant, concerned. They don't trust this mirror.

I pick the mirror up and set it on top of the bureau. Flash jumps on top of the bureau where he continues to watch the mirror with great suspicion.

The phone rings.

It's Johnny, the owner of the board-and-care home where my father has lived for the past six months. Whenever I stop by to visit, Johnny tells me how Dad has been doing and fills me in on details that I don't particularly want to know. I have learned about the need for stool softeners and socks with no-skid soles. I have discussed the merits of different varieties of walkers (one called, without irony, the "Merry Walker").

My father was once an archeologist. My father was once a member of Mensa. My father was once a very smart, very sarcastic, somewhat hostile man. Of all those attributes, only the sarcasm and hostility remain.

A few weeks ago, when I was visiting Dad, Johnny told me that my father had threatened to kick one of the other residents in the balls.

"He gets very angry," Johnny told me. "It's the Alzheimer's."

I nodded. It wasn't really the Alzheimer's. Dad had never suffered fools gladly. He considered most people to be fools. And he was always threatening to kick some fool in the balls.

I think Dad became an archeologist because dead people didn't talk back. Living people were far too troublesome.

Johnny prefers to blame my father's idiosyncrasies on Alzheimer's. Johnny is a sweet guy who chooses to believe that people are inherently nice. But tonight, Johnny is facing a challenge. "Your father won't stop talking," he says.

I can hear my father's voice in the background, but I can't make out the words.

"He's been at it for two hours. I've told him that it's time for bed, but he won't stop." Johnny sounds very tired.

"Let me talk to him," I tell Johnny.

I hear my father as Johnny approaches him. He is delivering a lecture on burial customs. "A barrow is a home for the dead," he is saying. "In its chamber or chambers the tenant is surrounded with possessions from his life."

"Your daughter needs to talk to you," Johnny says.

Dad doesn't even pause. "A shaman would be buried with his scrying mirror; a warrior with his weapons," he continues. "A fence or trench separates the barrow from the surrounding world."

"It's important," Johnny says. "She really needs to talk to you."

"Yes?" my father growls into the phone. His tone is that of a busy man, needlessly interrupted. "I'm teaching just now."

"This is Jennifer, your daughter. I called to tell you that it's late. Class is over."

"What are you talking about?"

"This is your daughter. You're running late. It's time for class to be over."

"I was just wrapping up."

"You'd better let the students go." Wrapping up could take hours. "They have to study for finals."

"They'd better study." His voice is that of a demanding instructor. Then a pause. "I have to get ready myself," he says, as if suddenly remembering something.

"Get ready? For what?"

"I'm leaving tomorrow."

Several times over the last few months, my father has mentioned that he is going on a trip. Sometimes he's going to an important excavation. Sometimes he's leaving because the conference he was attending is over. Sometimes he's not sure where he's going. I've learned not to ask.

"You can pack in the morning," I say. "You'll have time then."

"All right," he says. "In the morning."

In the morning, he will remember none of this.

While I'm waiting for the train at the 22nd Street Station, I walk along the tiny stream that's just a few steps away from the concrete platform. It's a muddy trickle, enclosed in a culvert for part of its length, then widening to shallow puddles that support clumps of wild iris surrounded by pigweed.

Frogs live in that stream—I hear them croaking in the evening. But they're hiding now. No matter how hard I look, I never catch a glimpse of them.

The steep slope above me is covered with tall grasses and wild fennel, with a few blackberry bushes working their way up to becoming a thicket. Toward the end of the platform, some city workers have been clearing the brush. I glance down at the bare ground.

It's an old habit, developed over many summers spent at archeological digs. Out in the field, I'd be looking for shards of broken pots or chips of worked stone, indications of ancient settlements. Here in the city, I'm just looking, not expecting to see anything more than the glitter of broken beer bottles.

But the morning light reflects from the edge of a pebble. I stop, pick up the stone, and examine it more closely. It's very tiny worked flint—about a centimeter long. I can see miniscule circles, each just a couple of millimeters across, where someone has flaked away the stone to make a sharp edge.

I hear a rumble in the distance. The train is coming. I put the tiny tool in my pocket, no time to examine it further. I hurry back to the platform.

As the train pulls away, heading south, I look out the window at the brush-covered slope. The city is filled with wild things. I once saw a family of raccoons crossing a major thoroughfare on their way to check out the dumpster behind a fast food joint. A possum with a wicked grin (way too many teeth) and a naked, ratlike tail regularly strolled through my father's backyard. Coyotes live in Golden Gate Park.

If there are frogs and raccoons and opossums and coyotes, why not other creatures? Small, wild, living in the gaps, in the gullies, in the ravines, in the half-hidden places underneath.

At today's meeting, Tiffany wants to establish the specifics of our particular fairies. Tiffany believes in fairies that fly on shimmering wings (made of child-safe Mylar, I think). Her fairies are similar to Tinker Bell, but not so similar that they'll trigger a cease-and-desist order.

Jane wants the fairies to hearken back to the classics. Think *Midsummer Night's Dream* and Yeats. Her fairies wear elegant green dresses. They have a queen, of course. At fabulous parties, they dance all night. Like me, Jane lives alone. Unlike me, Jane seems to mind.

Rocky's fairies sleep late. They are dark-eyed and sultry, dressing in black and looking for trouble. I think some of them are transgender, which makes sense if you really know *Peter Pan*. When Wendy returns from Neverland, she tells her mother that new fairies live in nests on the tops of trees. "The mauve ones are boys and the white ones are girls," she says. "And the blue ones are just little sillies who are not sure what they are."

That's from the book, not the movie. I don't think Disney believes in transgender fairies.

The way I figure it, you can choose what kind of fairies you want to believe in. I finger the stone tool in my pocket. In the foggy chill of San Francisco's summer, my fairies wear clothing made of tanned mouse leather. They are grimy, hardscrabble fairies that chip tools from stone and drink from the stream. They hunt in the marsh with stone blades and feed on frogs' legs. They'd mug Victorian flower fairies and take their stuff.

"What do you think? Forest or village?" Tiffany is polling the meeting, getting each member of the team to vote. Rocky says city; Jane says forest. It's my turn.

Wild or civilized. "Can't we have it both ways?" I ask.

Why not? Dirty little fairies, crouching in the litter by the stream, chipping stone into knives, strapping blades onto spear handles made of pencils and pens that commuters had dropped. My kind of fairy.

I spend the rest of the afternoon working on visual concepts for the fairy forest. For the fairy huts, I figure I should use all natural materials.

The traditional Celtic huts have stone walls, and I just can't see the fairies going to all that effort. After some online research, I settle on huts that looked like ones built in eastern Nigeria. The walls are made of bundles of straw, tied side by side. The roof is made of reeds.

The shape of the huts reminds me of acorns—smooth sides, textured cap. I figure Tiffany will like that. And I think the fairies could manage to build huts with straw.

In my sketch, the huts are tucked among wild blackberry brambles. Poison oak twines among the blackberry branches. I don't think these fairies want company.

After work, I go to the board-and-care home to visit my dad. I stop by the grocery store on my way and buy a basket of fresh raspberries. These days, I always bring something to eat. Finger food is best. Grapes, raspberries, blueberries. Something he can pick up and eat, no utensils required.

We sit in the living room, my father in a recliner and I in a straight-back chair. We eat raspberries.

I've learned not to ask many questions. Questions are difficult. More often than not, he has no answers. Or his answers relate to the distant past. Or halfway through an answer, Dad forgets what he was saying.

I tell my father many things these days. He likes to listen. When he listens, it does not matter that words are slippery and sentences betray him.

"I found this on the path to the train station," I tell him. I hold out the tiny stone tool. I've been carrying it in my pocket since I found it. "I can see tiny chips where someone has been working the stone, flaking away bits to make an edge."

My father examines the blade. His hand shakes. The skin of his arm is marked with dark purple age spots. He gives the stone back. "Microlith," he says. Basically, that's a technical term for "tiny worked stone." Not saying much I didn't already know.

"I found a mirror the other day," I say.

"That's good," he says. A complete sentence. Short enough that he can get through it without losing his way. Sentences are trickier than you realize, long and twisty. It's easy to get lost.

"I need…." he begins. He's pushing his luck now, working on a longer sentence. What does he need? "I need a mirror."

"Really? I'll bring you the one I found," I tell him. Does he really need a mirror or is that just the word that came most quickly to mind?

He nods. "Don't forget." Another easy sentence.

I care about my father in a grudging sort of way. My mother died when I was nine. She committed suicide, jumping off the Golden Gate Bridge. Even as a child, I recognized that she was a drama queen, a flamboyant woman given to grand gestures, to great joys and great depression. Today, she might be identified as bipolar.

My father, on the other hand, is solid and unemotional. After my mother's death, Dad took care of me in an awkward, casual, ham-handed sort of way. I never went hungry and I never got hugged. It was a balance, of sorts.

I take after my mother. I understand drama, I understand depression, and I understand the appeal of the dark and foggy waters below the bridge.

"Don't forget," my father says again.

We eat raspberries in companionable silence.

Godzilla is sleeping on top of the mirror, which is lying flat on the bureau. He was there this morning when I left for work. He is there when I get home. Usually, he supervises when I open a can of cat food for him and his brother. But tonight he jumps down from the bureau only after I set the food on the floor. He eats quickly, then returns to the mirror, gazing into it intently, sniffing it carefully, and then lying down on top of it once again. Curled up, he completely covers the glass surface.

When I sit down at my desk, I pat my lap and call to him. He lifts his head and regards me with that slit-eyed look that one of my friends says is how cats smile. He's not about to leave his post.

His brother, Flash, is prowling the apartment restlessly. Every once in a while, he walks past the bureau and looks up at his brother. Then he resumes his patrol.

Cats have theories. Every cat owner knows that. The cats can't and won't tell you their theories. You must deduce the theories from their behavior. Then you have theories about the cats' theories. If you modify your behavior in response to your theories about their theories, you may change their theories. It is an endlessly recursive loop. The viewer affects the system. It's Heisenberg's uncertainty principle with cats.

I let Godzilla sleep.

I am doing online research about fairy fashions. To draw convincing fairy clothes, I figure I'd better know what people think fairies wear. It's edging up on ten PM, and I have to be up at six in the morning to catch the train, but I'm not sleepy at all. When I'm insomniac, I find doing research online very comforting. I used to walk on the Golden Gate Bridge at night—but doing research online is safer.

I find information on Conan Doyle's belief in fairies. I find a discussion of pygmy flints, blades of worked stone that some claim are made by the little people. I find hundreds of images of Victorian fairies—pretty ladies with delicate wings.

Somewhere along the way, I find Rocky's blog.

Mostly it is one of those extremely tedious personal blogs that I am amazed that anyone writes and even more amazed that anyone reads. A description of an art opening he attended. Photos of his friends (all in black, of course). Discussion of his plans to attend Burning Man. And a long list of fairy links.

Rocky, it turns out, has done a lot research that he has not shared with the rest of the team. He has links to fairy porn. (Yes, of course there is fairy porn.) He has links to sites considering the connections between fairies and alien abductions, as well as sites about the original Celtic fairies—amoral creatures that are capable of great malevolence. In Celtic tradition, when someone died people said that they went to be with the fairies. Being touched by a fairy, according to one site, was commonly recognized as the cause of a stroke.

No sweet and beautiful fairies. No gossamer wings.

At the next meeting of the fairyland team, Tiffany gathers ideas for the portal to our fairy site. At Disney's fairy site, the splash screen has a sprinkling of fairy dust and the words: "Believing is just the beginning." Then pictures of fairies appear. Tiffany asks the group for an image and words that will capture the essence of our site.

"A black mirror," I say. "A portal to another world. And the words—clap if you believe in fairies."

I don't see the need to specify the type of fairy you might believe in. Dark-eyed and sultry; sweet-faced and dressed in pink. That doesn't matter to me. Clap if you believe.

Rocky smiles a little. "That could work," he says.

After the meeting, Johnny calls to tell me that my dad is in the hospital. Apparently Dad forgot that he could not walk without a walker. He stood up, and then fell down, fracturing his hip.

I go to the hospital after work. I bring the mirror and set it on one of the chairs in my father's room. He won't remember that he said he needed a mirror, but I do.

Dad is sleeping. The nurse says that he was cursing all day. He said he was going to kick the doctor in the balls. "It's the Alzheimer's," she says.

I nod, letting her believe what she wants to believe. Clap your hands if you believe that my father doesn't really want to kick the doctor in the balls.

I am not clapping.

I explain to the nurse that we have a DNR, a "do not resuscitate" order for my dad. No heroic measures, I explain. Just keep him comfortable.

Clap your hands if you believe in death.

Believing in fairies is much easier, I think. Death is an end, an emptiness, a darkness. People want to believe in the light. Go to the light, they say. We fear the darkness and the unknown, the fairies in the ravine, the world behind the mirror.

I set the stone tool beside the mirror. I sit by my father's bed and watch him breathe. His arms are loosely strapped to the rails of the hospital bed. The nurse had told me that they had to strap him down. He kept trying to get out of bed. His hip was broken and he couldn't walk, but he was still trying to get out of bed.

My father's life has been shrinking over the past few years. After I went to college, he lived alone in his Victorian home. When he couldn't get by on his own, I helped him move to an apartment in a senior residence. Then he moved from that apartment to his room in the board-and-care home. Then he moved from that room into this shared room in a hospital, where all he has is a bed and a table and a curtain that separates his space from that of another old man with a table and bed.

My father is not conscious. He is lying on his side, his spine curved, his legs bent. A sheet covers him, but I can see the outline of his body through the fabric. He looks smaller than he ever has before. The tube that snakes from beneath the sheet is dripping a cocktail of painkillers into his veins.

My father is dying. That's clear.

Here's a question. Do I stay and keep watch? Sit by his bed and do what? Read a magazine? Think about his life? Not such a happy life, by my lights.

What would I like, if I were the one lying on the bed?

I would like to be left alone.

So I go home, leaving the mirror and the stone tool on the table by the bed.

Clap your hands if you believe in death. Clap your hands and my father will die.

Actually, I'm kidding about that. My father will die no matter whether you clap your hands or not. My father will die, I will die, and someday you will die. You can applaud or remain silent and death won't care. You can choose to speed up your death—by plunging from a balcony, from a bridge—but all the clapping in the world won't put death off forever.

Some discussions of death make it sound all soft and warm, like falling asleep in a feather bed. But falling asleep implies waking up again, and Death means not waking up.

Not being here.

Being with the fairies.

An hour after I leave the hospital, a nurse calls to tell me my father has passed away.

Here's what I think happened: My father curled up into the fetal position. He curled up as small as he could. Then he curled up even smaller, then smaller, then smaller still. You might not think a person could shrink, but my father had been shrinking over the last year, growing shorter with each passing day. So he shrank until he was small enough to slip into the fairy mirror. When the time was right, the fairies came through the mirror and took him away with them.

You see, new fairies are not born. They are transformed through the fairy mirror.

Flash and Godzilla could see that the way was open. Cats notice that sort of thing. So they blocked the way—sleeping on top of the mirror to keep the fairies in and to keep me out. They were protecting me. They aren't stupid. They know who opens those cans of cat food.

My father left his worn out body behind, dressed in the unfortunate hospital gown. Like a snake abandoning its skin, my father slipped out of his body and emerged in the mirror. He felt better. All the life energy that remained in him was concentrated in his smaller form.

Right now, he's hunting for mice among the stalks of fennel and the blackberry brambles. He took the stone tool with him. He'll scavenge a pencil dropped by a commuter, lash the stone blade to the end to make a spear, and go hunting for frogs.

That's what I choose to believe.

I stop by the hospital to make arrangements for the body that my father has left behind. A kindly social worker helps me, giving me the name of a mortuary, telling me where to call to get copies of the death certificate, offering words of sympathy. Eventually I leave, taking the mirror with me. There's no sign of the stone tool among my father's things.

Late that night, I take the mirror to the train station. Light of a half-moon is shining down on Pennsylvania Street. I walk down the steps to the 22nd Street train station, alert to every noise around me.

When I reach the train tracks, I head south. No one is there. The graffiti artists are taking a night off. Their past creations look gray and black, the colors invisible in the moonlight.

A short distance from the benches and ticket machine, the tracks go into a tunnel. I lean the mirror against the wall beside the tunnel entrance. Somehow it seems right to put it by the tunnel mouth, near the entrance to the underworld. Well, maybe not quite the underworld—it isn't a very long tunnel. But it's the closest thing to an underworld there is around here.

My father had smoked when I was young. My early memories of him are tobacco-scented, wreathed in smoke. The father in those memories is strong and tall and energetic. He could sweep me up and toss me in the air, swing me by my arms until my feet left the ground.

I take a pack of cigarettes from my pocket and I tear the cigarettes open, one by one. I scatter the tobacco on the ground in front of the mirror. I am mixing my magic systems, I know. Native Americans offered tobacco to the spirits. The frogs call; something rustles in the bushes. An opossum? A raccoon? Something else?

I sit by the train tracks near the mirror for a time and think about death. Every now and then, someone will commit suicide by walking in front of a train. Such a noisy, messy, industrial way to go.

I leave the mirror and head for home. That night, I surf the web.

On Rocky's site, I find that he has been working on a fairyland. When I log in, I am given an avatar.

This is not a fairyland that would meet with Tiffany's approval. Yes, there are leafy groves, but the trees are gnarled and menacing, draped with Spanish moss. Little light reaches the forest floor and I have the sense the creatures other than fairies lurk in the shadows.

There's a fairy village, but the mud huts are neither elegant nor appealing. The carcass of a mouse, marked with the wounds that killed it, hangs curing in the shadows. There are no fairies in residence.

I explore Rocky's fairyland carefully. In the dark bole of a hollow oak I find a tunnel that goes down, down, down into the underworld.

I move my avatar through the darkness, the way illuminated by faintly glowing marks on the tunnel walls. I reach a dead end. A wooden door, closed with a bar and a large padlock, blocks my way.

I lay my hand on the door and the words "THIS WAY CLOSED" glow on the bar in neon green. I know what to do.

I reach out to the letters and touch the D, then the E, then the A, T, H. Death. Each letter winks out when I touch it. When I touch the H, the padlock and the bar dissolve. The door opens.

I stand by the open doorway, looking into a dark and misty world. I listen—and in the distance, I hear the low wail of a train's horn, the rumble of metal wheels on tracks. I catch a faint scent of wild fennel and tobacco.

Listening to the train rumble in the distance, I know the way is open, but I don't need to go there. I close the door.

At work the next day, I see Rocky in the lunchroom and pull up a chair next to him. "I visited Fairyland last night," I tell him.

He glances at me, startled.

"I particularly liked your attention to detail in the hollow oak," I continue.

He can't help himself—he is smiling now. A little smug, more than a little arrogant.

"Nice trick on the password."

That surprised him. "You opened the door?"

My turn to nod. "Obviously, I didn't go in."

He is considering me now—eyes narrowing. "Maybe later," he says.

"That goes without saying." I study him for a moment—face soft as a boy's, the arrogant confidence of the young in his eyes. Forever young. "I've been wondering where you got the name Rocky," I say. "Nobody names their kid Rocky."

I've been thinking about Rocky, a twenty-something web designer with an attitude and an obsession with death. Could he be something more?

Do you believe in Peter Pan? A boy who never grows up, a boy who knows his way to fairyland and back, a boy with the power of death in his hands. When Disney made a movie of *Peter Pan*, they kept the happy moments, but left out the essence. When Wendy's mother thinks about Peter Pan she remembers this: when children die, Peter Pan goes partway with them. Partway to fairyland where the dead people are.

The next day, at the 22nd Street train station, I look for the mirror. It's gone. Perhaps someone who needed a mirror picked it up. I hope they have a cat.

I sit on the bench by the tracks, sketching in my notebook as I wait for the train. In my sketch, two fairies crouch beneath the feathery fronds of a fennel plant. They wear war paint, stripes of color on their cheeks that help them blend with the shadows. One holds a spear made from a chipped stone point lashed to a pencil. He looks a bit like my father when he was younger and happier. The other fairy wears a Tinker Bell skirt, but she has a stone knife at her belt. Her face is in the shadows, but she has dark hair like my mother. It is sunny where they are. I'm glad of that.

These two are hunting for mice, I think. Tiffany's fairies drink dewdrops and sip nectar from flowers. Mine prefer protein.

The fairies look purposeful, but content. They have a simple existence: a hut to live in, mice and frogs to hunt. But that's enough.

The sun shines on the hillside covered with fennel and blackberries, on the concrete marked with messages that are not for me. In the stream, the irises are blooming.

LET MAPS TO OTHERS

KJ PARKER

K. J. Parker was born long ago and far away, worked as a coin dealer, a dogs-body in an auction house, and a lawyer, and has so far published thirteen novels (the "Fencer," "Scavenger" and "Engineer" trilogies, and standalone novels The Company, The Folding Knife, The Hammer *and* Sharps*), three novellas ("Purple And Black," "Blue And Gold" and "A Small Price To Pay For Birdsong," which won the 2012 World Fantasy Award) and a gaggle of short fiction. Married to a lawyer and living in the southwest of England, K. J. Parker is a mediocre stockman and forester, a barely competent carpenter, blacksmith, and machinist, a two-left-footed fencer, lackluster archer, utility-grade armorer, accomplished textile worker, and crack shot.*

K. J. Parker is not K. J. Parker's real name. However, if K. J. Parker were to tell you K. J. Parker's real name, it wouldn't mean anything to you.

There is such a place. And I have been there.

They all say that, don't they? They say; I met someone once who spent five years there, disguised as a holy man. Or; the village headman told me his people go there all the time, to trade timber and flour for spices. Or; the priest showed me things that had come from there—a statuette, a small, curiously fashioned box, a pair of shoes, a book I couldn't read. Or; from the top of the mountain we looked out across the valley and there it was, on the other side of the river, you could just make out the sun glinting off the spires of the temples. Or; I was taken there, I saw the Great Gate and the Forbidden Palace, I sat and drank goat-butter tea with the Grand Master, who was seven feet tall and had his eyes, nose and mouth set in the middle of his chest.

You hear them, read them. The first, second, third time, you believe. The fourth time, you want to believe. The fifth time, you notice a disturbing pattern beginning to emerge—how they were always so close they could hear the voices of the children and smell the woodsmoke, but for this reason or that reason they couldn't go the last two hundred yards and had to turn back (but it was there, it is there, it's real, it really exists). The sixth time breaks your heart. By the seventh time, you're a scholar, investigating a myth.

I am a scholar. I have spent my entire life investigating what I now firmly believe to be a myth. But there is such a place. And I have been there.

"The duke," she said, "is watching you."

Bearing in mind where we were, who she was and what we'd been doing, I sincerely hoped she was talking figuratively. "You don't say."

"Oh yes." She tugged at the sheet. Women feel the cold. "He's very interested in you."

Another thing women do is say things that aren't entirely true. Men do this, of course; but usually for a reason, usually a reason you can perceive; a shape hidden under the lies, like a body under a blanket. You see a blanket, but you can trace where the arms, legs, chest are. Women, by contrast, say untrue things just to see where the path will lead. "I doubt it," I said. "He won't have heard of me."

"Of course he's heard of you."

I yawned. I didn't feel like conversation. "My father, possibly," I said. "Maybe, just conceivably, my brother, because of the lawsuits. Me, no. Nobody's heard of me."

She cleared her throat.

"Outside of the Studium," I amended. "And the scholarly fraternity at large. I confess, I'm reasonably well known among my brother scholars. That fool who believes, they call me. Outside of that, though—"

She nuzzled against me, purely for warmth. "The greatest living authority on Essecuivo," she said.

"Exactly. That fool who believes. What on earth could that possibly have to do with the duke?"

"He's bought the Company."

I felt a shiver that had absolutely nothing to do with the temperature of the room. "Then he's an idiot," I said. "Even if he only paid a penny for it."

"He doesn't think so."

"Well, he wouldn't."

"And it was rather more than a penny," she went on, talking to the ceiling. "He's mortgaged Sansify and Gard Hardy and sold his half share in the tin mines to raise the money. He's serious about it."

I frowned; it was dark, so she couldn't see me. "I feel sorry for his sons," I replied. "It's miserable, being the poor son of a rich father. You never quite manage to get away from it. Mind you, there's a substantial difference in scale. My father was *well-off*, but nothing at all like—"

"He thinks it's a good investment."

I really wasn't in the mood for talking about the duke; especially since the conversation also appeared to involve Essecuivo, a subject I talk about incessantly among scholars and never to outsiders. In fact, I didn't want to talk at all. I just wanted to go home; but you can't, can you? Not straight away. "Well," I said, "I hope his faith turns out to be justified, naturally. If so, I'll be as pleased as I'll be amazed."

I felt her turn towards me. "It does exist, doesn't it?" she said. "There is such a place."

I sighed. "Yes," I said. "I believe it exists. Aeneas Peregrinus went there, and he was real enough. But we don't know where it is."

"You don't know?"

"And I'm the greatest living authority." I sighed. "One of the greatest living authorities. Professor Strella, in Aerope, would dispute that last statement, but he's a fraud. Carchedonius of Luseil—"

"You must have some idea."

I stretched. Time to get up and go. "It exists," I said. "Somewhere. Beyond that, your guess is as good as mine. I'd better go."

"No."

"I'd better. He might come back early, you never know."

"It's the second reading of the Finance Bill," she said irritably, "he won't be back till the morning. You never want to stay."

"I really should go."

"Fine. That's fine." You see what I mean. They're always saying things they don't mean. "Tomorrow?"

"Not sure about tomorrow," I said, "I may have to dine in Hall. And then I've got a lecture to prepare. The day after tomorrow would be better."

"Suit yourself."

I slid out of bed, felt for my trousers in the dark. I always find that sort of thing exquisitely distasteful. "Is the House sitting next week?"

"I don't know."

Of course she knew. But I could look it up in the gazette. I pulled on my shirt, then hesitated. "Is the duke really interested in me?"

"Yes."

I shrugged. "Maybe he'll be good for a few marks toward the chancel fund," I said. "It's getting pretty desperate, the rain's coming in under the eaves."

I was born in the City. My father was a junior partner in the Eastern Sea Company, which at that time was a cross between a bank and a munitions factory. He was on the munitions side of things; he ran the ordnance yard where they cast the cannons and mortars that would be mounted on the ships that would make the journey to Essecuivo, to sell woolen cloth, tin plates, mirrors, shovels, whatever in return for cinnamon, mace, nutmeg, fine red pepper and the curious root that cures plague, syphilis and baldness. Because nobody had discovered Essecuivo yet, there wasn't exactly a hurry; so, in order to keep the cash flow moving along, the Company sold the cannons and mortars my father made to the kings and dukes of neighboring states, who always managed to find a use for them. Back then, money was still pouring in to the Company (because everybody knew it was only a matter of time before someone found Essecuivo), and the directors invested it sensibly in worthwhile projects, to build up the capital against the day when the crucial discovery was made and the Company could launch its first fleet. It was called the Eastern Sea Company because, on the balance of the evidence then available, it was generally held that Essecuivo was somewhere to the east. But if it had turned out to be in the west, they wouldn't have minded. They were practical men, back then.

My father was a practical man. He wasn't convinced that Essecuivo would simply fall into our laps like an overripe pear; it would need finding, so someone would have to find it. Ordinarily he'd have done it himself (he was a great believer in if-you-want-something-done-properly) but he was too busy with supervising the cannon-founders and doing deals with foreign princes to find the time, so it seemed logical to keep it in the family and give the job to his spare son (me). Accordingly, from the age of nine I was tutored in geography, history, languages and book-keeping (for when I'd found Essecuivo and established our first trading post there). When I was sixteen, I was sent to the Studium, which possesses a copy of every book ever written, to continue my studies. And there I stayed, becoming the youngest ever professor of Humanities at age thirty-two.

Every book, I discovered, except one.

I first encountered Aeneas Peregrinus when I was twelve. I read about him in Silvianus' *Discourses*. Aeneas Peregrinus had been to Essecuivo, three hundred years ago. He set off from the City with a cargo of lemons, heading for Mesembrotia, but was blown off course by a freak storm. The storm lasted for nine days, and when the wind dropped, nobody had any idea where they were; even the stars were different, Aeneas wrote. For four weeks they drifted, until another storm, even more ferocious than the first, picked them up and carried them at terrifying speed for eight days, then died away as suddenly as it had arisen. On the skyline, they could see land. They sat becalmed for a further three days, until a gentle breeze carried them to what turned out to be Essecuivo, where the soil and climate are the best in the world, the people are gentle, sophisticated, wealthy beyond measure and wildly generous, and where they'd never seen a lemon.

Aeneas sold his cargo for its weight in gold, then spent a month or so travelling round the country talking to noblemen, priests and scholars, finding out everything he could about the wonderful country he'd stumbled across. Most of all, naturally, he wanted to find out where it was. That, apparently, was no problem; the Essecuivans are exceptionally learned in astronomy, geography and all related sciences, and taught him the principles of latitude and the techniques of advanced navigation using the astrolabe, compass and sextant (all previously unknown outside Essecuivo) which every ship's captain uses to this day. With this knowledge, it was a simple matter for Aeneas to fix the relative positions of Essecuivo and the City and plot a course home. The return journey took him three weeks, partly because he was held up by contrary winds a third of the way over. He arrived home with his cargo of gold ingots, and immediately sat down to write his two great books. The first of these, *A Discourse on Navigation*, he presented to the Council, who made him a Knight of Equity and set up a ten-foot-high statue in his honor in what is now Aeneas Square. The second book, a complete description of Essecuivo, including precise directions for finding it again, he kept to himself, although he occasionally showed selected passages to his close friends. After all, he reasoned, he was determined to go back there and make a second massive fortune, and quite possibly a third, fourth, fifth and sixth, for as long as the Essecuivans were prepared to pay ridiculous prices for lemons. Only an idiot would disclose the secret of unlimited wealth, and risk a flooding of the market.

Aeneas Peregrinus died suddenly, at the age of forty-six, three hundred and seven years ago. At the time of his death, the whereabouts of the manuscript of his second book were not known. It hasn't been seen since.

I'm not sure if I'm a geographer or a historian, or whether geography's a humanity or a science. What I do know is that, if I really am smart enough to deserve a chair at the Studium, I should've asked myself what a senator's young trophy wife ever saw in me, long before that casual mention of the duke. Still, better late than too late.

I walked home slowly through the back alleys, and every turning and doorway was crawling with the duke's men, watching me, taking notes, except that I couldn't quite see them. By the time I reached the lodge I was exhausted. The porter got up from his nice warm fireside and handed me a note.

Must see you at once. My rooms.
Carchedonius

That's not his real name, of course. Before he came to the Studium he was Liutprand Thiostulfsen. It cost me twelve angels to find that out, and I never could think of a good way of using it against him. Just knowing it made me feel better, though.

I should explain about Carchedonius. He's a fine scholar. He's painstaking, insightful, clear-headed, occasionally brilliant, always worth listening to. His work on the manuscript tradition of Thraso's *Dialogues* was what started me on the road to my finest hour, the deciphering of the Sunao Codex. Between us, we know everything there is to know about Aeneas, and Essecuivo. All in all, it's a shame we hate each other the way we do.

But that can't be helped, anymore than you can get an injunction to stop the winter. The stupid thing is, neither of us can account for it. I've never done him any real harm, though not for want of trying, and all his wild schemes to encompass my downfall have failed or backfired on him. Apparently he has some kind of grudge based on some relative of his losing a lot of money when the Company went under. If that's really the case, he must've nursed it like a shepherd's wife with an orphan lamb. I think I hate him so much because he hates me, though I'm not sure I didn't hate him first. In any case, it's been going on since we were both seventeen-year-old freshmen. I guess it's an interest for both of us; cheaper than collecting pre-Mannerist miniatures, slightly more exciting than watching the donkey-cart races.

Must see you in my rooms at once presumably meant the latest in a long line of labored, over-elaborate stratagems; presumably it hadn't occurred to him that I might simply decide not to turn up. He'd make a lousy spider; the patience and dedication to spin a good web, but not a clue about luring flies. His idea of subtlety would be a big notice; WEB THIS WAY. He'd starve.

I nearly didn't go. Nearly. If I was a fly, I'd be dead by now.

Here I go, rattling on about myself and my own inconsequential history. I'm ashamed of myself, as a historian. My part in the sequence of events is significant but limited. I shouldn't have talked about myself or even acknowledged my own existence for at least another ten pages.

The Company; the Eastern Ocean Company; actually, the correct name is the College of Merchant Adventurers for the Promotion and Regulation of Trade with the Nations of the Eastern Ocean. It was founded, coincidentally, in the year of my birth—here I am, intruding again—by three clockmakers and a goldsmith, affluent men with a taste for abstruse literature who'd been brought up on secondary accounts of Aeneas Peregrinus, and who could afford to indulge their scientific pretensions by chartering and outfitting a small ship (the *Squirrel*, 90 tons) to look for Essecuivo. That was all. But, being businessmen, they thought it would be common sense to spread the risk a little. Accordingly, they issued a prospectus, which they hired a couple of layabouts to give away free in the tea-houses around the Golden Carp.

The year I was born was also the year of the great gold strike in Eroine. For the first time in centuries, the City was awash with money; newly coined gold angels, tumbling like raindrops, looking for channels, gutters and conduits to drain off the flood. Men who'd been wise enough to take an early stake at Eroine and then sell before the strike worked out were looking around for the next good thing; preferably something a bit more substantial than gold-mining, up and down like a peacock's tail, as my father used to say. Essecuivo was exactly the sort of thing they were after; a solid, long-term venture yielding rich dividends for ever and ever. In a matter of days, copies of the free prospectus (the clockmakers had only printed two hundred) were changing hands for an angel each.

At this point, something strange and wonderful happened. The clockmakers, in order to keep track of who was investing what, had some more papers printed; not prospectuses this time, but shares. It wasn't a brand new idea, but it had never really caught on before. That all changed. The first subscription, at one angel a share, sold out in a week. The second subscription, three angels, went in a single morning; meanwhile, in the tea-houses, the disappointed investors who'd missed out on the subscriptions were cheerfully paying six angels apiece for second-hand shares. Twelve subscriptions later, Company stock stood at a hundred and six, and only the clockmakers had any idea how many shares were in circulation. At this point, they quietly sold out their own interests and retired to vast country estates in the Naquite, leaving the Company in the hands of its newly elected Board, one member of which was my poor father.

What nobody realized at that moment was that just under a third of the entire value of the Republic was now invested in the Company; whose assets, apart from money, consisted of a fine neo-Archaic mansion house in Widegate, a fair collection of maps and books put together by the clockmakers, four remaining years of a six-year charter of the *Squirrel* and some second-hand barrels. I think it was this that led my father to decide that someone really ought to find Essecuivo as quickly as possible.

I walked in and he didn't look up. "Tea?" he asked.

"Yes, why not?" I looked around. I hadn't been in his rooms for some time. Mind you, nothing had changed; the same heaps of junk everywhere. I decided to assume that the offer of tea implied an invitation to sit down, so I moved a stack of books and perched on a chair. He swung the kettle arm over the fire and peered back at me over his shoulder.

"I saw that thing you did in the *Proceedings*," he said.

"Did you now."

"Very good." He pawed the lid off the tea caddy and measured out three spoonfuls. Black tea, the cheap sort. I could smell the bergamot oil they use to mask the poor flavor. "I think you're right about Psammetichus. It makes sense of the western tradition, and it fits in with Hiero in the *Summary*."

"Thank you."

"Of course, you were wrong about Arcea," he went on, with his back to me. "The foundation date is fixed by the Lelantine War."

I frowned. He had a point. "That's a terminus post quem."

He shook his head. "Hiero lists Arceus among the dead at Limma," he said. "If he died at Limma, he couldn't have founded Arcea the year after, could he?"

Six months of agonizingly hard work gone up in smoke. I could have cried. Instead, I said, "If you're prepared to follow Hiero."

"You were," he replied. "Can't have it both ways." He turned round, holding a teapot and two small wooden cups. He loves to make a show of poverty, although his family owns half the Neada valley. "Lemon?"

I shook my head. "That's what you wanted to see me about."

"No." He sat down, not bothering to shift the books first; he sort of settled in beside and on top of them, like cement. "No, I've already written a note for the *Review*." He smiled. "Sorry."

I made a show of shrugging. "Just as well you spotted my careless oversight," I said. "The human race should be properly grateful."

He leaned forward to pour the tea. "Oh, the hell with that," he said. "I never could be doing with slipshod scholarship, is all." He frowned. "Did you say you wanted lemon?"

"Not for me, no."

He sipped his tea and pulled a face. "No," he went on (he starts most of his sentences with *no*), "it was something quite other. How are things with you, by the way? It's been a while since we had a chance for a civilized conversation. How's your father getting on?"

"He died," I said. "Last spring."

"That's a shame, I'm sorry. He can't have been out for long."

"Six months."

He shook his head. "Well," he said, "at least he didn't die in prison. That must be a terrible thing, don't you think?"

Sometimes, the best way of fighting is not to fight. I sat still and quiet. He drank his tea.

"No," he said eventually, "what I wanted to see you about was—" He stopped, put his cup down and folded his hands neatly in his lap. "You heard that Count Dorcellus is dead."

"No, actually."

He nodded. "The family's deep in debt, so they had to sell up. The whole place, including the library."

In spite of myself, I was mildly interested. The Dorcelli are one of those old families who used to be everywhere a few hundred years ago, and haven't done a damn thing since. Also, they were always notoriously mean-minded about allowing scholars to use their library. As a result, nobody had any idea what they'd got in there.

"It just so happens," he went on, looking over my shoulder, "that my uncle bought a few cases of books at the sale." He grinned, still not looking at me. "When I say cases, that's quite accurate. He bought four large crates, sight unseen. He's a clown, my uncle. Still."

I had a feeling of being taken on a guided tour of the torture chamber.

They do that, apparently, to make people confess. This is the wrack, that's the iron maiden, and over here we have the thumbscrews. "Anything interesting?" I asked.

"Some bits and pieces." He frowned again, then lifted his head and looked at me. "Oh, before I forget. They sent me your latest on Aeneas Peregrinus. They want to know if it's any good."

I felt cold all over. They, in this context, meant the faculty board, to whom I had submitted an outline of my researches in the hope of getting funding for another five years. Through ignorance or malice they'd given it to Carchedonius for peer review. I swallowed. "What did you think?"

"Splendid."

Oh, but you can't tell, really you can't. He always says *splendid* or *excellent*, just before he wields the knife. I waited. He made the moment last.

"No," he said, "I went through it all very carefully, and I'm forced to admit, I do believe you're right. And I've been wrong all these years. You convinced me. Congratulations."

Still I waited. These are the red-hot irons, that cage thing over there is for bending your arms backwards until your elbows burst. "And?"

"And nothing." The smile faded. "You know I can't stand you," he went on. "You're arrogant, sloppy, careless and full of shit, and the way you carry on with married women is a disgrace to the Studium. But, on this occasion, you've produced a piece of work of real quality. And put me in my place in the process." He picked up his teacup and put it down again, his fingertips still surrounding the rim. "I know now that you were right about the latitude of Essecuivo, and I was wrong. I'm trying to be graceful about it, but I'm probably not succeeding. It's not really in my nature."

It suddenly occurred to me to be glad I hadn't touched the tea he'd poured for me. Bergamot oil would mask any number of unusual flavors. "Well—" I said.

"Anyway." He stood up, crossed to the fireplace and gave the logs a sharp poke. Little red stars got up, like flies off a turd. "I've written to the faculty recommending that you get your money. I had no choice," he said. "After all, we're scholars, aren't we?"

I took a deep breath. "Is that what you—?"

"No."

I looked at him. People have mistaken us for each other. We're both tall and skinny, with very similar long faces and straight noses. Two scholars. "Fine," I said. "So?"

He sat down again, this time carefully moving the books, like miners clearing the fallen rocks behind which their friends are trapped, until he unearthed a long brass tube. He laid this across his knees and covered it with his forearms. "One small point in your work that I'd take issue with. Very small," he added quickly. "It hadn't occurred to me either until very recently. It's about the manuscript of the *Discovery*."

(The *Discovery of Essecuivo*, by Aeneas Peregrinus. Of course there was no manuscript.)

"You and I," he went on, "have both spent a large part of our adult lives trying to figure out what became of the manuscript when Aeneas died. Both of us assumed that it would have been inherited by his son. We traced every living descendant, we sorted through indices and cartularies wherever there's a library that might have received papers or books from Dives Peregrinus or his heirs. It's all been—" He grinned. "A complete waste of time. Oh, we've found books and papers. Just not the one we were looking for. Agreed?"

I nodded.

"We assumed," he went on, "that, because Dives inherited the land and the money and the house, he'd have had the papers too. After all, Aeneas was planning on going back. He died suddenly. The papers would have been with the rest of his property."

He seemed to want me to say something. "Yes," I said.

"Naturally enough. It was a fair assumption. But what—" He stopped, as though he'd walked into an invisible door. "What if Aeneas and his son quarreled about something, and Aeneas gave the papers to somebody else? The land and the money; well, he didn't really have a choice, people didn't just disinherit their only sons back then, so Dives got them all. But the papers—"

A hot, bright light inside my head. "The niece," I said.

He gave me a beautiful smile. "Precisely," he said. "His sister's daughter, whose name we don't even know. What if *she* got the papers, while he was still alive?"

I was ashamed. I really, really should have thought of it before. But I was too excited to let that get in the way just then. "The niece—"

"Married into the Dorcelli family," he said quietly. "Who, being at that time wealthy enough not to need to sully their hands with trade and commerce, filed the papers safely away in the archives of their beautiful library at Touchevre and forgot all about them. Probably never bothered to look to see what was in them. Meanwhile Dives, having ransacked his father's house searching for the old fool's last book and failed to find it, concluded that it must have been destroyed, and told people so. Naturally, they believed him. He was, after all, Aeneas' son."

Suddenly I could scarcely breathe. "Your uncle."

He smiled. "Bought four large crates, sight unseen. Including—" He pointed the brass tube at me, like a weapon. "This."

He held on to the tube. I unscrewed the cap. I could see the end of a roll of parchment. My hand was frozen solid. I couldn't move.

"Allow me." He pinched the parchment between forefinger and thumb and drew it out. It was stiff and brown. It looked like a stick. "Now, then," he said. "You're the greatest living expert on Essecuivo. You've just proved that, to my satisfaction. Would you care to take a look?"

My enemy, my one and only true enemy, holding in his hand the one and only manuscript. Would I care to take a look? I nodded. He leaned across, took my hand, opened the cramped fingers and pushed the scroll in between them. "Take your time," he said. "I'm in no hurry."

You know the story of Saint Aguellinus; how, every morning since he was nine years old, he climbed the mountain just before dawn and prayed to be allowed to look into the face of the Invincible Sun. For ninety years he prayed; then, one day, his prayer was granted. The Sun, rising above the Techenis mountains, burst upon him as he prayed and spoke to him, saying, Follow me. Whereupon Aguellinus, his prayers answered, was consumed by the fire that leaves no ash and ascended bodily into Heaven—

Me, I'm not religious. I can see the Sun any time I like. But this—

"Go on," he said. (I'll never forget how he said it.) "It won't bite you."

I unrolled it. The parchment creaked; I was suddenly terrified in case it snapped or crumbled into dust before I could read it. But it rolled out, smooth and springy, the surface hard under my fingernails. It was hand-written, of course, and of course I recognized the handwriting. I'd spent hours poring over the nine authentic surviving letters written by Aeneas Peregrinus—to his land agent, his son, the sheriff of his shire concerning the window tax.

Concerning the True Discovery of Essecuivo, being a faithful account—

"Go on," he said gently. "Read it."

I thought; if only my father was still alive. He died, as Carchedonius so thoughtfully reminded me, only a short while ago, after ten years in prison. He'd done nothing wrong; at least, not the things he was accused of doing.

But when the bubble burst and millions of angels were wiped out overnight, as suddenly and irrecoverably as snow melting, someone had to take the blame. My father, who'd done nothing wrong and therefore saw no need to leave the country with a small valise filled with precious stones, put up a strong case at his trial. He always was a good speaker, and he couldn't resist arguing the toss, even when it was clearly not the smart thing to do. I can imagine (I wasn't there) him arguing with Death, scoring five or six good solid debating points; the last thing he'd have seen before his eyes closed for ever was the panoramic view you get from the moral high ground.

But if he'd lived just a little longer, and seen this—

He'd have scolded me for not finding it earlier. The niece, he'd have said, shaking his head in that insufferable way of his, any idiot would've thought to investigate the niece. And he wouldn't have said *you failed me, you always were a bitter disappointment to me*, because he wouldn't have had to.

I read the manuscript. I could have written it myself.

That was the extraordinary thing. All my life I'd been speculating about Essecuivo, making educated guesses, extrapolating castles from grains of sand. From a tiny handful of dubious fragments of recollections in old age by men who'd heard their grandfathers talking when they were children; from observations based on ancient artifacts that may possibly have been copied more or less faithfully from things that may or may not have been smuggled back by Aeneas' men in their sea-chests; half the time I was pretty much making it up, on the balance of probabilities, and the rest of the time I was working from evidence you wouldn't rely on to convict a fox of killing chickens. The thing was, though, I was *right*. Uncannily so; even my wildest reaches and most vertiginous leaps to conclusions were borne out by the tall, thin, looped brown letters on the page. It was enough to make you weep. I hadn't needed the manuscript, except as proof. I knew it all already.

—But *proof*; oh, there's a world of difference, isn't there? I felt like a man accused of murder who's made up a wild and totally false alibi, only to have it corroborated by a perfect stranger of flawless integrity. *I was right*. About everything; the height of the mountains (which I'd calculated based on an almost certainly apocryphal story about how Aeneas had spilt a kettle of boiling water over his hand on a mountaintop, and not been scalded), the source of the great river that washes the gold dust out of the northern heights, which province the red-and-yellow parrots come from. Every damn thing.

"I expect you're feeling pleased with yourself," he said.

I'd forgotten all about him. I'd been gazing at the illuminated capital letters. Aeneas hadn't done them himself, he'd have hired a local scrivener or law-writer. They were typical of the period, quickly but well executed, the letters shadowed in red and embellished with leaf-and-scroll; standard decoration for title deeds, leases and contracts. Every paragraph started with one. A small touch of vanity, from a man who could afford it. "Sorry?"

"I imagine," he said, "that you're feeling quite happy just now. I would be, in your shoes."

"Yes," I said. "Of course. And you too."

He smiled. "Very much so. You know," he went on, "I've never had much in the way of good luck in my life. When things have gone well for me, it's because I made it happen. Not very often," he added with a grin. "But this is something quite different. I feel—well, *justified*, if you know what I mean."

I wasn't quite sure that I did, but I didn't want to spoil the mood. "Splendid," I said. "What do you intend to do?"

He leaned across and took it gently from me. I didn't want to let go, but I was afraid of tearing it, so I opened my fingers wide and let it slip through. "The only thing that's missing," he said, "is map references. Co-ordinates. But most people agree Aeneas must've known them, because he used them to plot his course home. Odd, don't you think?"

I thought about it. "I guess that was the one secret he didn't want to commit to writing," I said. "After all, he was planning on going back, like you said."

He nodded. "I'm glad we agree," he said. Then he leaned back a little and put the manuscript into the fire.

Anyway. Back to the real history.

For about five years, the Company continued to thrive. True, no progress whatsoever had been made in finding Essecuivo. I don't think anyone even tried. They were too busy.

To begin with, the money that poured in to the Company's coffers came from the gold miners and bullion dealers, who had, essentially, too much money and nothing to spend it on. Before long, however, the old landowning families started to invest, and then the established City merchants; and then, as the stock price kept on going up, anyone who could find or borrow the cost of a share or two. Land was easy to raise money on; canny investors who'd already made a pile sold out and bought estates, farms, forests, only to mortgage or sell them again to reinvest when the temptation grew too great to bear. The Council started buying stock with public money—why not? Each share issue was bigger than the last, and the price kept on rising steadily.

My father's side of the business—making artillery—was an early diversification. It came about because the *Squirrel* had twelve gun-ports but no guns. One of the original clockmakers knew a bell-founder who was going through a slow patch; he leased a space in his yard and had a dozen cannon made. They happened to turn out pretty well (cannon are notoriously hard to cast), and a friend of the clockmaker who was outfitting a ship of his own asked if he could buy eight pieces just like them. Before long, the Company had bought out the bell-founder and was turning out three dozen premium demi-culverins a week.

My father's fellow directors, who were starting to worry, realized that there was a lesson to be learned from what was essentially a commercial accident. They had enormous sums of money at their disposal. One day, it would be needed for Essecuivo. In the meantime, however, there was no sense in it just sitting there. They looked around for good ideas, like my father's cannon, to put money into.

At first, they didn't have far to look. They invested in shipyards, lumber yards and forestry—all quite logical, since once Essecuivo turned up, they'd be needing ships; lots of ships, well-built, properly fitted out, the right size and tonnage, at a sensible price. Then they figured that once they got to Essecuivo, they'd need goods to trade with. So they invested in woolen mills, sheepwalks and hill-country grazing; they bought land on the Sieva river and planted a thousand acres of lemon trees; they put money into cutlery, tinware and mining; all so as to be as well prepared as possible once Essecuivo eventually rose out of the sea, shining and inviting as the Goddess of Love.

The lease on the *Squirrel* ran out and somebody forgot to renew it; but the Company's investments were all doing quite well. So, quite accidentally, were the citizens of the Republic. Every month, hundreds of people left the farms and ranches where they'd been accustomed to scrape a meager living, and headed for the City, to work in the new foundries and factories. With the money they earned, they were able to buy the cheap goods the Company's trading partners produced; families who'd always eaten off wooden trenchers now had fine pewter plates, and wore good broadcloth instead of homespun. Thanks to the three per cent tax and its own investments in Company stock, the Council had funds for all sorts of magnificent projects; public buildings, paved roads, a dam on the Deneipha river to drain the marshes to provide more land for more lemon trees. They also commissioned the Republic's first fleet of publicly owned warships, built in the Company's yards and armed with my father's cannon. They were reckoned to be the most advanced warships in the world, and more than a match for anything they'd be likely to meet, in our own waters or beyond. They would even—people reckoned—give the antiquated galleys and galliots of the Empire a run for their money, if it ever came to it.

The war lasted three years. The immediate cause was the Evec peninsula. It seemed quite logical at the time. The Evec was notionally Imperial territory, but there was nothing there; just a few sheep ranches occupied by a handful of peasants, primitives (about as primitive as we'd been, before the Company came along). The Empire wouldn't waste money and resources defending an obscure and distant outpost, it wouldn't be cost-effective. We, on the other hand, could plant the whole lot out with lemon groves. It was the obvious thing to do.

The first action of the war took place off Cape Acuela. Two squadrons of antiquated Imperial galliots sent the Republic's magnificent new fleet to the bottom in just over an hour.

When the news reached the City, it sparked off a reaction of incandescent rage. Addressing the huge crowd gathered in Aeneas Peregrinus Square, the First Citizen vowed that we would never yield, not if it took every penny, every man. The replacement fleet was ready to sail in three weeks; it was twice the size and twice as heavily armed. The third, fourth and fifth fleets were even better. But not, unfortunately, good enough.

Once the Articles of Surrender had been signed and the Imperial fleet raised its blockade of the City harbor, the newly appointed provisional government sat down and looked to see what was left. There wasn't much. I have figures somewhere for the total cost of the war, in men and money. I can't recall them offhand. Some things are too uncomfortable to store in your head for any length of time. There was a debate about whether to dissolve the Company or to leave it as a sort of midden for the national debt. They couldn't decide, so they referred the matter to committee. That was eleven years ago. They haven't reported yet.

At first, I must have thought he was prodding the fire with the poker.

That's what the brain does. It takes images and tries to interpret them in accordance with a sane, rational view of reality. I'd seen a man poking a sluggish fire back to life a thousand times. It was something that made sense. Burning the manuscript made no sense at all.

But I looked again and saw what he was really doing, and I froze. I've been over it in my mind time and time again. If I'd reacted at once, could I have pushed him out of the way and saved the manuscript? It's almost like a game, a tennis match or something. Roughly four times out of ten, I win; I drag him back from the hearth, I wrestle the manuscript out of his hand and stamp out the fire, the damage is sometimes quite bad and sometimes minimal, but at least I save *something*. The other six times I don't make it; he shoves me out of the way, or we're struggling over it and the flames surge up and burn our hands, and I let go. It burnt surprisingly quickly, I remember that. Possibly something to do with how the parchment was originally cured, I think they may have used saltpeter back then.

Anyway, the parchment burned. I stared at him. I couldn't speak. He looked at me. When the flames reached his fingers, he opened them and let go.

"Now look what you've made me do," he said.

He explained. He told me that love and hate are as similar as brother and sister, both of them forms of the same obsessive fixation on another; love and hate both lead people to do extravagant acts, to make sacrifices, to subordinate themselves to the other. He told me that when the manuscript first came into his hands, he'd more or less made up his mind to kill me, because he couldn't bear the thought that I continued to exist. He'd had his reservations, nonetheless. In killing me he'd be giving his own life, because he would inevitably have been found out, arrested and hung. This troubled him, because in a very real sense (he said) it would have meant that I'd have *won*. I would be remembered as an innocent victim, he'd be condemned as a criminal, therefore he'd have handed the moral victory to me on a plate. That, he said, struck him as a gross crime against natural justice and ultimately self-defeating.

Nevertheless (he said) he'd resolved to go through with it, to make the ultimate sacrifice—his reputation, his moral soul; to give his life and his honor, greater hate hath no man than this—when quite suddenly and out of a blue sky, the manuscript arrived, along with a load of other junk, from his uncle. It could only have been, he said, a sign, sent by the Invincible Sun, in Whom he'd never believed until then.

It was particularly significant because at that precise moment he had my dissertation open on his desk. He read the manuscript and my dissertation side by side. At first, he was crushed. The manuscript proved that I was *right*, had been all along—in which case, I was right, a better scholar, I was the more worthy, I had prevailed and beaten him. But then (he said) the Invincible Sun's true design slowly revealed itself to him, and he understood why the manuscript had come to him at exactly that moment.

I was, after all, a scholar. Unsatisfactory and unworthy in every respect, but a scholar. Nothing mattered more to me than my work, science, the truth, to be proved right. What better punishment, therefore, than for me to know I was right, know beyond any shadow of a doubt, and *never to be able to prove it*. He and I would know; we two only, joined inseparably by our shared bond of mutual obsession. But the definitive proof, which I would have seen and read, would be lost forever. When in due course, as was inevitable given the nature of scholarship, some other scholar came along with the mental strength and agility to cast doubt on my research and question my findings, I would have no defense. I would know the truth, but not be able to prove it.

And that, he said, was why he'd done it. It was, of course, entirely up to me what I did next. I could kill him in an access of entirely justified rage. He wouldn't mind that in the least; because then I'd be the one dragged through the streets on a hurdle and pushed off a stool with a rope round my neck, to die with the jeers of common people in my ears. No? Ah well. In that case, I could go to the faculty and denounce him, tell them exactly what he'd done. He hoped I'd do that. He would deny it strenuously, I'd have no proof, and (given the history between us) my accusations would be dismissed as a deranged attempt to blacken his name, I'd be disgraced, and all my work would be discredited with me. And if I did neither—well, then, I'd have to spend the rest of my life reflecting on how he'd beaten me, out-thought me, used his superior intellect to devise the perfect snare; which thought would gradually eat me up over the years, like a tapeworm, growing commensurately bigger and stronger as I faded and became weak.

I said nothing. There was nothing to say. I drank my tea, which had gone cold, and went home.

Once I met an old man who told me he reckoned he was happier in his eighties than he'd ever been in his youth. I told him that was hard to believe. He grinned at me. I'm free, he said, of my worst enemy. Myself. My past (he explained). All the stupid things I've done and said, all the lies I told, everything that makes me cringe or weep when I think of it. You see, everyone I ever knew is dead, so there's no witnesses. Only I know the truth, and my memory's so bad these days, I can't rely on it worth a damn. So, all the bad things, for all I know, they may never have happened. And that (he said) is freedom.

History, science, scholarship; the art of extracting the truth from unreliable witnesses. Nine times out of ten, the best you can hope to do is make out a case that convinces on the balance of probabilities. Your jury—fellow-scholars, minded and motivated just like you—will be persuaded by the most plausible argument, the most probable version. Thus we create a model of the past governed by common sense, rational thought, considered actions, reasonable motives. Now think about the decisions you've made and some of the things you've done over the years.

History, therefore, will have every right to be skeptical about my account of the destruction of the Aeneas manuscript. No sane man, history would argue, would do something like that for such a reason. Logically, therefore, Carchedonius could only have done such a thing if he was insane. Indeed; and it's proverbial among historians that if your argument depends on such and such a key player being insane, it's probably untrue or at least deeply unsound. Go away and think of a more plausible explanation, we say. Insanity just isn't that common.

We've now reached the point in this narrative at which I can justifiably start talking about myself. From now on, my actions and their consequences are significant enough to be worth recording. I am, of course, an unreliable witness, simply because most of what I'm about to assert can't be proved by reference to external sources. You'll have to form your own judgment of my professed motives and the credibility of my account. That doesn't bother me unduly. I invite an appropriate degree of healthy skepticism. Besides, I'm presumably dead by now, and out of it, and so I couldn't really give a damn.

As it happens, I don't remember much about the week after Carchedonius burned the manuscript. People tell me I was wandering around in a sort of daze, either not answering or biting people's heads off when they spoke to me. Everyone assumed there'd been a death in the family.

No such luck. For what it's worth, I hadn't spoken to my mother since my father's trial. She seemed to think that I could've done something. I have no idea what she had in mind. Perhaps she thought I could pull Essecuivo out of my sleeve like a conjuror. The last I heard of my brother, he was in Mescarel, trying to sell diamonds and small, high-value works of art in a seriously flooded market. Either of them, or any of my relatives—I'd have shed a tear, of course, but life would have gone on. The *True Discovery*, on the other hand, was another matter entirely.

The eighth night after the burning, I was sitting in my rooms. I had a copy of Vabalathus' *Late Voyages* open on my desk; I was chasing down an obscure reference that might be taken as evidence to support the view that Essecuivo's climate was temperate enough to support olive trees. Ridiculous; I knew they had olives in Essecuivo, because Aeneas had written about them in the book. But the garbled fragment in Vabalathus was open to at least two other interpretations, which meant I couldn't substantiate my hypothesis, which meant that I had no solid foundation for my assertion that Essecuivo must lie below 62 degrees, the upper limit of cultivation of the olive. I was tempted to throw Vabalathus on the fire, except that for some reason I hadn't lit one for the past eight days. Stupid; it was just starting to get cold.

That made me realize that I couldn't go on. It was as though I'd reached an impassable barrier; a river in spate, a ravine, the sea. I could see where I wanted to go all too clearly. I could smell the woodsmoke, and hear the voices of children playing. But, having come so very far, I couldn't cross the last hundred yards. I didn't have enough provisions to go back the way I'd come. I was stranded.

The hell with that. I poured myself a large dose of brandy and made myself think long and hard about the nature of truth.

Take, for example, the concept *authenticity*. It's crucial, seminal, to the business of scholarship. However, like, say, brandy, it can tolerate a certain degree of dilution. A translation, for example; the words you read aren't the words the author wrote, but a translation can be allowed to possess qualified authenticity. Quotation and reporting; a substantial part of what we do is picking out nuggets of lost texts from the works of later authors who've quoted from them. Source-hunting, a favorite academic pastime; read a historian and try and figure out which of his facts and assertions were copied out from the earlier authority A (held to be accurate and reliable) and which were taken from B, who's generally believed to have made it up as he went along. Manuscript tradition; we have very few very old manuscripts. Most of the works of the great authors of classical antiquity exist only in the form of later editions, copies of copies of copies of copies of the original. As soon as a page is translated, quoted, edited, it ceases to be truly authentic. But the snippet of Archelaus I'd been looking for in my relatively modern edition of Rocais' translation of Vabalathus' *New Voyages* was, by all relevant criteria, authentic *enough*;

and if only it had said what I wanted it to say, I'd have adduced it as proof of my assertions without a moment's hesitation.

Well, then.

First, I needed something to write on. That wasn't too hard. There's plenty of three-hundred-year-old parchment around, if you know where to look. Fortuitously, I have a cousin who's a lawyer. In the cool, dry cellar under his place of business there are thousands of packets of title deeds, many of them so old as to have lost any semblance of relevance years and years ago. I made up some story and he gave me a Deed of Rectification—something to do with sorting out a boundary dispute between two neighbors who subsequently both sold out to a third party, rendering the Deed entirely obsolete—which bore the countersignature of a Council official who'd been in office the year after Aeneas Peregrinus came back from Essecuivo. Perfect. How more authentic can you get?

Back then, they used soot and oak-apple gall, ground fine, for ink. It comes off quite cleanly if you damp the parchment slightly and rub it down with a pumice stone. Naturally, you lose a tiny amount of thickness, but that's not a problem; six out of ten old documents you come across have been written on pumiced-off parchment. The stuff cost money, after all, and people were thriftier back then. In fact, it was entirely in keeping with what we know about Aeneas that he'd have used second-hand parchment. He didn't, in fact, but he could have. Should have, even.

Soot-and-oak-apple-gall ink is no trouble to make, if you happen to have read Theogenes' *On Various Arts*; it's two centuries earlier than Aeneas, but nothing much changed in the intervening time. There's a fine old oak in the Studium grounds that's been there for at least two hundred and fifty years. It still drops acorns. Attention to detail, you see. Authenticity. For soot, I climbed up onto the leaded roof of the Old Hall and scrabbled around inside the chimney-cowls. I mined deep and came up with a rich vein of soot that could well have been there since Aeneas was a lad. I'm not sure I needed to go that far, but if a thing's worth doing—

Style and handwriting. No problem. After all, I'm the world's leading authority. If someone wanted to authenticate a piece of writing attributed to Aeneas, they'd come to me. Also, I've always had a gift for copying other people's handwriting. Because my father was less than generous with my living allowance when I was an undergraduate at the Studium, I was forced to make ends meet by reproducing his signature on Company bills of exchange. Now my father's handwriting was so bad that occasionally *his* bills were questioned by the clerks, but all of mine were cleared without question.

I made a trip to Corytona, where they've got two of the surviving Aeneas letters, and studied them carefully. I knew for a fact that Aeneas had written his book using a pen with a new-fangled (at that time) steel nib. But most authorities agree that steel nibs didn't come in to general use for another twenty years or so, so I used an ordinary goose-quill.

Carmine, for the red illuminated capitals, was a serious headache. Back then, they made it by crushing dried beetles—not just any beetle, but a special kind only found in Maracanto, which is why it was expensive, which is why it was so fashionable as a decoration in manuscripts. These days we get carmine from grinding up a sort of rock they find at certain levels in the mines. Everyone says you can't tell the difference. I can't. But by that stage I was in no mood to take chances. Also, I felt a sort of *obligation*. If what I was doing was justified and right, it had to be done *properly*. As luck would have it, in the chemistry stores in the East Building, where nobody goes anymore, I found a tiny, dusty old bottle containing six shriveled, desiccated carmine beetles. For all I know, they could well have been there for three hundred years. With Theogenes open in front of me on the bench, I pounded them very carefully in a pestle, added the other bits and pieces, and came up with a beautiful deep red paste. Genuine authentic carmine ink.

Unfortunately, authentic genuine carmine ink fades over time. The color I'd seen in the manuscript that Carchedonius had burned was more a sort of reddish-pink. As far as I know, there's no way of artificially fading the stuff. In the end, I had to mix in finely ground barley flour and a few drops of aqua orientalis, which gave me precisely the color I wanted. It wasn't right, of course. It was an entirely authentic, genuine and period-correct reddish-pink (the recipe is in Theogenes) and therefore, inevitably, a lie. I felt very bad about that, but really, I had no alternative.

As for the words themselves; once again, I was in the invaluable position of being the acknowledged expert. I've read every surviving word Aeneas wrote, many times. I know his turns of phrase, his verbal eccentricities, the rhythms and cadences, the pet phrases. That, and I have a really good memory for the written word; if I read something through once, I can usually regurgitate large chunks of it weeks or even months later. From my reading of the *True Discovery* I guess I could remember about a third of it word-perfect. I got that down on paper straight away, then set about filling in the gaps. As far as content goes, I was on pretty firm ground, since so much of what I'd seen in the manuscript was little more than a pre-emptive paraphrase of my own various papers, essays and dissertations. There were one or two things in the original that I couldn't recall clearly or accurately enough to feel safe about including them, so, reluctantly, I left them out. I resisted the temptation to put in stuff from my own research that Aeneas had somehow neglected to include. I was proud of myself for that. I can see how easy it must be for a diplomat, say, or a commercial agent to overstep his authority in the heat of negotiations. I'd have loved to have put in my pet theory about the little cedarwood box full of crumbly red dust preserved in the archives of the Serio-Beselli at Anax; the family tradition says it was brought back by Aeneas' ship's doctor, and I'm convinced it's a sample of rottenstone (whose properties were unknown until shortly after Aeneas' return) It'd have been so easy to drop a casual mention of rottenstone, and how my friend the surgeon brought some home with him in a small box. That's just the sort of throwaway anecdote Aeneas goes in for. But no. That would've been wrong, I'd never have forgiven myself.

From start to finish, re-creating the manuscript took me seven weeks. I then put it up in the rafters in the roofspace above the Great Hall kitchens; there's a flaw in the chimney lining, and smoke gets in there. Also, the air up there is very slightly damp and greasy. I've noticed that old manuscripts are often a bit clammy to the touch; the *True Discovery* hadn't been, but I needed a provenance. It had to be something to do with the niece—after all, that had been what actually happened, and the manuscript tradition is in itself a valid subject for scholarship—but I couldn't think of a convincing way of explaining how I'd got hold of something from the Dorcelli auction. After all, the auctioneer's clerk would have records of who'd bought what, and my name would be conspicuously absent from it. That meant I'd have to invent a fictitious middleman, or else suborn a dealer in old manuscripts as an accomplice, which I was very reluctant to do. Instead, I decided to work backwards from a passing reference in the Ancusi diaries, which I'd known about for years but never gone into properly; Ortygia Ancusa, about a hundred and seventy years ago, talked about visiting the Dorcelli and expressing interest in some old maps and charts, which Lollius Dorcellus gave her as a gift. Ortygia was an amateur Essecuivo scholar (not a very good one). My theory would therefore be that the bundle of old maps that Lollius gave her included the *True Discovery*. It works, because Ortygia died of pneumonia not long after the visit, so wouldn't have had time to go through the papers she'd been given and recognize the *True Discovery* for what it was. The papers would've been bundled away in the house archive and forgotten about. I'd been given permission to go through the Ancusi papers several years ago, but never got around to it; I happen to know, however, that the bulk of the archive is stored in a loft directly above the main kitchens.

All right, answer me this. If the person you loved the most in the whole world died, and you somehow managed to catch that person's soul in a bottle; and suppose you then went round all the graveyards, digging up the newly buried bodies, carefully choosing a part here and a part there; and suppose you could stitch all the bits together so skillfully that it didn't show; suppose you'd built a body that looked so exactly like the person you'd loved that even you couldn't tell them apart; and you sucked the soul out of the bottle and blew it into the composite body's mouth and brought it back to life—

Well?

I confess I was looking forward to meeting Carchedonius again, though I didn't go out of my way. I didn't have to wait too long. He was there as a guest when I was awarded the Imperial Medal. I wasn't surprised to see him there. I'd insisted his name was on the guest list.

He was standing in a corner. That was what he did, at any kind of social gathering. I walked up to him and smiled. He gave me a long, grim look.

"Congratulations," he said.

Not quite what I was expecting. "Thank you."

I was prepared for anger (prepared? I was looking forward to it) but not to that degree of intensity. It took me a moment to decode it. He wasn't angry with me. He was absolutely furious with the entire world.

"I've got to hand it to you," he said. (He was wearing his green-with-age black Matriculation gown, over a shirt with frayed cuffs and flogged-out black boots that would've been very expensive twenty years ago. The rest of us were in frock-coats and lace ruffs. I think he was trying to look genuine.) "You're lucky."

I frowned. "Am I?"

It was rather frightening, watching him keep the anger down. I could see, it wanted to flow into his arms and hands, but he was keeping it bottled up in his head. "Oh, I grant you, it was a masterly piece of scholarship. You followed a clue the rest of us had overlooked, and it led you straight to the prize. I'm not for one moment suggesting you didn't deserve the medal."

I was puzzled by that. "Excuse me?"

"Oh, you did. You do. If you look at the nomination papers, I'm the fourth signature from the top." He paused to take a very deep breath; I could see him exploding, if he wasn't careful. "What I never anticipated was that there could possibly be a second manuscript." He gave me a three-second glare. "Now that's luck."

I could've burst out laughing. Instead, I nodded my head towards the door. "Come outside," I said. "I need to tell you something."

He shrugged and followed me. Outside, it was dark and just starting to spot with fine rain. "Well?"

I told him.

For a moment, I was sure he was going to attack me. I was worried. As a boy I learned fencing—good at it, though I hated it—but that's as close as I've ever got to anything in the way of physical violence. I'm taller than he is, but he's got arms like a bear. No idea why, since he's been a scholar all his adult life.

"You faked it."

I nodded.

"I see." I could almost hear him think. He was having trouble keeping his mind clear, because of the anger. "And of course I can't tell anyone, because then I'd have to explain how I know."

"That's the general idea."

Suddenly he went blank. "I examined it," he said. "My first thought was, it's a fake, he's got someone to forge a copy for him." Then he frowned; puzzled. "But it's perfect," he said.

"Thank you."

"Who did you—?"

"I did. Myself."

"Good God." He raised both eyebrows. "Seriously?"

"Of course. You don't think I'd be stupid enough to trust an accomplice."

"The capitals," he said. "You can't fade red carmine."

"I used Theogenes' recipe for pink."

I could tell from his face he'd never have thought of that. "Congratulations," he said. "I'm impressed. I never imagined you had a creative streak."

"Hardly that. That's the point. I didn't invent anything. I just copied."

He shook his head. "I've always wanted to be able to draw and paint, that sort of thing. But I'm useless at it. You could be an artist."

"I've never wanted to be anything else but what I am."

I've never seen so much contempt on a human face. He moved his head so he didn't have to look at me. I felt I had to defend myself, even though I'd so obviously beaten him. "It's not so different from how all the classics survived," I said. "The original is lost, but someone made a copy. If you look past the immediate deception, the end product is as authentic as the Gigliami Codex. In a thousand years it'd be just a footnote in the manuscript tradition, if anyone ever knew."

The blank look was back. "Last month I was offered the chair at Euphrosyne," he said. "It's more money, and I'd be head of department. I think I'll accept."

I was stunned. Euphrosyne. I imagine there must be people up there who can read—a few of them, clerks and customs officials—but Euphrosyne, after the Studium. It'd be like starving yourself to death over the course of thirty years. "Why?"

"Because you've won," he said. Then he turned and walked away, and I've never seen him since.

Who was it said that the only thing sadder than a battle lost is a battle won? Not my period, so I'm not going to bother checking the reference. Anyway, it's garbage. Once you've got past the initial frisson of guilt, victory is wonderful.

I had every reason to be pleased with myself. Faced by a reverse which would've broken most men in my position, I'd rallied and struck back. I'd routed the enemy, and my cause had been just. As a result, I was feted and lionized; promoted to the vacant Gorgias chair of commercial history, elected to Chapter, honorary doctorates from a slew of provincial universities; rock-solid tenure, more money, better lodgings, reduced teaching duties leaving me more time for research. True, the victory I was being rewarded for wasn't quite the victory I'd actually won, but you don't have to go too far back to find precedents of the very highest quality. After all, everybody says it was Palaechorus who defeated the White Horde. Garbage. He was a thousand miles away at the time, busily breaking down the Sueno bridges so the Aram Chantat couldn't get across. He saved the Republic, no possible doubt about that, but not in the way the man in the street thinks he did.

The only negative aspect to total victory is that once you've achieved it, the war is over. Having spent my adult life trying to recreate the lost manuscript of Aeneas Peregrinus, I was in the depressing situation of having succeeded, totally. The question *now what?* was written across the top of every new day, and I found it rather hard to answer. Of course, I didn't have to do *anything*. That's the point of being the Gorgias professor. You don't have to teach or publish, all you're called on to do is lounge around looking wise, maybe as a special favor explaining to selected admirers just how very clever you used to be. Gorgias professors are usually men in their mid-seventies. At that time, I was thirty-seven.

"The duke," she said, "would like to meet you."

I bet he would, I thought. Who wouldn't? "It'd be an honor," I said. I didn't specify who for.

"Fine," she said briskly, "I'll set something up. He wants to move quickly, so make sure you're available."

"That shouldn't be a problem," I said. "I'll have finished the paper for the General Conclave by this time next week, and then I'd better get something down for the Alixes Lecture, but after that, I should be—"

"No," she said. "This is important."

I'd have engaged her in a discussion of the true meaning of the word *important*, but just then we heard her husband's voice down below in the entrance hall. Her room has a balcony, and there's a hundred-year-old grapevine on that wall. I hate climbing.

The duke came to see me. Appreciate the significance. He came to me. An honor. One I could have done without.

I was in my rooms, as usual. For some reason, I was spending a lot of time there, in the book room, at my desk, just sitting. I had one oil-lamp—the habits of a lifetime of frugality die hard—and Diodorus' *General Discourse* open in front of me. In theory I was chasing down a reference, but really I think I was doing what the wild boar do in the woods; building a nest where I could curl up during the hours of daylight and not be seen.

There was a bang on the door, and before I could get up, it flew open and two kettlehats came bursting in. I assumed they were there to arrest me. Naturally I froze. But they stopped and took up position on either side of the doorframe, and the duke came in.

It wasn't so long ago that everywhere you looked, there was a portrait. As a scholar, I can tell you that ninety per cent of them are copies of the Treblaeus portrait, which used to hang in the atrium of the House chapel. I could also be very interesting about the subtle changes in the iconography of the mass-circulation portraits—the significance of the white rose in the top left field, or the changes in the political undercurrents that led to the wren perched on the windowsill quietly metamorphosing into a robin. The duke himself was, of course, an artifact, a thing created, reinvented, adapted and updated, until by the time I met him there's a plausible argument for saying that he was pretty much a forgery of himself. Bear in mind, this was just after the Secession debate but before the White Glove scandal. The duke had lost about a third of what he'd owned or controlled at the height of his ascendancy, but he was still the second richest and third most powerful man in the Republic. People like that are generally too big to fit inside rooms like mine, even if they are only five feet tall.

No, you don't see that in the portraits, but it's true. What the Invincible Sun had in mind when he made him that way, I have no idea. In the paintings you see what's essentially the perfect human being; classical proportions, perfect muscle tone if it happens to be a Classical or post-Mannerist portrait, and the face of an emperor off the old coinage, back when the die-cutters really knew what they were doing. Naturally people assume that in real life he looked nothing at all like that. Not true. The portraits are for the most part surprisingly accurate; authentic, genuine copies of the original. Except that he was five feet tall, which meant, when I rose to greet him, he just about came up to my shoulder.

"Please," I said. "Sit down."

He didn't move, and I realized that the only other chair in the room was piled up with books. I grabbed them and spilled them on the floor. It was the gesture of an idiot. He sat down. I looked round for something to offer him, but both decanters were empty, which was probably just as well.

I sat down opposite him, with the desk between us, for all the world as though he was a student in a tutorial. Just like a student, he sat there still and quiet—I hate it when they do that; I'm not one of your natural showmen. I never really know where to start.

I cleared my throat. "What can I do for you?" I said.

He looked at me. His nose really was quite thin at the bridge, as in the Corolles portrait. Treblaeus, of course, got round that by painting him three-quarter face; how to lie and tell the truth at the same time. "Allow me to congratulate you," he said.

What the hell was I supposed to say to that? "Thank you."

He slid his elbows out onto the arms of the chair. It should have been a magnificent gesture denoting confidence and power, but the chair was my father's, and he was a big man. Therefore, the arms were a bit too wide apart, and made the duke look like a chicken. Of course, there's never a mirror when you need one. "As you may know," he went on, "I've been a keen amateur student of the Essecuivo question for many years. I've read your work on the subject. I find it impressive."

The Invincible Sun leans down out of the clouds, pats you on the head and says *well done*. That's nice, and you hope he'll go away quickly. But the duke had settled in my chair like a besieging army. I kept my face shut. He peered at the books on the shelf opposite, then looked back at me. "The manuscript," he said. "A triumph."

"Thank you."

"I've taken the liberty of bringing it with me."

Now that really did knock me sideways. When I discovered it in the Ancusi archives, quite naturally they went berserk. The thought that something like that, something worth such a very, very large sum of money, had been sitting in their damp loft for three hundred years drove them wild. They moved it to the jewelry safe, hired forty armed guards and immediately opened negotiations with the Treasury with a view to making sure this priceless treasure stayed in the Republic. I believe the discussions stalled at two hundred thousand angels. Meanwhile, apart from me and scholars with my personal accreditation, *nobody* was allowed near it.

Almost nobody. He wiggled a fingertip, and a third kettlehat I hadn't even noticed sprang forward holding a silver-gilt tube. It was a real work of art, embossed with Essecuivo personified handing a cornucopia to the Spirit of the Republic. He must've had it made specially, probably overnight.

The kettlehat made a show of pulling on a pair of brand new white cotton gloves. Then he brushed all my books and papers off the desk onto the floor—the duke gave him a dirty look for that, but I don't see what else the poor man could've done—opened the tube and laid my manuscript out on the desk.

Not the first time it had been there, of course. In fact, I'd grown used to seeing it there, while I was making it, and I had to tell myself, this is the first time it's left the Ancusi, this is a special moment. It felt strange, though; like being formally introduced to your son and having to pretend you don't know him.

"Now then." The duke put his hand inside his coat and produced a pair of gold-framed pince-nez. I was stunned. As soon as he put them on, he changed out of all recognition. "Ah yes." He'd thrust his hand out over the parchment; he was touching it, no white cotton gloves. I was appalled. How dare he. Not appalled enough, mind you, to say anything.

He looked up at me. "No map reference," he said.

"No."

"Which I confess I found rather strange." He took the pince-nez off and put them down *on the manuscript*. I twitched, but kept still. I could see the kettlehats watching me. In their line of work, of course, you have to be able to interpret the smallest warning signs. "Because in the *Navigation*, Aeneas explicitly states that he calculated the co-ordinates of Essecuivo in order to plot his course home."

Not true, in fact. He implies, but doesn't state. For some reason, I didn't put him straight.

"Therefore," he went on, "you would expect to find detailed map references in the manuscript."

Pause. My cue. I nodded.

He leaned back in the chair. It made a sort of soft creaking noise. Like I said, my father was a big man and he used to tip it onto its back legs. There's only so much abuse tenons and wood glue can stand. I prayed to the Invincible Sun without moving my lips. "I've been studying Aeneas—in an entirely amateur capacity, of course—for twenty years," he went on, "during which time I evolved a theory of my own about the circumstances in which this book was written, and the reason why it wasn't with the rest of Aeneas' papers at his death. Would you care to hear it?"

"Oh yes."

He smiled. I'd said the right thing.

Shortly after his return from Essecuivo (the duke said), Aeneas quarreled with his son Dives. The cause of the disagreement was Dives' refusal to marry the daughter of a neighboring landowner, a match desirable for dynastic and territorial reasons but not to Dives' taste, since his affections were engaged elsewhere. This quarrel is evidenced by passing references in the letters of the neighboring family, which had lain in obscurity for centuries until the duke, whose tenants the family were, recognized their importance. (He had brought along transcripts for me to see; he'd even had them notarized, so I'd know they were genuine.) As a result of the quarrel, Aeneas took legal advice from the leading lawyer of the day (whose files the duke had been allowed to see, since the lawyer's descendants acted for him in property transactions) and was told that although he couldn't prevent his son from inheriting all his land and real property, because of a complex entail I didn't really understand, he was at liberty to disinherit him with regard to movable goods, ready money and choses in action—

Choses in action (the duke seemed disappointed that I needed to ask) means valuable but insubstantial assets—debts, promises to pay, the benefit of contracts, that sort of thing. Aeneas' principal chose in action was, of course, his knowledge of the whereabouts of Essecuivo. Not only was this knowledge valuable as a potential resource, it had immediate value in that Aeneas had entered into a partnership with six leading merchants (exhibit three; a notarized copy of the agreement) for the exploitation of Essecuivo and division of the profits. Aeneas was to get sixty-six per cent of the net, but he hadn't put in any money. Instead, he'd agreed to disclose the map reference.

From what he knew of his partners, so he told his lawyer, he didn't trust them to honor the agreement. They were perfectly capable, if they contrived to find the co-ordinates from some other source, of cutting him out and keeping all the profits themselves. Furthermore, they would have no scruples about suborning Aeneas' clerks, servants or even family members in order to get the information they needed.

Therefore (the duke went on) Aeneas had a very good reason for not committing the co-ordinates to paper, or at least not in any document liable to be read by anyone he couldn't absolutely trust—into which category his son no longer fell. On the other hand, it would have been the height of folly to rely on his memory alone. He had to write it down, but in such a form that only he would be able to read it. In other words, he'd have written it in code.

(I wanted to object at this point, but I got looked at and decided not to.)

As I myself had proved (the duke went on) Aeneas gave the manuscript to his niece; a silly, frivolous girl, according to the traditions of the family she married into; just the sort of featherbrain who'd let her cousin Dives look at or even take away the manuscript if he asked her nicely enough. And yet, where else would the co-ordinates be but in the book itself? Aeneas had written it principally as an aide-memoire—not for publication, since the information it contained needed to be kept secret, because of his agreement with his partners. Therefore the coded information must be in the text somewhere.

And that, the duke said, was as far as he'd been able to go without the manuscript itself; except for one final fragment, which he'd come across two years ago in the library of the Connani.

(I couldn't help myself. "The Connani let you look at their archives?"

He frowned. "Of course."

"Scholars have been trying to get access for *centuries*."

He looked at me down that long, thin nose. "Well," he said. "They're quite particular about that sort of thing.")

He'd found a letter—notarized copy herewith—from Manius Connanus to a friend of his I'd never heard of, some long-forgotten country squire, in which he mentioned in passing that his cousin Orthosius had lent the services of one of his clerks, a specialist in illuminated lettering, to none other than the celebrated Aeneas Peregrinus—you know, the bounder who came back from abroad with all that money. For some unexplained reason, Peregrinus was obsessed with finding a clerk of unimpeachable integrity and discretion, bribe-, blackmail- and threat-proof; Orthosius' man had been with the family for fifty years, and Orthosius owed Aeneas rather a lot of money. In exchange for a day of the clerk's time, Aeneas forgave Orthosius the debt. What an odd thing to do, can you credit it &c.

"And that," the duke said, his voice suddenly urgent, "was the clue I'd been looking for. Suddenly it all made sense."

I was still reeling from all of that. Fury at the thought that there was all that wonderful Aeneas material out there, and the selfishness and arrogance of the aristocracy had kept me from knowing it even existed; pure unalloyed lust at the thought of the paper I could write, if only I could persuade the duke to leave those notarized copies with me. "Excuse me?" I said.

"The capitals," the duke said impatiently—surely I'd figured it out for myself, a clever fellow like me. "The red illuminated capital letters at the start of each paragraph." He scowled at me, the way my tutors used to do when I was being particularly slow on the uptake. "I don't need to remind you of all people of the intense interest in numerology in educated circles at that time."

He was quite right, of course. In Aeneas' day, it was the latest fashion. Society necromancers would tell you your fortune by adding up the numerical value of your name—A is one, B is two and so on—adding it to your birthdate, subtracting your eldest child's middle name, multiplying by the distance in miles between your birthplace and the Golden Temple— whatever it took, in fact, to arrive at an auspicious number which would enable the soothsayer to give you the fortune you wanted in the first place. I believe they still go in for it now in the country.

And yes, just the sort of thing Aeneas would've been interested in. He had a superstitious streak (black cats, magpies, all that nonsense) and just enough of the scientific mindset to make him an easy touch for all the astrologers, alchemists, metaphysicians and other chancers who passed for scientists in those days. Now I came to think of it, he owned Priscian's *True Mirror*, Stellianus' *Many & Diverse Arts* and a couple of other numerological texts; they're mentioned in an inventory made just before he sailed. Of course, the duke must've known that.

Even so. "Excuse me?"

He sighed. "I believe," he said, "that if you were to find the numerical values of the illuminated capitals in the manuscript, taken together they'd prove to be the co-ordinates of Essecuivo—hidden, you might say, in plain sight. Why else would he hire a scribe specializing in illuminated capitals, at extraordinary expense, insisting on a man of flawless integrity?" He paused, watching me like a terrier beside a hayrick. "Well?"

The true horror of my position broke in on me like the dawn. For one thing, I wouldn't be at all surprised if he was right—in which case, he'd pulled off a coup of scholarship I'd have gladly sold my soul for a few weeks earlier. As a scholar, I could feel the excitement bubbling up inside me, in spite of everything. I was also acutely aware that the illuminated capitals in the manuscript, so painstakingly created using only the finest and most authentic materials, had been chosen by me—not exactly at random, but the effect was bound to be the same.

"Well?" he repeated.

At that moment I longed for a counterargument. All through my academic life, I've had a special knack of being able to come up with quibbles, objections, plausible doubts, even when I know the hypothesis I'm arguing against is rock-solid correct. It's a gift to which I owe my rapid advancement, a weapon I've used unsparingly against better men who happen to be marginally less mentally agile than me. And now, at the moment when I needed it most, it deserted me.

I did my best. I called into question the reliability of the sources, the value of hearsay evidence, the timings, the prosopography, certain fine points of semantic interpretation. The duke fended off each attack with the calm patience of a master, supporting each refutation with arguments and citations that made me all the more convinced that he was perfectly correct. After half an hour of this sorry performance, he'd backed me into a corner and I could dodge and weave no longer. I surrendered as gracefully as I could, and he actually smiled at me.

"Thank you," he said. "As you know, I place the highest possible value on your opinion. If, as you say, you feel that I have made out a case to answer—"

I nodded heavily. He nodded back. We understood each other.

"In that case." He picked up his pince-nez and fitted them solidly to his nose. "I suggest we proceed. Would you happen to have a pen and something to write on?"

A voice, a calm and beautiful voice, spoke to me in the back of my head just then. It said; Have no fear, the numbers he comes up with will turn out to be a meaningless jumble, whereupon he'll sadly conclude that his theory was wrong after all, he'll go away and never bother you again. It was the sort of voice, speaking in the sort of quiet, calmly reassuring way, that you instinctively trust. I passed him a pen (I very nearly gave him the goose-quill I'd used for my forgery; it was nearer, in the drawer of my desk) and an inkwell and a whole half-sheet of brand new pressed-linen paper. He wrote very much in the manner of a time-served clerk or scrivener, not looking down at his hand as he moved the pen, peering down at the figures through the top half of his pince-nez. But he pressed too hard, and bent my best Capo Latto nib.

Then he did the calculations; first in his head, then by writing out the alphabet with a number next to each letter. He'd made one mistake the first time. He wrote the result at the bottom of the page. I have to admit, it did look remarkably like a map reference; the right number of digits, and the appropriate order of magnitude. That gave me a twinge in the pit of my stomach, but I thought, So what? So much the better. He'll be happy, and go away, and when he gets home and looks at a map and sees there's no such place, he'll be in no hurry to advertise his failure. No more will be said about it, and everything will be fine.

"Would you have such a thing," he asked, "as a map of the world?"

I stared at him. Of course, in the circles he was used to moving in, it was probably a perfectly reasonable request. I've been to great houses where they have such things painted on walls, with the stars and constellations on the ceiling to match. "I'm afraid not," I said.

He frowned, then his eyebrows shot up. "The map room," he said.

Oh, I thought. The Studium does, of course, have as fine a collection of maps as you'll find anywhere. I floundered. "It'll be locked up for the night," I said. He didn't need to remind me that I was a senior member of the faculty. He just looked at me briefly. "I'll go and get the key from the porter," I said.

You will never have seen the map room. I'd been in there maybe a dozen times, looking up various points to do with my researches. I always think it looks like a giant haberdashery, the walls covered in shelves filled with rolls and bolts of cloth. You take down your roll and spread it out on a twelve-foot table, with heavy ivory and ebony ornaments to keep it from curling back up again. They had a map of the world; in fact, they had sixty-six of them, all subtly different. That's the thing about learning and scholarship. The more you learn, the less you actually know.

He chose Aurunculeius' Sixth Projection; a mildly unorthodox choice, but the one I'd have made myself, in his position. I didn't ask him why, mostly because I was afraid he'd tell me that I'd argued strongly for it in a paper about three years earlier. For some reason, Aurunculeius chose to mark his latitude and longitude lines in red, and they've faded a bit over the years. It makes them a trifle hard to follow over the green and brown land, but against the blue sea they're still reasonably clear.

"Here." He was pressing a fingertip on the middle of the Southern Ocean.

There's nothing there, I didn't say; because he'd have pointed out that we were, after all, looking for an undiscovered country. So, naturally, it'd be an empty spot in the middle of the sea. I felt another of those twinges. Why couldn't it have been slap-bang in the middle of the Cian mountains, or the Great Central Desert? But no, the voice told me, that's perfect. He's found himself a plausible spot on a map, he'll go away now. He might even give you money. In any event, it's over and you've survived.

"I wish," he said suddenly, "your father could have lived to see this moment."

I felt as though I'd been punched in the head. "You knew him?"

He shook his head. "Only very slightly," he said. "I visited him twice, when he was in the Citadel."

News to me. But of course he'd have been wonderfully discreet, money would've changed hands, the right people would've looked the other way. I didn't say anything.

"I needed to ask him a few questions about the Company," he went on, and suddenly I remembered. He'd bought it, hadn't he? For a ridiculous amount of money. Presumably it hadn't been a mere whim; he'd been planning it for years, meticulously researching every relevant issue. And so, reasonably enough, he'd been to see my father.

"I liked him," he said. "I believe he was an honest man."

He could have said it to make me like him; but why bother? I felt as though my heart had stopped. "Thank you," I said.

He didn't need my thanks, and he was too well-mannered to say so. "He would have been pleased to know that Essecuivo had been found at last," he went on. "It mattered to him, even in that dreadful place."

Had it? I'd never thought to ask him about it, or even wondered if he'd had an opinion. My father as idealist, dreamer, believer in wonderful lost lands beyond the sea. Not the man I knew, but—it occurred to me then for the first time—I didn't really know him all that well. Only as someone performing the office Father; not as a person, not as a man. But the duke had met him twice, and probably understood him better than I did.

"I have a copy of the Sixth Projection at home." (Well, he would.) "First thing tomorrow, I'll cross-reference with Carchedonius on tides and currents."

That threw me for a moment, until I realized he was talking about Carchedonius the book, not the man. Actually, Carchedonius on tides and currents (properly, *A Discourse On The Practicalities of Sailing To Essecuivo*) is a fine piece of work; he's taken every last scrap of evidence about Aeneas' voyage and compared it to what's known about tides, currents, prevailing winds and all that sort of thing in all the areas where Aeneas might possibly have gone. If I wanted to know whether the freak storm could conceivably have blown Aeneas to the spot on the map the duke's finger was pressed against, Carchedonius is where I'd look.

All I could think of at that moment was how to get rid of him. "I'll have a look at it myself," I said, and realized that it didn't sound right; however, I couldn't face trying to rephrase, and he didn't seem to be listening. I wondered if he'd notice if I simply backed quietly out of the room, and decided not to risk it.

Again, in my hour of greatest need, the little voice came to me. It said, There still isn't a problem. The mad nobleman's got what he wanted, and he's pleased with you. In the morning, Carchedonius will prove beyond a shadow of a doubt that Aeneas' ship couldn't have reached this arbitrary intersection of lines, because of the prevailing nor'-easterly trades, or some such nautical gibberish. The duke will then conveniently forget that he ever did anything so undignified as make a mistake, and it'll all be over, and you'll still be Gorgias professor. For now, though, play along. Pretend to be enthusiastic. There's still time for him to give you money.

"Of course," said the duke, "you'll have a copy of Carchedonius. We'll go and look it up right now."

So we did that; and, as was only to be expected, my enemy betrayed me. Not only was the arbitrary intersection a feasible destination, it was also, on the admittedly limited evidence available, a strong contender. If Aeneas, sailing on his original course, had been caught up in the prevailing south-westerly trade winds, which can reach gale force at that time of year, he'd have been blown at that spot on the map like an arrow from a bow.

The duke smiled, and closed the book. My input wasn't required, so I sat still and quiet. I'd decided I didn't want any money, even if he offered.

"Excellent," he said at last. "Well, I think we have everything we need. Can you be ready to sail in, say, three days?"

I was not at home to the little voice for quite some time after that. I felt, not unreasonably, that it hadn't advised me well. Indeed, I might have been forgiven for suspecting that it had deliberately led me on, encouraging me to make matters worse for myself. But it kept on whispering quietly, and on the second day I grudgingly allowed it to say its piece.

True, said the voice, you've let yourself in for a long sea voyage, which is never pleasant and can be extremely dangerous. But think; you'll be sailing with the second richest man in the Republic; a man who, like you, has never previously set foot on a ship in his life. You can at least be moderately certain that all the proper preparations will have been made, that the ships and crew will be of the highest quality, and that for the passengers at least, the journey will be made in circumstances of comfort and quite possibly luxury. He's agreed to pay you three hundred angels, which is nice, together with a pro rata share of the treasure (ah well, never mind). And, when you get there and there's nothing to be seen except empty blue ocean, it won't be your fault. It's a nuisance and a dreadful waste of time, but the chances are you'll survive and come home none the worse.

The preparations—oh, you should've been there.

Our fleet was to consist of five ships—*five*; this one man owned *five* ships. The lead ship, or admiral, was the *Lion*, 400 tons burden, three-masted galleon, seventy guns. Also; the *Lion's Whelp*, 150 tons burden, two-masted ketch, twelve guns; the *Attempt*, 200 tons, frigate-built two-masted brigantine, twelve guns; the *Heron*, 90 tons, two-masted galliot, forty guns, previously the property of the Empire, one of the very few prizes taken by our side during the War; and the *Squirrel*, 90 tons, two-masted sloop, six guns; not the original *Squirrel* but named, for some reason that escaped me, in her honor.

The duke and I, needless to say, would be on the *Lion*, along with sixty men-at-arms, the military stores and most of the gunpowder. The *Attempt* was the supply, carrying nearly all the food and water. The *Whelp* had the tools, surveying equipment, spare masts, lumber, ironmongery and so on. The *Heron* and the *Squirrel*, as far as I could see, were basically just sea-going footmen, their only function being to look impressive and top-and-tail the convoy.

The military stores came first. There was a cart jam in Longacre. Presumably the idea was that, in the event that we were called upon to fight at any stage in the venture, every man in the expedition could be fitted out as an archer, or an arquebusier, or a pikeman, with full black-and-white armor and all the bits and pieces. We had a thousand muskets, best quality; three hundred wheel-lock pistols, at four angels each; eight hundred longbows, six hundred crossbows, something like 400,000 arrows (they're sold by weight, so the precise number wasn't available), twelve hundred pikes, a thousand swords, Type 18, six hundred swords, Type 15—After a while, I simply didn't want to know. We had a hundred horses—a whole deck on the *Lion*—with hay, oats, rolled barley, all that sort of thing. My thought was that they definitely had horses in Essecuivo—Aeneas says so—and it'd have been much easier to take one small chest full of gold coins and buy horses when we got there, if we needed horses at all. But that, evidently, wasn't the way the duke's mind was working. If (I was beginning to think) it was working at all.

Rather more to my taste was the surveying equipment, though I didn't get a chance to look at it as closely as I'd have liked. I watched them loading it, but mostly it was crated up, and one enormous pine box looks pretty much like another. All I could tell for sure was that there was a lot of it, though not nearly as much, by weight or volume, as the weapons. Another bulk item, which came as a surprise, though a relatively pleasant one, was the musical instruments. I was nearly pushed off the gangplank into the bay by three strong men carrying between them the biggest spinet I've ever seen in my life, followed by other men with harpsichords, violas, cellos, two harps and a tuba. At least, if we were going to suffer, it wouldn't be in silence.

Most of the food, as I said just now, went on the *Attempt*. But the duke's personal rations travelled aboard the *Lion*, and it took half a day to get them on board and properly stowed. I can appreciate the difficulties the duke's people must've faced. How on earth can you store two hundred bottles of exquisitely fine wine on a ship without running the intolerable risk of them getting shaken up, exposed to potentially lethal extremes of temperature, theft by unauthorized persons and spoilage by seawater? Nobody seems to have considered that until the last moment; so the whole operation had to be suspended while the carpenters converted the front half of the middle deck into an emergency wine cellar.

Don't ask me about the voyage. I wasn't there; at least, my body was, but the rest of me was somewhere else. My body—poor abused, long-suffering flesh—spent three weeks in a tiny box, curled up on a wooden shelf with nothing but a sack stuffed with moldy feathers between my aching joints and the rough-planed planks. Occasionally someone remembered me and brought me food; rather better food than I'd have had back at High Table, but I didn't want to eat it. Why bother? It wasn't going to stay down very long, and when it came back up again, it just added to the misery.

I don't suppose I missed very much. The sea is, after all, the sea. From time to time I asked the steward if we were nearly there yet, but he only smiled. Once, after a particularly violent episode in the course of which I was repeatedly hurled off the shelf against the side of the box, I asked him if the ship had taken much damage from the storm. "What storm?" he said. I'd have told him about it, but he chose that moment to take the cover off a plate of scrambled eggs, so of course I was sick all over his shoes.

There came a day when the ship seemed to have been sitting still for rather a long time. I didn't mind that in the least. The thing I'd been dreading most about the voyage was boredom; how naive I was, back then. When you've been subjected to twenty-one days of incessant torture, with your guts trying very hard to force their way up through your mouth, a prolonged interval of nothing at all strikes you as the sort of bliss reserved by the Invincible Sun for the blessed elect. In fact, for a while I wondered if I'd died. But no. No such luck.

I was just nerving myself to sit up when the door opened and the duke came in.

He, of course, had proved to be a natural sailor. He'd divided his time between standing on deck looking magnificent in gold braid and sitting in his cabin doing precise calculations with mathematical instruments. He looked at me and winced, and covered his nose with a linen handkerchief.

"You might care to come up on deck," he said, and left the room.

The light hit me like a hammer as soon as I stuck my head through the hatch.

"Thank you for joining us." I could hear the duke's voice, but all I could see was blinding clouds of orange, yellow and red. "I thought you might like to be present at this extraordinary moment. After all, it's your dream too, and your father's."

He wasn't making any sense. I groped my way forward until my hand connected with something I could hang on to. It proved to be a man's arm. I let go quickly, staggered, and slumped against what turned out to be the mast. The firework display was thinning out a little. I could see the deck of the ship, a clear blue sky, dark blue sea. Nothing extraordinary about that.

"Essecuivo," the duke said.

Don't be silly, I wanted to say, there's nothing out there, just too much sky and water. But he was pointing—to be precise, he was posing for the statue that would presumably one day be cast to commemorate this moment; back straight, side on like an archer drawing, right arm outstretched at right-angles to his body, pointing. At what? I looked. There wasn't anything, apart from a grayish blur of clouds on the horizon.

"Excuse me?" I said.

He didn't reply. There were four or five other men, too clean and well-dressed to be sailors, and they were looking at the clouds too. Humoring the great man, who'd finally flipped. Maybe not.

They weren't clouds. Instead, I was looking at a mountain range, a very long way away. Land.

"Captain," the duke said. "Be so kind as to show our guest the chart."

Meant nothing to me, of course. Lots of pale blue, with pencil lines; some zig-zags, with dates scribbled beside the angles in tiny neat handwriting. The longest line stopped abruptly in the middle of nowhere. Something told me to look up and trace the latitude and longitude.

"Exactly where Aeneas said it would be."

No, I thought. No, please. Not even the Invincible Sun, that incorrigible practical joker, who designed the human digestive and reproductive systems, gave Man the brain of a god and half the lifespan of a beech tree, could be so cruel, so capricious. I stared, longing for the mountains to be clouds, but they weren't. They were mountains, just like the mountains Aeneas had described, in words that had gone up in smoke on Carchedonius' hearth, that you see as you approach Essecuivo from the north-west; the Aoidus mountains, at the foot of which sits the mighty city of Aos.

No good will come of this, said my little voice. Indeed. There are times when I wonder whose side I'm on.

The wind had died away completely almost as soon as we came within sight of land. The sails were flat, dead, and the smoke from the galley fire went straight up into the air, like a pine tree.

We sat there for two days. We couldn't quite hear the children's voices or smell the woodsmoke, but we were that close; but not quite close enough to launch a boat and row over. So we sat. The duke managed to keep his composure, but he spent most of the time peering at the distant bump through a colossal brass telescope, which he didn't offer to share. As far as I was concerned, the total stillness of the ocean more than made up for the frustration of being stuck. I was able to eat food, get up and walk about. I found a quiet place on deck not apparently required for seafaring purposes, snuggled down on a coil of rope, and read a book.

In the small hours of the morning of the third day, the wind got up. I began to suspect that something was wrong when I was thrown off my shelf and bounced off the *ceiling*. I didn't land terribly well, and I was lying there wondering if I'd been killed—I honestly don't know about all that stuff; how are you supposed to know the difference between a fractured skull and a nasty knock?—when someone barged in, dragged me off the floor and bundled me out through the door. I assumed I was being arrested and taken to be executed—it didn't require much imagination to supply a possible reason—but it turned out that we'd been holed on submerged rocks and they needed everybody to work the pump.

Everybody. The duke was there, leaning all his weight on the lever. It didn't seem to be working. It was a while before I noticed, but I remember looking down and not being able to see my knees because they were under water. That made me forget about my poor soft hands and pulled muscles, and I dragged on my allotted area of lever as though I was pulling myself up out of a snake pit. It was only when we stopped that I realized I was so blown I could scarcely breathe.

We pumped until well after dawn, at which point the wind suddenly died away, the ship stopped moving, and we all collapsed like empty clothes for a while. When eventually someone came down to tell us what was going on, the news wasn't good.

The storm had blown us almost to shore. We weren't quite there because the captain and the helmsman had fought like lunatics to keep us back, otherwise we'd have been crunched against the reefs like corn in a mill. The *Lion's Whelp* and the *Attempt* hadn't been so lucky. The lookout had seen them go down, and there wasn't any point looking for survivors. Where the *Squirrel* had got to, nobody knew. The *Heron*, fifty years old and built in the Imperial yards, had bobbed about like a bit of stick on a fast stream and was more or less unharmed. The *Lion*, however, was looking pretty sick. All three masts had gone (all the spares were in the *Whelp*, remember), she was badly holed below the waterline, two ribs had cracked through and she was only holding together through ignorance and force of habit. There was a chance—say one in ten—of getting her onto the beach, in which case it might have been possible to fix her up if we still had the tools and materials that had gone down in the *Whelp*; but only if we ditched as much superfluous weight as possible. Superfluous weight, in this context, meant the guns, the powder, the horses and their fodder, the arms and armor, the duke's wine, and all personnel not absolutely essential to the handling of the ship.

They had a devil of a job throwing the horses into the sea. They didn't want to go. So we had to hood them, hamstring them and tip them off the side using spars as levers. It took a long time. I was still part of the emergency workforce, though all I was fit for was fetching and carrying spars. I was too tired to think, which was a blessing. We worked all day and well into the night, spurred on by the pleasant thought that the wind could get up again at any time. The duke stayed till early evening before transferring to the *Heron*, which stayed with us through the night. I think I fell asleep standing at the windlass. I woke up in a sort of sprawl on the deck, and every bit of me hurt.

Come dawn, we were stuck again. They'd taken a mast off the *Heron* and jury-rigged it so that, with any luck, it'd get the *Lion* to shore, assuming a very gentle wind in precisely the right direction. Which was what, about halfway through the morning, we got. The ship, what was left of it, sort of slid lazily across the water at more or less walking pace. Just as it got dark, they dropped anchor and lowered the boats. Wherever the hell we were, we'd arrived.

The duke had drawn a map while we'd been becalmed, before the storm. It was one of a handful of things he'd managed to take with him, stuffed down the side of his boot. It was based on Aeneas and the rest of the available material, and if I hadn't known better, I'd have believed in it.

He stood on the beach with this thing in his hands, looking up at the mountains. They took me to him; I was, apparently, necessary. I'd come in on the *Lion*, which very nearly made it all the way, close enough that we were able to get nine-tenths of the passengers and crew off in longboats. The rest were picked up by boats from the *Heron*, which was shallow-bottomed enough to ride in close.

"That," the duke was saying, looking up from his extrapolated map, "must be the Ieria bluffs."

I knew all about them; the foothills of the Aoidus mountains, to which (in Aeneas' day) the suburbs of Aos were just starting to extend. He was measuring distances with a pair of dividers, doing calculations; his lips were moving. I looked for myself, and felt obliged to point something out.

"If that's the Ieria," I said, "where's the city?"

I maintain that it was a valid point. Aos was visible from the ocean; Aeneas saw it on his way in, sailed right up to the splendid granite quay, which stuck out a quarter of a mile into the bay. We'd landed on a sandy beach, and there was nothing man-made to be seen anywhere.

He ignored me. "In that case," he went on, "the mouth of the river should be no more than six hundred yards to our left." He lowered the map and turned his head. I looked with him, and saw, on the surface of the sea, the score-marks and ripples of an undertow. Exactly where he'd said it would be. But; no city.

"Follow me," he said, and we all set off up the beach, the wet sand sucking at our heels. A few minutes later, we were standing beside a fast-flowing river at the point where it emptied out into the sea. The duke looked as though he'd just been personally awarded the Order of Merit by the In-vincible Sun, in a gold-and-pearl tiara. "The river," he said. "This is where the piazza used to be."

Used to be—I stared at him. That thought hadn't occurred to me.

"I imagine what happened," the duke said, "is that over time the bay silted up and became useless, which is why it was abandoned." He smiled gently. "The circumstances of our own arrival would tend to support that view, don't you think?" He turned aside and poked at the ground with the tip of his sword. "I assume that the piazza is somewhere under the sand here. A pity. I was looking forward to seeing the great bronze statue of the Founder." He shrugged. "Presumably they moved it when they left here, so we'll see it in due course."

I think, as a scholar, that the text of Holy Scripture has been corrupted during the course of manuscript tradition, in some places. For example, I think the famous line should read; Blessed are those that have seen, and still believe.

One of the others started whacking the undergrowth with his sword. I looked at him, and heard the clinking noise of steel on stone. He knelt down, yanking out handfuls of weed and stuff. The duke came and stood behind him. "There," the man said. "Look."

It was worked, finished stone, peeping out between the stubble of hacked-off green shoots.

We searched for an hour or so, but didn't find anything else. Then the captains of the *Lion* and the *Heron* came looking for the duke and led him gently but firmly away. They had to talk, they insisted, about what was to be done.

Basically, we had nearly three hundred people on the beach, the crews of both ships plus the duke's party and the soldiers. There was enough food left on the *Heron* to feed them all once, maybe twice if we all went a little hungry. A hundred and fifty people could probably crowd on board the *Heron* without sinking her, but it'd be a tight squeeze, and obviously she wouldn't be able to go anywhere like that. Something had to be done about food and shelter. Instructions, please.

The duke wasn't particularly interested. He told them to do whatever they thought fit. Then he left them to it and walked away up the beach, his nose in the map. I wanted to stay and eavesdrop on the captains, but they made it fairly clear that I wasn't needed, so I left them and trotted back to the duke.

He'd found what he reckoned was the point where the main street—so wide, according to Aeneas, that four grand coaches could run side by side without scraping wheels—came down to the harbor. Follow it up—he pointed at the dense forest that swept down off the hills—and we'd come to the Great North Road, which ran from Aos to the capital, Eano, through a narrow pass in the mountains. If we set off straight away, he said, we could be in Eano by noon next day. At Eano, they'd give us all the food and shelter we could ask for, and we could open negotiations for shipping to take us home, or, at the very least, materials to build a ship to carry the rest of our people. I was the leading authority, he said, lifting his head from the map and looking straight at me. What did I think?

(What did I think? Let's see. I thought; this isn't Essecuivo, it can't be. Through a combination of uncanny coincidence and extreme wishful thinking, we've all perceived a resemblance; but, please note, the map the duke is holding was drawn *after we got here*; after he'd spent a long time peering fixatedly at the coast through his monster telescope. The map is therefore not evidence. Discount the map, and we're back to interpretations of the text. For all I know, there may be a thousand bays and natural harbors with rivers running down to them all over the world. Maybe it's an abundant form in nature, something you always get wherever there's a confluence of certain factors—estuary plus mountains plus prevailing winds and certain sorts of tides equals something more or less like this. Therefore, the professor regrets to inform you that your hypothesis has not been adequately proved and your paper cannot be accepted for publication.

And whether or not it's Essecuivo, unless we find some food and somewhere to shelter, we're going to *die*. If we go plunging into the forest, instead of digging for turtles' eggs or whatever the hell it is people do, we'll lose our little snippet of time, and we'll starve.

If I explain, perhaps he'll listen.

If—)

We followed the road. To be fair, there was a distinct line through the undergrowth and rubbish; a straight line, of the sort that rarely occurs in nature. And that man had found worked stone. It could once have been a road, at that.

Three hundred yards or so on, the straight line vanished into the trees. The duke had a compass, a beautifully dainty little thing in a silver gilt case, that hung around his neck on a blue silk cord. Eano, according to Aeneas, was thirty-two miles due north of Aos. I salved my conscience by telling myself that we were more likely to find edible animals and birds in the woods than on the beach. I had no basis for such an assertion. I'm not a true scholar.

I'm in no mood to tell you about that walk in the woods. On the first day, someone took a shot at something that could have been some kind of pig. He missed. The noise put up about a million small black birds, which flew off screaming. After that, the only living thing in the woods was us.

We spent the night in a bramble thicket. We chose it as a camp ground because it was too dense to hack a way through with what little energy we had left. I fell asleep as soon as my back hit its unsatisfactory mattress of crushed brambles, and didn't wake up till somebody kicked me. I'd have let them leave me there, because I ached so much I'd rather have died than try to move, but they wouldn't allow it. Tempers were getting short, and fools weren't being suffered gladly. I did as I was told.

It's usually cooler inside woods than outside them; in which case, I shudder to think what the temperature must've been outside, if there was an outside—for all I know, the forest covered the entire country. In any event, it was savagely hot, and we hadn't brought any water, for the excellent reason that we didn't have anything to carry it in. Around mid-afternoon we stumbled across, nearly fell into a river, of sorts. The duke immediately claimed it was the Aloura. I agreed. I was past caring.

That night was bitter cold. We lit fires, which didn't really do anything. In the morning, about twenty of the men had fevers, stomach cramps, various symptoms. There was no food. We told the sick men we'd come back for them. By nightfall, another thirty-odd were reporting the same symptoms; we left them, too. A part of me, the part that wasn't triple-checking my body temperature every minute or so for the slightest sign of incipient fever, was doing mental arithmetic; fifty from three hundred leaves two-fifty; the *Heron* could carry seventy of us, at a pinch, and still get home. By the next evening, we were down to one-eighty and I was still all right. Now (that little part of me said) if only the duke were to catch this unknown disease and die, we could all—

The duke took ill on the afternoon of the fourth day. We'd stopped because we'd found a huge spread of flat-topped green fungi, which none of us definitely knew to be poisonous. There was a bit of a free-for-all. I'm not big, strong and assertive. I didn't get any. Some people have all the luck.

Over half the fungus-poisoning victims died during the night. By daylight, none of the survivors could move. They were sweating, twitching, bleeding from the nose. The duke somehow managed to haul himself up against the trunk of a tree, presumably so he wouldn't die sprawled in the leaf-mould. I sat and watched him for about three hours. His breathing was slow and shallow, but he kept on and on doing it. After that I'd had enough. I got up and stumbled off, crashed around in the holly, brambles and brash until my foot caught in something and I fell over. When I opened my eyes, I found I'd landed on top of a big, fat creamy-white fungus, the sort they call Chicken-in-the-woods. You're supposed to cook it first. The hell with that.

By the time I'd finished stuffing my face it was getting dark. I tried to retrace my steps, got completely lost, gave up, looked around for somewhere to sleep and caught sight of a man's feet sticking out from behind a tree. It turned out I'd been going in circles, or a freak storm had blown me off course, or something like that. Anyway, I was back at the camp. I went to look at the duke.

Ninety-six men died from eating the poison mushrooms. The duke survived. By the time I got back he was sitting up straight, the map on his knees, though it was already too dark to read. He looked up at me as I trudged towards him and said, "If I'm right, those hills over there are CataAno."

I stared at him. "Excuse me?"

"CataAno. Where Aeneas changed horses on the post road to Eano. In which case, Eano is twelve miles dead ahead."

"I've been thinking," I said. "I might head back to the ship."

He smiled at me. "What, and miss all the fun? I don't think so."

"I think I'll go back," I said.

He shrugged. "You'll sail the ship all by yourself back to the Republic," he said. "What an exceptional fellow you are. And on an empty stomach, too."

I didn't tell him about the Chicken-in-the-woods. I said; "I don't think Eano's there anymore. If it's the capital, and it's only twelve miles away—"

He raised a hand, and I shut up. "I think I'd like to be proved right before I die," he said. "What about you? Aren't you just a little bit curious?"

I thought; he's going to die, and he's talked himself into believing, so why not let him die happy? But, if we all turned round and went back, maybe we could catch fish or something. If he said go back, they'd go back, wouldn't they? "There's something I need to tell you," I said.

"Really?"

"Yes." And I told him.

I shall never forget the look on his face. Hard to describe. The nearest I can get is, he didn't believe me, and he was deeply puzzled at why I should choose to make up such an improbable story. When I eventually ground to a halt, he gazed at me for a while, then looked down at the map. "From Eano," he said, "we should be able to row down the Pelanaima, assuming we can hire boats, and follow the coast back to Aos. That'll save us having to walk back the way we came."

I shook my head. "You're forgetting," I said. "There's a waterfall at Deudo. Aeneas said it was as high as the steeple of the New Year Temple."

"There'll be a portage," the duke replied.

"Aeneas never mentioned one."

"There'll be one by now," the duke said. "After all, that was three hundred years ago."

So I went looking for someone else in authority. That proved to be difficult. The captains and first mates of both the *Lion* and the *Heron* were dead; three from mushrooms, one from fever. The helmsman of the *Heron* was still alive, but delirious and shouting at people who weren't there. At least that explained why there'd been no mutiny; nobody left to lead it.

I wandered round the camp, counting heads. By now I was feeling considerably better, thanks to the chicken-fungus. I counted sixty-one, of whom probably fifty-eight would still be alive in the morning. Then I sat down under a tree with my head in my hands and burst into tears. Nobody objected, commented or seemed to notice.

While I was bawling my eyes out, it occurred to me that there was still one high-ranking officer still alive; me. I was, after all, the Gorgias professor of humanities at the Studium, which made me an *ex officio* member of the Lower Conclave and standing delegate to the College of Deacons. I wasn't sure if my jurisdiction extended to the ends of the earth, however. Also, I didn't want to be a leader. It's bad enough dying; dying when it's your fault must be so much worse.

Twice during the night I got up, with the intention of walking away, back down the trail we'd blundered through the forest. I didn't, of course. Too scared. It had all happened so fast—the deaths, the disaster, the sudden falling-apart of everything. I tried to put my finger on the moment when we'd lurched from in control to doomed, but I couldn't. The obvious truth, which I found I couldn't hide from no matter what I did, was that by this point there really wasn't anything I or anyone else could do. There was definitely no hope if I went back. We'd come too far. If we went on—well, who knows? We might just stumble to the edge of the forest, or meet with friendly savages, or kill a very large, stupid, slow-moving, half-witted animal.

In the morning, nobody was in any hurry to move on, not even the duke. We spent a while looking at the dead—we didn't have the energy or the tools to bury them, so we left them where they lay, but we looked at them, as being the only sign of respect we could still afford. Gradually, in twos and threes, we hauled ourselves to our feet, hesitated; then, without orders or words of command, we silently turned to face due north and began picking our way.

I don't know how long we'd been going—the canopy was high and dense, so we rarely saw the sun—when the man next to me, I never did find out his name, grabbed my shoulder and pointed. He wasn't the only one to have noticed. On the skyline, in a fortuitous gap between the trees, was a human outline, standing straight and perfectly still.

Someone yelled out; we all joined in. The human outline didn't move. We surged forward, howling, pleading. Actually, I'd sort of figured it out before anyone got close enough to see. Accordingly, I slowed down and walked while the others broke into a run.

Aeneas had liked most things he saw in Essecuivo, but he was mildly scathing about their works of art. Their paintings, he said, were simplistic and garishly colored, and their sculptures were stiff and unnaturalistic. But, he added, you can't help but be impressed by the sheer size of some of them. There was one, he said, a mile outside Eano on the main road to Aos, an advancing draped female in basalt, that had to be fifteen feet high—

Well, it was too badly weathered and worn to be sure what it was supposed to be, other than a human being, walking forward. We gathered under it, staring up. There was no face. But on the pedestal—too low to catch the wind and sheltered from the rain—was an inscription, in an alphabet I'd never seen before.

The duke crouched down to peer at it, then got up slowly and painfully.

"Nearly there," he said.

History demands absolutes. History would like to say that, at three minutes past the tenth hour of the seventeenth day of the sixth month, twelve hundred and seventy-one years after the foundation of the Republic, the duke entered Eano by the west gate. History, of course, is written by people like me.

As a historian, however, I'm at an overwhelming disadvantage. I was there. Accordingly, if I want to cling on to the few tattered scraps of intellectual honesty I have left, I'm forced to say, I don't know. I couldn't tell you what time it was, because the forest canopy was so high and dense I couldn't see the sun. I can guess at the date, but I suspect I've lost a day somewhere in my recollections; other survivors I've talked to remember another day before we reached the statue, which I have no memory of whatsoever. I can be reasonably sure of the year (but bear in mind Suavonius' recent and highly persuasive paper arguing that the Republic wasn't founded in Year One, but two years earlier) As to where we made our entrance, who knows? We walked between what looked like two ivy-smothered dead trees, which turned out to be the broken stubs of stone columns. The duke reckoned they were the remains of a gate, but for all I know they were the back door of a very large tannery. And as for the name of that city; well, ask someone else. Thanks to my lifetime of exhaustive study, I'm the least qualified man in the world to offer an opinion.

We spent the rest of that day and most of the next wandering round in a sort of daze, like country people on their first trip to town. We tripped over the fallen remains of walls, fell into gutters, cisterns, fountains and what may just possibly have been Aeneas' great central open-air bath (but it was filled with a tangle of vines, briars and creepers, so there was no way of knowing how deep it once was). At one point, we definitely walked across the flat roof of a large building. My guess is that something like twelve feet of leaf-mould had built up over what used to be ground level, so we were at least two stories high; in which case, we most likely marched straight over the suburbs without knowing they were there. We found about two dozen inscriptions in the same unknown script; the duke was desperate to copy them down, but nobody had a pen or a pencil; someone tried lighting a fire and charring the end of a stick, but it didn't work.

I forget the name of the man who found the window. He was one of the soldiers, a short, cheerful man with the unusual ability to sleep standing up; I'd exchanged a few words with him from time to time, until his optimism got on my nerves. He was poking about in the undergrowth when he came up against what looked like a huge anthill, except that under all the forest-floor garbage there was stone. He poked some more, and was mildly shocked when his questing boot shattered a pane of glass. The noise brought the rest of us, and we crowded round; there was just a chance, after all, that a relatively intact building might have been used as a food store by people coming this way.

The window proved to be big and round, and when we looked inside, there was just enough light to see that what we'd stumbled across was a rose window in a tower. Someone found a stone and pitched it through. We listened for the sound of it hitting the floor, but there was nothing. Then, just as we'd given up, we heard a faint, distant plink. The soldier stuck his head through as far as it would go, then wriggled back out in a hurry. The stink, he explained, was unbearable. What was down there? No idea. But the window was a very, very long way off the ground, and it was a sheer drop all the way down. If we had a lot of strong rope—But we didn't, and even if we had, we'd have lacked the strength to hold a man's weight, all of us put together.

How much of the city we explored I really couldn't say, because mid-afternoon on the second day we made a discovery that put everything else out of our minds, and accounts for me being here to tell you this story.

It was just as well we had a couple of farm boys with us. They recognized the yellowy-green turd-shaped things dangling from the trees as plantains; a cheap, low-grade animal fodder that we import by the flyboat-load from Scheria. You can eat plantains.

Later, we decided that they must have been the fifth- or sixth-generation descendants of a grove of ornamental plantains (the tree's quite nice to look at, apparently) planted to decorate some public space or building. Mercifully, they'd bred more or less true, which most cultivated fruits don't. What we ate was unripe and decidedly bitter, but somehow or other we rose above that and gorged ourselves till we could barely stand. Then, having learned at least a small part of our lesson in commissariat management, we crammed every pocket and aperture in our clothing with plantains, strung bunches of plantains together on creepers and slung them over our backs. There were still a few desolate survivors hanging from the trees when we left, but only because they were too high to reach.

Next morning, after we'd slept off the effects of the plantain orgy, we got up and started walking back the way we'd come. Nobody gave an order or made a decision; nobody objected. The feeling was a bit like a theatre at the end of a rather boring play; everybody stands up and slowly files out, not saying much. I'd expected the duke to make a scene; I imagined he'd want to stay and carry on exploring. Maybe he had more sense than I credit him for; if he'd tried to stop us from going back at that point, I don't imagine he'd have lived very long. I don't think so, though. I believe that he found still being alive after his apotheosis moment of entering the lost city came as such an anticlimax that he simply gave up and couldn't be bothered anymore. True, the next day he was showing signs of coming back to life. He put himself at the head of our pathetic little column and made a point of leading (which meant we got lost twice). He went round asking everybody who they were, an unfortunate thing to do in the circumstances, since it emerged that of the fifty-four of us still alive, only seven were sailors; and later, two of them died of a resurgence of the unknown fever, along with three others. That only seemed to energize the poor fellow. He started making plans for the five remaining sailors to train the rest of us in the maritime arts, so we'd be able to sail the *Heron* back home. Nobody paid him much attention.

We still had masses of plantains left over when we emerged from the forest into the light, to find ourselves on a shingle beach we'd never seen before. We weren't unduly upset about that. Getting out from under those horrible trees more than made up for being somewhat lost. We spent a night on the beach in more or less total silence; then, at dawn, the duke pointed left up the beach and said, Follow me. We didn't move. He said it again. We stayed put. Then he shrugged and walked right, down the beach, and we followed. We reached the bay a couple of hours later.

For some reason, I'd spent most of the walk back through the forest trying to prepare myself in advance for the shock of finding that the ship wasn't there anymore; that something had happened, it'd sunk or been burnt or carried off by passing buccaneers. Nice, just for once, to be wrong; because as we rounded a headland and saw the bay, there was the *Heron*, drawn up on the beach, exactly where we'd left it. More remarkable still, it wasn't alone.

The crew of the *Squirrel* had had, they told us, a pretty miserable time. The storm that sank the *Whelp* and the *Attempt* and effectively did for the *Lion* had blown them past rather than into the bay, and shoved them into the path of a strong current that swept them two days' sail down the coast. They'd lost their masts, so there wasn't much they could do, until the current eventually petered out, leaving them stuck on a sand bar. The next tide floated them free, and they'd sent the longboat ashore to cut two tall trees to make into new masts. No sooner had these been shaped and fitted than another sudden wind picked them up and threw them back out to sea. They weathered the storm, just about, and slowly picked their way back to shore, only to find the *Heron* beached and deserted, and no sign of life to be seen anywhere. They spent the next day fishing, being fortunate enough to hit a monster shoal of a sort of dark blue sardine; and then we showed up, looking like death; and where the hell was everybody else?

The captain of the *Squirrel* was the son of one of the duke's tenants in Rhiopa; he'd been in the duke's service since he was twelve, and regarded him as a sort of middle-order god. When the duke put him in charge of the expedition and said he wanted no further part in it, the poor man was temporarily stunned. Once he'd come round, however, he set about sorting out the mess, and by and large he did a pretty good job.

On closer examination, the damage to the *Squirrel* from the various storms proved to be worse than originally thought. Given time and a shipyard, she'd have been fixable. As it was, our new leader decided to abandon her and transfer the lot of us onto the *Heron*. We were short of pretty much everything—sailors, food and, worst of all, barrels for storing water—but there didn't seem to be much we could do about it with the resources available. He therefore decided to make a run for home as quickly as possible. Accordingly, at first light the next day, we sailed out of the bay and almost immediately picked up a very useful wind blowing north-west, precisely the direction we wanted. I can't remember seeing anybody look back as we left the coast behind us. The feeling was more one of sneaking away before the bastard woke up and had another go at killing us.

A word about plantains. Don't let the frost get on them, or they spoil and start to rot. Therefore, don't store them in nets on the deck of a ship.

We didn't know that. Accordingly, we ran out of food with at least six days still to go. I remember thinking, how perfectly ridiculous, to have survived so much, only to be killed by a cold snap. The *Squirrel* people tried casting their net, but it kept coming up empty; we were in a sea with no fish, which struck me as entirely in keeping. I'm not sure what we'd have done if we hadn't spotted a sail, far away on the horizon.

Odd, isn't it, how things turn out. If we hadn't lost the *Lion* and the rest of the fleet and all ended up squeezed together into the *Heron*, we wouldn't have been able to sail up to within boarding distance of an Imperial carrack, bristling with heavy guns and loaded down with nutmeg, mace, pepper, walrus ivory and lapis lazulae. Reasonably enough, they assumed we were the relief escort they'd been told would be meeting them at precisely those co-ordinates to make sure they got home safe without being attacked by privateers from the Republic.

I have a note somewhere of how much the cargo of the *Fortitude and Mercy* made at auction when we got home. To give you a rough idea, the twenty per cent claimed by the Treasury in payment for a retrospective privateering license amounted to slightly more than the government's entire annual revenue from other sources. The remaining eighty per cent was topsliced to pay off the mortgages the duke had taken out, reimburse him for the entire cost of the expedition and pay the death-in-service benefits of everyone who didn't make it back. The balance was divided pro rata between all the rest of us, the duke taking fifty per cent. I got four hundred and seven angels, which at that time was more money than I'd ever had at one time in my whole life.

I wondered about that. The ocean, after all, is a very big place, and the *Fortitude and Mercy* had made a point of staying well clear of the usual shipping lanes, for obvious reasons. Furthermore, what were the odds against us turning up, in an Imperial ship, at the exact place in all that sea where the carrack was expecting to rendezvous with an Imperial warship? I'm no mathematician, but they can't be very much greater than the odds against finding a new continent or large island at a set of co-ordinates randomly generated by adding a bunch of letter-values together. The fact remains, however, that the *Fortitude and Mercy* was only the fourth largest prize ever taken by Republican privateers; consider the *Roebuck,* the *Flawless Rays of Orthodoxy,* the *White Swan*, all chance encounters, and the biggest haul of all time, the *King of Beasts*, which Orlaeus stumbled into after both ships, following courses over two hundred miles apart, had been caught in a freak storm and carried to within a few hundred yards of each other in the exact centre of nowhere.

Not only was the *Fortitude* laden with treasure. They had salt beef, salt pork, biscuit, flour, fruit, water-casks, even six dozen live chickens (though not, after we'd caught up with them, for very long). Under other circumstances, we'd have been hard put to it to find enough men for a prize crew for a ship so much bigger than our own. As it was, we were able to secure the prize for the journey home and alleviate the overcrowding on the *Heron*

1

6 »» k. j. parker

at the same time.

From that moment on, things couldn't have gone more smoothly. We had a mild following wind all the way home, the weather was warm, and two of the men who'd been at death's door with the unknown fever quite suddenly snapped out of it and were fine, as soon as we crossed the 17th parallel. By the time we saw the Belltower, the duke was very nearly back to normal. He called me up on deck and gave me a lecture on how, all things considered, the expedition had been a success. We'd found Essecuivo. True, the two cities we'd visited had been abandoned at some point in the three centuries dividing us from Aeneas. There were all sorts of possible reasons for that, all of which he'd be analyzing in the book he'd already started to write. But there was no earthly reason to suppose that the entire country was like that; and when we went back again, next year—

"The duke?" she said. "Oh, he's out of it completely. Nobody even mentions him anymore."

I had a slight headache. "I thought—"

"The money?" She smiled at me, as if at a simple-minded child. "All gone. As soon as he got back, he took a massive gamble on wheat futures. But it was a record harvest, so he's back home in the country licking his wounds. Meanwhile, the Viscount Eretraeus—" Her small black eyes lit up as she said the name. "Now there's someone you should definitely get to know."

Shortly after that, I stopped seeing her.

I am, above all, a scholar. Just because I'm a bad human being, it doesn't necessarily follow that my scholarship is proportionately deficient. I can analyze evidence, draw conclusions and formulate plausible hypotheses.

So; as I think I mentioned, I have one of those see-it-once-and-it's-there memories. What I must've done was remembered, deep in some remote part of my mind, which letters were illuminated red in the original manuscript. When I came to make my true-as-possible-in-the-circumstances copy, I remembered which letters to start the paragraphs with.

The duke's theory about Aeneas' cipher was correct. The place we went to was Essecuivo. A lot can happen in three hundred years. Think about it. Three hundred years ago, Macella was a mighty kingdom, as big and strong as the Republic. What's there now? The bases of a few statues, what's left of a handful of buildings, after the locals plundered the worked stone to build pigsties.

As for our incredible luck in running into the carrack; when we asked the captain where he'd come from with all that valuable stuff, at first he refused to tell us, quite properly. But then we explained how big and wet the sea was, and asked him if he was a really good swimmer; and he told us he was returning from the annual spice harvest at Mas Agiba, an Imperial outpost whence the Empire derived the bulk of its spices. It had been Imperial property for well over two hundred years, and no, he wasn't going to tell us the map reference, not even if we threw him to the sharks.

Mas Agiba could just about be the same word as Essecuivo, phonetically speaking; or, more likely, they're both corruptions of the real name. Now, if the Imperial carrack had started from a different point on the same land mass as we had, going in more or less the same direction, it's rather more likely that we'd have run into each other in the way we did. It was still an exceptional piece of luck—good for us, bad for them—but at least it's possible. Imperial occupation would, of course, be a good reason for the destruction and abandonment of Aos and Eano. When the Empire makes a new friend in the colonies, it likes to play rough games. I imagine the captain is still being interrogated, somewhere in the State House cellars, assuming he's still alive. I am therefore quietly confident that additional data will become available in due course, and the matter will be cleared up to everyone's satisfaction.

There was another expedition. Not the duke; he sold the Company to clear his debts from the wheat speculation, and a consortium of City merchants took over. They went to Essecuivo in an orderly, businesslike manner, with precisely one object in mind, and were more or less successful. They'd heard the story of the rose window and the appalling smell and taken a chance, which proved to be entirely justified. The smell, they guessed, was guano (bat-shit, as it turned out; the very best material for the manufacture of saltpeter, which as you know is the prime ingredient of gunpowder). They brought back a caravel filled with the stuff, and they plan on going back every year until it's all gone.

That worked out well for me. Leafing through my copy of Emulaeus one day, I found a sheet of paper I'd folded to use as a bookmark, many years ago. It was my father's certificate for ten shares in the Company, which he'd bought on a tumbling market as an act of solidarity shortly before the crash. I sold my shares to the consortium for two thousand angels. So I'm all right.

One piece of evidence I nearly suppressed; but I find I can't. It wakes me up in the night sometimes, and I have to drink rather too much brandy to get rid of it.

I said that the carrack's cargo included fruit. So it did. What I neglected to mention was that it was carrying three tons of premium, freshly harvested lemons.

JOKE IN FOUR PANELS

ROBERT SHEARMAN

Robert Shearman [www.justsosospecial.com] *is probably best known for bringing back the Daleks in a Hugo-Award nominated episode of the first series of the BBC's revival of Doctor Who. But in Britain he has had a long career writing for both theatre and radio, winning two Sony awards, the Sunday Times Playwriting Award, and the Guinness Award for Theatre Ingenuity in association with the Royal National Theatre. His first collection of short stories,* Tiny Deaths, *won the World Fantasy Award; its follow-up,* Love Songs for the Shy and Cynical, *received the British Fantasy and Shirley Jackson awards, while third collection,* Everyone's Just So So Special, *spawned his craziest idea yet. His most recent book is collection* Remember Why You Fear Me.

Snoopy is dead. They found his body lying on top of his kennel, wearing those World War I fighter pilot goggles he liked, and there must have been a foot of snow on him. Charlie Brown told the reporters, "At first I just thought it was one of his gags. That up out of the mound of snow would float a thought bubble with a punchline in it." He went on to admit that he hadn't cleared the snow off the body for hours, just in case he did something to throw the comic timing. But Snoopy was dead, he was frozen stiff, it's a cold winter and the beagle was really very old. The doctors say it might have been hypothermia, it might have been suffocation, he might even have drowned if enough snow had got into his mouth and melted. Charlie Brown is distraught. "I can't help but think I might be partially responsible." But no one blames Charlie Brown, we all know what Snoopy was like, you couldn't tell Snoopy anything, Snoopy was his own worst enemy.

Everyone's being nice to Charlie Brown. No one's called him a blockhead for days. Lucy Van Pelt has offered him free consultations at her psychiatry booth, and the kite-eating tree has passed on its condolences. And all the kids at school, the ones who never get a line to say or a joke of their own, all of them have been passing on their sympathies. You admit, you immediately saw it as an opportunity. That if you went up to Charlie Brown and said something suitably witty, maybe it'd end up printed in the comic strip. You came up with a funny joke, you practiced the delivery. You'd find him in recess, maybe, or that pitcher's mound of his, and you'd say, "It's a dog-gone shame, Charlie Brown!" That's pretty funny. That's *T-shirt* funny. That's funny enough to be put on a lunch box. But when it comes to it, you just can't do it. When you see Charlie's perfectly rounded head, and the expression on it so vacant, so *lost*, it's not just a sidekick who's dead but a family pet—no, you *won't* do it, you have some scruples.—Besides, you can see that all the kids have had the same idea, he's being harangued on all sides by the bit part players of the *Peanuts* franchise, and their gags are better than yours.

Your name is Madalyn Morgan, although none of the readers would know that. Your name has never been printed. You've appeared in quite a few of the cartoons, whenever they need a crowd of kids to watch a baseball game or something. Once you got to be in a cartoon in which Charlie Brown and the gang were queuing up to see a movie, and you were standing just three kids in front! You didn't get to say anything, but you were proud anyway, you cut out the strip from the newspaper, and framed it, and now it hangs on your bedroom wall. You think Madalyn Morgan is a good name. It's better than Patricia Reichardt, she had to change her name to Peppermint Patty just to get the alliteration, and you have the alliteration already, they should have used you in the first place. And Peppermint Patty's friend is called *Marcie*, that's so close to *Maddie*, oh, it's infuriating. Some of the supporting characters have a gimmick, and you've been working on some of your own. Schroeder has a toy piano; you're learning how to play the harp. You think there's room for a harp in the *Peanuts* strip. Linus carries a security blanket everywhere with him, and believes in the Great Pumpkin. You've experimented with towels and Mormonism.

You're sorry that Snoopy is dead, of course, but you can't say that you'll miss him. He was a self-obsessed narcissist, that's the truth of it. And all those fantasies he had, that he was fighting the Red Baron on a Sopwith Camel, that he was the world's greatest tennis coach or hockey player or novelist, that by putting on a pair of sunglasses he could be Joe Cool and hit on the girls—is it just you that thinks these delusions aren't charming? But actually the symptoms of a sociopathic mental case? He was only kind to one of the characters, that little yellow bird called Woodstock, and you suspect that's because Woodstock can't speak English, and with no jokes of his own he'd never rival the dog in popularity. Snoopy is dead, and the world is in mourning, and you're *sorry*, but you can't pretend you care. But you admit that without his comic genius there's a cold wind now blowing through the funny pages.

There's a funeral for Snoopy, but it's only for close friends and stars of the strip. You're not invited. It's quite a big send-off, all over town everyone can hear it. There are fireworks. You like fireworks.

The *Peanuts* franchise has been marketed to the hilt, and it doesn't take you long to track down a full size Snoopy costume. When you try it on you're pleased that it's so woolly, that'll keep you snug during the cold winter months ahead. Your hair is quite distinctive, and you're worried that the head piece won't cover it up properly, but it's fine, it's better than fine, it pads out all the crevices nicely and helps give Snoopy's head that soft squidgy shape that's so endearing.

You put the supper bowl between your teeth, the way you've seen the real Snoopy do countless times in countless strips. You go up to the front door of Charlie Brown's house. You kick against it three times, loud, insistent.

You know this is a classic opening to many a *Peanuts* cartoon. Suppertime at the Charlie Brown house, and Snoopy banging on the door, demanding to be fed. And you can already imagine it on the page, this is panel one.

Charlie Brown opens the door. He stares at you. He doesn't say anything. He doesn't know *what* to say. And this is the crucial moment, you know this—if he accepts you, then you're okay, and the strip can continue, but there'll be a million and one reasons why he wouldn't *want* to accept you: for a start, you're some strange kid he doesn't know pretending to be his dead dog. His eyes water. Is he going to cry? You think he might cry. Or will he be angry? Charlie Brown doesn't do anger well, his character is sold on that essential wishy-washiness of his, but if ever a boy is going to get angry, it's now, surely—and you're suddenly aware of just how *obvious* the costume looks, the zips and fasteners exposed for all the world to see, you're some ill-fitting parody of a best friend he only buried last week.

And then his face softens. He has made the decision to play along, you can see it. Or has he been fooled? Is he really that much of a blockhead? "Snoopy, where have you been? We thought you were gone for good!" he says. The speech bubble appears to his side, you can read the words clearly, his response is now official. And that is panel two.

In panel three you're both walking to the kennel. Charlie Brown is now carrying the supper bowl. You're following behind, on hind legs, of course. You wonder whether you should be doing the happy dance, when Snoopy's fed his supper he sometimes does the happy dance, but you think that maybe it's a little ambitious. And it might break the comic focus—if there's one thing you've learned on your long stint on *Peanuts* it's that you mustn't smother the gag with extraneous detail. Always focus on what the story is *about*. This isn't a strip about Snoopy doing a happy dance. It's a strip about Snoopy coming home and Charlie Brown accepting him. Keep it simple. Charlie Brown says, "I threw out all your dog food, all I've got left are these old vegetables…"

And he's gone. And you're into panel four. The final panel on a weekday *Peanuts* strip is panel four, and it has a special job—it needs to sum up the world weariness and despair that is the hallmark of the cartoon at its best. To take all the hope that was present in the first three panels and show that it is wanting. To demonstrate that at best life is an awkward compromise we all just have to buckle down and accept. You don't know how to convey all that. All eyes are on you. You stare down at the awful food in your supper bowl. You roll your eyes. You send up a thought bubble. "Good grief," you think.

And it's a wrap.

The strip is printed in the newspapers the very next day. The world is glad to see that Snoopy is back again, even if he's sporting a zip.

You soon find out, in the absence of a really good punchline, rolling your eyes and thinking "Good grief" tends to work pretty well.

Sometimes the supporting cast come to see you. Linus says, "You are exploiting the grief of someone who is suffering, don't you feel ashamed?" And then quotes some Bible verses at you, and that's so *very* Linus—and you want to say, if you're so smug and sanctimonious, why do you carry a security blanket? No, you don't feel ashamed, because *Snoopy* wouldn't feel ashamed—that was the point of Snoopy, can't they see that, he had no conscience at all. You just lie on the roof of the kennel and let their criticisms wash right over you. Lucy is more direct, as usual; she says she wants to slug you; she says she wants to pound you. The best way to deal with Lucy is to call her "sweetie" and kiss her on the nose, that never fails to infuriate her.

Incidentally, it's hard to sleep on the roof of a kennel, especially one that tapers into such a very sharp point. It took you a week to learn how to do it without falling off. And even now, you haven't found a way of lying there without the pain, it jabs right into your spine, it's agony. Thank God your contorted face is masked beneath that Snoopy head. Thank God your Snoopy head is fixed in that expression of cute self-satisfaction.

Woodstock comes by only the once. He jabbers at you, and he's angry, but you've no idea what he's saying, his speech bubbles are full of nothing more than vertical lines. And you tire of him, and you punch him—you thwack him with your paw, and it says, "Ka-pow!"—and Woodstock is lying still on the grass for ages, and you wonder whether you've killed him. (And wonder whether it would matter; if the *Peanuts* strip can survive the death of the original Snoopy, who cares about the fate of a little bird that wasn't even given a name for the first twenty years of syndication?) But Woodstock *does* revive. And he flies away. And you never see him again.

The only one you need to keep happy is Charlie Brown. And Charlie Brown is *very* happy; he brings you fresh bowls of dog food every day, and you wolf them down, and dance the happy dance for real. He's the butt of all your jokes, but he has faith in you, and you have faith in him—life will knock the stuffing out of Charlie Brown each and every day, but he rolls with the punches, he keeps coming back for more. It's harder to be a Charlie Brown than a Snoopy. You have to admire him a bit for it.

You try out Snoopy's tried and tested specialty acts. You fly your kennel into World War I, and fight the Germans. The first time you strap on your goggles you think maybe something magical will happen, that you'll really take off into the air, that you'll really have to dodge the bullets of enemy fire. And you feel a bit disappointed at first that it's all pretend, of course it's all pretend, and it always was. But there's a certain thrill to it, that you have a nemesis, the Red Baron, even if it's just a made-up nemesis. And every time he shoots you down you shake your fist up to heaven and curse him, and it's fun, even though you know there's no one up there listening and that no one really cares.

You try to introduce some of your own skills into the act. For a few strips Snoopy begins to play the harp, with hilarious consequences. For a week or two he becomes a Mormon. The last storyline is seen as a noble failure, and is never repeated.

Sometimes you forget you're Madalyn Morgan at all. Sometimes you think you really were born at Daisy Hill Puppy Farm. And when your head itches, and once in a while you're forced to pull off your mask, you see that that hair of yours has just kept on growing, there's so much of it now, and you stare at it in the mirror with horror.

You don't see why a dog would try so hard to be human. Being human doesn't look that remarkable to you.

A kid pretending to be a dog, that's eccentric. But a kid pretending to be a dog pretending to be a kid? To coin a phrase, that's barking mad.

So, you tire of Snoopy and his anthropomorphistic ways. You want to be a real dog.

You try to tell Charlie Brown. But real dogs don't have thought balloons. You bark, you wag your tail in urgent manners. Charlie Brown looks very confused, but then, that's a default setting for Charlie Brown. You find a leash, drop it in front of him on the floor. At last he gets the hint.

He puts your leash on warily. He's waiting for the punchline. He's waiting for your ironic sneer, the little bit of humiliation you'll make him suffer. "Good grief," says Charlie Brown. His hands are shaking.

He takes you out to the park. That's where most people take their dogs, but he's never done it before. Now you're there, he hasn't the faintest idea what to do.

In your mouth you pick up a stick, and offer it to him. He takes it suspiciously.

His hands are still shaking.

You realize he's scared of you. Not scared that you'll bite him, like an ordinary dog might. But that you'll bully him. That you'll point at him and laugh. He was once the star of his own comic strip, and the wacky dog took that away from him, and reduced him to a stooge.

He throws the stick for you.

And, as Snoopy, so many options come into play. You could bring him back the stick, but have already fashioned it into some exciting piece of woodwork, a model boat, maybe, or a pipe rack. You could bring him instead an entire branch, an entire log, an entire tree. You could just roll your eyes, say "Good grief," and walk away. That would be the most hurtful.

You bring him back the stick. And not in your paws, as if you're a human. And not with a little gift bow on top, in sarcastic overenthusiasm. You bring it back properly, as a loyal dog would.

He takes the stick from you. He doesn't trust you. He's still waiting for the joke.

There is no joke. And each time he throws it, you bark, and race after it, and bring it back to your master. And each time, Charlie Brown's face breaks into an ever larger smile, and the smile is sincere and free, and it's not a smile for the newspaper readers at home, it's a smile for you, just for you, his faithful canine pal.

The supporting cast come back to see you again. Lucy Van Pelt says, "What are you doing, you blockhead?" and then she starts on about wanting to slug you again. Linus tells of how selfish it is that you are putting the needs of one above the livelihood of many, and finds some bit of scripture to emphasize the point. The truth is, the *Peanuts* readership is dwindling fast. No one wants to read about Snoopy, if Snoopy's just an ordinary dog. No one wants to read about a Charlie Brown who's happy.

It's easy to ignore Lucy and Linus, because you're a dog, and dogs aren't supposed to understand what humans say.

And not everyone minds. All the kids at school, the ones who never got names, the ones who never felt valued—they're free now, they can do whatever they want. Maybe they'll become proper kids now, with real lives, and real futures, and dreams that they have the power to fulfill. Maybe they'll find some other comic strip to knock about in. It's up to them.

And Charlie Brown one morning is excited to find something growing on his chin. "Look, boy, it's stubble! I think I'm growing a beard!" He's spent so many years trapped as an eight-year-old, and now even the banalities of ageing seem wondrous to him.

You wrap up your storylines. Snoopy the would-be novelist puts aside his typewriter; he finally has to admit that he was never good enough to get published. Snoopy throws away his tennis racquet, his Joe Cool sunglasses, his stash of root beer.

You put on your goggles for the last time, and climb aboard your kennel. It's time you put an end to the Red Baron once and for all. The engines roar into life, and you can feel the Sopwith Camel speeding up into the clouds. Kill the Red Baron, shoot him in cold blood if you need to, and the war will be over. You circle the sky for hours, but you can't find anyone to fight. There's no enemy aircraft up there. Because the First World War was such a long time ago. And the Red Baron, if he even existed, is dead, he's already dead—maybe he was a dachshund, or a German shepherd, and he was a dog in Berlin who used to climb aboard his own kennel and fantasize about being a hero—and by now the poor animal will be long dead, maybe he died of old age, maybe he died peacefully in the arms of some round-headed little German boy all of his own.

Panel one. And you're indoors. And your head is on Charlie Brown's lap. And he's scratching at your ears, and you like that. It makes you feel dizzy, it makes you feel you could just let go of this world altogether and drift off somewhere magical. And Charlie Brown says to you, "It was never what I wanted. I didn't want fame. I didn't know what I was agreeing to. I was just a little kid. What's a little kid to know? And do you sometimes feel that you just want to change, to be a different person, but you can't be? Because you're surrounded by people who know you too well already, and they don't mean to, but they're going to hold you down and keep you in check, there'll be no second chances because you can't escape their expectations of you—and the whole world has expectations of me, they're looking at me and know who I am and how I'll fail at every turn. And then the second chance comes. Impossibly, the second chance is there. I never wanted a dog who was extraordinary. I wanted a dog who was ordinary to the world, but extraordinary to *me*, who'd love me and be my friend. I didn't want a dog like Snoopy. I wanted a dog like you." And this was all far too much to fit inside one speech bubble, but it didn't matter, this is what Charlie Brown said to you.

Panel two. And he's still scratching at your ears. But, no, now he's tugging. He's tugging at your ears. He's tugging at your head. And you want to say, no, Charlie Brown, no, you blockhead! Because he's going to ruin everything. Because Charlie Brown was never supposed to be happy, because this isn't the way it's meant to be—and he should leave your fake dog head alone, the two of you work like this, it's *nice* like this, isn't it? It's neat. And if he pulls your head off and reveals the girl beneath there's no going back, it'll all change forever—and maybe the head won't come off anyway, maybe it isn't a costume any more, maybe at last you've turned into a real dog—but still he tugs, he just keeps tugging, and there's give, you can feel the weight lift from your shoulders—oh, you want to shout out, tell him to stop, good grief, Charlie Brown!—but you can't speak, a dog can't speak, you can only bark.

Panel three. And the head's off. The head's off. The head's off. And there's your hair everywhere. It's spilled out all over the frame, there's so much of it, how it has grown, how ever did you manage to stuff it all away? And its color is so vivid, bursting out of a black and white strip like this, it's wrong, it's rude. Rude and red, the brightest red, the reddest red, red hair everywhere. You stare up at Charlie Brown. And he stares down at you. The round-headed kid, and the little red-haired girl.

You stare at each other for a long time.

You wonder whether you'll move on to panel four. What the punchline will be, the thing that'll bring you both crashing down to earth. But there doesn't have to be one. There never has to be.

REINDEER MOUNTAIN

KARIN TIDBECK

Born in 1977 in Stockholm, Sweden, Karin Tidbeck [www.karintidbeck.com] *lives in Malmö where she works as a project leader and freelance creative writing instructor. She has previously worked as a writer for role-playing productions in schools and theatres, and written articles and essays on gaming and interactive arts theory. She's an alumna of the 2010 Clarion San Diego Writers' Workshop. She has published short stories and poetry in Swedish since 2002, including a short story collection,* Vem är Arvid Pekon?, *and the recent novel* Amatka. *Her English publication history includes the short story collection* Jagannath, *as well as stories in* Weird Tales, Shimmer Magazine, Unstuck Annual *and the anthologies* Odd? *and* Steampunk Revolution.

Cilla was twelve years old the summer Sara put on her great-grandmother's wedding dress and disappeared up the mountain. It was in the middle of June, during summer break. The drive was a torturous nine hours, interrupted much too rarely by bathroom- and ice cream breaks. Cilla was reading in the passenger seat of the ancient Saab, Sara stretched out in the back seat, Mum driving. They were travelling northwest on gradually narrowing roads, following the river, the towns shrinking and the mountains drawing closer. Finally, the old Saab crested a hill and rolled down into a wide valley where the river pooled into a lake between two mountains. Cilla put her book down and looked out the window. The village sat between the lake and the great hump of Reindeer Mountain, its lower reaches covered in dark pine forest. The mountain on the other side of the lake was partly deforested, as if someone had gone over it with a giant electric shaver. Beyond them, more shapes undulated toward the horizon, shapes rubbed soft by the ice ages.

"Why does no one live on the mountain itself?" Sara suddenly said, pulling one of her earphones out. Robert Smith's voice leaked into the car.

"It's not very convenient, I suppose," said Mum. "The hillside is very steep."

"Nana said it's because the mountain belongs to the vittra."

"She would." Mum smirked. "It sounds much more exciting. Look!"

She pointed up to the hillside on the right. A rambling two-storey house sat in a meadow outside the village. "There it is."

Cilla squinted at the house. It sat squarely in the meadow. Despite the faded paint and angles that were slightly off, it somehow seemed very solid. "Are we going there now?"

"No. It's late. We'll go straight to Aunt Hedvig's and get ourselves installed. But you can come with me tomorrow if you like. The cousins will all be meeting to see what needs doing."

"I can't believe you're letting the government buy the land," said Sara.

"We're not letting them," sighed Mum. "They're expropriating."

"Forcing us to sell," Cilla said.

"I know what it means, smartass," muttered Sara and kicked the back of the passenger seat. "It still blows."

Cilla reached back and pinched her leg. Sara caught her hand and twisted her fingers until Cilla squealed. They froze when the car suddenly braked. Mum killed the engine and glared at them.

"Get out," she said. "Hedvig's cottage is up this road. You can walk the rest of the way. I don't care who started," she continued when Cilla opened her mouth to protest. "Get out. Walk it off."

They arrived at Hedvig's cottage too tired to bicker. The house sat on a slope above the village, red with white window frames and a little porch overlooking the village and lake. Mum was in the kitchen with Hedvig. They were having coffee, slurping it through a lump of sugar between their front teeth.

"I've spoken to Johann about moving him into a home," said Hedvig as the girls came in. "He's not completely against it. But he wants to stay here. And there is no home here that can handle people with... nerve problems. And he can't stay with Otto forever." She looked up at Cilla and Sara and smiled, her eyes almost disappearing in a network of wrinkles. She looked very much like Nana and Mum, with the same wide cheekbones and slanted grey eyes.

"Look at you lovely girls!" said Hedvig, getting up from the table.

She was slightly hunchbacked and very thin. Embracing her, Cilla could feel her vertebrae through the cardigan.

Hedvig urged them to sit down. "They're store-bought, I hope you don't mind," she said, setting a plate of cookies on the table.

Hedvig and Mum continued to talk about Johann. He was the eldest brother of Hedvig and Nana, the only one of the siblings to remain in the family house. He had lived alone in there for forty years. Mum and her cousins had the summer to get Johann out and salvage whatever they could before the demolition crew came. No one quite knew what the house looked like inside. Johann hadn't let anyone in for decades.

There were two guest rooms in the cottage. Sara and Cilla shared a room under the eaves; Mum took the other with the threat that any fighting would mean her moving in with her daughters. The room was small but cozy, with lacy white curtains and dainty furniture, like in an oversized doll's house: two narrow beds with white throws, a writing desk with curved legs, two slim-backed chairs. It smelled of dried flowers and dust. The house had no toilet. Hedvig showed a bewildered Cilla to an outhouse across the little meadow. Inside, the outhouse was clean and bare, with a little candle and matches, even a magazine holder. The rich scent of decomposing waste clung to the back of the nose. Cilla went quickly, imagining an enormous cavern under the seat, full of spiders and centipedes and evil clowns.

When she got back, she found Sara already in bed, listening to music with her eyes closed. Cilla got into her own bed. The sheets were rough, the pillowcase embroidered with someone's initials. She picked up her book from the nightstand. She was reading it for the second time, enjoying slowly and with relish the scene where the heroine tries on a whalebone corset. After a while she took her glasses off, switched off the lamp and lay on her back. It was almost midnight, but cold light filtered through the curtains. Cilla sat up again, put her glasses on and pulled a curtain aside. The town lay tiny and quiet on the shore of the lake, the mountain beyond backlit by the eerie glow of the sun skimming just below the horizon. The sight brought a painful sensation Cilla could neither name nor explain. It was like a longing, worse than anything she had ever experienced, but for *what* she had no idea. Something tremendous waited out there. Something wonderful was going to happen, and she was terrified that she would miss it.

Sara had fallen asleep, her breathing deep and steady. The Cure trickled out from her earphones. It was a song Cilla liked. She got back into bed and closed her eyes, listening to Robert sing of hands in the sky for miles and miles.

Cilla was having breakfast in the kitchen when she heard the crunch of boots on gravel through the open front door. Mum sat on the doorstep in faded jeans and clogs and her huge grey cardigan, a cup in her hands. She set it down and rose to greet the visitor. Cilla rose from the table and peeked outside. Johann wasn't standing very close to Mum, but it was as if he was towering over her. He wore a frayed blue anorak that hung loose on his thin frame, his grime-encrusted work trousers tucked into green rubber boots. His face lay in thick wrinkles like old leather, framed by a shock of white hair. He gave off a rancid, goatlike odor that made Cilla put her hand over her nose and mouth. If Mum was bothered by it, she didn't let on.

"About time you came back, ståårs," he said. He called her a girl. No one had called Mum a girl before. "It's been thirty years. Did you forget about us?"

"Of course not, Uncle," said Mum. "I just chose to live elsewhere, that's all." Her tone was carefully neutral.

Johann leaned closer to Mum. "And you came back just to help tear the house down. You're a hateful little bitch. No respect for the family."

If Mum was upset, she didn't show it. "You know that we don't have a choice. And it's not okay to talk to me like that, Johann."

Johann's eyes softened. He looked down at his boots. "I'm tired," he said.

"I know," said Mum. "Are you comfortable at Otto's?"

Cilla must have made a noise, because Johann turned his head toward her. He stuck out his hand in a slow wave. "Oh, hello there. Did you bring both children, Marta? How are they? Any of them a little strange? Good with music? Strange dreams? Monsters under the bed?" He grinned. His teeth were a brownish yellow."

"You need to go now, Johann," said Mum.

"Doesn't matter if you move south," Johann said. "Can't get it out of your blood." He left, rubber boots crunching on the gravel path.

Mum wrapped her cardigan more tightly around herself and came inside. "What was that about?" Cilla said.

"Johann has all sorts of ideas."

"Is he talking about why we have so much craziness in the family?"

"Johann thinks it's a curse." She smiled at Cilla and patted her cheek.

"He's very ill. We're sensitive, that's all. We have to take care of ourselves."

Cilla leaned her forehead against Mum's shoulder. Her cardigan smelled of wool and cold air. "What if me or Sara gets sick?"

"Then we'll handle it," said Mum. "You'll be fine."

What everyone knew was this: that sometime in the late nineteenth century a woman named Märet came down from the mountain and married Jacob Jonsson. They settled in Jacob's family home, and she bore him several children, most of whom survived to adulthood, although not unscathed. According to the story, Märet was touched. She saw strange things, and occasionally did and said strange things too. Märet's children, and their children in turn, were plagued by frail nerves and hysteria; people applied more modern terms as time passed.

Alone of all her siblings, Cilla's mother had no symptoms. That was no guarantee, of course. Ever since Cilla had been old enough to understand what the story really meant, she had been waiting for her or Sara to catch it, *that*, the disease. Mum said they weren't really at risk since Dad's family had no history of mental illness, and anyway they had grown up in a stable environment. Nurture would triumph over nature. Negative thinking was not allowed. It seemed, though, as if Sara might continue the tradition.

Sara was sitting under the bed covers with her back to the wall, eyes closed, Robert Smith wailing in her earphones. She opened her eyes when Cilla shut the door.

"Johann was here." Cilla wrinkled her nose. "He smells like goat."

"Okay," said Sara. Her eyes were a little glazed.

"Are you all right?" Sara rubbed her eyes.

"It's the thing."

Cilla sat next to her on the bed, taking Sara's hand. She was cold, her breathing shallow; Cilla could feel the pulse hammering in her wrist. Sara was always a little on edge, but sometimes it got worse. She had said that it felt like something horrible was about to happen, but she couldn't say exactly what, just a terrible sense of doom. It had started about six months ago, about the same time that she got her first period.

"Want me to get Mum?" Cilla said as always.

"No. It's not that bad." said Sara, as usual. She leaned back against the wall, closing her eyes.

Sara had lost it once in front of Mum. Mum didn't take it well. She had told Sara to snap out of it, that there was nothing wrong with her, that she was just having hysterics. After that, Sara kept it to herself. In this, if in nothing else, Cilla was allowed to be her confidante. In a way, Mum was right: compared to paranoid schizophrenia, a little anxiety wasn't particularly crazy. Not that it helped Sara any.

"You can pinch me if it makes you feel better." Cilla held out her free arm. She always did what she could to distract Sara.

"Brat."

"Ass."

Sara smiled a little. She looked down at Cilla's hand in hers, suddenly wrenching it around so that it landed on her sister's leg.

"Why are you hitting yourself? Stop hitting yourself!" she shouted in mock horror.

There was a knock on the door. Mum opened it without waiting for an answer. She was dressed in rubber boots and a bright yellow raincoat over her cardigan. "I'm going to the house now, if you want to come."

"Come on, brat," said Sara, letting go of Cilla's hand.

The driveway up to the house was barely visible under the weeds. Two middle-aged men in windbreakers and rubber boots were waiting in the front yard. Mum pointed at them.

"That's Otto and Martin!" Mum waved at them through the window.

"I thought there were six cousins living up here," said Sara.

"There are," said Mum. "But the others aren't well. It's just Otto and Martin today."

They stepped out into cold, wet air. Cilla was suddenly glad of her thick jeans and knitted sweater. Sara, who had refused to wear any of the (stupid and embarrassing) sweaters Mum offered, was shivering in her black tights and thin long-sleeved shirt.

The cousins greeted each other with awkward hugs. Otto and Martin were in their fifties, both with the drawn-out Jonsson look: tall and sinewy with watery blue eyes, a long jaw, and wide cheekbones. Martin was a little shorter and younger, with fine black hair that stood out from his head like a dark dandelion. Otto, balding and with a faraway look, only nodded and wouldn't shake hands.

This close, the old house looked ready to fall apart. The red paint was flaking in thick layers, the steps up to the front door warped. Some of the windowpanes were covered with bits of white plastic and duct tape.

Mum waved towards the house. "Johann's not with you?"

Martin shrugged, taking a set of keys from his pocket. "He didn't want to be here for this. All right. We'll start with going through the rooms one by one, seeing what we can salvage. Otto has pen and paper to make a list."

"You haven't been in here until now?" said Mum.

"We've been cleaning a little. Johann only used a couple of the rooms, but it was bad. The smell should be bearable now."

Otto opened the door. Johann's unwashed stench wafted out in a sour wave. "You get used to it." He ducked his head under the lintel and went inside.

Johann had used two rooms and the kitchen on the ground floor. Neither Cilla nor Sara could bring themselves to enter them, the stench of filth and rot so strong it made them gag. By the light coming in through the door, Cilla could see piles of what looked like rags, stacks of newspapers, and random furniture.

"There was a layer of milk cartons and cereal boxes this high on the floors in there," said Martin, pointing to his knee. "The ones at the bottom were from the seventies."

"I don't think he ate much else," Otto filled in. "He refuses to eat anything but corn flakes and milk at my house. He says all other food is poisoned."

Otto, Martin, and Mum looked at each other.

Mum shrugged. "That's how it is."

Otto sucked air in between pursed lips, the quiet *jo* that acknowledged and ended the subject.

The smell wasn't as bad in the rest of the house; Johann seemed to have barricaded himself in his two rooms. The sitting room was untouched. Daylight filtered in through filthy window panes, illuminating furniture that looked hand-made and ancient: cabinets painted with flower designs, a wooden sofa with a worn seat, a rocking chair with the initials O. J. and the date 1898.

"It looks just like when we were kids," said Mum.

"Doesn't it?" said Otto.

Cilla returned to the entryway, peering up the stairs to the next floor. "What about upstairs? Can we go upstairs?"

"Certainly," said Martin. "Let me go first and turn on the lights."

He took a torch from his pocket, lighting his way as he walked up the stairs. Sara and Cilla followed him.

The top of the stairs ended in a narrow corridor, where doors opened to the master bedroom and two smaller rooms with two beds in each.

"How many people lived here?" Cilla peered into the master bedroom.

"Depends on when you mean," Martin replied. "Your grandmother had four siblings altogether. And I think there was at least a cousin or two of theirs living here during harvest, too."

"But there are only four single beds," said Sara from the doorway of another room.

Martin shrugged. "People shared beds."

"But you didn't live here all the time, right?"

"No, no. My mother moved out when she got married. I grew up in town. Everyone except Johann moved out."

"There are more stairs over here," said Sara from further away.

"That's the attic," said Martin. "You can start making lists of things up there." He handed Cilla his torch, a pen, and a sheaf of paper. "Mind your step."

The attic ran the length of the house, divided into compartments. Each compartment was stacked with stuff: boxes, furniture, old skis, kick-sleds, a bicycle. The little windows and the weak light bulb provided enough light that they didn't need the torch. Cilla started in one end of the attic, Sara in the other, less sorting and more rooting around. After a while, Mum came upstairs.

"There's a huge chest here," said Sara after a while, pushing a stack of boxes to the side.

Cilla left her list and came over to look. It was a massive blue chest with a rounded lid, faded and painted with flowers.

"Let me see," said Mum from behind them.

Mum came forward, knelt in front of the chest, and opened it, the lid lifting with a groan. It was filled almost to the brim with neatly folded white linen, sprinkled with mothballs. In a corner sat some bundles wrapped in tissue paper.

Mum shone her torch into the chest. "This looks like a hope chest." She carefully lifted the tissue paper and uncovered red wool. She handed the torch to Cilla, using both hands to lift the fabric up. It was a full-length skirt, the cloth untouched by vermin.

"Pretty," said Sara. She took the skirt, holding it up to her waist.

"There's more in here," said Mum, moving tissue paper aside. "A shirt, an apron, and a shawl. A whole set. It could be Märet's."

"Like what she got married in?" said Cilla.

"Maybe so," said Mum.

"It's my size," said Sara. "Can I try it on?"

"Not now. Keep doing lists." Mum took the skirt back, carefully folding it and putting it back into the chest.

Sara kept casting glances at the chest the rest of the morning. When Cilla caught her looking, Sara gave her the finger.

Later in the afternoon, Mum emptied a cardboard box and put the contents from the hope chest in it. "I'm taking this over to Hedvig's. I'm sure she can tell us who it belonged to."

After dinner, Mum unpacked the contents of the hope chest in Hedvig's kitchen. There were six bundles in all: the red skirt with a matching bodice, a red shawl, a white linen shift, a long apron striped in red and black, and a black purse embroidered with red flowers. Hedvig picked up the purse and ran a finger along the petals.

"This belonged to Märet." Hedvig smiled. "She showed me these once, before she passed away. That's what she wore when she came down from the mountain," she said. "I thought they were gone. I'm very glad you found them."

"How old were you when she died?" said Sara.

"It was in twenty-one, so I was fourteen. It was terrible." Hedvig shook her head. "She died giving birth to Nils, your youngest great uncle. It was still common back then."

Cilla fingered the skirt. Out in daylight, the red wool was bright and luxurious, like arterial blood. "What was she like?"

Hedvig patted the purse. "Märet was… a peculiar woman," she said eventually.

"Was she really crazy?" Cilla said.

"Crazy? I suppose she was. She certainly passed something on. The curse, like Johann says. But that's silly. She came here to help with harvest, you know, and she fell in love with your great-grandfather. He didn't know much about her. No one did, except that she was from somewhere northeast of here."

"I thought she came down from the mountain," I said.

Hedvig smiled. "Yes, she would say that when she was in the mood."

"What about those things, anyway?" Sara said. "Are they fairies?"

"What?" Hedvig gave her a blank look.

"The vittra," Cilla filled in helpfully. "The ones that live on the mountain."

"Eh," said Hedvig. "Fairies are cute little things that prance about in meadows. The vittra look like humans, but taller and more handsome. And it's *inside* the mountain, not on it." She had brightened visibly, becoming more animated as she spoke. "There were always stories about vittra living up there. Sometimes they came down to trade with the townspeople. You had to be careful with them, though. They could curse you or kill you if you crossed them. But they had the fattest cows, and the finest wool, and beautiful silver jewelry. Oh, and they liked to dress in red." Hedvig indicated the skirt Cilla had in her lap. "And sometimes they came to dance with the local young men and women, even taking one away for marriage. And when a child turned out to have nerve problems, they said it was because someone in the family had passed on vittra blood…"

"But did you meet any?" Sara blurted.

Hedvig laughed. "Of course not. There would be some odd folk showing up to sell their things in town, but they were mostly Norwegians or from those *really* small villages up north where everyone's their own uncle."

Sara burst out giggling.

"Auntie!" Mum looked scandalized.

Hedvig waved a hand at her. "I'm eighty-seven years old. I can say whatever I like."

"But what about Märet?" Cilla leaned forward.

"Mother, yes." Hedvig poured a new cup of coffee, arm trembling under the weight of the thermos. "She was a bit strange, I suppose. She really *was* tall for a woman, and she would say strange things at the wrong time, talk to animals, things like that. People would joke about vittra blood."

"What do you think?" said Sara.

"I think she must have had a hard life, to run away from her family and never speak of them again." Hedvig gently took the skirt from Cilla and folded it.

"But the red…"

Hedvig shook her head and smiled. "It was an expensive color back then. Saying someone wore red meant they were rich. This probably cost Märet a lot." She put the clothes back in the cardboard box and closed it.

Cilla stayed up until she was sure everyone else had gone to bed. It took ages. Sara wrote in her journal until one o' clock and then took some time to fall asleep, Robert Smith still whining in her ears.

The cardboard box was sitting on the kitchen sofa, the silk paper in a pile next to it. Cilla lifted the lid, uncovering red wool that glowed in the half-dawn. The shift and the skirt were too long and very tight around the stomach. She kept the skirt unbuttoned and rolled the waistline down, hoisting it so the hem wouldn't trip her up. She tied the apron tight around her waist to hold everything up, and clipped the purse onto the apron string. The bodice was too loose on her flat chest and wouldn't close at the waist, so she let it hang open and tied the shawl over her shoulders.

It was quiet outside, the horizon glowing an unearthly gold, the rest of the sky shifting in blue and green. The birds were quiet. The moon was up, a tiny crescent in the middle of the sky. The air was cold and wet; the grass swished against the skirt, leaving moisture pearling on the wool. Cilla could see all the way down to the lake and up to the mountain. She took her glasses off and put them in the purse. Now she was one of the vittra, coming down from the mountain, heading for the river. She was tall and graceful, her step quiet. She danced as she went, barefoot in the grass.

A sliver of sun peeking over the horizon broke the spell. Cilla's feet were suddenly numb with cold. She went back into the house and took everything off again, fished her glasses out, and folded the clothes into the cardboard box. It was good wool; the dew brushed off without soaking into the skirt. When Cilla slipped into bed again, it was only a little past two. The linen was warm and smooth against the cold soles of her feet.

They returned to the family house the following day. Sara decided that wading through debris in the attic was stupid and sulked on a chair out-side. Cilla spent the day writing more lists. She found more skis, some snowshoes, a cream separator, dolls, a half-finished sofa bed, and a sewing table that was in almost perfect condition.

Johann showed up in the afternoon. Martin and Otto seemed to think he was going to make a scene, because they walked out and met him far down the driveway. Eventually they returned, looking almost surprised, with Johann walking beside them, his hands clasped behind his back. When Cilla next saw him, he had sat down in a chair next to Sara. Sara had a shirtsleeve over her nose and mouth, but she was listening to him talk with rapt attention. Johann left again soon after. Sara wouldn't tell Cilla what they'd spoken about, but her eyes were a little wider than usual, and she kept knocking things over.

When they returned to Hedvig's house, Sara decided to try on Märet's dress. On her, the skirt wasn't too long or too tight; it cinched her waist just so, ending neatly at her ankle. The bodice fit like it was tailor-made for her as well, tracing the elegant tapering curve of her back from shoulder to hip. She looked like she'd just stepped out of a story. It made Cilla's chest feel hollow.

Sara caught her gaze in the mirror and made a face. "It looks stupid."

She plucked at the skirt. "The red is way too bright. I wonder if you could dye it black? Because that would look awesome."

Cilla looked at her own reflection, just visible beyond Sara's red splendor. She was short and barrel-shaped, eyes tiny behind her glasses. There were food stains on her sweater. "*You* look stupid," she managed.

Mum was scrubbing potatoes in the kitchen when Cilla came downstairs.

"Who's getting the dress, Mum? Because Sara wants to dye it black."

"Oh ho?" said Mum. "Probably not, because it's not hers."

"Can I have it?" Cilla shifted her weight from foot to foot. "I wouldn't do anything to it."

"No, love. It belongs to Hedvig."

"But she's *old*. She won't use it."

Mum turned and gave Cilla a long look, eyebrows low. "It belonged to her *mother*, Cilla. How would you feel if you found my wedding dress, and someone gave it away to some relative instead?"

"She has everything else," Cilla said. "I don't have anything from great-gran."

"I'm sure we can find something from the house," said Mum. "But not the dress. It means a lot to Hedvig. Think of someone else's feelings for a change."

Sara came down a little later with the same request. Mum yelled at her.

Maybe it was because of Mum's outburst, but Sara became twitchier as the evening passed on. Finally she muttered something about going for a walk and shrugged into her jacket. Cilla hesitated a moment and then followed.

"Fuck off," Sara muttered without turning her head when Cilla came running after her.

"No way," said Cilla. Sara sighed and rolled her eyes. She increased her pace until Cilla had to half-jog to keep up. They said nothing until they came down to the lake's shore, a stretch of rounded river stones that made satisfying billiard-ball noises under Cilla's feet.

Sara sat down on one of the larger rocks and dug out a soft ten-pack of cigarettes. She shook one out and lit it. "Tell Mum and I'll kill you."

"I know." Cilla sat down next to her. "Why are you being so weird? Ever since you talked to Johann."

Sara took a drag on her cigarette and blew the smoke out through her nose. She shrugged. Her eyes looked wet. "He made me understand some things, is all."

"Like what?"

"Like I'm not crazy. Like none of us are." She looked out over the lake. "We should stay here. Maybe we'd survive." Her eyes really were wet now. She wiped at them with her free hand.

Cilla felt cold trickle down her back. "What are you on about?"

Sara rubbed her forehead. "You have to promise not to tell anyone, because if you tell anyone bad stuff will happen, okay? Shit is going to happen just because I'm telling *you*. But I'll tell you because you're my little sis." She slapped a quick rhythm on her thigh. "Okay. So it's like this—the world is going to end soon. It's going to end in ninety-six."

Cilla blinked. "How would you know?"

"It's in the newspapers, if you look. The Gulf War, yeah? That's when it started. Saddam Hussein is going to take revenge and send nukes, and then the U.S. will nuke back, and then Russia jumps in. And then there'll be nukes everywhere, and we're dead. Or we'll die in the nuclear winter, 'cause they might not nuke Sweden, but there'll be nothing left for us." Sara's eyes were a little too wide.

"Okay," Cilla said, slowly. "But how do you *know* all this is going to happen?"

"I can see the signs. In the papers. And I just… know. Like someone told me. The twenty-third of February in ninety-six, that's when the world ends. I mean, haven't you noticed that something's really really *wrong*?"

Cilla dug her toe into the stones. "It's the opposite."

"What?" There was no question mark to Sara's tone.

"Something wonderful," Cilla said. Her cheeks were hot. She focused her eyes on her toe.

"You're a fucking idiot." Sara turned her back, demonstratively, and lit a new cigarette.

Cilla never could wait her out. She walked back home alone.

On midsummer's eve, they had a small feast. There was pickled herring and new potatoes, smoked salmon, fresh strawberries and cream, spiced schnapps for Mum and Hedvig. It was past ten when Cilla pulled on Sara's sleeve.

"We have to go pick seven kinds of flowers," she said.

Sara rolled her eyes. "That's kid stuff. I have a headache," she said, standing up. "I'm going to bed."

Cilla remained at the table with her mother and great-aunt, biting her lip.

Mum slipped an arm around her shoulder. "Picking seven flowers is an old, old tradition," she said. "There's nothing silly about it."

"I don't feel like it anymore," Cilla mumbled.

Mum chuckled gently. "Well, if you change your mind, tonight is when you can stay up for as long as you like."

"Just be careful," said Hedvig. "The vittra might be out and about." She winked conspiratorially at Cilla.

At Hedvig's dry joke, Cilla suddenly knew with absolute certainty what she had been pining for, that wonderful *something* waiting out there. She remained at the table, barely able to contain her impatience until Mum and Hedvig jointly decided to go to bed.

Mum kissed Cilla's forehead. "Have a nice little midsummer's eve, love. I'll leave the cookies out."

Cilla made herself smile at her mother's patronizing remark, and waited for the house to go to sleep.

She had put the dress on right this time, as well as she could, and clutched seven kinds of flowers in her left hand—buttercup, clover, geranium, catchfly, bluebells, chickweed, and daisies. She stood at the back of the house, on the slope facing the mountain. It was just past midnight, the sky a rich blue tinged with green and gold. The air had a sharp and herbal scent. It was very quiet.

Cilla raised her arms. "I'm ready," she whispered. In the silence that followed, she thought she could hear snatches of music. She closed her eyes and waited. When she opened them again, the vittra had arrived.

They came out from between the pine trees, walking in pairs, all dressed in red and white: the women wore red skirts and shawls and the men long red coats. Two of them were playing the fiddle, a slow and eerie melody in a minor key.

A tall man walked at the head of the train, dressed entirely in white. His hair was long and dark and very fine. There was something familiar about the shape of his face and the translucent blue of his eyes. For a moment, those eyes stared straight into Cilla's. It was like receiving an electric shock; it reverberated down into her stomach. Then he shifted his gaze and looked beyond her to where Sara was standing wide-eyed by the corner of the house in her oversized sleeping t-shirt. He walked past Cilla without sparing her another glance.

The beautiful man from the mountain approached Sara where she stood clutching the edge of the rain barrel. He put a hand on her arm and said something to her that Cilla couldn't hear. Whatever it was, it made Sara's face flood with relief. She took his hand, and they walked past Cilla to the rest of the group. The fiddle players started up their slow wedding march, and the procession returned to the mountain. Sara never looked back.

Cilla told them that Sara must have taken the dress, that she herself had gone to bed not long after the others. She told them of Sara's doomsday vision and her belief that she could tell the future by decoding secret messages in the newspaper. When the search was finally abandoned, the general opinion was that Sara had had a bout of psychotic depression and gone into the wild, where she had either fallen into a body of water or died of exposure somewhere she couldn't be found. Up there, you can die of hypothermia even in summer. Cilla said nothing of the procession, or of the plastic bag in her suitcase where Märet's dress lay cut into tiny strips.

She kept the bag for a long time.

DOMESTIC MAGIC

STEVE RASNIC TEM AND MELANIE TEM

Steve Rasnic Tem and Melanie Tem's [www.m-s-tem.com] *collaborations include the multi-genre story collection* In Concert *and the award-winning novella and novel* The Man on the Ceiling. *They are past winners of the Bram Stoker, British Fantasy, and World Fantasy awards. Melanie Tem is also a published poet, an oral storyteller, and several of her plays have been produced. Steve Rasnic Tem's latest books include the novel* Deadfall Hotel, *and the collections* Ugly Behavior *and* Onion Songs.

Felix didn't hate his mother, but got so mad at her so often she probably thought he did. Sometimes his anger scared him, that she might be right when she said thoughts could make things happen.

That was what made him so mad—that she said and believed ridiculous stuff and she almost got him believing it, too. And she didn't take care of Margaret right. Why'd they have to get a mother like her?

He'd skipped school again today to run errands with her. She'd never ask him to miss school, she was worried he'd get behind like she had when she was a kid. But she just let him do it. What kind of mother let her son skip school? Wasn't that against the law? What kind of mother made her son worry about her so much he didn't want her leaving the house without him? At his age you were supposed to be thinking about friends and music and video games and sex, not whether your mother was capable of crossing the street by herself or taking care of your little sister. He was almost grown now; it was too late for him. But Margaret was little.

He couldn't remember his mom ever saying no. He was the good kid, which was kind of sickening but it was easier than doing stuff that made his mother cry and chant and cook weird stuff in the Crock-pot that stank up whatever crappy apartment or homeless shelter they were living in at the moment.

Margaret was not a good kid. Felix tried to tell her what to do because somebody had to, but she just ignored him or laughed or threw a fit. When she was a baby she'd cried all the time because her world wasn't perfect, and Mom had fussed and worried and chanted and rubbed goop on her chest and the soles of her feet.

When Margaret had started crawling and toddling she got into everything, Mom's stuff and Felix's stuff, dangerous stuff and stuff you didn't want ruined. One time because of a hunch he looked into the dirty playroom of the shelter and she was coloring in his school books, copying one of Mom's so-called secret designs over and over again in the margins, crossing out words and underlining other ones, and he had to pay for the books. Another time when they lived in a studio apartment he had a feeling and found her on a chair reaching into a cabinet and dipping into Mom's jars of herbs and tinctures and sticking her fingers into her mouth, and he grabbed her and yelled at her and she threw up all over everything.

Mom would explain why she shouldn't do whatever she'd just done, and Margaret listened and then did the same thing again or worse because now she had more information. Felix yelled at her but it didn't make any difference. The minute she'd started talking she'd been whining, sassing, lying, chanting, telling you her dreams whether you wanted to hear about them or not, which he didn't.

So he had a crazy mother and a bratty sister who was probably crazy, too. It was like living with aliens. Everywhere else Felix felt like the alien, but he was the most normal one in this family, which was scary.

Mom patted his shoulder and said in order for powers to be most efficacious we have to meet people where they are and not wish they were somebody else. What about somebody meeting *him* where he was for a change? The only thing Felix ever got from his mother's advice was knowing what words like "efficacious" meant in case they showed up on some standardized test.

Practically the minute Margaret could run she'd started running away. Not like she was going somewhere; more like she was just *going*. Mom would chant and throw cards and do divinations until she thought she knew where Margaret was. Then she'd send Felix to get her. Felix got mad when she was wrong because she'd wasted his time. He got mad when she was right because Margaret was such a pain and Mom wouldn't punish her. She said it was Margaret's nature and the rest of the world, including him, would just have to get used to it. Well, what about *his* "nature"?

Wasn't that child neglect? Was there somebody Felix could report it to without having to tell everything else about his nutso family? Like that Mom really was a witch? She preferred "seer" or "person of powers," so he made a point of thinking "witch" in case she could maybe read his mind.

So far today there'd been no calls or texts from the school that Margaret had escaped. So here Felix was with his mother in a thrift store doing his best to act as if he'd never seen this crazy lady before. Being anywhere in public with her sucked. The older she got the weirder she became, and if anything bad happened to her he'd be stuck with Margaret by himself.

She talked to junk. Out loud. Who does that? Now she was holding up some old jar thing and speaking to it. "What have you held inside you? If I put some quarters for the laundromat into you, will you help me make them multiply?"

Great. Felix had been saving quarters for a couple of weeks so he could wash his and Margaret's clothes. He almost had enough. Maybe the jar would cough up a couple more. If they walked around much longer in dirty clothes somebody would surely call Social Services. Maybe that would be a good thing. Maybe not.

When the tone of Mom's voice told him she was about to start chanting, he walked over to the other end of the store and pretended to be looking at men's shoes. He needed shoes. So did Margaret. But who knew where this stuff had been, who'd touched it, what they'd used it for? Felix didn't believe in evil spirits but he did believe in germs. Donated clothes like from churches and clothing banks were safer but still embarrassing.

His mother bought the jar for herself—for the family, she'd say—and a long curved knife for Margaret. A knife for an eight-year-old? One more thing he'd have to get rid of, preferably before Margaret saw it and thought it was cool. Nothing for him. He didn't want anything, but it was another reason to be mad, along with the fact that she'd wasted $2.78 they didn't have. Sometimes people paid Mom for tomatoes or rhubarb, spells or potions or readings, and she got food stamps and checks from the government, but it still seemed there was never enough money for good food. Nobody should live like this, especially a kid like Margaret who didn't have a choice. But Felix was almost old enough to have a choice.

Next stop was an organic grocery where everything cost a fortune. Mom had been sick a lot lately, and she said it was because she had to wait for money to come in before she could buy what she needed. But obviously it was the crap she ate from places like this and from her garden and the woods and streets. He wasn't going to put any more of that crap into his body no matter how Mom tried to hide it in orange juice or disguise it as real food. Give him burgers and fries any day. "The government removes essential nutrients from our food," she told him cheerily for like the thousandth time as they went into the store. "Who knows what they replace them with?"

It was one thing to practice voodoo medicine and hoo-hoo eating on yourself. But not getting real food or health care for your kids made it other people's business. What would've happened if he'd told the school counselor that time Margaret had a fever for days that made her blue eyes shine like wet lilacs and Mom had refused to take her to the ER but she'd made her dolls dance?

When Felix came home from school that day every doll in Margaret's room, every figurine, every picture of a human or beast, even stuff that only vaguely looked like it had a head and legs was gyrating, hopping, waving, dancing. Margaret was laughing, and then she was out of bed and trying to make them dance the old-fashioned kids' way, moving them with her hands and pretending. She got frustrated and Mom wouldn't do it again because she said it wasn't right to be frivolous with your powers, and Margaret threw a fit. To shut her up, and because he was happy she wasn't sick any more, Felix played puppets with her and showed her how to put life into them or pull it out of them or whatever. The puppets had tugged at his hand and Margaret's hand, and she'd hugged him and said he was the best big brother in the world and he had to teach her how to do that, and he did his best but she never did learn.

So maybe Mom had cured her, but maybe Mom had made her sick in the first place. Felix never got around to telling the school counselor and pretty soon they'd moved anyway.

Margaret had the only clean, relatively nice room in their new house. Every other space, including half of his basement man-cave, was full of the witch's projects. Her clay sculptures and things that looked like body parts floating in colored liquids had mingled with and seeped into his ships in bottles and crushed leaves and sketches of things he knew about but couldn't name yet, couldn't quite make move, and everything got ruined. He'd given up having projects after that.

Seeing her plop another grape into her mouth, he whispered, "Mom!" She raised her eyebrows. The produce guy was heading their way (again) to tell her to quit shoplifting. What kind of role model was this for Margaret? Felix hurried around the corner and pretended to be interested in free-range eggs. More than once Mom had explained to him what "free-range" meant, but he refused to remember it and picturing the top of a stove full of brown eggs running around free like hamsters out of their cages made him laugh.

Mom chatted away at the bored checkout clerk. Felix just wanted to get out of there before she did something else embarrassing, and he almost made it. He had picked up the grocery bags—why was it his job to carry the bags?—when Mom reached over, stroked the bananas, and sang out, "Thank you, my little curved friends, for letting us eat you." The clerk stared at her, then stared at Felix, the poor kid with the crazy mother. Maybe somebody would call the authorities. Could you lose your kids for talking to bananas?

Mom wouldn't quit until she'd checked out at least one used bookstore. Felix wanted to tell her to carry her own damn groceries, but her back or shoulder or arm was giving her trouble. He thought about leaving her there and going to what they were calling home this week in order to be there when Margaret got out of school. Wasn't it illegal to leave a little kid alone? But when he compared who was more likely to get into trouble on her own, Mom or Margaret, Mom won by a landslide. He thought about pulling a Margaret and walking away as far away as he could get.

But he'd never do any of that because he was a wimp and a mama's boy and her enabler, and somebody had to watch out for Margaret, which made him mad at both of them. Too bad he couldn't just think Margaret into a safer place. Mom could probably do that, so why didn't she? Personally, Felix didn't have any magic.

Mom and the bookstore guy said hi to each other like they were buds, except that Felix heard the OMG! in his voice. She got out her list, longer every time because nobody could ever find any of the books she wanted. The bookstore guy tried, or pretended to try, until a couple of actual customers came in. Then Mom wandered around. With the bags Felix couldn't fit between the shelves unless he turned sideways. The plastic handles dug into his hands. There were chairs but they all had books on them, and even though the bookstore people always said it was okay to move the books if you wanted to sit down, Felix couldn't bring himself to do that, and it would be embarrassing to sit on the floor. He leaned against the end of a bookcase, willing it not to roll, and tried to think about things other than his mother or his sister.

She'd be here for a while, looking up weirdness like the fourteenth word on the sixty-seventh page in twenty-one different books. She'd write those words down in a tattered notebook and study them for weeks. She never bought anything—on her way out she'd grab some random book out of the freebie bin. When he edged around the towering books crowding the apartment he'd pretend to cast a protective spell so they wouldn't collapse on Margaret, but it was just making fun of Mom. Every time they moved there were more boxes of books to carry, except you couldn't bring extraneous stuff like that to a shelter, which was the only good thing about being homeless.

Feeling like a homeless person again with all the crap he was carrying, Felix almost wished for a grocery cart. The thrift store bag had the name of the store in enormous letters so there was no way to disguise where they'd been shopping, and the jar was heavy against his leg and who knew what would be released or destroyed or pissed off if he dropped it and it broke. Naturally the natural-foods store wouldn't use plastic so he had to deal with a flimsy cloth bag, and something in it smelled weird. The not one but three books Mom had grabbed out of the free bin without even looking had slick dust jackets and kept sliding out of his grip. He couldn't reach his phone to see what time it was, which at least meant he didn't have to deal with Mom's dumb comments about how cell phones introduced foreign energy into your brain.

"You about done?" he asked her. "Margaret'll be home soon."

But she was communing with the spirit of a piece of trash out of the gutter. Felix didn't want to know what it was or what she thought she was doing, but as she gently deposited it into the bookstore bag he couldn't help hearing its voice and seeing that it was a piece of broken pink plastic with sharp edges that would probably tear the plastic so everything would fall out and he'd be the one who had to retrieve it all and figure out how to carry it. "What is that?"

"That's Tinkerbell. A piece of Tinkerbell. You know how your sister loves Tinkerbell."

He had no clue what Tinkerbell was or if his sister loved it. "What's it for?"

Mom smiled. "I don't know yet. But it told me it could help us."

"Right." He didn't sound half as sarcastic as he wanted to.

She reached up and actually patted his head. He hated when she did that. She was the one who didn't understand the world and had to be taken care of and have things explained to her but wouldn't listen. He might be the kid, but he was the grown-up around here. "If you have a talent you should use it," she told him, like he hadn't heard that a million times. Like she was talking about a good pitching arm or being able to fix cars. "Sometimes there's just a thin line between survival and disaster. Sometimes it's so thin you can't even see it. Remember that, son. My abilities help this family stay afloat."

"Terrific, Mom. That's really nice. Can we go? Margaret'll be home and I gotta take a leak." The second part was very true. He hoped the first part was.

If he started off first there was a good chance she'd get distracted and stop following him and he'd have to go looking for her and Margaret would either be at home alone or not at home and wandering around somewhere by herself. Finally they were heading more or less toward the apartment. Felix sometimes worried that Margaret would forget where they lived today, or that he would. Mom seemed at home everywhere, which was really annoying and kind of creepy.

He was tired of walking but most of the time they couldn't afford bus fare and he couldn't get a job to buy himself a car because he had to watch out for his sister and his mother. When he complained Mom just twirled her fingers at him and said walking was good for your mind and your soul. She had her arms stretched out and her head thrown back, singing high and loud, and people on the sidewalk were detouring around her, even the homeless people. She actually squatted by one of them and invited him to sing with her, and he swore at her and walked off. Too crazy for the crazies. Felix trudged along, lugging her bags of junk and worrying about Margaret and hating it that he had to lug and worry.

They could be wearing decent clothes, eating good food, living in a nice house—still living in that house where he'd actually had a little space of his own. But no. She'd rather shop in thrift stores and wear smelly old clothes and eat obnoxious things and mumble under her breath. "Why can't we have a better life?" he'd say.

"It's a resource," she'd say. "Like clean water. You have to be careful or you might use it up."

"Why do you let people think you're crazy? Just *show* them what you can do—it'll shut them up!" Never mind that she *was* crazy.

"It's an art, that means it's personal, and nothing you can really explain. You don't know why it works, it just works. And what may work for me may not work for you. That's what people don't understand. They try it out, it doesn't work for them, and they stop believing."

"Why do we have to live this way?"

"It's all about luck. You try to line everything up proper, and the luck runs your way. But when it runs your way, you got to remember that means it runs against somebody else. So you have to be careful. You have to be responsible. You don't want to hurt people, but sometimes you have to just to survive, just to make do for you and yours. And sometimes maybe you let go of the luck so that it'll work for somebody else, because that's the right thing to do. You'll figure it out, Felix. I have faith in you." Just what he needed.

Could you go to the media with a story about a mother who was a witch and had special powers but wouldn't use them for the betterment of her children? Devising what he'd say and quietly rehearsing the interviews he'd give to the press occupied his mind so he could tolerate the rest of the walk back to the apartment.

Where Margaret was not.

Felix knew she wasn't there before Mom opened the door. Something about the energy. He didn't like noticing energy. He also knew Margaret was in danger. He didn't know how he knew that. Maybe he was wrong. Maybe he was just imagining the worst, and that would not make it happen. He wasn't the witch of the family.

Just as he dropped the bags onto the already-full couch, the handle of the health-food bag broke. It wasn't his job to chase after the bottles that rolled across the floor. Mom talked to them as she gathered them up. She didn't seem worried about Margaret. She seemed kind of excited or something. He didn't have time right now to try to figure her out.

On Margaret's bed in the corner, her lunch bag was open on top of homework papers. So she'd been home after school. She hadn't been doing her homework, though. Toys were out of the trash bag she kept them in. Crayons and colored pencils were scattered around, and papers with drawings on them of her stuffed animals and dolls with legs going this way and that, kicking at the big empty spaces on the page.

"She didn't eat her sandwich." Mom was digging through the bag.

He took the neatly wrapped sandwich away from her. "Mom, she *never* eats her sandwich. And nobody will trade with her. She throws it away at school or on the way home. Maybe today she was—distracted." Maybe she was kidnapped. Maybe she was—

"Why not?"

He unwrapped it, took it apart, spread the halves like a biology lab dissection. "Look at this—broccoli, grapefruit slices, and what's this paste made out of—honey and hummus? And I used to think this was bean sprouts, but it's that weed from the backyard, right? Gray bread, like chunks of papier-mâché. Who eats like this, Mom?" He thought about keeping it for evidence.

"It's full of essential nutrients! What has she been eating, then?"

"I give her money. From little jobs I get. And sometimes I just take it from your purse."

"Stealing is bad karma." She was looking at the floor.

"Like you never steal. And starving your kid—I bet that's bad juju too." He'd heard that word in an old Tarzan movie on TV and had just been waiting to use it on her. "She's gone, Mom. We've gotta go find her."

She didn't try to pretend Margaret might be at a friend's. Margaret didn't have any friends, because she didn't want anybody coming here. Felix had been the same way, so by now he didn't know how to make friends. Once Margaret was back safe, he might just point that out to Mom.

Mom said suddenly, "You look around the room, think about where she might have wandered to. You're smart, you'll figure it out before I can. I'm going out to get a tattoo."

Felix stared at her. "Mom. Margaret's gone *missing*."

"And we'll find her."

When she rolled up her left sleeve Felix realized it had been years since he'd seen her bare arms. It was covered by a series of mostly geometric tattoos, some maybe professional, a lot of them obviously amateur—it wouldn't surprise him if she'd done it herself with a sewing needle dipped in plant-based ink. Gross.

"Look." He didn't want to, but he looked. There was a tattoo of a sailing ship. "Look," and there was a fairy with a wand. "I've been tattooing pieces of your and your sister's lives, your passions, your dreams, maybe a lot of things you aren't even aware of, onto my body since before you were born. It's my map to my children. Once I add her disappearance, I'll know right where she is."

He found himself focusing on her tattoos, or they focused on him. They were changing, developing, growing longer and thicker, joining and crossing over to display twisted passages and dance-like movements.

He jerked his gaze away. "Aren't there some practical things, more *normal* things we should be doing? Like walking down the street, searching the park, knocking on doors? Maybe even calling the police?"

"No need for that. Don't you understand that the authorities poison us against the natural magic of the world? But go ahead and do that "normal" stuff. Watch and listen. Pay attention to your feelings and let them guide you. I have great faith in you, Felix." She hurried out.

For the next few minutes he searched the room. He picked things up gently and put them back where he thought they'd been. Tearing things apart would've just made him more scared, and Margaret would be furious when she came home. Books facedown to hold her place didn't tell him anything. None of her zillion unicorn and castle and enchantress and Harry Potter posters had anything to say to him, either. Real magic was a sham—hard to access, hard to control, crazy and arbitrary and unfair. It promised everything but never gave you what you really needed.

In her lunch bag he found a slip of paper. Mom used to leave notes in his lunch, too—stupid advice like YOU CAN DO IT! And REACH FOR THE STARS! This note had a silly fairy sticker on it that said Tinkerbell, plus a lot of weird designs, circles mostly, with various spokes in them, and scribbles connecting them. If he glanced at them a certain way the circles turned and the scribbles danced. Right beside Tinkerbell, under the glow of her tiny wand, was GO FIND THE MAGIC! in Mom's one-of-a-kind handwriting.

Tinkerbell told him what it meant, which was a clue to how upset and out of it he was. Mom had sent Margaret away on some impossible quest.

One of his sister's drawings crinkled under his hand, tingling his skin. He pulled the drawing up against the light and watched as the lines of the furiously dancing doll vibrated.

Felix had no idea what he was doing. Like his mother always said, he let himself be led. With various pencils, pens, crayons, he extended the lines on the paper so that they wrapped, cocooned, buried the dancing doll in a hard shimmering tunnel. Then the spiral spread off the paper to contour the folds of sheets, comforter, pillow, until he dropped everything, hands shaking, and stood back.

Vaguely he recognized the park by that shelter they'd stayed in for a few weeks last year, elaborate slide system with a tower where kids waited their turn. On the wall of the playground was a mural he couldn't see in the drawing, wizards and fairies, gnomes in fur coats like rats escaping a sewer, that had always creeped him out when he'd taken Margaret there. So had all the old guys hanging around like wizards who'd lost their powers, or who'd just hallucinated them, now convinced all the tasty magic was there in the bodies of the playing kids. Margaret had always wanted to say hi, and Felix hadn't let her. The lines didn't show anything but the dancing of the kids and a space of no-dancing, no-motion, watching.

The deep-shadowed tangle behind the playground hid the entrance to a secret cavern, or something more every day. The sewer. He'd yelled at Margaret to keep away.

When Felix got into the park it felt like dusk although he didn't think it was that late, hoped Margaret hadn't been left alone that long, didn't stop to check the time on his phone. Homeless guys were sitting on the wall. There was the mural, more faded and dirtier than he remembered, layered in a graffiti of filthy, hysterical requests. The opening of the sewer pipe was huge, protective mesh broken into fringe. It quivered like it was singing.

Margaret was in there. Looking for a magic place. Because she was a kid, and magic could be anywhere her mother said it was.

Felix dropped onto hands and knees and, without allowing himself to think about it, started into the pipe. Then the darkness detached into a ragged bulk of shadow backing out. The man grunted, hit his head and swore. The seat of his pants was muddy. He had Margaret. Her pale face popped up on one side and then disappeared.

Felix's first impulse was to block the exit, trap the guy inside the pipe and call the police. He fumbled for his phone. Then he thought he might have a better shot at saving his sister if he moved out of the way. The guy kept coming, dragging Margaret, his fist swallowing her hand. Felix grabbed at the guy's shirt and was about to throw himself at him when Margaret yelled, "No! Felix! He's my friend!"

The big, red-faced, dirty guy was all the way out, and he reached back into the pipe with both hands and pulled Margaret out. She hugged him before she hugged Felix. The homeless guy growled, "You better tell somebody, dude."

Into Felix's neck Margaret said, "I'm scared, Felix."

"Of him? What'd he—"

He felt her shake her head. "Of Mom. She makes me do stuff. She doesn't take care of us. My friend says it's not right, kids shouldn't be treated like that."

"Felix, you found her!" Mom went to hug Margaret but Margaret turned away. "I knew you could do it—I've always had faith in you." To the homeless guy she said, "Thanks, Woody," and kissed his cheek.

"You sent her out here, right?" Felix didn't care who heard. "A test for me."

Mom looked at Margaret and lowered her voice. "She loves magic but she didn't inherit my abilities. You did."

"I want it!" Margaret wailed. People were looking at them. Woody patted her head, told Felix again to tell somebody, and shambled off to find saner company. Felix finally found his phone.

"You have great talent, son. And if you didn't find her, I was your back-up." She was actually proud of herself.

She'd think he hated her, but he didn't. He just didn't have anything more to say to her. He waved his hands once, twice, and the lines danced around them. He didn't know if Mom couldn't see them, but she definitely couldn't see him or Margaret. He called 911.

SWIFT, BRUTAL RETALIATION

MEGHAN MCCARRON

Meghan McCarron's [www.meghanmccarron.com] *stories have recently appeared in* Tor.com, Strange Horizons, *and* Unstuck, *where she has since become an assistant editor. She lives with her girlfriend in Austin, Texas.*

Two girls in wrinkled black dresses sat in the front pew at their older brother's funeral. They had never sat in the front pew in church before, and they disliked how exposed they felt. Behind them stood their brother's entire eighth-grade class, the girls in ironed black dresses and gold cross necklaces, the boys in dark suits, bought too big so they could get another use. Few expected more funerals, but the suits would serve for graduation in May—which, after all, was a funeral, too.

The girls' aunt gave the second reading, which was one of the letters of Saint Paul to the Corinthians. The younger sister, Brigid, loved the rhythm of those words, "Saint Paul to the Corinthians." She didn't know who the Corinthians were, but she imagined a small, dusty town, the people crowded around the town square as someone stood, just like her aunt, and read the latest letter from Saint Paul. This letter informed the Corinthians that though their outsides were wasting away, their insides were filling with the light of God. Life was a wobbly tent, but God had built a sturdy house in heaven. The older sister, Sinead, thought this God-house probably sounded good to people in the desert two thousand years ago, but her brother's house wasn't just sturdy: it had a pool. Also, her brother's insides had not grown stronger. He had wasted away, all of him. This stupid reading confirmed her suspicions that God was like any other adult who lied and told you horrible things were for your own good.

Sinead and Brigid felt as alone as it was possible to feel while smushed up against someone on a pew, unaware that the other person was also furiously contemplating God. They were doing their best not to be aware of anything. Noticing things, they had discovered, was dangerous. Was that Ian's English teacher sobbing three rows behind them? Was that the priest saying Ian's name in the homily? Were those flowers already wilting on the coffin in the early-September heat? Before, Sinead would have gotten angry about these things. Brigid would have tried to figure out their meaning. Now, the sisters found it safer to sink into the fog of mourning, though they didn't know to call it that. They were just trying to be very still, in hopes that events would pass them by.

A few pews back, two of Ian's classmates trailed out, sobbing. The reading had ended, and the cantor began to sing "Alleluia." The congregation rose to their feet, and their mother's hymnal slipped out of her black lap. She chanted along in a low, flat voice neither of them had heard before. Their father did not stand, but sat upright at the edge of the pew so stiffly he almost looked funny. His suit was rumpled and he'd slathered himself in cologne to hide the scent of alcohol. Sinead and Brigid were used to the cologne, but they had never seen their father look so small before. They had done a good job ignoring their surroundings, but their strange, frightening parents dragged them back into reality. They stared hopelessly at Ian's fat, luminous coffin.

The reception after the funeral filled the house with earnest thirteen-year-old girls bearing food made by their mothers. Every girl in Ian's class brought food, and most of it was lasagna. Lasagna with beef, lasagna with pork and spinach, "garden lasagna" featuring broccoli and Alfredo, Mexican lasagna with hot peppers and tortillas, and one particularly vile concoction made with whole-wheat pasta and dairy-free cheese. All of the lasagna piled up in the kitchen, since the girls' parents had brought in caterers. Their mother didn't have the heart to throw it away, so she shunted it to the refrigerator.

The sisters spent the reception hiding in plain sight, or trying to. They glued themselves to their grandmother, who had flown in for the occasion. Their grandmother was a sour old lady who smelled like cigarettes and gin fumes. But she was also tall and heavyset, so they could literally hide behind her as she talked to second cousins and great-aunts and even a step-something, the girls didn't catch what. Sometimes the sisters held hands. Brigid was the one who did the hand-seeking-out, but Sinead was secretly glad for something to hold on to when strangers stooped down to say they were sorry. Where were they when Ian was sick? Sorry? Sinead would make them sorry.

There were still people in the house that night, straggler aunts and loud neighbors. One of Ian's coaches was out back with their father, smoking cigars and laughing too loud. At some point, their mother noticed the girls scavenging in the kitchen and sent them up to bed. Sinead made Brigid go up first, since her bedtime was an hour after her sister's, but once Brigid was gone Sinead felt unmoored. She was too proud to give up her older-sibling right to a later bedtime, but she also didn't want to be in the room with the loud, sad adults. She found herself contemplating the whole-wheat dairy-free lasagna. Their mother had left it out to rot, and the faux cheese was buckling and sweating.

Sinead heard Brigid turn on the shower in her bathroom. Brigid had only started showering before bed a few months earlier, to imitate her older sister. This infuriated Sinead generally; tonight it felt like a slap in the face. Sinead snatched up the casserole dish and took the withering lasagna up to Brigid's messy pink room. She carved it up with a butter knife and hid the uneven squares under Brigid's pillow, beneath her covers, in her shoes, under her dresser—anywhere it would either squish or rot. This was a cruel thing to do after Sinead had spent all day comforting and being comforted by her sister. But the comforting also served to remind Sinead that it was just the two of them now, and that she could no longer enjoy the position of invisible middle child. She had embraced this identity with gusto—her favorite book was *The One in the Middle Is the Green Kangaroo*—but now she was the *oldest*. In the books she'd read, the oldest was bossy and bullying, or foolish and frivolous. In their family, the oldest was either sick, or played pranks.

As Sinead stashed the lasagna in the tradition of her dead brother, she began to feel as if she were being watched. She whirled around, sure that she would find Brigid in her pink bathrobe, her hair piled on her head in a towel, like women in old movies and their mother. But the shower was still roaring, and Sinead found herself staring at her reflection in the mirror.

Except it wasn't her reflection. The face was Ian's.

Then it wasn't. Sinead took several gulping breaths. One of her aunts had sent her books about grieving, so she'd known that she might end up hallucinating. She must be hallucinating.

This did not stop her, however, from snatching up the dirty pan, running into her room, and locking the door behind her. She threw the pan beneath her bed, jumped under the covers, and turned off the light. Then she switched it on again and covered her mirror with a sheet. But that really made her room look haunted, so she took the sheet down and stared at her reflection, willing her brother's face to appear. The reflection remained her own, which made her feel stupid. Stupid was a familiar, oddly comforting feeling.

Brigid sat on her floor in the dark, drawing a picture. She used her tiny reading light, which was designed for airplanes, though Brigid had gotten far more use from it during long waits in the dim, fluorescent hospital. She almost missed sitting in the boring corridors, compared to funerals and evil sisters. Bits of lasagna were still mushed into her hair, and Brigid was drawing a picture of her sister's head on fire. Sinead's curly hair stuck out in all directions, like she'd been hit by lightning. Brigid added her parents to the picture as little stick figures, off in the distance. They didn't do anything about the flames.

Brigid felt bewildered and hurt by the lasagna bombing. She did, however, recognize that a prank war had begun, and she had to respond in kind or risk humiliation. Unfortunately, she had the younger sibling's handicap of not having seen as much television or read as many books as her older siblings, so she was reduced to deflecting the same prank back at them. For a time, Brigid had experimented with turning the other cheek, but this had only resulted in more spiders in her bed, more covert arm-twists, and more stuffed animals fed to the neighbor's dog. Clearly, Sinead was attempting to take over Ian's turf, and the only effective response was swift, brutal retaliation.

Brigid completed three more meditative, vengeful pictures of her sister before quiet settled over the house. When she was sure everyone was asleep, she slid open her door and crept down to the kitchen. The clean, shiny counters reflected the blue light thrown off by the oven clock. Brigid was old enough to understand that her house was full of "nice" things, though "nice" to her meant "alienating and not to be touched." When Brigid opened the fridge, a chill crept along the back of her neck, like someone was blowing on it. But the kitchen was empty and silent and blue.

The white light of the fridge was warm and calming, so Brigid left the door ajar after pulling out Sinead's special orange-mango juice. No one knew why Sinead liked this juice so much—their mother blamed their father, other mothers, television ads—but everyone else in the house thought it was nasty, and only Sinead ever touched it. Brigid left the juice on the counter, then got up on a stool to retrieve salt and hot sauce from an upper cabinet. She shook in as much hot sauce as she could, then poured in some salt. After shaking the mixture together, she examined its color and consistency in the fridge light. Satisfied, Brigid placed the bottle back on the top shelf exactly how she'd found it, with its label facing the milk. She took a moment to admire her handiwork and shut the door with a *schuck*.

Ian stood on the other side of it. Brigid stumbled away from him, and put her back against the counter. He had hair again, the straight, tufty blond stuff he'd grown in after the first time he'd gotten better, not the curls from the pictures before Brigid was born. He wore shorts and a polo shirt, like he was on his way to the country club. But his face was pallid and green, and his eyes were ringed by the deep, scary circles that had appeared right before he died. Brigid didn't feel fear, or even shock. All she could think was, *I thought I'd never see you again.*

Brigid became aware of a soft hissing sound. Her elbow had knocked over the salt, and it was pouring onto the floor. When she looked back up, Ian was gone.

Brigid forced herself to go to the closet, find a dustpan and broom, and sweep up every last grain of salt. Seeing her ghost brother was terrifying, but having her father find salt all over the floor was equally scary, if not more so. Once the floor was clean, her terror surged back and she sprinted up the stairs.

As she rounded the bend, she nearly crashed into her mother. For a flicker of a moment, Brigid was sure she'd been caught, but then her mother looked over Brigid's shoulder and said, "Ian, you better go wash the fishes."

Brigid realized her mother was back on Ambien. She had foolishly hoped her mother would sleep better once she stopped spending every waking hour at the hospital, but apparently not. She pressed herself to the wall and let her mother sleepwalk down the stairs.

Despite the fact that she was furious with Sinead, Brigid jimmied open her door—Sinead kept it locked, though they had figured out how to break into each other's rooms years ago—and jumped into her bed. Sinead woke with a groan and Brigid hissed, "Shhhhhh!"

"Euh?" Sinead said.

"I saw Ian," Brigid said.

Sinead stiffened, then put her arms around her little sister. She noticed her hair smelled like tomato sauce. "I saw him too," Sinead said.

"What are we going to do?" Brigid whispered.

Sinead thought about the brave older sisters she'd read about in books and said, "We're going to help him."

Sinead didn't actually believe in her own bravery, but her borrowed stock phrase seemed to calm Brigid. It calmed Sinead a little bit, too. When Ian was alive, there had been very little either of his sisters could do for him. When he was well, they had tortured him, or tortured each other; as a result, when he was sick, every earnest gesture had felt forced. They had loved their brother, but they hadn't *liked* him much. Now here he was, turning to *them*, of all people. Of course they would do right by him. Of course they would help.

Sinead woke early and cleaned up Brigid's room while Brigid caught up on sleep in Sinead's bed. She shook lasagna out of Brigid's shoes and scraped off everything that remained under Brigid's covers. Then she stripped the bed and took the whole mess downstairs. She put the sheets in the washing machine, pushed the rotting lasagna down the garbage disposal, and scrubbed the pan until her fingers hurt. Finally, when the evidence of her crime had been thoroughly erased, she let herself have breakfast. She poured herself some Rice Krispies, sliced up a banana, and sat down at the kitchen table with her laptop.

Technically, it was a school day, but Sinead and Brigid were taking a "leave" of a few weeks. This was supposed to help them recover from the trauma of Ian's death, though Sinead suspected it was actually so the other students wouldn't have to deal with their uncomfortable grief. Sinead had felt miserable and adrift in the days following Ian's death, but now that she had a purpose, those feelings disappeared. She felt happy, even privileged, to be sitting at home in the morning eating cereal and a banana and googling "ghost brother," though this only brought up television-show recaps and one site about "Haunted Gettysburg."

Brigid found her sister poring over her computer in the kitchen, a half-eaten banana by her side. Brigid had been deemed too young for a laptop, which filled her with uncharacteristic fury. She casually opened the fridge and found that the mango juice hadn't been touched. Brigid appreciated that Sinead had cleaned up her room, but she felt uneasy letting her sister off entirely. She let the mango juice be.

"A ghost comes back because of unfinished business," Sinead said, without looking up from the screen.

Brigid tried and failed to think of what unfinished business their brother might have. In all the books *she'd* read, "unfinished business" meant things like buried treasure or unsolved murders, which she didn't suppose Ian had any of. "We should search his room," Brigid said.

The sisters went up to Ian's room, which no one had opened since he went back to the hospital for good. Sinead carried a thermometer and a compass, which the internet had told her were useful for detecting paranormal presences. The thermometer was to register sudden drops in temperature. It was less clear what the compass was supposed to do, but Sinead imagined it would spin wildly, like in movies about the North Pole.

Ian's room had always been neat and uncluttered, utterly unlike his sisters'. His dresser was lined with soccer trophies, and his sneakers stood in matched pairs beneath his bed. The clock still blinked midnight from a late-summer power outage. His bed was made. It looked like a display room.

"Anything?" Brigid said, nodding toward Sinead's tools. Sinead shook her head in what she imagined was a curt, professional manner. The thermometer did not reveal any strange differences in temperature, and the compass did not point anywhere but a woozy north.

Sinead remembered reading somewhere, or maybe seeing in a movie, that you had to ask ghosts what they wanted. They went into Brigid's room, where Sinead had first seen Ian's ghost. Brigid's bed lay bare, and a few of her stuffed animals were piled to the side of it, wounded with tomato-sauce stains. Sinead took this in and finally offered a mumbled "Sorry about that." Brigid shrugged and said nothing, trying to hide the anger over the lasagna and guilt over the mango juice warring inside her.

Not that Sinead was paying attention. She seemed satisfied by their stupid exchange and had turned her full attention to the mirror.

Sinead stared for a long time. Her eyes glazed over, which blurred her features, but she never saw her brother's face looking back. Occasionally Brigid would ask, "Anything?" and Sinead would blink her eyes, rub them, and say, "Nothing."

Sinead and Brigid went to the kitchen next, the site of Ian's second appearance. Brigid opened and closed the refrigerator door a few times, making sure that didn't summon him, but she was too terrified Sinead would ask why she was in the kitchen to keep up the investigation for very long. Sinead blithely assumed Brigid was sneaking snacks.

For lunch they microwaved giant chunks of Mexican lasagna and leftover caterer chicken fingers. Their mother was home, but it didn't even occur to them to ask her for lunch. During Ian's last few months, their mother was usually busy taking care of him. When he died, they had briefly hoped she would recover her interest in their well-being, but instead her caring engines shut down completely. She spent whole days in her room; the girls had no idea what she did in there. If they put their ears to the door, they heard the television, but they had the eerie feeling it wasn't being watched.

When the leftovers were ready (re-ready?), Sinead opened up her laptop and logged on to Facebook. Sinead never used her account, since she was already sick of everyone at their school and couldn't imagine spending her free time reading their stupid updates. But Ian had been obsessed with Facebook, forever adding friends and commenting on pictures and taking polls. None of his own status updates ever had to do with chemo, or the hospital, or his family, which were just annoying distractions from being normal and popular. His updates were bizarre hypothetical questions about Batman or the *300* or *Boondock Saints*. Any comments pertaining to "good thoughts!" or "HUGZ" were deleted, unless they were posted by someone really hot.

"I'm going to send him a message," Sinead announced.

"On Facebook?" Brigid said.

"Ian loved Facebook," Sinead said. "Maybe he'd rather communicate that way."

Ian and Sinead were not Facebook friends, but he let anyone who went to their school see his profile. Even though his last update was weeks old, his page was full of activity. New wall posts filled in the top. Someone had posted a picture of Ian with his arms around two girls Sinead didn't even recognize, sitting in a hot tub at someone's pool party. He was grinning like he'd gotten away with something. Was he already sick by then? Or did he still think he was in remission? There were also messages on the page, "IANO WELL MISS U!!!" and "I KNOW UR A REAL ANGEL NOW!" The "angel" messages were a million times worse than "good thoughts!" or "HUGZ." Sinead felt an overpowering urge to tell these kids exactly which species of idiot they were, but the most insightful commentary she could come up with in her blind fury was "FUCK U." She moved to post it, but she felt Brigid staring at her. She looked at Brigid, who shook her head.

Sinead sighed and started a new message. She typed, "Ian, r u haunting the house?" She pressed send. Then she opened another one and added, "Why?"

They ate their Mexican lasagna very slowly, watching Sinead's Facebook inbox like it was extremely boring television. No new messages arrived.

The girls were in Sinead's room creating an altar out of Ian's trophies when they heard their mother banging dishes in the kitchen. If it had been their father making angry sounds, they would have stayed put. But with their mother, it was better to get the confrontation over with.

"You're not on vacation," their mother said as they came down the stairs. She wore glasses, a rumpled blue sweat suit, and, weirdly, makeup. She shoved their dirty dishes across the counter. "What if Daddy came home?"

Brigid immediately pulled her stool in front of the sink and started scrubbing the lasagna pan. Sinead stared very hard at her mother, trying out her telekinetic powers. She had just hit puberty, right? Maybe Ian wasn't Ian at all, but a poltergeist that had been unleashed by her hormones.

Her mother stared back at her, looking both dazed and furious. The side of her neck quivered, and there were huge circles under her eyes. Her mouth tensed, like she was about to say something nasty. Instead, her thin face collapsed, like a building imploding, and she started to cry.

Shame burned Sinead like poison. She snatched a dish from Brigid and rubbed it dry with a towel. Their mother went into the bathroom and both girls pretended not to hear her sob. When Ian was home, their mother never acted like this. It was only when he was at the hospital. Now, instead of Ian's death breaking the spell, he would be at the hospital forever. Brigid kept washing dishes, which Sinead dried and put away. They took a long time doing this, to kill time until their mother finally emerged from the bathroom.

That night, the sisters convened in Sinead's room to watch clips from *Real Ghosthunters*, a YouTube show Sinead had found. They were huddled in the dark around the laptop, taking mental notes about plasma, when they heard the garage door open. They held their breath, praying for their father to just come upstairs. Instead, his footsteps stomped around the kitchen. The master bedroom door opened, and their mother rushed out. After a moment of loaded silence in the kitchen, their voices exploded. The girls made out single words: "pigsty," "brats," "son." Their father pounded up the stairs, thundered past Sinead and Brigid, and slammed the bedroom door. Their mother's footsteps came next. They were slow and quiet. They heard her go into Brigid's room; then there was a knock at Sinead's door.

Their mother's arms were full of Brigid's white sheets, which Sinead had put in the wash and then forgotten. She had only added detergent, not bleach, and the soggy sheets were still covered in smears of red tomato sauce and greasy faux-cheese blots.

"What is this?" she said. Her voice was tight and quiet, the worst possible tone.

Sisterly solidarity was running strong, but it was still vulnerable to attack. If neither of them said anything, both would be punished. Traditionally, this had been the route the siblings took, because Ian believed in, and enforced, a no-ratting policy. The one time Sinead ever bucked it, Ian told everyone at school she wet the bed. For a month, everyone called her "Pee-nead." But the one time Brigid had told on Sinead, both Sinead and Ian conspired to punish her, first by locking her in the attic, then by tricking her into eating a bag of their father's favorite cookies. When he found the bag in Brigid's room, she lost snacking privileges for a month. As a result, Sinead had come to view the policy as a necessary evil, but Brigid *hated* it. If there was a moment for Brigid to change the status quo, this was it. It didn't matter how nice Sinead had been to her today; she had spent every other day being mean, and if Brigid did nothing things would go back to the way they'd been.

"Sinead put lasagna in my bed," Brigid said.

Sinead stiffened next to her sister, and Brigid shrank away. The instant the words were out of her mouth, she regretted them terribly. Their mother stared at Sinead with murder in her eyes, but the look she gave Brigid was not much kinder.

"Your father will speak to you tomorrow, Sinead. Brigid, come with me."

Their mother led Brigid out of the room, and Sinead was left alone, equal parts terrified and furious. She couldn't stop imagining all the terrible things that would happen now that her father knew. She also couldn't stop thinking about hitting Brigid, or kicking her, or pulling her hair. Sinead got up and started pacing, but this only made her anger worse. Brigid's insubordination could not stand, and since they weren't going to school, the only way to punish her was with another prank at home. But if her father caught her doing something bad again….

She needed a quick, deniable solution.

Sinead rooted through her desk drawer until she found a stiff, moldering stick of gum and chewed it until she couldn't even remember what flavor the gum had been. She found Brigid lolling facedown in a fresh set of sheets, her hair tousled against the pillow. Sinead's fingers delicately removed the gum from her mouth and nestled it into Brigid's hair.

Sinead marched out into the hallway, flushed with triumph, only to find Ian staring forlornly at the door to his room. The sight was so sad that her adrenaline-and-anger high crashed, and shame surged in its place. What was she doing torturing her sister when their brother needed help? Ian turned to face her and cocked his head, as if he sensed her regret. She'd never received such a look of understanding from her brother. People had told them they'd get along when they were older, but Sinead had always written that off as the same kind of adult bullshit as telling her that she'd look prettier after the braces came off, or the kids would be nicer next year. Now, under the weight of Ian's look, she felt the loss not just of her brother, but of their friendship. Their future.

Tears spring to Sinead's eyes. She hadn't cried since Ian went back into the hospital, and even then she had been crying for poor Sinead, who had to endure Ian's disease ripping her family apart. Now she was crying for her brother, who'd been bludgeoned by cancer and rewarded with a confused, silent afterlife.

This was no time for emotions, however. Ian needed her help. She swallowed her tears and whispered, "What do you want?"

She wasn't sure what she expected. He was waiting outside his room. Maybe he needed her to open the door? Instead, Ian looked at her with hurt confusion. He mouthed something at her, but there was no sound. She wondered how long it took to learn to read lips. Probably more than twenty-four hours.

"I can't hear you," she whispered.

Ian mouthed it again. And again. When Sinead shook her head, his face colored with unfamiliar anger. Ian had a temper, but Sinead had never seen fury like this. Ian spat a silent evil phrase at her, then disappeared.

A loud thump came from the kitchen downstairs, then a rustling. Something soft hit the floor, over and over. There was a crash, then the sound of footsteps, running.

Sinead rushed to the kitchen. When she flipped on the light, she found the entire floor covered in lasagna. It was strewn on the floor in messy goops, stuck to the cabinets, mashed on the fridge. The trash can had been tipped over, as if by a dog they didn't have; the rest of the lasagna lay inside in one red mass. The pans were still stacked in the sink and on the counter, crusted with burnt cheese products. One of them had shattered on the floor.

Her mother must have thrown the lasagna in the trash, though Sinead couldn't imagine her doing it—she hoarded food like a squirrel. Or maybe their father had decided he didn't like it filling the fridge. Their father wouldn't like all the dirty dishes in the sink, either, but perhaps her mother had staged her own tiny rebellion and refused to clean up after him.

But now, the lasagna was smeared across the entire kitchen, which definitely wasn't her parents' doing. Brigid was fast asleep, and anyway, she never would have made a mess like this. But blaming it on her angry ghost brother wasn't going to cut it with her father, so it was up to Sinead to fix it.

Sinead got out a mop to push all the lasagna toward the trash can. It slithered along the floor, leaving a streak of sauce behind it. Sinead scooped the lasagna into the trash with a dustpan and thanked God that her mother took sleeping pills and her father drank whiskey. Then she reminded herself that she didn't believe in God. Praying was a hard habit to break, though. She wished she could ask God to explain her brother to her. Why was he so angry? What was she supposed to learn from his punishment? But God wasn't listening, and she had to mop the floor.

Brigid marched down the stairs the next morning and threw the clump of her gum-wadded hair at Sinead. There were perhaps more sophisticated or more covert ways of handling her anger, but Brigid did not want to employ them. She hated her sister, and she wanted her to know it.

"Bitch," Brigid said. Ian had taught her all the curse words when she was five, but she'd never used one before. The anger behind it burnt her mouth.

Sinead flinched at the word, but also seemed strangely impressed. "I'm sorry," Sinead said. She didn't do the looking-away-and-shrugging routine that usually accompanied her apologies. But she didn't seem that sorry, either. Or, she seemed to feel she'd already paid the price.

Brigid stood there, fuming. Then she turned on her heel and marched into the pantry to look for something to eat.

"I saw Ian last night," Sinead called to her. "After I did it. He tried to talk to me, but I couldn't hear him, and he got mad."

"I don't care," Brigid said. This was not true, but she was sick of doing things Sinead's way. She took an entire box of cookies and marched back up to her room.

Brigid spent the entire day in her room, making herself sick on Chips Ahoy and reading through every book she owned that featured ghosts. But the ghosts in these stories were either too evil, or too good. The kids had friends, or adult helpers, or siblings who didn't put gum in their hair. None of them told you what to do when you were alone, and scared, and haunted by your mean, sick brother.

Brigid was sitting on her floor, staring at her pile of useless books and tugging on the newly gum-shortened chunk of hair when an epiphany broke: They had only seen Ian when they were pulling a prank.

She found herself perversely glad that Sinead had put gum in her hair. That meant she needed to get revenge on Sinead. And when she did, perhaps she could finally help Ian.

When Brigid heard her mother go downstairs to start dinner, she stole down the hallway into her mother's bathroom. She enjoyed spelunking in the cabinets when her parents weren't home, and the dusty bottle of Nair was right where she remembered. She'd seen a commercial that suggested it had something to do with summertime and shorts, but people also made jokes about using it for pranks on TV. Brigid was used to not understanding things, but she'd filed the idea away for when it was needed.

Brigid took the Nair into Sinead's bathroom and got out her honey-vanilla-mango shiny-hair shampoo. She unscrewed both caps and prepared to pour the white Nair into the conveniently white shampoo. But in the bright bathroom light, the clamor of words on the bottle—"patch test" and "doctor" and "burning"—gave her pause. Burning? Brigid was furious with Sinead, but was she furious enough to set her hair on fire—which, as far as she could tell, was what this concoction would do?

Brigid unscrewed the cap and watched herself in the mirror as she raised the bottle. She moved in slow motion, raising it, then placing it over the shampoo bottle, then tipping it in. When the first bit of Nair poured out, Ian was standing next to her.

Brigid set the Nair bottle down on the counter without taking her eyes off her brother. In the mirror, Ian snatched it up and tossed it between his hands in the languid, confident way he'd moved when he was alive. Her throat tightened; this bottle-tossing was the most Ian-like thing she'd seen the ghost do, and it made her ache for her brother. Brigid sensed he was waiting for her to do something.

"Hi," Brigid said.

Ian nodded in response and continued to toss the bottle back and forth.

Brigid tried to remember the plan she and Sinead had come up with for this encounter. "Do you…W—what do you want?" she said.

Ian's face darkened at that question, and Brigid fumbled for a new, non-angry-making one. She couldn't think of anything. Instead, she blurted out the only other question she had. "Is it better? Now that it's over?" she said.

Ian snatched the bottle out of the air and froze.

"I'm sorry! I didn't mean to say it like that. But, I just…people said, when you died, that it was a blessing, because you were suffering but now you're here, and I don't understand—"

Ian's face had changed when Brigid said the word "died," but she couldn't stop herself from talking, even as he looked at her with angry confusion, like Brigid had just told him a lie out of spite.

"Don't you know?" Brigid said. "Ian, you're—"

The scary anger returned to Ian's face, and his hands began to twitch. They flew up to his head and grasped the tufty blond hair that grew there. He pulled on it, and a chunk came away in his fist. He opened his hand and watched it float to the ground. Then he pulled out another chunk. And another. The chunks of hair floated down all around him, like the leaves of a dying plant.

"Stop!" Brigid said. His eyes darted between his head and Brigid's, then to the bottle of Nair. He snatched up the bottle and poured it all over Brigid's head. The thick liquid gushed down in a white stream, covering Brigid's messy brown hair, her forehead, eyes, nose, and mouth. Her eyes burned and she choked for breath. She watched her reflection in horror as Ian pulled her long brown hair from her head in sickly, dripping strands.

Brigid bolted out of the bathroom and down the stairs. She nearly knocked her mother over when she burst into the kitchen.

"Brigid!" her mother said, grabbing her daughter by the shoulders. "What are you doing?"

Brigid tried, and failed, to hide the terror in her eyes as her mother scrutinized her. She wasn't sure what her mother saw, but she seemed to think it required no more than a comforting hug. She held her daughter for a brief, sweet moment. Then she turned her attention back to the kitchen.

"Daddy will be home for dinner," she said. Her mother's hand on her shoulder tightened at the mention of Daddy. Brigid felt trapped. "Could you set the dining room table?"

The last thing Brigid wanted to do was touch the good china with her shaking hands. No, that wasn't the last thing she wanted to do. The last thing she wanted to do was sit in her room, alone, and wait for Ian's ghost to find her. She didn't think they should be trying to help him anymore. She wondered if she and Sinead were actually keeping him here.

The dishes in the china closet trembled when she approached it, and Brigid caught sight of herself in its mirrored back wall. Between the mirrored backs of the dishes, her reflection had all its hair. Brigid searched the corners of the mirror for Ian, but he was nowhere to be seen.

After Brigid finished setting the table, her mother discovered her newly short chunk of hair and yelled at her for ruining her haircut. Brigid didn't rat Sinead out this time, not because she was cowed by the stupid gum prank, but because she was afraid Sinead's revenge would provoke more terrifying Ian episodes.

Sinead was hiding in the basement in an attempt to put off her interview with her father, but she also had important work to attend to. Sinead had decided after the events of the previous night that Ian was lost, and being lost made him angry, so he needed to be guided to heaven, or wherever he was supposed to go—Sinead was pretty sure heaven was a part of the whole God-lie. Sinead had not made the prank connection, since she didn't know about all of Brigid's pranks; in fact, she was convinced that Ian was seeking them out, unable to let go. She had spent the afternoon acquiring the necessary tools: salt, an important memento, a tiny bell. The next time she saw him, she intended to send him off to eternal peace, whether she believed in it or not.

Sinead refused to come up from the basement to cut the potatoes, or polish the silver, or put out the glasses. She didn't even respond to their mother's calls for assistance, which made her sound as if she was shouting down the stairs at no one. By the time Daddy came home, their mother was crackling with irritation, and it fell to Brigid to make the appeasing niceties required whenever her father joined the family for dinner. When he asked her how she had spent her day, she told him she had watched cartoons.

The rest of the family was already seated by the time Sinead emerged, the little bell tinkling in the pocket of her hoodie. Her parents' half-empty bottle of wine sat on the kitchen counter and reminded Sinead that she wanted juice. She dug into the refrigerator for her orange-mango concoction, which she had secretly started to get sick of. But it inexplicably annoyed her father, so it would serve well as a final act of defiance before her punishment.

When Daddy came home for dinner, the family always ate in the dining room, with the gold-edged china and the freshly polished silver. The candles were always lit, and the girls' mother made food that was cooked in the oven, not the microwave. Tonight there were small, bloody steaks freshly seared in the broiler, roasted fingerling potatoes, and garlicky greens. Each of the women handed a plate to Daddy, and he dropped on greens and potatoes and a single, wobbly steak. Brigid got half a filet, both because she was the youngest and because she was considered by the whole family to be fat. Then Daddy served himself a filet and Brigid's leftover half, and the women listened to him talk about his day, and everyone enjoyed a nice family meal.

When Sinead sat down at the table with the mango juice, Brigid banged her knife on the table to get her attention, but Sinead refused to look up from her plate. She took a bite of her potatoes, then took a sip of her juice. She didn't even register the taste; all she knew was that it had to be out of her mouth, *now*. Sinead spat orange liquid all over the white tablecloth, splattering the green beans and extinguishing one of the candles. The silence afterward was so complete that when Brigid took a breath, it sounded like the rush of the ocean.

"What," their mother began with a sharp, clipped tone, "was that." She clearly hoped to derail their father by taking on the scolding herself, but he spoke over her before she could get out her next word.

"Is there something wrong with your drink, Sinead?" he said. He said it so gently that all three women at the table tensed.

Sinead said nothing as she stared at Brigid, who looked at her with wide, helpless eyes. Brigid had never felt regret like this before, not even when she told Ian that he was dead. That had been an accident. This was something she had done on purpose, and it had worked exactly as she had planned. As terrifying as Ian's reaction had been, he had stayed trapped in the mirror. Sinead and her father were here in the room.

Sinead kept staring at Brigid as she said, "Just went down the wrong tube."

Their father considered this answer, folding his hands like the girls imagined he did in complex negotiations. "Take another sip," he said—then added, as if it had just occurred to him, "so we know you're all right."

As she brought the glass to her lips, Sinead thought of the people who ate bugs on television. The horrid hot-salty flavor of the juice burned her throat, and her stomach turned and gurgled when it hit bottom. She put down the juice in a way she hoped was ladylike, then covered her mouth for one tiny cough.

Sinead could not tell if her performance had any effect, because now their father was looking between them, as if trying to spot an invisible thread. "Brigid, why don't you take a sip?" he said.

Brigid should just take it. Just take the glass, choke the whole thing down, and spare Sinead. But she would spew juice everywhere or, worse, throw it up. "I hate that weird mango stuff," she said. She pathetically hoped this would win his sympathy, since he, too, hated the weird mango stuff.

"Give it another try," their father said. "Go get the bottle."

Brigid rose from her seat as slowly as she possibly could, and shuffled into the kitchen. She pulled out the orange-mango juice and a glass and shuffled back into the dining room like a prisoner headed to the gallows. The three members of her family stared at her with anger as she approached, though their anger was confused, and directed at different people. Her sister was angry with Brigid for pranking her and furious with their father for toying with them. Her mother was angry with the girls for provoking her husband, though her constant, simmering anger at their father boiled up from beneath the other, safer emotion. And her father—her father was angry at his children, and at his wife, but his ideas of who they were and what they represented were so distorted that the anger might as well have been at different people entirely. He'd been furious at Ian when he got sick again. Brigid had seen him slap him. Their father's anger made no sense.

All these competing angers made Brigid angry, too. Hers was not mixed with denial, however, or directed at someone who didn't exist. She was angry at everyone, and she was going to make this stop. When she crossed the threshold, she slid her foot underneath the rug and elaborately, comically, tripped. The glass went flying out of her hands, and the juice bottle crashed to the floor. Their parents stared at Brigid, frozen, but Sinead leapt to her aid, making sure to knock over her juice glass in the process. Sinead slid her hands beneath her sister's arms and drew her to her feet.

Then their parents started screaming about the rug and broken glass and carelessness and disrespect. Sinead and Brigid couldn't make the words out, exactly. They were too distracted by Ian's reappearance. Sinead saw him standing next to their father, arms crossed. Brigid saw him staring out from the china-cabinet mirror, hovering.

"—disrespect that should have died with your son!" their father shouted, just at the moment when their mother fell silent. Then everything was silent, taut with the ugly truth that had just been unleashed. Ian was dead. And each member of the family had wished for that death in the hope that life would be better without him.

The first dish in the cabinet broke like a gunshot. The one closest to it went off next, then another, and another, the dishes exploding like targets in a carnival game. Sinead saw Ian pick them up and hurl them. Brigid saw his face in the mirror behind each dish. Their parents were screaming again, and the sisters watched the carnage unfold before them like spectators, rather than two people intimately involved in the situation. Then Sinead remembered the bell in her pocket, and Brigid remembered the look on Ian's face when she told him he was dead, and they both began to shout, too.

"You can leave!" Sinead shouted. She rang her little bell at the dish cabinet, then pulled out her salt and shook it around the floor. "You don't have to stay here! You can leave!"

"Ian, I'm sorry!" Brigid said. "I'm sorry you died! I'm sorry!"

The dishes kept exploding, and every member of the family kept shouting, and the sisters weren't sure if they had unleashed something cathartic or something terrible. Sinead believed Ian just needed to release this anger to move on. Brigid wondered if their family had poisoned him with their selfishness, and now they were paying the price. Either way, all they could do was cower under the table, holding hands, until it had run its course.

NAHIKU WEST

LINDA NAGATA

Linda Nagata [www.mythicisland.com] *is the author of multiple novels and short stories including* The Bohr Maker, *winner of the Locus Award for best first novel, and the novella* "Goddesses," *the first online publication to receive a Nebula award. Though best known for science fiction, she writes fantasy too, exemplified by her* "scoundrel lit" *series* Stories of the Puzzle Lands. *Her newest science fiction novel is* The Red: First Light, *published under her own imprint, Mythic Island Press LLC. She lives with her husband in their long-time home on the island of Maui.*

A railcar was ferrying Key Lu across the tether linking Nahiku East and West when a micrometeor popped through the car's canopy, leaving two neat holes that vented the cabin to hard vacuum within seconds. The car continued on the track, but it took over a minute for it to reach the gel lock at Nahiku West and pass through into atmosphere. No one expected to find Key Lu alive, but as soon as the car repressurized, he woke up.

Sometimes, it's a crime not to die.

I stepped into the interrogation chamber. Key had been sitting on one of two padded couches, but when he saw me he bolted to his feet. I stood very still, hearing the door lock behind me. Nothing in Key's background indicated he was a violent man, but prisoners sometimes panic. I raised my hand slightly, as a gel ribbon armed with a paralytic spray slid from my forearm to my palm, ready for use if it came to that.

"Please," I said, keeping the ribbon carefully concealed. "Sit down."

Key slowly subsided onto the couch, never taking his frightened eyes off me.

Most of the celestial cities restrict the height and weight of residents to minimize the consumption of volatiles, but Commonwealth police officers are required to be taller and more muscular than the average citizen. I used to be a smaller man, but during my time at the academy adjustments were made. I faced Key Lu with a physical presence optimized to trigger a sense of intimidation in the back brain of a nervous suspect, an effect enhanced by the black fabric of my uniform. Its design was simple—shorts cuffed at the knees and a lightweight pullover with long sleeves that covered the small arsenal of chemical ribbons I carried on my forearms—but its light-swallowing color set me apart from the bright fashions of the celestial cities.

I sat down on the couch opposite Key Lu. He was a well-designed man, nothing eccentric about him, just another good-looking citizen. His hair was presently blond, his eyebrows darker. His balanced face lacked strong features. The only thing notable about him was his injuries. Dark bruises surrounded his eyes and their whites had turned red from burst blood vessels. More bruises discolored swollen tissue beneath his coppery skin.

We studied each other for several seconds, both knowing what was at stake. I was first to speak. "I'm Officer Zeke Choy—"

"I know who you are."

"—of the Commonwealth Police, the watch officer here at Nahiku."

The oldest celestial cities orbited Earth, but Nahiku was newer. It was one in a cluster of three orbital habitats that circled the Sun together, just inside the procession of Venus.

Key Lu addressed me again, with the polite insistence of a desperate man. "I didn't know about the quirk, Officer Choy. I thought I was legal."

The machine voice of a Dull Intelligence whispered into my auditory nerve that he was lying. I already knew that, but I nodded anyway, pretending to believe him.

The DI was housed within my atrium, a neural organ that served as an interface between mind and machine. Atriums are a legal enhancement—they don't change human biology—but Key Lu's quirked physiology that had allowed him to survive short-term exposure to hard vacuum was definitely not.

I was sure his quirk had been done before the age of consent. He'd been born in the Far Reaches among the fragile holdings of the asteroid prospectors, where it must have looked like a reasonable gamble to bioengineer some insurance into his system. Years had passed since then; enforcement had grown stricter. Though Key Lu looked perfectly ordinary, by the law of the Commonwealth, he wasn't even human.

I met his gaze, hoping he was no fool. "Don't tell me anything I don't want to know," I warned him.

I let him consider this for several seconds before I went on. "Your enhancement is illegal under the statutes of the Commonwealth—"

"I understand that, but I didn't know about it."

I nodded my approval of this lie. I needed to maintain the fiction that he hadn't known. It was the only way I could help him. "I'll need your consent to remove it."

A spark of hope ignited in his blooded eyes. "Yes! Yes, of course."

"So recorded." I stood, determined to get the quirk out of his system as soon as possible, before awkward questions could be asked. "Treatment can begin right—"

The door to the interrogation room opened.

I was so startled, I turned with my hand half raised, ready to trigger the ribbon of paralytic still hidden in my palm—only to see Magistrate Glory Mina walk in, flanked by two uniformed cops I'd never seen before.

My DI sent the ribbon retreating back up my forearm while I greeted Glory with a scowl. Nahiku was my territory. I was the only cop assigned to the little city and I was used to having my own way—but with the magistrate's arrival I'd just been overridden.

Goods travel on robotic ships between the celestial cities, but people rarely do. We ghost instead. A ghost—an electronic persona—moves between the data gates at the speed of light. Most ghosts are received on a machine grid or within the virtual reality of a host's atrium, but every city keeps a cold-storage mausoleum. If you have the money—or if you're a cop—you can grow a duplicate body in another city, fully replicated hard copy, ready to roll.

Glory Mina presided over the circuit court based out of Red Star, the primary city in our little cluster. She would have had to put her Red Star body into cold storage before waking up the copy here at Nahiku, but that was hardly more than half an hour's effort. From the eight cops who had husks stashed in the mausoleum, she'd probably pulled two at random to make up the officers for her court.

I was supposed to get a notification anytime a husk in the mausoleum woke up, but obviously she'd overridden that too.

Glory Mina was a small woman with skin the color of cinnamon, and thick, shiny black hair that she kept in a stubble cut. She looked at me curiously, her eyebrows arched. "Officer Choy, I saw the incident report, but I missed your request for a court."

The two cops had positioned themselves on either side of the door.

"I didn't file a request, Magistrate."

"And why not?"

"This is not a criminal case."

No doubt her DI dutifully informed her I was lying—not that she couldn't figure that out for herself. "I don't think that's been determined, Officer Choy. There are records that still need to be considered, which have not made their way into the case file."

I had looked into Key Lu's background. I knew he never translated his persona into an electronic ghost. If he'd ever done so, his illegal quirk would have been detected when he passed through a data gate. I knew he'd never kept a backup record that could be used to restore his body in case of accident. Again, if he'd done so, his quirk would have been revealed. And he never, ever physically left Nahiku, because without a doubt he would have been exposed when he passed through a port gate. The court could use any one of those circumstances to justify interrogation under a coercive drug—which is why I hadn't included any of it in the case file.

"Magistrate, this is a minor case—"

"There are no minor cases, Officer Choy. You're dismissed for now, but please, wait outside."

There was nothing else I could do. I left the room knowing Key Lu was a dead man.

I could have cleaned things up if I'd just had more time. I could have cured Key Lu. I'm a molecular designer and my skills are the reason I was drafted into the Commonwealth police.

Technically, I could have refused to join, but then my home city of Haskins would have been assessed a huge fine—and the city council would have tried to pass the debt on to me. So I consoled myself with the knowledge that I would be working on the cutting edge of molecular research and, swallowing my misgivings, I swore to uphold the laws of the Commonwealth, however arcane and asinine they might be.

I worked hard at my job. I tried to do some good, and though I skirted the boundaries now and then, I made very sure I never went too far because if I got myself fired, the debt for my training would be on me, and the contracts I'd have to take to pay that off didn't bear thinking on.

The magistrate required me to attend the execution, assigning me to stand watch beside the door. I used a mood patch to ensure a proper state of detachment. It's a technique they taught us at the academy, and as I watched the two other officers escort Key Lu into the room, I could tell from their faces they were tranked too, while Key Lu was glassy-eyed, more heavily sedated than the rest of us.

He was guided to a cushioned chair. One of the cops worked an IV into his arm. Five civilians were present, seated in a half circle on either side of the magistrate. One of them was weeping. Her name was Hera Poliu. I knew her because she was a friend of my intimate, Tishembra Indens—but Tishembra had never mentioned that Hera and Key were involved.

The magistrate spoke, summarizing the crime and the sanctity of Commonwealth law, reminding us the law existed to guard society's shared idea of what it means to be human, and that the consequences of violating the law were mandated to be both swift and certain. She nodded at one of the cops, who turned a knob on the IV line, admitting an additional ingredient to the feed. Key Lu slumped and closed his eyes. Hera wept louder, but it was already over.

Nahiku was justly famed for its vista walls which transformed blank corridors into fantasy spaces. On Level 7 West, where I lived, the theme was a wilderness maze enhanced by faint rainforest scents, rustling leaves, bird song, and ghostly puffs of humidity. Apartment doors didn't appear until you asked for them.

The path forked. I went right. Behind me, a woman called my name, "Officer Choy!" Her voice was loud and so vindictive that when the DI whispered in my mind, *Hera Poliu,* I thought, *No way*. I knew Hera and she didn't sound like that. I turned fast.

It was Hera all right, but not like I'd ever seen her. Her fists were clenched, her face flushed, her brows knit in a furious scowl. The DI assessed her as rationally angry, but it didn't seem that way to me. When she stepped into my personal space I felt a chill. "I want to file a complaint," she informed me.

Hera was a full head shorter than me, thin and willowy, with rich brown skin and auburn hair wound up in a knot behind her head. Tishembra had invited her over for dinner a few times and we'd all gone drinking together, but as our eyes locked I felt I was looking at a stranger. "What sort of complaint, Hera?"

"Don't patronize me." I saw no sign in her face of the heart-rending grief she'd displayed at the execution. "The Commonwealth police are supposed to protect us from quirks like Key."

"Key never hurt anyone," I said softly.

"He has now! You didn't hear the magistrate's assessment. She's fined the city for every day since Key became a citizen. We can't afford it, Choy. You know Nahiku already has debt problems—"

"I can't help you, Hera. You need to file an appeal with the magistrate—"

"I want to file a complaint! The city can't get fined for harboring quirks if we turn them in. So I'm reporting Tishembra Indens."

I stepped back. A cold sweat broke out across my skin as I looked away.

Hera laughed. "You already know she's a quirk, don't you? You're a cop, Choy! A Commonwealth cop, infatuated with a quirk. "

I lost my temper. "What's wrong with you? Tishembra's your friend."

"So was Key. And both of them immigrants."

"I can't randomly scan people because they're immigrants."

"If you don't scan her, I'll go to the magistrate."

I tried to see through her anger, but the Hera I knew wasn't there. "No need to bother the magistrate," I said softly, soothingly. "I'll do it."

She nodded, the corner of her lip lifting a little. "I look forward to hearing the result."

I stepped into the apartment to find Tishembra's three-year-old son Robin playing on the floor, shaping bridges and wheels out of colorful gel pods. He looked up at me, a handsome boy with his mother's dark skin and her black, glossy curls, but not her reserved manner. I was treated to a mischievous grin and a firm order to, "Watch this!" Then he hurled himself onto his creations, smashing them all back into disks of jelly.

Tishembra stepped out of the bedroom, lean and dark and elegant, her long hair hanging down her back in a lovely chaos of curls. She'd changed from her work clothes into a silky white shift that I knew was only mindless fabric and still somehow it clung in all the right places as if a DI was controlling the fibers. She was a city engineer. Two years ago she'd emigrated to Nahiku, buying citizenship for herself and Robin—right before the city went into massive debt over an investment in a water-bearing asteroid that turned out to have no water. She was bitter over it, more so because the deal had been made before she arrived, but she shared in the loss anyway.

I crossed the room. She met me halfway. I'd been introduced to her on my second day at Nahiku, seven months ago now, and I'd never looked back. Taking her in my arms, I held her close, letting her presence fill me up as it always did. I breathed in her frustration and her fury and for a giddy moment everything else was blotted from my mind. I was addicted to her moods, all of them. Joy and anger were just different aspects of the same enthralling, intoxicating woman—and the more time I spent with her the more deeply she could touch me in that way. It wasn't love alone. Over time I'd come to realize she had a subtle quirk that let her emotions seep out onto the air around her. Tishembra tended to be reserved and distant. I think the quirk helped her connect with people she casually knew, letting her be perceived as more open and likeable, and easing her way as an immigrant into Nahiku's tightly knit culture—but it wasn't something we could ever talk about.

"You were part of it, weren't you?" she asked me in an angry whisper. "You were part of what happened to Key. Why didn't you stop it?"

Tishembra had taken a terrible chance in getting close to me.

Her fingers dug into my back. "I'm trapped here, Zeke. With the new fine, on top of the old debt... Robin and I will be working a hundred years to earn our way free." She looked up at me, her lip curled in a way that reminded me too much of Hera's parting expression. "It's gotten to the point, my best hope is another disaster. If the city is sold off, I could at least start fresh—"

"Tish, that doesn't matter now." I spoke very softly, hoping Robin wouldn't overhear. "I've received a complaint against you."

Her sudden fear was a radiant thing, washing over me, making me want to hold her even closer, comfort her, keep her forever safe.

"It's ridiculous, of course," I murmured. "To think you're a quirk. I mean, you've been through the gates. So you're clean."

Thankfully, my DI never bothered to point out when *I* was lying.

Tishembra nodded to let me know she understood. She wouldn't tell me anything I didn't want to know; I wouldn't ask her questions—because the less I knew, the better.

My hope rested on the fact that she could not have had the quirk when she came through the port gate into Nahiku. Maybe she'd acquired it in the two years since, or maybe she'd stripped it out when she'd passed through the gate. I was hoping she knew how to strip it again.

"I have to do the scan," I warned her. "Soon. If I don't, the magistrate will send someone who will."

"Tonight?" she asked in a voice devoid of expression. "Or tomorrow?"

I kissed her forehead. "Tomorrow, love. That's soon enough."

Robin was asleep. Tishembra lay beside him on the bed, her eyes half closed, her focus inward as she used her atrium to track the progress of processes I couldn't see. I sat in a chair and watched her. I didn't have to ask if the extraction was working. I knew it was. Her presence was draining away, becoming fainter, weaker, like a memory fading into time.

After a while it got to be too much, waiting for the woman I knew to become someone else altogether. "I'm going out for a while," I said. She didn't answer. Maybe she didn't hear me. I rearmed myself with my chemical arsenal of gel ribbons. Then I put my uniform back on, and I left.

All celestial cities have their own municipal police force. It's often a part-time, amateur operation, but the local force is supposed to investigate traditional crimes like theft, assault, murder—all the heinous things people have done to each other since the beginning of time. The Commonwealth police are involved only when the crime violates statutes involving molecular science, biology, or machine intelligence.

So strictly speaking, I didn't have any legal right or requirement to investigate the original accident that had exposed Key's quirk, but I took the elevator up to Level 1 West anyway, and used my authority to get past the DI that secured the railcar garage.

Nahiku is a twin orbital. Its two inhabited towers are counterweights at opposite ends of a very long carbon-fiber tether that lets them spin around a center point, generating a pseudogravity in the towers. A rail runs the length of the tether, linking Nahiku East and West. The railcar Key Lu had failed to die in was parked in a small repair bay in the West-end garage. Repair work hadn't started on it yet, and the two small holes in its canopy were easy to see.

There was no one around, maybe because it was local-night. That worked for me: I didn't have to concoct a story on why I'd made this my investigation. I started collecting images, measurements, and sample swabs. When the DI picked up traces of explosive residue, I wasn't surprised.

I was inside the car, collecting additional samples from every interior surface, when a faint shift in air pressure warned me a door had opened. Footsteps approached. I don't know who I was expecting. Hera, maybe. Or Tishembra. Not the magistrate.

Glory Mina walked up to the car and, resting her hand on the roof, she bent down to peer at me where I sat on the ruptured upholstery.

"Is there more going on here that I need to know about?" she asked.

I sent her the DI's report. She received it in her atrium, scanned it, and followed my gaze to one of the holes in the canopy. "You're thinking someone tried to kill him."

"Why like this?" I wondered. "Is it coincidence? Or did they know about his quirk?"

"What difference does it make?"

"If the attacker knew about Key, then it was murder by cop."

"And if not, it was just an attempted murder. Either way, it's not your case. This one belongs to the city cops."

I shook my head. I couldn't leave it alone. Maybe that's why my superiors tolerated me. "I like to know what's going on in my city, and the big question I have is *why*? I'm not buying a coincidence. Whoever blew the canopy had to know about Key—so why not just kill him outright? If he'd died like any normal person, I wouldn't have looked into it, you wouldn't have assessed a fine. Who gains, when everyone loses?"

Even as I said the words my thoughts turned to Tishembra, and what she'd said. *It's gotten to the point, my best hope is another disaster.* No. I wasn't going to go there. Not with Tishembra. But maybe she wasn't the only one thinking that way?

The magistrate watched me closely, no doubt recording every nuance of my expression. She said, "I saw the complaint against your intimate."

"It's baseless."

"But you'll look into it?"

"I've scheduled a scan."

Glory nodded. "See to that, but stay out of the local case. This one doesn't belong to you."

The apartment felt empty when I returned. I panicked for the few seconds it took me to sprint across the front room to the bedroom door. Tishembra was still lying on the bed, her half-closed eyes blinking sporadically, but I couldn't *feel* her. Not like before. A sense of abandonment came over me. I knew it was ridiculous, but I felt like she'd walked away.

Robin whimpered in his sleep, turned over, and then awoke. He looked first at Tishembra lying next to him, and then he looked at me. "What happened to Mommy?"

"Mommy's okay."

"She's not. She's wrong."

I went over and picked him up. "Hush. Don't ever say that to anyone but me, okay? We need it to be a secret."

He pouted, but he was frightened, and he agreed.

I spent that night in the front room, with Robin cradled in my arm. I didn't sleep much. I couldn't stop thinking about Key and his quirk, and who might have known about it. Maybe someone from his past? Or someone who'd done a legal mod on him? I had the DI import his personal history into my atrium, but there was no record of any bioengineering work being done on him. Maybe it had just been a lucky guess by someone who knew what went on in the Far Reaches? I sent the DI to search the city files for anyone else who'd ever worked out there. Only one name came back to me: *Tishembra Indens.*

Tishembra and I had never talked much about where we'd come from. I knew circumstances had not been kind to her, but that she'd had to take a contract in the Far Reaches—that shocked me.

My best hope is another disaster.

I deleted the query, I tried to stop thinking, but I couldn't help reflecting that she was an engineer. She had skills. She could work out how to pop the canopy and she'd have access to the supplies to do it.

Eventually I dozed, until Tishembra woke me. I stared at her. I knew her face, but I didn't know her. I couldn't feel her anymore. Her quirk was gone, and she was a stranger to me. I sat up. Robin was still asleep and I cradled his little body against my chest, dreading what would happen when he woke.

"I'm ready," Tishembra said.

I looked away. "I know."

Robin wouldn't let his mother touch him. "You're not you!" he screamed at her with all the fury a three-year-old could muster. Tishembra started to argue with him, but I shook my head, "Deal with it later," and took him into the dining nook, where I got him breakfast and reminded him of our secret.

"I want Mommy," he countered with a stubborn pout.

I considered tranking him, but the staff at the day-venture center would notice and they would ask questions, so I did my best to persuade him that Mommy was Mommy. He remained skeptical. As we left the apartment, he refused to hold Tishembra's hand but ran ahead instead, hiding behind the jungle foliage until we caught up, then running off again. I didn't blame him. In my rotten heart I didn't want to touch her either, but I wasn't three.

So the next time he took off, I slipped my arm around Tishembra's waist and hauled her aside into a nook along the path. We didn't ever kiss or hold hands when I was in uniform and besides, I'd surprised her when her mind was fixed on more serious things, so of course she protested. "Zeke, what are you doing?"

"Hush," I said loudly. "Do you want Robin to find us?"

And I kissed her. I didn't want to. She knew it, and resisted, whispering, "You don't need to feel sorry for me."

But I'd gotten a taste of her mouth, and that hadn't changed. I wanted more. She felt it and softened against me, returning my kiss in a way that made me think we needed to go back to the apartment for a time.

Then Robin was pushing against my hip. "No! Stop that kissing stuff. We have to go to day-venture."

I scowled down at him. "Fine, but I'm holding Tishembra's hand."

"No. I am." And to circumvent further argument, he seized her hand and tugged her toward the path. I let her go with a smirk, but her defiant gaze put an end to that.

"I do love you," I insisted. She shrugged and went with Robin, too proud to believe in me just yet.

Day-venture was on Level 5, where there was a prairie vista. On either side of the path we looked out across a vast land of low, grassy hills, where some sort of herd animals fed in the distance. Waist-high grass grew in a nook outside the doorway to the day-venture center. Robin stomped through it, sending a flutter of butterflies spiraling toward a blue sky. The grass sprang back without damage, betraying a biomechanical nature that the butterflies shared. One of them floated back down to land on Tishembra's hand. She started to shoo it away, but Robin shrieked, "Don't flick it!" and he pounced. "It's a message fly." The butterfly's blue wings spread open as it rested in his small palms. A message was written there, shaped out of white scales drained of pigment, but Robin didn't know how to read yet, so he looked to his mother for help. "What does it say?"

Tishembra gave me a dark look. Then she crouched to read the message and I saw a slight uptick in the corner of her lip. "It says Robin and Zeke love Tishembra." Then she ran her finger down the butterfly's back to erase the message, and nudged it, sending it fluttering away.

"It's wrong," Robin told her defiantly. "I don't love Tishembra. I love Mommy." Then he threw his arms around her neck and kissed her, before running inside to play with his friends.

Tishembra and I went on to my office, where Glory Mina was waiting for us to arrive.

When Tishembra saw the magistrate she turned to me with a look of desperation. I told her the truth. "It doesn't matter."

A deep scan is performed with an injection of molecular-scale machines called Makers that map the body's component systems. The data is fed directly into police records and there's no way to fake the results. Tishembra should have known that, but she looked at me as if I'd betrayed her. "You don't have to worry," I insisted. "The scan is just a formality, a required response in the face of the baseless complaint filed against you."

Glory Mina watched me with a half smile. Naturally, her DI would have told her I was lying.

I led Tishembra into a small exam room and had her sit in a large, cushioned chair. After Glory came in behind us, the office DI locked the door. I handed Tishembra a packet of Makers and she dutifully inhaled it. At the same time my DI whispered that Hera Poliu had arrived in the outer office. Sensing trouble, I looked at the magistrate. "I need to talk to her."

"Who?" Tishembra asked anxiously. "Zeke, what's going on?"

"Nothing's going on. Everything will be fine."

Glory just watched me. I grunted, realizing she'd come not to observe the scan but to gauge the integrity of her Nahiku watch officer, which she had good cause to doubt. "I'll be right back."

The office DI maintained a continuous surveillance of all rooms. I channeled its feed, keeping one eye on Tishembra and another on Hera as she looked around the front office with an anxious gaze. She appeared timid and unsure—nothing at all like the angry woman who had accosted me yesterday. "Zeke?" she called softly. "Are you here?"

When the door opened ahead of me, she startled.

"Zeke!" Hera's hands were shaking. "Is it true Tishembra's been scheduled for a scan? She didn't have anything to do with Key. You have to know that. She hardly knew him. There's no reason to suspect her. Tishembra is my best engineer and if we lose her this city will never recover... Zeke? What is it?"

I think I was standing with my mouth open. "You filed the complaint that initiated the scan!"

"Me? I..." Her focus turned inward. "Oh, yesterday... I wasn't myself. I took the wrong mood patch. I was out of my head. Is Tishembra...?"

The results of the scan arrived in my atrium. I glanced at them, and closed my eyes briefly in silent thanks. "Tishembra has passed her scan."

Against all expectation I'd made a home at Nahiku. I'd found a woman I loved, I'd made friends, and I'd gained trust—to the point that people would come to me for advice and guidance, knowing I wasn't just another jackboot of the Commonwealth.

In one day all that had been shattered and I wanted to know why.

I sent a DI hunting through the datasphere for background on Key Lu. I sent another searching through Hera Poliu's past. I thought about sending a third after Tishembra—but whatever the DI turned up would go into police records and I was afraid of what it might find.

Tish had used a patch to calm herself, resolved to go into work as if nothing was changed. "I'm fine," she insisted when I said I'd walk with her. She resented my coddling, but there were questions I needed to ask. We took the elevator, stepping out into a corridor enhanced with a seascape. The floor appeared as weathered boardwalk; our feet struck it in hollow thumps. Taking her arm, I gently guided her to a nook where a strong breeze blew, carrying what I'm told is the salt scent of an ocean, and hiding the sound of our voices. "Tish, is there anything you need to tell me?"

Resentment simmered in her eyes. "What exactly are you asking?"

"You spent time in the Far Reaches."

"So?"

"Did you know about Key Lu?"

I deserved the contempt that blossomed in her expression. "There are hundreds of tiny settlements out there, Zeke. Maybe thousands. I didn't know him. I didn't know him here, either."

The DI returned an initial infodump. My focus wavered. Tishembra saw it. "What?" she asked me.

"Key Lu was a city finance officer, one who signed off on the water deal."

"The water deal with no water," she amended bitterly. Crossing her arms, she glared at the ocean.

"Someone tried to kill him," I told her, letting my words blend in with the sea breeze.

She froze, her gaze fixed on the horizon.

"There was never a micrometeor. His railcar was sabotaged."

I couldn't read her face and neither could the DI. Maybe it was the patch she'd used to level her emotions, but her fixed expression frightened me.

She knew what was going on in my head, though. "You're asking yourself who has the skill to do that, aren't you? Who could fake a meteor strike? If it were me, I'd do it with explosive patches, one inside, one outside, to get the trajectory correct. Is that how it was done, Zeke?"

"Yes."

Her gaze was still fixed on the horizon. "It wasn't me."

"Okay."

She turned and looked me in the eye. "*It wasn't me.*"

The DI whispered that she spoke the truth. I smiled my relief and reached for her, but she backed away. "No, Zeke."

"Tish, come on. Don't be mad. This day is making us both crazy."

"I haven't accused you of being a murderer."

"Tish, I'm sorry."

She shook her head. "I remember when we used to trust each other. I think that was yesterday."

The second DI arrived with an initial report on Hera. Like an idiot, I scanned the file. To my surprise, I had a new suspect, but while I was distracted, Tishembra walked away.

Glory Mina was waiting for me when I returned to my office. She'd tracked my DIs and copied herself on their reports. "You should have been a municipal cop," she told me. She sat perched on the arm of a chair, her arms crossed and her eyes twinkling with amusement.

"It's not like I had a choice."

She cocked her head, allowing me the point. Reading from the DI's report, she said, "So Hera Poliu had a brother. Four years ago he was exiled from Nahiku, and a year after that he was arrested and executed for an illegal enhancement."

"Hera lost her brother. She's got to resent it. Maybe she resents anybody who has a—" I caught myself. "Anybody she *thinks* might have a quirk."

"Maybe," Glory conceded. "And maybe that's why she made a complaint against your intimate, but so what? It's not your case, Zeke. Forward what you've got to whoever had the misfortune to be appointed as the criminal investigator in this little paradise and let it go."

I made compliant noises. She shook her head, not needing the DI to know I wasn't being straight. "Walk with me."

"Where?"

"The mausoleum. I'm going home. But on the way there, you're going to listen to what I have to say about the necessity for boundaries." She crooked her finger at me. I shrugged and followed. As we walked past the vistas she lectured me on the essential but very limited role of the Commonwealth police and warned me that my appointment as watch officer at Nahiku could end at any time. I listened patiently, knowing she would soon be gone.

As we approached the mausoleum, I sent a DI to open the door. Inside was a long hallway with locked doors on either side. Behind the doors were storage chambers, most of them belonging to corporations. The third door on the left secured the police chamber. It opened as we approached, and closed again when we had stepped inside. One wall held clothing lockers. The other, ranks of cold storage drawers stacked four high. "Magistrate Glory Mina," Glory said to the room DI. She stripped off her clothes and hung them in one of the lockers while the drawers slid past each other, rearranging themselves. Only two were empty. One was mine. The other descended from the top rank to the second level, where it opened, ready to receive her.

Glory closed the locker door. She was naked and utterly unconcerned about it. She turned to me with a stern gaze. "You tried to pretend Key Lu was a victim. This once, I'm going to pretend you just missed a step in the background investigation. Zeke, as much as you don't like being a cop, being an ex-cop can be a lot worse."

I had no answer for that. I knew she was right.

She climbed into the drawer. As soon as she lay back, the cushions inflated around her, creating a moist interface all across the surface of her skin. The drawer slid shut and locked with a soft snick. Very soon, her ghost would be on its way to Red Star. Once again, I was on my own.

No matter what Glory wanted, there was no way I was going to set this case aside. Key Lu was dead, while Tishembra had been threatened and made into a stranger, both to me and to her own son. I wanted to know who was responsible and why.

Still, I knew how to make concessions. So I set up an appointment with an official who served part-time as a city cop, intending to hand over the case files, if only for the benefit of my personnel record. But before that could happen a roving DI returned to me with the news that the city's auto-defense system had locked down a plague outbreak on Level 5 West. The address was Robin's day-venture center.

It took me ninety seconds to strip off my uniform and wrap on the impermeable hide of a vacuum-capable skinsuit, police black, with gold insignia. Then I grabbed a standard-issue bivouac kit that weighed half as much as I did, and I raced out the door.

We call it plague, but it's not. Each of us is an ecosystem. We're inhabited by a host of Makers. Some repair our bodies and our minds, keeping us young and alert, and some run our atriums. But most of our Makers exist only to defend us against hostile nanotech—the snakes that forever prowl the Garden of Eden, the nightmares devised by twisted minds—and sometimes our defenses fail.

A general alert had not been issued—that was standard policy to avoid panic—but as soon as I was spotted on the paths wearing my skinsuit, word went out through informal channels that something was wrong. By the time I reached the day-venture center people had already guessed where I was going and a crowd was beginning to form against the backdrop of prairie. The city's emergency response team hadn't arrived yet, so questions were shouted at me. I refused to answer. "Stay back!" I commanded, issuing an order for the center's locked door to open.

In an auto-defense lockdown, a gel barrier is extruded around the suspect zone. The door slid back to reveal a wall of blue-tinged gel behind it. I pulled up the hood of my skinsuit and let it seal. Then I leaned into the gel wall, feeling it give way slowly around me, and after a few seconds I was able to pass through. As soon as I was clear, the door closed and locked behind me.

The staff and children were huddled on one side of the room—six adults and twenty-two kids. They looked frightened, but otherwise okay. Robin wasn't with them. The director started to speak but I couldn't hear him past the skinsuit, so I forced an atrial link to every adult in the room, "Give me your status."

The director spoke again, this time through my atrium. "It's Robin. He was hit hard only a couple of minutes ago. Shakes and sweats. His system's chewing up all his latents and he went down right away. I think it's targeted. No one else has shown any signs."

"Where is he?"

The director looked toward the nap room.

I didn't want to think too hard, I just wanted to get Robin stable, but the director's assessment haunted me. A targeted assault meant that Robin alone was the intended victim; that the hostile Maker had been designed to activate in his unique ecosystem.

I found him on the floor, trembling in the grip of a hypoglycemic seizure, all his blood sugars gone to fuel the reproduction of Makers in his body—both defensive and assault—as the tiny machines ramped up their populations to do battle on a molecular scale. His eyelids fluttered, but I could only see the whites. His black curls were sodden with sweat.

I unrolled the bivouac kit with its thick gel base designed for a much larger patient. Then I lifted his small body, laid him on it, and touched the activation points. The gel folded around him like a cocoon. The bivouac was a portable version of the cold storage drawer that had enfolded Glory. Robin's core temperature plummeted, while an army of defensive Makers swarmed past the barrier of his skin in a frantic effort to stabilize him.

The city's emergency team came in wearing sealed skinsuits. I stood by as they scanned the other kids, the staff, the rooms, and me, finding nothing. Only Robin was affected.

I stripped off my hood. Out in the playroom, the gel membrane was coming down and the kids were going home, but inside the bivouac Robin lay in stasis, his biological processes all but stopped. Even the data on his condition had been pared to a trickle. Still, I'd seen enough to know what was happening: the assault Makers were attacking Robin's neuronal connections, writing chaos into the space where Robin used to be. We would lose him if we allowed him to revive.

I checked city records for the date of his last backup. I couldn't find one. Robin had turned three a few weeks ago. I remembered we'd talked about taking him in to get a backup done… but we'd been busy.

The emergency team came back into the nap room with a gurney. Tishembra came with them. One glance at her face told me she'd been heavily tranked.

At first she didn't say anything, just watched with lips slightly parted and an expression of quiet horror on her face as the bivouac was lifted onto the gurney. But as the gurney was rolled away she asked in a defeated voice, "Is he going to die?"

"Of course he's not going to die."

She turned an accusing gaze on me. "My DI says you're lying."

I cursed myself silently and tried again, determined to speak the truth this time. "He's not going to die, because I won't let him."

She nodded, as if I'd got it right. The trank had turned her mood to smooth, hard glass. "I made this happen."

"What are you talking about?"

She turned her right hand palm up. A blue prairie butterfly rested in it, crushed and lifeless. I picked it up; spread its wings open. The message was only a little blurred from handling. On the left wing I read, *You lived*, and on the right, *so he dies*.

So someone had watched as we'd dropped Robin off that morning. I looked up at Tishembra. "No," I told her. "That's not the way it's going to work."

The attack on Robin was a molecular crime, which made it my case, and I was prepared to use every resource of the police to solve it.

Tishembra nodded. Then she left, following the gurney.

I could work anywhere, using my atrium, so I stayed for a time. First I packed up every bit of data I had on Robin's condition and sent it to six different police labs, hoping at least one could come up with the design for a Maker that could stop the assault on Robin's brain cells. The odds of success would go up dramatically if I could get the specs of the assault Maker—and the easiest way to do that was to track down the twisted freak who'd designed it.

Easy steps first: I sent a DI into the datasphere to assemble a list of everyone at Nahiku with extensive molecular design experience. The DI came back with one name: mine.

So I was dealing with a talented hobbyist.

It could be anyone.

I sent the DI out again. No record was kept of butterfly messages—they were designed to be anonymous—but surveillance records were collected on every public path. I instructed the DI to access the records and assemble a list of everyone who'd set foot on Level 5 at any time that day, because the blue prairie butterflies could only be accessed from there. The list that came back was long. Name after name scrolled through my visual field, many that I recognized, but only one stood out in my mind: Hera Poliu.

I summoned the vid attached to her name. It was innocuous. She'd been taking the stairs between levels and had paused briefly on the landing. Still, it bothered me. Hera had been involved with Key Lu, she'd filed the complaint against Tishembra, and now I had her on Level 5. Coincidence maybe... but I remembered the chill I'd felt when she accosted me in the corridor... and how confused she'd been when I reminded her of the incident.

I went by my office and changed back into my uniform. Then I checked city records for Hera's location. She was at the infirmary, sitting with Tishembra... Tishembra, who'd been a quirk just like Hera's brother except she'd eluded punishment while Hera's brother was dead. Maybe it was baseless panic, but I sprinted for the door.

The infirmary had a reception room with a desk, and a hallway behind it with small rooms on either side. The technician at the desk looked up as

I burst in. "Robin Indens!" I barked.

"Critical care. End of the hall."

I sprinted past him. A sign identified the room. I touched the door and it snapped open. The bivouac had been set up on a table in the center of the room. Slender feeder lines descending from the ceiling were plugged into its ports. Tishembra and Hera stood alongside the bivouac, Hera with a comforting arm around Tishembra's shoulders. They both looked up as I burst in. "Zeke?" Tishembra asked, with an expression encompassing both hope and dread.

"Tish, it's going to be okay. But I need to talk to Hera. Alone."

They traded a puzzled glance. Then Hera gave Tishembra a quick hug— "I'll be right back"—and stepped past me into the hall. I followed her, closing the door behind us.

Hera turned to face me. She looked gaunt and worn—a woman who had seen too much grief. "I want to thank you, Zeke, for not telling Tishembra who filed that complaint. I wasn't myself when I did it. I don't even remember doing it."

She wasn't lying.

I stumbled over that fact. Had I gotten it wrong? Was there something more going on than a need for misguided revenge?

"When was the last time you had your defensive Makers upgraded?"

She flinched and looked away. "It's been a while."

I sent a DI to check the records. It had been three years. I pulled up an earlier report and cross checked the dates to be sure. She hadn't had an upgrade since her brother's execution. My heart rate jumped as I contemplated a new possibility. No doubt my pupils dilated, but Hera was still looking away and she didn't see it. I sent the DI out again.

We were standing beside an open door to an unoccupied office. I ushered Hera inside. The DI came back with a new set of records even before the door was closed. At my invitation, Hera sat in the guest chair, her hands fidgeting restlessly in her lap. I perched on the edge of the desk, scanning the records, trying to stay calm, but my DI wasn't fooled. It sensed my stress and sent the paralytic ribbon creeping down my arm and into my palm.

"Let's talk about your brother."

Hera's hands froze in her lap. "My brother? You must know already. He's dead… he died like Key."

"You used to be a city councilor."

"I resigned from the council."

I nodded. "As a councilor you were required to host visitors… but you haven't allowed a ghost in your atrium since your brother's arrest."

"Those things don't matter to me anymore."

"You also haven't upgraded your defensive Makers, and you haven't been scanned—"

"I'm not a criminal, Zeke. I just… I just want to do my job, and be left alone."

"Hera? You've been harboring your brother's ghost, haven't you? And he didn't like it, when you started seeing Key."

The DI showed me the flush of hot and cold across her skin. "No," she whispered. "No. He's dead, and I wouldn't do that."

She was lying. "Hera, is your atrium quirked? To let your brother's ghost take over sometimes?"

She looked away. "Wouldn't that be illegal?"

"Giving up your body to another? Yes, it would be."

Her hands squeezed hard against the armrests of the chair. "It was him, then? That's what you're saying?" She turned to look at me, despair in her eyes. "He filed the complaint against Tish?"

I nodded. "I knew it wasn't you speaking to me that day. I think he also used you to sabotage Key's railcar, knowing I'd have to look into it."

"And Robin?" she asked, her knuckles whitening as she gripped the chair.

"Ask him."

Earlier, I'd asked the DI to bring me a list of all the trained molecular designers in Nahiku, but I'd asked the wrong question. I queried it again, asking for all the designers in the past five years. This time, mine wasn't the only name.

"Ask him for the design of the assault Maker, Hera. Robin doesn't deserve to die."

I crouched in front of her, my hand on hers as I looked up into her stunned eyes. It was a damned stupid position to put myself into.

He took over. It took a fraction of a second. My DI didn't catch it, but I saw it happen. Her expression hardened and her knee came up, driving hard into my chin. As my head snapped back he launched Hera against me. At that point it didn't matter that I outweighed her by forty percent. I was off balance and I went down with her on top of me. Her forehead cracked against my nose, breaking it.

He wasn't trying to escape. There was no way he could. It was only blind rage that drove him. He wanted to kill me, for all the good it would do. I was a cop. I had backups. I couldn't lose more than a few days. But he could still do some damage before he was brought down.

I felt Hera's small hands seize my wrists. He was trying to keep me from using the ribbon arsenal, but Hera wasn't nearly strong enough for that. I tossed her off, and not gently. The back of her head hit the floor, but she got up again almost as fast as I did and scrambled for the door.

I don't know what he intended to do, what final vengeance he hoped for. One more murder, maybe. Tishembra and Robin were both just across the hall.

I grabbed Hera, dragged her back, and slammed her into the chair. Then I raised my hand. The DI controlled the ribbon. Fibers along its length squeezed hard, sending a fine mist across Hera's face. It got in her eyes and in her lungs. She reared back, but then she collapsed, slumping in the chair. I wiped my bloody nose on my sleeve and waited until her head lolled against her chest. Then I sent a DI to Red Star.

I'd need help extracting the data from her quirked atrium, and combing through it for the assault Maker's design file.

It took a few days, but Robin was recovered. When he gets cranky at night he still tells Tishembra she's "wrong," but he's only three. Soon he won't remember what she was like before, while I pretend it doesn't matter to me.

Tishembra knows that isn't true. She complains the laws are too strict, that citizens should be free to make their own choices. Me, I'm just happy Glory Mina let me stay on as Nahiku's watch officer. Glory likes reminding me how lucky I am to have the position. I like to remind her that I've finally turned into the uncompromising jackboot she always knew I could be.

Don't get me wrong. I wanted to help Hera, but she'd been harboring a fugitive for three years. There was nothing I could do for her, but I won't let anyone else in this city step over the line. I don't want to sit through another execution.

Nahiku isn't quite bankrupt yet. Glory assessed a minimal fine for Hera's transgression, laying most of the fault on the police since we'd failed to hunt down all ghosts of a condemned criminal. So the city won't be sold off, and Tishembra will have to wait to get free.

I don't think she minds too much.

Here. Now. This is enough. I only wonder: Can we make it last?

FADE TO WHITE

CATHERYNNE M. VALENTE

Catherynne M. Valente [www.catherynnemvalente.com] *is the* New York Times *bestselling author of over a dozen works of fiction and poetry, including* Palimpsest, *the "Orphan's Tales" series,* Deathless, *and the crowd-funded phenomenon* The Girl Who Circumnavigated Fairyland in a Ship of Her Own Making. *She is the winner of the Andre Norton Award, the Tiptree Award, the Mythopoeic Award, the Rhysling Award, and the Million Writers Award, and has been nominated for the Hugo, Locus, Spectrum, and World Fantasy awards, and was a finalist for the Pushcart Prize. Her most recent novel,* The Girl Who Fell Beneath Fairyland and Led the Revels There, *is a* Time *magazine book of the year. She lives on an island off the coast of Maine with her partner, two dogs, and an enormous cat.*

Fight the Communist Threat in Your Own Backyard!

ZOOM IN *on a bright-eyed Betty in a crisp green dress, maybe pick up the shade of the spinach in the lower left frame. [Note to Art Dept: Good morning, Stone! Try to stay awake through the next meeting, please. I think we can get more patriotic with the dress. Star-Spangled Sweetheart, steamset hair the color of good American corn, that sort of thing. Stick to a red, white, and blue palette.] She's holding up a resplendent head of cabbage the size of a pre-war watermelon. Her bicep bulges as she balances the weight of this New Vegetable, grown in a Victory Brand Capsule Garden. [Note to Art Dept: Is cabbage the most healthful vegetable? Carrots really pop, and root vegetables emphasize the safety of Synthasoil generated by Victory Brand Capsules.]*

Betty looks INTO THE CAMERA and says: Just because the war is over doesn't mean your Victory Garden has to be! The vigilant wife knows that every garden planted is a munitions plant in the War Fight Struggle Against Communism. Just one Victory Brand Capsule and a dash of fresh Hi-Uranium Mighty Water can provide an average yard's worth of safe, rich, synthetic soil—and the seeds are included! *STOCK FOOTAGE of scientists: beakers, white coats, etc.* Our boys in the lab have developed a wide range of hardy, modern seeds from pre-war heirloom collections to produce the Vegetables of the Future. *[Note to Copy: Do not mention pre-war seedstock.]* Just look at this beautiful New Cabbage. Efficient, bountiful, and only three weeks from planting to table. *[Note to Copy: Again with the cabbage? You know who eats a lot of cabbage, Stone? Russians. Give her a big old zucchini. Long as a man's arm. Have her hold it in her lap so the head rests on her tits.]*

BACK to Betty, walking through cornstalks like pine trees. And that's not all. With a little help from your friends at Victory, you can feed your family *and* play an important role in the defense of the nation. *Betty leans down to show us big, leafy plants growing in her Synthasoil. [Note to Casting: make sure we get a busty girl, so we see a little cleavage when she bends over. We're hawking fertility here. Hers, ours.]* Here's a tip: Plant our patented Liberty Spinach at regular intervals. Let your little green helpers go to work leeching useful isotopes and residual radioactivity from rain, groundwater, just about anything! *[Note to Copy: Stone, you can't be serious. Leeching? That sounds dreadful. Reaping. Don't make me do your job for you.]* Turn in your crop at Victory Depots for Harvest Dollars redeemable at a variety of participating local establishments! *[Note to Project Manager: Can't we get some soda fountains or something to throw us a few bucks for ad placement here? Missed opportunity! And couldn't we do a regular feature with the "tips" to move other products, make Betty into a trusted household name—but not Betty. Call her something that starts with T, Tammy? Tina? Theresa?]*

Betty smiles. The camera pulls out to show her surrounded by a garden in full bloom and three [Note to Art Dept: Four minimum] kids in overalls carrying baskets of huge, shiny New Vegetables. The sun is coming up behind her. The slogan scrolls up in red, white, and blue type as she says:

A free and fertile tomorrow. Brought to you by Victory.

Fade to white.

The Hydrodynamic Front

More than anything in the world, Martin wanted to be a Husband when he grew up.

Sure, he had longed for other things when he was young and silly—to be a milkman, a uranium prospector, an astronaut. But his fifteenth birthday was zooming up with alarming speed, and becoming an astronaut now struck him as an impossibly, almost obscenely trivial goal. Martin no longer drew pictures of the moon in his notebooks or begged his mother to order the whiz-bang home enrichment kit from the tantalizing back pages of *Popular Mechanics*. His neat yellow pencils still kept up near-constant flight passes over the pale blue lines of composition books, but what Martin drew now were babies. In cradles and out, girls with bows in their bonnets and boys with rattles shaped like rockets, newborns and toddlers. He drew pictures of little kids running through clean, tall grass, reading books with straw in their mouths, hanging out of trees like rosy-cheeked fruit. He sketched during history, math, civics: twin girls sitting at a table gazing up with big eyes at their Father, who kept his hat on while he carved a holiday Brussels sprout the size of a dog. Triplet boys wrestling on a pristine, uncontaminated beach. In Martin's notebooks, everyone had twins and triplets.

Once, alone in his room at night, he had allowed himself to draw quadruplets. His hand quivered with the richness and wonder of those four perfect graphite faces asleep in their four identical bassinets.

Whenever Martin drew babies they were laughing and smiling. He could not bear the thought of an unhappy child. He had never been one, he was pretty sure. His older brother Henry had. He still cried and shut himself up in Father's workshop for days, which Martin would never do because it was very rude. But then, Henry was born before the war. He probably had a lot to cry about. Still, on the rare occasion that Henry made a cameo appearance in Martin's gallery of joyful babies, he was always grinning. Always holding a son of his own. Martin considered those drawings a kind of sympathetic magic. Make Henry happy—watch his face at dinner and imagine what it would look like if he cracked a joke. Catch him off guard, snorting, which was as close as Henry ever got to laughing, at some pratfall on *The Mr. Griffith Show*. Make Henry happy in a notebook and he'll be happy in real life. Put a baby in his arms and he won't have to go to the Front in the fall.

Once, and only once, Martin had tried this magic on himself. With very careful strokes and the best shading he'd ever managed, he had drawn himself in a beautiful gray suit, with a professional grade shine on his shoes and a strong angle to his hat. He drew a briefcase in his own hand. He tried to imagine what his face would look like when it filled out, got square-jawed and handsome the way a man's face should be. How he would style his hair when he became a Husband. Whether he would grow a beard. Painstakingly, he drew a double Windsor knot in his future tie, which Martin considered the most masculine and elite knot.

And finally, barely able to breathe with longing, he outlined the long, gorgeous arc of a baby's carriage, the graceful fall of a lace curtain so that the penciled child wouldn't get sunburned, big wheels capable of a smoothness that bordered on the ineffable. He put the carriage-handle into his own firm hand. It took Martin two hours to turn himself into a Husband. When the spell was finished, he spritzed the drawing with some of his mother's hairspray so that it wouldn't smudge and folded it up flat and small. He kept it in his shirt pocket. Some days, he could feel the drawing move with his heart. And when Father hugged him, the paper would crinkle pleasantly between them, like a whispered promise.

Static Overpressure

The day of Sylvie's Presentation broke with a dawn beyond red, beyond blood or fire. She lay in her spotless white and narrow bed, quite awake, gazing at the colors through her Sentinel Gamma Glass window—lower rates of corneal and cellular damage than their leading competitors, guaranteed. Today, the sky could only remind Sylvie of birth. The screaming scarlet folds of clouds, the sun's crowning head. Sylvie knew it was the hot ash that made every sunrise and sunset into a torture of magenta and violet and crimson, the superheated cloud vapor that never cooled. She winced as though red could hurt her—which of course it could. Everything could.

Sylvie had devoted a considerable amount of time to imagining how this day would go. She did not worry and she was not afraid, but it had always sat there in her future, unmovable, a mountain she could not get through or around. There would be tests, for intelligence, for loyalty, for genetic defects, for temperament, for fertility, which wasn't usually a problem for women but better safe than sorry. Better safe than assign a Husband to a woman as barren as California. There would be a medical examination so invasive it came all the way around to no big deal. When a doctor can get that far inside you, into your blood, your chromosomes, your potentiality and all your possible futures, what difference could her white gloved fingers on your cervix make?

None of that pricked up her concern. The tests were nothing. Sylvie prided herself on being realistic about her qualities. First among these was her intellect; like her mother Hannah she could cut glass with the diamond of her mind. Second was her silence. Sylvie had discovered when she was quite small that adults were discomfited by silence. It brought them running. And when she was angry, upset, when the world offended her, Sylvie could draw down a coil of silence all around her, showing no feeling at all, until whoever had affronted her grew so uncomfortable that they would beg forgiveness just to end the ordeal. There was no third, not really. She was what her mother's friends called striking, but never pretty. Narrow frame, small breasts, short and dark. Nothing in her matched up with the fashionable Midwestern fertility goddess floor-model. And she heard what they did not say, also—that she was not pretty because there was something off in her features, a ghost in her cheekbones, her height, her straight, flat hair.

Sylvie gave up on the fantasy of sliding back into sleep. She flicked on the radio by her bed: *Brylcreem Makes a Man a Husband!* announced a tinny woman's voice, followed by a cheerful blare of brass and the morning's reading from the Book of Pseudo-Matthew. Sylvie preferred Luke. She opened her closet as though today's clothes had not been chosen for years, hanging on the wooden rod behind all the others, waiting for her to grow into them. She pulled out the dress and draped it over her bed. It lay there like another girl. Someone who looked just like her but had already moved through the hours of the day and come out on the other side. The red sky turned the deep neckline into a gash.

She was not ready for it yet.

Sylvie washed her body with the milled soap provided by Spotless Corp. Bright as a pearl, wrapped in white muslin and a golden ribbon. It smelled strongly of rose and mint and, underneath, a blue chemical tang. The friendly folks at Spotless also supplied hair rinse, cold cream, and talcum for her special day. All the bottles and cakes smelled like that, like growing things piled on top of something biting, corrosive. The basket had arrived last month with a bow and a dainty card attached congratulating her. Until now it had loomed in her room like a Christmas tree, counting down. Now Sylvie pulled the regimented colors and fragrances out and applied them precisely, correctly, according to directions. An oyster-pink shade called *The Blossoming of the Rod* on her fingernails, which may not be cut short. A soft peach called *Penance* on her eyes, which may not be lined. Pressed powder (*The Visitation of the Dove*) should be liberally applied, but only the merest breath of blush (*Parable of the Good Harlot*) is permitted. Sylvie pressed a rosy champagne stain (*Armistice*) onto her lips with a forefinger. Hair must be natural and worn long—no steamsetting or straightening allowed. Everyone broke that rule, though. Who could tell a natural curl from a roller these days? Sylvie combed her black hair out and clipped it back with the flowers assigned to her county this year—snowdrops for hope and consolation. Great bright thornless roses as red as the sky for love at first sight, for passion and lust.

Finally the dress. The team at Spotless Corp. encouraged foundational garments to emphasize the bust and waist-to-hip ratio. Sylvie wedged herself into a full length merry widow with built-in padded bra and rear. It crushed her, smoothed her, flattened her. Her waist disappeared. She pulled the dress over her bound-in body. Her mother would have to button her up; twenty-seven tiny, satin colored buttons ran up her back like a new spine. Its neckline plunged; its skirt flounced, showing calf and a suggestion of knee. It was miles of icy white lace, it could hardly be anything else, but the sash gleamed red. Red, red, red. *All the world is red and I am red forever*, Sylvie thought. She was inside the dress, inside the other girl.

The other girl was very striking.

Sylvie was fifteen years old, and by suppertime she would be engaged.

Even Honest Joe Loves an Ice-Cold Brotherhood Beer!

CLOSE-UP on President McCarthy in shirtsleeves, popping the top on a distinctive green glass bottle of BB—now with improved flavor and more potent additives! We see the moisture glisten on the glass and an honest day's sweat on the President's brow. [Note to Art Dept: I see what you're aiming at, but let's not make him look like a clammy swamp creature, shall we? He's not exactly the most photogenic gent to begin with.]

NEW SHOT: five Brothers relaxing together in the sun with a tin bucket full of ice and green bottlenecks. Labels prominently displayed. A Milkman, a TV Repairman, a couple of G-Men, and a Soldier. [Note to Casting: Better make it one government jockey and two soldiers. Statistically speaking, more of them are soldiers than anything else.] They are smiling, happy, enjoying each other's company. The Soldier, a nice-looking guy but not too nice-looking, we don't want to send the wrong message, says: There's nothing like a fresh swig of Brotherhood after spending a hot Nevada day eye to eye with a Russkie border guard. The secret is in the thorium-boosted hops and New Barley fresh from Alaska, crisp iodine-treated spring water and just a dash of good old-fashioned patriotism. The Milkman chimes in with: And 5-Alpha! They all laugh. [Note to Copy: PLEASE use the brand name! We've had meetings about this! Chemicals sound scary. Who wants to put some freakshow in your body when you can take a nice sip of Arcadia? Plus those bastards at Standard Ales are calling their formula Kool and their sales are up 15%. You cannot beat that number, Stone.] TV Repairman pipes up: That's right, Bob! There's no better way to get your daily dose than with the cool, refreshing taste of Brotherhood. They use only the latest formulas: smooth, mellow, and with no jitters or lethargy. *G-Man pulls a bottle from the ice and takes a good swallow.* 5-Alpha leaves my head clear and my spirits high. I can work all day serving our great nation without distraction, aggression, or unwanted thoughts. *Second G-Man:* I'm a patriot. I don't need all those obsolete hormones anymore. And Brotherhood Beer strikes a great bargain—all that and 5.6% alcohol! *Our soldier stands up and salutes. He wears an expression of steely determination and rugged cheer. He says:* Well, boys, I've got an appointment with Ivan to keep. Keep the Brotherhood on ice for me.

QUICK CUT back to President McCarthy. He puts down his empty bottle and picks up a file or something in the Oval Office. Slogan comes in at hip level [Note to Art Dept: How are we coming on that wheatstalk font?]:

Where There's Life, There's Brotherhood.

Fade to white.

Optimum Burst Altitude

One week out of every four, Martin's Father came home. Martin could feel the week coming all month like a slow tide. He knew the day, the hour. He sat by the window tying and untying double Windsor knots into an old silk tie Dad had let him keep years ago. The tie was emerald green with little red chevrons on it.

Cross, fold, push through. Wrap, fold, fold, over the top, fold, fold, pull down. Make it tight. Make it perfect.

When the Cadillac pulled into the drive, Martin jumped for the gin and the slippers like a golden retriever. His Father's martini was a ritual, a eucharist. Ice, gin, swirl in the shaker, just enough so that the outer layer of ice releases into the alcohol. Open the vermouth, bow in the direction of the Front, and close it again. Two olives, not three, and a glass from the freezebox. These were the sacred objects of a Husband. Tie, Cadillac, martini. And then Dad would open the door and Faraday, the Irish setter, would yelp with waggy happiness and so would Martin. He'd be wearing a soft gray suit. He'd put his hat on the rack. Martin's mother, Rosemary, would stand on her tiptoes to kiss him in one of her good dresses, the lavender one with daises on the hem, or if it was a holiday, her sapphire-colored velvet. Her warm blonde hair would be perfectly set, and her lips would leave a gleaming red kiss-shape on his cheek. Dad wouldn't wipe it off. He'd greet his son with a firm handshake that told Martin all he needed to know: he was a man, his martini was good, his knots were strong.

Henry would slam the door to his bedroom upstairs and refuse to come down to supper. This pained Martin; the loud bang scuffed his heart. But he tried to understand his brother—after all, a Husband must possess great wells of understanding and compassion. Dad wasn't Henry's father. Pretending that he was probably scuffed something inside the elder boy, too.

The profound and comforting sameness of those Husbanded weeks overwhelmed Martin's senses like the slightly greasy swirls of gin in that lovely triangular glass. The first night, they would have a roasting chicken with crackling golden skin. Rosemary had volunteered to raise several closely observed generations of an experimental breed called Sacramento Clouds: vicious, bright orange and oversized, dosed with palladium every fortnight, their eggs covered in rough calcium deposits like lichen. For this reason they could have a whole bird once a month. The rest of the week were New Vegetables from the Capsule Garden. Carrots, tomatoes, sprouts, potatoes, kale. Corn if it was fall and there hadn't been too many high-level days when no one could go out and tend the plants. But there was always that one delicious day when Father was at home and they had chicken.

After dinner, they would retire to the living room. Mom and Dad would have sherry and Martin would have a Springs Eternal Vita-Pop if he had been very good, which he always was. He liked the lime flavor best. They would watch *My Five Sons* for half an hour before Rosemary's Husband retired with her to bed. Martin didn't mind that. It was what Husbands were for. He liked to listen to the sounds of their lovemaking through the wall between their rooms. They were reassuring and good. They put him to sleep like a lullaby about better times.

And one week out of every four, Martin would ask his Father to take him to the city.

"I want to see where you work!"

"This is where I work, son," Father would always say in his rough-soft voice. "Right here."

Martin would frown and Dad would hold him tight. Husbands were not afraid of affection. They had bags of it to share. "I'll tell you what, Marty, if your Announcement goes by without a hitch, I'll take you to the city myself. March you right into the Office and show everyone what a fine boy Rosie and I made. Might even let you puff on a cigar."

And Martin would hug his Father fiercely, and Rosemary would smile over her fiber-optic knitting, and Henry would kick something upstairs. It was regular as a clock, and the clock was always right. Martin knew he'd be Announced, no problem. Piece of cake. Mom was super careful with the levels on their property. They planted Liberty Spinach. Martin was first under his desk every time the siren went off at school. After Henry's Announcement had gone so badly, he and Mom had installed a Friendlee Brand Geiger Unit every fifteen feet and the light-up aw-shucks faces had only turned into frowns and x-eyes a few times ever. There was no chance Martin could fail. Things were way better now. Not like when Henry was a kid. No, Martin would be Announced and he'd go to the city and smoke his cigar. He'd be ready. He'd be the best Husband anyone ever met.

Aaron Grudzinski liked to tell him it was all shit. That was, in fact, Aaron's favorite observation on nearly anything. Martin liked the way he swore, gutturally, like it really meant something. Grud was in Martin's year. He smoked Canadian cigarettes and nipped some kind of homebrewed liquor from his gray plastic thermos. He'd egged Martin into a sip once. It tasted like dirt on fire.

"Look, didn't you ever wonder why they wait 'til you're fifteen to do it? Obviously they can test you anytime after you pop your first boner. As soon as you're brewing your own, yeah?" And Grud would shake his flask. "But no, they make this huge deal out of going down to Matthew House and squirting in a cup. The outfit, the banquet, the music, the filmstrips. It's all shit. Shit piled up into a pretty castle around a room where they give you a magazine full of the wholesome housewives of 1940 and tell you to do it for America. And you look down at the puddle at the bottom of the plastic tumbler they call your chalice, your chalice with milliliter measurements printed on the side, and you think: *That's all I am. Two to six milliliters of warm wet nothing.*" Grud spat a brown tobacco glob onto the dead grass of the baseball field. He knuckled at his eye, his voice getting raw. "Don't you get it? They have to give you hope. Well, I mean, they have to give *you* hope. I'm a lost cause. Three strikes before I got to bat. But you? They gotta build you up, like how everyone salutes Sgt. Dickhead on leave from the glowing shithole that is the great state of Arizona. If they didn't shake his hand and kiss his feet, he might start thinking it's not worth melting his face off down by the Glass. If you didn't think you could make it, you'd just kill yourself as soon as you could read the newspaper."

"I wouldn't," Martin whispered.

"Well, I would."

"But Grud, there's so few of us left."

The school siren klaxoned. Martin bolted inside, sliding into the safe space under his desk like he was stealing home.

The Shadow Effect

Every Sunday Sylvie brought a couple of Vita-Pops out to the garage and set up her film projector in the hot dark. Her mother went to her Ladies' Auxiliary meeting from two to four o'clock. Sylvie swiped hors d'oeuvres and cookies from the official spread and waited in the shadows for Clark Baker to shake his mother and slip in the side door. The film projector had been a gift from her Father; the strips were Clark's, whose shutterbug brothers and uncles were all pulling time at the Front. Every Sunday they sat together and watched the light flicker and snap over a big white sheet nailed up over the shelves of soil-treatment equipment and Friendlee Brand gadgets stripped for parts. Every Sunday like church.

Clark was tall and shy, obsessed with cameras no less than any of his brothers. He wore striped shirts all the time, as if solid colors had never been invented. He kept reading Salinger even after the guy defected. Sometimes they held hands while they watched the movies. Mostly they didn't. It was bad enough that they were fraternizing at all. Clark already drinking Kool Koffee every morning. Sugar, no cream. Clark was a quiet, bookish black boy who would be sent to the Front within a year.

On the white sheet, they watched California melt.

It hadn't happened during the war. The Glass came after. This thing everyone did now was not called war. It was something else. Something that liquefied the earth out west and turned it into the Sea of Glass. On the sheet it looked like molten silver, rising and falling in something like waves. Turning the Grand Canyon into a soft gray whirlpool. Sylvie thought it was beautiful. Like something on the moon. In real life it had colors, and Sylvie dreamed of them. Red stone dissolving into an endless expanse of dark glass.

"There are more Japanese people in Utah than in Japan now," Clark whispered when the filmstrip rolled up into black and the filmmaker's logo. Sylvie flinched as if he'd cut her.

They didn't talk about her Presentation. It sat whitely, fatly in their future. Once Clark kissed her. Sylvie cried afterward.

"I'll write you," he said. "As long as I can write."

The growth index for their county was very healthy, and this was another reason Clark Baker should not have been holding her hand in the dark while men in ghostly astronaut suits probed the edges of the Glass on a clicking filmstrip. Every woman on the block had a new baby this year. They'd gotten a medal of achievement from President McCarthy in the spring. The Ladies' Auxiliary graciously accepted the key to the city. She suspected her Father had a great deal to do with this. When she was little, he had come home one week in four. Now it was three days in thirty. His department kept him working hard. He'd be there for her Presentation, though. No Father missed his daughter's debut.

Sylvie thought about Clark while her mother slipped satin-covered buttons through tiny loops. Their faces doubled in the mirror. His dark brown hand on hers. The Sea of Glass turning their faces silver.

"Mom," Sylvie said. Her voice was very soft in the morning, as if she was afraid to wake herself up. "What if I don't love my Husband? Isn't that… something important?"

Hannah sighed. Her mouth took a hard angle. "You're young, darling. You don't understand. What it was like before. We had to have them here all the time, every night. Never a moment when I wasn't working my knees through for my husband. The one before your Father. The children before you. Do you think we got to choose then? It wasn't about love. For some people, they could afford that. For me, well, my parents thought he was a very nice man. He had good prospects. I needed him. I could not work. I was a woman before the war, who would hire me? And to do what? Type or teach. Not to program punchcard machines. Not to cross-breed new strains of broccoli. Nothing that would occupy my mind. So I drowned my mind in children and in him and when the war came I was glad. He left and it was *me* going to work every morning, *me* deciding what happened to my money. So the war took them," she waved her hand in front of her eyes, "war always does that. I know you don't think so, but the program is the best part of a bad situation. A situation maybe so bad we cannot fix it. So you don't love him. Why would you look for love with a man? How could a man ever understand you? He who gets the cake cannot be friends with the girl who gets the crumbs." Sylvie's mother blushed. She whispered: "My Rita, you know, Rita who comes for tea and bridge and neptunium testing. She is good to me. Someone will be good to you. You will have your Auxiliary, your work, your children. One week in four a man will tell you what to do—but listen to me when I say they have much better manners than they used to. They say please now. They are interested in your life. They are so good with the babies." Hannah smoothed the lacy back of her daughter's Presentation gown. "Someday, my girl, either we will all die out and nothing will be left, or things will go back to the old ways and you will have men taking your body and soul apart to label the parts that belong to them. Enjoy this world. Either way, it will be brief."

Sylvie turned her painted, perfected face to her mother's. "Mom," she whispered. Sylvie had practiced. Listened to the makeshift radio spitting half-garbled broadcasts from the other side of the world. A dictionary Clark found at a transfer station. Her mother. Whispering while she slept. Practiced until her lips hurt. So much, so often. She ordered the words in her head like dolls, hoped they were the right ones. Hoped they could stand up straight. "Watashi wa anata o shinjite ī nā." *I wish I could believe you.*

Hannah's dark eyes flew wide and, without a moment's hesitation, she slapped her daughter across the cheek. It wasn't hard, not meant to wound, certainly not to leave a mark on this day of all days, but it stung. Sylvie's eyes watered.

"Nidoto," her mother pleaded. "Never, *never* again."

Gimbels: Your Official Father's Day Headquarters!

PANORAMA SHOT of the Gimbels flagship store with two cute kiddos front and center. [Note to Casting: get us a boy and a girl, blonde, white, under ten, make sure the boy is taller than the girl. Put them in sailor suits, everyone likes that.] The kids wave at the camera. Little Linda Sue speaks up. [Note to Copy: Nope. The boy speaks first.] It's a beautiful June here in New York City, the greatest city on earth! *Jimmy throws his hands in the air and yells out:* And that means FATHER'S DAY! *Scene shift, kiddos are walking down a Gimbels aisle. We see toolboxes, ties, watches in a glass case, barbecue sets. Linda Sue picks up a watch and listens to it tick. Jimmy grabs a barbecue scraper and brandishes it. He says:* Come on down with your Mom and make an afternoon of it at the Brand New Gimbels Automat! Hot, pre-screened food in an instant! Gee wow! *[Note to Copy: hey, Stone, this is a government sponsored ad. If Gimbels want to hawk their shitty Manhattan Meals they're going to have to actually pay for it. Have you ever tried one of those things? Tastes like a kick in the teeth.] Linda Sue:* At Gimbels they have all the approved Father's Day products. *(Kids alternate lines)* Mr. Fix-It! Businessman! Coach! Backyard Cowboy! *Mr. Gimbel appears and selects a beautiful tie from the spring Priapus line. He hands it to Linda Sue and ruffles her hair. Mr. Gimbel:* Now, kids, don't forget to register your gift with the Ladies' Auxiliary. We wouldn't want *your* Daddy to get two of the same gift! How embarrassing! That's why Gimbels carries the complete Whole Father line, right next to the registration desk so your Father's Day is a perfect one. *Kids:* Thanks, Mr. Gimbel!

Mr. Gimbel spreads his arms wide and type stretches out between them in this year's Father's Day colors. [Note to Art Dept: It's seashell and buttercup this year, right? Please see Marketing concerning the Color Campaign. Pink and blue are pre-war. We're working with Gimbels to establish a White for Boys, Green for Girls tradition.]

Gimbels: *Your One Stop Shop for a One of a Kind Dad*.
Fade to white.
   Flash Blindness
   Martin wore the emerald green chevroned tie to his Announcement, even if it wasn't strictly within the dress code. Everything else was right down the line: light gray suit, shaved clean if shaving was on the menu, a dab of musky *Oil of Fecunditas* behind each ear from your friends at Spotless Corp. Black shoes, black socks, Spotless lavender talcum, teeth brushed three times with Pure Spearmint Toothpaste (*You're Sure with Spearmint!*). And his Father holding his hand, beaming with pride. Looking handsome and young as he always did.
   Of course, there was another boy holding his other hand.
   His name was Thomas. He had broad shoulders already, chocolate-colored hair and cool slate eyes that made him look terribly romantic. Martin tried not to let it bother him. He knew how the program worked. Where the other three weeks of the month took his Father. Obviously, there were other children, other wives, other homes. Other roasting chickens, other martinis. Other evening television shows on other channels. And that's all Thomas was: another channel. When you weren't watching a show, it just ceased to be. Clicked off. Fade to white. You couldn't be jealous of the people on those other channels. They had their own troubles and adventures, engrossing mysteries and stunning conclusions, cliffhangers and tune-in-next-weeks. It had nothing to do with Martin, or Rosemary, or Henry in his room. That was what it meant to be a Husband.
   The three of them sat together in the backseat of the sleek gray Cadillac. An older lady drove them. She wore a smart cap and had wiry white hair, but her cheeks were still pink and round. Martin tried to look at her as a Husband would, even though a woman her age would never marry. After all, Husbands didn't get to choose. Martin's future wives—four to start with, that was standard, but if he did well, who knew?—wouldn't all be bombshells in pinup bathing suits. He had to practice looking at women, really seeing them, seeing what was good and true and gorgeous in them. The chauffeur had wonderful laugh lines around her eyes. Martin could tell they were laugh lines. And her eyes, when she looked in the rear-view mirror, were a nice, cool green. She radioed to the dispatcher and her voice

lilted along with a faint twinge of English accent. Martin could imagine her laughing with him, picking New Kale and telling jokes about the King. He imagined her naked, laying on a soft pink bed, soft like her pink cheeks. Her body would be the best kind of body: the kind that had borne children. Breasts that had nursed. Legs that had run after misbehaving little ones. He could love that body. The sudden hardness between his legs held no threat, only infinite love and acceptance, a Husband's love.

When I think about how good I could be, my heart stops, Martin thought as the space between his neighborhood and the city smeared by. The sun seared white through dead black trees. But somewhere deep in them there was a green wick. Martin knew it. He had a green wick, too. *I will remember every date. Every wife will be so special and I will love her and our children. I will make her martinis. I will roast the chicken so she doesn't have to. When I am with one of them I will turn off all other channels in my mind. I can keep it straight and separate. I will study so hard, so that I know how to please. It will be my only vocation, to be devoted. And if they, the women of Elm Street or Oak Lane or Birch Drive find love with each other when I am gone, I will be happy for them because there is never enough love. I will draw them happy and they will be happy. The world will be green again. Everything will be okay.*

It all seemed to happen very fast. Thomas and Martin and a dozen other boys listened to a quintet play Mendelssohn. The mayor gave a speech. They watched a recorded message from President McCarthy which had to be pretty old because he still sported a good head of hair. Finally, a minister stood up with a lovely New Tabernacle Bible in her one good hand. The other was shriveled, boneless, a black claw in her green vestments. The pages of the Bible shone with gilt. A ribbonmark hung down and it was very red in the afternoon flares. She did not lay it on a lectern. She carried the weight in her hands and read from the Gospel of Pseudo-Matthew, which Martin already knew by heart. The minister's maple-syrup contralto filled the vaults of Matthew House.

"And when Mary had come to her fourteenth year, the high priest announced to all that the virgins who were reared in the Temple and who had reached the age of their womanhood should return to their own and be given in lawful marriage. When the High Priest went in to take counsel with God, a voice came forth from the oratory for all to hear, and it said that of all of the marriageable men of the House of David who had not yet taken a wife, each should bring a rod and lay it upon the altar, that one of the rods would burst into flower and upon it the Holy Ghost would come to rest in the form of a Dove, and that he to whom this rod belonged would be the one to whom the virgin Mary should be espoused. Joseph was among the men who came, and he placed his rod upon the altar, and straightaway it burst into bloom and a Dove came from Heaven and perched upon it, whereby it was manifest to all that Mary should become the wife of Joseph.”

Martin's eyes filled with tears. He felt a terrible light in his chest. For a moment he was sure everyone else would see it streaming out of him. But no, the minister gave him a white silk purse and directed him to a booth with a white velvet curtain. Inside, silence. Dim, dusty light. Martin opened the purse and pulled out the chalice—a plastic cup with measurements printed on it, just like Grud said. With it lay a few old photographs—women from before the war, with so much health in their faces Martin could hardly bear to look at them. Their skin was so clear. *She's dead,* he thought. *Statistically speaking, that woman with the black hair and heart-shaped face and polka-dotted bikini is dead. Vaporized in Seattle or Phoenix or Los Angeles. That was where they used to make pictures, in Los Angeles. This girl is dead.*

Martin couldn't do it. This was about life. Everything, no matter how hard and strange, was toward life. He could not use a dead girl that way. Instead, he shut his eyes. He made his pictures, quick pencil lines glowing inside him. The chauffeur with her pink cheeks and white hair. The minister with her kind voice and brown eyes and her shriveled hand, which was awful, but wasn't she alive and good? Tammy, the girl from the Victory Brand Capsule Garden commercials in her star-spangled dress. A girl with red hair who lived two blocks over and was so pretty that looking at her was like getting punched in the chest. He drew in bold, bright lines the home he was going to make, bigger than himself, bigger than the war, as big as the world.

Martin's body convulsed with the tiny, private detonation of his soul. His vision blurred into a hot colorless flash.

Blast Wind

Sylvie's mother helped her into long white gloves. They sat together in a long pearl-colored Packard and did not speak. Sylvie had nothing to say. Let her mother be uncomfortable. A visceral purple sunset colored the western sky, even at two in the afternoon. Sylvie played the test in her head like a filmstrip. When it actually started happening to her, it felt no more real than a picture on a sheet.

The mayor gave a speech. They watched a recorded message from President McCarthy's pre-war daughter Tierney, a pioneer in the program, one of the first to volunteer. *Our numbers have been depleted by the Germans, the Japanese, and now the Godless Russians. Of the American men still living only 12% are fertile. But we are not Communists. We cannot become profligate, wasteful, decadent. We must maintain our moral way of life. As little as possible should change from the world your mothers knew—at least on the surface. And with time, what appears on the surface will penetrate to the core, and all will be restored. We will not sacrifice our way of life.*

A minister with a withered arm read that Pseudo-Matthew passage Tierney had dredged up out of apocrypha to the apocrypha, about the rods and the flowers and Sylvie had never felt it was one of the Gospel's more subtle moments. The minister blessed them. They are flowers. They are waiting for the Dove.

The doctors were women. One was Mrs. Drexler, who lived on their cul-de-sac and always made rum balls for the neighborhood Christmas cookie exchange. She was kind. She warmed up her fingers before she examined Sylvie. *White gloves for her, white gloves for me,* Sylvie thought, and suppressed a giggle. She turned her head to one side and focused on a stained-glass lamp with kingfishers on it, piercing their frosted breasts with their beaks. She went somewhere else in her mind until it was over. Not a happy place, just a place. Somewhere precise and clean without any Spotless Corp products where Sylvie could test soil samples methodically. Rows of black vials, each labeled, dated, sealed.

They took her blood. A butterfly of panic fluttered in her—will they know? Would the test show her mother, practicing her English until her accent came out clean as acid paper? Running from a red Utah sky even though there was no one left to shoot at her? Only half enemy, half threat, born in San Francisco before the war, white enough to pass. A woman who spent her life curling her hair like it would save her. Lining her eyes so heavy, so they would look like magazine eyes. Sylvie shut her own unlined eyes. She said her mother's name three times in her mind. The secret, talismanic thing that only they together knew. *Hidaka Hanako. Hidaka Hanako. Hidaka Hanako. Don't be silly. Japan isn't a virus they can see wiggling in your cells. Mom's documents are flawless. No alarm will go off in the centrifuge.*

And none did.

She whizzed through the intelligence exams—what a joke. *Calculate the drag energy of the blast wind given the following variables.* Please. Other girls milled around her in their identical lace dresses. The flowers in their hair were different. Their sashes all red. Red on white, like first aid kits floating through her peripheral vision. They went from medical to placement testing to screening. They nodded shyly to each other. In five years, Sylvie would know all their names. They would be her Auxiliary. They would play bridge. They would plan block parties. They would have telephone trees. Some of them would share a Husband with her, but she would never know which. That was what let the whole civilized fiction roll along. You never knew, you never asked. Men had a different surname every week. Only the Mrs. Drexlers of the neighborhood knew it all, the knots and snags of the vital genetics. Would she share with the frosted blonde who loved botany or the redheaded math genius who made her own cheese? Or maybe none of them. It all depended on the test. Some of these girls would score low in their academics or have some unexpressed, unpredictable trait revealed in the great forking family trees pruned by Mrs. Drexler and the rest of them. They would get Husbands in overalls, with limited allowances. They would live in houses with old paint and lead shielding instead of Gamma Glass. Some of them would knock their Presentation out of the park. They'd get Husbands in gray suits and silk ties, who went to offices in the city during the day, who gave them compression chamber diamonds for their birthdays. As little as possible should change.

Results were quick these days. Every year faster. But not so quick that they did not have luncheon provided while the experts performed their tabulations. Chicken salad sandwiches—how the skinny ones gasped at the taste of mayonnaise! Assam tea, watercress, lemon curd and biscuits. An impossible fairy feast.

"I hope I get a Businessman," said the girl sitting next to Sylvie. Her bouffant glittered with illegal setting spray. "I couldn't bear it if I had to live on Daisy Drive."

"Who cares?" said Sylvie, and shoved a whole chicken salad triangle into her mouth. She shouldn't have said anything. Her silence bent for one second and out comes nonsense that would get her noticed. Would get her remembered.

"Well, *I* care, you *cow*," snapped Bouffant. Her friends smiled behind their hands, concealing their teeth. *In primates, baring the teeth is a sign of aggression,* Sylvie thought idly. She flashed them a broad, cold smile. *All thirty-two, girls, drink it in.*

"I think it's clear what room *you'll* be spending the evening in," Bouffant sneered, oblivious to Sylvie's primate signals.

But Sylvie couldn't stop. "At best, you'll spend 25% of your time with him. You'll get your rations the same as everyone. You'll get your vouchers for participating in the program and access to top make-work contracts. What difference does it make who you snag? You know this is just pretend, right? A very big, very lush, very elaborate dog breeding program."

Bouffant narrowed her eyes. Her lips went utterly pale. "I hope you turn out to be barren as a rock. Just *rotted away inside*," she hissed. The group of them stood up in a huff and took their tea to another table. Sylvie shrugged and ate her biscuit. "Well, that's no way to think if you want to restore America," she said to no one at all. What was the matter with her? *Shut up, Sylvie.*

Mrs. Drexler put a warm hand on her shoulder, materializing out of nowhere. The doctor who loved rum balls laid a round green chip on the white tablecloth. Bouffant saw it across the room and glared hard enough to put a hole through her skull at forty yards.

Sylvie was fertile. At least, there was nothing obviously wrong with her. She turned the chip over. The other side was red. Highest marks. *Blood and leaves. Red on white. The world is red and I am red forever.* One of Bouffant's friends was holding a black chip and crying, deep and horrible. Sylvie floated. Unreal. It wasn't real. It was ridiculous. It was a filmstrip. A recording made years ago when Brussels sprouts were small and the sunset could be rosy and gentle.

FADE IN on Mrs. Drexler in a dance hall with a white on white checkerboard floor. She's wearing a sequin torchsinger dress. Bright pink. She pumps a giant star-spangled speculum like a parade-master's baton. Well, hello there Sylvia! It's your big day! Should I say Hidaka Sakiko? I only want you to be comfortable, dear. Let's see what you've won!

Sylvie and the other green-chip girls were directed into another room whose walls were swathed in green velvet curtains. A number of men stood lined up against the wall, chatting nervously among themselves. Each had a cedar rod in one hand. They held the rods awkwardly, like old men's canes. A piano player laid down a slow foxtrot for them. Champagne was served. A tall boy with slightly burned skin, a shiny pattern of pink across his cheek, takes her hand, first in line. In Sylvie's head, the filmstrip zings along.

WIDE SHOT of Mrs. Drexler yanking on a rope-pull curtain. She announces: Behind Door Number One we have Charles Patterson, six foot one, Welsh/Danish stock, blond/blue, scoring high in both logic and empathy, average sperm count 19 million per milliliter! This hot little number has a reserved parking spot at the Office! Of course, when I say "Office," I mean the upper gentlemen's club, brandy and ferns on the thirty-fifth floor, cigars and fraternity and polished teak walls. A little clan to help each other through the challenges of life in the program—only another Husband can really understand. Our productive heartthrobs are too valuable to work! Stress has been shown to lower semen quality, Sylvie! But as little as possible should change. If you take the Office from a man, you'll take his spirit. And what's behind Door Number Two?

Sylvie shuts her eyes. The real Mrs. Drexler was biting into a sugar cookie and sipping her champagne. She opened them again—and a stocky kind-eyed boy had already cut in for the next song. He wore an apple blossom in his lapel. For everlasting love, Broome County's official flower for the year. The dancing Mrs. Drexler in her mind hooted with delight, twirling her speculum.

TIGHT SHOT of Door Number Two. Mrs. Drexler snaps her fingers and cries: Why, it's Douglas Owens! Five foot ten, Irish/Italian, that's *very* exciting! Brown/brown, scoring aces in creative play and nurturing, average sperm count 25 million per milliliter—oh *ho!* Big, strapping boy! *Mrs. Drexler slaps him lightly on the behind. Her eyes gleam.* He's a Businessman as well, nothing but the best for our Sylvie, our prime stock Sylvie/Sakiko! He'll take his briefcase every day and go sit in his club with the other Husbands, and maybe he loves you and maybe he finds real love with them the way you'll find it with your friend Bouffant in about two years. Who can tell? It's so *thrilling* to speculate! It's not like men and women got along so well before, anyway. Take my wife, please! Why I oughtta! To hell with the whole mess. Give it one week a month. You do unpleasant things one week out of four and don't think twice. Who cares?

Someone handed her a glass of champagne. Sylvie wrapped her real, solid fingers around it. She felt dizzy. A new boy had taken up her hand and put his palm around her waist. The dance quickened. Still a foxtrot, but one with life in it. She looked at the wheel and spin of faces—white faces, wide, floor-model faces. Sylvie looked for Clark. Anywhere, everywhere, his kind face moving among the perfect bodies, his kind face with a silver molten earth undulating across his cheeks, flickering, shuddering. But he wasn't there. He would never be there. It would never be Clark with a cedar rod and a sugar cookie. Black boys didn't get Announced. Not Asians, not refugees, not Sylvie if anyone guessed. They got shipped out. They got a ticket to California. To Utah.

As little as possible should change.

No matter how bad it got, McCarthy and his Brothers just couldn't let a nice white girl (like Sylvie, like Sylvie, like the good floor-model part of

Sylvie that fenced in the red, searing thing at the heart of her) get ruined that way. (If they knew, if they knew. Did the conservative-suit warm-glove Mrs. Drexler guess? Did it show in her dancing?) Draw the world the way you want it. Draw it and it will be.

Sylvie tried to focus on the boy she was dancing with. She was supposed to be making a decision, settling, rooting herself forever into this room, the green curtains, the sugar cookies, the foxtrot.

QUICK CUT to Mrs. Drexler. She spins around and claps her hands. She whaps her speculum on the floor three times and a thin kid with chocolate-colored hair and slate eyes sweeps aside his curtain. She crows: But wait, we haven't opened Dooooooor Number Three! Hello, Thomas Walker! Six foot even, Swiss/Polish—ooh, practically Russian! How exotic! I smell a match! Brown/gray, top marks across the board, average sperm count a spectacular 29 million per milliliter! You're just showing off, young man! Allow me to shake your hand!

Sylvie jittered back and forth as the filmstrip caught. The champagne settled her stomach. A little. Thomas spun her around shyly as the music flourished. He had a romantic look to him. Lovely chocolate brown hair. He was saying something about being interested in the animal repopulation projects going on in the Plains States. His voice was sweet and a little rough and fine, fine, this one is fine, it doesn't matter, who cares, he'll never sit in a garage with me and watch the bombs fall on the sheet with the hole in the corner. Close your eyes, spin around three times, point at one of them and get it over with.

IRIS TRANSITION to Mrs. Drexler doing a backflip in her sequined dress. She lands in splits. Mr. and Mrs. Wells and Walker invite you to the occasion of their children's wedding!

Sylvie pulled the red, thornless rose and snowdrops from her hair and tied their ribbon around Thomas's rod. She remembered to smile. Thomas himself kissed her, first on the forehead and then on the mouth. A lot of couples seemed to be kissing now. The music had stopped. *It's over, it's over,* Sylvie thought. *Maybe I can still see Clark today. It takes time to plan a wedding.*

Voices buzzed and spiked behind her. Mrs. Drexler was hurrying over; her face was dark.

ZOOM on Mrs. Drexler: Wait, sorry, wait! I'm sorry we seem to have hit a snag! It appears Thomas and Sylvie here are a little too close for comfort. They should never have been paired at the same Announcement. Our fault, entirely! Sylvie's Father has been such a boon to the neighborhood! Doing his part! Unfortunately, the great nation of the United States does not condone incest, so you'll have to trade Door Number Three for something a little more your speed. This sort of thing does happen! That's why we keep such excellent records! CROSS-REFERENCING! Thank you! *Mrs. Drexler bows. Roses land at her feet.*

Sylvie shut her eyes. The strip juddered; she was crying tracks through her Spotless Corp Pressed Powder and it was not a film, it was happening. Mrs. Drexler was wearing a conservative brown suit with a gold dove-shaped pin on the lapel and waving a long-stemmed peony for masculine bravery. Thomas was her brother, somehow, there had been a mix-up and he was her brother and other arrangements would have to be made. The boys and girls in a ballroom with her stared and pointed, paired off safely. Sylvie looked up at Thomas. He stared back, young and sad and confused. The snowdrops and roses had fallen off his rod onto the floor. Red on white. Bouffant was practically climbing over Douglas Owens 25 million per milliliter like a tree.

In four years Sylvie will be Mrs. Charles Patterson 19 million per. It's over and they began to dance. Charles was a swell dancer. He promised to be sweet to her when he got through with training and they were married. He promised to make everything as normal as possible. As little as possible should change. The quintet struck up Mendelssohn.

Sylvie pulled her silence over her and it was good.

Fade to white.

CLOSE-UP of a nice-looking Bobby, a real lantern-jaw, straight-dealing, chiseled type. [Note to Casting: maybe we should consider VP Kroc for this spot. Hair pomade knows no demographic. Those idiots at Brylcreem want to corner the Paternal market? Fine. Let them have their little slice of the pie. Be a nice bit of PR for the re-election campaign, too. Humanize the son of a bitch. Ray Kroc, All-American, Brother to the Common Man. Even he suffers symptomatic hair loss. Whatever—you get the idea. Talk to Copy.] Bobby's getting dressed in the morning, towel around his healthy, muscular body. [Note to Casting: if we go with Kroc here we'll have to find a body double.] Looks at himself in the mirror and strokes a 5-o'clock shadow.

FEMALE VOICE OVER: Do you wake up in the morning to a sink full of disappointment?

PAN DOWN to a clean white sink. Clumps of hair litter the porcelain. [Note to Art Dept: Come on, Stone, don't go overboard. No more than twenty strands.] *Bobby rubs the top of his head. His expression is crestfallen.*

VOICE OVER: Well, no more! Now with the radiation-blocking power of lead, All-New Formula Samson Brand Hair Pomade can make you an All-New Man.

Bobby squirts a generous amount of Samson Brand from his tube and rubs it on his head. A blissful smile transforms his face.

VOICE OVER: That feeling of euphoria and well-being lets you know it works! Samson Pomades and Creams have been infused with our patented mood-boosters, vitamins, and just a dash of caffeine to help you start your day out right!

PAN DOWN to the sink. Bobby turns the faucet on; the clumps of hair wash away. When we pan back up, Bobby has a full head of glossy, thick, styled hair. [Note to Art Dept: Go whole hog. When the camera comes back put the VP in a full suit, with the perfect hair—a wig, obviously—and the Senate gavel in his hand. I like to see a little more imagination from you, Stone. Not a good quarter for you.]

VOICE OVER: Like magic, Samson Brand Pomade gives you the confidence you need. *[Note to Copy: not sure about "confidence" here. What about "peace of mind"? We're already getting shit from the FDA about dosing Brothers with caffeine and uppers. Probably don't want to make it sound like the new formula undoes Arcadia.]*

He gives the camera a thumbs-up. [Note to Art Dept: Have him offer the camera a handshake. Like our boy Ray is offering America a square deal.]

Bold helvetica across mid-screen:

Samson Guards Your Strength.

Fade to white.

Ten Grays

Martin watched his brother. The handsome Thomas. The promising Thomas. The fruitful and multiplying Thomas. 29 million per mil Thomas. Their father (24 million) didn't even try to fight his joyful tears as he pinned the golden dove on his son's chest. His good son. His true son. For Thomas the Office in the city. For Thomas the planning and pleasing and roasted chickens and martinis. For Thomas the children as easy as pencil drawings.

For Martin Stone, 2 million per milliliter and most of those dead, a package. In a nice box, to be certain. Irradiated teak. It didn't matter now anyway. Martin knew without looking what lay nestled in the box. A piece of paper and a bottle. The paper was an ordnance unknown until he opened the box. It was a lottery. The only way to be fair. It was his ticket.

It might request that he present himself at his local Induction Center at

0900 at the close of the school year. To be shipped out to the Front, which by then might be in Missouri for all anyone knew. He'd suit up and boot it across the twisted, bubbled moonscape of the Sea of Glass. An astronaut. Bouncing on the pulses from Los Alamos to the Pacific. He would never draw again. By Christmas, he wouldn't have the fine motor skills.

Or it would request just as politely that he arrange for travel to Washington for a battery of civic exams and placement in government service. Fertile men couldn't think clearly, didn't you know? All that sperm. Can't be rational with all that business sloshing around in there. Husbands couldn't run things. They were needed for more important work. The most important work. Only Brothers could really view things objectively. Big picture men. And women, Sisters, those gorgeous black chip girls with 3-Alpha running cool and sweet in their veins. Martin would probably pull Department of Advertising and Information. Most people did. Other than Defense, it was the biggest sector going. The bottle would be Arcadia. For immediate dosage, and every day for the rest of his life. All sex shall be potentially reproductive. Every girl screwing a Brother is failing to screw a Husband and that just won't do. They said it tasted like burnt batteries if you didn't put it in something. The first bottle would be the pure stuff, though. Provided by Halcyon, Your Friend in the Drug Manufacturing Business. Martin would remember it, the copper sear on the roof of his mouth. After that, a whole aisle of choices. Choices, after all, make you who you are. Arcadia or Kool. Brylcreem or Samson.

Don't worry, Martin. It's a relief, really. Now you can really get to work. Accomplish something. Carve out your place. Sell the world to the world. You could work your way into the Art Department. Keep drawing babies in carriages. Someone else's perfect quads, their four faces laughing at you forever from glossy pages.

Suddenly Martin found himself clasped tight in his Father's arms. Pulling the box out of his boy's hands, reading the news for him, putting it aside. His voice came as rough as warm gin and Martin could hardly breathe for the strength of his Father's embrace.

Thomas Walker squeezed his Brother's hand. Martin did not squeeze back.

Velocity Multiplied by Duration

Sylvie's Father was with them that week. He was proud. They bought a chicken from Mrs. Stone and killed it together, as a family. The head popped off like a cork. Sylvie stole glances at him at the table. She could see it now. The chocolate hair. The tallness. Hannah framed her Presentation Scroll and hung it over the fireplace.

Sylvie flushed her Spotless trousseaux down the toilet.

She wasn't angry. You can't get angry just because the world's so much bigger than you and you're stuck in it. That's just the face of it, cookie. A poisoned earth, a sequined dress, a speculum you can play like the spoons. Sylvie wasn't angry. She was silent. Her life was Mrs. Patterson's life. People lived in all kinds of messes. She could make rum balls. And treat soil samples and graft cherry varieties and teach some future son or daughter Japanese three weeks a month where no one else could hear. She could look up Bouffant's friend and buy her a stiff drink. She could enjoy the brief world of solitude and science and birth like red skies dawning. Maybe. She had time.

It was all shit, like that Polish kid who used to hang around the soda fountain kept saying. It was definitely all shit.

On Sunday she went out to the garage again. Vita-Pops and shadows. Clark slipped in like light through a crack. He had a canister of old war footage under his arm. Stalingrad, Berlin, Ottawa. Yellow shirt with green stripes. Nagasaki and Tokyo in '45, vaporizing like hearts in a vast, wet chest. The first retaliation. Seattle, San Francisco, Los Angeles. Berlin and Rome swept clean and blank as pages. Clark reached out and held her hand. She didn't squeeze back. The silent detonations on the white sheet like sudden balloons, filling up and up and up. It looked like the inside of Sylvie. Something opening over and over, with nowhere to burn itself out but in.

"This is my last visit," Clark said. "School year's over." His voice sounded far away, muffled, like he didn't even know he was talking. "Car's coming in the morning. Me and Grud are sharing a ride to Induction. I think we get a free lunch."

Sylvie wanted to scream at him. She sucked down her pop, drowned the scream in bubbles.

"I love you," whispered Clark Baker.

On the sheet, the Golden Gate Bridge vanished.

Sylvie rolled the reel back. They watched it over and over. A fleck of nothing dropping out of the sky and then, then the flash, a devouring, brain-boiling, half-sublime sheet of white that blossomed like a flower out of a dead rod, an infinite white everything that obliterated the screen.

Fade to black.

And over the black, a cheerful fat man giving the thumbs up to Sylvie, grinning:

Buy Freedom Brand Film! It's A-OK!

SIGNIFICANT DUST

MARGO LANAGAN

Margo Lanagan [amongamidwhile.blogspot.com.au] *has published five collections of short stories*—White Time, Black Juice, Red Spikes, Yellow-cake *and* Cracklescape—*and more than ten novels, most notably* Tender Morsels. *She is a four-time World Fantasy Award winner for best collection, short story, novel, and most recently for a novella, "Sea-Hearts," which she has since expanded into a novel,* The Brides of Rollrock Island (Sea Hearts *in Australia).* Black Juice *and* Tender Morsels *are Michael L. Printz Honor Books, and Margo's work has also been nominated for the Los Angeles Times Book Prize, the Frank O'Connor International Short Story Award, and the Commonwealth Writers' Prize, and twice been placed on the James Tiptree, Jr. Award honor list, and the Shirley Jackson shortlist, as well as being shortlisted for Hugo, Nebula, Sturgeon, Stoker, Seiun, International Horror Guild, and SBritish Science Fiction awards. Margo lives in Sydney, Australia.*

…no significant dust was observed on the vehicle as presented for inspection.
— Lab report on the car involved in the Mundrabilla UFO encounter,
Western Australia, 1988.

"**S**o what's your plan, Vanessa?" says Dave.

Everyone turns from the fire to look at her. The light from the floodlit yard cuts hard, peculiar shadows across all their faces.

"Plan? I have a plan?"

"Course you do—you're a girl."

"What?" A nervous laugh pops out of her. "Why would—"

"I tell you, every bloke who comes out here, they're runnin away from somethin—kids, wives, the rat race, you name it. Every chick, they come because they've got a plan, and this is part of the plan. So where d'you go from here? What's your plan?"

She takes a sip of her lime and soda. Under the barbecue plate, the fire is a cozy orange cave. She'd like to crawl in there, lie and glow awhile.

"Well," she says. "All I thought was, I'd earn some money, and there'd be nothing to spend it on, so I'd save." She didn't think anything of the sort, but what business is that of Dave's, or anyone here's?

"Nothing to spend it on? Haven't you seen Kim's mail order catalogues?"

Huh—they'd have to pay *her* to buy any of that crap. She doesn't want to be rude, though, so she shrugs.

"What'll you buy, then? Car? Trip overseas?"

"Maybe." The idea of driving-and-driving appeals, of flying-and-flying. "Maybe travel."

"Where'd you *most* wanna go? Which country?"

Which country? He might as well ask which *star*. Look at them up there, all the same, all more or less bright. She makes a face and shakes her head. She can tell she's a disappointment in the conversation stakes, in the being-colorful stakes. Well, too bad.

"I think that's admirable," says Joe. It's still early enough for his kinder, sober self to show through. "She doesn't have to have a plan worked out yet. But when she does, she'll have a bit of money to put behind it."

Everyone nods, a bit bored. Good. They'll move on from her soon.

"Maertje's got a plan, haven't you, Maertje?" says Dave.

"To see as much of Australia as I ken, in two years," says Maertje like a calm little wind-up doll, "wurking my way from place to place. Then, going back to d'Nederlands and…well, it's not much of a plen, going straight beck to where I was six munss ago, with no more good prospects den det."

"Oh you won't be going back," Joe says kindly. "Not right back. You'll have more worldly experience. Your mind'll be broader."

"Joe's finding a *lot* of things to admire about the ladies tonight, aren't you, Joe?" Theo's young and handsome and everything Joe's not. He won't stay long here; there's not enough adventure for him. Not enough girls to go through.

"Aargh." Even this early, it doesn't take much to set the drink snarling in Joe. "They've got more bloody sense than us blokes, mostly."

They start arguing that, outdoing each other with examples for and against, leaving Vanessa alone under the stars, the girl with no plan. Or so they think. She *had* a plan, but it's done and dusted now; she got out of Perth, away from the coast, away from that beach, and from what she did, and everyone who saw. The disaster she brought down, that's still there, but at least she doesn't have to bear people's looks and silences any more. And no one here needs to know about all that back there. Ever.

The sun's not up yet, but the sky is light. Vanessa opens the restaurant for the day. No cars wait outside. But she's barely back in the kitchen when the bell rings over the door.

She keeps her face neutral when she sees him. "Morning." There's only him and her, here in this morning. If he's trouble, she hasn't got a lot of options.

He looks as if he's waited hours for opening, slept in his car, slept in his clothes—a great fat parka on him here in the middle of summer. He's brought in a smell—bad, sweetish, like that time the freezer died and the sausages broke out in green wounds. And he's tracked in filth, a black dust like cartoon gunpowder. All the way from door to counter he's dropped it, across the tiles that Maertje mopped last night. It showers out of his hair onto the glass-topped counter, and off his arms, which he sets one on top of the other like a rampart in front of himself, rigid, his hands fisted.

"Cup of tea?" he says, with a touch of hilarity, as if he can hardly believe in such a thing—and if it did exist, how could he possibly deserve it? He examines everything behind her, the cheap paneling, the clock, the tubes of liquid soap, insect repellent. It all seems to surprise him, as if every few seconds he's been freshly woken up.

"White?" says Vanessa.

"Sorry?" Woken again, he drags his gaze down to her. His eyes are like coal-miners' eyes in old photos, pale gray in his dust-blackened face.

"White tea? Milk in your tea?"

He processes the question. Will he faint or break out raving? But then, "Thanks," comes out of him, as if he coughed it up accidentally. "Yes. I better have it takeaway."

"It's fine," she says—why's she being kind to him, when he smells so bad, when there's clearly something wrong? "You can sit here." She waves grandly at the empty restaurant. "We've got plenty of room."

He looks pointedly down at himself and the sprinkled counter. She waggles her head that that doesn't matter. "Nothing to eat?" she says.

"Oh, no." The rampart comes apart and he looks at his filthy palms.

He has money; he lays it on the counter doubtfully, watches as if he expects her to call his bluff. She tries to shake the dust out of it without him seeing. She rings it up and counts the change out of the drawer. It feels as if she's rescuing him. She wishes someone would do this for her, reel her back into herself, back into the world.

"Take a seat." She puts the change into his shaking hand. "I'll bring your tea. I won't be a minute."

"What day is it?" he says.

"Wednesday."

His cogwheels try to grind again, but they can't get a grip on that word.

"Wednesday, the ninth of January, 1982." She waits for the moment he'll admit that he's joking.

He flinches, checks *her* for signs of lying, looks away. "But '82 was when *Riley* was born." Back come the pale eyes. "My boy."

She only wants to keep him from breaking things—from breaking *her*, yes, while there are no men about and no Kim, but mainly from hurting himself, by word or action. "Well," she says slowly and calmly, "I guess you've got that to look forward to, then."

That seems to make sense to him for a few seconds. Then it doesn't, and he turns bewildered towards all the empty tables and chairs.

She goes to the kitchen, makes the tea. When she comes back, he's sitting head in hands by the window, at the first table, right at the carpet edge. He's realized about the parka and taken it off; powerful body odor has joined the dead-meat smell. She'll have to air the place out, spray Glen 20 around.

He straightens as she comes, sees the blackness he's shed on the table, brushes some of it into his lap.

"Here we go." The pot crunches as she sets it down, the milk jug, the cup and saucer.

"Good on you." He doesn't tell her to sit down so he can explain. Just as well; she doesn't want to know about his boy, about his confusion, about anything. And besides, she's got a lot of chores still to get through.

Holidays. She sits on the wall at the end of the row of them, Tash and Tash's friends. Her own mates have left town or gone straight into summer jobs. *Come with us,* Tash said, not realizing what she was inviting, and now Vanessa sits swinging her legs and eating an ice-block, next to her sister, included in her sister's group.

She stepped on her sunglasses yesterday and broke them, so the world is bleached-out like an old home movie. Happy families, handsome surfers, bikini girls, big old tums-on-legs men with white chest-hair—all these people are arranged along the beach like ornaments, like props in a movie about how free she is now, how school's finished, and the world is waiting, and she might go anywhere from here.

What are she and Tash talking about? They don't talk, really, when they're out with people; they only hunt for things to say that will start everyone on long series of jokes at each other, the girls leaning about laughing, the boys shouldering each other. Once Brett even tumbled Brendan off the wall, dropped after him to the sand and wrestled him there. Everyone laughed; everyone cheered them on. Which is why, when Tash beside her tips back with the giggles and wobbles and shrieks, Vanessa gives her that little elbow-nudge that sends her backwards, over.

That little nudge. Nobody made her do it. It was completely her own idea. She wouldn't have been surprised if Tash, better balanced than she seemed, had righted herself, pushed her back—if she herself, Vanessa, had fallen. That would have been fairer.

She runs through the saltbush—or the bluebush. She can't tell the difference in the dusk, and does she care anyway? She runs because she can, running away from the fact that she can—running is the problem and the cure both at once, the same mess as everything.

The bushes grow well apart, but they're only knee-high; she can just jump over them if they get in the way. Jumping is good, dodging is good; it gives her just enough to do to keep her from thinking. If she runs far enough, she leaves the roadhouse and all its nosy people behind her. The moon seems less as if it's watching. The escarpment stops hulking and goes back to the dream it was having before she burst out here and pitched herself at the distance, disturbing the silence with her melancholy rage.

Tash upside-down, falling, irreversible. Tash's neat bottom, perfectly tanned thighs. The wall-edge has pressed red marks into the skin—has pressed some sand, too, which glitters in the sunlight, either side of the triangle of bikini-bottoms, sun-yellow, printed with crimson hibiscus flowers. Afterwards, hibiscus were everywhere. They shouldered forward on their bushes out of every park and garden, thrust themselves at Vanessa, reminding her. Everything reminded her, everything accused her.

The pretty bum, the neat bikini parcel—they're a snapshot portrait of everything that's on its way out: dressing for summer, or even *caring* what season it is; sex, ever; color; *flowering*; this group, carefree like this, because afterwards it'll turn into a competition for who's the goodiest two-shoes, and then fall apart from the strain of the *tragedy*. Everyone'll fly off in different directions—as *she's* flown off (but she's different, has different reasons).

Beside these great losses, what Vanessa's lost—sound sleep, unstained optimism, the last shreds of childhood—looks like nothing. She can lose all that and still be the lucky one. She can be an embarrassment to everyone, and disgusting to herself and a complete waste of space, life and moving parts, and still she can walk away.

Tony Tripp, the copper from Eucla, comes in for a can of drink and a toasted sandwich, because they're there, because they're the closest road-house. They might have seen something—that's his excuse. What he really wants is to gossip.

He stretches his legs out under the tea-room table. They always look too big for this room, men in uniform, even just the Greyhound drivers. Their stiff, crested epaulettes command more space than the curling, often-washed ones on the Boss's khaki work shirts.

"Slewed off the road just near the first cattle grid there, down by Dave's." Tony shows with his hands how the car ended, facing the highway ninety degrees on. "Hasn't rolled or anythink. There's no dammidge."

"And no one around?" says Kim. She's the Boss's girlfriend, tough as nails. Never had a moment's doubt in her life.

"Not a soul. Walked all over. Cooee'd. Sounded the siren. Drove up the top past Dave's and checked it out from up there."

"Send a chopper over?" says Theo. "Bloke could've collapsed in the scrub miles off. Never get found."

"Could've hitched out of there," says Kim. "Could've set the whole thing up to disappear himself. Or *her*self, some crazy broad."

Vanessa leafs through a magazine unseeing. The pages are soft with use, soothing to turn. Film stars smile strenuously; chicken pieces lean in enticing piles in gluey apricot sauce.

"Exactly," says Tony. "Might not wanna be found." He tilts his head at an engine sound from the west. "Here comes Jonesy now. Come and have a squizz. Don't touch anythink, but."

A lot of dusty cars roll up here—not often on a tilt tray, though. And this isn't orange desert dust; this is that black stuff again, gunpowder-grit, still whispering onto the tray from this curve and that crevice. The stink of it fills up the driveway.

"Gawd, what is it? I won't touch, don't worry." Covering her mouth and nose, Kim walks up and scowls into a wheel-rim. "Did he try to torch it or somethink?"

"Looks like that, dunnit?" says Tony. "But you look at the akshul car, none of it's burnt? It's like someone burnt something *else,* then come and dumped the ashes of *that* on him."

Vanessa stands halfway to the truck, within smell of it and not wanting to go closer. *A daggy blue sedan,* she thinks, *for a dirty gray-eyed man. / A half a pot of tea / was all that was left to see.*

She was surprised to find him gone, and disappointed—she'd been going to offer him a shower in the campground block, fetch him a towel and everything. She would have washed the used towel with her own things so no one would remark on any dust on it, any smell; she'd had it all worked out. She didn't know why. He was troubled, that was all, and she would have been glad to be able to help him in some little way—not too much, not to get *involved.* And she would have been glad to show—to show *whom,* if she was going to keep it so quiet?—that she could respect his silence.

But he went. He must've gone out with that couple who came in while he was drinking his tea, or she'd have heard his separate bell. She cleared the table, wiped it down, and the gritty chair; she went at the black spillage on the carpet with a dustpan and brush to get the worst off. He wasn't out in the driveway, or down the highway either way with his thumb out, or under the awning keeping a lookout for a ride. He must have *driven off* with that couple, though she hadn't heard them talking. They must have come to their agreement outside.

"And no luggage no nothing," says Kim, sauntering hands in pockets back to Tony.

"Not a sausage. Who knows who the bastard is?"

As she tips, Tash holds Vanessa's gaze, her face changing from giggles to fear and back to laughter, cueing Vanessa to stop laughing, start again, to clutch her face in theatrical terror. She can feel her hands again any time she wants, hot, rough with dried salt, the right one tacky with ice-block melt.

You bitch! Tash shouts on the way down. Vanessa treasures that shout more than anything, the sharing-in-the-joke tone, the edge of *I'll get you back for this!* The trust. *Tash* believed, just as much as Vanessa did, that everything would be all right.

What were glimpses, reassuring, have stretched out to forever in Vanessa's memory. Tash turns slowly head-down, still in a sitting position, her arms out, left wrist pretty with bangles, right hand holding the ice-block stick. Her hair and shirt, weightless as an astronaut's, flag out, and still she smiles. Her golden legs kick from the knee, as if she could swim her way out of trouble; the shine of her lacquered toenails claws a little light into one side of Vanessa's vision.

Idly Vanessa looks ahead of Tash's fall. It's shady down there; that will be nice for Tash, to be out of the glare. And look at that sand, so soft, mounded all aglow in reflected sunlight. It's almost as good as falling into a pile of feather pillows.

She lies awake a lot of nights; whether she runs or not doesn't make much difference. She leaves the blind and the window a quarter open for any breath of breeze. Cars and trucks from the west make faint, gray window-squares on her wall, doubled up and overlapping if both headlights work. They rise first on the wardrobe and creep across it slowly-slowly, slowly. Engine noise joins in at some stage, steady sometimes, sometimes just wafts, swipes of sound, depending on the wind. Then the engine reaches its peak, and the light-squares rush along the wall up to her head; the lights cut out and the noise drops by half as the vehicle roars past beyond the roadhouse and rumbles on eastward.

If two cars travel together, the lights of the one behind throw shadows of the driver and passenger into the mix of rectangles on the wardrobe. These heads never talk to each other, or sing, or laugh, or glance across. The driver grips the wheel and they both look ahead at the highway with its nothingness either side. From one horizon they labor across to the other, then drop out of sight and hearing, out of Vanessa's world, out of the night altogether.

Between these events—these leisurely minutes of come and come on, and go, and gone—hours can pass, lit only by the glow from the walkway outside, travelled only by Vanessa's perfectly circular thoughts spiraling on towards dawn.

A bright fog descends, sunlit, an old family movie with only patchy sound. Sometimes it rushes, sometimes it freezes, mis-catching on the spinning spokes that play it. It closes Vanessa in, hollows out the earth underneath her. She's very stiff; she doesn't want to move, not until Tash moves. Through all the *Oh God Tash Tash Say something Tash* and *Don't touch her!* and people running and sand kicking up into the sunlight, and the lifeguards, and Brett dashing for the phone box—through all that, she stands watching, hugging herself and the fog hugging her. Every detail burns itself into her brain—the faded tag sticking up at the back of Dan's

T-shirt collar as he bends over motionless Tash; Tash's eyelids fluttering and her eyes looking out, trying to put it all together from a very long way away; a crumpled Sunny Boy tetrapak, worn and bleached, wedged into a crack of the wall. She picks up Tash's green thong from the concrete, where it dropped when Tash fell; it seems like the only thing she can do to help.

The escarpment—scrubby on the lower slopes, bare on the upper ones, scrubby again along the rim—hides all the country to the north. Southward the saltbush and bluebush speckle the flat spread of dull-orange ground; eventually, out of sight but not too far beyond that, the country drops in sheer cliffs to the Bight. Famous cliffs, they are, although Vanessa had never heard of them before she came here.

Dave drove all the roadhouse girls there in his ute once. It was something he thought that Maertje should "have a look-see of," being a tourist.

Along the way they saw trees—"Actual trees!" crowed Nora beside Vanessa—a few thin-legged things throwing feeble shade over a grayed caravan, a dead fireplace. A dogger's camp, said Dave. The dogger had gone to Norseman; one of his wife's relatives had died.

The scrub went on as before, and they arrived above the sea. The dust of their driving floated off the cliff top, pale against the blue-green ocean and its trailing dabs of cream. After all the weeks of baked-hard land, of blazed-clean sky, the sea was a breathing thing—it almost *mused*, full of mysterious depths.

Maertje peered along the cliffs. "Broken off like a cookie."

"Like a *biscuit*," said Nora. "We say 'biscuit' here, not cookie. You and your crazy Yank English lessons."

Maertje and Nora took pictures of the cliffs east and west, then made the group stand together for a photo with the western cliffs angling out into the Bight behind them. "Like a tour group!" said Nora, and everyone made the right faces and was boisterous for the cameras. Then there was nothing left to do: look at an indigo horizon instead of a scrubby orange one, kick a pebble off the cliff, lean on the ute bonnet. Some joke of Nora's set Dave off on one of his long, unhurried stories, this one about a feral cat that wouldn't die; behind his dry delivery, his cobbled-together not-sentences, Vanessa heard his whole life in huge landscapes like this, hardly any people and all of them a bit mad from the emptiness. Plenty of room here for madness to flap around in.

Vanessa felt more foreign even than Maertje. The girls laughed and bowed around Dave, hardly believing the awfulness of the staggering staved-in-headed cat. Dave kept on delivering, pleased and embarrassed together, near motionless, elbows hooked back on the tray side. Vanessa smiled to show she wasn't a snob, or in a mood, or in a hurry to go. It *was* a good story. She could picture a different Vanessa, a *truly* lucky Vanessa, carrying it into her future and retelling it, and people laughing, her unimaginable friends.

"Can you believe that guy?' Nora said when Dave dropped them back at the roadhouse. "You can see how much he loves this place."

Vanessa loves it too, but only for what it's *not*. Everything, she can pretend, is wiped off the slate. There's only the one shelter in the entire landscape, if you don't know about the dogger's van; there's only the one possible livelihood, and everything is spelt out in the chores list. There's the desert up there, then this shelf of scrubland, and away down south the sea. The world skims at you along the highway, manageable parcels of it. It stands around for a while stretching its legs, refreshing itself, marveling at the absence of everything, then climbs into its vehicle and beetles away.

The ambulance glides down the ramp and sits there flashing; a crowd gathers. *What happened? She fell off the wall.* Everyone's voices are foggy. The ambulance officers—she loves them. They wear crisp uniforms, they're paid to be grown-up, they know what they're doing, they'll *fix* things. *Natasha?* they say, *Tash?* They speak conversationally, as if they've known her for years. *Wriggle your toes,* they tell her. *Squeeze my hand.*

I am, Tash says through her teeth. *I'm squeezing.* But she isn't; Vanessa can see her hand in the officer's and it's not moving. Vanessa presses her hipbones against the wall above, hugging the thong, watching. If she pays attention to all these details she's collecting, gathers the full picture, she might be able to reach in and change it, like editing a movie. She doesn't blink through the whole thing. Clare has an arm around her—it's just what she needs, but it's also a cold weight, a terrible necessity. Clare doesn't know yet, none of them know. They don't know to feel so terribly *awkward* around Vanessa. They don't know yet that they should cast her out. That'll all come later. No one will say anything, of course, no one will mean to be mean. It'll just happen that way, that she'll find herself alone.

She knows about the other light, too—without noticing, without worrying or understanding or caring very much. How often has she seen it? Maybe she dreams it, and dreams its recurring-ness, too.

It's never surprised her, this different light. Yellower, brighter than car lights, it throws a larger, softer-edged rectangle onto the wardrobe—so it must be closer, no? Does that matter? It doesn't follow the same path as the others; it moves as if something's veered off the highway and is bashing about in the scrub for the way back.

She welcomes it, even, maybe. Every time she sees it, it leads into a dream that ought to be a nightmare, but isn't. The landscape ought to be daubed and shuddering with anxiety, but instead it sits back patiently while the gnarled giant carries his lamp about searching for his sheep; while the lost family in the car, the kids clinging wide-eyed to their parents' seatbacks, throw frantic advice, the scrub rearing into the beams, roos bounding across; while Tony and his team from the city, with their special elaborate mobile light from HQ, cast about grim-faced for a body; while a great golden eye peers and peers, seeking something more to alight on than saltbush, than bluebush, than dust.

"In the bar, of a night," Kim said, trying to unlock Vanessa's room, "first drink's free but you pay for any after." She swapped keys and tried again.

"I don't drink," said Vanessa, still dazed from the bus trip, from arriving here, from the emptying-out of the world. She heard Mum's sigh of relief in her head; she realized, then, that this was why Mum sent her away: so that she could say that, and hear it as her own words, not Mum speaking through her.

"My God," Kim said. "There'll be bugger-all for *you* to do in your off-time." And she stepped into the hot-box of the room, threw the folded sheets onto one of the two beds, pushed the key at Vanessa and left.

A broom stood in the corner, and the floor crunched underfoot. So as not to just lie down on the unmade bed and pass out, Vanessa swept. The bed was low, and she had to get down on her knees to reach right back under it. Modest spiderwebs bridged three of the corners between the bed-legs and the base, and in each sat a small black spider with a clear dab of red on its back. She blew on the nearest one; it scrambled in its web like a fist assembling, then stilled. She would leave them there, she decided.

She swept the dirt over the doorsill, moved her case onto the floor and shook out one of the sheets. It had a small hole in it; it was a cast-off from the Smoking rooms in the motel. Grabby from being washed in bore water, it smelt strong and sweetly of detergent with an overlay of rotten eggs. She flung it over the sad bed and began to straighten and smooth.

Libby brings the other thong up from the sand, following the ambulance officers and their trolley, with Tash on the trolley neck-braced and blanketed.

She gives the thong to Vanessa; someone else brings Tash's beach bag, with the towel slopped through the bamboo handle. Vanessa takes these brightly colored items and hugs them. Let them not be relics; let Tash use them again.

"This is her sister." Tash's mates push Vanessa forward at the ambos.

"You better come too, love. Hop in the front," says the officer, backing past Tash's sandy foot-soles into the complicated room of the van.

Vanessa amazes herself, dealing with the door handle, climbing in, strapping herself to the seat. She's a wonder of self-propulsion and coordination. The driver gets in opposite, gives her a small serious smile that tells her: This won't be all right. Quiet, incomprehensible murmurs and tinkering happen in the back. They move off as smoothly as a limousine. Vanessa stares straight ahead at the dodging holiday-makers, at the picnickers, at the world she's leaving behind.

She's been in that ambulance ever since, really, its slow quiet glide, her sister in the back silent, being attended to, everything bright beyond the glass, and the weight of her own foolishness on her shoulders, bearing down, crushing.

Drinking used to be fun, part of the great joke of life. She and her mates did it, and it only made the girls more dazed and pretty, the boys more recklessly handsome. It brought them closer as a group; they propped each other up, helped each other home if they'd had too much, told the stories afterwards. She heard of bad things happening because of drink, but none of her mates ever really lost it and hurt themselves. Everyone came back fresh as daisies next day. Or looked a little more tousled, a little paler, held their head and groaned to get a laugh. Then someone gave them a couple of Panadol and they were okay.

But Joe and some of the others who work at and visit the roadhouse, some of them are really old and still grogging on hard, and she sees how un-pretty it is, clearly and coldly through her lemon-lime-and-bitters. Kim gets loud and argumentative and only talks to the men; Joe snarls; that truckie Arnold Ofie who brings the Frigmobile through, he turns into this horrible soppy weeping creature. You have to keep away from him; he paws the girls or flings his arm around the blokes, bellowing in their ear and crying. The conversations grow more passionate the less relevant they are to anything out here—private schools, the Labor Party, the new Princess of Wales. Effortfully, people grasp after the second halves of sentences. Beyond them, the windows show the lit-up gravel drive, the insects dancing around the lights, then black nothing. The clean empty distance that feels so wonderful during the day is gone, and Vanessa's trapped in a box with a bunch of slippery minds half off their leashes. Only the Boss, combed and sober behind the bar, holds everyone back from making some savage attack on each other, or on themselves, or on her—why not? She's here. Only the rawest luck protects her, the merest custom of politeness, and why shouldn't it run out, at any moment?

She goes to her room—some nights, she's been in her room all along—to read a book, or just lie in the dark and watch the lights on the wardrobe. Only her watch on the drawers next to the water jug and glass shows that this room's hers.

She thought there'd be silence out here; she hoped for it. But the generator roars on; Joe'll shut it down at one in the morning. The air-conditioners rattle out over the beaten dirt yard, cooling the Boss's house and the bar. Maertje's taken charge of some kittens, horrible half-feral things that have developed mysterious dry warts all over their bodies, and they squeal and mewl in the next room most of the night, Maertje herself cooing over them now and again. Silent as Vanessa might be here in her room, life keeps going on beyond it.

The first few days, she couldn't stop crying. It was too unfair, how little she'd meant by that elbow-nudge, how much she'd ruined, the blind bad luck of it, the pointless cruelty.

Then there came a moment, her in Mum's arms and Dad behind her saying in the coldest of cold voices, "Crying won't help. Just buck up and do what you can. Show you're sorry with concrete action. Nobody's counting your tears."

"Gary," Mum said.

"There's no getting past it. One moment's silliness, four lives stuffed. She has to face what she's done, what it is."

"Well, it's only natural to be *distressed* by it." Mum drew back and held Vanessa's shoulders, her own face red and eyes dewy.

"We're all distressed. Who's got time to cry? *Tash's* distressed, but she's got rehab to get through. *We're* distressed, but all this new stuff has to be sorted out. Don't waste everyone's time, Ness, I'm telling you. Just be as big a help around the house as you can."

And she had stood there, the sobs stopped in her throat but the tears still crawling down, and Mum looking at her all concerned and yet agreeing, somehow, with Dad—not telling him off, anyway, not telling him to go away and let Mum handle this. Things had changed, in that moment. All Vanessa's fear and franticness and beating up of herself had turned as rocklike and cold as Dad's voice. She had stopped being a silly girl and had turned instead into a bitter old woman, instantly, at Dad's bidding.

She likes the evening shift best. It quietens as it goes, rather than building to the panic of the lunch rush. And at the end is her favorite bit. She closes the restaurant and turns the sign around. Vacuuming is tedious around all those table legs and the noise is horrible, but then the worst's over. Back in the kitchen, she sprinkles Bon Ami generously along the counters, and scrubs them with a damp square of toweling, putting her back and arms into the job. The powder melts and leaves blue streaks, which she scrubs away to white. Then she takes a new towel, clean and dry, and rubs it all even harder to get the residue off, leaving each bench polished spotless behind her. The fluorescent lights show that she's done a perfect job, again. She sweeps the floor. She mops it with bleach-water. All the while the bar buzzes and muzaks on the other side of the double doors, but she doesn't have to go there if she doesn't want to.

  She lets herself out and crosses the beaten-dirt yard. Halfway across, she stops, because all that awaits her is the room, the heat there, the kittens mewling through the wall. She stands in the cloud of sweet chemical air she's brought from the kitchen, turns her face up. Night has thrown open its black door and sprayed its milk-bucket of stars across the dark. She could reach up and pull out a chunk of thousands of them, dislodge thousands more; she could stand here in the cold sparkling cataract of them. They might cleanse her, of smells, clothes, flesh. Finally, perhaps, the ground underfoot would weaken and crumble and fall away. She would owe no one anything, no work of her hands, no bite of her conscience. She would just be tumbling bones with the rest, pouring darkness, thoughtless, memory-free.

The worst thing had been how useless she was. Nobody needed her help to do all the things necessary to deal with what she'd caused. She couldn't fix anything, and she didn't know what to organize. All she could do was obey orders: clean, shop, try to get better at planning and cooking dinners. She sat over cookbooks and worried and made lists, and tried not to bother Mum with nervous questions, while everyone else rushed about doing appallingly adult things that she was incompetent to do.

The house had to change shape. There had to be ramps, and a lift put in, and doorways had to be widened to get the wheelchair through. Tash had to have the main bedroom; equipment had to be installed for getting her in and out of bed. Everything cost staggering amounts of money; Mum would have to work full-time again. Tash would have to have a caregiver, and Mum and Dad and Vanessa would have to be trained too, in all the equipment, and Tash's new rituals. Vanessa didn't think she could bear that; at the same time, it seemed like the most perfectly, exquisitely calculated form of punishment, that her own limbs should be put to the work that Tash's could no longer do. It's only fair, after all, she thought with dread.

She always starts her run along the highway, in the cool of the evening or the cool of the morning, depending on her shift. But if any vehicle lifts itself onto the plain, ahead of or behind her, first she runs onto the shoulder and then, well before the driver can spot her, into the scrub. She doesn't want to be buffeted by their passing, or their noise, or to meet anyone's eye, or hear anyone's horn, or be waved at.

"You can use my Walkman if you want," says Nora. "With ear plugs. They won't fall off you like a thing." She mimes a headset on herself. "And *heaps* of cassettes you can choose from. You've seen my collection."

Vanessa wrinkles her nose for a second and shakes her head. "Thanks, though." It'll sound weird if she says she can't *stand* music, anything passionate, anything with singing particularly, anything in English. It's exhausting, other people's emotions, especially piped straight into her head. It makes her want to curl up into a ball.

"Don't you get bored, just you and the wind?" says Nora.

"I guess. It's okay, though; it doesn't bother me."

"Kind of like a meditation, I guess."

"Oh, no," says Vanessa. "I'm not chewing over anything."

"That's what I mean. A meditation. Where you try and empty out your head of all thoughts."

"Oh." That doesn't sound right, but "Yeah, pretty much," she says.

Nora smiles at her. Her steady eyes make it a smile of sympathy, of curiosity, an invitation to confide.

"Thanks anyway," says Vanessa. She doesn't want any of *that*, either.

Vanessa approached the bed. Tash was immobilized by the neck brace, but awake. Her eyes met Vanessa's upside-down in the mirror. "Oh, it's you."

In a cold little silence Mum went forward and kissed Tash's cheek. Vanessa watched Tash not react, the mirror eyes unblinking.

"I suppose," said Tash, "you expect me to give a *shit* whether you're sorry or not."

"Natasha!" said Mum.

Deep in her wormiest, weaseliest insides Vanessa found a piece of ammunition. "It's not my fault you forgot how to fall."

"Vanessa!"

"All those extracurricular gym lessons, they were a waste of money, weren't they?"

Tash's upside-down eyes widened, all but flaming.

"Vanessa, I cannot believe how in*sensitive*—"

"It's all right, Mum—" and Tash spluttered there, and then the two of them, Tash and Ness, were convulsed by a horrible, painful laughter. Tears ran out the sides of Tash's eyes, first from the laughter and then from something else—they set Vanessa off too, and she blundered past all the equipment to sit the other side. She couldn't grab Tash's hand—what would be the point? She couldn't touch her sister's head—that would be weird. "I *am* sorry!" she choked out hopelessly.

"Shut up, I *know* you are. But a fat lot of good that does *me*, you know?"

And they sat there, lay there, ragged and wretched inside the situation, with Mum not quite understanding beside them, just letting them work it out as they would.

"Wipe my *eyes*, for God's sake!" Tash said. "Get me a *tissue* to blow into!" And Mum leapt into action.

"This's how it'll be, huh?" Vanessa tried to laugh, mopping her own eyes. "Everyone running round doing your bidding?" Her tone finished up all resentment.

"Oh, don't worry." Tash had given a bitter smirk. "I promise not to enjoy it any more than you do. Oh, and if it starts getting to you?"

She slid her eyes towards Vanessa, couldn't quite see her, couldn't even resettle her own head to make it possible. "You can always *walk away!*" she breathed. The high giggle she gave lodged in Vanessa's head, and from then on chimed out over her whenever self-pity threatened, burning it off like so much waste gas from the top of a polluted pond.

She wakes and the room is lit gold, almost unbearably hot. A puff of dust comes in under the near-closed blind, a puff of death. The thing whines in the otherwise complete silence, summoning or questioning—*investigative.* Vanessa pushes up very slowly off the bed, swings her feet down, stands facing the windows and the moving light.

It attaches to the roof softly, determined, crackling the thin metal—and to the hot fibro wall, which shudders and pops. Heat pours through, and a sense of the thing's heaviness, its care not to bear down too hard, not to break what it needs to touch.

"Maertje!" she calls out, because she feels she ought to, although she *wanted* this thing to visit, would have invited it if she knew how. Her voice comes out low, a slowed-down murmur, hardly more than a sigh. Maertje will never hear it through the whining. The dust churns in the window, rains onto Vanessa's pillow, slides into the crater her head left there.

"Maertje!" She tries to force her voice loud, to force it high, to force it to be *her voice,* but instead it sounds like some man's, some creepy, slow-talking, joking man's. *Maaaaairtyerrrrr*—like an engine turning over without catching.

Nothing touches her but her own night-dress and the lino underfoot, but she's being tugged on, gently, preliminary to being hauled sideways out of this existence. It's strong; even as it tests her she sees her senses *back there*, and the reality of the body she's used to, and feels herself forsaking them. It's powerfully interesting, the crumpled handkerchief of her self-left-behind, the illusions it had of being all there is, or at least at the centre round which it all revolved. Her back, front, scalp run with sweat; the room, the bed, will *foomp!* up in flames any minute.

But the heat cuts out, the questioning and the pull. She slips back into her old arrangement, ordinary again, alive, ongoing. She darts to the wall and presses her hands to the fibro. The thing disengages from the other side. The room should fly apart now, but it only darkens. She pulls roughly on the blind to open it, but it's old and delicate and it jams. She scrabbles it away from the window, pushes herself to the glass, her knee in the death-dusty pillow, stirring up the smell of smoking flesh.

Something bright snatches itself away at the top of the window. The glass is even smudgier now; the dust-clad smudges are almost all she can see, the glare of the walkway lights on them. She may as well be in the city, for all she can see of the sky.

She runs out, and around the building. A ring of the gunpowder-dust marks the sun-faded pink wall. With her arms wide she can just touch both edges. She examines the sky, brushing the dust from her fingertips, from her knee and night-dress. Nothing up there, only the moon, unexpectedly low, scooting through wisps of cloud.

She can never run far enough to get lost. She could lose sight of the road-house, run east or west over the horizon, or north up the escarpment and on and on—but there would always be the highway to bring her back, or the sun to direct her, or the stars, whose key clumps, whose tiltings through the night, she's beginning to know.

She could run south. She could do it at night, choose a moonless night so that she wouldn't see the edge when she came to it. She'd only know when, eyes on the sky, the earth refused to meet her last step and the stars snatched themselves away and then spun—underfoot, overhead, underfoot. Then the water would welcome her, or the rocks wipe out her whole past self.

She hasn't got the courage for it. She hasn't even self or shape enough to take that much control. With a kind of inner lip-curling, she watches herself fill her water-bottle at the tank before her run, notes on each outing the moment when she turns, when she heads back, when she seems to have decided to continue. How vain it is of her, how smug, how insufferably lightweightedly *teenaged*. The legs run, and dodge, and carry her; the little spare water sloshes in the bottle.

She hears the Boss's story in pieces as she takes the dinners out of the fridge in their cling-wrap, microwaves them one by one and ferries them through to the staff dining room. She hears enough from these fragments: the mother babbling, making the Boss come and look at the car; the big dirty circle on the roof, and how she made him pick up some of the dust with his finger; the boys stinking of fear; the mother's burnt hand, red one side, dust-blackened the other.

"So then we have this big fight. 'Friday!' she says. 'It's Friday! Tuesday night we were in Melbourne, Wednesday night Adelaide, Thursday we're coming along here hoping to make Norseman, weren't we, boys? When *this* happens!' So I say, 'You sure you didn't get a bit of a bump on the head, lady, in among all these shenanigans?' Well, she goes to deck me! So I come in the bar and grab the newspaper, so's I can show her *Tuesday* written there—"

When Vanessa finally sits down herself, the Boss is repeating about the light and how *evil* they'd said it felt—he smiles at that and everyone around the table smiles too, because he's that kind of man, unflappable, knowing blank terror when he sees it. First they chased it and then, when it chased them, they spun the car and drove back as fast as they could—*I was goin two-twenty k's, mate!* said the son. As fast as they could, and still they couldn't outrun it.

"And she was so *angry* with me!" the Boss says laughing, and they all imagine him standing there, taking the woman's scolding as politely as he can. "You'd've thought I *organized* this thing to go after them. Or at least I must know who did. All you crazy hicks must be in on this together! She didn't say that, but that was what she was thinking, all right."

Christmas came and went, all but uncelebrated among the half-finished renovations. Mum and Dad went out to a couple of dinners with friends; Vanessa stayed home—in disgrace, she felt, although "Pat says you'd be very welcome," Mum said, pinning her hair up into its "evening" style around her tired face. "It might be better than drinking yourself into a stupor here at home." Which is what Vanessa's taken do doing, quietly steadily knocking herself out every evening.

New Year's Eve crept up. There was a party; Vanessa was invited—by mistake, she suspected, or out of charity, in the hope that the crowd would diffuse her aura of shame. She dressed for the evening grimly, concentratedly. She'd lost weight—it was like dressing a skeleton—and nothing she could do would fix her eyes.

"You look nice," Mum said when she came downstairs to the loungeroom. Mum had been at work; she was tired, it went without saying. Stocking feet tucked in beside her, glass of cask wine at her elbow, TV wittering away in front.

"I do not." Vanessa threw down the little clutch bag, kicked off the silly shoes. "I look like a gargoyle. I don't think I'll go." She lay down on the couch, closed her eyes.

Sudden silence, of Mum turning off the TV; sudden falling-silent of the voice that had been whinging inside Vanessa, *But what'll I say? How do parties go, again? How will I ever last until midnight?* She didn't cry—*Nobody's counting your tears. You can always* walk away! She only lay there looking down the open throat of the year ahead.

"Ness, you need to get some kind of work," Mum said, quite gently. "Any kind. And anywhere, but probably... I hate to say it, but probably away from this town."

Vanessa opened her eyes a moment, stared at Mum half-accusing, half-surprised. Saw herself understood. Hid her face again.

"You just need to break out of here," Mum's voice went on, even more gently, "break away. You just need to put some—" She paused as if winding up to the effort of putting the words out. "Plain old geographical distance between yourself and this thing."

"This thing," Vanessa said, her voice blurry and rough. "This thing that I did."

Silence, because there was no denying it.

"But I can't help, if I'm away," Vanessa said muddily. "I can't, you know, *attend to my duties*. Cook and stuff, be useful—well, *try* to be. I s'pose I could send money home—"

"Don't worry about that," said Mum. "It'll help enough just to know that you're…" After another pause the phrase came out, toneless, dry, like foreign words tried for the first time: "Pursuing happiness."

Early hours, generator off, no engine-noise on the highway. Only this rectangle of light wavering on the wall, yellow, soft, preoccupied.

She gets up, dresses for running, lets herself out of the room. She steps lightly around everyone else's sleep, past the dark staff quarters, the dark Boss's house, along the crunching drive to the highway. When she gains the sealed road she sets off westward.

It's up ahead, not on the highway but a little north of it, over the scrub. It looks like a flat mushroom cap seen side-on, with a stub of stem left underneath, glowing brightest of all. It doesn't pulse or stretch; it moves about like something sensitive, like something apprehending every small feature and movement below it, adjusting in response.

She runs, with longer strides than usual, but at a pace she can keep up for a while. This is the best time to run—the coolness, the clarity, the star-frosted sky. It feels good to leave the roadhouse, the workplace, all those humans, feuding, griping, looking for laughs or oblivion. It's good to just run, not think, to move like a machine through the night, across the plain, towards any possibility at all

MONO NO AWARE

KEN LIU

*Besides writing and translating speculative fiction, Ken Liu [kenliu.name]
also practices law and develops software for iOS and Android devices. His
fiction has appeared in* The Magazine of Fantasy & Science Fiction, Asimov's,
Clarkesworld, Strange Horizons, TRSF, *and* Panverse 3, *among other places.
His story "The Paper Menagerie," which appeared in last year's volume, is
the only work ever to receive the Hugo, Nebula, and World Fantasy awards.
He lives near Boston, Massachusetts, with his wife, artist Lisa Tang Liu, and
they are collaborating on their first novel.*

The world is shaped like the kanji for *umbrella*, only written so poorly,
like my handwriting, that all the parts are out of proportion.

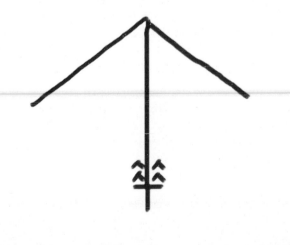

My father would be greatly ashamed at the childish way I still form my characters. Indeed, I can barely write many of them anymore. My formal schooling back in Japan ceased when I was only eight.

Yet for present purposes, this badly drawn character will do.

The canopy up there is the solar sail. Even that distorted kanji can only give you a hint of its vast size. A hundred times thinner than rice paper, the spinning disc fans out a thousand kilometers into space like a giant kite intent on catching every passing photon. It literally blocks out the sky.

Beneath it dangles a long cable of carbon nanotubes a hundred kilometers long: strong, light, and flexible. At the end of the cable hangs the heart of the *Hopeful*, the habitat module, a five-hundred-meter-tall cylinder into which all the 1,021 inhabitants of the world are packed.

The light from the sun pushes against the sail, propelling us on an ever widening, ever accelerating, spiraling orbit away from it. The acceleration pins all of us against the decks, gives everything weight.

Our trajectory takes us toward a star called 61 Virginis. You can't see it now because it is behind the canopy of the solar sail. The *Hopeful* will get there in about three hundred years, more or less. With luck, my great-great-great—I calculated how many "greats" I needed once, but I don't remember now—grandchildren will see it.

There are no windows in the habitat module, no casual view of the stars streaming past. Most people don't care, having grown bored of seeing the stars long ago. But I like looking through the cameras mounted on the bottom of the ship so that I can gaze at this view of the receding, reddish glow of our sun, our past.

"Hiroto," Dad said as he shook me awake. "Pack up your things. It's time."

My small suitcase was ready. I just had to put my Go set into it. Dad gave this to me when I was five, and the times we played were my favorite hours of the day.

The sun had not yet risen when Mom and Dad and I made our way outside. All the neighbors were standing outside their houses with their bags as well, and we greeted each other politely under the summer stars. As usual, I looked for the Hammer. It was easy. Ever since I could remember, the asteroid had been the brightest thing in the sky except for the moon, and every year it grew brighter.

A truck with loudspeakers mounted on top drove slowly down the middle of the street.

"Attention, citizens of Kurume! Please make your way in an orderly fashion to the bus stop. There will be plenty of buses to take you to the train station, where you can board the train for Kagoshima. Do not drive. You must leave the roads open for the evacuation buses and official vehicles!"

Every family walked slowly down the sidewalk.

"Mrs. Maeda," Dad said to our neighbor. "Why don't I carry your luggage for you?"

"I'm very grateful," the old woman said.

After ten minutes of walking, Mrs. Maeda stopped and leaned against a lamppost.

"It's just a little longer, Granny," I said. She nodded but was too out of breath to speak. I tried to cheer her. "Are you looking forward to seeing your grandson in Kagoshima? I miss Michi too. You will be able to sit with him and rest on the spaceships. They say there will be enough seats for everyone."

Mom smiled at me approvingly.

"How fortunate we are to be here," Dad said. He gestured at the orderly rows of people moving toward the bus stop, at the young men in clean shirts and shoes looking solemn, the middle-aged women helping their elderly parents, the clean, empty streets, and the quietness—despite the crowd, no one spoke above a whisper. The very air seemed to shimmer with the dense connections between all the people—families, neighbors, friends, colleagues—as invisible and strong as threads of silk.

I had seen on TV what was happening in other places around the world: looters screaming, dancing through the streets, soldiers and policemen shooting into the air and sometimes into crowds, burning buildings, teetering piles of dead bodies, generals shouting before frenzied crowds, vowing vengeance for ancient grievances even as the world was ending.

"Hiroto, I want you to remember this," Dad said. He looked around, overcome by emotion. "It is in the face of disasters that we show our strength as a people. Understand that we are not defined by our individual loneliness, but by the web of relationships in which we're enmeshed. A person must rise above his selfish needs so that all of us can live in harmony. The individual is small and powerless, but bound tightly together, as a whole, the Japanese nation is invincible."

"Mr. Shimizu," eight-year-old Bobby says, "I don't like this game."

The school is located in the very center of the cylindrical habitat module, where it can have the benefit of the most shielding from radiation. In front of the classroom hangs a large American flag to which the children say their pledge every morning. To the sides of the American flag are two rows of smaller flags belonging to other nations with survivors on the *Hopeful*. At the very end of the left side is a child's rendition of the Hinomaru, the corners of the white paper now curled and the once bright red rising sun faded to the orange of sunset. I drew it the day I came aboard the *Hopeful*.

I pull up a chair next to the table where Bobby and his friend, Eric, are sitting. "Why don't you like it?"

Between the two boys is a nineteen-by-nineteen grid of straight lines. A handful of black and white stones have been placed on the intersections.

Once every two weeks, I have the day off from my regular duties monitoring the status of the solar sail and come here to teach the children a little bit about Japan. I feel silly doing it sometimes. How can I be their teacher when I have only a boy's hazy memories of Japan?

But there is no other choice. All the non-American technicians like me feel it is our duty to participate in the cultural-enrichment program at the school and pass on what we can.

"All the stones look the same," Bobby says, "and they don't move. They're boring."

"What game do you like?" I ask.

"*Asteroid Defender!*" Eric says. "Now *that* is a good game. You get to save the world."

"I mean a game you do not play on the computer."

Bobby shrugs. "Chess, I guess. I like the queen. She's powerful and different from everyone else. She's a hero."

"Chess is a game of skirmishes," I say. "The perspective of Go is bigger. It encompasses entire battles."

"There are no heroes in Go," Bobby says, stubbornly.

I don't know how to answer him.

There was no place to stay in Kagoshima, so everyone slept outside along the road to the spaceport. On the horizon we could see the great silver escape ships gleaming in the sun.

Dad had explained to me that fragments that had broken off of the Hammer were headed for Mars and the Moon, so the ships would have to take us further, into deep space, to be safe.

"I would like a window seat," I said, imagining the stars steaming by.

"You should yield the window seat to those younger than you," Dad said. "Remember, we must all make sacrifices to live together."

We piled our suitcases into walls and draped sheets over them to form shelters from the wind and the sun. Every day inspectors from the government came by to distribute supplies and to make sure everything was all right.

"Be patient!" the government inspectors said. "We know things are moving slowly, but we're doing everything we can. There will be seats for everyone."

We were patient. Some of the mothers organized lessons for the children during the day, and the fathers set up a priority system so that families with aged parents and babies could board first when the ships were finally ready.

After four days of waiting, the reassurances from the government inspectors did not sound quite as reassuring. Rumors spread through the crowd.

"It's the ships. Something's wrong with them."

"The builders lied to the government and said they were ready when they weren't, and now the Prime Minister is too embarrassed to admit the truth."

"I hear that there's only one ship, and only a few hundred of the most important people will have seats. The other ships are only hollow shells, for show."

"They're hoping that the Americans will change their mind and build more ships for allies like us."

Mom came to Dad and whispered in his ear.

Dad shook his head and stopped her. "Do not repeat such things."

"But for Hiroto's sake—"

"No!" I'd never heard Dad sound so angry. He paused, swallowed. "We must trust each other, trust the Prime Minister and the Self-Defense Forces."

Mom looked unhappy. I reached out and held her hand. "I'm not afraid," I said.

"That's right," Dad said, relief in his voice. "There's nothing to be afraid of."

He picked me up in his arms—I was slightly embarrassed for he had not done such a thing since I was very little—and pointed at the densely packed crowd of thousands and thousands spread around us as far as the eye could see.

"Look at how many of us there are: grandmothers, young fathers, big sisters, little brothers. For anyone to panic and begin to spread rumors in such a crowd would be selfish and wrong, and many people could be hurt. We must keep to our places and always remember the bigger picture."

Mindy and I make love slowly. I like to breathe in the smell of her dark curly hair, lush, warm, tickling the nose like the sea, like fresh salt.

Afterwards we lie next to each other, gazing up at my ceiling monitor.

I keep looping on it a view of the receding star field. Mindy works in navigation, and she records the high-resolution cockpit video feed for me.

I like to pretend that it's a big skylight, and we're lying under the stars. I know some others like to keep their monitors showing photographs and videos of old Earth, but that makes me too sad.

"How do you say 'star' in Japanese?" Mindy asks.

"*Hoshi*," I tell her.

"And how do you say 'guest'?"

"*Okyakusan.*"

"So we are *hoshi okyakusan*? Star guests?"

"It doesn't work like that," I say. Mindy is a singer, and she likes the sound of languages other than English. "It's hard to hear the music behind the words when their meanings get in the way," she told me once.

Spanish is Mindy's first language, but she remembers even less of it than I do of Japanese. Often, she asks me for Japanese words and weaves them into her songs.

I try to phrase it poetically for her, but I'm not sure if I'm successful. "*Wareware ha, hoshi no aida ni kyaku ni kite.*" *We have come to be guests among the stars.*

"There are a thousand ways of phrasing everything," Dad used to say, "each appropriate to an occasion." He taught me that our language is full of nuances and supple grace, each sentence a poem. The language folds in on itself, the unspoken words as meaningful as the spoken, context within context, layer upon layer, like the steel in samurai swords.

I wish Dad were around so that I could ask him: How do you say "I miss you" in a way that is appropriate to the occasion of your twenty-fifth birthday, as the last survivor of your race?

"My sister was really into Japanese picture books. Manga."

Like me, Mindy is an orphan. It's part of what draws us together.

"Do you remember much about her?"

"Not really. I was only five or so when I came onboard the ship. Before that, I only remember a lot of guns firing and all of us hiding in the dark and running and crying and stealing food. She was always there to keep me quiet by reading from the manga books. And then…"

I had watched the video only once. From our high orbit, the blue-and-white marble that was Earth seemed to wobble for a moment as the asteroid struck, and then, the silent, roiling waves of spreading destruction that slowly engulfed the globe.

I pull her to me and kiss her forehead, lightly, a kiss of comfort. "Let us not speak of sad things."

She wraps her arms around me tightly, as though she will never let go.

"The manga, do you remember anything about them?" I ask.

"I remember they were full of giant robots. I thought: *Japan is so powerful.*"

I try to imagine it: heroic giant robots all over Japan, working desperately to save the people.

The Prime Minister's apology was broadcast through the loudspeakers. Some also watched it on their phones.

I remember very little of it except that his voice was thin and he looked very frail and old. He looked genuinely sorry. "I've let the people down."

The rumors turned out to be true. The shipbuilders had taken the money from the government but did not build ships that were strong enough or capable of what they promised. They kept up the charade until the very end. We found out the truth only when it was too late.

Japan was not the only nation that failed her people. The other nations of the world had squabbled over who should contribute how much to a joint evacuation effort when the Hammer was first discovered on its collision course with Earth. And then, when that plan had collapsed, most decided that it was better to gamble that the Hammer would miss and spend the money and lives on fighting with each other instead.

After the Prime Minister finished speaking, the crowd remained silent. A few angry voices shouted but soon quieted down as well. Gradually, in an orderly fashion, people began to pack up and leave the temporary campsites.

"The people just went home?" Mindy asks, incredulous.

"Yes."

"There was no looting, no panicked runs, no soldiers mutinying in the streets?"

"This was Japan," I tell her. And I can hear the pride in my voice, an echo of my father's.

"I guess the people were resigned," Mindy says. "They had given up. Maybe it's a culture thing."

"No!" I fight to keep the heat out of my voice. Her words irk me, like Bobby's remark about Go being boring. "That is not how it was."

"Who is Dad speaking to?" I asked.

"That is Dr. Hamilton," Mom said. "We—he and your father and I—went to college together, in America."

I watched Dad speak English on the phone. He seemed like a completely different person: it wasn't just the cadences and pitch of his voice; his face was more animated, his hand gestured more wildly. He looked like a foreigner.

He shouted into the phone.

"What is Dad saying?"

Mom shushed me. She watched Dad intently, hanging on every word.

"No," Dad said into the phone. "No!" I did not need that translated.

Afterwards Mom said, "He is trying to do the right thing, in his own way."

"He is as selfish as ever," Dad snapped.

"That's not fair," Mom said. "He did not call me in secret. He called you instead because he believed that if your positions were reversed, he would gladly give the woman he loved a chance to survive, even if it's with another man."

Dad looked at her. I had never heard my parents say "I love you" to each other, but some words did not need to be said to be true.

"I would never have said yes to him," Mom said, smiling. Then she went to the kitchen to make our lunch. Dad's gaze followed her.

"It's a fine day," Dad said to me. "Let us go on a walk."

We passed other neighbors walking along the sidewalks. We greeted each other, inquired after each other's health. Everything seemed normal. The Hammer glowed even brighter in the dusk overhead.

"You must be very frightened, Hiroto," he said.

"They won't try to build more escape ships?"

Dad did not answer. The late summer wind carried the sound of cicadas to us: *chirr, chirr, chirrrrrr.*

> "Nothing in the cry
> Of cicadas suggest they
> Are about to die."

"Dad?"

"That is a poem by Basho. Do you understand it?"

I shook my head. I did not like poems much.

Dad sighed and smiled at me. He looked at the setting sun and spoke again:

> "The fading sunlight holds infinite beauty
> Though it is so close to the day's end."

I recited the lines to myself. Something in them moved me. I tried to put the feeling into words: "It is like a gentle kitten is licking the inside of my heart."

Instead of laughing at me, Dad nodded solemnly.

"That is a poem by the classical Tang poet Li Shangyin. Though he was Chinese, the sentiment is very much Japanese."

We walked on, and I stopped by the yellow flower of a dandelion. The angle at which the flower was tilted struck me as very beautiful. I got the kitten-tongue-tickling sensation in my heart again.

"The flower…" I hesitated. I could not find the right words.

Dad spoke,

> "The drooping flower
> As yellow as the moon beam
> So slender tonight."

I nodded. The image seemed to me at once so fleeting and so permanent, like the way I had experienced time as a young child. It made me a little sad and glad at the same time.

"Everything passes, Hiroto," Dad said. "That feeling in your heart: it's called *mono no aware*. It is a sense of the transience of all things in life. The sun, the dandelion, the cicada, the Hammer, and all of us: we are all subject to the equations of James Clerk Maxwell and we are all ephemeral patterns destined to eventually fade, whether in a second or an eon."

I looked around at the clean streets, the slow-moving people, the grass, and the evening light, and I knew that everything had its place; everything was all right. Dad and I went on walking, our shadows touching.

Even though the Hammer hung right overhead, I was not afraid.

My job involves staring at the grid of indicator lights in front of me. It is a bit like a giant Go board.

It is very boring most of the time. The lights, indicating tension on various spots of the solar sail, course through the same pattern every few minutes as the sail gently flexes in the fading light of the distant sun. The cycling pattern of the lights is as familiar to me as Mindy's breathing when she's asleep.

We're already moving at a good fraction of the speed of light. Some years hence, when we're moving fast enough, we'll change our course for 61 Virginis and its pristine planets, and we'll leave the sun that gave birth to us behind like a forgotten memory.

But today, the pattern of the lights feels off. One of the lights in the southwest corner seems to be blinking a fraction of a second too fast.

"Navigation," I say into the microphone, "this is Sail Monitor Station Alpha, can you confirm that we're on course?"

A minute later Mindy's voice comes through my earpiece, tinged slightly with surprise. "I hadn't noticed, but there was a slight drift off course. What happened?"

"I'm not sure yet." I stare at the grid before me, at the one stubborn light that is out of sync, out of harmony.

Mom took me to Fukuoka, without Dad. "We'll be shopping for Christmas," she said. "We want to surprise you." Dad smiled and shook his head.

We made our way through the busy streets. Since this might be the last Christmas on Earth, there was an extra sense of gaiety in the air.

On the subway I glanced at the newspaper held up by the man sitting next to us. "USA Strikes Back!" was the headline. The big photograph showed the American president smiling triumphantly. Below that was a series of other pictures, some I had seen before: the first experimental American evacuation ship from years ago exploding on its test flight; the leader of some rogue nation claiming responsibility on TV; American soldiers marching into a foreign capital.

Below the fold was a smaller article: "American Scientists Skeptical of Doomsday Scenario." Dad had said that some people preferred to believe that a disaster was unreal rather than accept that nothing could be done.

I looked forward to picking out a present for Dad. But instead of going to the electronics district, where I had expected Mom to take me to buy him a gift, we went to a section of the city I had never been to before. Mom took out her phone and made a brief call, speaking in English. I looked up at her, surprised.

Then we were standing in front of a building with a great American flag flying over it. We went inside and sat down in an office. An American man came in. His face was sad, but he was working hard not to look sad.

"Rin." The man called my mother's name and stopped. In that one syllable I heard regret and longing and a complicated story.

"This is Dr. Hamilton," Mom said to me. I nodded and offered to shake his hand, as I had seen Americans do on TV.

Dr. Hamilton and Mom spoke for a while. She began to cry, and Dr. Hamilton stood awkwardly, as though he wanted to hug her but dared not.

"You'll be staying with Dr. Hamilton," Mom said to me.

"What?"

She held my shoulders, bent down, and looked into my eyes. "The Americans have a secret ship in orbit. It is the only ship they managed to launch into space before they got into this war. Dr. Hamilton designed the ship. He's my… old friend, and he can bring one person aboard with him. It's your only chance."

"No, I'm not leaving."

Eventually, Mom opened the door to leave. Dr. Hamilton held me tightly as I kicked and screamed.

We were all surprised to see Dad standing there.

Mom burst into tears.

Dad hugged her, which I'd never seen him do. It seemed a very American gesture.

"I'm sorry," Mom said. She kept saying "I'm sorry" as she cried.

"It's okay," Dad said. "I understand."

Dr. Hamilton let me go, and I ran up to my parents, holding onto both of them tightly.

Mom looked at Dad, and in that look she said nothing and everything.

Dad's face softened like a wax figure coming to life. He sighed and looked at me.

"You're not afraid, are you?" Dad asked.

I shook my head.

"Then it is okay for you to go," he said. He looked into Dr. Hamilton's eyes. "Thank you for taking care of my son."

Mom and I both looked at him, surprised.

> *A dandelion*
> *In late autumn's cooling breeze*
> *Spreads seeds far and wide.*

I nodded, pretending to understand.

Dad hugged me, fiercely, quickly.

"Remember that you're Japanese."

And they were gone.

"Something has punctured the sail," Dr. Hamilton says.

The tiny room holds only the most senior command staff—plus Mindy and me because we already know. There is no reason to cause a panic among the people.

"The hole is causing the ship to list to the side, veering off course. If the hole is not patched, the tear will grow bigger, the sail will soon collapse, and the *Hopeful* will be adrift in space."

"Is there any way to fix it?" the captain asks.

Dr. Hamilton, who has been like a father to me, shakes his headful of white hair. I have never seen him so despondent.

"The tear is several hundred kilometers from the hub of the sail. It will take many days to get someone out there because you can't move too fast along the surface of the sail—the risk of another tear is too great. And by the time we do get anyone out there, the tear will have grown too large to patch."

And so it goes. Everything passes.

I close my eyes and picture the sail. The film is so thin that if it is touched carelessly it will be punctured. But the membrane is supported by a complex system of folds and struts that give the sail rigidity and tension. As a child, I had watched them unfold in space like one of my mother's origami creations.

I imagine hooking and unhooking a tether cable to the scaffolding of struts as I skim along the surface of the sail, like a dragonfly dipping across the surface of a pond.

"I can make it out there in seventy-two hours," I say. Everyone turns to look at me. I explain my idea. "I know the patterns of the struts well because I have monitored them from afar for most of my life. I can find the quickest path."

Dr. Hamilton is dubious. "Those struts were never designed for a maneuver like that. I never planned for this scenario."

"Then we'll improvise," Mindy says. "We're Americans, damn it. We never just give up."

Dr. Hamilton looks up. "Thank you, Mindy."

We plan, we debate, we shout at each other, we work throughout the night.

The climb up the cable from the habitat module to the solar sail is long and arduous. It takes me almost twelve hours.

Let me illustrate for you what I look like with the second character in my name:

翔

It means "to soar." See that radical on the left? That's me, tethered to the cable with a pair of antennae coming out of my helmet. On my back are the wings—or, in this case, booster rockets and extra fuel tanks that push me up and up toward the great reflective dome that blocks out the whole sky, the gossamer mirror of the solar sail.

Mindy chats with me on the radio link. We tell each other jokes, share secrets, speak of things we want to do in the future. When we run out of things to say, she sings to me. The goal is to keep me awake.

"*Wareware ha, hoshi no aida ni kyaku ni kite.*"

But the climb up is really the easy part. The journey across the sail along the network of struts to the point of puncture is far more difficult.

It has been thirty-six hours since I left the ship. Mindy's voice is now tired, flagging. She yawns.

"Sleep, baby," I whisper into the microphone. I'm so tired that I want to close my eyes just for a moment.

I'm walking along the road on a summer evening, my father next to me.

"*We live in a land of volcanoes and earthquakes, typhoons and tsunamis, Hiroto. We have always faced a precarious existence, suspended in a thin strip on the surface of this planet between the fire underneath and the icy vacuum above.*"

And I'm back in my suit again, alone. My momentary loss of concentration causes me to bang my backpack against one of the beams of the sail, almost knocking one of the fuel tanks loose. I grab it just in time. The mass of my equipment has been lightened down to the last gram so that I can move fast, and there is no margin for error. I can't afford to lose anything.

I try to shake the dream and keep on moving.

"*Yet it is this awareness of the closeness of death, of the beauty inherent in each moment, that allows us to endure. Mono no aware, my son, is an empathy with the universe. It is the soul of our nation. It has allowed us to endure Hiroshima, to endure the occupation, to endure deprivation and the prospect of annihilation without despair.*"

"Hiroto, wake up!" Mindy's voice is desperate, pleading. I jerk awake. I have not been able to sleep for how long now? Two days, three, four?

For the final fifty or so kilometers of the journey, I must let go of the sail struts and rely on my rockets alone to travel untethered, skimming over the surface of the sail while everything is moving at a fraction of the speed of light. The very idea is enough to make me dizzy.

And suddenly my father is next to me again, suspended in space below the sail. We're playing a game of Go.

"Look in the southwest corner. Do you see how your army has been divided in half? My white stones will soon surround and capture this entire group."

I look where he's pointing and I see the crisis. There is a gap that I missed. What I thought was my one army is in reality two separate groups with a hole in the middle. I have to plug the gap with my next stone.

I shake away the hallucination. I have to finish this, and then I can sleep.

There is a hole in the torn sail before me. At the speed we're traveling, even a tiny speck of dust that escaped the ion shields can cause havoc. The jagged edge of the hole flaps gently in space, propelled by solar wind and radiation pressure. While an individual photon is tiny, insignificant, without even mass, all of them together can propel a sail as big as the sky and push a thousand people along.

The universe is wondrous.

I lift a black stone and prepare to fill in the gap, to connect my armies into one.

The stone turns back into the patching kit from my backpack. I maneuver my thrusters until I'm hovering right over the gash in the sail. Through the hole I can see the stars beyond, the stars that no one on the ship has seen for many years. I look at them and imagine that around one of them, one day, the human race, fused into a new nation, will recover from near extinction, will start afresh and flourish again.

Carefully, I apply the bandage over the gash, and I turn on the heat torch. I run the torch over the gash, and I can feel the bandage melting to spread out and fuse with the hydrocarbon chains in the sail film. When that's done I'll vaporize and deposit silver atoms over it to form a shiny, reflective layer.

"It's working," I say into the microphone. And I hear the muffled sounds of celebration in the background.

"You're a hero," Mindy says.

I think of myself as a giant Japanese robot in a manga and smile.

The torch sputters and goes out.

"Look carefully," Dad says. "You want to play your next stone there to plug that hole. But is that what you really want?"

I shake the fuel tank attached to the torch. Nothing. This was the tank that I banged against one of the sail beams. The collision must have caused a leak and there isn't enough fuel left to finish the patch. The bandage flaps gently, only half attached to the gash.

"Come back now," Dr. Hamilton says. "We'll replenish your supplies and try again."

I'm exhausted. No matter how hard I push, I will not be able to make it back out here as fast. And by then who knows how big the gash will have grown? Dr. Hamilton knows this as well as I do. He just wants to get me back to the warm safety of the ship.

I still have fuel in my tank, the fuel that is meant for my return trip.

My father's face is expectant.

"I see," I speak slowly. "If I play my next stone in this hole, I will not have a chance to get back to the small group up in the northeast. You'll capture them."

"One stone cannot be in both places. You have to choose, son."

"Tell me what to do."

I look into my father's face for an answer.

"Look around you," Dad says. And I see Mom, Mrs. Maeda, the Prime Minister, all our neighbors from Kurume, and all the people who waited with us in Kagoshima, in Kyushu, in all the Four Islands, all over Earth and on the *Hopeful*. They look expectantly at me, for me to do something.

Dad's voice is quiet:

> *The stars shine and blink.*
> *We are all guests passing through,*
> *A smile and a name.*"

"I have a solution," I tell Dr. Hamilton over the radio.

"I knew you'd come up with something," Mindy says, her voice proud and happy.

Dr. Hamilton is silent for a while. He knows what I'm thinking. And then: "Hiroto, thank you."

I unhook the torch from its useless fuel tank and connect it to the tank on my back. I turn it on. The flame is bright, sharp, a blade of light. I marshal photons and atoms before me, transforming them into a web of strength and light.

The stars on the other side have been sealed away again. The mirrored surface of the sail is perfect.

"Correct your course," I speak into the microphone. "It's done."

"Acknowledged," Dr. Hamilton says. His voice is that of a sad man trying not to sound sad.

"You have to come back first," Mindy says. "If we correct course now, you'll have nowhere to tether yourself."

"It's okay, baby," I whisper into the microphone. "I'm not coming back. There's not enough fuel left."

"We'll come for you!"

"You can't navigate the struts as quickly as I did," I tell her, gently. "No

624 »» ken liu

one knows their pattern as well as I do. By the time you get here, I will have run out of air."

I wait until she's quiet again. "Let us not speak of sad things. I love you."

Then I turn off the radio and push off into space so that they aren't tempted to mount a useless rescue mission. And I fall down, far, far below the canopy of the sail.

I watch as the sail turns away, unveiling the stars in their full glory. The sun, so faint now, is only one star among many, neither rising nor setting. I am cast adrift among them, alone and also at one with them.

A kitten's tongue tickles the inside of my heart.

I play the next stone in the gap.

Dad plays as I thought he would, and my stones in the northeast corner are gone, cast adrift.

But my main group is safe. They may even flourish in the future.

"Maybe there are heroes in Go," Bobby's voice says.

Mindy called me a hero. But I was simply a man in the right place at the right time. Dr. Hamilton is also a hero because he designed the *Hopeful*. Mindy is also a hero because she kept me awake. My mother is also a hero because she was willing to give me up so that I could survive. My father is also a hero because he showed me the right thing to do.

We are defined by the places we hold in the web of others' lives.

I pull my gaze back from the Go board until the stones fuse into larger patterns of shifting life and pulsing breath. "Individual stones are not heroes, but all the stones together are heroic."

"It is a beautiful day for a walk, isn't it?" Dad says.

And we walk together down the street, so that we can remember every passing blade of grass, every dewdrop, every fading ray of the dying sun, infinitely beautiful.

COPYRIGHT

"Mantis Wives" by Kij Johnson. © Copyright 2012 Kij Johnson. Originally published in *Clarkesworld* 71, August 2012. Reprinted by kind permission of the author.

"Bricks, Sticks, Straw" by Gwyneth Jones. © Copyright 2012 Gwyneth Jones. Originally published in *Edge of Infinity* (Solaris Books). Reprinted by kind permission of the author.

"Goggles (c 1910)" by Caitlín R. Kiernan. © Copyright 2012 Caitlín R. Kiernan. Originally published in *Steampunk III: Steampunk Revolution* (Tachyon Publications). Reprinted by kind permission of the author.

"The Education of a Witch" by Ellen Klages. © Copyright 2012 Ellen Klages. Originally published in *Under My Hat: Tales from the Cauldron,* published in the US by Random Childrens and in the UK & Commonwealth by Hot Key Books. Reprinted by kind permission of the author.

"The Color Least Used by Nature" by Ted Kosmatka. © Copyright 2012 Ted Kosmatka. Originally published in *The Magazine of Fantasy & Science Fiction*, January 2012. Reprinted by kind permission of the author.

"Significant Dust" by Margo Lanagan. © Copyright 2012 Margo Lanagan. Originally published in *Cracklescape* (Twelfth Planet Press). Reprinted by kind permission of the author.

"Two Houses" by Kelly Link. © Copyright 2012 Kelly Link. Originally published in *Shadow Show: All-New Stories in Celebration of Ray Bradbury* (William Morrow). Reprinted by kind permission of the author.

"Mono No Aware" by Ken Liu. © Copyright 2012 Ken Liu. Originally published in *The Future Is Japanese* (Haikosoru). Reprinted by kind permission of the author.

"Macy Minnot's Last Christmas on Dione, Ring Racing, Fiddler's Green, the Potter's Garden" by Paul McAuley. © Copyright 2012 Paul McAuley. Originally published in *Edge of Infinity* (Solaris Books). Reprinted by kind permission of the author.

"Swift, Brutal Retaliation" by Meghan McCarron. © Copyright 2012 Meghan McCarron. Originally published in *Tor.com*, 4 January 2012. Reprinted by kind permission of the author.

"About Fairies" by Pat Murphy. © Copyright 2012 Pat Murphy. Originally published in *Tor.com*, 9 May 2012. Reprinted by kind permission of the author.

"Nahiku West" by Linda Nagata. © Copyright 2012 Linda Nagata. Originally published in *Analog: Science Fiction Science Fact, October 2012*. Reprinted by kind permission of the author.

"Let Maps to Others" by K. J. Parker. © Copyright 2012 K. J. Parker. Originally published in *Subterranean Magazine*, Summer 2012. Reprinted by kind permission of the author.

"Jack Shade in the Forest of Souls" by Rachel Pollack. © Copyright 2012 Rachel Pollack. Originally published in *The Magazine of Fantasy & Science Fiction*, Jul-Aug 2012. Reprinted by kind permission of the author.

"Katabasis" by Robert Reed. © Copyright 2012 Robert Reed. Originally published in *The Magazine of Fantasy & Science Fiction*, Nov-Dec 2012. Reprinted by kind permission of the author.

"What Did Tessimond Tell You?" by Adam Roberts. © Copyright 2012 Adam Roberts. Originally published in *Solaris Rising 1.5* (Solaris Books). Reprinted by kind permission of the author.

"The Contrary Gardener" by Christopher Rowe. © Copyright 2012 Christopher Rowe. Originally published in *Eclipse Online*, October 2012. Reprinted by kind permission of the author.

"Joke in Four Panels" by Robert Shearman. © Copyright 2012 Robert Shearman. Originally published under the title "Madalyn Morgan," *One Hundred Stories*, 29 January 2012. Reprinted by kind permission of the author.

"Domestic Magic" by Steve Rasnic Tem & Melanie Tem. © Copyright 2012 Steve Rasnic Tem & Melanie Tem. Originally published in *Magic: An Anthology of the Esoteric & Arcane* (Solaris Books). Reprinted by kind permission of the author.

"Reindeer Mountain" by Karin Tidbeck. © Copyright 2012 Karin Tidbeck. Originally published in *Jagganath and Other Stories* (Cheeky Frawg Books). Reprinted by kind permission of the author.

"Fade to White" by Catherynne M. Valente. © Copyright 2012 Catherynne M. Valente. Originally published in *Clarkesworld* 71, August 2012. Reprinted by kind permission of the author.

"A Bead of Jasper, Four Small Stones" by Genevieve Valentine. © Copyright 2012 Genevieve Valentine. Originally published in *Clarkesworld* 73, October 2012. Reprinted by kind permission of the author.